The Secret of the Codex

Melissa Frey

Independently Published
in the United States of America

www.melissafrey.com

Book Layout © 2017 BookDesignTemplates.com

The Secret of the Codex / by Melissa Frey. —2nd ed.

Summary: When archaeology professor Kayla Harrington unearths a powerful Secret with colleague Grady McGready, she begins to realize that there's more to this discovery—and to him—than she thought.

ISBN 978-1-7324335-2-6

Reader,

Sometimes the journey itself is the adventure.

As I was writing this book—a book a decade in the making—the biggest lesson I learned was that I had to trust the process and embrace the journey.

And that's what Kayla discovers in this book—that sometimes the destination is just as important as who you become getting there.

My dream is that this book will keep you up at night, have you rooting for the heroes, and leave you breathless. Isn't that what we all want to get out of the books we read?

But more than that, I hope it makes you consider that the supernatural is possible, encourages you to find a love that takes your breath away, and nudges you closer toward the destiny you were created for all along.

<3 Melissa

The Secret of the Codex

Lightning

University of Central Florida, Anthropology Department

"DOCTOR HARRINGTON?"

Dr. Kayla Harrington looked up from the papers she had just finished grading to see a young blonde-haired, blue-eyed student standing in the doorway of her office with a messenger bag slung over her shoulder. She couldn't have been more than twenty. Kayla could almost remember being that young —when she wasn't trying to forget.

Kayla smiled and motioned her in.

The girl smiled timidly in return, tentatively entering the room. "I brought your mail."

Kayla nodded her thanks, reaching for the stack of papers and scanning the first few items with idle curiosity. Nothing good ever came in the mail anymore.

She'd gotten through a few pieces of mail before she noticed that the girl hadn't left yet. She slowly drew her eyes up to meet the girl's gaze. "Yes?"

The young student flashed another timid, almost apologetic smile before responding. "I know you're about to leave, but I was wondering if you had my final graded yet."

The flight! Kayla's heart skipped a beat. She'd nearly forgotten about it. Her eyes flew to the clock on the wall.

Her heart slowed down. She still had a few minutes. She offered the student a sheepish smile. "Sure, I should have it right here . . ." She shuffled the papers in front of her and quickly found the student's final. Sorting the students' papers alphabetically may be a little obsessive, but it did have its advantages.

After a brief once-over, she handed the paper across her desk with a wide smile. "You wrote a good paper. The conclusion was a little weak and didn't sound like you'd thought it all the way through, but all in all, good job."

The student smiled in return, more confident this time. She eagerly scanned the front page, her eyes quickly lighting on her grade. She looked happy with a B. "Thanks, Dr. Harrington. See you next semester."

Kayla offered a quick wave as the young girl rushed out of her office. She glanced over at the clock again. Ten minutes until she needed to leave for the airport. Enough time to finish looking through the mail.

Most of it was junk mail, magazines, and a stray bill that somehow got sent to her office instead of her home. But near the end of the stack, wedged between a magazine and a furniture ad, was a small, manila envelope.

Kayla's brow furrowed as she turned the package over in her hands. No return address. She reached for a letter opener and sliced open one end. Then she upended it, dropping its contents on her desk.

There, sitting atop the stack of newly-graded papers, was a silver charm attached to a long chain, almost like a necklace of sorts. Kayla leaned down without touching it, scrutinizing it for a moment, then picked it up, laying the charm in her left palm. From end to end, the charm nearly stretched the length of her palm. The metal was haphazardly chiseled into a crude rendering of the symbol for lightning. But the *way* it was rendered . . . something seemed oddly familiar.

She slowly stood, stepping around her large suitcase on her way to the overfilled and overflowing bookcases that lined the far wall of her small office. They were too big for the space, but she didn't care. They served their purpose. Barely.

She quickly found the book she wanted—she could always find things in her "organized clutter" as she called it, though no one else ever could—and she reached up to pull it out of its slot. It slid out easily, *too* easily—she had to jump under it to keep it from crashing to the ground. Her hands were the only thing that kept the large tome from hitting her in the head.

She flipped the book open quickly, stealing a glance at the clock. She needed to leave soon.

But not quite yet. She scanned the book, trying to find what she was looking for. Then, abruptly, she did. She laid the charm in the book, right beside the picture on the page, comparing the two. The distinctive way the symbol was drawn pointed to a very specific origin. She didn't know why she didn't recognize it immediately.

Now she really did have to leave. She returned the book dutifully to its proper place, draping the long necklace around her neck and dropping the charm beneath her shirt, then stepped over to the worn leather couch to retrieve her luggage. She leaned down and picked up her large suitcase by the handle, slung the strap of her smaller bag on her shoulder, and started for the door.

Then she remembered the papers she'd just graded and turned quickly to snatch them up—the way she kept her desk semi-organized in neat stacks ensured that she didn't grab anything else in the process—just before leaving and locking up her office. She placed the newly-graded papers on the front desk counter with a bright smile to the department's long-suffering receptionist before leaving the building for the summer.

Lamanai Archeological Project, Northern Belize Rainforest

Kayla stood up and stretched, yawning. Her long auburn hair fell down her back as she closed her eyes to the blinding glare of the sun. It had been a long day, and it wasn't even close to being over. She was fairly certain that this day still had quite a few more working hours in it.

Kayla blinked and shielded her eyes with one hand as she glanced down at the sandy ground where a dusty terracotta bowl was lying in pieces at her feet. After half a second's deliberation, she called over a nearby grad student to finish up the analysis. The monotonous portion of the work—though in truth she really didn't mind it—didn't need to be completed by the person heading up the dig; plus, it would give one of her favorite students much-needed field experience.

After letting the student know where she was going, Kayla trudged to her tent, pulling her gloves off on the way. She smiled serenely as she reached the entrance and eyed her cot.

Without stopping to remove her shoes, she flopped down on the makeshift bed.

After a few minutes of trying to sleep—though she'd known it would never happen before she'd even started trying—she reached for the necklace she still wore, the one she'd received just before she came here. She held the charm up to the light, turning it over and over, and stared intently at the lightning-shaped charm between her fingers. She had spent the entire plane ride here trying to figure out what it meant.

She didn't know why, but she couldn't shake the feeling that this was a warning of some kind. But a warning against what?

A polite voice interrupted her reverie. "Knock, knock."

Kayla sat up and smiled at the pretty young student she'd left with the terracotta bowl, the charm in her closed fist. "Hey, Jackie. Are you having trouble with the pottery piece?"

The girl called Jackie smiled back at her, flipping her long black hair out of her face. "Nope, all done." Her grin widened, and Kayla thought she saw her eyes begin to sparkle. "Dr. McGready is asking for you. I think they found something."

Kayla blinked. The dig had only been up and running for a few short months—and they had already found something? She hurriedly dropped the charm beneath her shirt and jumped up with a grin. "Coming."

"Jack, can you shine some light down there?" Kayla offered what she hoped was an overtly flirtatious smile in Jack's direction. A little light flirting always seemed to win their handyman over.

Her plan worked like a charm. Jack McFarland wheeled an industrial spotlight over to the correct spot. "Anything for you, sweetie." As the oldest worker on site, Jack was well-liked by everyone. He always had a nice word to say and a questionably interesting story to tell, if you had the time to stick around to hear it.

"I think we've hit the jackpot, Kayla," came from one of the dig's excavators.

Kayla gave a quick nod, but didn't look up to see who'd made the comment. She was too busy leaning over the shoulder of the computer tech on site, Dr. Grady McGready, trying to make sure the lighting was just right.

She watched as his deep blue eyes, eyes that complimented his short yet unruly dark brown hair perfectly, surveyed the scene expertly from behind his computer screen. A colleague of hers at the University of Central Florida and an expert in Mayan religious rites and traditions, Grady was now also filling the shoes of the dig's usual computer tech—the one who'd fallen violently ill just yesterday and had been medevacked to the States for treatment—thanks to his degree in computer science. One of his many degrees, if what she'd heard about him was true.

She took half a step back and looked at him more closely. They'd never really spoken to each other—excepting the occasional "hello" or nod as they passed in the hall and the usual business conversation at department meetings—and Kayla'd never really given him a second thought. But something about the way his sapphire eyes were examining the screen in front of them with such an understated confidence . . .

As she moved back toward the screen in front of them, she stole a glance at him out of the corner of her eye. He was only a few inches taller than her but easily outweighed her—though nothing about him made her think he was overweight. He just looked . . . strong. Like he spent a few hours a week running, maybe some occasional weight-lifting, but never spent much time at the gym.

Kayla didn't really think he needed to.

She chastised herself. He was her coworker, nothing more. No need to complicate things. She'd been down that road before, and it hadn't ended well. And that was an under-statement.

Grady's voice jolted her back to the present. "Shine that light a little to the left, Jack."

Kayla struggled to get her mind back on task. Thoughts like that would only distract her. She was here to do her job—nothing more. She leaned up close to Grady, checking the monitor to make sure the lighting was right. Once she was satisfied that everything was ready, she called out to their long-suffering handyman.

"Hey, Jack, we're all set. Thanks!" She waved him over.

Jack smiled at her as he headed their way. The group of people surrounding them—mostly the excavators that had made the discovery—now gathered behind Grady and Kayla to stare at the computer monitor.

The light illuminated a deep and narrow shaft. Though the light didn't reach the bottom, the widening walls of the shaft made Kayla think it was close. Embedded in centuries of dirt and debris, darkened skeletons lined the sides of the shaft. On one side, jutting out from between the layers of skeletal remains, were crude yet flat rocks that stuck out from the wall in a sporadic but oddly recognizable pattern.

"Hey, are those steps?" one of the onlookers queried, pointing at the screen.

Kayla's heart skipped a beat as she walked the ten yards to the shaft, taking the flashlight off her belt and pointing it down the hole. She broke into a grin. "I think so!" *This is great,* Kayla thought. *I've only been here a few days, and we find this!*

She could feel Grady's gaze on her back. "So what's the plan, Dr. Harrington?"

Kayla sighed, still gazing into the shaft. Then she looked up at the darkening sky and headed back toward Grady and the computer. "We're losing the light. Let's start on this first thing tomorrow. And please, it's Kayla." She smiled sweetly at him, then turned back to the group and raised her voice. "Okay, everyone, let's get some rest. We'll start on this as soon as the sun is up."

Grady grinned from behind the computer monitor as the crowd surrounding him dispersed. Kayla's tenacity was infectious—and quite endearing.

He started to join her at the edge of the shaft, but suddenly he couldn't move. As though his mind had opened a gateway to the future—one possible future, anyway—he could see them together. He saw their nondescript home back in Florida, saw them having breakfast in their small kitchen every morning, saw her lying next to him in bed with the sunlight streaming through the window, illuminating her cheek as she slept . . .

Grady shook his head violently, trying in vain to erase the idea of Kayla and him together. His inexplicable vision of them together was . . . well, unsettling to say the least. Where had those images come from?

He looked back at the monitor—hid behind it, more accurately—concentrating a little too hard on bringing his mind back to the present. He barely knew Kayla—she'd never given him a second glance, he was certain of that—but something was there, hiding just below the surface. Something he just couldn't quite put his finger on.

He'd never really considered dating her—not seriously enough to act on it, anyway. She'd only ever been a coworker in his eyes. Oh, she was attractive—beautiful, he'd thought more than once—but she always seemed out of reach. Like he wouldn't have anything close to a chance with her.

Life was cruel. Why had his mind conjured up those images of them together? He didn't—couldn't—have a future with her, not in this lifetime.

Then she was standing right next to him. "Dr. McGready, can I talk to you for a minute?"

Grady jumped. He hadn't said anything aloud, had he? That would be . . . unbearable. "Call me Grady." He shoved his hands in his pockets. "And yeah, what's up?"

Kayla looked over at him and smiled, leaning in just a little and lowering her voice. "Care to get started tonight? Our little secret?"

Grady grinned at her, feeling much more at ease. When he wasn't thinking about them together, she tended to have a calming effect on him. Odd. "Sure, I'd love to."

As the sun started to disappear behind the trees of the surrounding forest, they worked together getting the markers set up for the computer to read, sending a light down the middle of the shaft to help them better determine its length, and ensuring the lighting below would be sufficient enough for them to do some preliminary exploring.

Personal feelings aside, Grady was excited to have Dr. Harrington—Kayla—working with him on this project. He had been in Belize for the spring semester working on this site—one purported to be an important religious site for the ancient Mayans, though no one had yet determined why— and was glad to finally have another expert on the dig. And not just another expert, but *the* leading Mayan language expert in the U.S., if not the world.

"Okay," Grady said as soon as he'd checked the computer screen one last time, "we're all set. Let's go."

Kayla couldn't miss the hint of a smile on Grady's lips. She reached for the flashlight she'd laid by the mouth of the shaft and smiled back at him, pointing the light toward the hole in the ground. "You first."

Grady grabbed his own flashlight, attached it to his belt, and headed toward the illuminated shaft. Kayla felt a wave of warmth caress her skin at the sight of the brilliant smile he flashed her way before climbing down.

After he'd descended the first few steps, he peered over the edge of the hole. "You coming?"

Kayla grinned and snapped her own flashlight to her belt. "Wouldn't miss it."

CHAPTER 2

Discovery

AFTER WHAT SEEMED LIKE an eternity, Grady could finally see the sandy bottom. He jumped down, his landing sending up a cloud of fine brown dust. Just before the air cleared and Grady could see again, Kayla jumped to the sandy floor. Coughing, Grady strained to see something—anything—but all he could see was a cloud of dirt.

When the dust finally settled, Grady pulled out his flashlight. They hadn't been able to adequately illuminate this room from above, so the light from their flashlights and the small lantern he had clipped to his belt was the only light they were going to get tonight. Grady's beam searched the walls, the ceiling, the floor, looking for any clue as to where they were.

They had landed in a small room. With the exception of the shaft they had just descended, the room had only one exit —a tunnel that led further into the darkness. Grady shuddered. *Why on earth is this here?*

Grady suppressed the thought and went back to examining the room they currently found themselves in. Especially the floor. He wanted to be sure he knew where they were walking before they took their first step.

"Grady, look at this." Kayla's light was focused on the wall next to her.

Grady took a cautious step over to her, leaning down to examine the wall illuminated by Kayla's flashlight. He didn't see anything. Was he missing something?

"There's nothing here," Grady tentatively offered, hoping he wouldn't sound utterly stupid.

Kayla shook her head and pointed, seemingly oblivious to Grady's concern. "Look closer."

Now Grady saw it—saw *something*—but he couldn't tell what it was. Even from a foot away, he couldn't quite make sense of it. But then, he didn't read Mayan very well. Not as well as Kayla, anyway. "What does it say?"

Kayla's brow furrowed and she bit her upper lip as she concentrated on the tiny symbol etched into the wall. Grady studied her face closely, fighting a grin. The expression on her face was so . . . well, cute.

After a few lengthy seconds of confusion, recognition suddenly flashed across her face.

"What is it?"

Kayla drew a sharp breath, and Grady instinctively tensed. This couldn't be good.

Kayla exhaled pointedly before offering an explanation. "A few days ago, just before I left for the flight here, I received an anonymous package in the mail." She hesitated, frowning.

"What was in the package?" Grady prodded.

Kayla glanced back at the wall, eyes wide. "This symbol." She pointed at the small hieroglyph they'd been examining.

She didn't continue, but Grady waited. He sensed she wasn't done.

He was right. Kayla was reaching for a chain around her neck, pulling something out from underneath her shirt, something attached to the chain. She pulled the chain over her head, handing it to Grady. "This was inside."

Grady's eyes fell on the charm at the end of the chain, then shot to hers before he took the necklace. Kayla continued. "This is the Mayan symbol for lightning—well, the *universal* symbol for lightning, but the way it's chiseled definitely points to Mayan origins. That's what's here, on this wall." Kayla pointed again. "Can you see it?"

Grady leaned in closer to the wall. Suddenly he saw the image for what it was, a tiny replica of the shape in his hand. "Of course!" How did he miss that before?

Kayla cleared her throat. Grady thought she sounded almost . . . nervous. Why would she be nervous?

"This charm . . . what if it's a warning? To stay away? What if . . ." she swallowed hard. "Maybe we shouldn't be here." Grady saw something new flash across her face. It almost looked like . . . fear.

Grady abruptly felt an inexplicable urge to comfort her. "I'm sure we'll be fine. How would whoever sent this know we would find this room? It doesn't make any sense."

Kayla slowly nodded, but somehow she didn't look reassured.

Grady tried a different approach. "Look, let's not worry about it now, okay? Let's see what we can find down here tonight, and worry about the charm tomorrow. Agreed?"

Kayla looked past Grady and bit her lip.

He lifted a hand to touch her shoulder, then rethought it and lowered his hand. Instead, he moved directly into her line of sight and stared directly into her eyes, not moving until she met his gaze. "Agreed?" he repeated, refusing to back down. Something told him that Kayla wouldn't give in otherwise.

Kayla hesitated a moment longer, then sighed. She nodded once. "Agreed."

Grady smiled at her, then, without thinking, draped the necklace over her head. His hand brushed her forehead. For an instant, he took a half-step back. Then he steeled himself, took a deep breath, and stepped toward her, reaching for her hand.

The warmth of her hand caressed his skin. This was something he could get used to.

Before she could guess what he was thinking—he hoped—he pulled her toward the dark tunnel. "Come on. Let's see what we can find." He flashed a smile in her direction.

She attempted an answering smile. Grady's smile widened. At least she was trying.

Kayla ducked low to avoid a small stretch of low ceiling, wincing as she saw that Grady had to bend nearly in half to continue.

She hoped this tunnel opened up soon. It felt like they had been walking for hours, and she could feel claustrophobia slowly setting in.

Several long minutes later, the beam of Grady's flashlight was no longer illuminating the rocky walls of the tunnel in front of them. Instead, it seemed the walls were gradually moving away from them, opening into what appeared to be another room. Kayla sighed in relief.

Just before they reached the room, Grady stopped abruptly. Kayla had to jerk to a stop to avoid running into him.

"What is it?" she whispered, not sure why she felt the need to keep quiet.

Grady apparently didn't have the same need. "Look." His voice echoed back to them quickly, bouncing off the walls of the invisible room in front of them. A hand shot out to stop her from going any further. "The floor drops off." He shined his flashlight over the edge. The floor was a good twenty feet below them.

Kayla flashed her light around the opening and into the black room. There didn't appear to be a way through the room. With the aid of her light, she could just barely see an identical opening on the other side; they could get down, if they really had to, but couldn't get back up. Kayla didn't like that idea.

Kayla studied the space around her more closely, her light piercing the darkness erratically as she searched. A leaning, partially decayed wooden post was stuck in the ground just to her left. She leaned over to see the other side of the post, the side that faced the room. As she expected, a thin shred of rope dangled from the base of the post. There must have once been a bridge that crossed this room, but it had long ago rotted through.

She sighed. "I guess we'll have to bring a ladder in the morning." She started to turn around, but Grady was frozen in place. Something had caught his attention.

Grady stared at the room's ceiling, which was softly illuminated by his light. Hanging from it, at inconsistent intervals, were roots from the trees above. They dangled into the dark space like tendrils that would certainly catch a person in their grasp if anyone ventured too close. Grady shivered at the thought, quickly trying to put it out of his mind.

Because he had an idea.

"Kayla . . . how much do you trust me?" He smiled deviously as he said it, realizing as he did that there was probably no way she would trust him enough to follow his plan. Especially once she heard it.

To his amazement, Kayla just smiled back at him. She actually looked . . . excited. Like she was up for anything. She stood up straight in the small space and put a hand on her hip. "What've you got?"

Grady shook his head at her, still smiling, then chuckled before speaking again. "I had a crazy idea." He flashed his light at the roots hanging just above their heads. He reached out and grabbed the nearest one, then pulled on it, testing it. "You in?"

He didn't need to explain the plan—he could see immediately that Kayla understood. Despite her initial enthusiastic response, he saw a hint of apprehension flash across her face before she buried it. She shrugged. "Sure, I guess it's worth a shot. I just wish we had some rope or something." As she said it, the mask on her face slipped. Apprehension was back, not so quickly hidden this time.

Grady had to hide a smile as he handed her the first dangling root.

"You're loving this, aren't you?"

Grady's smile broke through; he couldn't help himself. "Of course. Adventure, mystery, a beautiful woman . . . what more could a guy ask for?"

Kayla released the root with one hand to punch him playfully in the arm. He pretended that it hurt. "Ow!"

Kayla wrinkled her nose at him, letting go of the root and stepping back from the ledge. She crossed her arms stubbornly and nodded toward the entrance. "You go first. Maybe you'll get lucky and the roots won't collapse and kill us both."

Grady just reached for the first root and grinned.

Kayla followed him out into the darkness, their flashlights stowed in their pockets, the lantern on Grady's belt swinging lazy circles around the room but offering little help in dispelling the suffocating blackness. Only Grady's steady breathing told her he was still there.

"How far across is this room?" Her whispered musings were swallowed up by the darkness as she stretched to reach the next hanging root. She struggled to remember how large the room had looked in the light. It hadn't been very big, had it?

A moment later, she thought she heard something—Grady's feet landing on the ground, maybe? She was sure it would've been accompanied with a yell if he'd fallen nearly thirty feet to the floor of the room, and besides, she probably would've heard him land. So did that mean he'd reached the other side . . . ?

Suddenly, there were no more roots in front of her to grab on to. Her heart raced as panic threatened to set in. What was she supposed to do now?

But then she remembered what she'd heard, and surmised that maybe Grady *had* reached the other side after all. She hoped. She tentatively stretched her hand out farther in front of her . . . and her palm hit a smooth and invisible rock face. She slowly ran her hand down the rocky surface until she found the upper edge of the opening, her heart pounding in her chest.

Then Grady's hand was there, pulling her into the tunnel. She let him pull her down, her breathing rapid as her heart tried to pound through her chest. Without thinking, she leaned into him. After only a second's hesitation, she felt Grady's arms slide around her as he pulled her to his chest.

Leaning heavily into Grady's embrace, Kayla felt herself relaxing. Her breathing started to slow down and she felt her heart start to return to a normal pace. Who knew she would be this—anxious—in the dark? It had never freaked her out before.

Once her breathing was back to normal and she realized what she was doing, she abruptly jerked away from Grady's chest. She coughed once as she took a step back and instinctively straightened her clothes. "Sorry," she muttered.

She could hear the smile in Grady's voice. He actually had the nerve to sound smug, too. "It's fine. It was . . . nice."

Kayla wanted to hit him for the second time in just a few minutes. Instead, she did the next best thing: she pulled out her flashlight and shined it in his direction. The sudden bright light blinded them both, but she took comfort in the fact that the light was directly in his face. *That's what he gets for being so smug about everything.*

"Sure, whatever." Kayla pushed past him when she could see again and headed down the tunnel. She heard him follow close behind, but she refused to turn around. She wouldn't give him the satisfaction of seeing the embarrassment most certainly plastered all over her face.

But as they continued down the tunnel, the embarrassment faded and Kayla began to remember what it felt like to be in his arms. How comforting it was just to have someone care enough about her to hold her until she calmed down.

She almost snorted. Her mind was playing tricks on her. Grady had no reason to care about her. He was probably just put in an awkward position and did the first thing that came to mind.

Besides, she'd been over this. She couldn't let herself get involved with anyone, especially anyone she worked with. Again. And not at this point in her life, when she had just gotten everything she'd ever wanted—a prestigious job in the field she loved, a nice condo near the university . . .

She sighed. She couldn't even think of anything else. She'd let her work consume her life, so much so that now she didn't even have one. Brilliant.

Kayla started to notice the tunnel opening up again. She braced herself for another drop-off, but one never came. Instead, the tunnel opened up into—well, blackness. Her light was swallowed up by it.

Thankfully, the floor of what had to be a huge room met up with the floor of the tunnel. No more climbing from hanging roots again. At least not until they had to head back. She swallowed hard, trying to suppress the less-than-helpful thought. *First things first.*

Grady came up next to her. They shined their lights into the room and tried to make sense of it, but their lights simply disappeared into the darkness.

Kayla shined her light on the one thing they could see well, the floor, and looked at it more closely. Nothing seemed out of the ordinary. Its sandy surface seemed safe to walk on.

But Grady had found something else. "Kayla, look at these walls." His voice echoed back to him as his light illuminated the nearby walls of the cavern. They curved away from the entrance. "We could follow these walls and try to meet up on the other side of the room. Maybe we can get some sort of idea of how large this room really is."

Kayla nodded. "I'm just glad we have a floor this time." She grinned.

Grady smiled back. "Me, too." He reached for the walkie-talkie he'd strapped to his belt before their descent and turned it on with a crackling sound. "Just make sure you keep your radio on. Don't want to lose you in this gigantic black hole."

Kayla clicked her radio on, testing it once before clipping it back on her belt. Just before she headed into the pitch-black room, she offered a "see you on the other side" to Grady.

Grady nodded once before heading to the right. "Be careful." Kayla watched him disappear into the room, then turned to start her own trek into the unknown.

Kayla made her way around the room, checking her watch frequently to make sure that she didn't miss her every-two-minutes check-in with Grady. She didn't think there was any reason to be worried, but she kept checking anyway. If something happened to him . . .

Grady's voice squawked through her radio just before the third check-in. "Hey . . . Kayla?"

She raised the radio to her mouth. "Yeah?"

"I'm . . . it looks like there's something just ahead of me. I think I'm starting to see some, uh, light . . . huh. That's weird . . ."

"What? What do you see?"

There was a long pause. Kayla could feel panic starting to rise in her chest. She held her breath for five infinitely long seconds. Then, as she slowly raised the radio to her mouth, his voice broke through the silence. Kayla jumped.

Grady's voice sounded a little odd. "I think you should come over here. This is really strange."

Kayla froze; she had to get to him, but she didn't want to leave the wall—she could get lost in this huge, dark place. And she hadn't really made much progress anyway.

Then she noticed something. Something that didn't make any sense. Something that shouldn't be there, something she shouldn't be able to see.

A boulder materialized to her right. Then another a few yards beyond that.

Kayla blinked a few times, trying to figure out why she could suddenly make out more of the room. Surely her eyes were playing tricks on her . . .

The room got even lighter. She could see to the other wall now. She scoured the room, her tensed shoulders releasing when she spotted Grady a good distance away from her, looking as though he'd made only a little more progress than she had. He was standing just in front of the far wall, his back turned to her. Something was . . . well, not really wrong. Off, maybe.

The wall behind Grady, the wall he now stood frozen in front of, seemed to be the source of the light. The wall glowed around Grady, casting a surreal halo of light around him. Shadows stretched toward the middle of the room. Kayla imagined his shadow was stretching to reach her, beckoning her to his side . . .

The room lightened further, almost as if the light was on a dimmer and someone was slowly turning it up. Now she could almost see the whole room. It was *gigantic*.

But she could only think of Grady. She could clearly see him across the room now, and he hadn't moved an inch. Had something happened to him?

She set off toward him, cautiously at first, then gradually breaking into a run. She reached him more quickly than she would have thought possible, coming up close beside him;

her short breaths were the only sound in the deafeningly silent room.

His deep blue eyes were wide; he stood motionless, just staring at the wall. Kayla followed his gaze.

The glow in the room, the glow that was now shining brightly and immersing the room in light, was coming from *behind* the wall. Kayla inhaled sharply and impulsively reached for Grady's hand.

As their hands met, the light behind the wall started glowing brighter—almost too bright to look at directly—yet Kayla was unable to look away.

Grady broke the silence. "Are you seeing this?"

Kayla nodded. "Amazing. How is it doing that?"

Grady shook his head. "No clue." He blinked once, then again, then faster. He seemed to be coming out of whatever spell the light had had him under.

Kayla turned to him, her eyes now as wide as Grady's had been. She opened her mouth to say something, but caught a glimpse of the room beyond him before she could. Her jaw dropped.

The vastness of the cavern was staggering; she hadn't fully taken it all in before. The ceiling towered over them, easily five or six stories above their heads—probably more like ten. Kayla couldn't believe they'd ventured so far below the surface.

The walls were roughly circular, and, at their widest point, stretched out to what had to be over a hundred and fifty yards. This room could hold an entire football field—and probably the stands, too.

But, as shocking as the size of the room was, it paled in comparison to the radiant light emanating around them.

The light, shockingly brilliant, nearly blinded them after traveling in the dark for so long. It exploded out like lightning rods from behind the glowing wall, reaching even the furthest edges of the room. Kayla was speechless.

Then something sparked inside of her, something instinctive, and she abruptly felt an overwhelming need to know *how* the wall was glowing. Without another thought, her scientific side took over and she turned back to the wall.

At first glance, the wall seemed unexceptional. But as Kayla looked closer, she began to see some . . . irregularities.

Grady leaned in, examining the wall with her. He hesitantly reached out and touched the wall lightly. "Look . . . this wall has a translucent top layer. The light must be coming from behind it." He carefully pressed a little harder, testing the strength of the rock. What appeared to be simply a thin layer of rock didn't move.

Kayla squinted, trying to examine the wall without looking directly into the middle of it. By now, the light was shining almost as brightly as the sun.

As she scrutinized the top layer of rock, she noticed small etchings on the surface. A strange pattern, nothing that made any sense . . . hmmm. Well, the symbols *did* make sense, kind of. The writings were of Mayan origin, she was almost certain of that, but they were . . . different. Almost . . . then it hit her. They were *backward*.

She stared more intently at the symbols. Something about the way the light was shining out from behind the wall . . . She slowly turned around. Her eyes widened. Again.

"Grady . . . look." Kayla pointed toward the middle of the room.

Grady's mouth fell open.

Cavern

GRADY WAS TRYING TO WILL his body to move, but to no avail. What on earth was he seeing? His mind kept telling him to sprint toward the middle of the room so he could make sense of what he was seeing, but his legs wouldn't move.

Then, excruciatingly slowly, his muscles began responding. And, finally, his body began listening to him again.

Once he was confident his legs would cooperate, Grady walked, ran, sprinted toward the middle of the room.

Directly in the center of the cavern, an enormous boulder—a monument, really—stood erect, blocking their view to the other side. Grady reached the boulder quickly then stopped to take it all in. There, on the side of the large rock, was writing—not etched in the rock, not written in ancient faded ink, but *reflected* on the rock from the brilliantly glowing wall behind him.

Kayla was coming up behind him, sprinting toward the center of the room—he could hear her frantic footsteps in the sand—but before she reached him, Grady heard her abruptly stop. He spun around. "What is it?"

She jabbed a finger at another part of the room, another wall. "Look! Those walls are shining, too." She moved to the right, taking a look at another side of the boulder. "Grady . . ." Her voice trailed off; Grady instinctively held his breath.

Kayla's next words were whispered. "These walls all have writing on them, too."

Grady looked past her to another part of the wall. It too was glowing, transposing symbols on another side of the boulder. Grady backed up a little, trying to see a little better.

Now he could see what Kayla was talking about. This was an amazing find. Soon his head was spinning with the possibilities.

Kayla had started circling the boulder. Grady followed close behind, always keeping her in sight, but making sure he didn't step in the way of the light's reflected words. She didn't seem to notice him in her exuberance. Grady just smiled as she gazed almost reverently at the symbols shining on the huge rock.

"Do you know what it says?" Grady was trying to make sense of the hieroglyphs with little success. He didn't know the language nearly as well as Kayla did; not many people did, after all. He found himself wishing he hadn't relied on his translators quite so much.

"Yes," Kayla mumbled, "but I'm not sure . . . I think these are stories, written histories of some kind." She paused as she read the ancient Mayan symbols. Her brow furrowed.

Grady watched the frown on her face deepen as she read. "It appears as though they're detailing random events in their history, stories of . . . hmmm. Something's not adding up."

Grady frowned. "What?"

"I don't know," she whispered. Then her expression abruptly changed.

"What is it?"

Kayla was grinning widely, all but jumping up and down. Grady smiled. She'd *definitely* found something.

"Yes! That's it!" Kayla's words came faster now, becoming jumbled in her excitement. "Here they're talking about a group of four men—they were referred to as the 'Old Ones' here . . ." she pointed at a small symbol, her hand briefly passing through the light, distorting the image, before she continued her explanation. "They ruled the Mayans for . . ." her voice cut off suddenly.

Grady inched closer. "For what?"

Kayla shook her head, blinking. "This says they ruled the Mayans for . . . *centuries*." She took a deep breath. "How is that possible? How have we never heard of them?"

Grady stared at the symbols shining on the boulder. "No one knows how to read K'iche as well as you, Kayla." Grady smiled, referencing the ancient Mayan language of this region. "Also, the ancient Mayan texts were always careful not to mention their royalty. They didn't even mention they *had* any royalty. Not for any significant period of time, anyway. Their gods were the only things they worshipped. At least, that's all we've ever uncovered." He shook his head. "This changes everything we know about the ancient Mayans."

Kayla was frowning again. "Grady . . . I think you need to hear this."

He leaned over her shoulder. "What?"

Kayla pointed at the rocky surface. "This says they ruled for *centuries*." She emphasized the word again.

Grady didn't get it. "So? Royal families have ruled for centuries throughout history."

"No." Kayla shook her head. "Not a family. *The same four men.*"

Grady froze. He just stood staring at the side of her face, trying to figure out if she was joking, trying to let what she'd just said sink in. After a few moments, he finally found his voice. "How can—" his voice cut off as he choked on the words. He cleared his throat and tried again. "How can that be?"

Kayla continued reading. "This part says—and I can't believe that I'm reading this—that they *never aged.*"

Grady smiled crookedly. "There's no way. That's impossible. Are you sure you didn't translate it incorrectly?"

Kayla shrugged. "I suppose I could have." She rechecked, frowning again. "But I don't think so. By these accounts, it sounds like these four 'Old Ones' ruled the Mayans absolutely, for centuries, and were never challenged. No one ever went up against them." She abruptly shuddered. Without thinking, Grady lightly rested a hand on her shoulder; something she'd read bothered her—he was certain of that. Grady watched her swallow hard before she continued. "Well, it's clear why they were never questioned. At least, they were never questioned *twice.*" She chuckled darkly. "The repercussions of insubordination came at a very high cost. Sounds like no one ever survived."

Grady cringed at the thought until he had another one. He cocked his head to one side. "How?"

Kayla turned to stare at him. "How what?"

Grady frowned. "I mean, how did no one survive their attacks? What made them so powerful?"

Kayla turned back to the hieroglyphs without a word, clearly searching for the answer.

After what seemed like an eternity, it seemed as though she'd found it. Kayla slowly stood, inching away from the wall almost imperceptibly. "Grady . . ." Her voice sounded strangled.

"What did you find?"

Kayla just squinted at the symbols in front of her. Grady felt his heart start to beat a little faster, though he didn't yet know why. He sensed he was about to find out.

"I think I know the how," Kayla whispered.

Grady just leaned in, so she continued. "These 'Old Ones' somehow found something that gave them absolute power. I think the story of what they discovered is here, I just haven't deciphered it yet."

"What *have* you deciphered?"

Kayla felt a pit forming in her stomach, getting larger by the second. "These men—they didn't just have power—they had *powers*, plural."

Grady's eyes widened as Kayla felt him freeze beside her. It took him several seconds to find his voice. "Powers? You mean like superpowers? X-ray vision, invisibility, comic book stuff?"

Kayla nodded gravely. "Basically, yes."

Grady smirked, just a little, and crossed his arms. "You can't be serious."

Kayla shrugged. "Normally, no. But maybe . . . It does explain everything. How they ruled absolutely, why no one who stood against them survived, why they never aged . . ."

Grady uncrossed his arms and held them out in front of her; Kayla thought he looked almost like he was begging. "But it can't . . . Kayla, superpowers don't exist. As a scientist, surely you have to know that."

Kayla bit her lip, unsure of how to respond. At any other time, on any other day—even just an hour ago—she would've had the same reaction. But she was here, this was now, and somehow she just *knew*.

Kayla drew a deep breath, releasing it before she spoke. "I don't know how I know, Grady, I just do. I'm sorry."

A long silence stretched between them before Kayla tried to clear the air. "Look, we don't have to figure this out tonight. I'm sure it's getting late, and we need to take these symbols down. Did you happen to bring a camera?"

Grady shrugged. "Left my phone in my bag—not much sense in keeping it charged around here. And the dig's cameras are so bulky I left them above ground. Sorry."

"Yeah, me too." Kayla sighed, not sure what to do. Everything still felt a little awkward with Grady, and she couldn't figure out how to fix it.

Then Grady spoke. "Kayla . . . I'm sorry. I had no right . . . If you believe these Old Ones had powers, who am I to say they didn't? You are pretty much the best K'iche translator in the entire world."

Kayla couldn't help but smile when Grady grinned at her. She almost even giggled. "Pretty much?"

Grady's grin widened as he turned back toward the boulder in front of them. "So we don't have any cameras down here, but we need to take these symbols down. Thoughts?"

Kayla nodded and grabbed a notepad from her shirt pocket. "Yup. We'll go old school." She winked at him before turning back toward the wall.

Grady grinned. Smarts and a sense of humor.

He knew he should follow her, help her, but instead he just stood there for a few seconds, watching as Kayla started circling the boulder. Something about the light in this room had gotten him thinking . . . where was it coming from? He knew there was some light coming from behind the walls, but it had brightened—seemingly in response to their presence—as one unit. Plus, now that he thought about it, the light had seemed to ebb once they walked away from the wall. There had to be a single source, a sort of catalyst that was sustaining it, right? It seemed to make sense. But what would such a thing even look like? And where on earth would it be?

Grady took a few steps back, scanning the formation in front of him as he went, barely noticing Kayla moving on to the next boulder face, off to his right. Where could . . .

Then he looked up.

Kayla was making good time. At this rate, she would have all four sides of the boulder transcribed in just another ten minutes or so. She wasn't translating everything as she went—this massive underground cavern was oddly getting more claustrophobic by the minute—but she was catching enough to start getting excited. This was an amazing find! She couldn't wait to get back to the work trailer, lay all these symbols out, maybe even get them scanned into the computer . . .

Then she felt it. Something was not right. Maybe it was just being in this room, but something was definitely off.

For the first time in who-knew-how-many minutes, she looked up from her work. Where was Grady? She'd all but forgotten about him.

Then she spotted him, several feet away from the base of the boulder, to her left. And staring toward the ceiling.

Could he even *see* the ceiling from here? She glanced upward, tried to see what he was gazing at so intently. Nothing out of the ordinary. Not even the ceiling, which was shrouded in shadow.

Kayla took a few steps toward him. She wanted to call out to him, ask him what was wrong, but she couldn't find her voice. She was worried that any sudden sound or movement could . . . well, she didn't know what. Maybe send him further into his trance?

She reached his side and faced the boulder, mimicking his stance. Then she looked up.

Sitting atop the largest boulder, barely visible from this vantage point, something was glowing. Kayla backed up to try to get a better view. From this angle, she could see the top of what appeared to be a golden sphere illuminated by the light in the room—or was it illuminating the room? The space around it was filled with an eerie glow.

"Kayla . . ." Grady's voice cracked.

"It's . . . amazing."

Kayla felt Grady come up beside her. "I can't even begin to explain how it . . ." his voice trailed off.

Kayla nodded slowly. "What is it?" She didn't really expect an answer.

Grady gave her one anyway. "I think this is the catalyst for the light in this room. Somehow it's giving off so much light that the entire room is illuminated."

Kayla's eyes widened. "Amazing," she repeated. After a few more seconds of awestruck silence, she shook her head and forced herself to look away. "We'll have to examine it tomorrow, when we can get a ladder down here." She smiled, then switched gears. "I haven't taken everything down yet.

Wanna help? I'd like to get back topside as soon as possible." She nodded toward the ceiling then offered a half-smile.

Grady smiled back, nodding. "Of course."

Grady fell into step behind Kayla, pulling out his own notepad and circling the boulder to take down the symbols she hadn't gotten to yet. He couldn't read them this quickly, not all of them, but he could copy them down. At least he could do *that*.

Kayla hurriedly followed Grady to the surface. Once their feet hit the ground, she stood very still for a brief moment, closing her eyes. She drew the cool night air into her lungs and felt it clear her head. Until now, most of her fieldwork at Lamanai had been above ground—and after tonight, she'd prefer to keep it that way.

But she had a job to do. Kayla deliberately focused her attention on what they'd found and went directly to the dig's primary work trailer, a portable, aluminum-sided refuge where they stored some of their more sensitive work equipment, those most susceptible to the weather. The one-room trailer housed a small library, a couple of microscopes, a handful of computers, and plentiful desk space. Aside from being on her stomach in the dirt unearthing her next treasure, this trailer was Kayla's favorite place to be—especially due to its comfortable, climate-controlled interior.

Kayla rolled a desk chair up to one of the tables and set to work. Opening her notepad, she tore out the pages she needed and began to organize the stories in chronological order as best as she could.

She barely heard the door open as Grady followed her in a few minutes later. Never taking her eyes off her work, she motioned to him with one hand. "Can I have your notepad?"

His notepad landed beside her on the table and she muttered a quiet "thanks" without looking up. She was barely registering anything beyond her work at the moment. That's how it always was.

She heard a scratching behind her then felt Grady come up beside her. Out of her peripheral vision, she saw him leaning over the table, peering at the papers she'd carefully assembled.

Kayla ignored him without really meaning to. She hoped he wouldn't take it personally.

Grady grabbed one of the two sandwiches he'd brought in—dropping the other on the desk next to Kayla—and started gnawing on it as he leaned back in his chair. He was only slightly hungry. He mostly just needed something to do.

After a few minutes—and only a small dent in the sandwich—Grady tossed the sandwich back on the table beside him. With a loud sigh, he rose and pulled his chair over to the dig's solitary desktop computer. After waiting for what seemed like an eternity for the dinosaur to wake up, Grady started searching the internet for information about the geographical area, blindly searching for anything that might give them a clue about who might've written the symbols in the cave—or maybe he'd get really lucky and find some info on the "Old Ones." He half-smiled. There was no chance of that.

He gave up only a few minutes later; the computer was just too slow, and it wasn't like he'd really find anything useful, anyway. He pushed away from the desk and moved to the dig's small library. Thorough research had been done on this site for more than a year before they'd decided the area warranted an archeological inquiry. He searched for those researchers' notes to see if they'd had any indication of what might have happened here or who may have written on the walls of the cavern below ground. A brief perusal of their lengthy notes turned up exactly what he expected. Nothing.

He glanced over at Kayla. She was still poring over the papers in front of her, but Grady was relieved to see a half-eaten sandwich in her hand. He watched as she blindly grabbed one-handed for a larger, well-worn, leather-bound notebook. It almost looked like a diary of sorts.

"What's that?" Grady asked, unable to remain quiet a second longer.

Kayla squinted at the notes in front of her, setting her sandwich down and reaching for a pencil without her eyes ever leaving the page. As she began scrawling frantically in the notebook, Grady wondered if she'd even heard him.

But she eventually answered. "My journal." She kept up her furious scratching as she continued. "I've been keeping a record of everything that happens here, everything we find. For my personal use."

She nodded at the table in front of her. "I think I have these in some sort of logical order. I'm transcribing them into my journal so they'll make more sense. Just a few more minutes." Grady couldn't help but notice her smirk at that last sentence. She'd noticed his impatience. Of course. It wasn't easy to miss.

A few minutes later, true to her word, Kayla set her pencil down, then picked up the journal in front of her. She motioned for Grady to move closer.

"Okay," she began, "this is what I have. It seems to be a first-person account from the perspective of one of the 'Old Ones.' Apparently these men ruled as dictators, taking what they wanted without regard for anyone else. They all but declared themselves gods, and anyone who stood in their way— anyone who dared question them—was *eliminated*." She winced. "It says here, loosely translated: 'I had more power than I could imagine, but I needed more. Our subjects were only a way to more of that power.' Nice guys, huh?"

"Ha." Grady offered a half-smile. *These 'Old Ones' had absolute power, that was obvious, but why? How? And why did everyone fear them so much, or allow them to rule in the first place? There had to be a reason.*

Then he had a thought. "Should we scan these into the computer?" He eyed the locked cabinet to his right that he knew held all four of the dig's laptop computers and the scanner, which could easily be set up in under thirty seconds. He also knew that both he and Kayla had a key.

Kayla yawned as if in response. Then she smiled. "We probably should." She glanced at her watch, which made Grady involuntarily check the clock on the wall. *Ten-thirty.*

"Maybe not; it's late," Grady offered.

Kayla nodded. "Tomorrow, then. It'll still be here tomorrow."

Grady nodded back, then came up beside her to help her clean up the papers in front of them. In no time at all, he felt his eyes getting heavier as a yawn escaped him.

Tomorrow was going to be a long day.

Later that night, long after everyone had gone to bed, a dark figure sprinted through the forest, weaving seamlessly through the weeds and undergrowth, covering hundreds of feet in mere seconds. He didn't even stop to catch his breath. He didn't have to.

Alerted by the dim lights that surrounded the archaeological compound, the stealthy figure slowed. He couldn't afford to be seen.

The Intruder cautiously approached the assorted collection of canvas tents and aluminum-sided trailers, careful to stay in the shadows. He peered through the dimly lit darkness in search of his mark.

There. The door flap of a nearby tent rustled slightly. Anyone else might've written it off as the wind, but the Intruder instinctively knew what was coming; this was why he was here.

A shrouded figure was suddenly hurtling toward him in a rush, keeping to the shadows. What they were meeting here to do could not be exposed. His counterpart knew it, too.

The other figure approached hurriedly but somehow carefully, silently. The Intruder grinned. This was just what they needed . . .

Then, suddenly, nothing more than a shadow was standing in front of the Intruder, its hands stretched out between them, a small object in its outstretched hands. The Intruder quickly swiped the object from his counterpart's hands, surprised at how light it was. He tossed it unceremoniously into his burlap bag, not even bothering to see what it was. It didn't matter.

The Intruder nodded his thanks at the dark figure, then retreated back into the comforting protection of the forest.

Kayla woke the next morning with anticipation fluttering in her stomach. What more would they find with the aid of their equipment, more people, and lights? She dressed quickly, donning her usual khaki pants and not-too-tight-but-still-flattering dark T-shirt. She draped a pocketed lightweight khaki work shirt over her shoulders and shrugged into it as she grabbed her watch and fastened it tightly. She subconsciously placed her hand over the charm she wore around her neck. She still didn't know what it meant, but she was going to keep it with her—and under wraps—until she and Grady could figure it out.

She reached for the notepad she always kept on the table by her cot, the one that she had filled up with the symbols from the cave, but her searching hand found nothing. Her eyes scanned the floor of her tent, the inside of her suitcase that lay open on the ground—she even rechecked the small table and shook out the light blankets on the cot—but the notepad was nowhere to be found. She sighed. She must've left it in the work trailer. She snatched up her now fully-charged phone instead; she supposed a camera would have to do.

With the help of Grady, Kayla headed up the expedition to explore the cave. Excavators swarmed the shaft and the caves underneath. At first, Kayla and Grady stayed above ground to keep tabs on their progress.

A few hours later, just before Kayla was about to head underground, Jack managed to get their floodlights safely down the shaft. Kayla was grateful she'd have more light than last night. Grady followed close behind her as they scrambled carefully but quickly down the shaft's haphazard staircase.

The room looked completely different in the blinding glare of a floodlight, the one Jack was just finishing setting up. When he was done, he started down the long tunnel carrying four other floodlights, with the help of a few other excavators. Kayla grinned at the array of lights he'd brought down with him. She had warned him how large the biggest cavern was, and he seemed determined to be prepared. One of the many reasons she liked him.

In the bright light, Kayla noticed something strange. The lightning symbol was everywhere. The ceiling, the walls—Kayla could even see symbols on the floor, peeking out from the sand on its surface. She made a mental note. Someone had thought this symbol was important enough to emblazon upon every surface; there must've been a reason. She reached for her pocket-sized notepad to make a note of her findings, then realized she'd forgotten to retrieve it from the work trailer. She reached into her pocket and pulled out her phone to snap a few pictures. She checked the small screen—the camera did not do this room justice in the slightest—but she was satisfied she'd recorded enough.

Once her analysis of the first room was complete—there was little left to see after her initial discovery—she followed Grady down the dimly lit tunnel. These floodlights sure beat flashlights. By a mile.

As the tunnel began widening, Kayla felt a familiar trepidation creep up in her stomach. Her former nemesis, this dark and seemingly floorless room, stretched out before her, beckoning her to continue, to fall into its depths.

She approached the room carefully, close enough to Grady that she could've reached out and touched his back. She slowed down to make sure she didn't run into him, thinking he would stop just before the entrance. But, unlike last night, Grady didn't stop. He took a step into the room as though nothing was wrong.

Kayla held her breath.

But Grady didn't fall; he bobbed up and down a few times, then seemed to stabilize a little. Abruptly, Kayla realized what kept Grady from falling. She felt like an idiot.

Their trustworthy excavators had strung a surprisingly sophisticated rope bridge across the room, complete with bright yellow rope and thick pieces of wood—ropes had even been strung on either side as handrails—creating a highly functional pathway to the tunnel beyond. On the bridge's side, at both ends of the room, the workers had strung sturdy rope ladders that nearly reached the bottom.

This was not the same room as the night before. The dangling roots still hung from the ceiling, but they now faded into the background as the more intriguing elements of the room came into view.

In the glare of the floodlight that illuminated the space— she was surprised that she hadn't noticed last night—Kayla saw that the room was dripping with water. The water dripped through the ceiling of the room, feeding the roots and turning the floor into a slick mud.

But that wasn't the most intriguing part. Interspersed throughout the piles of mud and dirt were pieces of . . . something. Kayla couldn't quite make it out.

She watched as an excavator pulled one of the pieces from the mud and began to carefully clean it off in a nearby water drip. Kayla immediately recognized what the man was holding. In his hand was a small clay pot. There were dozens of them littering the ground. But they weren't alone.

Kayla caught a glimpse of an unobtrusive, off-white fragment sticking out of the ground near one wall. Her eyes widened as she realized what it was. It wasn't pottery; it was a human skull.

As she surveyed the room, Kayla began to comprehend the sheer number of bones in this room. The floor was nearly *covered* in off-white bone fragments. The excavators would be busy for awhile.

But Kayla knew they could handle it. They would call in an anthropologist—the kind that dealt with human remains regularly—who would work to piece everything together and give them an idea of how these men and women died and how their remains ended up here.

So Kayla, realizing there was nothing more she could do here, decided to head further down the long tunnel. She followed Grady across the rope bridge—reluctantly at first—then into the tunnel that led to the cavernous room beyond.

The stadium-sized room was just as ominous as it had been last night, and, oddly enough, the floodlights Jack was busy setting up only made it more so. To Kayla, the bright LED lights juxtaposed against the otherworldly feel of the room reminded her of a basement morgue. She felt a chill run down her spine. What was it about this room that was so unnerving?

She eyed Grady. Given the way his eyes were darting around the room, he was feeling it too. She wrapped her arms around herself, feeling a chill that had nothing to do with the temperature.

Kayla tried to shake it off, to concentrate on the task at hand. She glanced around the room. The few workers that had made their way to this room were standing in odd clusters as if they were waiting for direction, eyes darting to, then away from each other.

She noticed Grady start heading toward the wall they'd discovered last night. Kayla followed automatically, wondering why the wall wasn't brightly lit up with all the people around. Last night, she and Grady seemed to have activated it, and the light had stayed on until they'd left the room. But today, even with all the people in here, the space behind the walls was lit only by a dim glow. Only the floodlights shed light in the room, but, despite their bright glare, they couldn't illuminate the entire space. The room was simply too massive.

As Grady approached the wall, Kayla saw the light in the wall start to glow. She touched his shoulder lightly as she came up next to him, and the light burned just as brightly as she remembered. *It must only light up when someone is directly in front of it,* Kayla mused.

Which gave her an idea. She called to one of the workers that stood huddled near the entrance. "Ramón, could you please bring us something to put in front of this wall?"

Immediately Ramón started moving, eager to please. He was soon at Kayla's side with a large metal stepladder. Grady and Kayla helped him set it up in front of the wall, then the three of them tentatively backed away from it. The light dimmed, but the room was still brighter than it had been. With the aid of the floodlights and the luminous walls, the room took on a bright yet eerie glow. At least now they had enough light to do some exploring.

Kayla called instructions to the rest of the workers, then leaned over to Grady as the workers dutifully started preparing the room for excavation. "So . . . did you notice how the light was a lot brighter when we stood in front of it together?"

Grady nodded, eyeing the workers just as Kayla had been doing. "Yeah. What do you think it means?"

Kayla made an effort to shrug nonchalantly. "Nothing good."

They both watched as one of the workers walked in front of the wall, stopping just in front of it to set up some equipment for testing. Kayla almost held her breath.

The light didn't waver.

"Weird," Grady breathed beside her.

Kayla nodded.

They fell into a comfortable silence as they observed the workers. Kayla wondered why only she and Grady brightened the light behind the wall. Whatever the reason, she wasn't sure she wanted to know. She was pretty sure she wouldn't like it.

Then it hit her, and Kayla shuddered. The way that light only really shined when they were near it, it was almost as if . . .

Almost as if it *recognized* them.

She pulled her arms tighter around her.

CHAPTER 4

Revelation

KAYLA WATCHED THE WORKERS finish prepping the area with indifference. Something felt *off*, but whatever was wrong—whatever was bothering her—would not be resolved until she started exploring. Something in this enormous cavern held the answers. She could feel it.

As if in answer to an unasked question, her attention was then inexplicably drawn to the large, towering boulder in the center of the room. She barely registered the prattling workers nearby, Jack securing the final floodlight, Grady double-checking the setup . . . her eyes were drawn to the tall boulder and the glowing sphere sitting on top of it. As she stood there, staring up at the globe from at least thirty feet below, it hit her. The sphere—the oddly illuminated but otherwise innocuous globe sitting atop the stately boulder—held all the answers she needed.

She needed to get up there.

Ignoring an excavator's tentative protest—just another benefit of being the boss—Kayla grabbed a long metal ladder off the wall and pulled it toward the center of the room. She smacked it against the boulder resolutely. Her scientific side was quickly taking over.

She scaled the ladder quickly, eager to find out what about the glowing ball had her so intrigued. Once she reached the top, she found herself staring directly into the center of the globe.

The light should have hurt her eyes. That was her first thought. Her second thought was that it could be too hot to touch. Her third thought was that although the sphere was large, it still looked small enough to carry. Ignoring her second thought, she braced herself against the side of the boulder and reached for the glowing ball. It wasn't hot at all.

But it didn't budge.

She tugged harder. It still didn't move.

Kayla sighed in frustration. If she pulled any harder, she risked breaking it, or knocking the ladder over. Reluctantly, she decided to simply do a cursory exam. No use wasting her time—or anyone else's time—when she was already up here.

Her hands traced lightly over the globe's surface. The feel of it reminded Kayla of the rocks she and her sister had frequently plucked from the creek behind their house—smooth and clean. Though she didn't know how the sphere had lasted this long down here without collecting a thick layer of dust.

Odd.

The top layer of the ball was translucent, allowing the light at its center to shine through, similar to the walls surrounding her. Kayla looked more closely at the glowing center, gazing into the luminescence inside. As she watched—with ever-widening eyes—the light began moving, swirling.

Something was happening.

Grady was busy analyzing one of the glowing walls. So far, he'd been unable to get a good picture of the area behind the wall, the part that was glowing, with their imaging equipment. The light from within seemed to be obscuring any attempts they made to see inside the wall. He was beginning to think that they may have to cut out a small piece of the wall and snake a small camera inside for a clear picture.

He cringed. Sampling the wall was the very last resort. He was an archaeologist first; he worked to preserve history, not destroy it. After a minute of internal debate, he sighed; he just couldn't bring himself to do it. Whatever picture they were able to get with their imaging equipment would just have to work.

He could discuss it with Kayla later and see what she wanted to do. Though, like him, he doubted she'd vote to destroy the wall, even a tiny piece.

Where *was* Kayla? She'd been only a few feet away a minute ago, hadn't she? Grady lifted his head to look for her.

"Grady?" A man called over to him from behind a nearby computer monitor.

Grady walked over to him, his search for Kayla temporarily abandoned. Something in the worker's voice made him think they might've finally gotten a clear picture of the inside of the glowing wall.

He was right. Grady stared at the full-color image on the monitor. His jaw dropped.

There, in sharp contrast with the dark brown background, was a white, brightly glowing globe, similar to the ball atop the boulder he'd noticed last night. Grady wondered if it was the same size. He glanced up at the top of the boulder behind him to compare.

Kayla was there, standing at the top of an impossibly tall ladder and staring at the lighted globe, her eyes only inches from it. She wasn't moving. What was she doing?

Kayla couldn't look away. She tried, but the attempt was actually physically painful. Something was stopping her—something intangible, but very, very real.

She stared at the globe, unable to do anything else. And then, as she gazed into its center, she felt something change, something she couldn't quite put her finger on. Fear pitted in her stomach.

Gradually, so slowly that she couldn't tell exactly when it started, the scene around her began to fade. The boulder she rested against, the glowing essence of the massive cavern, even the globe in front of her was fading away before her eyes. More than that, the sounds of the workers below her began to fade, too, until all she could hear was a quiet breeze that blew lightly around her. She shuddered as the breeze caressed her skin. What was going on?

She was no longer standing on a ladder three stories above the cavern's sandy floor—her feet were resting on a rocky surface; she could feel the jagged edges beneath her soles. She seemed to be on a small bluff, overlooking a large village. She smelled the smoke of several fires snaking up into the sky, felt the light breeze rustle her hair as it blew by, saw the off-white canvas coverings that composed the large collection of tents.

Then she was gone; the village disappeared from view. Now she was standing in a grassy clearing somewhere in the forest. Across the large clearing, several rugged, scantily-clad men were training in war games—grappling with each other, sparring with makeshift swords. They didn't seem to notice her.

The image faded again, into something else. She found herself transported to the edge of the forest on a sandy path, one that led out of the forest to a village just beyond, a village that looked just like the one she'd just seen from afar. Children ran by her into the darkness of the dense forest. They didn't even look up as they passed by.

She saw women scurrying about the village, towing baskets and pots from tent to tent, loading and unloading them in a frenzy. As Kayla stared at the sight, taking it all in, she felt a curious uneasiness creep into the pit of her stomach. Something was wrong.

The women started moving faster; the children whirred by her in a blur. Straw baskets and clay pots were being snatched up and thrown to the ground in rapid succession. But they weren't breaking.

Kayla couldn't understand what was happening. Why was everyone so rushed? And why didn't anyone notice that everyone else was speeding up?

Then, abruptly, Kayla realized what was going on. The *people* weren't moving faster—the *picture* was. The scene sped up, blurring around the edges. Kayla started to get a little dizzy.

Suddenly the scene was whirring by so quickly that all Kayla could see was a blur of gray, the colors swirling and indistinct. Kayla tried to grab onto something to keep her from falling over, but there was nothing within reach. Then there was just nothing.

Kayla would've fallen to the ground if there'd been ground underneath her—if there'd been *anything* underneath her.

She was frozen, staring straight ahead at images flying by so fast that all her brain could register was an eerie darkness. They were moving so fast that it almost seemed like they'd stopped.

Then, with a blinding flash, the images did stop. She was staring at a picture, an image forming out of the blackness. An image that stopped her heart.

In front of her, much too close and in grotesque detail, the people from before—all the people she'd seen in the village— were suddenly being horribly and gruesomely slaughtered. Tears ran down her face as the men, women, and children came against an invisible force, one that threw them to the ground with a vicious and relentless fury, leaving them spent and lifeless in pools of their own blood.

Kayla was choking, unable to catch her breath. The air was too thick, too repugnant to draw into her lungs. She was sobbing, fighting the growing darkness she felt welling up inside her.

The images dimmed, then blacked out completely. Kayla was exceedingly grateful. She couldn't stare at the faces of those brutally murdered people and continue to breathe.

Then Kayla was suddenly back in the cavern. The shock of it rocked her backward. The ladder teetered beneath her. She gasped and instinctively threw herself toward the boulder with so much force she was knocked breathless for a split second.

Her sudden adjustment had worked; she was no longer shaking atop the ladder. But her crash to the boulder had affected the boulder itself. Now, at the exact spot the ladder rested, the boulder was breaking apart.

Slowly at first, then gradually speeding up, tiny pebbles began to flow from the enormous rock to the floor below. The rocky surface that was holding Kayla up was disintegrating right in front of her. Kayla's eyes shot to the floor below. She wouldn't make it down fast enough.

She jerked her gaze back to the globe. It was still sitting atop the boulder, unmoving, but it wouldn't hold for long—the rockslide was growing. She had to do something, and fast.

Without thinking, Kayla reached for the globe. It came away from the rock easily, as if it had never been attached and had been simply resting on the rocky surface. As soon as she picked it up, the cascade of rocks abruptly stopped. For a split second, time itself stopped.

Then the rockslide began again, with a vengeance. Kayla jumped into action, tucking the globe awkwardly but carefully under one arm and starting down the ladder.

The ladder was moving beneath her; without the stabilizing force of the rock, the ladder was free to sway in the cavern's now dust-filled air. She struggled to hold on, struggled to descend; she couldn't do both. Doing just one was becoming increasingly difficult.

Then she was suddenly still. The earth wasn't moving beneath her. She almost laughed at how odd that felt.

She glanced down, and realized why she wasn't moving. Grady and all the workers in the room were huddled at the base of the ladder, stabilizing it. She'd have to give them all raises.

She climbed down quickly, flashing what she hoped was a reassuring smile. Grady, in particular, didn't look like he was buying it.

Once she was within reach, Grady stretched up to help her down, placing both hands on her sides to steady her on the last few steps. She'd reached the bottom much too slowly, but she'd reached it without injuring herself or dropping the globe. Point for her.

She handed the globe to Grady carefully. He took it only after hesitating for a split second. Kayla understood why; it was still glowing.

The light in the room was still shining, but was gradually dissipating. Kayla—well, technically the cascade of pebbles that she had caused—had removed the light's catalyst. The globe Grady now held, almost reverently, had been keeping the room lit. Kayla was almost sorry she'd removed the globe.

But not completely. She'd give up the light in the room to be able to get the sphere under a microscope. It was getting a little unnerving in here, anyway.

The workers dispersed, taking the ladder with them, satisfied that their boss was out of danger. Grady stayed close. Kayla knew he was just concerned, but there was nothing to be worried about. There wasn't a scratch on her, right?

Grady was looking her over. "You okay?" His voice was strained.

Kayla nodded quickly, a little *too* quickly. "Yeah, I'm fine. Nothing to worry about." She chuckled, trying to sound blasé. She just ended up sounding like she was trying to sound blasé.

Grady gingerly set the globe on the sandy ground. He tentatively drew Kayla to his side in a one-armed hug. "You sure you're okay? What happened up there?"

Kayla shrugged. She didn't want to explain it—honestly, she couldn't explain it. There weren't really words. Not ones that she was able to come up with, anyway.

Grady backed up and stared at her. He didn't look like he was buying it.

Kayla tried again. "Really, I'm fine." She managed what she thought was a believable smile.

He still didn't look like he bought it, but he returned her smile, albeit apprehensively. Kayla knew he wouldn't believe her until she explained herself. Which she would do, some-day, once *she* understood it.

As she watched Grady return to the workers, she felt something pull inside her. Only the brief stirrings of some-thing she couldn't put her finger on, but it was definitely there. Her experience with the globe had changed her. Some-thing inside of her had been awakened, like the flipping on of a light switch. Whatever it was, she had the distinct feeling that something was now set in motion, something she couldn't stop. She knew, with an unsettling certainty, that her life was about to change.

Kayla couldn't sleep. Her restless mind would not slow down long enough for her to relax. It was beyond frustrating.

After several hours of tossing and turning on her increas-ingly uncomfortable cot, Kayla eventually fell into an agitated sleep. But the disturbing dreams that filled her sporadic sleep did little to calm her down.

First, she was back overlooking the large village, the men training in the clearing, the women and children going about their daily tasks near their tents—everything was exactly as she'd seen it earlier, right down to the pair of dark-haired children running past her into the forest. Then, just as before, the images of the women sped up, and the world began to fly by in front of her eyes. She cringed as she fought the growing disorientation. She knew the pictures would stop flying by soon—but she also knew what was coming next.

The gruesome images again invaded her mind. She started to feel sick, even knowing it was only a dream. Somehow the blood seemed even thicker than before, the murders even more horrific. People—fellow humans with hopes, dreams, and aspirations—were being eviscerated right before her eyes by an unseen force, and there was nothing she could do to stop it.

She braced for the end of the dream, braced herself for something unseen to jar her awake. She didn't want to wake up. If she did, she might actually be sick, right off the edge of her cot. She fought to control the nausea.

But then something unexpected happened: the grisly images were suddenly gone, flashing into oblivion. Kayla felt a strong sense of relief for a brief second, but it didn't last long. Pain came back in a rush.

It wasn't the pain of nausea, or the pain of a physical wound. Her eyes involuntarily squeezed shut as the pain of a blinding white light glared in the space the images had once held only moments ago. Her mind's eye sought relief from a light as bright as the sun but found none.

The light was reminiscent of the brilliance in the cavern hundreds of feet below where she slept, but infinitely brighter. It glowed with an almost irreverent glory, shining so brightly that nothing could stand against it. The shining light was so pervasive that it seemed to take on a life of its own, a life essence that moved around her, clung to her skin.

Kayla shuddered in her sleep. The light was invading her dream, invading her body without her permission. She now wished she *could* wake up, but she couldn't fight her way past the light. Couldn't even shut it out.

Then, not nearly soon enough, the light quickly receded like a cloud imploding in on itself; the edges of the light flowed into its center until it swallowed its own essence. The sudden darkness was somehow comforting—but it wasn't dark for long.

Kayla, once able to see again, stared in wonder as a picture came into focus, fluctuating and quivering like an old movie.

Nothing about the wavering image in front of her carried any import, but Kayla's eyes were transfixed on it anyway. She couldn't look away.

The image remained constant, in motion but somehow still, unlike the scenes preceding it. Kayla took it all in.

In front of her was a breathtaking view of a windblown, snowcapped mountain, one surrounded by a forest of trees. She could almost feel the icy wind gusting through the trees, feel the blowing snow biting at her cheeks. She shivered at the scene before her. What was this place?

Kayla jerked upright on her cot, startled awake. The image was burned in her mind, as clear to her in waking as it had been in sleep. She bit her lip, contemplating the dream. What did it mean?

Then it hit her, as abruptly as a bolt of lightning. The mountain in her dream, the windswept scene burned into her memory—she recognized it.

She'd never been there before. There was no logical reason she should know that place. But she knew what it was, *where* it was—and that she had to go there. She knew—though she didn't know how—that something was there she needed to find.

CHAPTER 5

Na-um

Somewhere in the Belize Rainforest

THE HUNTER SPED THROUGH the forest, long black hair flowing behind him like a flag on the mast of an ancient battleship. His breathing settled into an easy rhythm, only slightly faster than normal despite his exertion. His ears, able to pick up every sound for miles despite his speed, tracked the beast in front of him. Though the beast was still a little over a mile away, he was closing the distance quickly.

Na-um, the one his people called "The Hunter," pushed harder, hurtling himself through the forest even faster. He barely noticed the trees that he effortlessly dodged, the fallen logs he easily catapulted over, or the swaying foliage that barely brushed his feet but never slowed him down. He loved running like this—the freedom and serenity of the forest calmed him, cleared his head as it flew by at lightning speeds.

Then, as though the dense forest in front of him split down the middle, he could see the beast ahead of him. His eyes peered through the trees, leaves, and bushes and spotted the massive animal, hundreds of yards away. Na-um grinned wickedly, then pushed himself to the breaking point to close the distance.

Na-um jerked to a stop, sending up a spray of dirt and mud that cascaded down the straps of leather that comprised his outfit and the darkly tanned skin of his muscular fore-arms and legs. He was still a good distance away from the beast; his small disturbance in the forest wouldn't attract his prey's attention.

He sunk into a crouch, inching his way closer to the oblivious beast. Then he stopped.

Just in front of him, the dense undergrowth of the forest was ending, disappearing into a grassy clearing. Every muscle in Na-um's body tensed. The beast nonchalantly lowered its muzzle to the ground, its jaws smoothly rotating as it fed on the tall grass of the clearing. Despite the apparent peacefulness of the beast, Na-um knew it wouldn't stay still for very long. He had to move fast, or he'd lose his chance.

Moving as few muscles as possible, Na-um slowly and deliberately stretched his hand to the back of his neck. Sheathed along his back was a handmade spear, a razor-sharp arrowhead attached to the end of a thick bamboo stalk with strong twine. The spear made no sound as Na-um carefully slid it out and held it at his side. He raised it soundlessly into position.

The beast, unaware of its imminent demise, grazed contentedly. Its head never left the ground as it enjoyed what would turn out to be its final meal.

The spear soared across the clearing.

A sickening wailing emanated from the beast as the arrowhead struck its side and burrowed deep in its chest. It howled, raising its head toward the sky. Its mournful cries pierced the tranquility of the forest. Na-um came out of his crouch and sprinted into the large clearing, crossing it in no more than two seconds. He approached the beast, which lay sprawled out on the ground, hind legs futilely kicking the air. Na-um watched as the beast pulled in one last, shuddering breath.

The Hunter had won.

"Na-um! Na-um!" A young boy, black hair cascading wildly around his shoulders, sprinted into the clearing. His bare feet slid across the damp grass as he tried to slow down. Na-um stifled a wide grin. He'd had trouble stopping when he'd first started running, too.

Once the boy had found his footing, he bounded over to Na-um. "Come home, Na-um!" He shouted in their native tongue. "We are ready to eat."

Na-um bent down and scooped the young boy up in his arms, squeezing him tightly. After a quick embrace, he set the boy back down on the damp grass. He crossed his arms and stood looking down at the boy, answering back in the only language he knew the boy would understand. This boy was too young to have learned much of the many languages those in the Clan were bred to speak. He would start mastering those a few years from now. "Oh, are we? And how did you even know to come look for me here?"

The child in front of him looked down at the ground. His words came out softly. "I heard you."

"What?" Na-um prodded, trying to get him to speak up. He shouldn't be ashamed of his powers.

The boy looked up suddenly, staring directly into Na-um's eyes, his lips tightening into a straight line. "I heard you running through the forest. I heard you stop here. I heard the beast fall. So I came to find you."

One side of Na-um's mouth turned up. He was pleased. This young boy was just coming into his powers, the powers he and the members of his Clan shared. This little man needed to know how to use his powers, certainly, but more importantly, he needed to be proud of them. They were a gift from the heavens. His people were given them to do good. They should all be sending up prayers that they were endowed with these powers, not hiding them.

Na-um patted the boy's head gently. "Good. You are learning quickly. Soon you will be able to hunt just as I can."

The boy looked up at him and beamed.

Na-um reached for his hand. "Let us return to the village. We will go eat."

The boy looked over at the fallen beast. "What about that?"

Na-um shrugged. "I will send someone for it. The Clan will be fed for many days."

A playful laugh burst from the boy's lips as they took off down the forested path.

As Na-um approached the village, he felt the hairs on the back of his neck stand up. He couldn't really see anything yet, just patches of khaki-colored canvas peeking through the trees at the edge of the forest, but he could tell something wasn't right. He slowed to a stop, halting the boy's progress as well. The child looked up at him and Na-um noiselessly shook his head. The boy's eyes grew wide, spreading to take up nearly half of his face, but he stayed quiet.

Na-um froze, listening to the sounds of the village—or, rather, listening *for* the sounds of the village. All was quiet save one voice, far away . . .

Still holding the boy's hand, Na-um ventured toward the still village. He'd never seen—or heard—his village like this. It could only mean one thing.

And it wasn't good.

Na-um, with a tighter-than-normal grip on the young boy's hand, crept through the large collection of canvas tents that housed his people. His eyes took in the eerie sight of a fire pit with flames burning brightly and a charred piece of what used to be meat spitted over the fire, still cooking. At his feet, an abandoned doll lay in the dirt. He squatted down and picked it up. The boy let go of Na-um's hand and walked out of sight, then returned a few seconds later holding a small wooden toy.

The boy whispered a question in Na-um's ear. "What happened?"

Na-um cocked his head, listening to something off in the distance, then set the doll back down in the dirt and stood up. He started to reach for the boy's hand, but both were clutched around his toy. Na-um laid a hand on his shoulder instead. He softly replied, "I do not know. Everyone is in the meeting hall."

The boy's eyes grew even wider. "What for?"

Na-um's eyes narrowed. "The Elders have called a meeting."

Na-um led the way through the village to the meeting hall, nothing more than six thick wooden posts holding up a thatched roof. The covered space was packed; everyone was in attendance. The Elders held regular meetings here, but very rarely called impromptu gatherings. Na-um had only seen it happen once—and that hadn't ended well.

Na-um approached the crowd quietly. Thankfully, nearly everyone was turned away from him and the boy. The only people facing them were the Elders, standing a head above the crowd on what was most likely the raised platform that usually sat at the head of the open-air meeting space.

Na-um sent the young boy through the crowd to find his mother, then stood near the back, trying to remain inconspicuous.

"Ah, our Hunter has returned!"

So much for being inconspicuous. The crowd began muttering in indistinct whispers as every neck craned to look back at him. Na-um gave a slight nod of his head. He knew that voice.

"Greetings, Chac." His voice rang out over the din of the crowd.

The man called Chac, the leader of the Elders, motioned Na-um forward. Na-um was fairly certain he hadn't been seen as he approached the gathering, so Chac must have sensed him. Or something. No one really knew everything the Elders could do. Sometimes they almost seemed to know things about the future, things no one should be able to know. Almost as if they could see the future for themselves. It made Na-um's hair stand on end when he thought about it.

Na-um made his way through the crowd, bodies parting for him as he passed. The effect was unsettling.

As was everything about this meeting. Na-um could sense it; something was coming, something big. Something Na-um wasn't sure he'd like.

Chac addressed the crowd in their native tongue as soon as Na-um reached the platform. "Brothers and sisters, as you well know, we have always been a peaceful people. We have never had reason to use our superior combative abilities. But still we trained, as those before us, to be ready to fight if the need arose.

"Today, regrettably, that time has come. The powers we have protected for so long are in danger of being unleashed. So we are calling all men to fight, to prevent this from happening." He barely took a breath as he switched gears.

"Are there any among you unable to fight?" Low murmurings again spread through the crowd, but no one dared answer. Na-um scanned the faces in the crowd; wide eyes and pale complexions greeted him from every side.

Chac continued. "Good." He smiled. "The power of our ancestors is in your blood. Do not be afraid, men; this is your purpose, your reason for being. There is nothing to stop you, nothing in your way but your own fear." He paused. Na-um winced internally. Chac really knew how to work a crowd. Much too superficial for Na-um's liking.

"So today we train. We prepare to fight. We prepare to win!" Everyone cheered, as if on cue. But Na-um could easily see the fear barely masked in their eyes. The men of this village were going into battle. And, despite Chac's confidence, Na-um knew some of them probably wouldn't make it back.

"Na-um," Chac said as soon as the crowd had quieted down. Na-um looked over at him, moving past the other elders to his side. Na-um faced the members of his Clan with a blank expression on his face. He knew what Chac and the rest of the Elders wanted. And he knew he was going to give it to them.

Chac turned back to the people, placing a hand on Na-um's shoulder. "Here is our leader in this fight. He is the best-trained fighter among us, and the strongest. His abilities are unmatched in our Clan. He will show us the way; he will prepare you all for the battle—for your Destiny."

A quiet murmur trickled through the crowd. Na-um knew what he had to do.

"I am honored to lead you in this fight. We will prevail!" His display of assurance was met with cheers and applause. Na-um flashed what he hoped was a confident smile.

Because he didn't feel confident at all.

"Chac, what is this about?" Na-um approached the leader of the Elders as soon as the crowd had dispersed.

"How are you, my son?" Zotz, the longest standing Elder, placed a genial hand on Na-um's shoulder. Na-um resisted the urge to shrug it off. He just wanted answers; no need to stall with useless trivialities.

Tohil, one of the more agreeable Elders, spoke up before Na-um could answer. "We have received word of a breach at the Lamanai site. Our source says that a few American scientists have uncovered a shaft in the dirt and have discovered the underground passage there."

Na-um blinked, expecting Tohil to continue. When he didn't, he said, "And?"

The one named Bacob took over. "Na-um, this underground passage contains important information, information that we are here to protect."

The picture was still a little hazy, but Na-um thought he was catching on. "Information about the Secret?"

All five Elders exchanged glances with each other. The youngest of the Elders, Kucumatz, continued. "All you need to know is that we need to stop them. If they continue down this path, the path they discovered in this underground tunnel, they will unleash a great evil on the world, an evil we must abolish."

Na-um sighed to himself. He wasn't going to get any more information out of them. The Elders were extremely tight-lipped about the "Secret." How apropos.

Na-um nodded in response. "Of course." Give them what they wanted now. He could do some research on what they were hiding later; right now he had a job to do. "When shall I begin the training?"

Chac smiled, a confident grin that put all his teeth on display. "Tonight."

Lamanai Archeological Project, Northern Belize Rainforest

Kayla tossed restlessly on her cot, unable to go back to sleep. After an hour of staring at the canvas ceiling, fidgeting until her light blanket was on the ground beside her, she gave up and got dressed. She left her tent with the sun still hiding behind the eastern horizon and headed for the mess tent. Might as well get some breakfast before the morning rush.

Morning rush. The thought almost made her smile. Almost. Maybe if she wasn't so tired.

She ducked under the blue tarp that covered the mess tent just as the rain was starting. Kayla wished she would have brought her rain jacket. Now she'd have to either wait for the rain to stop or get drenched running back to her tent. This day was starting off wonderfully.

Kayla grabbed an apple, a granola bar, and a glass of water from the communal water jug. Thankfully, whoever was in charge of bringing the purified water had done their job well. In this heat, even with the intermittent rainstorms, having clean drinking water readily available was a must.

Kayla dropped into a nearby chair and tossed her food on the white plastic tabletop gently. Still worn out from her dream and the subsequent lack of sleep, she opened the granola bar and picked at it, staring at the table. Usually, she was a morning person. Not today.

She didn't know how long she'd been staring at the table, but she suddenly noticed she could see the muted red skin of the apple in front of her clearly. The sun was finally up, fighting with the rain and mostly losing. The rain was coming down harder now, incessantly pelting the tarp above her head. A sigh escaped her. She'd be here awhile.

Just then, she heard staccato footsteps splashing toward her. She looked up to see Grady jogging through the rain toward the shelter of the mess tent. He stepped under the tarp and jerked his head quickly from side to side, sending a spray of water toward Kayla. Though the water was warm, she jumped in her seat, nearly knocking over her chair. Grady laughed.

"Not nice," she mumbled in his direction as she grabbed a napkin from the table dispenser and began drying herself off.

She stole another look at Grady as he grabbed some food for himself. Grady's hair hung in long spikes, water dripping from the ends. The royal blue shirt he was wearing clung to his chest, saturated with water. Kayla stared a little longer than she should have. She pulled her gaze back to the food in front of her with a little effort, hoping Grady didn't notice.

Grady dropped to the chair across from her, putting his own breakfast on the table between them. Kayla didn't dare look up. She wasn't sure she could avoid staring at his chest.

"Sorry for getting you wet."

Though Kayla wasn't looking at his face, she could picture his sheepish expression. She glanced up, careful to look him directly in the eye. His expression was just as she thought. She smiled bitterly in his direction. "Sure you are."

Grady chuckled. "Okay, so I'm not *really* sorry. Well, maybe a little. Just thought I'd be nice and apologize."

Kayla nodded. "Well, you needed to." A tiny smile escaped her lips, belying her words. For some reason, she couldn't stay angry at him.

Grady returned her smile. He still looked a little too cocky for her taste.

They sat in silence for a few minutes, Grady crunching on a granola bar of his own. Kayla, who had abandoned hers awhile ago, casually started on her apple.

"So how are you?"

Grady's question caught her off guard. Did she really look that terrible?

"What does that mean?" She shot back without thinking.

"You just look tired. Did you not sleep well last night?"

Kayla sighed, then shook her head. "Not really."

"Bad dream?"

Grady's intuition was a little too on point for this early in the morning. Kayla shifted in her seat and went back to staring at the table.

"You don't have to tell me if you don't want to," Grady offered.

If he'd pressed her, Kayla probably would have kept it to herself. But when he was being all nice . . .

"Yeah, it was a bad dream." She took a deep breath. Grady waited. "I can tell you, but you'll probably think I'm crazy."

Grady smiled sweetly, no hint of teasing. "Hey, we're all a little crazy."

She smiled, then, with a deep breath, began relaying her story. She first told him about her vision in the cavern, then about the eerily similar dream she'd had. Grady didn't interrupt, but Kayla watched his eyes widen more than once.

When she was done, Grady leaned back in his chair and crossed his arms across his chest. Silence stretched between them as she let him process all the information she'd given him.

One word broke the silence. "Wow."

Kayla's mouth turned up a little on one side. "I know."

"So what does it mean?"

She shrugged, her fingers playing with her granola bar wrapper. "I'm not sure."

Grady just nodded, a look of concentration on his face. Kayla had had at least twelve hours to process this, at least some of it, and she still was in shock. Grady could take all the time he needed.

But he needed to know everything first. Kayla drew in a deep breath. "I didn't tell you the last part," she whispered.

Grady's jaw dropped, just a little. "There's more?"

Kayla nodded once. "My dream was exactly like the vision I had—until the end."

Grady leaned forward in his chair. "What did you see at the end?"

She took a deep breath. "First, there was a blinding light. Then I saw one last picture." She didn't continue, even knowing what Grady would certainly ask next.

"What was the picture of?"

Yeah, that was the question. Kayla hesitated. This was the really crazy part. Was she ready for Grady to know just how insane she really had become?

She steeled herself, then continued. "The bright light faded into the picture of a mountain." She folded her hands on the table and stretched them out in front of her. Her eyes bored holes into them.

Grady laid his hands on top of hers. Kayla twitched at his touch, but didn't pull away. Her eyes flew to his, and he stared right back. "You can tell me."

Kayla held his gaze, suddenly feeling a little better. Something about staring into his sapphire eyes made her feel almost confident, a little more sure of herself. "I've never been there, never seen a picture of this place, but somehow I know where it is. And I don't know why, but . . ." she let her voice trail off as she looked back down at where their hands touched. Her next words were a whisper. "Something is calling me there."

She expected Grady to chuckle, or make some snide comment about her really being crazy, but when she didn't hear anything, she looked up. Grady was staring at her blankly. That couldn't be good.

Finally, he spoke. "Where is it?"

Kayla blinked. "That's it?"

Grady's eyebrows scrunched together. "What do you mean?"

"I mean, you're not going to tell me how crazy I am? How I should be committed, or, at the very least, sent home?"

Grady's forehead smoothed out and the beginnings of a smile pulled at his lips. "No. I don't think you're crazy."

Kayla sighed and sat back in her chair. "Then you're as crazy as I am."

Grady chuckled and leaned back himself. After a few moments, he said, "So are you going to tell me where we're going or not?"

"We?" Kayla couldn't keep the shock from her face.

"Of course." He sounded so sure of himself.

Kayla crossed her arms. Was she ready for this? Was she ready to travel across continents with the man in front of her?

She realized quickly and with little surprise that, since the moment she'd glanced over at him in front of that computer monitor less than two days ago, the answer had always been yes. She'd go anywhere with him. Or, in this case, take him anywhere with her.

Grady's voice broke into her thoughts. "So? Where are we going?"

Kayla grinned. "Alaska."

CHAPTER 6

Capture

Somewhere in the Belize Rainforest

THE ELDERS ASSEMBLED ALL the men of the Clan and sent them into the forest to train with Na-um. Such an overt display of confidence in his abilities made Na-um breathe a little easier. The Elders trusted that he could prepare these men for battle. Na-um was actually starting to believe it himself.

Na-um taught them all the ways of the Hunter. Some were skilled in archery or the way of the spear; Na-um gave them their arrows and oversaw their target practice. He taught them the art of weaponry-based combat, showing them how to stalk and capture their prey before their quarries even knew they were being pursued. He taught them well, and soon at least a dozen men were as skilled as he was in the hunt.

Others were skilled in hand-to-hand combat; these he trained personally, man to man. He showed them various combative maneuvers, both offensive and defensive, trying to simulate every possible scenario before pairing them off to train further.

To those who were new to the fight, to the training, he assigned tasks after a quick analysis of their strengths. He found a few men who were exceptionally strong; these he trained in hand-to-hand combat with the others, so they were able to use their strength to their advantage. The others were divided and sent to different groups according to their abilities.

The youngest man among the newer recruits was of a slighter build than the others, his long black hair unkempt and his clothes slightly more tattered than the rest. At first glance, he seemed to have little to offer their small force. Na-um studied him carefully, watching as he failed exercise after exercise. The young man, a boy called Holun, was barely old enough to fight, still a child.

Na-um studied him carefully for several days, trying to understand this boy's inept mannerisms. By the fifth day, he was about to give up on the boy and send him back to the village. He decided to allow the boy one more chance, one last chance to prove his worth.

He watched with idle curiosity as the boy fought with one of the other younger but clearly stronger men, something he'd not yet seen the boy Holun do. They grappled in the dirt for a few minutes, the other boy clearly holding a steady advantage.

The two fighters were eventually on their feet, locked in a face-off, waiting for the other to attack. The older recruit stood a foot taller than Holun; Na-um was surprised the younger boy had lasted this long. Na-um watched with steadily increasing interest, half expecting the same outcome as the exercises before.

But as he watched in growing disbelief, the strangest thing happened. The younger boy closed his eyes and froze, standing completely still for a split second—the pause was not even long enough for the other soldier to react. Na-um wondered for a moment if perhaps he had simply blinked.

When Holun came out of the momentary trance—after only a second—he opened his eyes just as the other boy lurched toward him to attack. Right before the other recruit could touch him, he jumped to the side, just out of reach. The older boy fell to the ground, stumbling as he missed his mark. Holun seized the opportunity, kneeling on his attacker and restraining him.

Na-um's mouth dropped open slightly. The youngest of their soldiers had won the fight despite the other boy's disproportionate advantage; Na-um was impressed.

As Na-um watched the boy's reaction to his unlikely victory, he saw something in his eyes, something he couldn't explain. He watched as Holun quickly composed himself, not bothering to rejoice in his success, then return to his place in the nearby formation. Na-um considered it for a moment, then called to him.

Holun hurriedly rushed to his superior's side, snapping to attention in front of him. *He's entirely too eager for his own good,* Na-um thought, fighting to contain his smile.

Na-um chose to start with an easy question. "How old are you, son?"

The young boy hesitated. Well, it *should* have been an easy question.

"Answer," Na-um demanded, his anger flaring.

"I'm sorry, sir. I don't know. My family was gone before I was old enough to remember them, and no one knows where

I came from. I have been staying with Tohil." Surnames were considered an unnecessary formality in the Clan.

Na-um nodded. He vaguely remembered such a story, of a young boy orphaned and taken in by the Elders. He rephrased his question. "Are you old enough to fight?"

"Yes, sir." Holun nodded vigorously.

"And given your performance of the past few days, do you believe you will be an asset to our force?" He didn't really try to hide his critical tone.

Holun hung his head, his eyes dropping to the ground. "I have tried my hardest, sir. It seems that my skills lie elsewhere."

Something about the way he said that last part piqued Na-um's interest. Maybe this boy would explain what he thought he had seen in the earlier scuffle. His eyebrows rose quizzically. "And what skills are those?"

Holun once again looked up at him, a blank expression crossing his boyish features. "It is hard to explain, sir. Perhaps I can show you?"

Na-um nodded once. "You may."

The young boy's eyes fell closed. Na-um felt an ethereal chill trickle down his spine. Though the gesture was simple, the effect was eerie.

After about half a minute, Holun opened his eyes. "Most of us will be training for at least a few more days, and in a rainstorm. The Elders are not ready for us yet. But a small contingent will be called upon soon for an important task."

Na-um was speechless—he hadn't told anyone of his plans to send a small group of soldiers to Lamanai in the near future . . . how could this young boy possibly know that?

Holun smiled at him unassumingly, as if he was expecting this reaction, and remained silent.

Na-um recovered quickly. "What was that?"

Holun shrugged nonchalantly. "I can see what's going to happen."

Na-um had seen too much in his life, heard too many legends to doubt this boy's words. "Impressive. How does it work?"

Holun smiled. "I just close my eyes and the visions come. The longer my eyes are closed, the farther out I can see."

Na-um returned his smile. What a fortunate turn of events! "Does anyone else know of your ability?"

Holun shook his head. "No, sir, I don't believe so. I just learned of it myself recently. I've been testing it in secret."

Na-um was ecstatic. As far as he knew, this was unprecedented in their Clan—and he was well versed in the Clan's histories. He ordered Holun to continue to keep his ability a secret, but knew he would take this new knowledge into account as he prepared for the impending conflict.

He continued to train his small but determined force as the rains came, just as Holun had predicted. He knew his people wouldn't have another chance for this to work, once the final battle began. They would all need to know how to fight as he could, so they would prevail.

The next few days were filled with constant practice and growing anticipation, and Na-um began to tire. He knew this training was necessary—vital, even—but he couldn't help but become impatient. When would the Elders give the order? When could they fight?

The answer came that night.

Lamanai Archaeological Project, Northern Belize Rainforest

The morning dawned bright and clear, and uncharacteristically cool for this time of year. The heavy rains that had drenched the dig for the last few days had fortunately stopped—for now, anyway—leaving the air thick but chilly.

Kayla was up with the sun. She dressed hurriedly, layering her light khaki pants and deep blue tank top with a light-weight tan work shirt. She knew that, despite the cool breeze blowing now, the day would heat up considerably in a hurry. She exited her tent early and couldn't help but smile brightly when she found Grady at breakfast, wearing khaki pants with a black polo shirt stretched across his chest. She noticed Grady's returning smile a second too late, but nothing in his expression told her he noticed her lingering glance at his chest. She was beginning to think he was either very unobservant or very gracious. She didn't think it was the former.

After breakfast, as she and Grady approached the off-road vehicle that would take them to the airport, Kayla surveyed the group loading their gear into the SUV.

Of the easily two dozen workers presented the opportunity to travel with them—Kayla and Grady had held a short meeting last night around the campfire to discuss their upcoming trip—only three people had shown up for the expedition that morning, one of whom had offered only to drop them off at the airport. Still, Kayla was grateful for the support they *did* have, and determined to make the best of it.

Kayla and Grady exchanged introductions and good mornings with the three men as they tossed their bags in the back of the vehicle. They took the front seats as their small group jumped in the back and began the long, bumpy drive to Belize City.

A few miles down the road, however, the SUV started sputtering, shaking and jerking all over the road. Kayla glanced over at Grady, who was clutching the steering wheel in an attempt to keep the vehicle under control. Just before she opened her mouth to ask what was going on, the SUV jolted violently, then stalled. Grady, groaning from the driver's seat, threw the vehicle in park and jumped out. "Everyone stay put for now; I'll see what the problem is."

Kayla ignored him. She hopped out of her side of the car, slinging her backpack over her shoulder. She still hadn't found her missing notepad—it hadn't been in the work trailer as she'd hoped—so she wasn't going to let anything else important out of her sight. "What is it, Grady? What happened?"

Grady was crouched down at the back of the SUV with one hand on the bumper to steady himself, looking underneath. "Great. It looks like something cut the gas line."

"What?" As Kayla leaned down to look, she saw a small object protruding from a rubber hose underneath the vehicle. "What is that?" she asked, pointing at it.

Grady had seen it too. He reached for it, dislodging the object.

"Be careful," Kayla breathed.

As he turned the small object over in his hand, Kayla shivered, realizing what the sharp object that Grady now gingerly held between his thumb and forefinger really was.

In his hand was a small arrowhead, one clearly handmade but also clearly very deadly. She looked toward the surrounding forest, contemplating what kind of person would do something like this, eyeing the foliage for any sign of trouble. It was then that she noticed something stuck in the back tire —another razor-sharp arrowhead, larger than the first but shaped just like it. A quiet gasp escaped her lips.

Grady's eyes shot to her face. Kayla could feel his eyes on her, but she couldn't look away. Her gaze was locked on the arrowhead jutting out of their back tire.

She knew when Grady saw it. "Okay, this can't be an accident."

Kayla was frozen, staring into space and trying to make sense of the situation, when suddenly she felt Grady jerk beside her. But before she could turn to him, she caught something out of the corner of her eye that looked a lot like a flame . . .

Then she heard Grady in her ear: "Kayla, run. Now. RUN!" He shoved her toward the trees, away from the SUV, then smacked the palm of his hand hard on the back door as he yelled to those inside. "GET OUT! NOW!" In the next moment, only seconds after he'd started running for the trees, the SUV exploded, shattering into a million pieces. The force of the explosion knocked Kayla forward and she crashed to the ground. She felt the heat of the blast scald the back of her legs as the flames licked the morning air.

It only took her a second to figure out what had happened. She leapt to her feet. "NO!" Kayla screamed, reaching back instinctively toward her new friends in the now unrecognizable vehicle. Grady grabbed her around the waist, holding her back. Another smaller explosion made them both jump and fall back to the ground. Kayla was sobbing, tears streaming down her face; she couldn't remember when she'd even started crying. "Why?" she wailed between sobs. "Why would someone do this?"

But Grady didn't have time to answer. Suddenly Kayla felt herself being torn from the ground. Before she could react, she felt a sharp pain at the back of her head; then everything went black.

University of Central Florida, Orlando
"Mandy! Phone!"

Mandy Carlson, a third-year student in UCF's graduate-level Maya Studies program, looked up from the suitcase she was packing and made a face. She flicked her mid-length strawberry blonde hair away from her neck in disgust. Though she loved her boyfriend of three years, Justin Stanford, she knew he knew it, too; that was the problem. He frequently took her for granted—and she hated the aggravating way this sometimes made him act. *I'm not an animal,* she thought. *You could've asked nicely. Or, heaven forbid, actually bring me the phone.*

She found her blond-haired, blue-eyed boyfriend in the living room, holding the cell phone she'd left on the coffee table. His eyes never left the TV as she snatched the phone away from him. She glared at him with her hazel eyes on her way to the kitchen, though he was too enthralled by the TV to notice.

"Yes? This is Mandy Carlson."

"Ms. Carlson, this is Dean Stewart." The caller wasn't really a surprise. Her "teacher's pet" reputation at school had begun to include the deans as well.

"Hello, how are you?" She kept it formal. The man was kind and gracious but Mandy still found him a little intimidating, even over the phone.

"Fine, fine. I have a request, if you don't mind."

"Sure, what is it?"

He hesitated almost imperceptibly, but she caught it. "Do you know Drs. Harrington and McGready?"

Her heart jumped a little. A knee-jerk reaction—a subconscious habit she couldn't suppress whenever she heard his name. "I was in one of Dr. McGready's classes last semester. Is he okay?"

Another moment of silence, this time glaringly obvious. When the dean didn't respond, Mandy asked another question. "What happened?"

She heard him sigh. "Ms. Carlson, Dr. Harrington and Dr. McGready are missing. They were at the Lamanai dig, working, and they seem to have found something. But as they were heading to the airport in Belize City this morning they were . . ." He paused, then tried again. "Well, by all accounts, it looks like they were *ambushed*."

Mandy's next word came out a whisper. "What?"

Dean Stewart sighed through the phone. "I'm sorry to drop this on you so suddenly, but I knew you were headed to Lamanai tomorrow, anyway, so I wanted to ask if you would head up the search party."

Mandy couldn't help but get a small bit of satisfaction from his request. Finally, her years of making nice with the teachers were paying off. And if *she* were the one to find them . . . "I would be happy to." In her sophomore year at the university, she had met Professor Grady McGready, immediately developing a crush. She had since matured and grown out of it, but was still concerned with his well-being—probably a little more than she should be.

Maybe she hadn't grown out of it as much as she'd like to think.

The Dean sounded exceptionally relieved. "Please find them. Our school can't afford to lose such great archaeologists—or such great people."

Mandy smiled. She knew Dean Stewart well enough to know he really did care about his people. "Justin and I were just packing for our flight in the morning. Should we leave sooner?"

"No, the morning's flight is the first one headed that way. Please let me know what you find out. We're all concerned for them; any news would be greatly appreciated."

Mandy smiled, her dimples making an appearance in the empty room. "Will do."

He hung up without another word.

Mandy's smile faded as she let the situation sink in; this news was particularly distressing. She always looked forward to Grady's classes—what was wrong with a little ogling? She vaguely remembered Professor Harrington—she thought she'd had a class with her a few semesters ago—but couldn't quite recall what she looked like. Mandy was always more attentive when it came to the opposite sex.

"Justin!" She yelled too loudly. She smirked as she returned his earlier favor. *See how you like it.*

Unfortunately, as she had come to expect, he didn't notice her subtle rebuke. He simply loped into the room, energy drink in hand. "What's up? What'd the dean want?"

She rolled her eyes at her always less-than-attentive boyfriend. "Something happened at the dig. Grady McGready and Professor Harrington were attacked on the way to Belize City. No one can find them, so they want us to head up the search."

Justin grinned. Mandy knew without asking that he would be overly excited about such an adventure—and though she would never admit it, it was one of the reasons she put up with him. "Cool!" He took a large final swig from his drink, then chucked it into the recycling bin with a large, dopey grin. "Let's go pack."

He sprinted ahead of her into their bedroom. She followed with the intention of finishing up her own packing. Of course, that happened eventually.

CHAPTER 7

Captivity

Rainforest, Location Unknown

KAYLA WOKE SLOWLY, her head throbbing. She was sitting up, slumped over in a chair. How had she managed to stay upright while asleep? She struggled to remember what had happened, but could only remember bits and pieces. Where was she? How did she get here?

She opened her eyes, but was met with nothing but darkness. She tried to move her hands to clear her vision. The movement sent sharp pain through her wrists and up both arms. Panic squeezed her chest until she could barely breathe as she realized why her arms weren't moving—her hands were tied behind her back.

Abruptly shaken from her stupor, she quickly realized something was obstructing her vision. She wanted to call out to Grady, try to see if he was nearby, but something was covering her mouth, too. It tasted like blood and sweat, and the salty flavor nauseated her. Though she didn't know where she'd go, she tried to get to her feet. But whoever had brought her here was thorough—her feet were bound to the legs of the chair she was sitting on, effectively binding her to her dark prison.

Someone was coming; she could sense it. She stopped struggling instinctively, hoping that whoever it was didn't intend to cause her additional harm. *Unlikely*, she thought.

The intruder ripped the shroud from her eyes, yanking out some of her hair in the process. Kayla yelped through the gag in her mouth; she couldn't help it. Her eyes adjusted to the light and she noticed Grady sitting a few feet from her, his head slumped over as if still asleep. Her loud howling did not seem to wake him; she figured that he must still be unconscious from whatever had knocked her out.

The man in front of her—bulky and by no means in shape —was barely covered in scant strips of what was probably homemade leather. His body seemed to fill the tent as he roughly wrenched the gag out of her mouth while shouting something at her in a language she didn't quite recognize. She stared at him, uncomprehending. He rolled his eyes, or some approximation of the gesture, then switched to broken English. "Why you here?"

Kayla didn't understand. "What?"

An enormous hand shot into the air just in front of Kayla. Her eyes instinctively squeezed shut, anticipating impact.

A quiet yet authoritative voice interrupted the angry man just as his hand was gaining speed. A small gust of wind blew across her cheek. Just one word in their captors' language had halted the man's attack, but the big man's hand had come very close. Way too close.

Kayla had to remind herself to breathe as the voice spoke again. Her eyes fluttered open, her gaze falling on the newcomer, the one who'd rescued her from almost certainly getting knocked out again.

The man was tall and muscular and was standing almost casually just inside the door of the tent, holding back the door flap with one hand, a clear invitation. He stared pointedly at the other man, who huffed loudly, then stormed out of the tent.

The newcomer was dressed very similarly to the previous man, but the strips of leather fell perfectly around his muscular arms, his tight chest, his thick legs. Black, unkempt hair fell around his shoulders, clearly unwashed but somehow managing to still look healthy. Kayla could appreciate the distinct line of his jaw and the intriguing sparkle just behind his deep brown eyes, but he wasn't her type. Of course, kidnapping her took him out of the running long before she'd ever met him.

The man spoke in accented, yet nearly perfect English, in sharp contrast to the previous man. "He meant, why are you in Belize?"

Kayla somehow managed to find her tongue. "I'm an archaeologist. So is he." She nodded to Grady, whose head was still slumped to his chest. The handsome man was still waiting, his barely covered chest heaving in unconcealed annoyance, so she continued. "We work for a university in the States, and are excavating the Lamanai site." She wasn't sure how much she wanted to tell this stranger, so she stopped, waiting for him to respond.

He took only a moment to assess what she had said. "And where were you going?" It was odd, but Kayla had the thought that he already knew the answer.

"Belize City, to the airport. We were headed back home for supplies." The lie slipped easily off her tongue. She didn't like it, but when she needed to she could convince even the least gullible of people. And something told her this man would need a lot of convincing.

He eyed her suspiciously. Kayla could almost see his mind working, deciding whether or not he would accept her explanation. Kayla stared back, unblinking.

Grady started stirring, slowly coming out of his fog as Kayla had. Their intimidating captor noticed. He ripped off Grady's shroud, then untied the gag. Grady turned his head and spit on the ground. The man stared at him, then asked, "Where were you going?"

Kayla cringed internally. Had Grady heard her? Would he inadvertently expose her lie?

"We were going to the airport. We needed supplies." He shrugged, seemingly nonchalant in the face of their frightening captor.

Apparently the man wasn't expecting that answer. Kayla could feel his eyes shift to her almost immediately, but hers were on Grady. She was putting on her best poker face, trying not to give the man in front of them any reason to doubt their charade. It seemed to be working. Maybe.

With the man preoccupied with Kayla, his back turned away from his other captive, Grady winked at Kayla. *So he was faking it*, Kayla thought, the first glimmer of hope welling up inside her. *He heard our conversation. He's a better actor than I thought he would be.* She wanted to sigh in relief, but she kept her emotions from her face. Better not to give anything away.

The man folded his arms across his muscular chest, stretching the thin pieces of cloth tight against his skin. "My name is Na-um. I am sorry for this unfortunate turn of events, but I cannot let you leave. There will be a man at the door at all times; please ask him if you need anything. He is under strict orders not to touch you." He said the last sentence loudly, as if making sure the man outside heard. "We will bring some food in soon." He reached down and untied Kayla's hands. She rubbed her wrists as he went to Grady and did the same. Then he turned abruptly and walked outside.

Kayla glanced sideways at Grady as she leaned down to free her legs. "Where are we? What happened?"

Grady shrugged, touching the back of his head gingerly to survey the damage. He pulled his hand back quickly, wincing. "I'm not sure. These people must've been the ones that stopped us on the road. Are you feeling lightheaded?"

Kayla thought for a second. "A little. The gag made me nauseous." Her legs freed, she straightened in her chair. "How long do you think we've been out?"

Grady smiled at her as he leaned down to untie the restraints around his own legs. Once done, he sat up and looked toward the door. "Looks like we've been out at least for the day," he said. "Seems to be nighttime out there. Wherever 'there' is."

Kayla gingerly touched the back of her head then quickly removed it, wincing just as Grady had. Just her light touch shot shockwaves of pain and nausea throughout her body. Hopefully there wouldn't be any permanent damage. "Great. Well, at least it stopped bleeding. Wish we had something to put on it, though. It's gonna be sore for awhile."

Grady frowned and was reaching up to touch the back of his head again just as a young woman came in with a large tray full of food. She pulled over a small table and set it between them, placing the tray on top. Kayla eyed the various vegetables, meats, fruits, and breads hungrily, not recognizing everything, but not caring. The woman left without a word.

"Do you think it's safe to eat?" Grady's voice broke into her musings.

Kayla shrugged, her eyes still trained on the food in front of her. Her mind and body were warring inside her, her body begging her to feed it, her mind telling her to be careful. "I think they could have killed us a few times already, but they didn't. I don't think they'd poison us at this point."

Grady paused for a minute, then nodded. "I guess you're right." Grady grinned, and for a split second, Kayla thought she saw the Grady she was beginning to know quite well. She grinned back, grabbing the first piece of bread she could reach and taking a huge bite.

Grady and Kayla devoured the food quickly. When they were finished—or, more accurately, when the tray was empty—Kayla leaned back in her chair and closed her eyes. "What are we going to do now?" she asked to no one in particular.

Grady sighed. "I don't have a clue."

The next day—just before dark by Kayla's estimation—after a horribly uncomfortable and restless night but a full breakfast, lunch, and dinner, Kayla and Grady heard a noise just outside their tent. They had both been casually sitting on the ground in the middle of the tent discussing their current predicament—Kayla was enjoying their intermittent conversation, despite their circumstances—but at the sound they were both suddenly alert. Kayla's eyes shot to Grady's.

As the noise came closer, they began to hear the sounds of a struggle and someone yelling in what sounded like heavily-accented broken English. Kayla and Grady stood at the same time, cautiously walking toward the door opening. Before they could get there, though, two nondescript beings fell —or were pushed—through the door. Their heads were obscured by black hoods similar to the ones Kayla and Grady had worn, and their hands were tied behind their backs. As they stumbled into the room, Kayla reached for the one closest to her, trying to keep whoever it was from falling. Grady reached for the other one. Kayla carefully began removing the shroud from the person in front of her. Grady followed suit.

"Justin? What are you two doing here?"

Kayla glanced at Grady curiously, then looked at the young woman in her grasp as she began untying her gag. She did look familiar, though she couldn't seem to remember her name.

"Mandy?" Grady seemed to know their fellow inmates.

Grady turned to her after removing the one called Justin's gag. "Kayla, this is Mandy Carlson and Justin Stanford. They are grad students in one of my classes."

A light bulb went off in Kayla's head. She remembered Mandy as a student from one of her classes a few semesters back. "Oh, yes. What are you doing here?" The question came out more harshly than she intended.

Mandy answered first. "Dean Stewart sent us to find you. He found out y'all had left for the airport but never boarded the plane, so we came to look for you." Kayla smiled at her slight Southern drawl. She'd spent some time in the South, for sure.

Justin interrupted, continuing the story. "We asked around the dig, and Jack told us you had left for Belize City but that they hadn't heard from you, so we followed your trail and found the truck." His eyes darkened. "These *mercenaries*"—Justin spit out the word—"picked us up there, and brought us here."

Justin's word for their attackers sparked something in Kayla, as if she'd heard it somewhere before, or maybe it reminded her of something . . . She couldn't quite put her finger on it.

Mandy coughed pointedly. "Um, can y'all get our hands untied? I think mine are starting to fall asleep."

Kayla nodded, hurriedly reaching for the rope that bound Mandy's hands together. Grady spoke as he began untying Justin's hands. "I'm positive that these are the same guys that disabled our Jeep, and set it on fire. We found these odd handmade arrowheads stuck in the gas line and in at least one of the tires just before we were taken." He paused, and Kayla spied a lone tear in the corner of his eye. "I just wish I could've saved them."

Kayla walked over to Grady and put her hand on his shoulder, ignoring the way her heart skipped a beat when she touched him. "You did everything you could. You saved *my* life."

Grady looked up, a sad smile on his lips. "Thanks," he mouthed.

Just then, the man called Na-um walked in. "Sit down." He glanced at the two women as he nodded to the chairs in the middle of the tent. *A gentleman for a kidnapper,* Kayla mused. *Lovely.*

Kayla and Mandy complied, knowing arguing would be utterly pointless. Justin moved immediately to Mandy's side as Grady came up beside Kayla. Na-um looked directly at Mandy, then up at Justin. "Now what are you two doing in Belize?"

Justin spoke up. "Looking for them." He nodded to Kayla and Grady. Mandy nodded vigorously in confirmation.

Na-um exploded. "Why do you all keep lying to me?!?" he growled.

Grady crossed the space between them and stared Na-um down. "We don't know what you want. We've told you all we know."

Na-um leaned in until he was inches from Grady's face. "I want the truth."

No one said anything as the men continued their masculine posturing, neither moving, their eyes boring holes into each other. With her only thought of Grady's safety, Kayla stood and took a few steps toward the men. She put a hand on Grady's chest, inching between him and Na-um. "Grady, stop. *Please.*"

Grady lingered for a moment, his eyes menacing. Then finally, with a glance at Kayla, he backed off.

Kayla turned to look at Na-um, her hand still on Grady's chest. "Listen, we really don't know what you're talking about. We were just going back to the States for supplies. When we didn't show up, these two came looking for us. That's all."

Na-um still seemed unsatisfied, but her words seemed to calm him down. He looked at all four of them, one at a time, probably trying to assess their story. He grunted loudly then turned and stormed out of the tent.

Once he was gone, Mandy turned questioning eyes to Kayla. "What was that all about?"

Kayla shrugged. "He's been asking us that since we got here. Wanting to know what we were doing in Belize."

"So where *were* you going?" Mandy's voice dropped to a whisper. "We know you weren't headed back to Florida. Dean Stewart wouldn't tell us anything; said we had to hear it from you," Mandy finished as she and Justin moved in closer to hear what Kayla had to say.

Kayla listened for a moment, checking for eavesdroppers before explaining. For all she knew, someone could be right outside, listening to their every word. "Well, soon after I got to Lamanai, some of the workers found a tunnel. Grady and I went down to explore it, and found a giant room with writings on the wall." She knew she wasn't explaining anything, not really, but she was trying to keep it short, keeping the detail to a minimum. She continued, keeping her voice low. "The writings were stories of ancient Mayans, of their rulers, things we didn't know before." She could feel Grady's eyes on her, but she was careful to avoid eye contact. She wasn't ready to share her insanity with anyone else. Not yet, anyway.

She glossed over the next part. "We . . . found something in the cave that indicated something might be . . . uh . . ." she let her sentence trail off, glancing at Grady before finishing her story abruptly. "So we were headed to Alaska." She lowered her gaze. She had intentionally omitted the weird part, the *real* reason they were headed to Alaska.

Mandy blinked. "What's in Alaska?"

Grady shot a pointed glance at Kayla, who shrugged and answered Mandy's question as well as she could. "Honestly, we're not sure." Silence fell between them for a long moment. Kayla wondered how crazy Mandy and Justin thought she was after that poor excuse for an explanation.

Justin broke the silence. "So what are we waiting for? Did you have a plan to get out of here?"

Kayla released the breath she hadn't realized she was holding.

"Not really," Grady chimed in. "I've been trying to assess the situation, but it hasn't been easy with everyone outside. They won't even let us look out of the tent to see what's out there. They blindfold us every time they take us outside. Plus, we weren't sure where to go once we did get out. We were both unconscious on our ride here." A slight smile turned up one corner of his mouth as he looked the newcomers over. "Looks like you both fared better than we did." He paused, his brow furrowing for a few seconds. "Did your trip here give you any ideas? How long did it take?"

Justin shrugged. "About four hours, from what I could tell." He looked over at Mandy, who nodded slightly. "We were traveling at a pretty good clip, too, considering the condition of the roads. I think we were headed south, but I can't be sure. The sun seemed to be on our left side for most of the trip, though."

Mandy spoke up, nodding again. "Yeah, I think that's right."

Just then, a massive blast sounded nearby. Grady jumped. "What on earth was that?"

Justin grinned. "Our escape."

Justin ran to the tent opening to try to get a glimpse outside. It was just as he had hoped: the blast had drawn everyone to it, and the clearing was deserted.

But before he could rush outside, he felt Grady's hand on his shoulder. "Justin, what's going on?"

Justin turned around, grinning. "Just a little present for our captors. Timed charge."

Grady just stared.

Justin shrugged. "When they grabbed us, they just threw us in the back of their truck with a blanket over us. I found the charges and stuck one in somebody's pack. Once the car stopped, I was able to set it before they tied us up, put hoods on us, and walked us both here. Glad it didn't go off sooner!" He grinned at Mandy's glare, then jabbed a thumb toward the opening. "Come on, we've gotta go." He spied some leftover food on a table in the corner and snatched it up, distributing it among Grady and Mandy. "Take these. Kayla"—he nodded to the left of the door—"grab those."

Kayla snatched up the two large containers of water their captors had left for them—both were fortuitously nearly full—and Grady, evidently realizing what was going on, sprang into action. He reached for the blankets he and Kayla had been given to soften the hard dirt as they slept and shook them out before wadding them up in his arms. He nodded to Justin. "After you."

The Rainforest Outside the Mercenaries' Camp

Once outside, the settling darkness seemed almost comforting to Kayla. Perhaps it just felt good to be outside—to *see* outside—in what felt like forever. Those had been the longest twenty-four hours of her life—not that she had really minded, given the company.

She breathed in the cool night air as they all quietly ran through the nearby jungle, away from a large cloud of smoke smoldering in the distance. Under the cover of the trees, the group began heading in a roughly straight line north, guided by Justin's compass that was somehow still tucked away deep in his pocket, a nod to either the arrogance of those men or their ignorance. And Kayla didn't think they were ignorant in the least.

Just outside the Mercenaries' Camp

At the sound of the explosion, Na-um spun around, looking for Holun. Where was that boy? Holun would most likely know who'd set off the blast. He probably had even seen it coming.

After a few minutes of searching, Na-um spotted him in the village, across the main clearing. The boy's face was white, his expression blank, his eyes closed. Na-um's heart thudded in his chest as he sprinted to his subordinate's side with very little effort. "Holun?"

As Holun's eyes blinked open, Na-um could tell immediately that the boy had seen something, something he didn't like—something he wouldn't want to share.

When Holun didn't speak up, Na-um commanded in their native tongue, "Tell me."

The boy's eyes were wide. "Our prisoners have escaped."

"WHAT?!" Na-um bellowed.

Holun backed away, almost bowing. "One of the two that joined them today formed the plan."

"Where are they?" Na-um growled, his chest heaving.

Holun cringed. "I can't see them, and I don't know why. While they were here, I could see them clearly. But once they left . . ." His voice trailed off. "Now they're just gone."

Great, that's just great. A lot of help you are, kid, Na-um vented silently. But he knew this wasn't the boy's fault—Holun hadn't asked for these visions. Na-um knew they were lucky to have Holun and his visions around at all, even if his foresight was limited. But still . . .

Na-um drew a deep breath. He didn't want to take his frustration out on the boy—in all likelihood, he would need Holun on his side someday.

As if that day hadn't already come.

"Thanks, Holun, that helps." His words were sincere, and Holun visibly relaxed. "We'll just have to find a way to catch up to them, so you can see them again."

Holun smiled at him. Na-um had realized quickly that Holun didn't take well to scolding; he responded better to praise and reassurance. No wonder he didn't fare well as a soldier.

Belize Rainforest, Location Unknown

The four ran until they were exhausted, then slowed to a walk. They walked through the night until Kayla saw the sun peeking over the horizon; she thought it wise to be as far away from Na-um and his men as they could until they stopped to rest. She couldn't be sure if—or perhaps more accurately *when*—their kidnappers would notice that they'd escaped, so she wasn't going to take any chances.

Mercenaries' Camp

Na-um cursed under his breath. The men he'd sent out to find their escaped prisoners—a group of his best trackers—had just returned empty-handed. His men were stronger, faster, and much more familiar with the rainforest than the Americans. So how did they get away?

CHAPTER 8

Captivated

Belize Rainforest

THE SMALL BAND OF RAGGED ex-prisoners seemed to be making good time. They would only stop for a few hours at a time, letting everyone get some sleep in shifts, taking turns keeping watch. Kayla wasn't entirely sure they weren't being followed, so she made sure they were taking all the necessary precautions. She didn't want to be surprised again.

A few nights into their trip—Kayla hoped they were over halfway to the dig, but there was really no way of being certain—they stopped to rest longer than usual. The constant walking was making everyone especially weary, so Kayla decided that, since it did not appear they were being tracked, they could allow themselves a reprieve.

As Mandy and Justin slept nearby on the blankets Grady had stolen from their captors, Kayla and Grady were on watch, sitting together on a log they'd found in front of a small fire—a calculated risk Kayla had been willing to take due to the chill in the air tonight. A good-sized pile of dirt stood next to it to snuff out the fire in a matter of seconds if the need arose, but, for now, the warmth was downright comforting.

Kayla, for the last hour or so, had been staring off into the dark trees trying to make sense of everything that had transpired. Not much of it actually *made* sense. She stole a glance at Grady out of the corner of her eye; he was staring into the fire, clearly deep in thought. Kayla thought she saw something in his expression—a look in his eyes that she was coming to know quite well. He looked like he was wrestling with something, maybe trying to make a decision. About what, she didn't know.

She really wished she did. Since that night in the cavern—a little over a week ago now—her mind had been driving her crazy with thoughts of Grady. How he looked, how he acted—everything about him had been suddenly on her radar, as if he had become the most important person in her life. She smiled. She supposed he had.

But, as she kept trying to remind herself repeatedly, she'd been down this road before. Her two-year relationship with one of her professors, Dr. Jonathan Cartier—the last, and by far the worst, in a string of heartbreaks—hadn't ended well, and that was a gross understatement. He'd left her in their shared apartment for a prestigious job across the country—abruptly—and Kayla, still young and finishing up her doctorate, had been devastated. Looking back, she knew her career was the only reason she'd survived. And now it was all she had.

For years, she'd been telling herself that she liked it that way, that her work was important and if she was going to be the best in her field, she didn't have time for anything else. Or anyone else.

Her work was certainly important, but, if she was being honest with herself, she was lonely. When her dad inevitably asked, she told him it was because she worked too much, or because she hadn't found the right person yet, but the truth was that she was scared. Scared to try something new, put herself out there again.

As much as she found herself attracted to Grady—and attraction was just the tip of the iceberg, again being honest with herself—she had to wonder: would Grady be the same? One of her many heartbreaks? She didn't know if she trusted herself enough to be able to put her heart on the line—yet another time—only to have it handed back to her in pieces. She had to take whatever this was with Grady very slowly. Wait for him to make the first move.

She doubted he was even interested. Or maybe, even if he was interested, he was a wiser person than she was and knew that it would never work.

That's when Grady's voice broke the silence with three words: "You captivate me."

His quiet, almost whispered sentence came out of nowhere. Kayla's eyes flew toward the sound. She never suspected—would never have thought in a million years—that his thoughts had headed that direction. Had he read her mind? As she stared out into the darkness, unable to keep the stunned expression off her face, she almost wondered if he had.

"What?" It seemed to be the only word she could choke out.

Grady shrugged beside her. "You always have, since that first night when we found the cave." He seemed unable, or unwilling, to raise his eyes, instead choosing to continue his staring contest with the flames in front of them. From the look on his face, he seemed determined to win.

Kayla drew in a shaky breath. She turned to him and stared at the side of his face, trying to make sense of what he had just said. Had she heard right? She had just told herself she would wait for him to make the first move, and in the next second he had—at least she thought he had. Maybe something—God, the universe—was trying to get her attention. Then again, maybe not.

Grady shifted on the log beneath them. "I've never really been able to understand you, Kayla, how your mind works. I've always wanted to know what's going on behind those intriguing brown eyes." He turned to look at her, catching her gaze and holding it.

Kayla attempted a shaky smile and tried to keep it light, an automatic reaction she hated but couldn't quite help. "Sorry to be so frustrating."

Grady smiled back at her. But, despite Kayla's unwitting attempt to save him from the conversation, he continued on, clearing his throat before speaking again. "You're not as frustrating as it would seem." Then his smile slowly faded, replaced by an uncertainty in his expression that made Kayla's heart beat just a little bit harder in her chest. "I would love to know what you're thinking, though, so I can bow out gracefully if I need to."

Kayla hesitated. Was she ready for this? She sighed in spite of herself. Ready for *what*, exactly? It wasn't like Grady was asking her to move in with him or anything. This was an undefined, open invitation to see where this thing might go. And she couldn't deny the admittedly strong feelings she had for him.

So she decided to take that leap of faith. "I actually don't think you're too far off at all." She bit her bottom lip for a moment, carefully contemplating her next words. She gazed off into the nearby woods, taking a deep breath before continuing, gathering every ounce of courage she had before turning back to him. This next part was going to be hard. Sometimes the truth was. "I find myself thinking of you when I least expect it. In the little time we've spent together you've become the most important person in my life." She drew another deep breath, shifting her eyes away from Grady. She found herself praying that he wouldn't throw this all back in her face, tell her she was crazy, play off what he'd said as a misunderstanding. She almost stopped talking, then steeled herself and finished. "I'm . . ."—she struggled with the next word—"*uncomfortable* with the thought of being without you." She timidly turned back toward him, keenly aware in that moment of exactly how much her heart was in his hands.

Grady caught her gaze and stared intently into her eyes. Kayla could see him struggling to catch his breath and found it suddenly hard to breathe herself. "I don't want to lose you either," he said breathlessly. Grady slowly raised his hand to her face, brushing her hair from her forehead. At his touch, Kayla felt her heart speed up, felt her skin start to tingle.

The fire crackled beside them as Grady held her gaze, his thumb lightly touching her forehead. For a brief, fleeting moment she felt a little uncomfortable, but the moment stretched on, and the discomfort was soon replaced by wonder. Kayla didn't want to look away. The significance of the moment stunned her. She was lost in his eyes—and by the look she saw in them, he was lost, too.

"So where do we go from here?" Kayla breathed, her voice barely a whisper.

Grady sighed, resting his hand on her cheek. Kayla's eyes slid shut. "I don't want to lose you," Grady repeated.

Kayla opened her eyes again, watching Grady's face as he lowered his hand and took both of hers in his, his eyes fixed on the spot where their hands met. She took another breath. "I'm not going anywhere."

Grady caught her gaze again and smiled, nodding slightly. "Neither am I."

Kayla smiled back at him, feeling something she knew was not physically possible, but felt very real nonetheless—she felt her heart expanding in her chest. In that moment, looking into Grady's deep sapphire eyes with even a small part of the truth of how they felt about each other out in the open, she suddenly felt a strange release, a strange *joy*. Kayla chewed on her lip—hard—to keep herself from grinning ear to ear.

Just outside the Mercenaries' Camp

Na-um still couldn't believe it. Over the past few days, he'd sent dozens of groups of soldiers into the surrounding forest. And every single man had returned with the same report: the Americans were gone. How could a group of four people elude them so completely? Na-um could accept one or two groups missing something, but by now he'd sent everyone he had—and not a single one had been able to track them down. Even Holun was still clueless.

Something was off; Na-um could feel it in the air. It was almost as if Destiny . . . no. He couldn't admit that, even to himself. They were right in their quest, he and his men. The Secret could not be released upon the world. It was much too dangerous.

But somewhere, deep in the recesses of his mind, that small voice repeated, over and over again: What if something *was* helping those four Americans, something bigger than all of them? Wouldn't that mean that *their* cause was just?

Not seeing another choice, Na-um returned all his men to their training. Let the Americans go now; he would catch them later on.

After all, he *did* know where they were going.

Belize Rainforest

Kayla's food supply was quickly depleting, and, even with rationing it, the water was almost gone. The long night of rest had helped them regain their strength, but Kayla was eager to get home. She wouldn't feel safe until they were back at the dig, or, better yet, out of the country. Maybe not even then.

On the morning of the fifth day, Kayla heard a muffled sound. The others had heard it, too; all four crouched instinctively, concealing themselves in the tall undergrowth. Who knew that five days in the wilderness would so drastically hone their survival instincts?

The sound was coming from in front of them, and seemed to be getting closer. Kayla glanced over at Grady, whose expression matched what she was feeling exactly. Had the Mercenaries been close all along, waiting for them to wear down, waiting for the perfect moment to attack? Had the menacing army of men finally tracked them down?

As the noise came closer, Kayla slowly began to recognize the sound—was that a car? All four remained frozen in their defensive positions, but began looking at each other with questions in their eyes. What now?

Then a Jeep came into view. They were well hidden in the trees, but from her vantage point, Kayla could see the driver of the vehicle. She exhaled, then heard the others follow suit as they recognized their savior. Jack McFarland drove up to them as they came out of the trees, waving him down.

Justin spoke first—a little too loudly, Kayla thought. They had been out here for far too long—her instincts were all off. Certainly the danger had passed. "Man, are we glad to see you!"

Jack grinned as he stopped and the four weary travelers climbed aboard. As soon as they were inside, he headed back the way he came, not wasting any time. "I thought I'd never find you guys! I've been out looking for days, hoping against hope that I would somehow find you. Looks like I was right."

Kayla tried to get her bearings, but after nearly a week in the forest, the trees had all started to look the same. "How close are we to the dig?" She desperately wanted to shower and get out of the clothes she'd been wearing for the past week.

"Only a few miles." They all groaned loudly. Jack laughed. "You've been gone awhile. We've all missed you." He patted the hand that Kayla was resting on the passenger seat.

She smiled over at him. "You have no idea how grateful we are. We've been walking for five days."

Jack whistled low in surprise. "No worries. We'll get you all cleaned up and feeling up to par in no time." Jack smiled, then his expression suddenly changed. "Oh! Kayla, I almost forgot. I've got a gift back there for you." He jabbed his right thumb between the seats toward the back of the vehicle. "Grady, a little help?"

Grady leaned back and reached for something stashed behind the Jeep's backseat. When he turned around, he was holding Kayla's backpack, the bag that held every one of her prized possessions—at least the ones that'd traveled with her to Belize.

"Oh, Jack, thank you so much!" She reached back and grabbed the bag from Grady, hoisting it between the seats while being careful not to hit Jack with it. "You don't know how lost I've been without this." She began rifling through it, utterly relieved to find everything still in its place, if a little worse for wear.

Jack smiled at her. "I thought as much. It was just laying there in the tall grass, near the Jeep . . ."

His voice trailed off and Kayla's mind immediately recalled that fateful explosion. When she thought of the men she'd really only met an hour or so before they were gone, she was grateful that Jack had declined their invitation to join them on the trip. The decision to stay had saved his life.

The remainder of the short ride was quiet. Kayla stared out the window while Mandy and Grady laid back, resting their eyes, and Justin sat with his eyes closed, rubbing his temples. Kayla glanced back at him and sighed. *Glad this whole mess is finally over.*

If she had been able to see what was coming, she wouldn't have jinxed it.

The mess was just beginning.

CHAPTER 9

Vision

Somewhere Between Belize City and Fairbanks

KAYLA SIGHED, THEN SET the sci-fi novel she was reading on the empty seat next to her. She couldn't concentrate, and being tens of thousands of feet above the ground didn't help. The events of the past few days had taken their toll, and she was exhausted.

She laid her head back on the headrest and closed her eyes; maybe she could sleep. Considering that she hadn't been able to sleep much at all last night—the previous day had been largely restful, but strange dreams she couldn't even remember now had made for a very restless night—she should have been asleep already, even despite the hundreds of tons of metal and steel beneath her, suspending her and her traveling companions in the sky. But something somewhere deep inside her was unsettled, and she couldn't relax.

She couldn't put her finger on it, didn't have the slightest clue what it was—she just knew that something was off.

Frustrating.

Kayla shifted in her seat and settled down deeper, trying to focus her thoughts solely on the rock music streaming through her earbuds—oddly enough, the only music that she could relax to; something about the incessant beat was soothing to her—hoping against hope that she could get comfortable enough to fall asleep.

Ha. Not in coach.

Then it happened.

Lamanai Archeological Project, Northern Belize Rainforest

"Mr. McFarland?"

Jack froze instinctively, wrench in hand, and stared up at the underside of the Jeep he was working on, as if the man calling his name couldn't see him if he didn't move. Yeah, right. That ship had already sailed. *What does this joker want now?*

Jack cringed as he scooted out from under the vehicle and sat up, leaning against the old Jeep's passenger door, knowing full well who was beckoning him. He pulled out a greasy used-to-be-red rag and began wiping his hands as he squinted up into the sunlight to see a dark-haired, tanned, middle-aged man in a monkey suit staring down at him. Surprise, surprise. "Yes, Mr. Barring, what can I do for you?" He asked, not bothering to hide his disdain.

The suited man, Lamanai's *liaison*—Jack used that word very loosely—from the Central American Institute of Archaeology, just kept staring down at him. "Um, I need to see some paperwork, and no one seems to be able to help me. I was told you're in charge around here, so I was hoping you would be able to find it for me."

Jack let out an exaggerated sigh, pausing before lumbering to his feet. He tucked the filthy rag into his pocket, smudging more grease on his dingy blue overalls, then headed off toward the work trailer.

Mr. Fancy Pants was mopping his forehead with his own rag, a white one that looked like it had come straight from the store. He probably had an entire suitcase dedicated just to rags such as these—though *rag* wasn't quite the right word. Handkerchief, probably. Just a day of using a *handkerchief* like that would certainly have destroyed it. Jack snickered to himself.

He led the way to the work trailer, the central hub of pretty much everything at the dig, including all the legal goings-on of this place. Jack referred to all the paperwork they kept as "a pile of worthless cow dung"—why did they need all that legal crap, anyway?—but apparently Mr. Barring here needed to see it, needed to make sure everything was in order. Jack wouldn't be able to make heads or tails of any of it. Hopefully Mr. Barring could, because he was on his own.

When Jack pulled open the curiously unlatched door to the trailer, he saw Jackie, his favorite student worker at the dig, sitting in front of the dig's only desktop computer. When he closed the door behind them, she jumped.

"Oh, Mr. McFarland! You scared me!" Jackie leapt to her feet, sending the wheeled office chair she was using crashing into a table a few feet away. "What are you doing here?"

A smug smile tugged at his lips as Jack crossed his arms. "I could ask you the same question." Kayla—who'd left with Grady and the other two Einsteins just this morning—had left him in charge in their absence. Sometimes having the authority card to play came in handy.

But Jackie had regained her composure, and seemed unfazed by Jack's reply. She smiled sweetly. "I was just sending an email to a friend back home. I hope I wasn't overstepping my bounds." Her brow creased in a worried line.

Jack let the smile he was fighting break through to his lips. "No, not at all."

Just then, Mr. Barring, hidden all this time behind Jack's large frame, coughed loudly. Jack stepped to one side, his eyes still on Jackie.

It was so small he could've missed it. If he hadn't been looking directly at her, he wouldn't have been able to tell. But in the split second that Jackie laid eyes on the man behind him, Jack saw something flash through her eyes. Something nearly imperceptible, yet utterly unmistakable.

Recognition.

Jack blinked, and Jackie's face was suddenly back to normal. "And who is your friend?" Her sweet smile had returned.

Jack blinked again, taking a little longer than he should have to answer her question. "Uh . . . um, this is Mr. Barring, with the Institute. He's here checking on our humble dig." He offered a silent "congratulations" to himself on his quick recovery.

Jackie crossed the space between them and offered her hand. Mr. Barring took it with what Jack could've sworn was confusion on his face.

Jackie spoke as soon as their hands met. "Pleasure to meet you, Mr. Barring. My name is Jackie."

The man still seemed a little flustered, but managed to find his voice. "Please, it's Alex. And the pleasure is mine, I'm sure." He finally eked out a smile.

Jack looked at both of their faces, one after the other. Their faces were both set in amiable smiles, perfectly normal. Had he been imagining things?

Jackie dropped the man's hand. "So, Mr. McFarland here says you're checking up on us. Is there anything I can help you find?"

Mr. Barring—Alex to Jackie, apparently—flashed a quick smile. "I believe so. I'm looking for the legal documents on the dig—permits and such—just to make sure all your files are up to date."

Jackie nodded. "Of course. They are right over here. Mr. McFarland, you don't mind if I show Alex around, do you?"

Jack, still a little stunned, simply nodded. Then he was suddenly outside the closed door of the trailer, not remembering how he'd gotten there.

What on earth was going on?

She was seeing it all again. All the scenes, all the pictures were flashing before her eyes, just as they had twice before. An overwhelming déjà vu inundated her mind as she stared in amazement at the images before her. She didn't bother trying to open her eyes; she was so lost in the images, the places—and the emotions they brought—that her surroundings had long ago faded away.

The scenes started speeding up, soon flashing by at lightning speed. Picture after picture, emotion after emotion—the visions were just as she remembered them.

The images stopped, just as they had in her dream, but this time they focused on the picture of the windswept mountain, the mountain she'd first seen what seemed like ages ago. As she stared at the picture that was now irrevocably embedded in her mind's eye, she realized she was expecting something else, something that followed the maniacal pattern of these visions. Something more she needed to see, to understand. Her mind anticipated it, waited for it, knew it was coming. Even if she didn't consciously know what "it" was.

And she wasn't disappointed. The picture of the mountain suddenly changed, as if she had been viewing it through a camera and the angle had shifted. In the scene before her, the sun was just setting below the horizon, casting muted shadows along the mountain's edge. Kayla gazed at the horizon. What was this vision trying to tell her?

She stared, eyes wide, as the picture zoomed in, rushing toward her at breakneck speed. Then, just before the mountain swallowed her, the picture abruptly froze, leaving Kayla a little dizzy.

Directly in front of her, an outcropping of rocks—a very specific set of rocks, Kayla knew without question—came into focus. Then, suddenly, she was in the scene. She was no longer viewing it as if through a camera lens. The entire scene surrounded her, as if a movie was playing in her mind's eye, but she was somehow experiencing it firsthand. She stood on the side of the mountain, taking in the scene before her. She felt, incredibly, the light wind blowing through her hair—she actually lifted her hand to brush it off her cheeks—and the warm sun caressing her skin.

She was here for a reason, and once the thought formed in her mind, she saw what she knew she'd come here to see. Her eyes widened again as the entrance to a cave, concealed in the rocks, seemed to materialize out of nowhere. She entered the cave, somehow walking though she knew she hadn't left her seat in the airplane. Her mind's eye was moving her through the vision. She didn't fight it, didn't try to rationalize it—she simply accepted it. She needed to see where this vision was taking her.

She ventured farther into the recesses of the cave, guided only by the light of the setting sun. She wasn't having trouble seeing in the near-dark; that fact alone reminded Kayla that she wasn't actually there. Everything else seemed so real.

The dark, uneven walls cast eerie shadows on the floor around her. As she traveled down the black tunnel, she realized that she was alone; none of her travel companions were with her. A lump formed in the pit of her stomach; this excursion was not something she had any desire to do alone. She hoped this part of the vision wasn't prophetic.

Then, with a dizzying rush, the vision ended. Suddenly she was back on the plane, staring at the back of the seat in front of her. She could only guess what the vision had meant. Was this vision, like her others, telling her where to look?

She abruptly shivered, though she wasn't cold. Another almost sinister thought had occurred to her: even if they could somehow find that dark tunnel, would they like what they found at the end of it?

She shrugged, mostly to tell herself to relax. *All part of the adventure, I guess,* she reasoned. She collected her things and glanced up at the not-yet-illuminated "fasten seatbelt" sign before standing and heading up the aisle.

She needed to talk to Grady.

CHAPTER 10

Alaska

Fairbanks International Airport

"SO WE'RE GOING *WHERE* EXACTLY?" Justin's voice carried in the nearly empty terminal as the four of them, stretched the width of the small carpeted hallway, headed to the baggage claim.

Kayla, half a step ahead of Justin, ignored him. She didn't want to deal with his questions right now. It was only about noon, but she'd been up all night and was eager to get out of the airport and into—hopefully—a nice, comfy hotel bed. Maybe a shower first. A long, hot shower.

"Kayla?" Justin's voice right beside her made her jump.

Kayla blinked, shook her head a few times, then offered what she hoped sounded like a sincere apology. "Sorry." She offered a sheepish smile over her shoulder but didn't slow down. "Just tired, I guess."

"So where are we going?" Justin persisted, hugging her left side. "Isn't this pretty much the middle of nowhere?"

Kayla could feel Grady's eyes on her. She glanced back at him and shot him her best "please save me" look, hoping he'd answer for her; she'd already filled him in on the plane.

Grady nodded once in her direction. "We're headed about two hours south of here." *Love that man.*

"Where?"

Kayla wanted to strangle Justin. She'd even have settled for snapping at him. But she bit her tongue, let Grady do the talking. And did her best to look exhausted, which wasn't at all hard at this point.

Grady hesitated. Kayla could guess why, as she herself suspected that giving Justin and Mandy the answer to that question would only lead to more questions. Questions she didn't know if she was ready to answer. At least not now.

Kayla sighed. She supposed it couldn't be avoided at this point . . .

"Denali," Kayla interjected matter-of-factly. She was simply too tired to fight the questions any longer, wherever they might lead.

"The mountain?" Mandy was struggling with her just-barely-carry-on-size suitcase. One of the wheels appeared to be broken. "How did you know to go there? And why did you wait to tell us until now?"

Would these two ever let up? Kayla sighed again. She supposed she'd brought this on herself. She so badly just wanted to sleep . . . was that too much to ask?

Kayla glanced over at Grady as they walked. The look in his eyes told her what she already knew, the truth she'd been avoiding: Mandy and Justin deserved to know.

Justin had apparently noticed the pointed look between them. "What?" He nudged Kayla's arm.

His touch broke her gaze with Grady. Kayla shrugged and adjusted the strap of her shoulder bag. "It's a long story."

Grady coughed beside her. She shot him her best "oh stop" look before turning back to Justin and Mandy. "Okay, okay. I'll tell you both the whole story on the way to the hotel."

True to her word, Kayla explained everything that she'd already told Grady, everything that Mandy and Justin had a right to know. She even added the vision she'd had on the plane. Kayla felt like she was baring her soul to complete strangers. This wasn't quite the same, but she nonetheless found herself fidgeting in the passenger seat as she neared the end of her story.

Mandy and Justin just stared from the backseat of the car, eyes wide. Once Kayla finished, they were silent the rest of the way to the hotel, save Mandy periodically uttering unintelligible words of astonishment at sporadic intervals. Justin, his eyes slightly wider than normal, just sat staring out the window, not saying a word. Kayla thought that was probably some kind of record for him.

Denali National Park and Reserve

Despite their sleepless night, the group met up only a few hours later, grabbing a quick dinner before heading out, eager to see what was at Denali. Kayla hoped she wouldn't be wasting their time.

They had all brought along their camping gear—Grady'd even had the foresight to pack a tent, though Kayla couldn't figure out how he'd gotten that past airport security—and stopped to purchase enough provisions to last them a few days at a grocery store on their way out. No one knew how long they would be in the Alaskan wilderness searching for whatever they had come here to find; it was best to be prepared for anything.

Kayla headed up the expedition once they reached the foot of the mountain. Since no one was really sure what direction they should be heading in, or where precisely they were going, Kayla had to feel it out. She hated it. She would much rather be following coordinates on her GPS, but her visions just weren't that precise. It was maddening.

They walked for hours, tracing a wide arc around Denali's base. They started heading higher as the terrain allowed, slowly making their way up the mountain. Kayla wondered how long they would be out here. Nothing she had seen today had come close to the images in her vision.

Though the sun was still up well past 11PM, they waited to set up camp until night fell. Kayla had hoped that sunset would have revealed the outcropping of rocks from her vision to her, but nothing happened, and the sun had disappeared along with her hopes for the day.

The group slept restlessly. Without anyone saying it aloud, the group seemed to designate shifts for themselves, and someone was always awake. Kayla figured they were just so used to it from their trek in the forest that it now came naturally. They couldn't be too careful, after all. Whoever had tried to kill her and Grady was still out there, and, in all likelihood, still trying to kill them.

The morning—though Kayla and the others slept through the better part of it due to their late night—broke unseasonably cold, and dew blanketed the grass around them. After a leisurely late breakfast, they packed up camp and headed out. They trudged through the wet grass in their warm fleece jackets—Kayla was thankful they'd had the foresight to purchase them before leaving the airport—and ventured further up the mountain. Again they walked for hours, stowing their coats as the sun began to warm the ground around them, chasing away the dew.

From time to time, Kayla could feel the eyes of the rest of the group fall on her, quite obviously looking for any signs of recognition or confirmation. Kayla could tell they were getting tired—and probably quite annoyed—but she was just as disappointed as they were when she found nothing.

She gazed at the sun, now low in the sky. Time was running out for today, just like yesterday, and she was getting tired. Kayla sighed, feeling despair start to taint her features. She felt Grady's light touch on her shoulder and smiled, slowly turning toward him. Under any other circumstances, Kayla's heart would've melted at the realization of just how much it pained him to see her upset.

She placed a hand on top of Grady's, hoping to reassure him, but her eyes didn't quite reach Grady's face. She stared past him, straining to see what had caught her attention.

Then she froze.

Grady jolted as his world came into sharp focus, his hand still on Kayla's shoulder. He reached out his other hand to steady her, grasping the tops of her arms gently; she looked oddly fragile, like she was having trouble standing.

Grady barely noticed as Mandy and Justin hurried to Kayla's side, searching her blank face for a sign—any sign—that she was okay. When they received no response, Grady could feel their eyes on him, but he had no explanation to offer. He simply stared at Kayla's expressionless face, his heart thudding loudly in his chest, and found himself praying that she was okay.

After what felt like an eternity, Kayla blinked hard, slowly coming out of her trance. Grady stared at her for a long moment, willing her to come back to reality. He knew Mandy and Justin would be staring at him, but he didn't care. He reached for Kayla's hand without looking away. He needed to know—needed to see in her eyes—that she was alright.

Kayla blinked again, looking away from Grady, and shook her head as if she were trying to clear it. Grady kept his eyes fixed on her face, still looking for a sign that she was okay. Kayla's eyes slowly met his, and, the second they did, Grady finally felt as though he could breathe.

Kayla smiled slightly, then she was gone again, staring past him.

Grady followed her gaze, his eyes widening as they fell on what had frozen Kayla in place. His breath caught. *Unbelievable,* he marveled. *She found it.*

CHAPTER 11

Tunnel

KAYLA REACHED THE OUTCROPPING in a matter of minutes with the others not far behind. She knew from her vision that an opening to a cave would be hidden in these rocks, but in the waning sunlight it was hard to see much of anything. Kayla continued her search mostly on instinct; as soon as she let her subconscious take over, the cave seemed to appear out of nowhere.

Kayla clicked on her flashlight as she led the way into the cold, damp cave. Though the sun was nearly gone—as nearly gone as it would get this time of year—the absolute darkness of the cave was still startling. Kayla clutched an arm over her chest. If it got much colder in here, she'd have to pull out her jacket again.

She trained her flashlight on the walls around her, pointedly ignoring the cold. As soon as she did, she let out a sigh of relief. The cave was just as she'd seen in her vision; she remembered it precisely. Her shoulders slumped as she finally began to relax.

But where was the rest of the group? They were being so quiet . . . She turned to look behind her, making sure the rest of the group was still following her.

"Ow," Grady muttered from two feet away, shielding his eyes with his free hand.

Kayla jumped and whipped her flashlight toward the side wall. She smiled sheepishly. "Sorry."

As she turned back around, she saw Grady smile in the dim light. She smiled to herself and reached back for Grady's hand, brushing it lightly as she continued down the tunnel. Grady caught her hand and held it, easily matching her stride as they ventured into the blackness of the cave. Kayla was grateful that, unlike her vision, she didn't have to do this alone.

A few surprisingly grueling minutes later, Kayla's light hit something up ahead. She couldn't quite make it out. She drew closer, slowing as she tried to make sense of what she was seeing.

Then she figured out what it was—and her stomach dropped.

They'd hit a dead end.

How could that be? Kayla was positive that this was the right cave. Was she missing something? "Hey, guys," she called to the group behind her. "Did any of you see any other tunnels off this main one?"

It was dark in here, even with all of their flashlights on, but she could still see Mandy shrug. "I don't remember seeing anything. And I was trying to pay attention."

Justin spoke up. "Yeah, I don't think there was another tunnel. I was looking for it."

Kayla nodded, hoping that the others could see it. This darkness was just so . . . thick, so stifling. Kayla fought off the feeling that the walls were closing in on her, and struggled to keep her breathing steady and even.

Grady, still holding her hand, pulled her a little closer. "Are you alright?"

Kayla swallowed hard, then nodded. "I . . ." She cleared her throat. "I'm okay. I just . . . I thought it would be here."

"Whatever 'it' is," Mandy mumbled under her breath, but Kayla didn't take offense. She knew exactly how her friend felt.

Grady took charge. "Everybody look around, see if you can find anything out of the ordinary." Just the sound of his voice, the sound of someone else taking charge, made Kayla feel a little bit better. She began to feel her heart returning to a normal pace.

After a few long minutes, Justin's voice echoed through the tunnel. "Hey, come look at this! I think I found something!"

Kayla hurried over to Justin, Grady just behind her. Justin was crouched down, peering at the bottom of one of the walls of the cave. Mandy was eyeing the wall from just behind his shoulder by the light of his flashlight.

Justin handed the light to Mandy, pointing to the spot where he wanted her to aim the light. He glanced back at Kayla and Grady, still pointing. "Look, here. Do you see it?" He sounded breathless.

Kayla leaned closer, straining to see what Justin was pointing to. Then she blinked, taking in the sight again; she recognized the familiar symbol, the one on the charm still hanging from her neck: the symbol for lightning. She shouldn't have been surprised.

"Amazing," Grady breathed from just behind Kayla. "It's just like the ones in the cave."

Mandy turned to him, wide-eyed. "What do you mean?"

Grady stood up, his eyes scanning the walls around him with the aid of his own light. A few seconds later, a low whistle escaped his lips. Instead of answering Mandy's question, he looked at Kayla. "Do you see it?"

She'd already seen it. A short chuckle escaped her lips. "Yeah. Incredible."

Mandy frowned. "What? I don't see anything." Kayla could imagine Mandy's younger self pouting.

"Look." Grady guided his light to illuminate the walls of the cave again. Slowly, Mandy's eyes followed the light. Then she gasped. "What does it mean?"

Justin looked over his shoulder at them, but didn't stand up. "What did you guys find?"

Kayla smiled. "That symbol you found there—it's all over the walls of the cave."

Justin just shook his head. "Crazy."

But then Mandy spoke up. "What did you mean before, about the cave? What cave? The one at Lamanai?"

Grady was still examining the walls as he nodded. "Yes. The cave just below the shaft we showed you"—Grady and Kayla had shown them the entrance to the cavern at Lamanai before they'd left for Alaska—"had this symbol all over its walls and ceiling."

Kayla took over. "We haven't been able to figure out what it stands for, not yet, but it means that we're on the right track. We must be close to something." She still hadn't told them about the necklace, and, because it still felt like a warning somehow, she wasn't sure she wanted to. No need to concern them unnecessarily. Although that man Na-um and his band of mercenaries just might force her hand sometime soon. She hoped not.

That's when she heard the crash.

Mandy shrieked, her heart pounding. "You could've warned me!"

Kayla was glaring at Justin. "What do you think you're doing?" She shouted.

He all but ignored her question. "Look, here . . . see?" He pointed near where he'd hit the wall just a few seconds ago. "This part of the wall is different than the others. There aren't any lightning symbols here. And the stone is a slightly different color! Plus," he grunted, smashing the butt of his light into the wall again, "this tunnel has to go *somewhere*. It seemed to me that this was the most likely spot. Considering . . ." Another hit, and a small piece of the wall went tumbling and crumbled to the ground. "There. Look."

Justin turned his light around, shining it on the wall where he'd just removed a piece of rock. Mandy didn't get it. "What? It's just more dirt."

Grady stepped closer, smiling slightly. "Yes, but it's not the same. It's finer, not as tightly packed." He reached in for a handful. The dirt wall gave way easily. Grady held up his hand, letting the dirt run through his fingers. "See?"

Mandy felt her jaw drop slightly as she looked closer. She could see the difference now in the color and texture of the dirt. "So now what?"

Grady flung his backpack off his shoulder, setting it on the ground and digging around for something. A few seconds later, he pulled out a small shovel, grinning. "We dig."

Elements

IN NO TIME AT ALL, the four of them had dug out a hole in the wall large enough to step through. Mandy bounced impatiently as she waited for the others to move out of the way; she needed to get inside. Something a little stronger than simple curiosity was building up inside her, something she couldn't explain. She had to find out what it was. And this room behind layers of centuries-old dirt held the key—she could feel it.

She stumbled through the opening and found herself at the top of what could only be described as an ancient staircase with long, wide, well-worn stairs descending into a darkened room below. Mandy hurried down them without a second thought. After only about six large stone steps, her feet landed on the sandy floor of what appeared to be a large room that stretched beyond the reach of her flashlight. Mandy was grateful for her five-foot-three-inch frame as her head barely cleared the smooth rock ceiling; she cringed as she noticed the others hunching over as they reached the bottom of the steps.

Before she could even figure out what to do next, Mandy heard Kayla and Grady beside her breaking several light sticks and placing them strategically around the room; the sticks glowed dimly in the expansive room, but illuminated it enough to explore. Mandy found herself grateful for their foresight; she'd have never thought of that.

Through the dusty green light, Mandy spotted a hole at the base of the rock wall to her left, and headed toward it with a wide smile on her face. She had to bend over to duck through the hole, but her smile grew even wider when she saw what was on the other side. "Hey, y'all, this looks like another room!" Mandy was unable to keep her excitement—or her Southern drawl—in check.

"Yeah, looks like I have one over here, too," Grady called back from across the room, out of sight.

Justin spoke up. "I found another one over here, too. I count three openings off this main room."

Mandy nodded to no one in particular. "Everyone please be careful—we don't know what we're walking into."

"Of course," came from Kayla, her voice muted, presumably by the thick stone walls surrounding them.

The room Mandy found herself in was small, nothing more than an innocuous cave. The ceiling was so high over her head that her light didn't reach it; the walls seemed to stretch higher and higher, never visibly reaching that extraordinarily high ceiling. The floor was the same sand of the connecting room, though the surface was not entirely uninterrupted. Mandy walked over to the far corner, kneeling down beside a pile of what appeared to be dark, old wood. She carefully picked up a long, narrow piece, turning it over in one hand while shining her light on it with the other. She reached for another piece, then another, discarding each one in turn. Could this pile of wood at one time have served a purpose? The wheels in her head started spinning, and she noted a twinge in her thoughts, like she was trying to remember something but it wasn't quite there . . .

Justin was suddenly at the entrance of her tiny room. "Find anything?"

His voice made her jump, the piece of wood in her hand clattering to the pile beneath it.

"Sorry." Justin shrugged as he entered, quickly crowding the space. Mandy stood to her feet, dusting her knees off before answering.

"Just this pile of wood here. And over there . . ." Mandy used her flashlight to point to a small pile of off-white scraps a few feet away. "That could have been some books or papers." She walked over for a closer look. "Yeah, that's got to be what that was." She leaned down, grabbing a handful of shredded cloth and lifting it closer. She frowned. "Doesn't look like there's any ink left on these scraps, if there was even any on here to begin with." She opened her fingers, letting the scrap cloth sift through her fingers like confetti. She wiped her hand on her leg. "Come on; let's go see what Kayla and Grady found."

Mandy didn't make it to the other side of the room. About halfway across the sandy floor, she froze. She couldn't explain it, but something was happening. Pieces were falling into place in her mind; everything was starting to make sense. The thing she was trying to remember before—but how could she be remembering when there was no way she could've known in the first place?—finally broke through the surface.

"Mandy, baby?" Justin's voice shook her out of her trance. She blinked a few times, coming back to the present, and stared at Justin's sheet-white face. For what may have been the first time in their relationship, she finally understood how much she meant to him, even if he never seemed willing to admit it aloud.

Mandy raised her hand, placing it briefly on his cheek, and smiled at him. "I was just thinking . . . this looks exactly like a crude home. That room there . . ." she pointed to the one Grady and Kayla had just exited at the sound of Justin's voice, ". . . could have been a bedroom or something, and the other one I found could have been a sort of library." She paused, realizing that her conclusions must sound crazy, but, oddly enough, she had never been more certain of anything in her life. "Someone used to live here."

For an excruciatingly long minute, everyone just stared at her, unmoving. Mandy doubted they were even breathing. *And now everyone thinks I'm crazy. Wonderful.* But regardless of the looks she was getting from everyone, she knew she was right.

Finally, mercifully, Justin spoke up. "Yeah, that makes sense." He smiled, draping a long arm around her shoulders. Kayla and Grady nodded in unison. Mandy was grateful that they weren't all mad at her—or convinced that she was insane. Mandy let out the breath she didn't realize she was holding and smiled.

"But we still have one unanswered question," Justin continued. "Where does that lead?"

The other three followed his pointed finger to the farthest wall. Mandy heard Kayla gasp just before she got close enough to recognize it. And her heart stopped.

Right in front of her, embedded in the rock so thoroughly it appeared as though it belonged there, was an enormous wooden door. She had missed it before in the dim light. They had all missed it.

Mandy hurried closer, stopping a few feet short of touching it, her neck craning to see the top. The monstrosity had to have been at least three stories tall; the ceiling curved up abruptly to accommodate it. The door stretched the length of the room, easily twenty feet across. Mandy searched her mind for a rational explanation as to how this door could've gotten here, how it was even possible that such a large piece of wood was in such a small cave, but came up blank. She stepped closer to the enormous door and began examining it in earnest.

The door was covered with strange markings ornately carved into the dark brown wood. Near each of the corners, four symbols stood out with stark clarity. Mandy stared at them blankly. She didn't really know much Mayan—or K'iche, as Kayla would say. She could almost hear her correcting her.

But the voice that reached her ears was Grady's. "What does it say?" Mandy glanced over at him to see him staring intently at Kayla. Made sense; Mandy didn't have a clue what the symbols on the door meant.

"These are ancient Mayan symbols, of the same era as the ones in the cave." Mandy didn't have to ask her which cave she was talking about. No one else seemed to have to, either.

But something was bothering Mandy. Kayla's voice sounded so odd, so foreign, that she wouldn't have even thought it was Kayla's had she not been looking right at her as she spoke. With everything going on around them tonight, not to mention all the events of the past week or so, the strangeness of Kayla's voice seemed particularly eerie. She just couldn't figure out why.

Justin didn't seem to notice. "So what do they mean?"

Kayla didn't answer right away, and Mandy was left contemplating what they could mean. Why were there four prominent symbols on this mysterious door—were they somehow significant in some way? She thought she kind of recognized the one on the top left . . . she strained to remember from class. *Was that the symbol for . . . what was it . . . wind? No, that's not right . . .*

Kayla interrupted her thoughts. "Air, fire, water, earth."

"What?" Grady's voice was a little louder than normal.

"The four elements of nature: air, fire, water, earth." Kayla reiterated, pointing at each symbol as she translated.

Mandy exulted. Of course! Air! That was the one she'd been trying to figure out.

Justin jumped in with characteristically excessive enthusiasm. "What does it mean, these four symbols together? What do the four elements of nature have to do with anything?"

Mandy wanted to roll her eyes.

Kayla answered him with what Mandy thought was the patience of a saint. "The four elements have to do with *everything*—especially to the Mayan people, I'd imagine, who by all accounts worshipped the earth. Everything in nature is comprised of some combination of the four elements. The significance of the four symbols together is remarkable. I haven't seen this combination together before in any of my Mayan research, but given the new information we found at Lamanai . . ." her voice trailed off.

Mandy's head was spinning.

Air, fire, water, earth.

The four elements.

What did it all mean? She peered at the symbol above her, the one she now knew stood for air. She stared at it for so long she could feel herself memorizing it.

Then, for no real reason that she could figure out, she took a few steps back, the low ceiling blocking her view of the symbol. The others were still close to the door and didn't seem to notice her.

But she was looking for something. And she knew the instant she saw it.

CHAPTER 13

Door

IT WASN'T READILY OBVIOUS, wasn't really obvious at all. Actually, it was just about invisible. In the dim light in here, her eyes couldn't decipher the difference between it and the wall around it. She couldn't explain how she'd found it, but she knew it was what she had been looking for.

"Um, y'all might wanna see this . . ." Mandy drawled. Though her voice had been barely a whisper, her words carried in the silent, echoing room.

She felt more than saw the other three come up beside her. As they approached, Mandy lifted her hand to a particular spot on the rock wall to the left of the door. She gently pressed her fingers to the rock, certain of what would happen next, nearly certain of how the others would react. But she didn't care; she knew she was right, though she had no idea how.

She took a deep breath then pressed a little harder, and the rock wall started to give way. A second later, the wall was crumbling beneath her hand. Tiny bits of stone broke off, tumbling through the wall and disappearing into a hidden cavity. After a few seconds, a hole the size of her fist had opened up. She stared through it, trying to see to the other side. For an instant, she thought she saw something—a symbol, maybe? But before she could comprehend what she was seeing, she saw a bright flash, then heard a small click.

Dirt and debris began raining down on their heads. Mandy and the others scrambled away from the door to avoid the rubble that now poured from the top and sides of the wooden door. They stared wide-eyed as the door impossibly dislodged itself from its stony confines where it had been imprisoned for what was likely centuries.

Gradually, the dirt waterfall cut off. Then, just as the last pebble fell to the ground, the door began to quiver, as if shaking loose from the wall. Mandy held her breath.

Suddenly, with a loud clap of finality, the door abruptly froze in place. For a long second, the silence rang in Mandy's ears. She stood in place, eerily still, eyeing the unmoving door. She didn't dare take her eyes off its surface.

Then, with a stunningly strong gust of warm air that threatened to knock her over, the door flew open, slamming against the wall behind it. Mandy lifted her arm to shield her eyes from the swirling sand.

When she lowered her arm, the door lay open with no indication of the chaos that had just transpired, save the scattered piles of dirt that had rained down on them moments before. Mandy stared into the room that lay behind the door and froze.

What she saw was inexplicable, terrifying. The room beyond the door was lit from an invisible source—shadows flickered, light dancing on the curved walls of what appeared to be a completely circular room, a dome of sorts where the walls stretched to meet the high, curved ceiling. Mandy couldn't believe what she was seeing, couldn't *let* herself believe. Clearly this room had been closed off for a very long time; how could a fire burn down here, beneath layers of dirt and stone? And wouldn't the wind from the opening door have blown out such a fire anyway?

With a deep breath that shook more than she would've liked, Mandy ventured into the curious room. As soon as she crossed the threshold, she felt that same twinge deep inside her—it was small but very distinct, and her breath caught. What was that?

She took another step, and she felt another . . . *something*—she could only describe it like a sharp prick inside her chest, though she felt no pain. What on earth was going on? Another step, and the feeling grew stronger. Another step, stronger still. She didn't understand it, but she had to find out more.

Mandy abruptly straightened and strode boldly into the room. She felt Justin reach out to stop her, but he was too far behind her. She was glad. She couldn't let him get in her way. She walked confidently to the exact center of the small room and stood with her back to the group. And something started happening.

Once Kayla saw that Mandy was unharmed, she cautiously entered the inexplicably fire-lit room, followed closely by Grady and Justin. Justin hesitantly crossed the threshold, but once he was through he ran to Mandy's side. "Mandy, baby, what are you doing?"

Mandy's back was to them, her face aimed toward the ceiling, eyes closed. Her arms were raised slightly, extended out on either side of her waist, palms up. She almost looked as if she were in a trance.

As she started across the room toward Mandy, Kayla noticed Justin had begun shaking. It was almost imperceptible, but Kayla immediately understood what was going through his head—she could sense how he was feeling. She was scared, too.

Kayla had reached Mandy and now moved in front of her friend, next to Justin. Then she froze. Kayla knew that expression—though she'd never actually seen it herself, she recognized it. Mandy's face epitomized what Kayla imagined her own face looked like during her visions. Kayla knew—though she didn't understand how it was possible—that Mandy was having one, too. She was sure of it.

She had hoped she'd be the only one in the group to go insane.

Grady was the last one to join the group in the middle of the room. He was scrutinizing the walls, the floor, the ceiling, looking for any clue as to why this room was here, why they could see it clearly by the light of a fire that shouldn't be there. After a quick, uninformative inspection of the room, he gave up, turning his attention to Mandy, who was just now slowly opening her eyes.

The sight sent chills down his spine. She looked *exactly* like Kayla did just after one of her visions. Had Mandy seen something, too? That seemed the only logical explanation. But how?

Justin's voice reached her ears. "Mandy, baby? Are you okay?"

Mandy blinked and lowered her chin to meet Justin's eyes. She saw him shudder.

She cocked her head a little to the side and furrowed her brow. Why would Justin be scared? She was feeling so many things: contentment, fulfillment, happiness—but definitely not fear. Not in the least. She opened her mouth to ask him, but he cut her off.

"Mandy, what's wrong with you?"

Mandy took a step back. "Nothing's wrong with me!" She couldn't help but snap at him. He had no right to berate her.

"That's not what I meant." Justin drew in a deep breath. "What happened?"

Mandy was pleased that his voice came out much quieter this time. She blinked, accepting his sort-of apology for now. "I saw something."

Kayla jumped in. "What did you see?" In those four simple words, Mandy knew that Kayla completely understood what had just happened to her. And for that, she was grateful.

Mandy closed her eyes again, remembering. "I saw—as if from someone else's eyes—this room, this place. Someone did live here; I saw everything as it would have been when they were here. This room . . ." she opened her eyes to look around, "was lit up, just like it is now, and over here . . ." she jogged to one side of the room while the others stayed frozen in place, eyes wide, "was a desk, a table of sorts, with all kinds of documents on them." She pointed across the room as she started back toward its center. "Over there was a crude bookshelf, with more manuscripts, and here, in the middle"—she had rejoined the rest of the group—"was a large book. And on its cover was a symbol, one of the ones we saw on the door."

Kayla interjected, as if she couldn't help herself. "Which one?"

Mandy smiled peacefully. "The symbol for 'air.'"

Mandy watched as the jaws of her companions dropped simultaneously. She chuckled, just a little, feeling like a weight she didn't even know she'd been carrying had been lifted off her shoulders.

Justin was the first to speak. "What does it mean?"

Mandy shrugged, though she suspected she knew the answer, at least part of it. "Not quite sure, but those symbols were important to the Mayans, as Kayla said. Clearly the word 'air' meant something to the person that lived here. Though I'm not exactly sure what . . ." Her voice trailed off as she tried to remember more of the vision.

Grady glanced over at the enormous door sitting near the room's entrance against the circular wall. "So, Mandy, how did you get that door open? I still can't figure out how that happened."

"I can't explain it." Mandy frowned. "I just . . . I don't know . . . *felt* something that drew me to that spot on the wall. I don't know what, or why, but somehow I just knew what to do. And this is the weird part—doesn't seem possible it could get any weirder, right?—I looked into that opening, and saw a symbol or something, but it was like . . ." she shivered, pulling her arms around her, ". . . like the door *recognized* me. Like me looking into that hole somehow opened the door. How is that even possible?"

Again, nothing from the group. Mandy was beginning to think she would always have that effect on them. It seemed to be happening so often lately.

When she didn't get a verbal response, she continued. "The door opened, and when I took a step into the room, something inside me responded to it. I'm not really sure what it was, but it kept getting stronger and stronger as I moved inside. Then, when I got to the center of the room, I closed my eyes, and I could see it: I was alone in this room, many, many years ago, seeing this room like it was back then."

She swallowed hard, trying to get rid of the lump that had just appeared in her throat. "But that book—the one with the symbol—was what we came here to find. I'm sure of it." She looked at Kayla, willing her to understand.

Kayla nodded, patting Mandy's arm. "I believe you." Then she smiled. "Head rush, isn't it?"

Mandy smiled. "Yeah." She was glad that Kayla understood. It was hard being crazy by yourself.

Justin jumped in. "So, Mandy, where is this book?"

Mandy scanned the room, then pointed. "There."

CHAPTER 14

Air

KAYLA FOLLOWED MANDY'S GAZE down to the floor beneath their feet. All four backed away from the stone slab below them as one, like some oddly choreographed play. Kayla stared at the sand at her feet intently, curious as to why Mandy would think the book would be here, under the ground . . . Then she saw it.

Peeking through a thin layer of light sand was gray stone, similar to the stone that comprised the walls and ceiling of this room. Kayla knelt down to examine the stone more closely; she could feel the stone slab digging into her knees.

There was more. She furrowed her brow, and reached down to dust some of the sand away. Her eyes widened slightly as the tiniest smile pulled at her lips. She began furiously uncovering the rest of the stone. Once they realized what she was doing, the other three bent down to help.

Before long, the four of them had completely cleaned off the stone slab. The slab was average in size—it was only about five or six feet in diameter—but formed a perfect circle. The four of them backed up again, retreating to the sandy surface just beyond the stone's outer edge. Kayla gasped as she fully absorbed the stone slab in its entirety for the first time.

Right in front of her, carved into the stone's light gray surface, was another set of Mayan symbols, identical to the ones on the door with one exception: the symbol for air was featured prominently in the middle of the stone. Surrounding the familiar signs was a carved ring of other Mayan symbols—a quick inspection revealed that they were the four symbols on the door plus the lightning symbol, repeated in a circular pattern—that marked the edge of the stone slab, where the stone ended and the sand floor began.

With a confidence that Kayla didn't understand, Mandy immediately stepped back onto the stone, kneeling near its center, just beyond the 'air' symbol. Without hesitation, Mandy deliberately stretched out her hand, palm down, and placed it directly in the center of the symbol. As she pressed, a perfectly circular section in the middle of the stone—the one embossed with the air symbol—started to give way. The sound of stone grinding stone reached Kayla's ears as the smaller slab began to sink into the floor. Before long, the grinding sound turned painful.

Mandy kept pushing for several more seconds until the hole engulfed her entire right arm and she was up to her shoulder in the opening. Then Kayla heard a sharp click coming from inside the hole and Mandy stopped. The stone had been pushed as far as it was going to go.

But the sharp click from below triggered something in Kayla. There was no logical reason for her to sense danger, but something inexplicable from deep inside her told her a very real danger was coming—and soon.

Right now.

"Mandy! Get out of the way! NOW!" Her shout echoed off the stone walls, hurting her ears, but she didn't care. She had to save her friend. She didn't need a repeat of the Jeep explosion. She couldn't live with herself if anything happened to this young woman.

Just as Mandy's hand cleared the hole, Kayla heard another awful grinding sound, but this time it seemed louder, more urgent. Her stomach dropped as she watched Mandy struggle to get off the stone slab. Without so much as a thought to her own safety, Kayla lurched toward Mandy, straining to reach her just as the stone slab beneath them started tilting. The stone was spinning on its axis, flipping itself over. Kayla didn't even have time to think about what was happening, or how. She just kept going.

In the blinding dust kicked up by the rotating stone, Kayla's hands miraculously found her friend. She yanked Mandy's arm as hard as she could, pulling her free of the stone just as it was reaching a vertical position, then stared in amazement as the stone continued turning until it fell back into place, completely upside down.

Kayla was speechless. Mandy's mouth fell open. Grady and Justin didn't make a sound.

Precisely in the middle of the slab, slightly larger than the hole Mandy had created on the reverse side, was a small, perfectly circular pillar. Atop the pillar was a book. And on the cover . . .

Kayla couldn't help but blink hard, check to make sure she wasn't seeing things. She opened her eyes after a few seconds and the book was still there. It was amazing enough that this book had somehow materialized out of that hole. But the thing that was stealing her breath was what was on the cover.

The Mayan symbol for air.

Before she could ask if the others saw it too, Mandy spoke. "Just like my vision . . ." she breathed.

The book itself was small—considerably thicker than a ruled notebook but about the same shape—but appeared to be light, with a brown leather cover. The symbol was pressed into the leather from behind, creating a sunken background in the negative space around it. It was astoundingly simple, yet majestically beautiful. Mandy ventured back onto the stone slab and reached for it.

As she touched the book, a faint light—so subtle that Kayla could barely see it in the settling dust—glowed unobtrusively around her fingertips. She began trembling, a slight shaking that rippled throughout her entire body, originating at the point where Mandy's hand was still touching the book's cover. The faint light traveled up her arm and encompassed her entire body until she was glimmering, shining. Her eyes rolled back in her head before they closed, and the tremors stopped. Then she slowly opened her eyes, her skin glowing only faintly.

"Wow, that was amazing," she whispered. Her words matched her tone exactly.

"Mandy, what happened?" Justin was behind her with both arms wrapped around her torso.

"I just felt . . . something . . . take me over. It was really intense."

"You were . . . *glowing*."

Mandy smiled serenely and leaned back against Justin's chest. "Yeah, I felt it."

Grady shook his head. Kayla could tell he was trying to clear away all the unsettling emotions of the past few minutes. She loved that she knew him that well.

Then he took charge. "Well, let's see what's in this book." He reached for it hesitantly, stepping in front of the stone pillar. Kayla watched his chest heave before he placed his hand on the book's cover. She found herself holding her breath, too.

When he touched the book, nothing happened. Kayla noticed his shoulders relax as she exhaled. She looked over his shoulder as he began to examine the book. Mandy and Justin leaned in for a better look.

The book itself looked easy enough to open, and, as the top cover fell to the side, Kayla noticed that the pages were filled with some of the same hieroglyphs from the cave. Grady took a step to the side, as if to give her room, and immediately she felt everyone's eyes on her. She ignored their speculative gazes and concentrated on the symbols in the book.

Kayla glanced pointedly at Grady, who seemed to know exactly what she wanted. He reached in a pocket and produced a small notebook and pencil, handing it to her as she turned her attention back to the book. She began translating the figures on the page as soon as the pencil was in her hand.

She ripped the first page from the small notepad when it was finished, not even bothering to look at her translation, handing it to Grady. She continued scribbling furiously on the next page of the pad, trying to get everything down.

Grady's brow furrowed as he read the hurriedly scrawled words on the page. Still staring at the page, he nudged Kayla's arm. "Uh, Kayla . . ."

She didn't even stop her feverish writing to look over at him. "Yeah?"

"This doesn't make any sense."

At this she stopped, leaning over to examine the words on the paper for the first time. Then she read them again. "Huh." She blinked. "I'm confused."

"What?" Grady handed her back the paper.

"Well . . ." she thought carefully, trying unsuccessfully to form a logical hypothesis in her mind before speaking it aloud. "These words seem to be in random order; it's just nonsense. Why would someone make a book like this? Where nothing makes sense?" She closed the book, frowning. Then she had a thought. There *might* be a scenario where that makes sense . . . But she couldn't share her idea with the rest of the group, not yet. It was too early to be making those kinds of assumptions. Besides, it was just crazy—though it seemed like crazy was becoming their specialty.

Justin rolled his shoulders, straightening his back. He reached over to pick up the book, pulling with a little force to dislodge it from the rock, but it wasn't budging.

Mandy smacked his arm. "Hey!"

"What?" Justin shrugged. "How else are we gonna get it out of here?"

Mandy reached over, placing both hands on either side of the book. As soon as she touched it, she started glowing again. Kayla just stared at her, trying to understand. Why did only Mandy glow when she touched the book? Why only her, and no one else? All of them had touched it, but nothing had happened to the rest of them.

Mandy clasped the book between her hands and lifted. As if the subtle glow of Mandy's skin wasn't enough to make Kayla think they were all going crazy, the book offered no resistance as Mandy picked it up. It simply lifted off the stone pillar as if it had only been resting there all along.

Justin snorted. "It can't be that easy."

Mandy flashed him a smug smile. "For you, maybe." Her soft chuckle echoed in the room as she gave it a final fleeting glance and headed for the exit. "Now who's up for some dinner? All this glowing is making me hungry."

Southern Belize Rainforest, Mercenaries' Camp

"Holun, can I talk to you?" Na-um strode to the door of his protégé's tent, calling out as he approached.

Holun appeared immediately in the doorway. "Of course, sir."

Na-um turned abruptly and headed off toward the nearby trees. He could hear Holun just behind him, scrambling to keep up. Na-um was glad again—as he often was—that Holun was so acquiescent. Helped keep the other troops in line.

Na-um and Holun strode through the town largely unacknowledged. Na-um knew the others noticed them—he could see the furtive glances of the townspeople as they went by—but they knew not to question them, wouldn't even dare say hello. What Na-um and his young second-in-command did was none of the townspeople's business. Though he'd never admit it, some days it made Na-um a little lonely. Today he was exceedingly grateful. What he had to say was not for prying ears.

Once they were a safe distance away from the camp, miles into the forest, Na-um spoke. "I just met with the Elders."

"Yes?" Holun was learning not to mince words.

"They've just received word—one of the books has been found."

Holun gasped. "No!"

Na-um nodded, his expression blank. "They are furious, understandably. They want to know what we are going to do about it."

"This is serious . . ." Holun stared off into the forest, but it was clear to Na-um that he wasn't fully understanding the severity of the situation. Na-um needed him to be more aware, and now.

"Holun!"

Holun blinked a few times, then his eyes shot to Na-um's. "Sorry. What can I do?"

Na-um hesitated. "Well, I have a few ideas, but . . ." his voice trailed off.

"What?"

Na-um sighed. "I've only ever seen them this . . . concerned . . . once before. Concerned enough that all five of them are attending the meetings. It worries me."

"When was that?"

Na-um cringed. He had never told this story to anyone, least of all his idolizing second-in-command, but Holun needed to know. He needed to understand exactly how much trouble they were actually in.

So Na-um drew in a deep breath, as if the extra air would give him some extra courage. He didn't think it helped.

For the first time since it happened, so many years ago, Na-um allowed himself to think about that day. Immediately, as if it had happened yesterday, the memories crashed down on him with an all-too-vivid intensity. As much as he wanted to run away from the pain, he knew he had to tell this story.

He felt himself reliving the ill-fated day as he began to tell Holun the whole story. "I once had a younger sister, one I loved very much. I did my best to protect her from everyone and everything—no one was allowed to touch a hair on her head without answering to me. Her name was Shani." Na-um took a shaky breath. He hadn't spoken that name in years, even when he was alone. He hadn't even allowed himself to *think* that name. "I swore that I would give my life to protect her. Then, one night, that all changed."

Na-um could see Holun's eyes widen just a little. "I was coming back from my training, much similar to what we're doing now, but with less intensity—the threat wasn't as near back then. I entered our large hut—I was regarded as the

Clan's most capable warrior even then, so my hut was one of the largest in the village, just as it is now—and I called out for her. I heard some shuffling, but couldn't tell where it was coming from. I didn't know if she was even supposed to be home."

Na-um's eyes drooped just a little. "I hurried through the hut, checking each room as I passed. The room she slept in was at the end of the long hall, the last room I had to check. I stopped for a second before I went in. The curtain was down, completely covering the entry. I knew something was wrong right away—we never let our curtains down. I got very angry—I didn't know why she wasn't answering me. So I tore the flap down. And there, standing next to the blankets laid out on her floor, was my young sister, the one I loved so much, pulling on and fixing her dress. Her long hair was down, nothing holding it up. But the worst thing, the thing that made me so angry, was the man in the room with her, straightening his clothes and standing just a few feet away from my sister. In a closed room! I couldn't see straight.

"She yelled at me to get out—back then our hut was away from all the others, so no one could hear her screams—but I couldn't move. I was shocked not only by the situation, but by the fact that she'd never yelled at me like that before. She spoke again, this time more quietly, almost sternly, telling me to leave. I was still in shock, but I somehow managed to ask who the man in the room with her was. I glared at him, somehow hoping I could just will him away. For a second I didn't recognize the man, but then the realization hit. He wasn't one of our Clan! And I told her that." Na-um had to fight back tears. *Not in front of Holun.*

"As soon as I said the words, Shani looked like she was about to cry. I wished that everything was okay, that I could go to her and wipe her tears away like I always did, but nothing was okay anymore." Na-um drew a breath. "Then she spoke only three small words: '*I love him.*'" Those three words had haunted him ever since.

And this was a lot harder to talk about than he'd thought it would be.

"She knew marrying outside the Clan was forbidden, just as it is now, but she just did not care! Somehow she had grown up and was making all the wrong choices while I was busy trying to keep her my little sister." Na-um's voice almost cracked.

"Shani also knew the consequences of betrayal, of trying to marry someone outside the Clan. She begged me not to say anything, that she would leave as soon as she packed and never return. I left the room, thinking. How could I turn in my sister? Sentence her to disgrace and servitude for the re-mainder of her young life? I knew she loved that man—I could see it on her face—and that she would be happy with him. But how could I break the very laws I'd sworn to pro-tect? I didn't know what to do."

Na-um paused, trying to decide how much he really want-ed to tell Holun. This could get quite dangerous for him. "Shani never came back, and though the Elders questioned me, they decided to let everything remain as it was, thinking that perhaps Shani had just run away." That wasn't the whole truth. Holun didn't need to know that Na-um had lied to the Elders to keep Shani's secret.

"So . . ." Na-um watched as Holun put it together. "The Elders all got together to discuss Shani, didn't they?"

Na-um nodded.

"Wow. They must've really been worried about her."

Na-um smiled. "We all were. But they would not be happy if they ever found out the truth about her." He gazed very pointedly at Holun, his smile fading.

Holun took the hint and nodded furiously. "Of course. I will take this secret to my grave."

"Good." Na-um slapped him on the back. "Now I need you to watch for anything out of the ordinary. Especially when it pertains to the Elders. I'm not sure what to tell you to look for . . . just watch for anything that might seem suspicious. Can you do that?"

Holun grinned. "Yes! That's much easier than trying to keep an eye on the Americans. I can at least *see* the members of the Clan."

Na-um smiled back, placing his hand on Holun's shoulder. "Thanks. You're doing a great job."

Holun beamed.

"The Elders suggested we keep an eye on the other locations, in case they turn up there. I'm dispatching some small groups today. You and I will stay here, to keep watch."

Holun nodded as they both turned and sprinted back toward the village.

CHAPTER 15

Kiss

Somewhere Near the Base of Denali

THE FOUR LEFT THE PITCH blackness of the tunnel behind them and stepped out into the starlit night. Grady had already scouted out a good location for a campsite, for which Kayla was eternally grateful. She was tired, hungry, and her feet hurt. A little relaxation was definitely in order.

But she was too wired to sleep—they all were. After a leisurely snack—dinner was ages ago—they all gathered around the campfire Grady had just built to discuss what they'd found.

Justin posed the first question. "So what does this discovery mean? Who lived in that cave we just found?"

Kayla looked over at Mandy. She would be the one who could best answer that question. When she didn't, Kayla interjected, glancing over at Justin before answering. "I'm not sure." She eyed Mandy again, who was staring at the fire with her legs stretched out and her hands tucked between her thighs, before continuing. "But I may have an idea."

At those words, Mandy's head came up, her eyes meeting Kayla's. She leaned forward, drawing her knees up toward her, and rested her elbows on her knees. "What?"

Kayla smiled. "I've found some interesting things in the stories we discovered at Lamanai."

Now Justin leaned in. "Like what?"

Kayla smiled wider as she felt Grady move just a little bit closer to her, as if to lend his support. She took a deep breath, then told them more about the hieroglyphs in the cave and the stories they told of the four Old Ones who had special powers, going into greater detail than she'd had time to before. Then she took a deep breath. "That's why I think that this is quite possibly the first of four books."

Mandy's jaw dropped. "Really? How is that?"

Kayla shrugged. "Well, those four Old Ones—they each had special abilities. They . . ." Kayla took a breath. Were the others really ready for this kind of crazy? ". . . they each had control over one of the four elements."

"Wow," Justin breathed.

"Yeah."

Grady was smiling next to Kayla. "It's pretty amazing."

Kayla nodded, eyeing Mandy, who was once again silent and staring into the flames. Kayla would have expected her to be excited, or even scared, at Kayla's revelation, but she seemed to have almost retreated into herself. Kayla was getting a little worried. "Mandy?"

Her friend raised her head ever so slowly. "So I have control over the air?"

Kayla didn't quite know how to answer that. "Well, maybe not—or maybe not yet? I don't know. The stories told of the four of them finding *one* book. Yet this book pertains to air exclusively—you all saw the symbol on the cover. That—plus the fact that the book was completely unreadable—leads me to believe that there are three more books for us to find. One pertaining to each of the other three elements."

A silence fell over the group. Kayla couldn't possibly begin to guess what they all were thinking. She knew it sounded crazy—it had sounded crazy in her head—but she knew in her heart that all of it was true.

"What was his name?" Mandy's soft voice broke the silence.

"I'm sorry?" Kayla asked.

"The name of the guy who controlled air. What was his name?"

Kayla reached for her journal. "His name was Kukulcan. He could control the air, which meant he could control what it did to people. And, surprisingly, he could read minds."

"What?" Mandy practically yelled. "How is that even possible?"

Kayla shook her head. "I'm not sure. But these accounts seem to be valid. And all the things I've seen, heard, and read in the past few weeks have only confirmed that."

Kayla fell silent, letting her words sink in. She watched as the expressions on her friends' faces changed as all the pieces fell together.

Finally, Grady let out a low whistle. "Amazing."

Mandy picked up the book they'd found—which had never left her sight since they'd found it—and clutched it to her chest. The glow of her skin was subtle, but still there. Kayla would've missed it if it had been any lighter out here. "What I felt today, the glowing, the vision . . . I think y'all are right. I already feel more . . . well, powerful, for lack of a better word."

Kayla nodded. "There's more."

Justin's mouth dropped open. "What more could there be after finding out that we might be getting superpowers?"

"Apparently the Old Ones didn't age."

Kayla watched silently as Mandy's expression swiftly matched Justin's. They stared at her and Grady, mouths open, frozen in place. Kayla had expected their reactions; she knew she would have to wait for her words to sink in. Grady caught her gaze and held it while Mandy and Justin just stared.

Justin characteristically found his voice first. "They didn't *age*?"

Kayla shook her head. "Nope, not from what I've read, at least initially." She took a breath. "The stories talk about how their loved ones died and they were powerless to stop it."

Justin started shaking his head—slowly at first, then speeding up until it was shaking furiously. Mandy placed her hand on his forearm. "Justin, it's okay. We're going to be fine."

"How can you say that?" He practically yelled. "We might get powers, sure, that's cool and all, but we won't age? How is that fine? Doesn't that mean we will essentially no longer be *human*?"

Grady responded first. "I'm not so sure. The Old Ones seemed to lose their humanity, given the fact that they enslaved and tormented their own people. But I think, on some level, they were still human. They just let their powers get the best of them."

Kayla nodded. "Yeah, makes sense to me. The powers just made them a little more than human, able to do more than normal humans can. But still human, all the same."

Mandy smiled whimsically, letting her eyes fall closed. Kayla was confused. "What is it, Mandy?"

Mandy opened her eyes, gazing around the fire at the rest of them. "I honestly believe we are going to be fine. When I stepped into that room, I instantly felt like . . . well, like I was *home*. Like this is exactly where I am meant to be. Something like Destiny, I'd imagine. This is what I was—what we all were—created for."

Justin snorted. "Really? I doubt it. I've never been made for more than studying and camping. And given our current surroundings . . ." his arm swept a wide arc, indicating the surrounding foliage, "I think there may not be any hope for me at all." He winked at Mandy, a smile turning up the corner of his lips.

Grady wasn't so sure. How could all of this even be possible? He knew what Kayla had read, all the stories, and she'd told him everything she'd seen in her visions. Sure, all that stuff was weird, and unexplainable, especially the stories about the Old Ones. But who's to say those stories weren't just a figment of some ancient Mayan's imagination?

But she was so sure. And she wouldn't lie to him, right?

Grady realized then that something was holding him back from believing it—believing her—completely. Doubt? Perhaps, almost certainly. But maybe something else, something deeper . . .

He looked over at Kayla. The instant he met her eyes, he knew exactly what had been holding him back. He had been hurt before—just once had been enough—and he was afraid to let himself trust her. But in that moment, in the split second of time that seemed like an eternity, he felt his heart let go, and knew that he trusted her completely.

Amazingly, he knew that he believed her, too. Everything she'd said that didn't make any sense to his logical brain became crystal clear to his heart. He knew he didn't have to understand it—he just had to accept it. And, with the last of his walls crumbling to the ground, he was finally able to admit it to himself: he loved her, completely and undeniably. He'd always loved her, but only now did he see the blinders he'd been wearing all this time. It was only when they were removed that he noticed they'd been there at all.

Kayla reached for his hand, squeezing it. Grady returned her reassuring smile. He desperately wanted to tell her what his brain had just figured out, what his heart had known all along—that he was in love with her, more absolutely than he'd ever thought possible. But he couldn't let himself hope that she felt the same way. Or could he?

Justin interrupted his thoughts. "So is that everything, Kayla?"

She hesitated. "Well . . ."

Grady gaped at her. "There's *more*?"

She chuckled. "Just more for us to figure out. I'm not sure where we're going next, just that there are more places to go. And what's really weird . . ." She nodded at the book Mandy was still clutching in her hands. "I think the only way this one will make sense is with the other three. Maybe it's some sort of code or cipher—where you need all of them together to read the entire message."

Grady shook his head, grinning. "Of course. I can't believe I didn't see that before."

The group fell silent and Grady stared into the fire, the warmth of Kayla's hand still in his sending electricity through his body. He felt like a teenage boy. *Keep your hormones in check.*

Mandy's voice spared his brain from going where that train of thought was headed. "Well, I think I'm finally tired. Anyone care if I get a few hours of sleep?"

Kayla rose, too, her hand sliding out of Grady's as naturally as she'd reached for it. "I need to get some sleep, too. You boys okay out here by yourselves?"

Grady rolled his eyes playfully. "I think we'll manage. Well, I will, at least," he joked, glancing pointedly at Justin.

Because his eyes were momentarily on Justin, who was blissfully oblivious to both him and Kayla, Grady was completely taken aback when Kayla leaned down, pulling his face toward her with both hands and kissing him squarely on the lips. She didn't linger, as much as Grady wanted her to. Instead, she straightened up with a quick "good night" then headed off to the tent.

Grady's mouth was still half-open—he was sure of that—but he couldn't help it. He was still reeling from her abrupt kiss, trying to figure out what it meant. Surely that wasn't an I'll-just-let-him-down-easy-by-telling-him-I-just-wanna-be-friends kiss, was it?

"Yeah, I knew it."

Grady cringed. Of course Justin had seen the whole thing. "What?" He was never good at feigning innocence. Made him a terrible liar.

"You guys *are* together, aren't you?"

Grady shook his head, whispering his response. "No."

"But you wish you were?"

Grady hesitated, eyeing the nearby tent. "It's really none of your business, Justin."

Justin grinned widely. Grady wanted to smack it off his face. "I know. You guys are hilarious. She's been acting the same way."

Grady rolled his eyes. "Give it up, Justin. We work together."

Justin chortled. "Yeah, like that matters. You know, I think she's into you, too. Why else would she kiss you, and in front of me, no less?"

Grady fell silent. He wouldn't give Justin any more reason to continue this conversation. Fortunately, Justin took the hint.

But his annoying friend's claims had started him thinking. Did Kayla really feel the same way he did? He had taken her silence on the subject as rejection, or at least indecision. Did it mean something else? Was she really just as interested as he was?

Grady closed his eyes and pinched the bridge of his nose. The events of the day were finally catching up with him.

"Do you mind if I get some rest, too? It's been a really long day." He yawned, effectively emphasizing his words.

Justin shrugged. "No problem." He reached down and picked up a hunk of wood. He pulled out a pocketknife and began whittling away at the piece of wood. "See? I'll have a horse by morning."

Grady chuckled then grabbed his sleeping bag. "Thanks. Wake me up if you get tired."

Justin waved energetically. "No problem." Then he gazed off into the distance, feigning wistful contemplation. "Maybe I'll do a self-portrait."

Grady stood, rolling his eyes again. He moved toward the tent then rolled out his sleeping bag in front of it. He was asleep within seconds.

Kayla slept uneasily that night, tossing around in her sleeping bag. She couldn't shake the eerie feeling she had from what they'd found in the tunnel, and from the odd revelations she'd had this evening.

Yet she knew she was right, knew Mandy was right, knew they *all* were right. Maybe, just maybe, this *was* her destiny, to receive these powers. Or perhaps she was just in the right place at the right time, and the others had unwittingly gotten in the way.

No, she didn't believe that. She had never believed in co-incidence—she believed that everything happened for a rea-son. Everything was predetermined, everything happened on purpose—including this.

But that didn't mean she wasn't worried about it.

After only a few hours of restless sleep, Kayla woke with a start. Her body jolted upright without her permission, and her eyes widened. An all-too-familiar feeling swept through her—she knew what was coming.

As soon as the internal slideshow was finished she darted out of the tent, nearly stepping on Mandy in her haste. "Grady!" She hissed, scanning the campsite for him.

Grady rolled out of the way before she could trip over him. "Kayla," he called, grabbing her hand as she rushed by, "I'm right here. What's wrong?"

Kayla, yanked to a stop by Grady's hand, spun and fell to the ground next to him, gasping.

Kayla could see he understood as soon as he saw her face; his next words came out matter-of-factly. "You had another vision."

Still trying to catch her breath, Kayla nodded furiously. "Yes. I know where we're going next."

CHAPTER 16

Attack

Mercenary Camp, Belize Rainforest

NA-UM NEEDED A PLAN. Oh, he'd sent contingency groups to all the locations, scouting platoons designed to keep watch, report back. So far, only the Northern Detachment had reported in with any news, and it hadn't been good, but the Americans were still far from revealing the Secret.

He needed to do something, to show he was in control, but he didn't know what to do. Killing the four Americans would be distasteful, and he was nearly certain he couldn't stomach it, anyway. But he didn't want to go to that extreme. Perhaps there was another way . . .

Then it came to him.

Kayla couldn't go back to sleep—and apparently Grady couldn't either. She hoped it was out of interest in her that he insisted on staying awake, but he still hadn't mentioned the kiss, so she didn't know what to think. Either way, it was sweet of him to keep her company.

Her brain was just too wired to sleep. She was starting to believe she might never sleep well again. Which seemed like an utterly exhausting proposition.

After several hours of unabashed flirting with Grady—she just couldn't help herself—Justin and Mandy woke up, ready to go. The four hurriedly packed, eager to get back to civilization. Once they found their cleverly stashed SUV—Justin apparently had handy camouflage skills; Kayla could barely see the vehicle until they were right on top of it—they started back toward Fairbanks, and hopefully toward a long, hot shower and a soft, warm bed.

The trip back to Fairbanks was mercifully short. After showers and a leisurely lunch surrounded by a variety of luscious foliage in the hotel restaurant—complete with sweeping views of the mountain—the group set to making their travel arrangements before settling in for the night. As Kayla had suspected, their superiors at the university were ecstatic to learn of their discovery and offered them nearly unlimited access to their funds set aside for archeological digs and the like.

With early morning flights scheduled and a quick check-in with Jack at the dig—he assured her that he had everything under control, and not to worry—Kayla decided to leave the guys in the lobby and head back to her room. Perhaps she could go over the notes she'd taken of the book, see if she could recognize any patterns, see if anything made sense. Anything was better than just sitting here, listening to the guys chatting it up on the phones, bored out of her mind.

Maybe she could even examine the book itself . . .

Kayla looked around for Mandy, who she knew would have the book, but didn't find her in the lobby. She caught a glimpse of the back of her friend's head heading down a side hallway, toward their rooms. Kayla stood and headed toward her, hoping to ask to borrow the book, even if only for a few minutes. Maybe she could make more sense of the writings inside.

Kayla stopped Mandy just before she'd reached her room, the book in her hand. "Hey, glad I caught you."

Mandy turned tired eyes in her direction and offered a sleepy smile. "What's up?"

Kayla got right to the point. "I was wondering if I could borrow the book for a little while. I thought I might be able to glean a little bit more from it, maybe compare it to the hieroglyphs at Lamanai, try to make sense of everything."

Mandy nodded, extending the large tome toward Kayla. "No problem. Won't be much good to me while I'm sleeping anyway." Her smile widened.

"Thanks. I'll take good care of it, I promise." Kayla grinned. "Sleep well."

As Mandy opened her door and stepped inside, Kayla turned to continue down the hallway to her room a few doors down. She was hoping to get this curious book under a figurative microscope, dissect all she could from it. Maybe it would give them some answers. Kayla shrugged to herself as she reached in her back pocket for her room's keycard. That didn't seem likely.

She set the book down on the small room's sole table, eager to study it. Then she remembered—she hadn't told Grady where she'd be, just in case he needed her for something. She reached for her phone to let him know where she was, quickly realizing she'd left it in the lobby with the guys. Ugh.

Kayla snatched the room key off the table, shoved it back in the pocket of her jeans, and threw open the door.

On her way back to the lobby, Kayla noticed some odd sounds coming out of one of the rooms across the hall. Was that someone fighting? Kayla stopped, leaning closer toward the noise.

That was Mandy's room.

"JUSTIN!" Her scream, which could have easily been heard on the floors above the open lobby, sent Justin and Grady hurtling down the hall. They reached her in record time, their eyes wild.

"We have to get in there, now," she hissed through clenched teeth.

Justin hurriedly unlocked the door, throwing it open and bounding through. His eyes scanned the room anxiously. Then he froze.

Kayla—Grady wasn't too far behind her—pushed past him, unwilling to give Justin time to adjust. In all likelihood, they did not have the time to wait.

Kayla's breath caught in her throat. The main room was empty, but something had definitely happened here—something Kayla wasn't so sure she wanted to discover. She bit down hard on her lower lip and fought for her scientific side to take over.

The small-for-a-queen bed to her far left was all but stripped, its crisp white but thread-bare sheets strewn in a haphazard line across the floor. The out-dated bedside lamp lay shattered into a hundred little pieces now littering the heavily carpeted floor on the side of the bed closest to the door. White gauzy curtains flanking the open window had been torn and shredded; tiny specks of red dotted them and the floor beneath them as they rustled in the slight breeze.

Kayla's chest tightened. "Grady . . ." she choked, unwilling to let herself consider what had happened here. She reached out her hand, grasping his forearm with less strength than she would've liked.

"I know, I know." He laid his hand on hers then called out tentatively, "Mandy?"

At that moment, Kayla heard a barely perceptible choking sound coming from around the corner to their right. She recognized it immediately—it was the same sound she'd heard through the door—but thankfully much less urgent this time. Just as she started to head around the corner, Justin pushed past her, brushing her shoulder rather harshly, with no signs of caring about her welfare. There was someone else he cared about more.

Kayla ran toward the bathroom just behind Justin and Grady, who quickly crowded the small space. What she saw in the bathroom put a knot in her chest. Mandy was sitting on her knees, hunched over, her loose clothes clinging to her in patches where they were wet. Leaning against the edge of the bathtub, she covered her mouth with the hand that she wasn't cradling in her lap, trying in vain to conceal the coughing fit that didn't seem to be stopping any time soon. Justin was already on the floor with one arm wrapped around her when Kayla stepped into the room.

"Baby, are you okay? What happened?" Justin's voice came out more harshly than Kayla would've liked.

Mandy nodded, her constant choking and coughing impeding her speech. Her hair, wet and stringy, clung to her face and neck. Justin gently pulled her hair away from her face with what Kayla thought was incredible control, especially given the rage she could see just under the surface. She watched his breath catch as he pulled the last dripping strand out of his girlfriend's face.

Kayla's eyes immediately followed Justin's gaze. The entire left side of Mandy's face was red. Kayla could make out a handprint; she cringed as she realized the pain her friend must have been in—must still be in.

Justin growled out his next question. "Who did this to you?"

Mandy simply shook her head and let out a short cough, finally finding her voice. "I . . . I don't know who it was. One of the Mercenaries, I think, given his features and his long, black hair." She touched her hand gingerly to her cheek then winced. Kayla grabbed a towel and ran from the room to find ice. She pushed through the crowd of people in the hallway just outside Mandy's door without a second glance. *Go back to your rooms, people. Nothing to see here.*

When she returned less than thirty seconds later, Grady was kneeling at Mandy's side and Justin, chest heaving, was pacing just outside the bathroom door. Kayla could imagine quite easily the scenario that landed Justin outside of the bathroom, but instead she focused on the task at hand, handing the makeshift icepack to Grady and kneeling beside him, directly facing Mandy. Her courageous friend took the towel-wrapped ice from Grady and gingerly put it to her face, wincing at the cold for a split second before looking up at Kayla. Her expression was vastly different than it was just seconds ago.

"What is it?" Kayla ventured, curious as to the change in Mandy's demeanor.

Mandy tried to smile, but winced again at the pain. "I just wanted to say thank you. He left when you screamed . . . he could've—he would've killed me." Her eyes tightened.

Kayla frowned, near tears. She hadn't known Mandy for very long, not really, but her heart went out to this young woman. She wished she could make it better somehow, but knew the only way to fix this would be to assess the damages, address them, and keep whoever did this from doing it again. Kayla leaned over to get a closer look at Mandy's face. The area around her left eye was slightly bruised and she had a long but shallow cut on the right side of her forehead, which was still bleeding. Her nose was trickling blood as well; fortunately, it looked like the worst of it had stopped. Kayla tucked a stray piece of hair behind Mandy's ear, wanting to cry; instead, she smiled, trying to be reassuring. She hoped Mandy was buying it.

Just then, Justin came back into the room, looking as though he had control of himself. "Mandy, baby—what happened?"

Mandy sighed, laying her arm on the side of the tub and resting her head on it. She blinked a few times before she spoke. "I was almost asleep when I heard someone. I didn't even open my eyes because I assumed it was Justin." She stopped abruptly. "He must have already been in here. I never heard the door open . . ." Mandy shivered subconsciously. Justin reached for a towel and laid it across her shoulders.

Mandy attempted to smile up at him as she adjusted the towel tighter around her. "Thanks." She took a breath. "I don't remember much. He somehow got me off the bed and into the bathroom, where he . . ." She tried to shift her weight, then winced at the movement, turning her gaze to Grady and Kayla. "There was already water in the tub and he tried to hold me under . . ." Her voice trailed off as her eyes tightened, then widened in the next instant as something else occurred to her. "He'd already put water in the tub . . ." her voice caught.

Kayla placed her hand on Mandy's shoulder. "I'm *so* sorry, Mandy. I'm so sorry we didn't stop this."

Mandy shook her head again, and shifted her legs out from under her, turning to sit with her back against the tub, and pulling her knees up against her chest. "This isn't your fault. You *did* stop him. It just happened so quickly . . ." She laid her forehead on her knees. Grady picked up the ice-filled towel she had discarded halfway through her explanation and pressed it to the side of her face lightly. She smiled tiredly and raised her head just a little to give Grady better access to her cheek.

As she did, Mandy seemed to notice Justin, who was still standing just inside the bathroom door. Kayla followed her gaze, not understanding the expression on Justin's face. Then Mandy spoke. "Justin, baby—it's okay. I'll be fine." She attempted a half-smile that didn't reach her cheeks, and Kayla instantly understood. Mandy and Justin, despite their occasional bickering, knew each other quite well.

Justin squeezed his eyes shut, shaking his head frantically. "No. I should have been here to stop this. I'll never forgive myself for that."

Mandy put her hands on the edge of the tub and slowly lifted herself to her feet, staggering a little. Kayla helped her steady herself before letting her stand on her own.

Mandy took a few unsure steps to reach Justin's side. She put her arms around his waist, leaning into him for support. "Don't beat yourself up about this, baby," she said into his chest, his shirt muffling her words. "It could've been a lot worse. I really will be fine."

Justin wrapped his arms around her shoulders, hugging her tightly and resting his chin on the top of her head. "I'm just so very sorry." Justin kissed her hair, then led her out of the tiny bathroom.

Kayla grabbed a cloth, wetting it to start cleaning up. She wiped the blood off the side of the tub and the floor, effectively erasing all reminders of the assault—the physical ones, anyway. After draining the tub, she gathered the excess dirty rags into a pile and threw them in an innocuous corner of the room, purposely out of sight.

After wiping up the excess water from the floor, Grady rose to his feet, stepping just outside the bathroom and placing a hand on Mandy's back with a smile. "We're really glad you're okay."

Kayla nodded emphatically as she came out of the bathroom. "Please, Mandy . . . let me know if you need anything."

After offering to take Mandy to the nearby E.R.—Justin insisted they needed some quiet before that happened, but promised he would take her soon—Kayla leaned down to pick the blankets up off the floor and set them on the bed before she and Grady headed out the door. Mandy and Justin would definitely need some alone time to sort all this out. Kayla knew the physical scars would eventually heal, but someone doesn't just instantaneously get over an attack like that. She found herself praying that Mandy would be alright. She really hoped Someone was listening.

If asked, she would say she believed in God, but she knew that faith—real, true faith—required trust. And she just wasn't sure she was ready to give up that much control.

She pushed the thought to the back of her mind, trying to focus on something else. She didn't want to consider such deep issues at the moment. She didn't have the time right now. Or, perhaps more honestly, she didn't want to take the time.

They had nearly reached the door next to hers, the one leading to Grady's room, when Kayla suddenly realized she didn't want to be alone. The words just spilled out before she could stop them. "Grady . . ." he turned to look at her. "Would you mind . . . I don't . . ." she glanced at the still-closed door.

"I won't be any trouble. I have a book I started earlier—I'll stay out of your way. I just . . ."

Grady cut her off. "Kayla, it's okay, I promise. I don't want to be alone, either." He offered a kind smile. "Go grab your book, use the adjoining door. Give me five minutes?"

Kayla nodded, turning toward her room quickly to hide her reddening cheeks. What had she just done? She'd been hurt so many times before, rushed into relationships that always ended in disaster—she knew she needed to take this slow for it to work. She wasn't sure she was ready for this to be given a sharp jolt right past friendship into something a whole lot more.

But didn't she want more? Hadn't she been wishing that Grady would . . .

Oh geez, she thought. *Let's not go there.*

She'd better get this stuff sorted out in her head, and fast; Grady wouldn't wait around forever. And she didn't want to mess this thing up.

CHAPTER 17

Spark

GRADY WAS THE PERFECT GENTLEMAN. He pulled out a novel of his own—he'd made considerably more progress on his gigantic tome than she'd made on her tiny-by-comparison novel—and reclined against the bed's headboard, giving Kayla the comfy easy chair in the corner.

Kayla found it a little hard to concentrate at first—just being in the same room with Grady was intoxicating—but after reading the same paragraph what had to be fifty times, her brain finally started registering the words and she slowly began to make progress.

But as good as the book was, she soon found her eyes getting heavy. It'd been a long few days with little sleep—she couldn't remember the last night she'd slept peacefully, or had slept through the night. Her dreams, though helpful, were wearing her out.

She leaned her head against the back of the chair and let her eyes slide shut. Maybe she could just rest her eyes for a minute or two . . .

She woke to find Grady leaning over her, nudging her shoulder. "Kayla? Kayla, wake up."

She blinked then stood up slowly, peering around the room. She ran her hand across her hair. "What time is it?"

Grady smiled at her, pushing her hair out of her face. His hand lingered near her chin. "You've only been sleeping a few minutes, but you didn't look very comfortable. Thought you might want to get out of that chair."

She winced, then closed her eyes and leaned into his touch. "Sorry." She smiled sheepishly and opened her eyes to look at him, her expression apologetic. But she was so comfortable here, next to him, that she made no move to leave the room.

Grady didn't seem eager for her to go, either. His hand traced her jawline as he caught her gaze and leaned toward her.

Time stopped. Kayla's heart started sputtering erratically, and suddenly she couldn't remember how to breathe. She stared into Grady's eyes, willing him to close the distance. Her breath caught and her eyes slid shut the instant before their lips met.

The kiss was nothing like the night before. His lips were soft, lightly caressing hers slowly. His breathing was as sporadic as hers.

His hand reached under her hair and closed around the back of her neck, pulling her closer to him. As he did, Kayla reached her hand up to his jaw, cupping her hand around it.

Her fingers massaged his cheek, stroking it tenderly as she eagerly kissed him back.

Then Kayla felt the kiss change, become more intense. Grady's lips felt more urgent on hers, more insistent. In an instant she felt her passion for him increase exponentially, and she struggled to keep her emotions in check. She pressed closer to him eagerly, feeling a nearly tangible electricity radiate through her veins.

Kayla reluctantly pulled away to catch her breath. Grady, unwilling to release her, brushed his lips lightly against her forehead before pulling her to his chest. He was breathing unevenly, his frantic heartbeat pounding in Kayla's ears. Kayla stayed buried in his chest, strangely self-conscious. She hadn't done anything like that in a long while.

Grady slowly stroked her hair as their breathing steadied. Only after Kayla had completely composed herself did she pull away. She sheepishly met Grady's gaze with her own, trying desperately to mask the vulnerability she was sure was emblazoned across her face. She wondered what Grady was thinking.

Then his lips parted to form a single word. "Wow."

Kayla nodded soundlessly, swallowing hard.

Grady smiled peacefully. "That was amazing."

Kayla released the breath she didn't know she'd been holding. "It was," she breathed. She smiled back at him, gazing into his sparkling blue eyes.

Grady grinned. "Wanna try it again?"

Kayla threw her arms around his neck and pushed him down on the edge of the bed. Their lips met with a spark; Kayla heard his breath catch with a gasp and she grinned in spite of herself. She had been waiting for a moment like this —though until this moment, she hadn't even known that this was what she'd been waiting for—for what felt like forever. And it was even better than she'd imagined.

Grady brought both hands to her neck, tangling both of them in her hair. After a minute he pulled away to lightly trace his lips down her neck, sending new sensations throughout her body. She could feel the blood pulsing through her veins, making her skin tingle. She had never felt this way before; those in her past had never kissed her like this. So carefully, yet with so much passion. His lips returned to hers as he let out a small moan, causing her to shudder. She never wanted this to end.

She let Grady pull her down on top of him, her body pressing against his as they eagerly devoured each other. Every touch, every new feeling was addicting, pulling them toward an inescapable conclusion. She knew she wanted this, had even dared to hope for it in the depths of her heart.

But on top of all that, she realized she'd been lying to herself. She knew she loved him, without a doubt, but until this moment she hadn't known its full extent. She was *in* love with him, so completely and so absolutely that she didn't want to screw it up. She couldn't bear to hurt him . . . or lose him. And if she did this now, before she was certain how he felt, what he really wanted . . . She sighed and pulled away, sheepishly finding his gaze.

Grady reluctantly followed suit, but his eyes told Kayla he didn't understand. She lay down next to him and looked away, resting the back of her wrist on her forehead. She desperately hoped that Grady would understand that she was sorry, that she hated this as much as he did.

Their breathing slowly returned to normal again as they both stared at the ceiling, then Grady rolled on his side and rose up on one arm to look at her. She slowly met his gaze as she propped her head up with her hand, hoping against hope that he would understand.

"Everything okay?" Grady brushed a stray hair from her forehead.

Kayla's stomach dropped at the uncertainty she heard in Grady's voice. She quickly tried to explain. "Of course. I thoroughly enjoyed that." She flashed a genuine grin in his direction, then looked away as the smile faded. She sighed. "I just . . . I don't want to mess this up. I have a tendency to do that. I don't want to jump into anything too soon, before we're ready."

Grady visibly relaxed. "I get it. I promise."

Kayla smiled.

"I'm just glad it wasn't me or anything."

"Of course not!" Kayla's eyes flashed at him until she saw the laughter in his. She almost hit his shoulder, but she couldn't stop smiling, so there really wasn't any point pretending to be mad at him. She chuckled, unable to contain her elation.

Grady chuckled, too, but not as easily. Kayla thought he sounded almost . . . nervous.

"Kayla . . ." he started, then paused.

Kayla bit her lip to keep from interrupting him. *Let him get it out, just let him get it out,* kept repeating in her head.

A few moments later, Grady lifted his hand to Kayla's cheek and stroked it gently. Then three soft words broke the silence. "I love you."

Kayla's heart thudded in her chest. She had been waiting for this, waiting for this perfect moment. Waiting for confirmation of his reciprocated feelings, confirmation that she now had.

So she didn't hesitate. "I love you, too."

Grady sat up then, pulling her up with him. They sat on the edge of the bed facing each other as Grady spoke. "I've known for a while now. I just didn't know what to say, how to tell you. Or how you felt." He shrugged.

Indescribable joy swept through Kayla, and she grinned. "I've been trying to find the right way to tell you how I felt. I was . . . scared, I guess."

Grady grabbed her hand. "Well, now it's out in the open." Then he added, "I suppose Justin will be happy."

Kayla laughed quietly and rolled her eyes. "He really gets on my nerves sometimes."

Grady chuckled. "Tell me about it."

Kayla yawned reflexively and Grady noticed. "I'd better let you get some sleep."

She nodded tiredly and rose. "Sorry I fell asleep in your room."

Grady stood up next to her, still holding her hand. "Anytime." The loaded meaning of Grady's one-word statement made Kayla's mind go to another place, one to which she was certain she wasn't ready to go. Grady leaned down for a quick kiss—a welcome distraction—lingering for just a brief moment before kissing her forehead. "Good night, Kayla. Sweet dreams. I mean that."

Kayla smiled then headed toward the door, grasping his hand as long as possible, stretching it out between them. "You, too. See you tomorrow." She dropped his hand and opened her adjoining door, passing through it with one more glance back before pulling it shut. She paused on the other side with her back against it, taking slow, deliberate breaths to try to clear her head.

Only minutes later, she smiled as she sunk into bed, crawling between the sheets. Sleep found her quickly and, as if

God Himself had heard Grady's wish for her, she slept undisturbed until morning.

CHAPTER 18

Bozeman

"JUSTIN, FOR THE THOUSANDTH TIME, will you *please* tell me where we're going?" Mandy threw the red dress she'd discarded for the light blue one she was wearing in her suitcase, then crossed her arms and stared directly at Justin and his army-green duffel bag sitting barely packed on the bed. She was getting sick of this stalling. Out with it already.

But Justin was clearly enjoying himself. He grinned as he pulled on a dark red v-neck over his light khakis. "Nope."

Mandy playfully punched his arm, quickly regretting it. She was still quite sore from the fight in her room yesterday. "Come on, tell me! I can't be the only one in the dark." She stuck out her lower lip.

Justin simply grinned too widely in her direction. She threw a pillow at his head. He ducked, deftly avoiding the flying projectile.

"You know that's not fair." She began cramming clothes in her bag, throwing her belongings a little too harshly into her suitcase.

Justin shrugged as he grabbed a wadded up a pair of khakis and stuffed them in his bag. "Life's not fair."

"Ugh! You can be so aggravating sometimes."

"You know you love me." Justin strolled around the bed and hugged her from behind. She shrugged him off, choosing instead to stomp toward the bathroom.

Grrr! That man is insufferable sometimes, Mandy thought as she put both hands on the counter and stared at her reflection in the mirror. The bruises were worse today—though not as bad as she supposed they should have been; they appeared to already be healing—so she dabbed some concealer on her cheek and under her eye until she could barely make them out.

Then Mandy sighed. *I wish there was a way to make him tell me.* Then she had a thought. *Worth a try . . .* She grinned, started filling her toiletry bag with just about everything on the counter, then called out, "It's okay, I'll find out eventually. Kayla will tell me." She threw her toothpaste into the small bag then froze, waiting for Justin's response.

He was at the door immediately. "No! Don't do that. I want to surprise you."

Mandy turned to look at him, cocking her head to one side. She hadn't been sure that would work. "Surprise me? That doesn't sound good. Tell me."

Justin paused for a brief moment, then walked back into the main room. Mandy grabbed her packed toiletry bag and followed him to the bed, sitting down next to him. She threw the bag into her suitcase then grabbed his hand, staring into his eyes. "Come on. You know I hate surprises."

Justin sighed. *Finally,* Mandy thought.

"So you know I'm not from Florida," he began.

Mandy nodded but stayed quiet.

"I grew up in Montana, near Yellowstone."

Mandy blinked. "And?"

Justin stared at her pointedly, waiting.

Then, suddenly, she got it. She grinned. "We're going to Yellowstone!"

Justin smiled at her. "Yes, but . . ."

"But what?"

He hesitated. "Well . . . we've been together for a few years now."

"Yeah . . ."

"And we're pretty serious, right?"

Mandy raised an eyebrow. "What's this about, Justin?"

Justin took a deep breath. "You wanna meet my parents?"

Mandy shoved his arm. "You were going to just *surprise* me with this? You were just going to let me go into that blind?"

"I don't know. I just . . . I guess I didn't really want to find out what you thought, in case you didn't want to."

She smiled at him, a smile she could tell reached her eyes in spite of the pain in her cheek. "Of course I'll meet them. But only if you want me to."

Justin shrugged. "Sure."

Mandy leaned over and kissed him. "Don't worry. People love me."

"Right," Justin mumbled sarcastically, kissing her cheek lightly before they both turned to finish packing.

Bozeman Yellowstone National Airport

"Hey, Dad." Justin threw his duffel bag over his shoulder and turned to hug his tall and barely graying father, who stood with the back of his large, jet-black SUV open and empty, ready for luggage. Justin was glad—traveling with two women wasn't a simple task when you considered the amount of luggage they carried.

"Hey, Mom. Thanks for coming to pick us up." He leaned in to kiss the cheek of his short, slightly overweight blond mother, who all but pounced on him before he got the chance.

"Justin! We haven't seen you in forever!" His mom flipped her chin-length, bone-straight hair out of her eyes and threw her arms around him in one motion, hugging him tightly to her. Just feeling her too-thick-for-summer knit vest with crocheted pine trees and blue birds emblazoned on it through his thin T-shirt made Justin feel hot.

Justin squirmed out from under her embrace, throwing her an apologetic half-smile. "Yeah, sorry. I've been . . . busy."

Grady came around the back of the SUV with a large wheeled suitcase in each hand. Kayla followed just behind him with a smaller wheeled suitcase and a shoulder bag with the broken strap she'd been struggling with the entire trip here.

"So, Justin, who are your friends?" his mom inquired, eyeing them almost playfully as her muscular husband hoisted the first of the suitcases Grady was carrying into the back. She moved to stand right in front of Kayla and Grady.

"Mom, this is Dr. Kayla Harrington and Dr. Grady McGready, two of my professors at UCF."

Grady offered his right hand to Justin's mother just as Mr. Stanford took the second large suitcase out of his other hand. Kayla nodded a quiet "Nice to meet you" to both of them, her hands still full of luggage.

Justin's mom enthusiastically shook Grady's hand, pulled Kayla into a quick and slightly awkward one-armed hug, then glanced pointedly at the last member of the group, who stood just behind Kayla. Mrs. Stanford caught her son's gaze and cocked her head toward Mandy.

Justin grabbed Mandy's hand, pulling her out from behind Kayla and in front of his mother. He slung an arm around Mandy's shoulders and drew her close to his side. "Mom, Dad, this is Mandy Carlson. My girlfriend."

Mandy extended her hand with a large and polite smile. "I'm very pleased to meet you both."

Justin's mother took a step toward Mandy and swept her into an exuberant hug, pulling her away from Justin and ignoring her outstretched hand deftly. "I'm Jan, this is Roger." She pulled away slightly as she nodded toward her husband, her hands still on Mandy's shoulders. She offered Mandy a brilliant smile. "It's so nice to finally meet you."

Roger stuck his head out of the back of the SUV, offering a smile matching his wife's. "She's a cute one, Justin." Justin rolled his eyes as his father turned to Mandy. "Good to meet you, sweetie."

He slammed the door to the back hatch shut. With the bags securely loaded, the six of them all climbed into the SUV, grateful for the extra row of seats in the back. Roger slid behind the driver's seat and pulled out into the evening airport traffic.

After a few minutes in the airport parking lot and fighting their way through the parking gates, they made the turn onto the main thoroughfare, taking it twenty minutes southeast before coming to a small, sleepy town. From the back seat, Mandy gasped as 360-degrees of larger-than-life mountains came into view.

Roger grinned into the rearview mirror, sweeping his hand across the windshield with a flourish. "Mandy, Kayla, Grady—welcome to Bozeman."

Just outside Bozeman, Montana

After another fifteen minutes of driving away from the setting sun, the Stanfords pulled up to their charming home, which was covered on all sides in dark gray driftwood with an even darker roof.

But Kayla could clearly see Jan's personality shining through in all her cheery attempts to brighten the home's facade. The largely unremarkable entrance was enhanced by a wide porch that stretched the length of the house. The opening to the covered porch was flanked on either side by vividly green flower boxes filled with a vibrantly colorful array of native flowers that sat atop the stark white railing.

Large, flat stones in varying shades of gray led the way across the semi-short field of grass to the front door. The group followed them from the gravel driveway in front of the garage to the front steps.

Roger pulled open the screen door then leaned down to unlock the bright white front door, theatrically swinging it open for the group to enter. Kayla smiled as she crossed the threshold in front of the others and got her first look at the upbeat interior.

"Your home is beautiful, Mrs. Stanford. Thank you both for letting us stay here." Kayla set the suitcase she was carrying off to her left, in front of the entrance to what looked like a formal living room, to get it out of the way of the others coming through the front door. As she did, she surveyed the small front room to the right, cheerfully decorated in a homey country motif overflowing with various floral patterns in deep blues and bright yellows. The staircase, painted a bold deep green, was positioned just across from the entrance. Bright silk flowers dotted the handrail at irregular intervals. A small hallway next to the stairs, festooned with dozens of family pictures, led the way to the back of the house, presumably to the kitchen.

Mrs. Stanford stepped through the door last, letting the screen door fall shut behind her. "Please call me Jan. And thank you. We enjoy having company." She moved toward the small hallway next to the stairs, then glanced at Kayla and Mandy. "The men will get your suitcases. Roger knows where they should go. Mandy, Kayla, follow me."

Mandy and Kayla followed their affable host to the back of the house and into the quaint, bright kitchen as the men hoisted their bags upstairs. "Please make yourselves at home. I'm sure you must be hungry, coming off airplane food and all." She smiled at her subtle joke.

Mandy smiled back. "Sure. What can we do to help?"

As Kayla filled glasses with homemade lemonade on the kitchen island and Mandy grabbed the plates, Mrs. Stanford checked on the contents of the oven. The smell wafted into the kitchen as soon as the oven door was open.

Kayla took a deep breath and smiled. "That smells wonderful."

"My mother's old recipe: Hawaiian pot roast." Jan grinned then pushed the door closed. "Almost ready."

The men joined them just as the roast was coming out of the oven, already laughing and joking amongst themselves. Kayla could clearly see where Justin had inherited his easygoing personality.

With a good-natured "behave yourselves, boys" to her husband and son, Jan set the roast on the table, nodding for everyone to take their seats. Roger and Justin quickly took over the conversation as they ate, cracking jokes between the two of them without breaking a stride. Soon even Jan was laughing so hard she had tears in her eyes.

Kayla enjoyed the Stanfords' welcoming hospitality just as much as the delicious food, for which she was exceedingly grateful; she couldn't remember the last time she'd had a home-cooked meal. Or laughed this much. Roger's colorful—and questionably truthful—stories of growing up on a ranch had everyone laughing until their sides hurt.

As the conversation and laughter lingered well into the night, Kayla realized she hadn't felt this relaxed in a long while. Grady squeezed her hand under the table, a wide smile on his face. He winked at her and she giggled like she was a kid again.

She could get used to this.

Kayla rose early, wanting to get a head start on the planning, careful not to wake Mandy sleeping beside her. But Mandy was soon awake anyway, followed shortly by Grady and Justin, who the women could hear stirring in the other room.

The four of them were soon getting ready, in and out of the single upstairs bathroom, ducking into walk-in closets and between the two bedrooms, trying to find a private place to change clothes, brush hair, dab on makeup. Justin and Grady were done first and headed downstairs, followed soon after by Kayla and Mandy.

The Stanfords were just coming out of their first-floor suite as Kayla came down the stairs. After some heartfelt "good mornings" and smiles for everyone, Jan set out to create a large spread.

They made their plans in the brightly-lit dining room over pancakes, eggs, and bacon coupled with diced fruit and freshly-squeezed orange juice. Roger and Jan ate with them, assisting where they could with their knowledge of the local area.

They even offered their off-road vehicle—their second SUV, a few years older than the one they'd driven to and from the airport but only slightly worse for wear—for the group's use.

"So where exactly are you headed?" Roger interjected as the group was discussing their plan to head to the nearby Yellowstone National Park.

Justin pointed to the map spread out on the table among their dishes, circling Yellowstone with a wide arc. "Somewhere in this general area. We're not exactly sure where." He glanced at Kayla surreptitiously.

Kayla frowned. She wished her vision would've been more specific. She'd just seen pictures in her head of the park. She wasn't entirely positive where specifically they should look. She shrugged subtly in apology.

Grady patted her leg under the table. Kayla smiled, just a little.

Justin's mom didn't miss anything. She looked over at Kayla speculatively. "Just how did you get this information? We understand you came from Alaska . . . ?" She let her voice trail off, hoping for an explanation.

Kayla spoke quietly. "We were at the dig at Lamanai, in northern Belize, when Grady and I found something. We were . . . kidnapped . . . on our way out of the country." Jan gasped but Kayla continued her story. "That's when Mandy and Justin found us, and rescued us." She smiled at the couple, happy to be able to praise them both in front of Justin's parents. She omitted the part about them being kidnapped as well.

"We headed out of the country as soon as we could. We'd found something at the dig that sent us to Alaska, then found something in Alaska that led us here." Kayla shifted in her seat.

"When you say you found something . . ." Jan persisted.

Kayla glanced at Grady. Grady smiled back, squeezing her hand under the table, and spoke for her. "It's hard to explain, rather complicated. We should know more later today."

Kayla's shoulders dropped ever so slightly as she silently sighed. Once again, Grady came through.

And Jan got the hint. She dropped her line of questioning with a nod, then changed the subject. "So is everybody packed up? For the hike, I mean."

Their discussion turned to the more mundane details of their trip, such as the best places to park for overnight stays, some of the best campsite options, and the weather, which was unseasonably warm, even for June. They packed again for a few days, prepared to stay overnight if necessary.

But Kayla hoped they would be done before nightfall. She was enjoying sleeping in an actual bed—in an actual home—and eating homemade food for once. A second night in a cozy, welcoming home and a warm bed wasn't too much to ask, was it?

CHAPTER 19

Yellowstone

Yellowstone National Park

THE FOUR OF THEM—with Grady driving—made the almost two-hour trip to the park entrance, where they immediately received a warning from the park ranger: the National Weather Service was predicting a storm, so the ranger suggested they make their visit quick. Kayla agreed with him vehemently. *We can always hope.*

They headed south on the main road, for lack of any more specific place to go. Justin was spouting off useless trivia as they went; he had quite apparently spent many summers here as a child. "We're coming up on Mammoth Hot Springs, almost like the hub of Yellowstone, at least coming in from the north . . .

"Many of the attractions of Yellowstone exist because of its supervolcano, which created the many calderas of Yellowstone, including the largest, the Yellowstone Caldera. Many scientists believe it's the largest active supervolcano in the world. All the thermal activity—like the geysers—are evidence of this as well."

Kayla had all but tuned him out, and she could see Grady was doing his best to ignore him, but Mandy was keeping up. At Justin's mention of a volcano, she snorted. "Active? Yeah, right. I suppose that means it'll erupt while we're here?"

Justin smiled. "Not likely. The last major explosion was hundreds of thousands of years ago, according to most scientists. They classify the volcano as 'active' because of the thousands of earthquakes each year and all the thermal activity."

"Thousands?"

Justin grinned, nodding. "A couple thousand are recorded each year. You know, many people believe . . ."

He continued his incessant prattling, and Kayla stopped listening altogether. She was trying to concentrate, trying to will a vision into her head. It wasn't really working.

They passed through the Mammoth Hot Springs area, past the Historic Fort Yellowstone—from the days the army controlled Yellowstone, Justin interjected—past the Amphitheater, past the Albright Visitor Center. Justin didn't know how the visitor center got its name.

Kayla held her breath as they left the small semblance of civilization, hoping that maybe leaving "town" would make it easier for her to see something, divine something. *Anything.*

Nothing.

Kayla sighed, looking out over the majestic mountains, sparkling lakes, vast forests. It reminded her of her childhood in Seattle. *Mom would have loved this.*

Always the adventure-seeker, Marci Harrington had loved hiking Mt. Rainier in the summers, kayaking along the San Juan islands in the fall, and scuba diving in Puget Sound year-round. Growing up, Kayla frequently went along with her to discover the nature that surrounded the city.

Kayla loved it; she supposed her mother was one of the reasons she loved the discovery of archaeology. Nature had so many stories to tell if you knew where to look.

"Hey, Grady, pull over here." Justin's voice interrupted her musings, and she sighed. It seemed Justin was determined to do the tourist thing until they got more information out of her.

Kayla rolled her eyes as they drove past yet another landmark she could've sworn they'd already seen at least once today and pulled into a roadside parking lot; she found herself hoping for a vision to get them out of this particular excursion. All she could think about at the moment—besides the underlying sadness at the thought of her mother—was the next elusive location. She knew they were close—they *were* at Yellowstone, after all—but she still felt lost.

Justin hopped out of the vehicle, slamming his door shut. The other three imitated him—Kayla with considerably less enthusiasm—and followed him to a nearby trail.

"This shouldn't be too long of a hike; we should be able to leave our gear here," Justin shouted back to the group as he sojourned on.

Mandy trailed after him, excitedly sputtering questions as she went. Kayla brought up the rear, folding her arms across her chest as her tennis shoes scuffed the ground. Grady slowed and put his arm around her.

"You okay?"

Kayla attempted a smile as she looked over at him. "Yeah. I just wish we had a better idea of where to look. It's so irritating that I can't force these visions into my mind. I wish so much that I could."

Grady hugged her to his side as they sauntered after Justin and Mandy. "Don't worry about it. You've done so much already—you've gotten us *this* far. Let's just enjoy ourselves until it comes."

Kayla nodded at him and swallowed hard, trying to talk herself into it. She slid her arm around his waist, grateful for the contact. Grady grinned and kissed the top of her head as they sped up to try to catch the chattering couple ahead of them.

"Come on, you two. No time for dawdling." Justin called back to them with a smile, winking. He fell into the role of tour guide easily, much to Kayla's amusement. She started laughing at him, feeling the laughter calm her nerves, release her anxiety. For a fleeting moment, she thought that perhaps she *could* relax and enjoy spending the day with the man she loved.

Then, suddenly, Kayla felt her body jerk violently before crashing abruptly to the ground.

Grady tried to catch her but she slipped too quickly out from under his arm. Instantly he fell to his knees at her side. Grady shook her—hard—but her eyes seemed welded shut. He yelled her name repeatedly, but somehow knew she couldn't hear him.

His frantic screams sent Mandy and Justin running back.

"What happened?" Mandy rushed over to Grady and fell to the ground on Kayla's other side.

"She just shook—hard—then collapsed. I couldn't stop her from falling. And now she won't wake up." Grady heard the panicked strain in his voice, but barely registered it. He was having trouble breathing.

Mandy's heart went out to him. She knew, in that moment, that Grady loved the unconscious woman lying between them. Mandy frowned, wishing she could ease his pain. She could only imagine how she would feel if anything happened to Justin . . .

She gulped, forcing the thought away. She couldn't allow herself to be distracted now. Kayla was in trouble.

Mandy moved closer to Kayla and cradled her friend's head in her lap. She understood—granted, on a much smaller scale—how Kayla felt; she remembered how she'd felt when it had happened to her. But Kayla's unresponsiveness worried her. Her visions were getting worse, starting to hurt her. Mandy wished she knew why—and how to stop them.

Then Kayla blinked once and her eyes opened wide. She sat up quickly, seemingly unharmed. She stared only at Grady and spoke with such assuredness that Mandy could not doubt her for a second. "I know where to look."

Grady nodded, but there was pain etched in his features. Kayla cringed at the sight. "What's wrong, Grady?"

Grady forced a smile to his lips, but it didn't reach his eyes. "You fell." His two small words said everything Kayla needed to know, everything she hated to know.

Kayla rested her hand on his cheek. "I'm fine, really. Nothing hurts." She shifted her weight and winced. "Well, it only hurts a little. Just minor bruises." She smiled sheepishly as Grady took her hand, carefully helping her to her feet. She took a few shaky steps down the trail before her feet finally steadied beneath her. "Come on, we're almost there."

Mandy and Justin were only a few feet behind Grady, who was right on Kayla's heels. Mandy glanced through a break in the foliage to take in the view of Golden Gate Canyon—that's what Justin had called it in the car—for a split second, then heard some leaves rustling just in front of her. Her eyes shot back to the trail in front of them. Kayla was nowhere to be seen.

She whispered "Where'd she go?" to Justin just as Grady took a few steps backward, then turned a sharp left into the dense, thick forest. From the noise he was making, he was running. Fast.

Mandy ducked into the forest, Justin right beside her, but they were too far behind their friends to see them. "Grady? Kayla?" Justin called out.

Grady's answering call was ahead and slightly to the left of them, but closer than Mandy would've thought. This overgrowth was really thick.

Mandy started running toward Grady's voice, but Justin got there first—and nearly ran into Grady. Kayla was just a few feet away from him, frozen in place, staring straight ahead. Grady was off to her side, staring at the side of her face. Mandy could only guess what he was thinking.

She walked up to Kayla, placing one of her hands on her friend's shoulder. "Kayla? Where is it?" Mandy shook her gently, hoping to shake a response out of her. She didn't bother asking *what* was going on—she already knew that. What she didn't know was the *where*.

Kayla raised her arm slowly and pointed to an insignificant spot on the ground. Mandy understood immediately. She dropped to her knees near the spot at the same time Kayla did, no questions asked.

Kayla looked up at Grady, her eyes asking a silent question.

Grady reached in his pocket for his flashlight. Mandy was amazed at how well they could already sense each other's thoughts in just a few short weeks. She had a hunch that Grady and Kayla already knew how much they cared for each other; when they would let her and Justin know was the only question now.

She smiled, then turned back to the task at hand, watching as Grady and Kayla began digging with the crude tool, making very little progress. Grady addressed Justin without looking up. "Justin, I think there are a few shovels in the back of the truck."

Justin nodded and took off. Mandy heard a rush of leaves and a gust of wind; her eyes shot up to find he was already gone. That man was *fast*.

He was back in what had to be no more than a minute. How could he have come back so quickly? That trip would've easily taken her between five and seven minutes through this thick forest. How did he do it?

She pushed the thought to the back of her mind; there were more pressing things at hand. Turning her attention back to the dirt in front of her, she grabbed one of the shovels and started digging. Kayla and Grady knelt on either side of her and did the same while Justin wiped away what dirt he could with his hands. Mandy rolled her eyes. He never did mind getting a little dirty.

The group had been digging for a good five minutes before the metal head on Kayla's shovel struck a solid object with a dull thud. Throwing a glance at the others, she set down her shovel then lay down on her stomach to start dusting off whatever was buried here. With the others' help, whatever it was soon lay uncovered. The four of them peered over the edge of the hole.

The large metal object they saw reminded Kayla of a small, thin safe, about the size of a few shoeboxes laid side by side. Grady reached down into the deep hole to retrieve it, lying down next to Kayla so he could use both hands. Kayla watched as he struggled to lift it out of the hole; that box had to be much heavier than it looked.

Its surface was a shiny silver—impossible by Kayla's estimation, given they'd just pulled it out of the dirt—that brilliantly refracted the few afternoon sun's rays that made it through the canopy of trees above them. Weird.

Kayla moved to sit next to Grady and pulled the box between them, setting it on the ground in front of the hole they'd just made. She searched for an opening, a keyhole, *any* way inside. But the box appeared to be sealed shut—well, sealed wasn't exactly the right word. The box had absolutely no holes, no *seams*. It was one hard, impenetrable piece.

Kayla turned the box over to examine it. Its surface was completely smooth, devoid of markings of any kind, including the ones her shovel should have made.

As she flipped the box back over, something inside knocked against its interior and she jumped, dropping the box on the ground.

Mandy, standing nearby, picked up a shovel and slammed it down on the hard metal, but the box remained unaffected; its exterior showed no indication that she'd even struck it.

"We could try to find something stronger; maybe something to cut through the metal?" she suggested.

Kayla shrugged, almost certain it wouldn't work. She glanced at Grady, who shrugged back. Mandy continued to examine the metal box, running her hands over the smooth surface again and again.

Then Justin reached for the box.

As soon as his hands touched each side of the box, his body wrenched violently, then straightened as Justin jerked abruptly to his feet as if by an invisible force. The quiet of the forest was then viciously breached by a sharp grinding sound —the sonorous, grating sound of metal against metal. Kayla cringed away from the screeching, involuntarily squeezing her eyes shut for a few seconds. When she opened them, a hauntingly familiar sight made her mouth drop open.

Justin was *glowing*. The ambient light flowed in ripples along the surface of his body, and he was trembling faintly. His eyes were closed peacefully, despite the turmoil readily evident on his skin. Then the shaking stopped, and an eerie stillness took its place. Justin stood perfectly still, motionless; his hands were flat but still clutching the metal box on either side, looking as though they were glued to the surface. His face was raised to the sky as if he were simply enjoying the warmth of the sun on his skin.

The metallic shrieking subsided slowly. Kayla's eyes were glued to the box in Justin's hands; they widened as a fissure tore the box in two. A blinding light shot out from the crack; its exodus took with it the screeching cacophony, leaving a thundering silence in its place.

Kayla stared wide-eyed at Justin, unable to form any appropriate words. Grady was frozen, mouth open. Mandy gasped.

In Justin's hands, where the metal box had been, was a book.

Finally coming out of his trance, Justin lowered his head, opening his eyes. His gaze immediately rested on Mandy, and his lips widened into a gleaming smile. Mandy jumped to her feet and ran into his arms. He hugged her tightly with his right arm as he shifted the book into his left in one smooth motion. Their eyes closed contentedly as the embrace lengthened, neither moving away.

Kayla's brow furrowed as she shot Grady a quick glance. What was going on?

Mandy was the first to talk, looking up at Justin. "You feel it, don't you?"

Justin nodded.

Then Kayla understood. "Amazing," she breathed.

Grady leaned over to her and whispered, "What'd I miss?"

Kayla smiled. "He's feeling the power now. Just like Mandy."

Justin overheard her explanation and nodded excitedly. "That was *incredible.*"

Mandy smiled up at him. "I remember."

The couple finally broke their embrace—though Justin kept Mandy's hand in his, seemingly unable to let her go— and dropped to the ground around their newly dug hole. As soon as they hit the ground they began jabbering rapidly to each other, and everything else seemed to fall away.

"Do you feel it still? The power coursing through you . . ."

Mandy nodded vehemently. "Barely, but it's still there." She swallowed quickly. "You were glowing. I was, too, wasn't I? It's so hard to believe . . ."

"I can't believe it, either. I don't know what it all means. I feel so—"

"—powerful, but like you don't know how to release it?"

"Yeah. Like I don't know what to do with it. Kind of like I *should* know what to do with it, but I don't."

"Like something's missing."

"Yeah."

Justin's one-word response finally silenced them. They stared at each other briefly, then slowly, almost comically, simultaneously turned to stare at Kayla and Grady, finally acknowledging the rest of their group. Kayla wanted to laugh aloud at their identical reactions, but their suddenly solemn expressions stopped her short.

"What's wrong?" Grady asked, reaching for Kayla's hand.

"Well, we just—I don't know how to explain it." Mandy looked at Justin.

Justin attempted. "I almost . . . well, *heard* what Mandy was thinking, but it wasn't really like that." He glanced over at Mandy.

Mandy took over. "It was kind of like I just knew what Justin was thinking, and I'd had the same thought, too. Like we had one mind."

Kayla, not even sure what to address first, felt her mouth drop open. "What was it?"

Mandy paused. "You two are what we're missing."

"What?!"

Justin answered Grady's question. "We have the power now, but for some reason—don't ask us how we know, we just know—we can't fully access it before the two of you, well . . ." he glanced over at Mandy for a split second before looking back at Kayla and Grady. "Before you . . . get yours."

Kayla just stared. She'd heard what he'd said, but it wasn't really registering. They'd all discussed the four of them getting powers as a possibility, sure, but what Mandy and Justin were saying now somehow threw it into the realm of reality. How could they be so certain—how could they just *know*?

Kayla bit her bottom lip. Maybe the same way she just *knew* that the first book would be in Alaska, and that the second book would be here?

Kayla shivered.

CHAPTER 20

Stanfords

Just outside Bozeman, Montana

JUST UNDER TWO HOURS LATER, Grady turned the SUV into the driveway of Justin's parents' home. The house stood silent in stark contrast to the bright, late afternoon sky; the storm starting just before they'd left Yellowstone hadn't reached Bozeman yet—if it ever would.

Kayla expected to see Jan in the garden at the side of the house, or Roger in the garage tinkering on his next project. Though young, both were retired—Kayla inferred they'd made a large sum of money in the .com boom or something, but they'd never said—and their various pursuits usually centered around their beloved home.

So the eerie stillness that greeted them now made her hair stand on end. The house showed no signs of life, gave no indication that anyone was home. Kayla tensed; something was not right.

Grady pulled right up to the closed garage door slowly; the only sounds reaching Kayla's ears were the crunch of gravel beneath their tires and the low hum of the Jeep's engine. Grady purposefully placed the car in park and turned the key. The silence that met Kayla's ears through their open windows was even more pronounced without the crunching gravel or the rumbling motor.

Though she could hear Mandy and Justin opening their doors and getting out behind her, Kayla stayed where she was, glued to her seat. She just really didn't want to get out of the car.

Justin squinted in the brightly lit landscape as he carefully exited the vehicle, barely shutting his door to keep silent—an automatic reaction to perceived danger. Justin led the group —he noticed Kayla following a good distance behind Mandy and Grady—and found each breath he took coming more quickly than the last. He cautiously approached the front door, tapping on it gently. The door gave way under his light touch and Justin heard Mandy gasp from behind him. His eyes drifted down to the broken latch; someone—someone uninvited—had been here.

Justin entered the house, and, as he did, he felt a knot start to form in the pit of his stomach. On an imperceptible signal that no one was in the house, Justin rushed down the hall to the kitchen, calling for his parents as he went.

Before she got to the kitchen, Mandy ran into a wall—Justin stood frozen in the hallway. Mandy leaned around him, her eyes never leaving his face, careful not to look at the scene his blank eyes were taking in. She'd never seen Justin's countenance so . . . nondescript. Like he was no longer there.

Her eyes slid to the side unwillingly but she forced her head to remain frozen. She did not want to know what Justin was seeing—it had to be something so horrific that he now stood unmoving, staring—but she could guess. She tried to force the image she knew she was about to see from her mind, but to no avail. She stared harder at Justin's face, brows furrowing, eyes narrowing. She didn't dare move.

Out of the corner of her eye, Mandy noticed Grady lean around her to survey the room. Kayla cried out a second later. Mandy saw Kayla grasp the edge of the doorway in an attempt to remain standing as her knees buckled beneath her.

Unable to fight it any longer, Mandy turned ever so slowly, first taking in the horrified look on Grady's face, then Kayla gasping for breath on her knees, before she turned completely around. Her breath stopped.

The sunny kitchen, which had, just hours ago, been a place of warmth and happiness, was now the exact opposite, the antithesis of home and family. The bright curtains above the sink, once cheerfully splashed with vibrant blue and yellow flowers, were now stained with red. Darkening red streaks covered the edge of the kitchen sink, smeared down the side of the cupboard.

Mandy's eyes followed the crimson line to the floor. She screamed.

On the floor, lying side by side with hands barely touching, were Justin's parents. Their eyes seemed dull, unseeing. Scarlet pools collected on the ground beneath their heads; their throats were cut with a perverse precision. They didn't appear to be breathing.

Justin fell to his knees. The spattered kitchen in front of him epitomized the most vicious of crime scenes, its horror reserved for only the most unlucky of visitors. And these victims—guilty of nothing, certainly nothing that warranted this—were his parents.

He was choking, unable to catch a breath. Mandy dropped to her knees in front of him, putting herself between him and the gruesome sight. She gripped his face fiercely, willing him to look at her. His eyes, which had been fixed on the gory scene, slowly turned to meet Mandy's. They stared intently at each other, sharing this moment of abrupt and devastating grief in silence. A single tear escaped down Justin's cheek.

"Jus . . . Justin . . ." a choking voice whispered.

Justin's eyes shot up. He flew to his feet then fell at his father's side. "Call 911!"

Kayla ran for the phone, quickly punching in the number.

"Dad? Dad, can you hear me?" Justin grasped his father's free hand, holding it in both of his as he strained for any response.

But his dad was unconscious again; his eyes rolled into the back of his head. Justin started CPR in a desperate attempt to revive his father. Justin leaned over, his ear to his father's mouth. His breathing was irregular, coming in shallow gasps, but still there. He sighed, shoulders relaxing, when his fingers found a faint but consistent pulse on his wrist.

He reached up to the counter, his hand finding a cloth. He pressed it to the wound on his dad's throat, pressing tightly to stop the bleeding, but not so tightly he couldn't breathe.

Mandy was already at his side, and now took over. Justin—sure then that his father was being taken care of—attended to his mother.

He moved around Mandy to his mother's other side, grabbing her wrist. He stared at his watch as he searched for a pulse. He leaned his ear to her mouth, listening for any signs of life. He found none.

He immediately began CPR, trying in vain to revive his mother. But his attempts were ineffective and he soon gave up; his mother was gone. He slowly laid his head on her stomach. He couldn't feel a thing.

Kayla returned the phone to its cradle and joined Grady who was carefully looking over the scene. Justin's eyes stared blankly, unseeing. Kayla walked over to him, resting her hand on his back for a brief moment, then drawing it back almost as quickly. Kayla could understand how he felt. She herself had been overwhelmed with grief once, and it never really went away.

It seemed like a lifetime ago.

As she took her place on the floor next to Grady, drawing her knees up to her chest and leaning back against the cupboard, she fought the ensuing onslaught of painful harsh images that she could never fully erase from her memory. She'd tried to forget, tried to shove the memories back to the furthest reaches of her mind, but the sight of Justin's parents just lying there in a pool of their own blood . . . a single tear escaped the corner of her eye, followed by another and another until she had to wipe them away with the back of her hand. She was fighting—but she was losing.

A sharp knock on the front door made Kayla jump, but she was exceedingly grateful for the distraction. She rose too quickly on her way to the front door, causing her head to spin. Lightheaded, she teetered slightly before stabilizing herself with the kitchen counter. Perhaps her fall at Yellowstone had affected her more than she'd like to believe. She blinked and shook her head to clear it before she took a few unsure steps toward the front of the house. She deliberately drew a deep breath as she reached the door.

Kayla threw the door open and immediately stood aside as the paramedics rushed through. She pointed toward the kitchen but stayed frozen in place.

She would've thought this would've been easier, having been through it before. Apparently experience doesn't help in this kind of situation. *Maybe it makes it worse. Because I know what's coming next for him.*

After making sure that the paramedics had plenty of time to get set up in the kitchen, she slowly made her way back to the room. She needed to see Grady right now, to feel him next to her. She needed the support. Literally.

She drew another deep breath before entering the room. She tried to prepare herself again for the scene, but knew her attempt was in vain. She didn't understand how the paramedics in front of her could walk into something like this all the time and still do their jobs.

The room was worse than her brain had remembered it, and the sight alone made her nauseous. Instead of letting herself fully absorb the gruesome scene in front of her, she turned her attention to Grady, focusing her eyes solely on him. She fought with all her strength to ignore everything else in the room as she walked over to him with slow, deliberate steps.

He looked up before she reached him. Once he saw the expression on her face, he jumped to his feet and ran to her side, pulling her to his chest. He couldn't begin to guess what she was thinking; he just knew she needed him now.

They stood there in the middle of the room and let everything else disappear for a few brief moments. They drowned out the sound of the paramedics frantically trying to revive Justin's mother, desperately trying to stabilize Justin's father, repeatedly moving Mandy and Justin out of the way so they could work. As the world fell away, Kayla and Grady simply leaned on each other, offered each other strength when they didn't have enough themselves.

After a few moments, Grady pulled away to look at Kayla's face. He couldn't make sense of the expression he saw there. He'd recently discovered Kayla to be a strong person, able to handle just about anything thrown her way; their kidnapping had proved that. What had happened to Justin's parents was beyond horrendous, but he sensed something else beneath the surface, something that told him there was more to the story.

Grady put his hand under her chin and raised her eyes to meet his. Her eyes were pleading with him through her tears —a silent but unmistakable plea to make her suffering go away.

He stole a glance around the horrifying kitchen, ensuring that they were not needed. Then he dropped his hand from Kayla's shoulder and grabbed her hand, leading her to the living room. He sat on the floral couch and pulled her down next to him, then put both hands on her shoulders and turned her to face him.

"Kayla, sweetie, what's wrong?"

Kayla's head dropped, and Grady's heart broke. She just looked so utterly and completely helpless.

But Grady wasn't going to let her deal with whatever this was alone. "Kayla?" He dropped his head until his eyes met hers.

Kayla sighed and clutched his hand tightly in both of hers. "Did I ever tell you about my family?"

Grady shook his head but remained silent.

Kayla took a breath. "When I was fifteen, growing up near Seattle, I came home from school one day and my mom and sister weren't home like they were supposed to be. At first, I didn't think anything of it, but then my dad came in the front door and I knew . . ." Her voice cracked. "I knew something was wrong." She wiped away a lone tear trailing down her cheek. "My mom and sister had been in a horrible car accident. My sister survived, with months of therapy. But my mom . . ." Her voice trailed off.

Grady understood. He reached his free hand around the back of her neck and pulled her head to his chest. "I'm so sorry." His heart ached for her suffering, for what she had lost. He could feel his own heart breaking again as he heard Kayla's muted sobs. He wished he could take her pain away.

Kayla broke the silence after a short time. "This just . . . brings back all those memories. I had them locked away nicely. I didn't want to think about them again." She kept her head on his chest.

Grady kissed the top of her head. "I am truly sorry you had to go through that—and have to go through it again."

Kayla raised her head to look at him, the tears still flowing. "I want Justin to know that I understand. But I . . . I just don't know what to say to him."

Grady caught and held her gaze. "Just think about what you needed to hear. Sincerity goes a long way."

Kayla nodded and stretched up to kiss his cheek. Her tears were drying; it seemed that for now, she was done crying. "I don't deserve you." She smiled faintly up at him.

Grady kissed her forehead. "I'm sure you have that backward." He rose to his feet, then helped Kayla to hers. "Are you okay now? Can you go back in?"

Kayla nodded, wiping under her eyes, then stood straighter as if to convince herself it were true. She grabbed Grady's hand once again, and let him lead her back to the kitchen.

After

IT HAD STARTED RAINING. That was all that Justin could think of as the paramedics wheeled Roger Stanford outside. Wouldn't his dad get wet?

He stumbled out of the kitchen—Kayla and Mandy were both very close on either side of him, but he couldn't figure out why—and collapsed on the couch in the living room. The rain was hitting the porch roof. It seemed really loud. Why wouldn't it stop?

He supposed it was fitting. Rain always accompanies sad occasions, doesn't it?

He idly noticed Mandy holding his hand; he didn't even feel it. He thought she seemed worried. The thought perplexed him. Worried about what? His dad? *Yeah,* he thought, *that would make sense.*

He closed his eyes and laid his head against the back of the couch. Kayla touched his shoulder lightly. He wanted to shrug it off, but what was the point? The rain just wouldn't stop coming, his dad was getting wet, and his mom . . .

No. He would think about hiking, camping, their recent trip to Yellowstone. It had been so beautiful there. So unlike here. Was that just this morning?

He heard a second stretcher coming down the hall, but didn't open his eyes. He didn't need to. He knew very well what he would see if he did.

His mom was gonna get wet, too.

"Justin?" A quiet voice barely got through. "Baby?"

He blinked and opened his eyes, but didn't move his head. Again, what was the point?

He felt Mandy's chest heave beside him. Why was she so upset? She barely knew his parents! He was the one who should be upset! He was the one who had been robbed of his family! No more heartfelt birthday cards, no more home-made Thanksgiving dinners, no more snowy Christmases . . .

Geez, stop it already.

"Justin." Mandy was still trying. He was listening, wasn't he? She was right here, right next to him. *Say it already! I can hear you, obviously.*

"Baby, are you okay?"

Of course I'm not okay! How could I possibly be okay? Justin made an attempt to sit up and eked out one word. "Yeah."

Mandy and Kayla both sighed beside him. Grady cleared his throat from the chair across the room. When did he get in here?

"Justin," Grady began, "what can we do for you?"

Justin straightened his back, sitting up rigidly. At least he felt rigid. "Where did they take my dad?"

Grady glanced through the closed window. "They gave me the name of the hospital. We can go there, if you'd like."

Justin nodded. He didn't have any other ideas, and all this talking was giving him a headache. Or was it just making the one he already had worse?

Kayla patted his shoulder. He felt like a dog.

Perhaps just to change the subject, he muttered, "I can't stay here tonight."

Grady nodded and jumped to his feet. Justin thought it might have looked funny under any other circumstances. He thought Grady looked eager to leave the room. He didn't blame him. Justin was eager to leave, too.

Kayla stood with him. "We'll go pack up our things. Meet you in the car?"

Justin felt Mandy nod beside him. "Yeah, we need some air, anyway."

Mandy stood and Justin followed, glad to step outside and finally be out of the house.

He didn't care if he got wet.

The Parkside Motel—Grady'd gotten the name from Roger's doctor, Dr. Coolidge, just before they'd left the hospital; Roger was still unconscious so Dr. Coolidge promised to call if he woke up—was moderately maintained, marginally clean, but in desperate need of an update. It certainly wasn't fancy, but Kayla was glad they at least had somewhere to stay. Somewhere that wasn't Justin's parents' house.

Nestled up close to the five-story hospital, the two-story motel was invisible from all but the hospital's north side. Though the hospital was large, the motel was not, and, except for a dismal four-pump gas station, the tiny motel stood alone on the back side of the hospital.

Knowing they would not want to be far from the hospital—and that they all needed some rest—Grady checked the four of them in for the night. Justin and Mandy sauntered off to their room in silence, oblivious to the diminishing rain still steady enough to soak through their shirts.

It was already seven thirty, so Kayla suggested she and Grady head out to find some food. When Mandy answered the door with bloodshot eyes, Kayla immediately realized that her friends weren't ready to be out in public. She quickly promised to bring back some food for the two of them. Mandy simply nodded then slowly turned and disappeared back into the darkness.

Grady drove to a nearby diner, a small, middle-of-nowhere establishment complete with a uniformed waitress behind the counter serving up endless refills of bad coffee from a stained carafe. Kayla headed toward the only available booth, one wedged between the front entrance and a side wall.

The other of the two booths was full of a group of white-haired men, chatting about the events around town loud enough for Kayla to hear. The three remaining tables were filled with a group of teenagers on their phones, a young mom and dad desperately trying to corral their two toddlers, and a gossiping group of older women who seemed to be keeping an eye on the group of older men.

Kayla slid into the booth as quickly as she could, avoiding eye contact with the locals who had all looked up when the bell on the front door shook and Kayla and Grady had stepped inside, shaking rain droplets from their jackets. Kayla was glad Justin wasn't here. Someone could recognize him here, and bring him unwanted attention. Just the two of them were getting enough unwanted attention as it was.

"Hi, I'm Kathy." The thin, bubbly waitress approached their table. "What can I get for ya?"

Kayla smiled at her appearance—it felt good to be allowed to smile, if just for a moment—and tried not to stare. Their waitress was smacking a large wad of gum and even had a pencil tucked behind her ear, which she now pulled out. Her curly red hair, unruly and short, clashed harshly with her unflattering yellow uniform.

Kayla looked at Grady, who was clearly fighting a grin. "A soda and a burger for me." He glanced at Kayla. "Hmmm . . . chicken for you?"

Kayla nodded in response, pleased that Grady was getting to know what she ate. "Chicken sandwich, please. No mayo. And a water, no ice." She handed the menus to the amiable middle-aged waitress who smiled as she collected them and left the table.

Kayla took a deep breath and released it slowly. "Big day, huh?"

Grady nodded slowly. "I would say so."

"Let's not repeat it, okay?"

Grady met her gaze. "Definitely." He reached across the table for Kayla's hand and she smiled at him as he slowly rubbed the top of it.

Then she noticed the slight slant of Grady's head and the furrow of his eyebrows and her smile fell. "We have work to do."

"Yes, we do."

Kayla reached in her backpack and pulled out Justin's book. She had kept it with her all day, knowing that Justin had more important things on his mind but wanting to keep it safe.

She opened the book, hoping to find something more than the gibberish that Mandy's book had held. She held her breath without meaning to as she opened the front cover.

Less than a minute later, Kayla exhaled loudly and frowned. The symbols were more of the same nonsense that Mandy's book had so infuriatingly displayed. Kayla flipped through the ancient pages slowly, checking each page to see if anything was readable. She began flipping a little faster—still with great care—searching for something she wasn't entirely sure she'd find.

Wait . . . what was that? Kayla stopped, then started flipping backward. She was sure her eye had caught something.

"What is it? What did you find?" Grady moved to the edge of his seat, his neck craning to see the page.

Kayla simply furrowed her brow, still searching. Then . . . Her hand stopped on the page that had caught her attention.

There, on a seemingly innocuous page, was a collection of hundreds, maybe thousands, of symbols. And in the middle— the exact middle, she was almost certain—was the symbol for *fire*. The same symbol that adorned the cover.

But the symbol itself was not what had caught Kayla's attention. The shape of it *and* the surrounding symbols seemed to form a bigger picture, something Kayla couldn't quite make out, but it was enough to catch the attention of her subconscious mind.

What *was* that?

She turned the book around to face Grady. "Do you see anything on this page? Anything unusual?"

Grady scrutinized the page, eyes squinting. He bit down softly on his bottom lip, which made Kayla smile, just a little. She loved when he did that. "What is it? What are we looking at?"

Kayla turned her attention to the page, viewing it upside-down while trying to understand what had stopped her in her tracks. She sighed as her smile slowly faded and her shoulders slumped. "I don't know."

Their enthusiastic waitress arrived with a beaten up brown tray full of food and drinks. Just as soon as the saucy woman set her plate down, Kayla politely moved it aside to continue to examine the book, which she turned around to face her again. She just stared at it until the waitress headed for the kitchen with her empty tray. "I think . . . I'm not sure, but I think these symbols are pieces of a larger symbol, or . . ." she took another long look at the page, then her eyes widened. Finally.

The seemingly random collection of symbols formed a picture.

Kayla almost laughed. "I know where I've seen this."

"Where?" Grady snagged a fry and munched on it, still on the edge of his seat as he leaned toward Kayla over the table.

"This looks like one of the images I've seen in my visions. A river, or a lake." Her fingers hovered over the page as she outlined the shape.

Grady turned the book around to get a closer look. After a minute, his mouth fell open and his deep blue eyes widened. "Amazing."

Kayla nodded, her smile widening. "I think this is a clue to the next location."

Grady grinned back and winked at her. "Excellent."

Kayla relaxed her shoulders and returned the book to her bag. She slid her plate in front of her, barely stretching her hand around the monstrosity they called a chicken sandwich before lifting it to her mouth. "Now let's eat before this gets cold."

CHAPTER 22

Gone

THE RAIN HAD STOPPED by the time Grady pulled into the hotel parking lot. On Kayla's lap were two white foam containers with whatever food was quickest to cook up at the diner before they left. At least Mandy and Justin would have the option of eating, even if they didn't feel like it.

Kayla could understand how they must be feeling, especially Justin. It had taken her months to even be able to catch a breath after the accident. It was nearly a year before she felt any semblance of normalcy. And even then, things were never the same, not really. She frowned, staring out the window at the overcast evening sky.

Grady pulled into a parking spot and slowly shifted the Jeep into park, then leaned back in his seat with an audible sigh. Kayla reached over and grabbed his hand. She could imagine that the thoughts going through his head were similar to her own: How should they act around Justin and Mandy? What should they say? She wished she knew.

As soon as their car doors slammed, the door to Mandy and Justin's room opened and their two friends stumbled outside, blinking in the waning sunlight. Mandy wiped a stray tear from her cheek with the back of her hand.

Kayla could tell the instant that Justin registered their presence. He smiled—a sad smile, but a smile nonetheless—and hurried over to her. He eyed the food she was still carrying. "Something for us?"

Kayla wanted to smile back, but was too confused to do anything but hold one of the white containers out for him to take. He muttered a quick 'thanks' before grabbing a plastic silverware packet from the small brown bag she held in her other hand and leaning up against the car. Mandy followed suit, the prospect of food seemingly lightening her mood as well. Kayla shook her head and raised her eyebrow at Grady, who simply shrugged.

After a few minutes, Mandy broke the silence as she chewed on a fry. "So what happened? You found something, right?"

Kayla had no idea what to say. Grady just stared.

"We felt it."

Grady found his voice, barely a whisper. "What?"

Justin, gnawing on a piece of bread, answered him with his mouth still half-full. "We were just sitting there, and we suddenly could *see* what you saw. It was in the book, right? A river or something?"

Kayla just nodded, staring.

Mandy jumped in. "It made us remember what brought us out here. Why we were here in the first place." She looked at Justin, reaching over to stroke his shoulder.

Justin nodded slowly, his expression softening as he gave Mandy a half-smile. "My mom would've wanted us to continue. She was excited for us, eager even. You all saw it. She wouldn't have wanted us to give up now."

Kayla fell silent, contemplating Justin's words. His whispered confession seemed sincere enough, but Kayla wondered at his newfound acceptance of his mother's death. Shouldn't he still be grieving? Had he *ever* let himself grieve? He didn't even look like he'd been crying.

Kayla glanced over at Mandy, the question in her eyes. Mandy simply met her gaze with less worry on her face than Kayla had seen since their discovery at Justin's home. The corners of Mandy's mouth turned up slightly, an obvious attempt to calm Kayla's worries about Justin.

It didn't work.

Mercenary Outpost, Location Unknown

"Sir?"

The Commander looked up from the map in front of him without lifting his head. "Yes?"

The Commander of the Western Detachment, a thick, steely man sitting on a collapsible stool behind a piece of plywood laid across two empty water barrels, appraised the tall, muscular soldier who'd just entered his tent. The soldier stood at attention, his gaze fixed on an unimportant spot on the tent's back wall. "The targets were hit, per your instructions. Clean attack, in and out."

One corner of the Commander's mouth turned up. He couldn't help it. "And the Americans?"

There was the slightest hesitation before the answer came. "We are still watching that develop. We are unsure of their next course of action. I do not think they have been able to form any plan to continue on their misguided quest."

"Good." The Commander looked back down at the papers he'd been working on. This was better than he'd expected. From the report, it sounded like his orders were carried out thoroughly. But one can never be too careful . . . He looked up again. "Were the targets confirmed dead?"

A longer pause, and the soldier shifted his weight. That couldn't be a good thing. "Well . . . I . . ." He cleared his throat. "I believe so, sir."

The Commander lifted his head and stared directly at the soldier, who still would not meet his gaze. "You *believe* so? Did you not confirm?"

The young man shook his head, slowly. "The Americans arrived sooner than we expected. We had to leave without solid confirmation. But we believe they were dead; neither one was breathing when we left." The last sentence was hurried, the words spilling out as fast as he could say them.

The Commander stared off into space, contemplating this news. After a few long moments, he nodded to himself. "Where are the others?"

The soldier's face visibly relaxed. "The men have returned. They are resting now; I assumed you would approve of them taking the rest of the day off."

The Commander nodded, uncertain of whether or not the soldier would even see it; he seemed fixated on that same spot on the back wall. "That's fine." Then he forced a smile, knowing that the soldier would be able to hear it in his voice. "I am happy to hear that the mission went well. Thank you."

The soldier's gaze met his for a split second before the younger man went back to his bothersome staring.

The Commander waved him off. "You are dismissed."

The soldier nodded once, then turned to leave.

But then the Commander thought of something. "Soldier?"

The man whipped around. "Yes, sir?"

His superior stood, coming out from behind his makeshift desk and crossing the small space to where his soldier stood. He placed his hand on the young man's shoulder as he spoke. "I want to commend you personally. This was good work."

The young soldier was beaming, but somehow managed to do so without smiling. "Thank you, sir."

The Commander nodded and released the shoulder of the other man, who promptly took his leave.

The Commander allowed himself a long, satisfying smile. This really *was* going better than he expected. The Elders would be pleased. Surely Fate must be smiling on them.

Then he remembered what his soldier had said, how unconvinced he was that the mission was one hundred percent successful, and the smile died on his lips. He abruptly turned, quickly storming out of the tent. He had to check in.

Bozeman, Montana

Kayla was awakened by a bright light shining in her eyes. She squinted, then sleepily raised her arm to shield her eyes. Where was she?

She sat up, blinked. What was that light? She noticed a blinding streak of light coming in the window to her left . . . Oh, yes. It must be morning. And that made this her hotel room. In Bozeman.

And it all came rushing back. She sighed, wiped her hands across her face and through her hair, blinked a few more times. She pulled her knees up to her chest under the blankets, resting her forearms on them and gazing around the room. It wasn't usually this hard to wake up. What time was it?

Early, according to the bedside clock. She groaned. This was way too early, even for her and her morning-person tendencies.

She lay back down and pulled the blankets up to her neck, turning away from the blinding sun. It was too early to get out of bed, even to close the privacy curtains.

A knock sounded at the door, and Kayla groaned again, mumbling "go away" to whoever was interrupting her sleep—er, waking.

The knock sounded again, more insistent. Kayla flung off the bed covers, swung her legs off the bed, then pushed herself up with both arms to a sitting position. With her feet finally on the ground, she opened her eyes.

There was that incessant knock again, followed by a "Kayla?"

Kayla jolted to her feet. Grady? What was he doing up this early?

"Coming!" she called as she reached for the sweatshirt laying on top of her suitcase. Grady didn't need to see the ratty T-shirt she slept in.

She swung open the door, probably a little too harshly. Groggy to wide awake in 1.9 seconds'll do that to a person. "Grady? What are . . . ?" Then she noticed the expression on his unshaven face, one she'd seen only twice before, both much too recently.

When Mandy had been attacked, when they'd first found Justin's parents . . . "Grady, what's wrong?" Her heart pounded erratically in her chest.

"It's Justin."

"What . . . is he okay?"

"He's missing."

Kayla didn't hesitate. "Give me ten minutes."

"Meet me in Mandy's room."

Kayla hurried back into the room to get the quickest shower on record—not overlooking that fact that Grady had said "Mandy's" room.

That didn't bode well.

"Mandy?"

Kayla, in khaki shorts and a loose T-shirt just nine minutes later, pushed open her friend's hotel room door, thankful that Grady'd had the foresight to prevent the door from closing with its own lock. As Kayla entered the still-dark room, Mandy lifted her tear-stained eyes to meet Kayla's gaze. Kayla crossed the room as fast as she could and took a seat on the bed next to Mandy, draping an arm across her friend's shoulders. "What happened?"

Mandy sniffed. "Justin's gone. I don't know where. I woke up and he was just . . . gone." A fresh gush of tears spilled down her cheeks. She buried her face in her hands.

Kayla pulled her closer and looked over at Grady, who was sitting across the room. She wished Grady could read her mind, though she wasn't even sure what she was thinking. She just knew they needed to do something, and fast. Mandy didn't need this, especially now.

For a second, Grady appeared to be just as lost as Kayla was. Then something in his eyes changed, and he ran out of the room.

What was he up to?

Fortunately, Grady returned what had to be only a few minutes later, though it seemed like an eternity to Kayla. "What's going on, Grady?"

Mandy looked up at the sound of Kayla's voice, her eyes flying to Grady's face. Kayla felt her friend's body tense under her arm. *Grady, please have something—anything,* she begged wordlessly.

Grady's look couldn't really be described as a smile, or a grimace, but Kayla definitely saw something there, something that released the tightness in her chest the slightest bit. "I just spoke with Dr. Coolidge. He said that Justin was there fifteen minutes ago." Mandy gasped. "He said that Justin had already left, but maybe we can start there. Not really sure how much we'll be able to find out, though." Grady frowned.

Mandy jumped to her feet. "What are we waiting for? Let's go!" Then she looked down at her pajama pants and top as if noticing them for the first time. "Uh . . . give me a few minutes." She offered a sad half-smile, then headed for the bathroom.

They rendezvoused at the Jeep in less than five minutes. Mandy appeared wearing dark jeans and a fitted black T-shirt, her hair thrown up in a messy ponytail. She jumped in the backseat before the rest of them could even open their doors. Kayla noticed a strange energy about her, almost as if she were bouncing up and down, but not quite.

Grady threw the vehicle into reverse, then headed to the entrance of the hospital.

The doctor was waiting for them. He rushed over to them as soon as they burst through the ICU doors, quickly leading them to Roger's room. Just before they reached the doorway,

Dr. Coolidge turned to them. "Justin was here less than thirty minutes ago. He seemed distant, distracted—understandably, I suppose." He sighed. "He went in to see his father. Then, a few minutes after he arrived, Justin just suddenly ran out. We don't know why."

Grady nodded for the group. "Thank you, Doctor. We appreciate you letting us know. We just really need to find him, and this was the first place we thought to look." He glanced over at Mandy. "We won't be long, I promise."

Dr. Coolidge nodded and headed back toward the lobby.

CHAPTER 23

Fire

KAYLA SWALLOWED HARD AS she entered the room behind Mandy and Grady. She struggled to keep her eyes on everything but the man lying unconscious on the cold sterile bed in the middle of the room. She stared at the plastic cushioned pastel-orange chair by the bed that Mandy quickly sank into, Grady's perusal of the nurse's chart on the side wall with all kinds of indeterminate scribbles on it, and the covered window on the far wall, the thick blinds letting in very little light. Which just added to the dismality of the whole situation, in Kayla's opinion. As did the incessant beeping of Roger's heart monitor.

After having looked at everything else she could think of, Kayla reluctantly turned toward the unconscious man in the middle of the room. Roger Stanford, who, just a day earlier, had been laughing and talking with her and the others, was now lying on a callously white hospital bed, fighting for his life.

Kayla's fists clenched at her sides. What kind of people could do this to another human being? What had the man lying motionless in front of her with a thick bandage on his neck ever done to deserve this?

The answer was simple: nothing. He *didn't* deserve this. Neither of them did.

A single tear escaped the corner of her eye.

She fought to keep the anger from her face, for Mandy. Kayla looked over at her friend with a compassion she had to force herself to feel until she really saw Mandy's face.

Mandy's cheeks were stained with tears, as had been the norm for the last twenty hours or so. But Kayla noticed another layer—the corners of her eyes had drooped, her light brown eyebrows were furrowed—that told a more intimate story.

She was in incredible pain. A sorrow so great for a man that she'd only known for a few days was evident in the way she sat hunched over in the chair, avoiding eye contact with everyone in the room. Evident in the way that one look at Roger set off another wave of tears.

Mandy cared for him—Kayla could see that. Perhaps she'd loved him since she'd met him—or would have, if she'd been given the chance. Kayla knew that Mandy'd cared for Justin's mother as well; that was just the kind of person Mandy was. Kind, compassionate, loving. Everything good in a person.

Kayla desperately wished she could take away the pain, even take it on herself. That someone so tender would have to go through something so harsh was almost unbearable. As Mandy broke down completely and fell out of the chair onto her knees, Kayla knelt down beside her and put her arms around her, let her cry.

As her friend struggled against the crushing weight of grief and loss, Kayla just held her. Because she'd been there.

Because she understood how Mandy felt. Because she knew that anything anyone said didn't make it right, no matter how good their intentions.

Kayla stared at a spot on the wall above Roger's head and thought of Justin's mother. She knew, rationally, that death was just a part of life. She knew, rationally, that her own mother had not left her intentionally, or by choice.

But sometimes it felt that way.

As a result, she never allowed herself to get close to anyone. How could she, when they would inevitably disappear? First her mother, then Jonathan, the only man she had ever loved before Grady, had left her. Why did everyone she loved leave?

So her new relationship with Grady terrified her. She let herself think about it again, in the context of such a great loss. Could she survive it if he left?

But something in the back of her mind—a small but persistent voice—gave her the faintest glimmer of hope. Her mind had gone dark, despair clouding it, but this voice seemed to light it up, shining the smallest flicker of light into the dark recesses of her mind. It steadily grew until it illuminated her every thought.

Suddenly, she felt no more despair. Only hope. She knew, without knowing why, that everything would be fine. Despite the tragedy of yesterday, she knew that things would work out.

And now her head was clear. She began to think about the situation, analyze it, figure it out.

She recalled the scene at the house, swallowing hard as she pushed through her unwillingness to recall something so horrible.

The blood on the cabinet—there had been a fight. It was too spread out to think any differently. Footprints in the pooled blood—too many to belong to just one or two people. There had been at least three attackers.

The "who" was obvious. The Mercenaries had attacked again.

But why? Simply for the fun of it? They had killed before, seemingly without remorse. And now, again, they killed someone close to the four of them. Another warning, as before?

Of course. That had to be it. Another warning, another attempt to thwart their search. Just like the charm still around her neck . . .

The tiny light persisted, filling her mind with hope despite her desolate thoughts. With her mind's eye, she stared at it. It bounced and flickered as though a fire. Where was this light coming from? Though it was in her mind, the light didn't feel like it was coming from within her, but somehow coming from *outside* of her.

Then, without warning, the light blinked out. Hopelessness once again flooded her mind. The tears again welled up in her eyes. She gazed through the watery haze at the young woman next to her.

Mandy had stopped crying. She was looking up at Kayla with questions in her eyes.

Upon meeting Mandy's gaze, Kayla reached down and squeezed her friend's hand.

Kayla wiped her eyes and tried to force a smile. She knew Mandy needed her to be strong right now. She tightened her hold on Mandy's hand and pulled them both to their feet.

Mandy graciously returned Kayla's forced smile with a genuine, albeit teary, one of her own. Mandy went over to Grady, who'd been looking at Roger's chart, and started asking him some questions about the gibberish on it. Surprisingly, Grady knew the answers to most of Mandy's questions.

Kayla wondered idly if he spent all his free time watching those medical shows, then smiled to herself at the thought. What free time would a man with multiple degrees really have?

Kayla stood watching the scene, taking it in. Her smile faded as the hopelessness she felt began to once again permeate her mind, clouding her thoughts, darkening her mood. Then, in an instant, that tiny sliver of hope returned, flashing to life in the back of her mind, and she realized in looking at Mandy and Grady that she had people who loved her, cared for her. Her heart swelled.

This time, the light danced and flickered, quickly growing into a blazing fire. She again stared at it through her mind's eye, her thoughts abruptly silenced as she gazed in awe at the fire's white-hot center.

The fire blazed, burning hot in her mind, devouring her every thought. A gentle warmth started in her head and soon encompassed her entire body, growing warmer with every passing second. It was soon uncomfortably hot. And getting hotter.

Kayla grabbed her head, knowing full well it wouldn't do any good, and squeezed her eyes shut. She sunk to the cushioned chair Mandy'd just abandoned, the one right next to Roger's bed, a small moan escaping her lips.

Grady whipped around at the sound, and ran to her side. Mandy was at her other side in the next instant.

Kayla couldn't speak. A wildfire was burning through her mind, as though trying to swallow up her entire consciousness.

She couldn't think. Couldn't even breathe. The fire was consuming her, traveling out of her brain and throughout her entire body.

Only one thought escaped the torture. It was not of Grady, Mandy, or even of wanting the burning to stop. It was only of Justin.

Justin?

She tried to ignore the burning as she considered the thought. Why Justin?

Then, as if on cue, the fire stopped burning. Oh, the light was there, blazing bright into every part of her body, but it was no longer hurting her, burning her from the inside. It was cleansing her, cleaning out every dark, desolate part of her being, replacing it again with hope.

Hope?

Grady just stood there, staring at Kayla with eyes wide and mouth hanging open. Then Kayla started smiling and he instantly froze, a huge lump suddenly in his throat. What was happening?

Kayla slowly opened her eyes. But her mind was far from the hospital room.

The fire was *speaking* to her. Not audibly, of course, but she knew what it was trying to tell her. She watched as it ebbed slowly, then ignited suddenly, then ebbed again, as though trying to relay a message that only her confused mind could decipher.

Unlike her visions of the past, she saw no pictures. She saw no easy path to take, no sure course of action. Instead, she *felt* it.

Justin was alive.

She blinked, opening her eyes this time to the small hospital room. She took stock of her limbs, her torso, her head. Everything seemed intact. Her left hand was resting on her lap; her right hand was clutching at her chest. She just stared at it.

Suddenly she realized her hand was cramping. She slowly released it, finger by finger.

As the feeling in her hand came back, she noticed something sharp poking her palm. What was that?

She turned her closed fist over and opened it. She was grasping the charm she'd had around her neck all this time.

But it was what she saw next that caught her breath in her throat.

Directly underneath the charm, the exact shape and size, was a red mark burned into her flesh. How on earth did she not feel that?

Her eyes shot to Grady's. He'd already seen the burn and stared back at her wide-eyed, crouching down beside her and reaching for her hand. His touch was so gentle Kayla almost forgot she'd even been injured.

"Grady . . ." she managed to choke out. "What . . . what happened?"

Grady was still examining her hand. "It started glowing while you were . . . unconscious. I didn't realize you'd grabbed it."

"I don't even remember doing it." Kayla shifted in her seat, still staring at her burned palm.

Grady set her hand back in her lap, then headed out of the room without another word.

Kayla didn't even realize Mandy was at her other side until she spoke. "Uh, Kayla? What is *that*?"

Kayla blinked, then remembered. She hadn't told Mandy about the necklace.

She met Mandy's gaze for the first time since she'd entered the room. "This was mailed to me in Florida, before we even knew of the Mercenaries, the Old Ones, any of it."

Mandy swallowed hard. "What does it mean?"

Kayla gingerly fingered the charm, then picked it back up once she was certain it wasn't hot. It was actually a little cold. "I honestly don't know. This . . ."

Mandy interrupted so swiftly that Kayla blinked. "What if this is the Mercenaries' symbol? With this symbol etched into the walls of those caves . . . maybe they are more connected to all of this than we think. Maybe that's why they're doing all of this—the car bomb, my attack, Roger and Jan—they're trying to protect the books."

Kayla stared at the wall a moment before nodding. "That makes sense. I always felt like this was a warning of some kind."

Mandy nodded back. "To stop us from ever finding those books, I would imagine." She glanced over at Roger, placing her hand on his. She began stroking the back of his hand gently. The silence in the room lingered a little longer than Kayla would've liked.

"Kayla?"

"Yes?"

Mandy hesitated for a moment. "What did you see? In your vision, I mean. That *was* a vision, right?"

Kayla nodded slowly. "Yes, but it was different than the others."

Mandy cocked her head to one side, her hand still on Roger's. "How so?"

Kayla gulped. "I didn't really *see* anything. I more like *felt* it."

Mandy's eyes widened. "Felt what?"

"Justin."

Mandy gasped.

"I felt him. It was like he was telling me he's okay." Kayla smiled at her friend.

Mandy was still gaping. "So you *heard* him?"

Kayla bit her bottom lip. "Not really. I can't really explain it; I just know he's alive. I just don't know where." She frowned.

Mandy nodded. "Then we keep looking. Dr. Coolidge said he was just here. Maybe when Grady gets back we should head to his parents' house. He may have gone back there." Then she gasped as something occurred to her. "Kayla . . . what if he went back there to try to track down the mercenaries?" Her next words were strangled. "They will kill him."

Kayla stood and put her arm around her friend's shoulders, forcing what she hoped was a reassuring smile. "We'll just have to find him first."

But despite her show of confidence, Kayla wasn't so sure they would be able to find him in time. What if Justin *did* go after the mercenaries? It sure seemed like something he would do.

And what if they didn't find him first?

CHAPTER 24

Secret

Belize Rainforest

"NA-UM." HIS WHISPERED NAME seemed to come out of the air. He was too confused to answer.

But then he saw Holun over with the other soldiers, clearly ignoring them and looking straight at him across the clearing. He nodded once, and Holun sprinted to his side.

Na-um turned to stalk into the forest, Holun on his heels, before stopping to talk. "What is it, Holun?"

Holun licked his lips. "I've been searching for the Elders, like you said. And I noticed that something is wrong."

Na-um leaned in. "What is it?"

"The Western Detachment . . ."

"Yes?"

"I can't see them."

Na-um blinked. "What?"

"I've been checking in with the four detachments, but I cannot see the Western Detachment. It's almost as if . . . as if someone is blocking me."

Na-um was breathing hard now. "Any idea who?"

Holun started to shake his head, then stopped. "What if . . ." he lowered his voice considerably. "What if it's the Elders?"

Na-um considered it. "It could be."

"What does it mean?" Holun's brow furrowed.

Na-um crossed his arms. "I think the Elders *are* blocking you somehow. We'll have to find a way around it." Na-um closed his eyes, calling out in his mind to his Commander in Montana. Nothing.

So he tried another man he knew was there. Still nothing. So he tried another—nothing. He kept going, tried to contact every man up there . . .

Finally. One man answered. "Yes, sir?"

Na-um addressed the soldier by name before continuing. "What is happening up there?"

Na-um could almost see the eager look on the man's face. "Well, sir, the plan was successful."

Na-um sensed he needed to choose his words carefully. "And which plan was that?"

"The plan to attack the Americans."

Na-um had to bite his lip to keep from yelling. "Were they hurt?"

He could almost hear the smile in the soldier's voice. A dutiful soldier, just following orders. "The older ones were. The parents of one of the Four were killed."

Na-um felt himself start to burn on the inside. He'd done his research; he knew exactly who this soldier was talking about. "The younger man's parents?"

"Yes, sir."

Na-um didn't know where to go from here.

"Uh, sir?"

"Yes?"

"Why are you not asking the Commander for the report?"

Na-um frowned. He didn't want to alert anyone—least of all one of his newest and most impressionable soldiers—to the fact that he didn't know what was going on. "He was not available; he must be very busy."

"Oh, yes, sir. I heard that the Elders were having him check in with them often." The man stopped abruptly. "Did they not check in with you as well?"

That was the wrong question. Na-um made an effort to handle it with a clear head. "I have not had a chance to talk to the Elders."

"Okay, sir."

Na-um forced a smile into his voice. "Please accept my congratulations on your successful mission."

"Yes, sir, thank you."

Na-um cringed as he severed the connection. Why were the Elders usurping his authority? What gave them the right? And why wouldn't they tell him?

And how dare they issue orders that directly defied his!

He sighed. He really couldn't do much, not against the Elders. They had given him this authority—now it seemed they wanted to take it away. As much as he hated it, this was not his choice to make.

He opened his eyes and turned back to Holun. "The parents of one of the Four have been killed."

Holun gasped.

Na-um continued. "It seems the Elders gave the order. And nearly all of my men up there are blocked from me. I was lucky to find the one I did."

Holun stared for a moment before finding his voice. "So what are you going to do now?"

Na-um drew a slow breath. "I am not certain. Perhaps the Elders thought my approach was too passive, too risky. I've never known them to supersede my orders, though. They must think the Secret is in danger of being discovered."

Holun's heart skipped a beat. He had heard the stories of the Secret throughout his childhood. The Secret was to never be revealed. The Clan was in existence solely to prevent this from happening.

Na-um broke into Holun's thoughts. "Assemble the men in the east clearing, the one a good distance from here." He paused. "We're starting a training exercise."

Holun eyed his superior, curious as to what he was going to do next, but Na-um wasn't sharing. He wondered why.

Na-um was seething, and he struggled to keep it from his face. The Elders had overridden him, ignored his authority— that they had given him!—and had commanded his men to perform horrible actions to stop the Americans. Na-um hated what his superiors had done, but hoped this would at least keep the Americans from continuing their misguided quest to uncover the Secret.

He needed to get out of here. Na-um bolted into the woods, away from Holun, running until he was out of earshot of his men. He needed to be able to think without distraction.

What really *was* his plan? Was he being too passive, allowing the Americans to get too close? He had started this fight as any other: prepared to use any means necessary to achieve the objective. So why was he backing off? Was he losing his ability to lead? Perhaps the Elders were right in relieving him.

No, he didn't—couldn't—believe that. He deserved to lead, deserved to fight. He'd built this army, trained these men. He *should* be giving the orders.

So why had the Elders gone against him? Perhaps his apparent inaction *had* seemed passive, but shouldn't they have talked to him first, asked him about it? Challenged his methods so they could work together to find a better solution?

After all, he was a warrior. He knew that in battle there were casualties. The men in the Jeep at Lamanai had been the first casualties in this war. So why was he now concerned about the parents of one of the Americans?

He growled aloud, but no one was around to hear. Surely he wasn't sympathizing with the Americans. He couldn't allow himself sympathy for his enemies.

And they were his enemies, weren't they?

Or were they?

His mind spun in circles, furthering his confusion with every whirling pass. He shook his head frantically, trying to get the barrage to stop.

Finally, after a few dizzying moments, they did. His thoughts calmed, and he was abruptly struck with the image of his sister.

Tears welled up in his eyes, threatening to spill over. He missed his sister, his only family, dearly. He wished he could see her, talk to her. He needed to know she was okay.

Wiping the tears from his eyes, a thought occurred to him. Was Shani the reason he was becoming soft? He hadn't thought of her in years, not until he had told Holun her story. Was allowing himself to remember her causing him to have sympathy for these people—and their families, too?

It made him angry. He couldn't afford—his *Clan* could not afford—to let the Americans uncover the Secret. Its continual concealment was of utmost importance. Not only to him and to his people, but to the world.

So perhaps the Elders were right, after all.

This was a war, and in war, there are casualties.

This was a war, and in war, there are sacrifices.

This is war.

And he decided, that very moment, that he would do whatever it took. He would fight. And he would win.

No matter the cost.

Bozeman Deaconess Hospital, Bozeman, Montana

Grady reentered the room with a white tube in his hand. He walked straight to Kayla's side, kneeling down next to her before pulling the tube from his hand and unscrewing the lid.

Grady reached for her hand. "Here," he started, squeezing the ointment onto Kayla's burnt palm, "this should help." Kayla winced and Grady pulled back, but only for a second. "Sorry."

Kayla nodded once, sucking in her breath as Grady rubbed in the ointment. His touch was gentle, somehow comforting. Despite the coolness of the gel on her burnt hand, she could feel the warmth of his touch. She smiled, just a little, then stood as soon as Grady was done.

"Wait," Grady went over to a nearby cart and pulled open the drawers, looking for something. He headed back to Kayla when he found what he was looking for and starting wrapping her hand in gauze. Kayla felt like an invalid.

"Grady, I don't . . ."

"For me, please."

Kayla hesitated, then nodded once. She shoved her good hand into her pocket when he was done. "So what do we do now?"

Mandy grabbed her purse. "We need to find Justin."

Kayla nodded. "His parents' house?"

Mandy nodded back. "That's the only place I know to look."

Without another word, the three of them headed for the door.

CHAPTER 25

Feeling

THIS WAS TAKING TOO LONG. Mandy couldn't sit still, and the bumpy ride in the Jeep's backseat wasn't helping. Why weren't they at the house yet? She needed to see Justin, needed to *feel* him, needed to know for certain that he was okay. She felt like she couldn't breathe. This not-knowing, this waiting was too much. How was she . . .

Then she had an idea.

"Kayla?"

Kayla turned to look at her from the passenger seat. "Yeah?"

Mandy held out her hand. "Could I see that charm?"

Kayla glanced at Grady before turning again toward the backseat. "Uh, Mandy . . ."

Mandy kept going. "Please; I don't know how to explain it, but it might help me find Justin. It helped you know he was okay."

Kayla could feel Grady's eyes on her, but she was careful not to meet his gaze. She would have to explain that one to him later.

"Kayla, please. This should work. It *has* to work," Mandy pleaded.

Kayla sighed, then reached for the necklace, pulling the chain and the charm from around her neck. Mandy quickly reached for it, holding it by the chain and letting the charm dangle in front of her eyes.

She stared at the charm, willing it to let her see Justin, hear Justin, somehow communicate with him. And the longer she stared, the more the world fell away. Time seemed to slow, and she could barely tell the car underneath her was still moving. She whispered one word, "Justin," and blinked in slow motion as the sunlight hit the charm at just the right angle, glinting across her face.

Mandy.

She swallowed hard, then started crying. *Justin . . .* The word felt strangled, even in her head.

Mandy?

Justin, baby, where are you?

Mandy, what's happening? How are you doing this?

Mandy sniffled. *Baby, please. I'll explain later. Where are you?*

Mandy could sense his hesitation.

Justin, where are you? Please tell me.

He still didn't answer, but Mandy knew their connection was still intact. So she changed her approach.

What are you planning to do?

Finally, he answered. But once she heard his response, a small part of her somehow wished he hadn't. *Mandy, they have to pay.*

The tears came harder. *Justin, baby, no . . .* she choked on the words, willing him to change his mind.

I . . . I can't just let this go.

Mandy paused, tears streaming down her face. She couldn't see Kayla or Grady, or even the car beneath her. Justin was all she knew in this moment. And if she couldn't stop him, she knew without question that this would be their last conversation.

That didn't work for her. *Justin,* she began, anger slowly drying her tears, *you* cannot *do this. Even if you can find them, they will* kill *you. Please hear me on this, because I know it to be true: if you go up against the Mercenaries now,* you will die.

Mandy—

No. The tears were gone, and her survival instinct had taken over. Because she couldn't survive without him. *You will stop this. I cannot lose you, too.*

Justin paused, then sent his next words in a whisper: *Mandy . . . you haven't lost me.*

If you do this, I will.

And, for the first time since she'd known him—though it was only in her mind—she heard Justin start to cry. *Mandy . . . please . . . I need . . .*

Mandy interrupted him. *I will be there soon.*

I'm at Mom and Dad's. She heard the tears coming faster now, and her heart broke into a million pieces.

Okay, sweetie; just hold on. I'm right here.

I need you, Mandy.

Mandy had started crying again. *I know, baby; I will be there very soon.*

Then she blinked, and she was once again in the backseat of Roger and Jan Stanford's Jeep, and the charm was once again a charm at the end of a long chain. She handed it back to Kayla, who Mandy could tell was trying not to stare at her tear-stained cheeks.

Mandy cleared her throat quickly, then leaned up toward Grady. "He's at the house. Hurry."

Grady stepped on the gas.

Justin wasn't used to crying. He couldn't remember the last time he had. All he knew in this moment was that he felt so weighted down that tears seemed like the only release. He sunk to the floor of the living room of his dead and comatose parents, his back against the wall, and buried his head in his lap, sobs wracking his body.

He just couldn't seem to stop.

"Justin!" Mandy screamed his name before she'd even made it out of the Jeep. She bolted across the Stanfords' front lawn and crashed through the front door, still calling his name. Where was he?

She stopped just inside the hallway, hesitant to venture toward the kitchen. She veered off to the right and entered the living room. That's when she heard him.

She found him sitting against the back wall of the living room, half-hidden by the couch, feet on the ground with his forehead resting on his knees. Mandy rushed to his side, kneeling beside him as she put an arm around his shoulders and pulled him close. "Justin, baby, it's okay . . . shhh . . . I'm here. It's okay."

Justin lifted his head to look at Mandy, his face red and tears rolling down his cheeks. Mandy's heart broke again. "Mandy . . ." he whispered.

She pulled his head to her shoulder. "It's okay, baby . . . you're okay."

His body was shaking, and Mandy didn't really know what to do. In the nearly four years she'd known him—including the two years of that that they'd lived together—he'd never cried in front of her. Not even once.

But that didn't matter now. Nothing mattered except Justin, Justin and his pain. She wished she could take it away, wished that someone she loved so much didn't have to go through this. Tears started running down her cheeks, her heart breaking with every sob that shook his body.

Kayla and Grady found them then, but, at Mandy's nod, stepped back outside to give them a little privacy. Justin needed to get this out. Ever since his mother had died and his dad had been sent to the hospital, he'd been numb; Mandy could tell. He'd tried to hide it, and had done a decent job doing so, but she knew him better than anyone, and she could see in his eyes the pain he'd buried deep inside. This release, here and now, was exactly what he needed.

Justin could feel his tears subsiding. He'd thought he'd cry forever, thought that all the tears he'd held in for years would all come out in an endless stream, but it seemed that, for now, he was finished. He sat up straight and leaned his head back against the wall, feeling completely spent.

He closed his eyes, then turned his head slowly and opened them to Mandy. "Hi."

Mandy chuckled a little. She always did that after she'd been crying. "Hi."

Justin smiled at her, cupping a hand around her cheek. He caught her gaze. "Thank you."

Mandy was staring into his eyes, staring into his *soul*, but he didn't care. In these last few minutes, something between them had disappeared—a wall had fallen or perhaps a dam had broken. Justin had never been that vulnerable with any-one—which terrified him—but the intimacy he felt in this moment, with this woman, surpassed anything he'd ever ex-perienced. Why had he been scared of this?

In that instant, he knew what he wanted, what his parents had wanted for him. Love, purpose, happiness. All of which he had found with Mandy, with Kayla and Grady and this quest. And he was overwhelmingly grateful.

He pulled Mandy gently toward him, his lips finding hers.

Then, in the same moment their lips met, something hap-pened.

He could hear her.

It shocked him to his core. It shouldn't have, but it did. He stood, bringing Mandy to her feet, and held her away from him only to stare into her eyes, his mouth hanging open.

Justin, I'm okay. We're okay. You're here, and nothing could be more right.

Justin nodded, and a stray tear slipped down his cheek. He quickly wiped it away with the back of his hand. Then, with what he knew Mandy would call his characteristic "Justin" grin, he scooped her up into his arms, reached a hand behind her head to cradle it, and kissed her with more abandon than he thought possible.

After a very productive day of reading—the giant tome he'd brought with him was nearly completed—and an edited-for-TV action movie, Grady showered and climbed into bed. When he didn't fall right to sleep, he lay on his back tracing the lines of the ceiling tiles with his eyes. Sleep refused to come, even after many long, frustrating, *grueling* minutes. It was aggravating.

She was aggravating.

No, that wasn't true. He couldn't be aggravated at her. She was scared; she didn't want to get too close too quickly. And on some level, he understood, or maybe wanted to understand. She was being cautious. Smart. And the guy in him hated it.

Aggravating.

He knew he loved her—with his entire being. He thought she knew that. Hadn't he told her as much—shown her in every way possible?

And she loved him. She'd told him, shown him in countless ways.

Could she still be unsure?

He lay there, staring at the ceiling tiles, arguing with himself. What should he do? He wanted more than anything to be with her, but he knew, deep down, that it wasn't quite right yet. He had to respect her wishes, only take them as far as she wanted to go. It would drive him crazy, but he could do it, for her. For them.

Every fiber of his being wanted to touch her, hold her, feel her close to him. He knew as soon as the thought crossed his mind that he would have her, all of her, one day. But only when she was ready, only when the time was right.

That's when he felt it. Just a small twinge in his chest, barely perceptible. But still there. What . . . ?

Another one, stronger this time. What was that?

Then it hit him.

Kayla.

He jumped up as if something had shocked him and flew to the door.

He threw it open before she could even raise her hand to knock.

CHAPTER 26

Love

"GRADY?" KAYLA FELT HER mouth fall open at the sight of him. His heaving chest and labored breathing immediately caused an alarm to go off in Kayla's head, and she nearly forgot why she was here in the first place. Wait—why *was* she here exactly? "Is something wrong?"

Without answering, Grady threw a hand around the back of her neck and pulled her to him. Her breath stopped as he pulled her into a passionate kiss. His lips were hard on hers; she pressed closer to him in response, drawing further into the room. She barely noticed as he effortlessly slung the door shut behind her.

As soon as the door closed, Kayla threw her arms around his neck. There wasn't an inch between them as she feverishly kissed him back, letting every part of her sink into his embrace. She so desperately needed this.

Kayla could barely breathe. Having Grady this close was all-consuming—stealing her every breath, her every thought.

Every move he made elicited an involuntary response in her. There was only feeling, only reacting, no time for thinking. It was the perfect state of blissful euphoria; even as she ached for more, she was thoroughly enjoying this moment with the man she so fiercely loved.

They stopped to catch their breath a few minutes later. They stood in the middle of the floor, foreheads touching. Their chests lifted and fell in unison as they tried to slow their breathing.

"Hi," Grady whispered, pulling back to see her face. One hand was lightly stroking her hair as the other wrapped around her waist.

Kayla smiled. "Hi."

Grady smiled back at her, and Kayla had never felt more at home. "Was there something you needed? Didn't mean to be rude."

She reached up on tiptoes for him, planting her lips briefly on his. "I only needed you."

Grady's smile widened and he picked her up. She wrapped her legs around his waist, as if she'd done it a thousand times before. "Glad to hear it."

Grady kissed her again, but this kiss was more playful, more comforting. As if all her worries were melting away at his touch. She wrapped her arms around his neck, smiling against his lips. He pulled back. "What?" He wasn't hiding his own grin very well.

Kayla just shook her head. "Nothing."

Grady set her down, but Kayla was glad his arms were still around her. She wasn't entirely sure she could stand on her own. Grady McGready was intoxicating. "Come on." Grady sat on the end of the bed and patted the bedspread next to him. "Sit with me."

It was exactly what she needed to hear. Kayla felt a single tear escape her eye and quickly turned to wipe it away, but Grady grabbed her hand and pulled her toward him before she could hide it. "Is something wrong?"

Kayla sniffled, then tried to laugh it away. "Nothing's wrong. Nothing at all. Everything is perfectly right."

Grady's smile melted her heart. She sunk to the bed next to him and laid her head on his shoulder. He pulled her close, held her against him. Kayla couldn't think of a single place in the world she'd rather be, or a single thing she'd rather be doing. Suddenly everything wrong in her life—her worries about what her visions were doing to her, when the Mercenaries would catch up with them, and even where her relationship with Grady would go once they got back to Florida—faded away in Grady's embrace. All the troubles of this summer seemed so distant yet so surmountable when he was with her. Basking in his love, she felt as though she could conquer the world.

She looked up at him after a few minutes. "Grady, this may sound . . . um, presumptuous . . . but could I sleep here tonight?"

Questions flashed in Grady's eyes before he could hide them.

She turned toward him, cupping her hand around his cheek. "I'm sorry. I just . . . need you tonight. I need to be close to you." Then a thought occurred to her. "I don't mean to be complicated." She shrugged and walked over to the window.

Grady was confused. What did Kayla want? It seemed as though something was wrong; he could see the conflict in her eyes. He ran his fingers through his messy hair—he hadn't exactly had time to smooth it out. He winced. It must look terrible.

Why had Kayla come here? He knew she wasn't ready to take their relationship any farther right now—and, truthfully, he wasn't sure he was either. Not that he wasn't ready to commit to her—every part of him wanted her and no one else, forever—but she deserved better. She deserved someone who would fully commit to her—body, mind, life, and soul—before asking her to give it all away. And he would strive every moment from now on to be that someone. He owed it to her. He owed it to himself.

Kayla needed to know, tonight, that she was safe with him, that there were no expectations. That when the time was right, when they were both ready for that next step, they would be together.

He looked up. Kayla's back was to him, but he could see her biting her nail as she stared out the partially opened window.

"Kayla?"

She turned, and Grady could see her bottom lip trembling. Something deep inside him knotted up at the expression on her face. He'd never seen Kayla so . . . not in control. It hurt his heart to see her like this.

"Sweetie, it's okay." He crossed the room and pulled her into a hug. He kissed the top of her head, then stroked her hair as he'd done just moments before. "You're safe here."

Kayla knew Grady's words were true, could feel the truth in the depths of her soul. And, suddenly, the dam broke. She let herself cry, releasing all the tension and control she'd kept bottled inside. She hadn't been feeling this at all, and couldn't figure out where all this was coming from. She felt stupid for even doing it, but she couldn't stop.

And that was okay. The revelation hit her in that moment, and her sobs began to subside. She could be herself with Grady, could be vulnerable. She'd never had that before. It was an enlightening and freeing experience, and suddenly her tears turned to laughter. She pulled back and looked up at Grady. "Sorry," she choked out between water-logged laughs, "I'm just a mess tonight."

Grady smiled at her, a smile so tender she felt her heart expand in her chest. "You're beautiful."

Kayla's laughter tapered off and she wiped at her eyes. Grady handed her a tissue from the box on the end table and she tried to clean up her tear-stained face. Thank God she wasn't wearing mascara, or she'd really look ridiculous.

Kayla offered a soggy smile. "Can I use your bathroom to clean up a little?"

Grady nodded, staring at her with a smile she'd never seen before. She couldn't quite be sure what it meant, but she could see an overwhelming love there. Her breath caught for just a second before she headed out of the room.

Kayla washed her face and instantly felt better. Then she kicked herself. What kind of woman comes to a man's room, uninvited, at night, and kisses him passionately, then just a few minutes later breaks down crying? She really was a mess.

She stared at herself in the mirror. How could she be so presumptuous? She wasn't ready to sleep with him, she was certain—well, *almost* certain. She was trying to talk her conscience out of it at the moment.

Stop it, she chastised herself. *You're not ready. And he will understand.*

She knew it was true, and loved Grady even more for it. She squared her shoulders, took one last look in the mirror—she looked good, considering—and opened the door.

Grady was on his side, stretched out near the end of the still-made bed, feet hanging off the end, flipping through a back issue of his favorite scientific magazine. He looked up at her entrance, and instantly she noticed a shift in his countenance—almost like . . . joy. She shifted her weight and looked away for a brief second, then straightened and walked over to him, sitting on the bed in front of him. "Whatcha reading?"

Grady closed the magazine. "Nothing important." He tossed it aside, then sat up. "Can I talk to you?"

Kayla drew in a breath, then had to tell herself to release it. "Sure." She wished her voice was steadier.

Grady ran his fingers through his hair. "Kayla, I just want you to know . . . I don't expect anything from you. You—" he stared at the side wall, just above the TV. "You're welcome to stay here tonight, no expectations."

Kayla could feel the blank stare on her face, but the muscles in her face weren't responding.

Grady continued, reaching for her hand and catching her gaze. "You *are* safe here, like I said. You are safe with me. I won't ever ask you to do anything you're not sure about." He paused, smiling at her. "We're not ready for that yet."

Kayla's heart thumped in her chest. She knew exactly what he was talking about without him having to spell it out. He was echoing her thoughts of thirty seconds ago, *exactly.*

She still couldn't seem to find her voice, though, so she just nodded.

Grady lifted his hand to rest on her cheek. Kayla's eyes fell closed briefly at his touch. When she opened them, all she saw was Grady. She gazed into his deep sapphire blue eyes and could see all the love there, but now she saw something else, something she'd never seen directed at her, from anyone. She saw respect there, and adoration. Grady was the kind of man she'd always wanted, but never believed existed. Yet here he was, right in front of her. And hers.

Kayla leaned close to him, and finally found her voice. "Thank you, Grady." She smiled and lightly kissed his cheek. "I love you."

Grady smiled, and pulled her to his side. "I love you, Kayla, more than you know."

She couldn't contain her elation at his words, and a smile stretched across her face. Grady leaned even closer to her, stopping only an inch short of a kiss. His lips brushed hers gently, sending sparks up and down her spine, out to her fingertips, down to her toes. Then, before she could catch a breath, he kissed her with a burning desire that had been building for an eternity.

When they resurfaced who-knows-how-many minutes later, Kayla couldn't stop smiling. That was fun. And that was an understatement. She felt like she did in middle school, with her first love. When no one was so preoccupied with sex that they could just enjoy being together. Innocent. And freeing.

She stared at Grady, who was now lying peacefully on his side, staring back at her. She'd commandeered one of his pillows and was enjoying just lying there on top of the still-made bed, being close to the man she loved. She scooted a little closer to him and he reached for her, stroking her side. She involuntarily shivered at his touch. "Are you cold?"

Kayla shook her head, but Grady was already reaching for a sweatshirt. "Maybe I turned the A/C up too high."

Kayla shook her head again, but accepted his sweatshirt, draping it over her shoulder. It smelled like him, which made her smile. "Thanks."

Grady turned to lie on his back. "Come here."

Kayla moved toward him and laid her head on his shoulder, then stared up at the ceiling with him. Staring at the ceiling was much better with Grady's arm wrapped around her, hearing his heart beat in his chest. "This is nice." Another understatement.

She felt Grady nod then kiss her hair. "Yes, very." He pulled her a little closer; she wouldn't have thought that possible, which pleased her greatly.

They laid there in silence for what could've been hours. Then, when sleep wouldn't come—surprise, surprise—Kayla raised one finger and began making lazy figures in the air. Grady chuckled beside her. "What are you doing?"

She twisted her head to the side to look at him, her arm stopping in mid-air. "I'm tracing the lines on the ceiling tiles." She resumed staring at the ceiling and her arm moved once again. "Can't sleep."

She could somehow feel Grady's grin. "Me neither." Then she saw his finger raise and start tracing the lines, too. She smiled, and it stretched across her face. They must really be a ridiculous-looking pair.

Then she froze.

CHAPTER 27

Lines

GRADY FELT KAYLA TENSE up beside him. "What is it?"

Kayla bolted upright, and Grady could see lines creasing her forehead. "Where's your map?"

"What?" Grady rose up on his elbows. What was she talking about?

Kayla was already halfway off the bed. "A map. I need a world map."

Grady sat up and reached inside the bag that was sitting next to him on the floor. "Here. Will this work?" He opened the map and smoothed it out on the bed.

Kayla scooted next to him and leaned over the map, her hair falling down the side of her face before she tucked it behind her ear. She nodded. "Yes, thanks." She fell silent as she scanned the map, and Grady watched her face intently. "Grady . . ." her voice trailed off, then suddenly her eyes widened.

"What, Kayla? What is it?"

She jumped up and started refolding the map. "Come on. We need to go talk to Mandy and Justin."

"Now?" Grady countered with an automatic glance at the bedside clock. Almost eleven thirty. Wow, they were in here for longer than he thought. Those were a good couple of hours . . .

Kayla's voice halted his reverie in its tracks. "Yes." She held the newly refolded map in one hand and reached for his with the other. He took it without question as she pulled him toward the door.

"They might be asleep."

Kayla shrugged but flashed him a smile as she opened the door. "Well, we'll just have to wake them up. This can't wait."

Mandy was halfway through a fashion magazine when she heard the knock on the door. Justin was preoccupied with whatever shoot-'em-up movie was on TV, so Mandy walked around the bed to get the door. She shot him an annoyed look as she walked between him and the set. He simply kept staring as if he had been able to see right through her. She rolled her eyes and opened the door.

Her exasperation with Justin vanished as soon as she saw her friends' faces. "Kayla? Grady? What are you doing here?"

Justin looked up at them from his position at the head of the bed. "Hey, guys. What's up? Is something wrong?"

"No, not really." Kayla moved past Mandy and laid her map out on the table near the door. Mandy came up right behind her, knowing better than to doubt Kayla when she was like this.

"What did you see?" Grady asked from her right.

The map was finally smoothed out, displaying a rendering of both North and South America. Kayla stood up, crossing her arms in satisfaction. "There."

Justin, who'd given up on his enthralling movie to join the party, spoke up. "Where?"

Mandy looked up at her from her position at Kayla's immediate left as she hunched over the map on the table. "What are we looking for?"

"No one sees it?" Kayla asked.

Grady gazed intently at the map. "No, I . . ." he cut off abruptly. "Wait . . ."

Kayla flashed a smile. "Yeah."

Grady whistled through his teeth, sinking slowly to a nearby chair. "I don't believe it."

"What?" Mandy asked.

"Look, here." Kayla jabbed a finger at Belize, where they had all met. "This is Lamanai, approximately." She lifted her finger off the map and pointed again, this time at Alaska. "This is where the first book was found, at Denali." Then, moving slowly, she dragged her finger from Alaska to Yellowstone. "And the second book—here, where we are now." She stopped briefly at their current location, then continued the line down toward Lamanai.

Mandy gasped. Justin's jaw dropped. Kayla and Grady just grinned at each other.

"*Now* you see it?" Kayla queried, still smiling.

Justin's words came out intermittently detached. He dropped to the edge of the bed, his eyes never leaving the map. "I . . . can't . . . it . . . doesn't . . . incredible. I . . . I . . ."

"Wow," was all that Mandy could say. She couldn't think of anything else.

Grady reached for the pen sitting on the bedside table. He circled the Alaska site, the Yellowstone site, and the Lamanai site. Then he drew a line between all three, a straight line connecting all three sites.

Mandy finally got out another word. "Amazing."

Kayla nodded. "Yeah."

Justin was the first to come out of his stupor. "So what does this mean? Besides the fact that it's a little . . . creepy."

Mandy answered. "It's too blatant to be coincidence."

Grady and Kayla nodded in unison, then Grady glanced up at Kayla. "It is. Which means that—"

Kayla finished his thought. "—we know where to find the next location."

Belize Rainforest, Mercenary Camp

"Na-um, are you sure about this?" Holun trailed behind his superior as the latter spun crazily through the interior of his hut, haphazardly stuffing a small canvas bag with essential items from around his home. From what Holun could tell, Na-um planned to be gone awhile.

Na-um simply grunted.

Holun kept going. "I mean, have you really thought this through? Are you positive you have to go to these extremes?"

Na-um abruptly stopped what he was doing with a loud sigh. He whirled around to meet Holun face to face. "Yes." With his abrupt one-word response delivered, he started to turn back around to continue his packing.

Holun wouldn't back down. "But . . ."

Na-um whipped his head around once again, this time stopping only inches from the tip of Holun's nose. "Holun!" He paused to take a breath, chest heaving dangerously. When he spoke again, his voice came more calmly, but through his teeth. "I know what you are trying to do, but I have made up my mind. This is the only way to stop the Secret from being revealed."

"I know that you think so, Na-um, but there *has* to be another way. This—it's too violent! I cannot, will not, commit such violent acts. On anyone." Holun stared Na-um straight in the eye, hoping his defiance would successfully underscore his insistence.

Na-um sighed, placing his hand on the boy's shoulder. Holun fidgeted a little—he couldn't quite help it. "And I won't ask you to. You will accompany me in the training and on the mission, but you will not be directly involved."

"Na-um!" Holun yelled in a final, no-holds-barred effort as Na-um turned away. "This is unspeakable!"

But Na-um was already headed for the exit. Before he threw the canvas flap aside, Holun heard him mutter under his breath: "This is war. And in war there are casualties."

The Parkside Motel, Bozeman, Montana

"You're gonna have to explain that."

Kayla, still hunched over the map, glanced over at Justin out of the corner of her eye before answering him. "We know where to look to find the next location."

Justin folded his arms across his chest. "And where is that?"

Grady stepped in, tracing the line on the map with his finger. "See? This line contains all three locations we've found so far—well, the two with the books and Lamanai, where this all began. Granted, it's not exact, but it's too close to be a coincidence. So the next location is probably—almost *has* to be—somewhere on this line." He straightened but kept his eyes on the map.

Mandy leaned in. "Okay . . . but where?" She traced her own finger slowly southeast from Alaska.

Kayla pulled Grady to the side while Mandy and Justin perused the map. "Grady, this line tells us basically where to look for the next location, but where exactly? That line covers a lot of ground."

Grady bit his bottom lip, hesitating before he answered. "Hmm. Well, think about it. Denali—high elevation, extreme cold, wind—and Yellowstone—one of the largest, if not *the* largest, supervolcanoes in the world . . ."

"Okay, right," Kayla interrupted. "So Denali, high winds, cold . . . that signifies air?" Grady nodded, so she continued. "One of the world's biggest volcanoes—that signifies fire." That one wasn't a question.

Grady finished the thought for her. "So we're looking for a pretty large and significant body of water. A river or a lake, almost certainly, like you saw in Justin's book. But something important, well-known. Or perhaps something with the earth, maybe mounds of earth—large mountains?" He glanced toward the table and sighed. "No, you saw a river in Justin's book. We should be looking for that."

Kayla nodded as they stared at each other for a brief second before their eyes widened simultaneously. They bolted for the map. Mandy jumped out of the way; Kayla deftly ignored the questions she saw in her friend's eyes.

Kayla traced the line Grady'd made with her finger, starting first at Alaska and moving southeast very slowly. She glared intently at every spot her finger touched, scrutinizing the map for any large river or lake. Her finger traced past the Canadian coast . . . perhaps the ocean? She quickly discarded the notion. It didn't feel right—they weren't looking for the ocean. The ocean wasn't a river or lake; it didn't fit.

She traced all the way down to Belize, to Lamanai, and still hadn't found anything that captured her attention. She sighed, removing her hand. She backed up and slumped into a nearby chair, discouraged.

Grady moved into her former place. She was still able to view the map from this angle, but she leaned forward to get a better view. What was he doing?

Soon she couldn't stand the waiting any longer. She stood up and drew close to him, eyeing his every movement. Justin and Mandy's eyes were trained on him as well as he continued his examination.

Grady leaned down and pointed at Lamanai. Kayla could clearly see what she was learning was his "thinking" look emblazoned on his face. She knew better than to interrupt him when he had that look.

Grady left his finger on Lamanai for a full minute as he scanned the rest of the map.

Kayla could tell the instant he had found what he was looking for. His eyes ceased their aimless scanning, focusing instead on one spot on the map. He very slowly—excruciatingly slowly, in Kayla's opinion—dragged his finger further down the map, continuing southeast from Lamanai at the same angle as the rest of the line.

As soon as Kayla saw where he was headed, she gasped, kicking herself for not thinking of it sooner. Grady smirked a little but continued his slow progression downward, stopping on the location both he and Kayla had seen.

Kayla knew when Mandy saw it; she heard a small gasp to her left.

"The Amazon?" Justin asked.

Grady nodded. "Yeah." He looked up at Kayla. "Makes sense, right?"

Kayla nodded frantically, a wide smile spreading on her face. "Perfect sense. That *has* to be it."

CHAPTER 28

Globe

SOMETHING WAS OFF.

She wasn't sure why, but as Kayla sat slumped in one of the cloth chairs near the table, gazing vacantly around the room at her friends, she had the unsettling feeling that something was . . . missing. Incomplete.

They were headed for the Amazon—but where? The river spanned the width of the entire continent. How would they know where to look?

She casually glanced over at Justin, who was pacing the floor near the bathroom door, on his cell phone. Kayla assumed he was making their travel plans—who else would he be talking to for so long, and in the middle of the night? Made sense. But where in the world were they headed? He could book them somewhere in South America, she mused, as if that narrowed it down. Kayla would've sighed aloud if her body would've responded, but her body had settled into a weird non-responsive state not long after they'd discovered the next location—just about the same time she realized she didn't really know where that next location was at all. She supposed her stoicism was due not only to her frustration over the situation, but also to a keen lack of sleep, the overwhelming weight of the whole situation, and the fact that a large, ruthless group of men wanted them dead. If she weren't so tired, she might've broken down crying again.

She shifted her eyes to Mandy, who was still standing over the map, gazing intently at it as if she could divine something from it. Good luck trying.

Justin tossed his phone on the bed. "We're headed to Atlanta, for now. From there, we'll . . ." he glanced at Kayla, briefly, but she still noticed. They all noticed. "Well, we'll just figure out where we're going when we get there." He smiled in her direction without looking directly at her. Kayla appreciated the gesture, but his thoughts were evident. Kayla didn't like it any more than they did. Probably a lot less.

Kayla forced herself to stand, pushing herself to her feet with the wooden arms of the chair. "We should get some sleep."

Grady nodded, rising from the bed where'd he been sitting for the past ten minutes or so and meeting her at the door. "Here's hoping for a good night's rest."

Kayla smiled, but as she and Grady retreated to their separate rooms—despite what Kayla's less cautious side was shouting in her head—she doubted she'd be able to sleep at all.

Much to her amazement, she actually managed to get a few hours of sleep. She woke again with the sun, which was gleaming through the thin curtains covering the room's one window. For one brief, blissful moment, she imagined what it would be like to wake up with Grady by her side, in her bed, every morning.

Then reality hit, as it always does, and came crashing down on her. She rose from the bed, suddenly grumpy as she stumbled sleepily into the bathroom and flipped on the shower. One of the few nice things about hotels, even this motel—unlimited hot water. Usually. Certainly much better than the four-minute average at the dig. Even in her sleepy state she was no dummy; she was going to let it get good and hot before climbing in.

She turned and caught a glimpse of herself in the mirror. *Ugh. I'm a mess. How could Grady have possibly been attracted to this?* She untwisted her hair and let it fall around her shoulders, shaking it out as she did. *Wow. Even worse.* She really *was* a mess.

She undressed and stepped into the steamy shower, letting the warm water soothe her tired joints. It had been a rough few days, and she was glad for the opportunity to take her time.

She stood there unmoving for a long while, just staring at the water trickling from the shower head. She began to see meaningless patterns in the water as it fell into the tub.

Gradually the patterns seemed less meaningless. Was that the same picture she'd seen in Justin's book? And what was— wait . . . what was *that?*

Before her, displayed through the cascading water, was the very clearly defined picture of a rainforest. Her mind started whipping through the possibilities of what the vision could mean. Were they supposed to go back to Belize?

But the picture didn't seem familiar. In fact, it seemed a little . . . off. Different.

Then, suddenly, she was *in* the rainforest. It was dark and dank, with very little light. She assumed that it must be nighttime. Why else would it be so dark? As she strained to take in her surroundings in the murky, thick air, she noticed that she was standing right in the middle of a cluster of trees. Her hot shower in the bathroom of her hotel room in Bozeman was a distant memory.

She attempted to move her feet to explore this new world, but they encountered a heavy resistance. Why wouldn't they move? She had to tell herself not to panic.

She looked down at the floor of the forest, glaring through the little light she had, searching for what was holding her in place. She quickly found what was arresting her legs.

She was thigh deep in water.

What?

She took in the rest of her surroundings, trying to get her bearings. She thought she saw a fading outline of tree-covered mountains off in the distance, through a small break in the dense foliage.

Mountains, flooded rainforest, definitely *not* Belize. Their location in the Amazon?

As soon as the thought crossed her mind, it was the only thing that made sense. She studied the vision more intently. She needed to find this answer, needed to know where they were headed.

Then, without any visible change in the vision, she knew where she was. They already knew they were going to the Amazon—Grady's assumption was now proven correct. But the place they needed to go—the *specific* place—was now right in front of her. The next book would be found here.

She grinned widely as the vision ended. The feeling that something was wrong—the one she'd been feeling since Grady'd made the connection on the map—was suddenly gone. In its place was a calm assuredness, the certainty Kayla had needed.

She quickly finished her shower and hurriedly dressed, then ran to find Grady. She had to tell him about her vision. They had to finalize their plans.

She already knew they were headed to South America. But now she knew where.

Belize Rainforest, South of the Mercenary Camp

Holun opened his eyes, then winced. For a fleeting second, he imagined ways he could get out of telling Na-um what he'd just seen—a fake seizure, perhaps? Or a real one? Or he could use the machete sheathed around his waist on his hand, cut it off . . . that'd distract him . . .

Holun shook his head to no one but himself, halting his macabre thoughts. He was being ridiculous. Na-um would be angry, sure, livid even, but Holun had never really been scared of him. Right?

Holun looked around for his superior. Great. Na-um was right in the middle of a training exercise with his men. Holun knew his boss hated to be interrupted while he was training, but he feared what Na-um would do if he found out Holun had held something back.

So Holun got up and walked toward the group of soldiers. "Na-um?" Holun hated how timid his voice sounded.

Na-um raised his hand to halt the exercise, then turned. Holun had to force himself to stand his ground, not shrink a few feet back like every muscle in his body was telling him to do.

Na-um led Holun a few feet away from the men, then raised an eyebrow. "Yes?"

Holun swallowed. Hard. "I've been watching the Americans, trying to follow their moves. It is a little easier since I've seen them before, but I'm still only getting bits and pieces."

Na-um growled a "yes" through his teeth. Holun moved on quickly.

"The Americans have found the third location."

Na-um looked as though he would have thrown anything he could have gotten his hands on. Fortunately, there wasn't much of anything out here, except . . . Holun took a step back. Then one more, just to be safe.

Without meaning to, Holun started babbling. "I was looking for the Elders again. Nothing new with them, they are still going forward with their plans. So I checked the Southern Detachment, and saw the Americans there." Holun swallowed again. "I am not certain that they will survive their attack." Holun squeezed his eyes shut and shrunk back a few inches without moving his feet.

When he didn't feel Na-um's hand strike his cheek, or clutch his neck, he ventured a look at his superior. What he saw in Na-um's face scared him so much more than Na-um's anger ever did.

Na-um was grinning ear to ear, and nearly snickering. There was something sinister about the smile, something almost . . . evil. Holun stared, his wide eyes never leaving Na-um's face.

"Good," Na-um began, the same wicked smile still stretched across his face, "if the Southern Detachment succeeds, our plans here may not be needed." Na-um crossed his arms, and Holun could've sworn his chest puffed out a good ten millimeters. "But we will still prepare, in the unlikely event that they fail."

Holun nodded absently. Na-um was even more scary than he'd been when Holun had defied him to his face, less than a day ago, and Holun was afraid of how Na-um might react to a dissenting opinion now.

Holun had never seen his superior like this, and wasn't sure he even recognized the leader he once revered. It had been there earlier, under the surface, but only now did Holun realize it, now that it had come to the surface and taken Na-um over. It was as if his leader was possessed; his visage and even his personality had changed. And the look in his eyes, like a lion stalking his prey, or a demon stealing someone's soul . . .

Holun had come to know Na-um as careful, calculating, and fearless, but compassionate. Never calloused. Never indifferent to the killing of innocents—and he seemed almost *excited* now!—despite his order to attack the Jeep leaving the dig a few weeks ago. Na-um had been visibly remorseful, but he'd said those men had been casualties of war—and Holun had almost understood his logic. But this? Where was the logic in this?

As Holun slunk back to his innocuous position away from the older, stronger men, he wondered if the Na-um he knew was ever coming back.

Na-um returned to his men, the grin still emblazoned on his face, as if it were stuck there. He wanted so desperately to remove it, to be able to talk to someone about how much all this was tearing him apart . . . but that would be a sign of weakness, and would undermine his leadership. The Elders had done enough to undermine his leadership already. His plans—the plans he'd made to stop the Americans—were nearly fool-proof. He should have been elated; he would, in all likelihood, win this war.

But instead he was worried, afraid, and more troubled than any other time in his life. Why, when he was only a few short steps away from victory, was he falling apart?

He was *born* for this. His entire life had been devoted to it. He knew what he believed, what the Clan had taught him from birth, what he had taught others himself.

The Secret must never be revealed.

And yet, as he continued training his men with the outward confidence every great leader should have, every fiber of his being was screaming, desperately pleading with his conscience to stop; something was extremely and utterly wrong.

Lamanai Archeological Dig

"Hey, Jack. Was that Grady checking in?" A voice called from just outside.

Jack set the satellite phone down, then smiled at the pretty grad student from his perch in front of the communication trailer's only desk. "No, that was Kayla this time. They're headed to South America."

Jackie's eyes widened as she stepped inside the trailer. "Cool." Her eyes glazed over and what looked to Jack like a dreamy expression came over her face.

Jack grinned. "Did you have something for me?"

"Oh, yes," she replied, blinking a few times. "We are finished cataloging the artifacts from the cavern. All three hundred plus," she added with a smirk.

"Good work."

Jackie beamed. "Anything else I can do here?"

Jack pursed his lips. "Well, I . . ." He paused, looking her over. "Okay, but this has to be kept quiet."

Jackie grinned conspiratorially. "Of course."

Jack leaned down, reaching under the desk. Jackie moved to his side, eyes sparkling.

Jack slid a cardboard box out onto the open floor.

"What is this?" Jackie ventured.

"This, Miss Jackie," Jack started with a theatrical flourish, "is something Kayla found that first day in the cavern." He leaned down and slowly—one at a time—opened the four cardboard flaps.

Jackie leaned over the box and peered inside.

What was that?

The interior of the box was bathed in a subtle yellow light. What was causing it?

She looked closer, squatting down and pushing aside the foam peanuts blocking her view of the object. The light brightened.

What—was it *glowing*?

She carefully reached inside the box to retrieve what she saw to be an intriguingly luminescent sphere. What was making it do that?

She slowly lifted the globe from the box, drawing it up to eye level. The area around the ball was illuminated with the yellow light emanating from its interior. Jackie just stared; her eyes danced in the soft light.

Jack smiled. "Cool, isn't it? I need you to find out everything you can about this globe without damaging it. No cutting, no samples. Think you can find anything?"

But Jackie wasn't listening. She just kept staring at the object she held in her hands.

"Jackie?" Jack reached out and touched her shoulder.

The light touch caused her to jump slightly, shaking her out of her reverie. Fortunately, though, she still managed to maintain her careful grip on the sphere. "Oh! Sorry." She offered him a placating smile. "This really is *very* intriguing."

Jack withdrew his hand and nodded as his face relaxed. "Well, you're the best grad student here. I figured you were the right one for the job." He returned her smile. "But you'll keep this quiet? Kayla doesn't want anyone to know."

Jackie nodded and gingerly replaced the object, then lifted the box and headed for the door. "You don't have to worry, Jack. I can keep a secret." She flashed him a final wide smile as she opened the trailer door, box on her hip. "You can trust me."

CHAPTER 29

Amazon

Just Outside Leticia, Colombia

"IT ISN'T HERE!" Kayla growled to no one in particular from where she was kneeling at the base of a large tree. After over twenty-four hours of flights—and precious little sleep— she was exhausted. Her feet, coated with mud from the damp ground, were sore, but as she leapt to her feet, angrily wiping at her mud-stained knees, she barely noticed. She *did* notice however that her neck and shoulders were sore—probably from all the sitting in the uncomfortable coach seats on the plane—er, *planes*—and that leaping to her feet like she was throwing a temper tantrum didn't help matters any. Not that she cared. She was breathing hard and felt like punching the tree in front of her, but had fortunately retained the presence of mind to stop herself from badly injuring her hand. Instead, she glared at the acres of greenery around her, looking for anything, seeing nothing.

Kayla was standing just outside a mid-sized town in southern Colombia called Leticia—a cozy hamlet nestled on the banks of the mighty Amazon. Grady'd easily found a clean hotel where they'd checked in quickly and dropped off their luggage. They'd ventured a small distance into the nearby rainforest a short while later in hopes that Kayla would be able to get a better idea of where they were supposed to be going the next morning.

Now the rest of the group was staring at her—unintentionally, she supposed, though it didn't feel that way—waiting for her to divine a more specific location. She could almost feel their expectant gazes boring into her. Now she really *did* want to hit something. Why was she always expected to find the next clue? Couldn't any of the others pull their weight at some point?

She sighed, deflated. That wasn't fair. She really needed to learn how to get her temper in check.

Kayla saw Justin look over at Grady, then, after a moment's hesitation, whisper something in his ear and leave with Mandy. Grady never moved, his eyes staying locked on her. If she didn't care about him so much, she would probably have yelled at him.

She chastised herself.

How could she be so angry? None of her companions really expected her to deliver good news at every turn. Sure, they all hoped for it, hoped that the next vision would be sooner rather than later, but they knew she was human—she could see the understanding in their eyes. There was only hope, pure and simple, no demands. Which meant she was really only angry with herself. And for what? For not knowing how to control her visions? Hmm. Maybe.

Grady came up beside her, his brow furrowed, eyes questioning but nonthreatening. "Kayla, honey, what's wrong?"

She slumped to a nearby moss-covered log, shoulders hunched forward. "I don't know. I was *so* sure that Leticia was the place." She leaned over, resting her elbows on her knees, and stared at the muddy ground. This up-and-down emotional rollercoaster was really wearing on her. "Now I'm not getting anything. I don't have a clue where to look." She dropped her head into her hands, covering her face.

Grady sat down beside her and pulled her to his side. He kissed the top of her head lightly but didn't let go. "You're putting too much pressure on yourself, Kayla. We can look tomorrow. No need to rush it."

Kayla's head, still buried in her hands, shook almost of its own accord.

"Kayla." Grady grabbed both her wrists and pulled her hands away from her face. He held them in her lap with one hand as he reached to turn her head toward him. She stubbornly refused to meet his gaze. After a long moment, Grady spoke. "Kayla, look at me."

She didn't want to look at him. He didn't need to see her cry. Again.

But he was still holding her chin resolutely, and he wasn't letting go. She slowly, reluctantly brought her eyes to his. He spoke quietly, almost silently, but his words came across loud and clear. She shouldn't have been able to hear him at that volume, but somehow she did. "This is not your problem. You don't have to fix this. Especially not today."

Kayla started to shake her head again, but Grady put both hands on either side of her face and held it firmly. "No." He held her gaze and waited.

Kayla sighed, but the weight of the world didn't lift off her shoulders. "Fine, you win."

Grady shook his head and smiled. "It's not about winning or losing, Kayla. It's about your peace of mind. And right now, it seems as though that's your last concern. When's the last time you slept through the night?"

Kayla tried to remember, she really did, then realized with a jolt that she couldn't.

Grady chuckled, Kayla supposed at the expression on her face. He kissed her forehead. "You need some sleep."

Kayla automatically shook her head, but then she yawned, widely.

Grady was laughing now. "Aw, honey, come on. You really *must* get some sleep. You're falling asleep just sitting here."

Kayla stood, a little too quickly, and staggered before Grady helped her right herself.

Grady wrapped his arms around her as he leaned in for a kiss. "You'll thank me later," he whispered just before his lips closed on hers, then he led her back to the hotel.

The next thing Kayla knew she was waking up to the sun shining brightly through the open balcony doors of her hotel room.

Amazon Rainforest, Southern Detachment Outpost

"Sir, our squad is ready and waiting for your command."

The Leader of the Southern Detachment nodded in satisfaction. "Excellent. The four Americans have arrived—the time will soon be upon us. Please notify me if your status changes."

"Certainly, Sir," the soldier replied, then turned and exited the Leader's tent.

The Leader surveyed his now largely empty tent, then turned his attention to the map on the table in front of him. His messenger had, only a few moments ago, confirmed that the four targets had arrived in Leticia but had been unable to make any further progress.

How are they able to find every location? These locations have been hidden for centuries, and these Americans just happen to find every one of them with little trouble. How is that possible? He scrutinized the map as he considered these questions and more, outlining the many plausible scenarios and plotting multiple escape routes for their ambush.

Not that it would matter. If everything went as planned—and there was no reason to think it wouldn't—there wouldn't be anyone left to see them escape.

He was doing everything he could to ensure a successful attack. The supplies they needed had been easy enough to procure in this country, but everything else needed to fall into place just as easily for the mission to succeed.

They couldn't risk another failed attempt at stopping the stubborn and seemingly invincible Americans. He would make certain they would not survive.

Downtown Leticia, Colombia

Kayla felt refreshed, relaxed. She never imagined she'd sleep until morning.

She smiled. She'd never be able to repay Grady for stabilizing her, so many times in the past few weeks, when she felt like she was spinning out of control. But she'd be willing to spend the rest of her life trying.

As Kayla showered and got ready to face the day, she dared to wish—hope even—that today would be the day they found the answers buried here.

Hopefully.

The Amazon River, just outside Leticia

Grady spoke the best Spanish among them, so with his rudimentary language skills he secured a guide to lead them along the river. He even managed to procure a boat of sorts—to Kayla it looked more like a large raft, but their guide assured them it would travel a substantial distance down the river. At least that's what Grady'd told her he said—her Spanish was spotty, at best.

Their "boat" was a collection of presumably—hopefully—waterproofed wood, secured side by side by large, thick ropes, with a weathered and beaten deck. Kayla hoped the logs—and the deck they supported—weren't really as old and fragile as they seemed to be. The craft stretched to a surprising twenty feet long and ten feet wide, but Kayla still found it oddly claustrophobic. Even without railings.

Kayla spied what could only be a small engine hanging off the back of the raft, but it wasn't in use. She realized it was only for taking them back upstream when the need arose, or if they needed to speed away. She didn't want to think of a reason why they might have to speed away, so she focused her attention more clearly on the only thing keeping her from falling into the muddy river. For now.

Flanking either side of the raft, Kayla saw something that looked like large coolers—she thought that perhaps they had been coolers at one time. Though old and faded now, she could easily picture the once bright red and blue colors emblazoned proudly on their sides. They appeared to be functioning as crude "cargo holds" with two hand-made clasps on each of them to help secure the lid. Mandy was using the blue one as a seat; Kayla decided to take the red one.

Near the front—what Kayla assumed was the front, anyway, given the direction they were heading—was a small cabin. The all-wood craft was barely accommodating a relatively large, enclosed structure, about the size of a small bedroom, with a worn but somehow still-holding tarp stretched across the top. Through the open door—yes, the "cabin" did, in fact, have a working door—she spotted a small cot and metal picnic table. The farthest wall encased thick windows and a small instrument panel stood in front of it. She imagined the wall she couldn't see held a tiny kitchenette. Did their guide actually live here?

She glanced through the door at their guide, the owner of this humble craft, and smiled to herself. His unkempt hair, unshaven chin, and sloppy clothes made her think that he definitely did live here, and probably had for longer than she cared to imagine. She was suddenly glad for the openness of the raft—and the light breeze. And glad she wasn't in that enclosed room with a man who looked like he hadn't showered in weeks. How was Grady able to stand it?

She saw Grady walk out of the cabin, and Kayla grinned at him. He shot her a harsh glare for a second, which made her laugh silently. She watched as he drew in a deep breath once on the open raft. Kayla covered her mouth to keep from laughing aloud.

Grady crossed the raft and moved to sit down next to Kayla. She moved her backpack full of supplies out of the way so he could sit.

"Better?" Kayla grinned at him.

Grady shot her a look, but couldn't hide his smile very well.

Kayla laughed, a lilting sound that surprised her. She hadn't thought she was as relaxed as the laugh insinuated.

"You're mean." But Grady wrapped one arm around her anyway and pulled her into a half-hug.

Kayla shook her head. "Sorry." But she was still smiling— she couldn't help it. Another laugh escaped her.

"And you're a bad liar," Grady dropped his arm and crossed both arms across his chest, pouting. Which made Kayla laugh harder.

As hard as she tried, she couldn't stop laughing, and soon Grady joined in. It felt good to laugh with him, even if at nothing at all. She felt her worries melt away with each passing second.

Then it happened.

Kayla jerked upright, so suddenly it made the raft quiver dangerously in the calm waters. Grady jumped but remained seated, his eyes flying to Kayla. What he saw there shouldn't really have surprised him, but it startled him anyway and his heart tightened, as if someone had reached inside his chest and started squeezing.

Kayla's head was swimming long after the vision was over. She pressed a hand to her forehead but her head wouldn't stop spinning. She squeezed her eyes shut. Was she really taking longer to recover than before, or was she just imagining it?

After a few minutes, thank God, the dizziness was replaced with a sudden and certain clarity. She lurched to her feet—nearly tipping the not-quite-big-enough raft over for the second time in less than ten minutes—and shrieked at the top of her lungs in the direction of their guide, forgetting momentarily that he couldn't understand a single word of English.

"YOU'RE GOING THE WRONG WAY!"

CHAPTER 30

Beacon

"KAYLA, HONEY, WHAT ARE you talking about?" Grady stood next to her, his hand absently stroking her hair. He couldn't remember when he'd started doing it.

"I mean . . . we're supposed to . . ." Kayla gasped, trying to catch a breath where she could. "We need to . . . go . . . that way." She jabbed at the air, pointing in the opposite direction they were going.

Grady glanced behind them, trying not to get frustrated. Couldn't she have figured this out before they'd wasted hours —and a considerable amount of money—floating aimlessly down this murky river?

Grady sighed then dutifully approached their guide—who was currently staring wide-eyed at the crazy American woman who'd just shrieked nonsense at him—and rattled off new instructions to him in what Grady thought was an admirable attempt at coherent Spanish. But he soon started getting angry as the little man started barking out his many complaints. Grady was certainly paying him enough money to do what he was asking without complaint.

But as the guide just stood there with his arms crossed, jaw clenched, Grady knew more would be required. He growled his dissatisfaction before jabbing another bill into the greedy man's greasy hand. Grady ordered him to hurry before heading back to Kayla.

That guy had better get moving.

Three hours later—the trip against the current took considerably longer than their first trip downriver—the group was nearly back to where they'd started.

Despite her calm and clarity directly following her latest vision, Kayla was now irritated. Why couldn't she have known the right direction to go *before* they wasted half the day on the river? What good were these visions if they wouldn't come when she needed them? Not hours later, after the group had spent a small fortune simply wasting time.

She glanced up at the bright sky, wishing that "Destiny" had never brought them to this humid rainforest. She was even beginning to wish she'd never had those first visions in the cave, that she'd never started on this quest.

The sun was nearly centered in the sky, only minutes away from midday. She squinted at the cloudless sky, shielding her eyes with her hand. Her eyes dropped slowly as a rather unwelcome lump settled in her throat. Yet again, she was clueless as to where they were headed. She fought the tears, fought the doubt creeping into her mind.

Then she saw it.

"Grady!" Kayla hissed under her breath. Grady was the only one close enough to hear her, anyway, and his wide eyes flew to hers.

Her gaze was trained on a singular point on the horizon. Grady followed her line of sight, searching for what had so completely captured her attention.

What he saw froze him in place.

Mandy wasn't paying much attention until she noticed out of the corner of her eye that Kayla and Grady weren't moving. Her gaze shifted away from the book she'd been reading—it was getting good, too—and up at Kayla and Grady's faces.

What she saw there made her forget about the book and just about everything else. She tapped Justin's arm lightly, nodding at their friends. Justin looked up, his forehead creasing as he glanced from Kayla and Grady to Mandy, then back, then back again.

Mandy stood and walked over to Kayla and Grady, examining their faces for any clue as to why they had become statues. Then she noticed their eyes—staring at the same spot, as though they couldn't look away.

Mandy turned slowly—she could sense Justin do the same only a few feet away—and followed their gaze, searching for what was so enrapturing, so captivating . . .

Then she saw it, too.

And instantly she knew, beyond the shadow of any doubt, that they had finally found it—the location of the next book.

Kayla stumbled off the raft, unable to move her eyes from the mystical spot on the distant horizon for more than half a second. She heard the others moving around her, even heard Grady mumble something to their guide—probably about why they were getting off—but she couldn't keep her eyes off the beckoning vision in front of her.

She felt the weight of her backpack at her right hand and took it from Grady without thinking—she knew it was Grady from the way he smelled, which was an ever-increasingly pleasant reminder of his nearness—and slung it on her shoulder, still staring at the indescribable sight before her.

Like a lighthouse guiding ships in a dark night, their own personal beacon shone brilliantly in the noonday sun, guiding them to their next destination. Atop a nearby mountain, inexplicable yet undeniable, a light gleamed so brightly that it nearly blinded her. Nevertheless, Kayla stared at, unable to look away. It almost seemed to be beckoning her forward.

And Kayla realized, the moment she felt the others join her to face that light, why they had wasted the morning on the river, why they hadn't been able to find anything yesterday afternoon.

Timing was the key.

That mountain had been nondescript this morning—she knew that because she'd seen it as they left this morning—but now, under the blazing glare of the hot sun, the location of the next book was calling out to her, to *them*, their path lit by this shining ray of light.

"There must be something on that mountain, something that reflects the sun, but only at a precise time of day," Grady postulated, under his breath. And, though Grady was several feet away from her, with Mandy and Justin between them, Kayla heard him loud and clear.

The realization broke her entrancement with the light. "What did you say?" She whispered, barely audible. Even Justin next to her shouldn't be able to hear her.

But Grady did. "Kayla?" There was no mistaking the shock in his voice, even at barely a whisper. "How can I hear you?" She felt Grady's eyes on her before she turned toward him.

Kayla smiled at the look on his face, his jaw nearly on the ground. She mouthed "come here" and grinned at him as he walked behind Justin and Mandy, who were still transfixed on the sight before them, seemingly oblivious to the exchange between Grady and Kayla.

Grady reached her and immediately drew her into a hug. "Kayla," he breathed, "I can hear you."

Kayla nodded into his chest, comfortable there despite the noonday heat. This was what home felt like, she was sure of it.

Grady pulled back and looked into her eyes. "You are *my* home."

Now it was Kayla's turn to be shocked, though she supposed she should've been more surprised that she could hear him speak below a whisper from many feet away. Her mouth and eyes dropped open at the same time. "Did you hear my *thoughts*?"

Grady looked her over. "Not really, I just said what I was thinking at the time . . . though, now that you mention it, I've never had a thought like that myself. Almost like—"

"—the thought wasn't your own."

Grady's eyes were wide as he nodded slowly.

Kayla nodded back, more resolutely than Grady. "I think that's all the confirmation we need . . ." . . . *that we're on the right track*, she thought, knowing Grady would somehow understand. She smiled and addressed the group, raising her voice. "Come on, let's go." Justin and Mandy glanced over at her with glassy eyes. She knew how they felt.

"I don't think it's far. Maybe we can get there by dinnertime." With that, Kayla led the way into the brightly lit rainforest that stood between them and their Destiny.

Less than an hour later, Kayla glanced up at where the beacon should be, but she didn't notice it from this vantage point. Somehow, though, she knew it was still there. It had called her, drawn her to that exact spot, at that exact moment. She could still see it in her mind's eye, could remember the precise location it pointed to. Or maybe she wasn't remembering—maybe she just knew.

As they bushwhacked their way through the overgrown rainforest, Kayla had begun to notice something, to feel something. It was subtle at first, but as they trekked up the mountain, the feeling became stronger, so much so that Kayla couldn't ignore it.

It was starting to worry her, having such an overwhelming feeling that just wouldn't go away. She couldn't tell if the feeling was good or bad, but it was definitely there. She swallowed hard, tried to shove away the lump in her throat, but it only seemed to get bigger.

And she knew, though how she couldn't tell—something was about to happen.

Good, bad, or indifferent, *something* was close.

To the east, less than a thousand meters away, a small group of five camouflage-painted men hurried silently through the thick foliage. On their leader's silent command—relayed with one abrupt fist pump—the men quickly froze in place. Upon seeing a quick but clear jabbing of their leader's hand in three different directions, the men spread out and found their positions, creating an arc with their leader in the center. They all intuitively ducked behind trees, rocks—any cover they could find—and raised their weapons in rapid succession. Simultaneously—almost as if rehearsed—the men lowered their heads and stared through their scopes to locate their marks.

The Four continued their seemingly endless hike to the foot of the mountain. Slowly but steadily, more sun was coming through the trees overhead and their trek through the forest was becoming easier, with less foliage underfoot to trip them up. But the thinning forest had Kayla on edge. And suddenly an errant thought ran through her mind: if there was danger lurking out there in the trees, they would be easy targets.

One rifle was trained on each of the four Americans. The camouflaged men stared at their targets through the long-range scope, waiting for the precise moment to take their shot. The Americans continued their trek, seemingly unaware of the very real threat concealed in the foliage. The Leader smiled ruthlessly as he surveyed the Americans through the scope of his rifle, one he shouldn't need if everything went as planned. *This will almost be too easy,* he thought as he started to raise his hand to issue the order to fire.

Then, suddenly, he couldn't see a thing.

The Four, oblivious to what was happening in the nearby forest, reached the base of the mountain. The foliage was still thin, but somehow heading up the mountain made Kayla feel a little bit better. Maybe it was because they were that much closer to their goal.

Or maybe it was because they were finally out of that unfamiliar and ominous forest.

The Leader squeezed his eyes shut, wincing. Where on earth had that light come from? Blinking furiously, he tried to assess the location of the rest of the team. Had they seen it too?

It took a few minutes for his sight to return; he quickly located the other members of his team. Every man was wincing, some were moaning, others were rubbing their eyes. After several moments their Leader could sense the question they all wanted to ask but were afraid to: what went wrong?

The Four headed up the mountain, Kayla at the helm, keeping in a roughly straight line to its peak. With any luck—and judging from where she thought the beacon might have been —Kayla thought they might not have to climb all the way to the top.

Apparently, luck was on their side. After a little over twenty minutes walking—and another five or six actually climbing—Kayla saw something come into focus in the midday sun, eerily materializing out of thin air.

A cave, nestled in the mountainside, was cleverly disguised by a carefully arranged outcropping of rocks. The mouth of the cave was small and only visible from their specific vantage point—the rock faces surrounding it created an ingenious optical illusion, effectively concealing the entrance from almost every angle except one.

This had to be it.

Justin rushed past Kayla, reaching the opening first. Apparently she wasn't the only one who'd noticed the cave.

"Hey! Hurry up!" He called down to the rest of the group as he began to explore the opening of the cave from the outside. As Kayla reached the entrance, she was grateful he'd had the foresight to check the entrance before blindly going in. There may be hope for him yet.

Grady was right behind her, and Mandy right behind him. Grady stepped in front of Justin to the mouth of the cave and clicked on his flashlight, glancing pointedly at Justin before entering. Justin took a giant step backward, raising his hands as if surrendering, then, with a flourish, swung his arms around as if he were presenting the opening to Grady.

Grady rolled his eyes, but headed into the blackness, ducking to avoid hitting his head on the top of the opening. Kayla hoped it would open up once they got inside.

She got her wish. Grady'd entered the mouth of the cave hunched over, but had gone only a few yards before the cave's ceiling disappeared, transforming the tiny cave into a massive cavern. Kayla was amazed that this cave had remained hidden for centuries despite its enormity, a large cavern just a few yards from the outside world. *Perhaps the right people just hadn't found it yet,* she thought with a smile as she followed Grady into the black abyss, her eyes—and flashlight—never leaving the back of his shirt.

Mandy followed behind Kayla while Justin brought up the rear. Easily the quickest of the four, Justin would be best able to keep them safe, to alert them of any danger before it got too close. Kayla was certain that if someone tried to sneak up behind them, they would never be able to get past Justin.

Grady agreed. She didn't know how she knew; she just did.

Which pleased her very much.

The light was gone, as quickly as it had come. The Leader began to wonder if he'd imagined it. And, judging by the looks on their faces, his men did, too.

Once the disorientation wore off, the Leader began a frantic search for their prey, swiftly snatching up his rifle and using the scope once again to scan the forest in front of him. He anxiously searched the face of the mountain only after thoroughly scrutinizing the forest before it.

But the Americans were nowhere to be found.

Grady slowly made his way through the pitch black cave. He pointed his flashlight in every direction, but was not finding much other than more darkness, from what Kayla could see. The other three followed suit, but even their combined light did little to dispel the pervasive blackness. Kayla fought the urge to hyperventilate as the ground started to lead them downward—the cavern's sheer enormity was becoming almost oppressive.

The sound of their footsteps echoed off the far-away walls of the cave, reaching Kayla's ears much later than she supposed it should have. Anything could be out there in the blackness. She shivered, though the air was quite warm, and moved just a little bit closer to Grady as they descended further into the ground.

"WHERE DID THEY GO?" The small contingent's Leader growled. How could they just vanish into thin air?

But none of his men had any response. They just stared at him blankly, then four sets of nervous eyes darted accusingly around the group.

The Leader reached for his rifle a second time, searching the area again, more thoroughly this time. When he didn't find them on his second scan of the mountainside—third, actually, since he'd already been through this twice before— he squeezed his eyes shut, hoping against hope that when he opened them again, the Americans would be right in front of him. Slowly, breathing a prayer to the gods, he opened the eye peering through the scope.

Nothing.

The Leader growled wordlessly, shoving the rifle back against the tree. He spun around, turning his back to his soldiers. He couldn't deal with them right now; he needed to think. *No, there's no time to think,* he thought. *I need to give my report.*

He cringed. The Commander wouldn't be happy.

He turned back to his soldiers. "Pack up; we're heading back to camp. I will return shortly." With that, he turned and stalked off into the forest to give the Commander the bad news.

Kayla drew a deep, wet breath with much more difficulty than she should have had. This underground hike seemed to be taking forever, and the air was getting thicker by the minute. She reached a free hand down to the leg of her shorts and pulled the sopping material away from her thigh. Gross.

And now the walls and ceiling of the cave seemed to be closing in on them; their lights had started hitting the top and sides of the tunnel they were traveling down. She should have found this comforting, given the oppressive blackness they'd been in since they'd entered this cave, but the ever-diminishing corridor was just adding to her claustrophobia. Her breathing became slightly labored as she tried to find unsaturated oxygen in the saturated air.

Then Grady froze. Kayla tried to stop, but the slippery incline of the sandy floor coupled with the distraction of her growing anxiety caused her to run right into his back before she could stop herself. Mandy and Justin, a little farther behind, came up behind them slowly, flanking Grady and Kayla on either side. Kayla came around to Grady's side and the four of them stood in a line—a small feat given the shrinking size of this cave—to see what had brought Grady to a standstill.

CHAPTER 31

Trust

K AYLA WAS THE FIRST to break the silence. "A dead end?" Her voice sounded less discouraged than she felt.

Grady reached out and touched the wall in front of them with his fingertips. "Looks like it. I was so sure . . ." A grating sound interrupted him just as his palm flattened on the rock face. Kayla suddenly felt a bewildering sense of vertigo. What was happening?

She looked over at Grady, whose hand was no longer on the wall. He was holding both hands out in front of him, and looked like he was about to lose his balance. Mandy was standing next to Grady; she too was rocking, as though she could fall over at any moment. Her eyes were wide, and Kayla didn't like the petrified terror she saw in them. Justin, standing on Kayla's other side, was nearly toppling over, his arms flailing frantically in an attempt to keep himself upright. In that moment, Kayla realized what was happening.

They were falling.

❋

The floor beneath their feet shattered into a million pieces as Kayla, Grady, Mandy, and Justin crashed to the ground below. Somehow the floor lying in pieces beneath them—the one that had only seconds ago been holding them more than fifteen feet above where they now lay—had given way and cascaded into the cave they now found themselves in.

Kayla heard Mandy groan from across the blackness. Then she yelped, and sucked in her breath. Kayla then heard shuffling, which she could only hope was one of the four of them moving in the utter darkness. Where was that flashlight?

"Ugh . . . I think my wrist's broken." From Mandy.

Kayla heard a more hurried scramble, toward where Mandy's voice had echoed, and assumed Justin was coming to her rescue. She hoped so, anyway. Half a second later, Mandy squealed again. "Be careful!"

Kayla found her misplaced flashlight, and, once her eyes adjusted and the beam of light found her friends, she noticed Justin at Mandy's side, wrapping her injured wrist with some gauze. Resourceful.

Justin deftly wrapped the wrist, then constructed a simple sling with the remaining gauze, gently placing it around Mandy's neck to secure her wrist. "I guess spelunking's not your thing." Kayla could hear the smirk in Justin's voice—she didn't need her flashlight for that.

Mandy slapped him with her good arm, and Kayla lifted her hand to cover her mouth, fighting a smile. He definitely deserved that.

Kayla heard a noise to her left, just out of the beam of the flashlight, and she jumped, whipping the light around. Then she sighed. Grady. Thank God.

He was already on his feet—there certainly was enough headspace in here—and reached out a hand to help her up.

Kayla gladly took it, brushing herself off once she was on her feet again. She mentally took stock of her body, noting a few bumps and bruises, maybe a few scrapes, but nothing warranting a second thought. She thought of Mandy, thinking that it could've been worse.

Grady had been looking her over and nodded at her in the light, and she somehow knew he'd heard her personal assessment. Then she heard him doing the same thing.

This was going to take a lot of getting used to.

Kayla started scanning their new prison—er, surroundings—hoping to find a way out. So far, nothing seemed promising. Grady was at her side, and had started scanning the room with his own light as soon as he'd heard her think about finding an exit. Mandy and Justin joined them, talking amongst themselves, looking a little worse for wear than their slightly older counterparts. Justin had a little limp and Mandy's makeshift sling made Kayla worry that they couldn't continue. She opened her mouth to ask if they were okay, but no sound ever made it out.

"Shhh!" Grady exclaimed in a hoarse whisper, effectively cutting Kayla off without really realizing he did so. A short break in Mandy and Justin's conversation had called something to his attention. "Do you hear that?" He asked no one in particular.

The room was silent for a moment as everyone else strained to listen. Grady could hear Kayla wondering what was wrong, and her concern for him was so endearing that for half a second he forgot everything and only wanted to take her across the room and kiss her for a very long time.

Then he remembered that their telepathy went both ways. And blushed. Thankfully, it was still very dark in here.

Kayla graciously seemed to ignore anything she'd heard, leaving Grady wondering exactly what she *had* heard in his head. "What do you hear?" Her voice was barely a whisper, but it carried in this nearly silent tomb.

Grady was back to listening, and his brow furrowed in the darkness. What *was* that?

Kayla came up to his side and took his hand. "What is it?" Again, a whisper.

Grady pointed into the blackness. "There. That's where we need to go." He took a step in that direction, pulling Kayla with him. She didn't pull back. Grady considered that a step in the right direction in the trust department. And that he didn't care if she heard.

Grady led the way out of the small, roughly circular room and into a small tunnel hidden almost completely from view, even with all of their lights shining on it. Kayla followed obediently, not saying a word, though she wanted to. She was fighting the urge to take over the whole time, but she let Grady lead. She'd realized that this was his book, his discovery, and it seemed only *he* would know exactly where to look. She would just have to trust that.

So she trudged forward, through the muddy dirt caking in and around the soles of her shoes, and kept her mouth shut. Even when they seemed to hit another dead end.

But then it wasn't a dead end. Grady took a sharp right and headed down another long hallway. Kayla's mouth dropped open slightly. He really *did* know where he was going, didn't he?

Did you ever have any doubt? came Grady's voice in her head.

Oh, shush, she shot back.

Grady could still hear that noise, the one that had called him down these hallways, growing louder with every step. The sound reverberated in the rock-encased tunnel and beckoned him further.

Now Kayla heard it, too. *What in the world is that . . . ?*

Grady smiled. He could get used to having her in his head.

Grady led the way further into the darkness and toward that sound, gingerly stepping on the wet rocky surface that was now under his feet. The floor was starting to angle downward, the ceiling with it, and now Grady had to stare at the ground to make sure he didn't slip. To make matters worse, the slick decline was slowing their descent, which Grady didn't care for at all.

After a few minutes, the floor sloped more sharply. The ceiling sloped with the floor, but was closing the distance between them ever so gradually. Soon they would be hunched over. Grady had to holster his flashlight to brace himself against the cave walls. The others followed suit, and soon their only light was shining in haphazardly swinging circles on the floor beneath them.

"Is that a river?" Justin asked no one in particular.

Grady just smiled again, though he knew no one would be able to see it. They were close.

Their slow progress made the journey seem infinitely longer than it actually was. After a short yet very long time, the floor sloped drastically, and Grady had to catch himself before he went tumbling headlong into the emptiness before him. Instinctively he reached back for Kayla, grabbing her elbow before she could fall and helping her regain her balance. She smiled at him in the ambient light of their downward facing flashlights and the smile warmed his insides. He'd never tire of her smile.

As Mandy and Justin came to a stop just behind Kayla, Grady turned his attention to the floor under him, bracing himself against the walls to free a hand and pull out his flashlight.

Now the floor wasn't sloping at all—it was just completely gone. The cave floor had opened into a massive hole. The sound of rushing water coming from it was loud enough that they had to raise their voices to be heard.

"Now what do we do?" Kayla queried.

Grady just grinned as he struggled against the wall and now constricting ceiling to find a better foothold, pressing his back against the smooth rock surface. He held his flashlight in one hand as he leaned carefully over the edge and pointed it down into the dark water. "Who's up for a swim?"

"Are you *completely* insane?" Mandy's voice reverberated off the suffocatingly close walls, and Kayla winced. Even the sound of the rushing tide below them did little to deaden the shrill outburst.

Kayla knew Grady had never been more certain of anything—she'd heard as much in his thoughts—but when she opened her mouth to defend him, Justin cut her off. "Grady, we don't know where this thing ends up. It could go underground for miles and we may never resurface! We don't have oxygen tanks or anything. This is *not* a good idea." If Kayla hadn't been so sure of Grady, seeing the lines creasing Justin's forehead would've made her stomach knot up. But it didn't, because she just knew.

"Stop." Kayla's command carried above the noise of the flood beneath their feet. She closed her eyes for a second, then opened them to find three pairs of eyes on her. "This is the way."

Justin leaned forward slightly. "Are you sure?"

Kayla smiled and looked over at Grady, who caught and held her gaze. "Positive."

But Justin didn't seem to be entirely convinced. He looked at Grady. As if to answer Justin's unvoiced question, Grady straddled the hole in the ground, drew a deep breath, then stepped off the side and disappeared.

Everything in Kayla's head told her Grady was crazy, and that she was crazy for trusting him, but her heart told her a different story. She could still hear the resolve in his thoughts, knew how certain he'd been—certain enough to jump into rushing water without any idea where it would lead —but her head still fought her, screamed at her, implored her to stop, to wait, to analyze, then make an informed decision.

But she couldn't. She looked up the long hallway they'd just come down and knew they would never make it back that way. The only way out was through. She just had to trust that Grady knew what he was doing.

So she jumped, backpack and all, into the swirling abyss, praying that Grady'd been right.

Mandy gasped as soon as Kayla hit the water and dropped out of sight. She turned wide eyes to Justin. "What do we do now?" She didn't like the panic she heard in the voice echoing around the small chamber.

Justin seemed to be frozen for a second or two, then blinked and few times and shrugged. "I guess we follow them." He started toward the hole.

Mandy thrust out her hand to stop him. "No!" She couldn't help but shout, which she regretted immediately. She winced as the shout rang in her ears.

But Justin turned to her and smiled. "Look, honey, I've learned to listen to Kayla—and Grady—in the past few weeks. I know they'd never do anything to hurt us. They believe so strongly that this is the way we have to go that they jumped in, no questions asked." He drew a shaky breath as he inched closer to the edge. "So now I think we need to believe them." He took one final step over the edge and disappeared just as Kayla and Grady had before him.

Mandy wasn't fully convinced. How could she put her trust in something she couldn't see? How could she be certain that this one decision wouldn't kill them all?

The short answer was: she couldn't.

She sighed, but was still unsure. How did she know they hadn't just slammed the coffins shut on their own watery graves? Why would they do such—then, out of nowhere, she heard a hurried shuffling echo off the cave walls. She jumped, almost losing her balance and stopping herself just short of hurtling headlong into the hole.

She saw something moving at her feet, and scrambled away from it as best as she could. Then, from what she hoped was a safe distance, she looked at it more closely . . . and recognized what it was.

A rat, just inches from her feet, scurried by and headed back up the tunnel.

That was it. This tunnel was getting way too creepy.

She took a deep breath and plunged into the rushing water.

CHAPTER 32

Water

GRADY HAD BEEN HOLDING his breath for what seemed like forever. A million questions were running through his head, but one prevailed: What had he just done?

Had he condemned himself and his friends to death? Had his one spur-of-the-moment decision cost all of them their lives? Would this river ever resurface?

Would *he* ever resurface?

His lungs were screaming for oxygen. His head was throbbing, desperately pleading with his body for air. He thought that this might be the end, that he might never see . . . no, he couldn't let himself think that. That was more than his mind could handle at the moment. He struggled against the urge to breathe, tried to hold on for just a little while longer. Tried to remember that Kayla was just behind him—he heard her decide to jump in but her thoughts had grown quiet after that. He hoped she was okay.

The river was rushing around him, catapulting his body down the tunnel while relentlessly battering it against the tunnel's edges. He was mentally kicking himself for this stupid decision. How could he have been so foolish?

But then he remembered how he'd felt before he'd jumped into this deathtrap. He had been positive—beyond the shadow of a doubt—that this was where they needed to go. The book was calling out to him, pleading with him to find it, and he'd been sure that this was the only way.

Then an odd realization hit him, and his mind started to clear. He suddenly felt as though he was about to find something he'd never known he was missing. Like the book already *belonged* to him—he had just misplaced it. And this river, this watery tunnel under the earth, was his way to what was rightfully his.

If he didn't drown first.

Kayla kept her eyes tightly shut as the torrent of water propelled her under the ground. She was *almost* certain that this was the way to the next book, but how could she be sure? She had no way of positively knowing, one hundred percent, that they wouldn't be dead in the next few minutes.

But Grady had been so sure. He had jumped in without hesitation.

And she'd followed him. She trusted him, and now she knew how completely. She trusted him absolutely, with her very life.

There, in the turbulent stream of water with her lungs begging for air, she realized just how much she needed him, just how much she loved him.

She just hoped she would have the chance to tell him.

Grady opened his eyes in the murky water, blinking as his eyes adjusted to the wet darkness. He thought he had sensed light just a few seconds earlier—now he was sure. There was light ahead!

His lungs were burning, but he no longer cared. He was seeing the literal light at the end of the tunnel—he wouldn't be underwater much longer.

His feet exploded from the watery shaft but touched nothing but air, and more water. The rest of his body followed, shooting him out of the tunnel. He flew through the air for what seemed like an eternity as water sprayed all around him. He struggled to hold his breath for just a few seconds longer.

He landed hard on his back on a sand-covered but rocky surface, which knocked the wind out of him. He sat up as soon as he could recover, coughing and gasping for air. The air here was very thick, saturated with water, but wonderfully breathable. He sat there for a little while, content to simply breathe again.

Kayla shot out of the tunnel a few moments later, and Grady quickly moved out of the way. Kayla landed hard, just as he had. Then, while caught in a coughing fit, she rolled over next to him to catch her breath. She had apparently figured out where Justin and Mandy were going to land.

Justin catapulted from the hole soon after Kayla—and Mandy soon after that—and they both lay on the ground gasping.

Mandy's sling was soaked, but it appeared that she had miraculously avoided landing on her arm.

Kayla squinted up at the hole they had just burst out of. It was easily twenty feet above the ground. She was amazed they didn't break their backs when they fell.

Water was violently spewing out of the hole in the wall, sending a misting spray around the entire room. The torrent flowed out of the hole and into another river, creating a beautiful yet volatile waterfall. The river continued out of the room, through another hole in the wall, this one at floor level. There didn't appear to be any other exit, which made Kayla frown without really meaning to. Would they have to risk drowning again? She hoped not. She certainly wasn't looking forward to it.

Then it suddenly occurred to Kayla that she was squinting. She looked around, her brow furrowed. Why would she be squinting in here? Kayla focused her attention on the ceiling, where a bright light was shining and filling the room. It seemed to be coming from directly above her. She blinked a few times, shading her eyes with her hand, trying to adjust her eyes to the light.

Once she could see again, she took Grady's offered hand and let him help her to her feet. She smiled to herself as she brushed herself off, then began to really take in their surroundings.

The room itself was large—but still much smaller than the cavern at Lamanai—a circular dome whose sides curved upward from the ground. At the apex of the domed ceiling, Kayla imagined a small hole—the light was so bright she couldn't see it, but a hole in the ceiling was the only explanation she could come up with—that allowed the midday sun to shine through freely. The entire room was brilliantly lit, and, as her eyes adjusted, Kayla found the sunlight comforting after the darkness of the watery tunnel. And the warmth, which had nearly dried her shirt and thin khaki shorts despite the mist surrounding them.

Grady snorted to her immediate left. "Well, that was fun." He shook his head rapidly, his sopping wet hair sending a spray of warm water over Kayla.

Kayla leaned over and playfully smacked his arm, noting the similarities to that rainy morning in the mess tent just a few weeks ago. Had it only been a few weeks? "Thanks for that." She theatrically wiped at her face.

He grinned widely at her, then pulled her to his side. "Oh, you were wet anyway. Quit complaining." He leaned down and kissed her forehead.

Justin rolled his eyes. "Geez, guys. Get a room."

Kayla laughed aloud.

"Wait a minute," Mandy spoke up, and Kayla noticed that her voice was missing the playfulness of the rest of the group's conversation.

"What?" Kayla frowned.

Mandy looked up at the ceiling, surveying the room. "There's no echo in here. But there should be . . ."

Grady nodded in agreement. "Yeah . . . that's definitely odd." He too began to survey the curving walls that led up to the hole in the middle of the ceiling.

Justin clearly didn't understand. "Why does that matter?"

Kayla tried to explain. "There should be an echo in here. These walls appear to be made of rock, so our voices should echo off them, but they don't, and, come to think of it, neither does the sound of the water. It doesn't make sense . . ." her voice trailed off as she started to walk toward the nearest wall, taking the first step away from the group. The wall appeared to be made of solid rock, just as the ground under their feet.

Then she reached out to touch it—and her hand disappeared. *Into* the wall.

Mandy let out a short cry as Kayla's mouth dropped open.

"But . . . how . . . how is that possible?" Grady stammered, staggering over to Kayla's side. "How are the walls even staying up?"

Justin and Mandy joined their friends, eyes and mouths wide.

Kayla pulled her hand back out of the wall and stared at it in astonishment, turning it over again and again, afraid it might disappear if she stopped looking at it—and unable to shake the unsettling spongy feeling of the interior of the pliable wall.

"Amazing," Grady breathed. He reached out his own hand to test the wall, but his fingertips never touched the wall. He froze. Kayla looked up to see his eyes glaze over, and the sight terrified her.

He began to walk away from the group robotically, heading down the wall about twenty feet before he abruptly stopped. He eerily turned toward the wall and reached out his hand, eyes wide but unseeing.

His fingers slid through the malleable substance that comprised the wall and Kayla held her breath. Grady extended his arm further and it vanished into the wall up to his elbow. He kept going, and soon his entire arm disappeared.

Then he stopped.

"What?" Kayla's stomach was churning as she ran over to him. Mandy and Justin were close behind.

Grady was still, his expression blank. Kayla was really starting to get worried. She put her hand on his shoulder and spoke softly. "What's wrong?" Her voice came out much lower than she expected, and she realized at once that she didn't want an answer to her question.

Then Grady's countenance suddenly relaxed, and a glow shone on his face. His eyes cleared and he slowly began to smile.

But Kayla couldn't relax. "Grady, tell me! What's wrong?"

Grady shook his head, blinking as though he was coming out of a trance. His next words came out barely above a whisper, but Kayla could hear the wonder in them. "I found it."

Mandy tilted her head and squinted. "What?"

Grady grinned now, and began to pull his hand out of the wall. Slowly his elbow reappeared, followed by his wrist, then his fingers . . . which held something tightly in their grasp.

Mandy gasped, the pieces coming together in a rush.

The third book.

Emblazoned on the distressed leather cover was the Mayan symbol for "water"—Grady remembered enough K'iche to know that—and his heart skipped a beat as he turned it over in his hands. He had found his book.

He stared at it silently for a moment, then sunk to the hard sandy ground, opening the book carefully, almost reverently. He felt Kayla drop to the ground beside him as his eyes took in the first page.

Mandy, having little knowledge of the Mayan language, got up and started exploring the rest of the room, looking for a way out. Justin—who knew even less of the Mayan language than she did, Mandy knew—followed suit; they headed in opposite directions, running their hands lightly against the wall as they walked.

Mandy was astounded. The wall—if it could even be called that; its consistency was completely permeable and lacked any substantial foundation that she could determine—gave way under the slightest touch. Only by dragging her hand along the wall with a feather-light touch did her hand not breach the surface.

What little she could feel under her fingertips felt surprisingly like rock, only thin and somehow pliable. She gazed up at the ceiling and wondered, as Grady had, how the walls were still standing.

Mandy was nearing the gushing waterfall from which they had all been propelled. She gazed at it as she approached, taking her hand off the wall without really realizing it.

The water was moving so rapidly that it saturated the entire area around it except the ground directly beneath, where the water couldn't reach. Mandy took the last few final steps and stood directly under the falling water, leaning over slightly to examine the floor and the wall next to her.

She slowly reached out her hand to test the wall beneath the opening. She touched it ever so lightly, anticipating that her hand would simply plunge through the thin outer layer and slide easily into pliant material.

But nothing happened.

She pressed her fingertips a little harder—applying only the slightest bit more pressure—and the wall started to give way. But instead of her hand contacting the sponge-like material that comprised the rest of the wall in this room, the wall crumbled in her hand. She retracted her hand quickly, as if a snake had snapped at it.

Then, to her horror, she heard a sharp crack.

She stared, frozen, at the wall in front of her and watched as a large fissure shot up from the small depression she'd made toward the large hole from which the water was gushing. She tried to back away, but jolted to a stop just before she was doused in a torrential waterfall; she'd forgotten about the rushing water behind her, which was now holding her in place.

For the moment. She turned and ducked to the side, sprinting back into the room, away from the deluge.

She didn't get very far. Just a few seconds later, a second, much louder cracking sound seemed to split the room in two and Mandy jolted to a stop. Kayla and Grady flew to their feet, eyes wide. Justin started running toward her.

Feeling as though she was in slow motion, Mandy turned around to gaze at the wall, which was now barely visible under the ever-increasing stream of water. Her eyes widened; as much as she wanted—and tried—to, she was unable to pull her eyes away from the terrible sight.

She sensed rather than saw Justin coming up next to her. Unable to think of anything else to do, she slowly reached for his hand.

His hand was trembling.

CHAPTER 33

Faith

KAYLA LOOKED ON, EYES WIDE, as the wall beneath the waterfall deteriorated with a grating sound so loud she had to clasp her hands over her ears. The water previously gushing from the relatively small opening was now spewing forth through a massive hole that had replaced an entire section of the wall. The small river bisecting the room was overflowing, slowly filling the room with an ever-rising flood.

"Time to move!" Grady shouted, snatching up the book just before the water reached their feet.

Yes, but to where? Kayla wondered, her eyes frantically scanning the room for an exit—any exit.

Out of the corner of her eye, she caught Grady running toward the flowing water. *Toward?* Was he insane?

Even though her instincts were screaming for a better solution, she headed toward Grady, toward the waterfall. Her feet sloshed through the rising water surrounding them, slowing her progress, but she closed the distance to Grady's side more quickly than she would have thought possible.

She trusted him completely. Implicitly. She knew he was the only reason she was now throwing herself headlong into certain danger; there couldn't be any other explanation. Kayla glanced over to take in his expression.

What she saw on Grady's face should have surprised her. It would have surprised anyone else. But she wasn't surprised; she was, instead, comforted. She smiled, an unfamiliar but gratifying warmth flooding her veins.

She saw in his face an expression she was certain now mirrored her own. One that displayed a strange and inexplicable peace, a calm assuredness that defied all logic and reason.

In that moment, nothing could touch her, nothing could harm her. As long as he was with her, nothing else mattered.

She reached over and grasped his hand with a slight smile on her face as they stared at the ever-rising water.

Justin just stared at his two friends. What were they thinking? What was left of the wall beneath the gushing water was certain to give way in a matter of seconds. This room would be completely flooded in only a few minutes. So why were they so eager to face the danger head on? Why were they now staring at the water pouring from the wall as though it was their salvation?

Grady smiled serenely as he looked at the waterfall before him. The water around them was rising; he could feel it lapping at his knees. He clutched the book to his chest and gripped Kayla's hand tighter. Then he waited.

For what, he wasn't entirely sure.

His brain—his logical side—told him that this was foolish. That they all would certainly die in this underground cave, and the mystery of the books would never be found out. The only smart thing to do now—the only logical thing—would be to search for a way out.

But another part of him—the part that was winning out, though for what reason he didn't know—was telling him to wait. Something was coming, something that would rescue them from this seemingly impossible situation. He just need- ed to wait, to trust.

So he did; he and Kayla stood for what seemed like an eternity just staring at the water flowing from the wall. Nei- ther of them moved, nor felt the need to move. He knew— and could sense that Kayla knew, too—that everything would be okay. This thing they were waiting for—whatever it was— would come soon, and it would save them.

Mandy didn't know what to think. She glanced at Justin, who was staring at Kayla and Grady with a scowl on his face, then looked over at Kayla and Grady. They were standing side by side, staring at the growing rush of water with an inexplicable look of complete peace on their faces, even as the water rose. What were they doing?

Shouldn't we all be looking for the exit? she thought, even as she found herself unable to move.

Mandy felt horrible. She had caused the rift in the wall, the crack that had split the wall in two and caused the water to overflow and begin to flood this room. She glanced toward the ground, heart beating harder in her chest, at the water rising beneath her. She extended her hand out to her side; it touched the surface of the water.

The water was now up to her waist.

She panicked. "Grady! Kayla! We need to move!"

She forced her legs to trudge through the water and started toward them, taking Justin's hand and pulling him along with her.

She kept yelling the entire way. "We have to go! We need to find a way out!" She could barely hear herself above the sound of the rushing water, but she had to try.

"Kayla!" She came up behind her friend, placing a hand on her back. Kayla didn't move, didn't even flinch.

Mandy was officially worried. She let go of Justin's hand to put both of her own on Kayla's shoulders. She shook her, trying to force her out of this odd trance.

But, again, Kayla didn't seem to hear her, or feel her touch. Mandy got angry and forcibly turned Kayla to face her, splashing in the waist-high water as they went. "Kayla! Talk to me! What are you doing?"

Kayla's mouth turned up ever so slightly. The effect was eerie.

"What are you doing?" Mandy demanded again, but the question came out nearly a whisper as her voice caught at the sight of the expression on Kayla's face.

Kayla's lips parted slightly as she turned back to the torrent, grabbing Grady's hand once again. Mandy came up beside her friend, pulling Justin along with her while trying to keep herself in Kayla's line of sight. She didn't hear the words that came out of Kayla's mouth, but Mandy could easily read her friend's lips. "We're waiting."

Mandy's mouthed response was desperate. "For what?"

Before Kayla could answer, a thunderous clap broke throughout the room, shaking it violently as though they were in an earthquake. Mandy looked over at Grady, whose vague smile was turning into a grin. He and Kayla seemed to snap out of their trance in the same instant.

"This is it!" Grady yelled as the thunderous earthquake subsided slightly. "Get ready!"

Mandy wanted to ask "for what?" again, but in that moment she couldn't get any words out. She couldn't even breathe.

Something had knocked the wind out of her.

They were falling—Grady was sure of that. He felt the water start to pull him under as the rocky surface beneath his feet crumbled and shattered into the space below.

Grady, Kayla, Mandy, and Justin plummeted beneath the surface, free-falling through the water as if being funneled down a massive drain. They landed in a heap on a hard surface below as an enormous waterfall poured down over them. Grady couldn't catch his breath.

Blindly he reached out his hand, trying to find Kayla. Somehow he had let go of her during the fall, and not knowing where she was now terrified him. Grady blinked as he strained to see through the falling water, coughing as he did, looking for some sign that Kayla was alive. He strained to hear her thoughts, but they seemed scrambled, incoherent. *Please be okay*, he thought, willing her to hear.

The water was now trickling over the side of the floor above them, and Grady was finally able to hear something other than rushing water. He could hear Justin and Mandy gasping for air behind him, and he *thought* he could hear a third person . . .

There. He finally saw Kayla lying a few feet away from him, quietly gasping for air. He rushed to her side, not caring about the trouble he was having breathing at the moment. He needed to touch her, to know she was real, to know she was okay.

But something was wrong, and he couldn't figure out what. Her thoughts were still jumbled and weren't making any sense. "Kayla," he breathed, brow furrowed.

"Grady," she whispered, reaching up to touch his face with what Grady could tell was a forced smile. Then she coughed, and the smile faded.

"Kayla, what's wrong? Are you hurt?"

Kayla looked confused for a moment. "What?"

"Are you hurt? Are you okay?" His questions came out so rapidly that he hoped she understood.

"I . . . I think so . . ." she tried to move, then winced.

Grady cringed. "Where are you hurt?"

"I . . . don't know . . ." she tried to move again, this time with more success. She lifted herself up on her elbow, testing her range of motion carefully. When that seemed to be okay, she rose to a seated position. Grady stayed with her, gauging her movements carefully. She started to stand.

She staggered, then fell over. Grady caught her before she hit the ground, hearing in her thoughts exactly what hurt.

"My ankle . . ."

Grady cringed again, then released the breath he hadn't realized he'd been holding. If only her ankle was broken—or, perhaps even better, sprained—there was no serious danger. Well, not really *better*, but she should be fine. He could easily carry her out of here if he needed to.

But how did they get out?

The room was an inky black, the light above absorbed by the darkness in this pit. Grady's eyes strained to take in his surroundings as something occurred to him. Where had all the water gone? The floor was barely wet, save a few small puddles here and there. All that water had to have gone somewhere.

He helped Kayla to her feet, letting her balance on her good leg and lean into his side. He welcomed the contact; he felt as though he had been too long without her.

Life after falling in love with her would never be the same—he knew that. It had altered him so completely that nothing else seemed to matter anymore. Nothing but her.

He knew Kayla could hear his thoughts—hers were clear now and he could almost hear her smiling in the darkness—but he didn't care; he was beyond that now. They were beyond that. If—when—they ended this journey still intact, he wouldn't hesitate to make her his own.

So the only thing that brought him back to reality, the only thing that could, was the reluctant change in her thoughts, followed immediately by the sound of her voice. "So how do we get out of here?"

Justin spoke up. "Well, while you two were fooling around I figured out where all the water went." His flashlight illuminated the tiny room surrounding them.

The room was small; it could barely even be called a room. It was really just a deep, circular pit in the ground, a dark and dank place where, apparently, excess water was expended. The four of them now stood on a circular piece of rock in the center of the pit. Around its edges, a small crack separated the floor from the wall. Apparently this was where all the water had gone.

The crack was only about six inches wide, but it was still disconcerting. The room left Grady with the feeling that they were stuck in the middle of a well with no way out.

He had to ask the question. "So . . . did you find an exit?"

Justin grinned, puffing up his chest. "Of course. I never disappoint."

Mandy rolled her eyes.

Grady looked over at the spot now illuminated by Justin's light. He stared wide-eyed at what shouldn't—what couldn't—possibly be real.

But there, in the most miraculous of places, was a hole in the side of the well, a small opening that led away from this damply saturated place. Grady stood frozen for half a second, then abruptly snapped into action. He handed his book to Kayla, knowing she would guard it with her life, then helped her stagger slowly toward what was sure to be their way out of this place.

Justin was the first to duck through the opening, hunched over. He came out on the other side just as Mandy ducked into the cramped passageway. Kayla, then Grady, followed quickly, their backs only inches from the ceiling.

As soon as Grady could stand up straight again, he looked up to see what the others were already gaping at: there, in the most unexpected and glorious place, was a staircase. The group gladly climbed it, letting it lead them up and away from the cave that had nearly been their tomb. At the top of the stairs, another tunnel stretched before them, but Grady could see daylight ahead. He couldn't wait to see the sun, to breathe fresh air again. He led the group toward the light, their beacon showing them the way out.

The four of them, injuries and all, broke out from the suffocating oppression of the mountain and stepped into the bright light of the afternoon sun.

Informant

Lamanai Archaeological Dig, Northern Belize

JACKIE TRUDGED SLOWLY DOWN the two steps in front of the work trailer, awkwardly reaching behind her to close the door. She absentmindedly began to head back to her own tent, where she was stowing the globe, as she contemplated the meeting she'd just had with Jack. Nothing really important was said—he'd only wanted an update on what she'd found out about the globe, which wasn't much—but something was up with Jack. Most of the time he'd just stared off into space, and didn't answer her questions right away . . . What could possibly have been bothering him? She knew him well enough to know that something was on his mind, but also knew that it wasn't her place to pry. As much as she wanted to. Needed to, really. Did he know her secret?

She forcibly shrugged for the mass of people surrounding her, in case they were watching, to try to mask the frown on her face. She couldn't let them see that she was concerned, even if they wouldn't read anything into it. A secret like hers could get her in trouble around here, and she'd gone this long without anyone suspecting a thing. Or so she thought. Did Jack suspect? Was that what was bothering him?

She was going to drive herself crazy with such thoughts. She decided right then, as her tent came into view, that she couldn't let what Jack might have been worrying about bother her. If she needed to know, Jack would tell her . . . right? She hoped so.

As her tent got closer, she made a conscious effort to think about something else, but it was proving difficult. With all the excitement of the past few weeks, she hadn't had time for thinking—or for much of anything, really. A novel she had fully intended to read lay unopened in her tent, and a few letters lay in a small stack under her cot, letters she hadn't had time to respond to, or even read thoroughly.

Remembering the letters brought a small smile to her face. Just thinking of who wrote those letters, what she remembered them saying of what little she'd had time to read . . .

She stopped abruptly as a thought occurred to her. She glanced around quickly, and checked her watch. *No one should be in there now . . .*

She turned a sharp left and headed for the communications trailer, by way of the mess hall and the main part of the dig—again, just in case people were watching and wondering where she was going. She needed to be seen going somewhere obvious, somewhere no one would question. Then she would steal away to her destination when she was sure prying eyes were elsewhere. She was probably being overly cautious, but she couldn't take any chances.

After a few frustrating minutes of being stopped by who she was certain was every single person at the dig to ask every inane question known to man, Jackie crept up to the door of the communications trailer and stole a few furtive glances to make sure she wouldn't be seen before ducking inside. She pulled the door shut behind her with a feather-light touch; despite her caution, she was fairly certain the sound of her entry would be masked by everything going on at the dig. No one would realize she was here. No one was even nearby.

She wasn't supposed to be in here; she knew that. The satellite phone was strictly for emergencies. But she couldn't help herself. She hadn't heard his voice in forever.

Downtown Leticia, Colombia

"So where are we headed next?"

Justin's offhand question at their late dinner elicited more of a response in Kayla than she would've liked. She was certain he didn't mean anything by asking, but lately she'd been taking personal offense to questions like that—which bothered her. Why did her mind keep bringing this up? She couldn't do anything about it, and her friends knew that. And they didn't care. She told herself to shut up and reached for her sparkling water.

Grady's voice broke into her thoughts. "Not sure. We could be going anywhere." The sound of Grady's voice made her jump, and she realized for the first time since they'd left the mountain that she couldn't hear his thoughts anymore. She frowned.

Grady set his fork down to reach over and squeeze her hand. "It's fine," he mouthed to her, offering a sweet smile.

Kayla thought her answering smile fell a little short.

Mandy spoke up. "That's fine with me." She drew a large swig of water from her straw. "It's so pretty here."

Kayla nodded absently at the observation, then glanced around the hotel's restaurant and lobby to fully appreciate their surroundings. All around them, the sandy-colored stone floors and walls were adorned with delicate, multi-colored tile inlays; gauzy white swatches of fabric hung from the high ceiling, waving ever-so-slightly in the breeze coming in the wall of open-air windows that afforded a panoramic view of the surrounding rainforest. A myriad of plants stood unobtrusively around the room in brightly colored, massive urns, giving such a cheerful place even more life. It was definitely beautiful.

"So what should we do while we wait?" Justin posed the question to the group.

Kayla raised her arms above her head and stretched. "I don't know about all of you, but I could use some rest." She pushed her chair back and stood.

Grady smiled. "Sounds good to me." He tossed some cash on the table as he rose to follow her out of the lobby.

"Grady?" Kayla stopped just before she reached her room and turned to the man she loved.

Grady reached for her hands and held them in his. "What is it?"

"I just . . ." Kayla began, unsure of where she was going with this. "I just wanted to give you a proper goodnight." Her lips turned up as she gazed into Grady's eyes. She stretched up to kiss him deeply, lingering for a few moments before pulling away.

Grady grinned. "You sure know how to say goodnight. Although I may not be able to sleep after that."

Kayla shrugged, her brows furrowing. "After what?"

Grady suddenly wrapped his arms around her waist and pulled her to him, pressing his lips on hers passionately but somehow gently. She loved when he took her by surprise. Kayla's head started spinning as she let him press her up against the door to her room.

When he pulled away—only slightly—minutes later, Kayla was still reeling. She didn't think she'd be able to sleep after that, either. She opened her mouth to invite him in when all of a sudden she couldn't move.

What was that? A highly unwelcome interruption scattered her thoughts, and she was intensely distracted. She frowned; something was messing with her thoughts. Was that Grady?

She placed her hands on Grady's chest, pushing him away and hating it every second, but unable to sort out her thoughts with Grady being so close. Grady's countenance changed as his eyes found hers and held them, and Kayla's heart broke at the confusion she saw in them. "Grady . . . I . . . I'm sorry."

"Is everything okay?"

Kayla tried to nod but she couldn't. Instead, she spoke the truth. "No."

Grady's hand flew to her arm. "What's wrong? What is it?"

Kayla shook her head, but it didn't help to clear it. It only seemed to make the confusion in her head worse.

Grady had both hands on her upper arms now. "Kayla. Talk to me." He was nearly growling now.

Kayla blinked hard, then stared directly into his eyes. And then, though she could still see him, she couldn't feel him anymore. She felt an immediate and pervading isolation—though she was staring right at him—right before it hit her.

It wasn't like her other visions; it was simply a feeling, but one so strong and overwhelming that she reached for Grady's forearm and gripped it tight. She couldn't feel his arm under her hand.

Then, as quickly as it had come, it was gone, replaced by a deep pit in her stomach. Something was very wrong.

She blinked at Grady then spoke, wincing at the sound of terror she didn't want to hear there. "We have to get back to Lamanai. Now."

Northern Belize Rainforest

Hours after everyone had eaten dinner and dispersed to their evening activities, a darkly clad figure reached the edge of Lamanai without a sound, barely visible in the thick under-growth. Taking a few steps forward, the figure stepped out from under the concealing cover of the rainforest, constantly peering through the holes in its highly-impractical-for-this-weather ski mask.

The shadowy outline headed directly for the mess tent, which backed up to the surrounding rainforest not far from where it had just appeared. As the figure entered the wall-less room, it reached into a cargo pocket and extracted three small vials. Immediately locating three large coolers of water, the figure crossed the short distance to stand in front of them. Silently the first top came off, followed by the other two. The contents of one vial trickled soundlessly into each cooler, then the lids were carefully replaced as if they'd never been removed.

The dark form stole out from under the cover of the tent, slipping silently past the unknowing inhabitants of the dig under the night sky.

Lamanai Archaeological Dig, Northern Belize

Jackie awoke with a start, jolting upright on her cot. Light streamed through the small opening in her tent and illuminated the space inside through the canvas walls. Her eyes darted around erratically, anxiously searching for her two tent-mates, but their cots were empty, the tent otherwise uninhabited.

She stepped into some sandals as she grabbed a nearby sweater out of habit. She pulled it on as she exited the tent.

The sun was hot already. She could feel it beating down hard on her face. She had taken only a few steps before she put a hand over her eyes and turned back to the tent to grab a wide-brimmed hat.

As she left the tent a second time, leaving behind the sweater but donning the hat, something occurred to her. Why was it so bright out here? And why was it so hot? She squinted up at the sky and saw the sun overhead, much farther from the horizon than she expected. What time was it?

She glanced down at her watch. Almost eleven. How had she slept this late without being woken up? Where had her roommates gone?

Then she noticed something, or rather, the lack of something—this place was much too quiet. This time of day, the dig should be bustling with activity. Especially this late in the morning.

So where was everyone?

Belize Rainforest, South of the Mercenary Camp

Holun yawned and tilted his head to either side. He was sitting at the edge of a large clearing, easily fifty yards away from where Na-um was briefing the troops. He played with a long blade of grass as Na-um administered his daily dose of sleeping medication in the form of troop movements, plans, and the like. Holun resisted the urge to stand up and visibly stretch. Even from this distance, he could clearly hear every word Na-um was saying. The exceptional hearing afforded a few of the more gifted members of the Clan usually came in handy.

But today, it was nearly nauseating.

Holun stared at the ground as he tried to focus solely on the single blade of grass in his hand in an unsuccessful attempt to drown out Na-um's wearisome speech.

"We will continue our training the rest of the week . . ." Na-um was saying. Holun rolled his eyes, careful to hide it from anyone who may be looking his way. *Training, ha. That's a joke.* Exasperated, he tossed the blade of grass to the ground in front of him. He was about to stand up when something unexpected reached his ears. He froze in place, now listening intently as his eyes bored holes in the ground.

"Na-um," the voice was whispering, "I have more news."

Holun stole a glance toward the formation, taking in the fifty-plus men standing at attention before his eyes stopped on Na-um.

And the young man now by his side.

Holun vaguely recognized the man—well, boy, really. He was almost as young as Holun himself. He had always just been one of the soldiers, nobody special. At least to Holun.

Apparently Na-um didn't share the same sentiment.

Holun tried to not stare, but he couldn't help but feel like something was wrong. Like someone was more important to

Na-um than he was. It was stupid. To feel like someone had taken his place by one simple conversation . . .

"I just came from Location Alpha," the boy continued. "The plan was executed nearly perfectly. All but a few should be dead by the end of the day."

Holun gasped, then mentally kicked himself. He quickly averted his eyes, hoping Na-um didn't suspect that he was listening in. Only a few in the Clan had exceptional hearing—and only those select few even knew about it.

But Na-um was one of them. He had undoubtedly heard Holun, which meant that he would have easily realized that Holun was listening. And, clearly, the secret conversation was not something Holun was meant to hear.

After all, if Na-um wanted him to know, wouldn't he have been told about this guy by now?

As the conversation ended and Na-um continued his brief, Holun sighed, feeling as though he had avoided a verbal lashing. His reprieve was short-lived, however, as he remembered what he had heard. Where was Location Alpha, and what plan had been executed there?

He plucked another piece of grass from the ground in front of him as he contemplated the possibilities.

The location could be Lamanai, the dig . . . or Leticia, where the Americans currently were. But given what the young informant had said—*all but a few should be dead*—he figured they were probably talking about the people at the dig. Plus, Na-um wouldn't be continuing his speech if the American foursome were dead. There would be no reason to continue.

So what was the plan? Did they have a small group go in last night and murder everyone in their sleep? He shuddered at the thought, realizing as a knot formed in his stomach that the scenario was entirely possible. Na-um had lost any semblance of humanity days ago; Holun wouldn't put the execution of innocent people past him. Except . . . didn't the boy say they should be dead *by the end of the day*? What did they do?

"Holun?"

Holun jumped at the sound of Na-um's voice. He hadn't even noticed his leader finish his brief and release his men. Holun's internal musings had successfully blocked out his superior's voice, and he found himself eternally grateful that Na-um couldn't read his mind.

Na-um now stood at his side, arms crossed. Holun shot to his feet instantaneously and snapped to attention. "Yes, Sir?"

Na-um smiled a little. "Sorry to startle you, Holun. At ease."

On the outside, Holun appeared to relax a little, but the knot in his stomach was multiplying into hundreds of little knots. He returned Na-um's smile with a little effort. "Yes, Na-um . . . sorry." His body relaxed even more as he composed himself further. "What is it?"

"Holun," Na-um began, placing a hand on Holun's forearm and leading him a few steps farther away from the group. "I heard you listening to my conversation a few minutes ago."

Holun pasted an apologetic look on his face. For appearances only. "Sorry," he said quickly. "Still haven't gotten this hearing thing under control." The lie came to him more easily than he would have thought possible, which surprised him. And worried him, just a little.

Na-um smiled and placed a hand on Holun's shoulder. Holun knew that Na-um intended the gesture to be reassuring, but the younger man just found it to be condescending. "That's fine, Holun." His superior took a deep breath and fell silent, his brow furrowing in concentration. With every second that ticked by, Holun grew more and more nervous.

Finally, Na-um sighed. "It's probably time for you to find out what's going on." He walked to a nearby boulder and sat down, motioning for Holun to do the same. Holun took a seat as Na-um began.

"When we first discovered our problem at Lamanai, I had Konae do some recon for us," he started, nodding toward the soldier Holun had overheard just moments earlier. He was currently running around with his friends like the adolescent he was. Holun had to stop himself from rolling his eyes. "He started reporting on their movements, on everything that was happening. He was the reason we knew when the Americans were leaving the dig, and why we were able to stop the vehicle from getting too far, at least the first time."

The memory of that day sickened Holun, but he was able to keep any telling expression from his face. He all too clearly remembered the day the Clan robbed those innocent men of life.

Na-um continued, apparently oblivious to Holun's displeasure. "Soon after he started the recon, he came across someone at the dig, a supporter. Someone sympathetic to our cause."

Holun couldn't believe what he was hearing. Someone at the dig was helping them? How could they live with themselves? "Who?"

Na-um shook his head. "I'm not sure. They apparently want to remain anonymous. No one knows who Konae's contact is but him."

"But why would they help us?"

Na-um shrugged, looking a little too pleased with the situation. "Who cares? We have someone on the inside, someone willing to help us defeat the Americans. Why question such a fortuitous turn of fate?"

Holun could think of many reasons, but he kept his mouth shut.

Na-um rose to his feet. "Konae's been keeping me apprised of any progress at the dig. We've found his contact to be extremely reliable. This should be over very soon." He smirked as he started to head back to his men. "Holun," he called back over his shoulder just before he was out of an average man's earshot, "let me know when you find something!"

Holun nodded slowly, trying to play along. Na-um knew Holun could've heard a whisper from a hundred yards away, so his last statement was obviously for his soldiers' benefit, soldiers who didn't know of Holun's special hearing ability. Holun stayed seated on the rock and—initially for appearance's sake—serenely slid his eyes shut.

Although Na-um hadn't directly mentioned anything about his visions, his comment made Holun realize it'd been awhile since he'd looked for any news. *Guess now is as good a time as any.*

He tried to concentrate, struggling to see the outcome of Na-um's imminent battle with the Americans. As anticipated, he was unable to see anything.

At first, it had been extremely irritating. He had wondered what was wrong with him, why he couldn't see the most important battle his people would ever fight. But after awhile, he came to expect the lack of information. Maybe something was blocking him again. Or maybe he wasn't supposed to know the outcome in advance—after all, why would they bother fighting if Holun saw the possibility that they might not win?

Holun sighed. *Well, I guess I can still try to check on the Americans.* He clenched his eyes tighter and tried harder to concentrate. He thought that perhaps if he could focus solely on their informant at the dig, whoever it was, he may be able to find a link to the Americans. He figured it was worth a try.

The plan worked like a charm. Holun smiled to himself as he began to tap into the consciousness of their informant, gleaning all the information he could from them. He found out about the plan at the dig, about why everyone was dying. And he saw the previously undiscovered whereabouts of the four Americans—the very ones that had so frustratingly eluded them so far.

Just before the vision cut off, he felt something, a twinge in his consciousness. Almost as if someone was pulling at his mind, trying to get in. The informant? Holun clenched his teeth as he fought to keep them from tapping into his mind, but that only seemed to make them stronger.

This had never happened before. Whoever this was—and he suspected it was their informant—was powerful, and knew how to control their mind. The thought made him shiver. He struggled to cut off the connection, fought to break the vision off. He couldn't let them take over . . .

Holun's eyes flew open. Sweat was pouring down his forehead as he stared at the ground, trying to compose himself before hurrying to tell Na-um the news. Good news, for once. Well, it would be to Na-um, anyway.

But as he rose and started walking toward his superior, he couldn't shake the eerie feeling settling deep inside him. Someone out there was powerful, perhaps even more powerful than Na-um himself. That person—if it, in fact, was their informant—was on the Clan's side, for now. But who knew where their loyalty would ultimately lie? Holun shuddered. He had a sinking suspicion that if this person was as strong as he feared, whoever got in their way probably wouldn't survive.

CHAPTER 35

Contagion

Lamanai Archaeological Dig, Northern Belize

KAYLA DREW AN UNSTEADY BREATH as she climbed out of their rental car. She pulled her shirt away from her stomach and tried to fan herself with it, but the fabric was heavy and saturated in the thick and visibly moist evening air. Thanks to the only car they could find to rent at such short notice being seriously lacking in air conditioning, her clothes were all plastered to her skin. Kayla rested her hands on her lower back and stretched, then rolled her shoulders and neck. She really wished she could just go get a cool shower and sleep for a good twelve hours before she had to do anything else.

Then she remembered why they'd traveled hundreds of miles to come here, and knew her wish was not coming true tonight. She sighed and reached for Grady's hand. She would need his strength to help her get through what she could only imagine lay ahead.

But, even with Grady at her side, the longer she was here, the more unsettled she felt. Something sinister, intangible but undeniably real, was reaching out for them, beckoning them toward certain demise. The air was thick, yes, but it wasn't just from the humidity. Something else, something almost evil, was here. She could feel it just underneath her skin.

Death.

Kayla squeezed Grady's hand and pulled him closer. He leaned over and kissed her forehead, but the smile he attempted fell far short of genuine happiness. Though she couldn't hear his thoughts anymore—which she found herself missing more and more—she knew him, and could still read him. And she knew that he was feeling the same way she was.

Then she spotted something, floating toward them out of the mist in the waning daylight like a ghostly apparition. Jackie's face came into view, hovering about five and a half feet off the ground before the rest of her body appeared. Kayla felt herself relax a little when she started to notice another person behind Jackie, then another, and another, gradually appearing out of the mist and walking toward them. Well, maybe relax wasn't the word. Relief, maybe? No, not quite that either, exactly. She *was* relieved that some people had survived whatever had happened here . . . but what exactly *did* happen here? She opened her mouth to ask, but Grady raised his hand and the words died in her throat.

Grady's simple gesture halted Jackie and her small band of refugees in their tracks. They stopped a good distance away, almost too far to be heard without raising their voice.

Grady pulled her slightly behind himself, and Kayla was glad for the barrier between her and the refugees. Something was off here tonight, and just seeing the bedraggled group made the feeling stronger, reminding her of why they'd spent nearly twenty-four hours in airports and on planes to rush here and—do *what*, she wasn't sure. She'd only known that they'd had to get here, and fast.

"Grady!" Jackie's shout abrasively broke the silence, a sound which grated on Kayla's nerves a little, like someone speaking too loud at a funeral home. Almost exactly like that. "We're not contagious—at least I don't think we are," she began. "We haven't touched or even gone near any of the . . . sick." Jackie paused briefly to take an abnormally short but deep breath, then pressed on. "Plus, none of us have shown any symptoms."

Grady's eyes flashed to Kayla's. "What are you talking about?"

Kayla could see Jackie blink hard, even from this distance. "You didn't get my message?"

Grady shook his head and reached instinctively for his phone. "We've been on a plane most of the day."

Jackie stared, then blinked again. "I thought that's why you came. Though I couldn't figure out how you got here so quickly. It's only been an hour."

Kayla couldn't stay quiet any longer. She had to know. "Since what?"

Jackie exchanged glances with her group. She drew another deep breath before explaining. "This morning—I think at breakfast; I skipped it this morning—everyone started getting sick. They just fell to the ground and looked like they were in a lot of pain."

"What happened to them?" Grady prodded.

Jackie shrugged, looking more nonchalant than Kayla would have liked. "We're not really sure. Somehow we didn't get sick, though, at least so far."

Grady simply nodded, hesitating for a moment before yelling across the distance between them. "Where are they?"

"They're spread out all over the dig. Like I said, we haven't gone close to them, which hasn't been all that easy. It seems like most of them are in the mess hall, though." The side of her mouth turned up in a humorless grin.

"And the medic?"

"I think Dr. Larson's sick,"—Kayla heard her voice catch even from this distance—"but only because I haven't seen him. I figured he would have found us if he wasn't."

Kayla ventured another question. "And Jack?"

Jackie's face fell, and Kayla felt her stomach drop. "I haven't seen him either." Jackie frowned as her brow furrowed. Kayla choked back tears.

Grady spoke up. "So what are the symptoms?"

Jackie shrugged. "No idea. We haven't gotten close enough to tell. At first, they were all moaning and holding their stomachs, but now they're quiet. We didn't know if they were . . ." her voice trailed off as she stared off into the murky darkness.

Grady's next question came out a little less harshly, for which Kayla was grateful. "Are you the only . . . survivors, Jackie?"

Jackie nodded quickly. "Yes, as far as we can tell. But there could be more, maybe . . ." She didn't sound hopeful.

Grady swallowed hard. "Do you have any ideas about what might have happened?"

Jackie paused before answering, and her eyes flitted around the group at her side. "Um, we're not really sure. We've been talking, and the only thing we thought sounded reasonable was poison . . ."

Grady nodded once, and cut her off. "Okay. If none of you have contracted the disease by now, it doesn't look like whatever happened here was contagious. So . . . wait. Have you called the Institute, the authorities?"

Jackie looked at the ground. "Our communications are disabled. Everything in the trailer is unusable. Which I guess means this wasn't an accident . . ." Kayla could see she was fighting back tears. "Who would do this to us?"

Grady ignored the question. "And the satellite phone? You were able to get a call out to me."

Jackie shifted her weight. "They didn't get that, at least not the phone itself. But it doesn't seem to be working now. We've been trying."

"How did they miss the phone? Wasn't it in the trailer?" Grady continued his interrogation, but Kayla could see that Jackie had reached her breaking point. She placed her free hand on Grady's shoulder. He understood, and changed the subject. "Well, we should be fine to look around. Jackie, can you find a place for your group to stay while we do some digging?"

"Sure," she said, stifling a yawn. "We've been in my tent since it happened anyway. We'll just go back there." She started to turn around.

"Keep trying the satellite phone. And can you put together a list of . . ." Kayla moved to where she was sure Grady could see her and gave him a look, effectively cutting him off. "Never mind. Just get some sleep." Kayla squeezed his shoulder.

Jackie nodded once, then turned completely around and plodded slowly back the way she'd come, the group behind her parting so she could once again be in the lead. One by one, the rest of her group followed solemnly. To Kayla, their somber trudge into the shadows looked exactly like what it may, in fact, turn out to be—a funeral march.

Once Jackie and her group had disappeared into the mist, Grady led the group to the nearby medical trailer. As soon as the trailer came into view, Grady felt a sudden knot in his stomach. Something was definitely wrong. The door—which was always locked when the trailer was unoccupied, one of the strictest rules at the dig given the strength of the meds it contained—was ajar.

"That isn't normal," Justin said to no one in particular.

But Grady answered him anyway. "No . . . why isn't it locked?" Grady rushed over to the door. Forgetting momentarily that there was a possibility he might actually need protection from whatever was making everyone sick, he ripped open the door and flew inside. "I don't know why it wouldn't be . . ." He cut off abruptly as soon as his eyes registered what was in the room.

They had found the medic.

Mandy was the last to step into the medical trailer. The first thing she saw was the three outlines of her friends, huddled around something in the dim light. The second thing she saw was the expression on Kayla's face.

The third thing she saw turned her stomach. She stumbled back out of the trailer and doubled over as she heaved, but nothing came out. Then she remembered they hadn't eaten in hours. *Good thing, too. That wouldn't have been pretty.*

She straightened up and drew a deep breath of fresh air. Summoning her last vestige of courage, she turned back toward the trailer. Warily climbing the steps, she braced herself for the sight inside.

The shock was gone the second time around, thankfully, but her stomach still churned inside her. Dr. Larson, the dig's medic, was lying on the ground. He was clutching his stomach, curled up in a tight ball. Mandy couldn't remember seeing such an excruciatingly painful expression before.

She felt her own face form a grimace as she approached the group that now filled most of the trailer. "What happened?" The question was ludicrous, but it was the only thing she could come up with at the moment.

Grady, who was on his knees wiping beads of sweat from the sick man's forehead, answered her. "As far as we can tell from what little he could tell us, Dr. Larson started to feel sick after drinking some water out of the coolers in the mess tent. He noticed other people were already feeling sick, so he came here to try to analyze the water. Looks like he got the test done before the pain got too . . ." His voice trailed off.

Justin was already looking over a computer printout, comparing it to something on the screen of the trailer's laptop computer, and mumbling to himself. "Okay, good . . . yeah, that should be fine . . . Grady?"

Grady looked up.

Justin pointed to the computer screen. "This poison has an antidote. And if I'm reading this right . . ." He pressed his finger against a clipboard that was posted on the wall over the trailer's lone desk. Mandy assumed it held the inventory list of all the medications they had. "What we have in stock should work. And—again, if I'm reading it right—we have a lot of it." He turned to look at Grady. "It might just be enough for everyone."

Grady nodded, jumping to his feet. "Hand me that."

Justin pulled the clipboard off the nail it was hanging on and handed it to Grady. Grady quickly looked it over, then *he* started mumbling. "Good. Yeah . . . should be enough. Looks like it's over here . . ." He headed over to a nearby cabinet, checking the list periodically as he searched. In less than fifteen seconds, he had located the correct cabinet and was removing its contents.

Some of the black liquid antidote was already in small test tubes, in what Mandy assumed were proper dosage amounts. Grady grabbed one tube from its holder and stepped over to the man still cringing on the floor. "Justin, does it say how much of the antidote to give the patient?"

Justin checked the computer screen again, his eyes scanning the page frantically. Then he shrugged, frowning. "Not sure. Think it depends on how long it was in their system." He eyed the tube in Grady's hand. "Dr. Larson would know best, but I'd say give him the whole tube."

Grady nodded. "Dr. Larson?"

The dig medic was still curled into a tight ball on the floor, writhing in pain. He barely acknowledged the sound, only able to turn slightly and with great effort toward Grady's voice. Mandy couldn't figure out how he'd managed to tell the others his story; he looked like he was barely functioning.

Grady was now at his side. "Take this." He uncapped the small vial and carefully cupped his free hand behind the doctor's head as he poured the vial's contents between the man's pursed lips. Dr. Larson quickly swallowed the liquid in the tube.

The effect was almost immediate. The doctor's face relaxed, and, though he was still lying on the floor, he was calming down. Mandy released the breath she'd been holding.

After several minutes, he sat up, leaning against a nearby cabinet. "Wow."

Grady sat down next to him. "How are you feeling?"

Dr. Larson just shook his head. "Fine. Amazing, considering. I thought for sure that wouldn't work."

Mandy had to ask. "Why?"

The doctor looked up. "Because I wasn't sure how much of the poison I'd ingested—or if I'd identified it correctly, it was really just an educated guess—and it's already been"—he glanced at the clock on the wall—"almost twelve hours. I must not have taken a lethal dose, just enough to make me really sick. And the poison must have had some anti-absorption agent attached to it, or maybe the water diluted it enough. It just . . . it shouldn't have worked." He sounded a little awestruck.

"So we can save the others?" Mandy asked tentatively. She didn't want to get her hopes up.

Dr. Larson actually smiled. "It's entirely possible, yes. Provided they took less than or as much as I did, or they drank the poison after I did." He looked back at the stock in the cabinet to his left. "Looks like we may just have enough to try, at any rate." He jumped up, and Mandy reeled a little at the abrupt turn-around in the doctor's condition. It gave her hope for the rest of her friends here.

Grady stood with Dr. Larson, grabbing his arm. "Are you sure you're okay, Doc?"

The medic's answering smile said everything. "Yes. I still have a little pain, but that should go away soon." He pulled out a large, covered glass carafe from the back of the cabinet Grady'd already opened. The bottom quarter of the carafe was filled with a black powder. "Mandy, Justin—can you help with this? Just fill it with water, mix, and pour—then fill up all the empty vials you can find. We will probably need all of it." He pulled a couple of trays filled with empty test tubes from a nearby cabinet. Mandy felt herself nodding at him while her brain was still trying to process everything that had just happened.

"Okay, thanks. Kayla, Grady, here," he said as he reached for the holders containing the full tubes and handed a few each to Kayla and Grady. After he grabbed a few trays for himself he closed the cabinet door and smiled. "Let's go perform miracles."

CHAPTER 36

Antidote

"So how are we doing?"

Kayla, who was in the mess tent tending to one of the recovering-more-slowly-than-she'd-like patients lying in the grass in front of her, smiled at the sound of Grady's voice before she looked up. As she stood, she set the clipboard she'd been holding on one of the tables nearby and stretched. "Good, so far." She nodded to the clipboard, which held the dig's personnel list. "Got another twenty or so checked off."

Grady smiled at her, then looked around at the group of people laying haphazardly on the ground around them. "How are they doing?"

"Okay." Kayla shrugged, then frowned. "They're taking a lot longer to recover than the group before them, and that group took longer than the group before them." She sighed. "Even giving them extra doses aren't helping speed up their recovery. I'm afraid that if someone hasn't been given the antidote by now, they may not recover."

Grady nodded, his mouth set in a straight line, his smile long gone. "And the list?" He eyed the clipboard, still sitting on the table.

Kayla offered a half-hearted smile and picked the list back up. "Good, I think. It's possible this last group completed it; there can't be many more left."

Grady came up next to her and perused it as she started to flip through the six pages of names. "Any missing?"

Kayla stared at the list in front of her. "Not so far. I'll check the rest. Can you . . . ?"

Justin's voice interrupted her from the other side of the tent. "Grady! I could use your help here." He struggled to hoist one of the newly filled backup water coolers onto the head table.

Grady placed a hand on Kayla's back. "You okay here?"

Kayla nodded, then placed her hand on the back of Grady's elbow and pushed him toward Justin. "Go. I'm just going to double-check the list."

Grady nodded back at her, then ran off to help with the second water cooler before Justin spilled it all over the ground.

Kayla sighed, then flipped back to the first page of the list. There, in black and white, were the names of all her friends, acquaintances, and co-workers, with checkmarks next to each of their names. She scanned the column of checkmarks, looking for any missing. Had they found everyone?

Kayla's heart started beating faster as she flipped to the second page, then the third, not finding any checkmark missing. She wanted to believe they'd found everyone, but something inside her, deep in the pit of her stomach, was telling her that someone was missing. She hoped to God she was wrong.

Good, everyone on the third page was accounted for, just like the first two. But instead of relaxing, she tensed up even more. Hoping against hope that the last half of the list was just like the first, she turned to the fourth page.

The clipboard tumbled soundlessly to the thick grass as she took off running.

Belize Rainforest, Mercenary Camp

Holun stood in the middle of the place he called home. He gazed at the thatched roof and mud walls, taking in everything that now seemed so foreign to him. It felt like it'd been forever since he'd been here.

Because everything had changed.

Na-um's men—the full army, save the few contingents still out in the field—were congregating in the town center at this very moment. Na-um was detailing their final assault on the Americans, outlining their heinous plans.

Holun sank to the floor in the middle of his small residence, despondency starting to take him over. *This isn't right,* he despaired. *These are innocent people. Even if they know what they are doing, they don't fully understand it all. Na-um has no right . . .*

Of course, he knew that Na-um fully believed that not only did he have the right to destroy the Americans, but he also believed it was his duty, his *Destiny.*

Holun hated the word. It had been thrown around so flippantly in the past few months. To Holun, the word seemed to have lost any real meaning.

And it didn't even make sense. How could he know what his Destiny was? How could he be certain—as Na-um always seemed to be—that this was the path chosen for him?

Maybe Destiny didn't exist. Maybe it was only a word Na-um used to justify his gruesome tactics. Maybe Na-um just needed his men to believe that this was their "Destiny" so they would fight without worrying about the consequences. Holun knew most of these men. He didn't believe they would really kill—murder—the Americans if they knew they were innocent.

But what could he do? He was only an advisor, and then only to Na-um. And he knew Na-um wouldn't listen; he had tried before, right?

As he sat in solemn contemplation, his hands lightly brushing the dirt, a horrible truth began to sink in. No matter what he did to stop it, the Americans would be attacked. And, if he knew Na-um like he thought he did, they would die.

He couldn't believe in Destiny, not if it was like this. It just wasn't fair, wasn't right.

How could Destiny be so cruel?

Lamanai Archaeological Dig, Northern Belize

Kayla ran, her legs pushing her faster than she ever thought she could go, across the dig to Jack's tent. There was no sign of him. She swallowed hard, wanting to cry but knowing she couldn't afford the waste of time. She sprinted out of the tent and headed for the secondary work trailer, the one located on the southern end of the dig. Jack liked to work in solitude, removed from the main commotion of the dig, so she knew he spent most of his time there.

As soon as she saw the work trailer, standing in stark contrast to the orange canvas tents nearby, she stopped in her tracks. The door hung ajar, nearly falling off its hinges. But nothing else seemed amiss at first, and Kayla, for the smallest fraction of a second, dared to hope.

But then she saw something—and realized immediately that the broken door wasn't nearly the worst of it. Slumped next to the steps leading up to the damaged door, curled up in a tight ball in the high grass, was Jack McFarland.

As soon as recognition hit, Kayla ran to his side, crashing to her knees beside him. She couldn't stop the tears now, and they started flowing freely.

"Jack!"

Jack's eyes fluttered open at the sound of her voice. His face was the palest of whites and his cheeks had sunken in, emphasizing the dark circles around his eyes. Kayla blinked hard, but she couldn't erase the horrific sight she was sure she'd remember for the rest of her life.

"Kay . . . la." He struggled to even say her name.

"Shhh, it's okay. Jack, we found the antidote for the poison you took. Here," she reached into her pocket and pulled out two vials. Just to be safe.

"No . . ." His chest heaved with every labored breath.

What?! "Jack, you *have* to take this! You'll . . . die." She choked on the last word.

He shook his head ever so slightly. "No, I . . . I have to tell you something." He coughed once.

"No, Jack. First take the antidote. Then you can tell me."

"No, it's . . ." A cough interrupted him. "It's . . . too late for me." Jack's eyes opened wide as he summoned the last of his strength. A feeble hand even clutched the edge of her shirt. "Kayla, listen to me." His voice was slightly stronger, urgent. "I saw . . ." He coughed, droplets of blood glistening in the palm of the hand he used to cover his mouth. Still he pressed on. "I saw who poisoned us. They are . . . helping . . . men who kidnapped . . . you and . . ." His voice trailed off as he started coughing again, but Kayla got the gist. And could only blink, and stare.

"Who would . . . Jack, who is it?" she asked once the coughing subsided.

Kayla's eyes widened as Jack, with his last breath, uttered his final word.

Belize Rainforest, Mercenary Camp

Na-um was pleased. This really was coming together.

He stood, arms crossed, in the middle of town and surveyed his army. His men were milling around the small collection of huts. Sounds of homecoming echoed in the air. Women crying, shrieking in joy; children clapping, jumping, running, shouting.

Only moments before, just as he was finishing up his speech, the Southern detachment had reported in. The Northern detachment had arrived a few hours ago, followed closely by the detachment from the East. The Western detachment would be arriving soon, after they'd performed the special task he'd ordered. Then, once everyone was here, they would finalize their plans.

And he'd been worried. What was there to worry about, really? Destiny was on their side; everything was falling into place, and soon the final battle would begin.

He couldn't wait.

Lamanai Archaeological Dig, Northern Belize

Grady ran a hand across his forehead as he slumped to the grass beneath the mess tent, exhausted. Slowly his eyes rose and he took in the pitch-black sky, wondering when this heat would let up. The sun had set hours ago; where was their reprieve?

Surely everyone had been given the antidote by now. He glanced around to find Kayla, to see if everyone on the list had been accounted for—just to make sure.

But she wasn't anywhere in sight. Where could she be? She had been right there just a few minutes ago . . .

Grady stood, moving to join Justin first, who was busy filling paper cups with uncontaminated water. People were starting to gather here, and Mandy was helping him pass out the cups of clean water to their thirsty guests.

When Justin barely seemed to notice him, Grady spoke up. "Have you seen Kayla?"

Justin shrugged as he set three more cups down on the table they'd moved to the front of the tent to function as a serving table. He arranged the cups already filling the table toward the front so Mandy could easily reach them. "I really haven't noticed anyone. I've been busy trying to get this water out. Everyone's probably dehydrated, both from the poison and the heat. But you can ask Mandy." He nodded as she approached the table with a tray.

"Mandy?"

Mandy looked up at Grady for a split second before setting her tray on the table to fill it up. "Hi," Mandy offered with a quick smile.

Grady surmised Mandy must've worked in the food industry before; she was masterfully positioning the full cups strategically around the tray—and quickly. "Have you seen Kayla?"

"No, sorry." She shot him a fleeting apologetic glance before hoisting the heavy tray to her shoulder and moving to the next table of thirsty recovering patients with graceful ease.

Grady sighed. Mandy and Justin were understandably busy; they didn't have the time to search for a grown woman

who, in all likelihood, was off attending to the sick somewhere else.

Grady glanced around the mess tent, to the tables full of
his friends and coworkers, to Mandy bustling around to all
the tables with trays of water, to Justin still setting the cups
full of water out . . . wait—what was that? Something shiny
had glinted in the light from the hanging construction pendant lights strung around the interior of the tent.

He walked over to the edge of the mess tent, almost exactly where he'd seen Kayla last. Was that . . . was something
lying on the ground? As he reached the spot, he recognized
the clipboard that he'd seen Kayla holding when he'd last
spoken with her. The one with the list on it. She'd been
checking to make certain everyone on the dig was accounted
for . . .

No. With a rush, Grady's mind put it together. Only half a
second later, he knew what'd happened. He snatched up the
clipboard and started tearing through the list, voraciously
searching for a name—any name—that wasn't marked off.
Then, on the fourth page, he saw it. And understood completely why she'd left so quickly.

A deep, gnawing, gut-wrenching dread filled the pit of his
stomach. He had to find her.

Where would she be? Grady was wracking his brain, trying
to think like Kayla, like Jack. He wanted to run, to go to her—
but where? If Jack was as bad off as he suspected, and was too
far gone, Kayla would need him to be there for her. But
where would she have gone? He hated that he couldn't think
of where to find her; the dig wasn't *that* big, right?

But instead of running frantically around the dig with no direction, he begrudgingly chose to wander quickly around the dig, systematically checking off every area in the dig they could be—provided she'd even found Jack yet—and asking every person he came across if they'd seen either of them. So far, no one had.

As he passed the communications trailer, he was ready to start throwing things; why couldn't he find her? *Think, Grady, think!*

He jumped as Jackie crashed out of the trailer out of breath, satellite phone in hand.

"Grady," she gushed, "we were able to fix the sat phone, and I finally got a call through to the Institute. They're having a team sent first thing in the morning to do a damage assessment."

"Good," Grady muttered, eyes wandering as he spoke. He wanted—needed—to continue his search for Kayla. "Jackie, have you seen Kayla?" He continued when Jackie shook her head. "How about Jack?"

Jackie shook her head again. "No, sorry—everything okay?"

Grady chose to be honest. "I'm not sure."

Jackie frowned. "I'm sure you'll find them. This dig is pretty small."

Grady forced what he imagined was an unconvincing smile. "Thank you."

"Sure." She opened her mouth to say something else—what, Grady wasn't sure—but the phone in her hand started to ring. "Oh, it's probably the Institute checking in."

Grady nodded. "Everyone I've seen has been given the antidote we found, and seem to be recovering well." He chose to leave the possibility of Jack's demise off the record, for now. No need to worry anyone unnecessarily.

Jackie nodded back at him once and started back toward the comm trailer as she answered the phone. "Hello?"

Jackie's voice quickly faded into the distance as Grady resumed his now more frantic search. What if something had happened to Kayla?

No. He couldn't let himself think that way. He couldn't allow himself to even imagine the possibility. He blinked furiously in an attempt to shut out the terrifying thought.

Then, as he rounded the edge of yet another trailer, he saw her. And, for a few eternal seconds, she was all he could see.

But then—all too soon—reality hit. And he *really* saw her.

She was a mess. Tears lined her cheeks as she stared at something lying on the ground; it looked like she was holding part of whatever it was in her lap. Grady couldn't quite see what it was in the darkness; she was sitting in the shadows. He squinted at the scene as he took a few steps forward.

Grady knew the second recognition hit, but it wasn't his brain that told him first. It was his stomach, suddenly roiling, and his chest, tightening into knots. He stumbled, trying to maintain his balance.

As soon as his legs received the command—much later than they should have—Grady ran to Kayla's side. He barely felt his knees bruise against the ground as he wrapped her tightly in his arms.

At first, Kayla didn't respond. She couldn't. All she could see through her tears was Jack's still body, lying limp and lifeless in her lap. It was all she could think about, all her brain could register.

But, after a few minutes of silence, she found herself able to blink a few of the tears away. Then, an eternity later, she pulled a hand out from under Jack's head and slowly placed it on Grady's leg. He offered no response except to softly kiss her hair.

She understood, though no words were spoken. And she knew he understood, too. She leaned into him, drawing strength from his embrace. Then she carefully, reverently, removed Jack's head from her lap and placed it softly on the grass. She backed away slowly, then stood.

Grady never left her side. "Kayla . . ."

Kayla shook her head, trying to clear it.

Grady misunderstood. "Okay. We don't have to talk about it."

"No, it's fine." She waved her hand. "I was just . . . trying to make sense of it all." She looked down at Jack as tears reappeared in her eyes, blurring her vision. "He really is gone, isn't he? Like the guys in the Jeep and Jan . . ."

Grady reached for her and pulled her to his chest, placing a simple kiss on her hair.

Kayla blinked hard, trying to make herself believe it, though not really wanting to. Then she remembered what Jack had told her just before he . . . She couldn't even think the word.

But Grady needed to know what Jack had told her. She pulled away to look up at him. "Grady, Jack had some information. Something important."

Grady blinked. "What did he say?"

"He told me that someone at the dig is helping Na-um and the Mercenaries. He said he saw who poisoned everyone here."

Grady's eyes widened. "Who on earth would do such a thing?"

In the next second, before she could even think her response, Kayla was keenly aware of what felt like a dozen knives stabbing through her skull. Her vision blurred for a split second, then the entire world went black.

CHAPTER 37

Hearing

"KAYLA!" GRADY SHOUTED as he reached to catch the woman he loved before she fell. She slumped in his arms, and Grady staggered as he helped her lifeless body to the ground. He cringed as the similarity between the two bodies in front of him struck him like a bolt of lightning. *No*, he reasoned with himself. *Kayla will be fine. She's not . . . She's still breathing.*

Much as Kayla had been doing with Jack only moments earlier, Grady dropped to his knees and cradled Kayla's head in his lap. He gently brushed a stray strand of hair from her face as he stared at her blank expression. He desperately hoped her face reflected what was going on inside her head—though his instinct told him that was far from the truth.

Kayla was unconscious. She knew that. And yet, for some reason, here she was, completely aware of her thoughts. She didn't understand. It didn't usually work this way—did it?

A picture flashed in front of her mind's eye, then vanished as quickly as it had come. Was that yet another mountain? She didn't recognize it from anything she'd ever seen.

Then, all of a sudden, she realized what was happening. This was another vision, yet unlike any she'd had before. Much stronger, more . . . insistent. Insistent enough to steal her consciousness.

Her head was still being invaded by a myriad of stabbing knives, a thousand times stronger than the worst headache she'd ever had, exponentially more painful than the visions of before. She wanted to cry out, to scream at the top of her lungs, but she couldn't. Her mind registered the pain, but she was excruciatingly unable to find release.

But she didn't have time to dwell on it. Suddenly her mind was filled with flashes of pictures, taking her through the same images she'd seen for the first time in the cavern, while staring into the globe. Then, with eerie continuity, she saw a repeat of her vision of Denali—precisely as she remembered it.

As the knives continued to pierce through her skull, Kayla saw every one of her previous visions in unrelenting succession. The effect was exhausting, only compounding the pain in her head. She knew she would be screaming for relief if only her body would respond to her commands.

And, unbelievably, the pain seemed to only be getting worse. With every repeated vision, the throbbing in her head intensified. She desperately searched for a way out of her inundated mind.

But how does one fight the subconscious?

No answer came. The seemingly endless parade of pictures was still flashing through her mind. But as the images from her most recent vision materialized in front of her, she hoped that the incessant visions would be coming to an end; and with them, the pain.

But it was not to be. As another set of images came into focus, the pain became so intense that she could barely remember how to breathe. Using all her concentration—and hoping her body would breathe for her—she struggled to focus on the new pictures. Perhaps this was the vision they were waiting for, the one that would reveal the location of the final book.

Or maybe there was something else she needed to see.

Mandy heard Grady shout from across the dig. Her eyes flew to Justin's as they both dropped what they were doing—literally in Mandy's case; a tray-full of water splattered to the grass beneath her feet. She was seconds behind Justin as they took off in the direction of Grady's voice.

They found him half a minute later, slumped on the ground with Kayla's head in his lap. Mandy, shocked that she'd been able to keep up with Justin despite his lightning-fast sprint here, stopped just short of running into Justin, who'd come to an abrupt stop just before he ran into Grady and Kayla.

But Grady didn't acknowledge their presence. He simply continued to stare into Kayla's expressionless face.

It was then that Mandy noticed that Grady and Kayla weren't alone. She stifled a gasp as her hand flew to her mouth. She placed a hand lightly on Justin's shoulder and nodded toward the body only a few feet away from where they were standing. He shook his head when he saw the body of Jack McFarland lying lifeless in the grass.

Mandy sunk to the ground beside Grady. Jack was clearly gone, beyond help. But what about Kayla? It seemed to her that her friend's latest vision had overloaded her mind. The corners of Mandy's lips turned down. She'd been afraid of this.

She felt for Grady. With all the pain she was feeling for Kayla in this moment, she knew Grady's pain would be at least a thousand times worse. She couldn't imagine if Justin was . . .

"Justin?"

The voice that broke into Mandy's thoughts seemed very loud and utterly out of place. She turned her head to see Jackie approaching, holding a strange object in her hand. In the darkness, Mandy couldn't quite make out what it was.

Justin turned at the sound of his name and moved to meet the new arrival. "Yes, Jackie, what is it?" His voice was subdued, respectful.

Mandy watched Jackie's eyes scan the scene before her; she knew when the girl understood. "I'm sorry, but there's a call for you, from the States," she whispered as she lifted what Mandy now recognized as the satellite phone toward him. "I think it's important."

Justin simply nodded once and took the phone from her hand. Mandy felt a gentle kiss on the top of her head before he headed off to take the call. She lifted her head to offer a teary smile in his direction, but he was already gone.

Justin took a deep breath. "Hello."

The voice on the other end was deep, almost solemn. "Justin, this is Dr. Coolidge."

Suddenly, Justin couldn't speak, couldn't breathe. He understood in that instant why Dr. Coolidge's voice was so somber, why his stomach had dropped when the doctor had started to speak.

But he asked the question anyway. "Is my father okay?"

He heard a pause. Then a breath. Then: "Justin, I'm sorry."

That's it. Three short words. Just three words, but Justin felt the last of his world crumble to pieces around him. "He's dead." So matter-of-fact, so certain.

"I'm so sorry for your loss, Justin."

Justin didn't know what to say. He stared across the darkness of the dig, unseeing. Was he even still breathing?

When Justin didn't respond, the doctor continued. "We lost him this evening. His heart stopped, and we couldn't revive him."

Justin nodded slightly, not even realizing that Dr. Coolidge couldn't see it.

"Justin, are you there?"

Justin coughed, only then realizing that the doctor expected a response. "Yes . . . this is just . . . sudden. How did this happen?"

He could hear papers rustling on the other end of the line. "Honestly, we're not sure. He was doing fine, then his heart stopped. We tried to restart it, but we couldn't." More pages flipping. "All his tests were fine, then . . . I'm sorry; we just don't know."

Justin nodded again to no one but himself. He didn't know what to say. "Okay."

"Is someone there with you, Justin?"

"Yes."

"Then please let me know if you need anything."

Justin cleared his throat. "Thank you, Doctor. I will." He hung up the phone.

After heading back to Jackie to return the phone to her then watching her walk away, Justin sauntered back toward the group, arms crossed. He knew Mandy would ask, but he wasn't ready to talk. All he could think about was his father, and what had happened to him.

He knew who was responsible. The Mercenaries had somehow gotten to his father, just like they'd gotten to his mother. How could someone take everything from him with such indifference? His parents had been innocent bystanders. Why would these men do this? Just to stop them from finding a stupid set of books? It wasn't fair, wasn't right.

Justin knew the second Mandy saw him. Her voice came at him in an urgent whisper. "Justin! Are you okay?"

He barely registered her question. He could only think of his father.

But still, he knew Mandy. He knew she would need an answering response, if only to know that she had been heard. He took a deep breath, then gathered what was left of his strength.

Eerily—with a feeling he couldn't quite comprehend—his eyes met hers.

The blank, empty stare she remembered from just after his mother died was back. Mandy's heart broke into a million pieces as she rose to meet the man she loved. Wrapping her arms around him, she pulled him close and held him tightly to her.

Within Mandy's embrace, he offered no response, no reciprocation. He simply stood there stiffly, waiting for her to move. But she refused to relent. She knew him completely, as much as anyone could, and he needed her right now—whether or not he was willing to admit it.

Something was terribly wrong. And, given everything they'd been through together in the past few weeks, Mandy could only think of one thing that would tear Justin apart this completely.

Roger Stanford was dead.

She released Justin only enough to gaze up at him. He stood staring at an obscure point on the horizon. She waited resolutely for a full minute until he lowered his gaze to meet hers.

"Justin, I'm so sorry."

"He's dead." The dispassionate finality she heard in his two small words tore through her already shattered heart. She desperately wanted to understand—really understand—how he felt. She wanted, more than anything, to be able to help him.

Mandy choked back tears. "I know. I'm so sorry." She couldn't think of anything else to say.

A short silence followed. Then, abruptly, Justin put a hand behind her head, pulling her back to his chest. "Thank you." He held her close, resting his head on top of hers.

Mandy blinked hard. Where had this sudden change come from? It scared her even more than the blank stare. An entirely expected yet wholly unwelcome shiver ran down her spine.

"Are you okay?" The question seemed inadequate, but she knew Justin would understand what she meant. At least she hoped he would.

"I'll be fine." As soon as he spoke the words, his brow furrowed, and his nostrils flared. Mandy didn't know what it meant at first.

Then, with a startling clarity, she knew everything.

It was as though Justin had entered her mind. But even more than that, Justin's *mind* had entered *hers*. She could hear his every thought, read his every emotion. She felt his consciousness enter hers with a swiftness that took her breath away.

She should have been resistant. She should have been downright terrified. But she wasn't scared; she felt his anger at the Mercenaries, his confusion at how unfair the situation was, but the thing she felt the most was grief. Grief that overpowered her thoughts and overwhelmed her consciousness. Her desire to empathize with the man she loved was answered in an entirely unexpected, largely unprecedented way.

Mandy raised her eyes to Justin's face, uncertain of what she would see there. She knew what he was feeling, but she needed to see it for herself to believe it was real.

What she saw in his face made her heart skip a beat. As soon as her eyes met his, she felt an overwhelming love—but it wasn't coming from her.

It was coming from Justin.

The grief she'd been feeling was temporarily overpowered by this new feeling. Channeling Justin's love for her, all she wanted to do was hold him and never let go.

This new sensation was consuming, more surreal than anything she'd ever experienced. She had never been this close to anyone in all her life; she supposed no one ever had been. And she'd never even suspected that he loved her this much.

Justin tenderly placed his hand on the back of her neck. Mandy's skin electrified at the touch as Justin leaned down to kiss her.

Mandy's mind overloaded with emotion as their lips met. Their combined emotion surged through her veins, making it nearly impossible for Mandy to think about anything else but Justin and how desperately she needed him—and how much he needed her. Mandy had to remind herself to breathe as the kiss intensified; she felt raw emotion take her over, and she knew that, in this moment, she and Justin were in complete agreement about one thing.

They were meant for each other.

It was a simple, almost obvious truth, but it hadn't even occurred to Mandy until this very moment. Something had been in the way, something she still wasn't able to put a finger on. Something she hadn't even realized *was* there. In this eternal moment, all the walls between them fell away. And all that was left was Justin.

After too short a time, Justin pulled away. Mandy heard him remember where they were, what was happening around them. It occurred to Mandy that she should be embarrassed, but she quickly realized that Grady didn't even notice they were here. The only person Grady saw—the only reality he knew in this moment—was the woman he loved.

Grady.

Grady's eyes shot up, instinctively searching for the source of the voice he'd just heard. He gazed at Mandy and Justin—realizing for what might have been the first time that they were standing there—but was only met with questioning eyes.

Grady. A familiar, comforting voice resounded once again in his head. A voice he now recognized, a voice he trusted, a voice he'd heard so many times before.

Kayla.

Grady, go get the globe.

Grady froze in place.

She wasn't sure what was happening. She only knew that she could now hear Grady's every thought, so she reasoned he could hear hers. And since her body wasn't responding to her commands at the moment, she figured it was worth a shot.

Ignoring the stabbing pain still torturing her brain, she concentrated on his name.

Grady.

She felt his confusion at once, realized he wasn't quite understanding. So she tried again.

Grady.

He understood that time, remembered how it had felt in Leticia, remembered her voice.

Grady, go get the globe.

Okay, that was unexpected. Her subconscious had somehow taken over. Why had she told him that? What good would the globe do?

But, for some unknown reason, she knew that the globe was what she needed to get out of this vision-induced coma.

Maybe something besides Grady had entered her mind.

Her body couldn't feel Grady leave, but she knew when he did. She could see everything he could as he ran back toward the main part of the dig, desperate to find the globe.

"Jackie!" Grady was still dumbfounded at what had just happened, but there was a reason Kayla could communicate with him again; there was no way he would question that now.

Jackie came running out of the communications trailer. "Sorry, Grady, we're still working on getting everything up and running again, but . . ."

"No, Jackie, that doesn't matter," he interrupted with a wave of his hand. "Do you know about the globe we found here a few weeks ago?"

"Sure. Jack had me examining it. I couldn't find out much, though."

"It's okay; it doesn't matter. Where is it now?"

Jackie nodded toward her tent. "I left it in the trailer with Jack originally, but I went back later and took it to my tent. I wasn't trying . . ."

"You mind if I grab it?"

Jackie blinked at him. "No, of course not."

Grady took off running. He yelled a quick "Thanks!" back in her general direction before she was out of earshot and left her frozen in place, eyes wide.

As soon as the tent came into view, Grady came to an abrupt stop. He shouldn't have been surprised at what he saw, given everything that had transpired in the past few minutes, yet somehow he was.

From every crevice, every opening in the khaki-colored canvas, brilliant rays of light shot out in every direction.

The entire tent was glowing.

Kayla could see the glowing tent in Grady's thoughts, shining brightly in the darkness. Yes! This was what she needed, what she knew would wake her from this painful slumber.

Go ahead, it's safe, she relayed to Grady when she felt his hesitation.

He took a few tentative steps toward the light.

It's okay, I promise. She was beyond doubting now.

Apparently Grady could sense her resolve. He broke into a run and batted aside the canvas door.

The light was blinding. Grady shielded his eyes the best he could as he entered the tent. Struggling to see anything in the radiant light, he searched for the globe.

After only a few short seconds, he was able to determine where the light was coming from—a simple cardboard box sat unassumingly in the dirt next to the tent's sole desk. He reached down and snatched it up, box and all, and exited the tent, nearly tearing the canvas door in two. The instant the box was out from under the canvas-lined abode, the tent went dark.

Night had long fallen on the dig, but the globe burned as bright as the sun and illuminated Grady's path. He had no trouble finding his way back to Kayla.

As he approached, he felt Mandy and Justin staring at him. He supposed their stares were warranted—no one could have missed the glowing box he held in his hands.

Bring it here.

Grady walked over to Kayla and set the box down next to her.

Pull it out of the box; put my hand on it.

Grady hesitated. This thing was shining like the sun; wouldn't it stand to reason that it was just as hot?

It's okay. Trust me; this is right.

Sighing, Grady acquiesced. He cautiously peeled back the cardboard flaps and reached inside. He took a deep breath before placing his own hands on the globe.

But, to his utter relief, it felt just like he remembered it—just like stone that had been buried in the ground for a thousand years. It was almost—*cold.*

Carefully he set it on the ground near Kayla's hand. Then he reached for her hand and, after gently kissing it, set it carefully on the shining globe.

The moment her hand touched the sphere, her back arched violently. She stayed that way for a full five seconds. Then, as her body started to shake with wild spasms, she started screaming.

CHAPTER 38

Traitor

THE ONLY THING HE COULD think was that he shouldn't be here. He should be doing something constructive, something useful. But nothing was coming to mind.

So instead he sat silently, frozen on the ground, staring ahead but seeing nothing. He couldn't figure out what he was supposed to do next. So he just let his mind wander, simply staring off into space and letting himself think about absolutely nothing.

It was a blissful experience, almost. With the mind completely devoid of thought, a person's consciousness becomes clear—and the next coherent thought is likely to be, in some manner, utterly profound.

A person just needs to give their subconscious mind time to figure things out.

So he continued to sit, unmoving, until something came to him. But it wasn't at all what he expected.

Instead of discovering a profound truth or philosophical revelation, his mind suddenly flashed into overdrive. Pictures flashed in front of him in rapid succession—a dizzying sensation that made him glad he was sitting down.

His first thought was neither earth-shattering nor novel; he simply thought that, on one level, this felt like a vision. Or what he imagined this sort of vision might feel like.

But on another level entirely, one he couldn't quite define, this felt completely foreign to him. And it scared him. Because he didn't know exactly what this was, or where it was coming from. He only knew—sensed, really—that he should pay attention.

At the precise moment he decided to focus entirely on this "vision"—if that's what this was—his brain was bombarded with immense pain. For the briefest of seconds, he thought that someone had come up behind him and rammed a knife through his skull. But as the seconds passed, he realized that the pain was coming from *inside* his head.

It shouldn't be this way. No vision should hurt this much —something was wrong. Very wrong.

He had to figure out a way to correct it, to fix it somehow . . .

He felt his eyes roll back into his head before his body violently started shaking.

Kayla felt herself wake up, but it was not the release she'd been expecting. Instead, her convulsing body threw her back into a harsh reality, one that seemed almost worse than the coma.

What was she thinking by having Grady bring her the globe? The thing was *glowing*—surely that couldn't have been a good sign. She should have trusted Grady's hesitance and found another way out. Because this was simply unbearable.

Now that she knew what was happening, now that she was more aware than ever, the pain in her head increased to the breaking point. The screaming she'd been wishing she could do only minutes before was spilling out of her like an avalanche. But, again, it was not the release she'd hoped for. Her piercing screams almost seemed to make things worse, compounding the stabbing pain in her head. Grady—and probably Mandy and Justin, too—had to be nearby, and her screaming was likely terrifying them.

So she tried to stop. She tried to eke a simple semblance of willpower from her shredded brain, but her entire essence was focused on the pain. She just couldn't silence the screaming, no matter how hard she fought. Her mind was crying for a way out, begging her subconscious for any release. So, though she knew it would be futile, she fought harder, tried harder, begged her mind for release from this pain.

But nothing happened. Why wasn't this stopping? Surely this couldn't go on forever.

She tried to think of something else besides the pain. Something—anything—to think about that might take her mind off what was happening. *Anything* to get her through this pain.

Nothing.

So she took the only other option available—she faced it head-on. The choice was simple: fight, or be destroyed.

The second choice wasn't an option.

Gathering every ounce of strength she possessed and collecting it in the center of herself, she focused that pinpoint of strength solely on the pain. She fought her subconscious for a minuscule amount of brainpower, and, with nothing now dividing her focus, she was finally rewarded. She began to recall her vision, the newest one, in tiny flashes. Nothing too spectacular, nothing too insightful. Just a brief, barely coherent flash of an image, which quickly faded to black.

But it was what she needed. Grasping on to what felt like the only thin strand of sanity she had left, she struggled to hold on until the images lasted longer and longer. They eventually started to overtake her brain, inch by inch.

And the agonizing pain, the pain she thought would surely last forever and swiftly kill her, began to subside. Slowly, *very* slowly, Kayla began to retake control.

The screaming subsided. The pain was lessening. Kayla was exhausted, her mind drained. Her first thought was of aspirin, the next of Grady. And that was when she noticed it. She was able to think of something other than the pain. Because the pain was gone. Completely.

He was waking up. That's that only way he could describe it. He knew he'd never been asleep, but somehow he was waking up. And the pain was slowly lessening, thankfully.

But much too slowly. This pain was so . . . intense. Blinding.

At least it was going away.

Now he had a bigger problem, a question that had been gnawing at him the minute the pain had started to subside: what did this vision mean? This wasn't like anything he'd ever felt before, so it had to have been shown to him for a reason, had to mean *something*.

But what?

Kayla sat up, blinking furiously. Where was she? And where were the others? She had sensed others around her, more than just Grady. They must still be here, right? So where were they? Her vision wasn't clearing nearly as quickly as she would've liked.

Nevertheless, she gradually regained her sight, and, by the light of the nearly full moon and a dim light over the work trailer, she began to make out blurry objects in front of her. Slowly, things came into focus. The trailer, a collection of canvas tents in the distance, and . . .

She swallowed hard, her memory coming back in a rush. A single tear escaped her eye for her deceased friend. Life wasn't fair, not in the least.

Then she remembered that she wasn't alone. She sniffed and wiped her eye as she turned to look for Grady.

Where was he?

The convulsions had apparently laid him out in the dirt. He slowly sat up, then carefully stood. He reached to wipe the dirt off his back before taking in his surroundings.

Good, no one was around. With any luck, no one had seen what had happened. That was the last thing he needed right now.

Holun closed his eyes, for once not looking for a vision.

He now knew what he had to do.

Grady.

When Kayla finally laid her eyes on him, she could only think his name. The trauma she had just endured was making any other thought difficult. Her brain was apparently still recovering.

So she met his gaze and flashed him a sweet smile. She knew he had been there, every step of the way. He had been by her side; he had kept his head when she needed him most.

I love you.

She waited, but heard no response. *Grady?*

Again, nothing.

She noticed the confused look on Grady's face in the same instant it occurred to her: she couldn't hear him anymore. Their telepathic connection, just like before, had been severed yet again.

She turned to him, holding out her hand. He took it and, being the complete gentleman he was, helped her stand up.

She was more stable on her feet than she thought she'd be, given what she'd just experienced. She kept a hold of Grady's hand as she turned to see Mandy and Justin standing nearby.

The looks on their faces made Kayla smile. "Hey." She heard Grady chuckle under his breath.

"Hey?" Mandy was the first to reply, her eyes abnormally large. She started gushing. "That's all you can say? Hey?! Are you crazy? I'm glad you're okay, but come on! Really? I was so worried!" She ran to Kayla and threw her arms around her friend.

Kayla laughed, loving the sound of it. "I'm fine. Now." She offered a half-smile, half-cringe in Grady's direction.

"Kayla, what happened?" Justin joined Mandy and placed a gentle hand on Kayla's shoulder.

Kayla shrugged, not wanting to go into the details. Her friends were worried enough. "Just another vision. I haven't really had time to make much sense of it, though."

Grady frowned. "It hasn't worked that way before. Usually you're so sure."

Kayla's shoulders slumped ever so slightly. "I know."

A brief moment of silence ensued. Kayla strained to remember what she'd seen while unconscious, but, like an elusive dream, the images had faded once she'd woken up. That worried her a little. Had she gone through all of that for nothing?

"So are we just not gonna talk about it?" Mandy's voice broke into her thoughts. Kayla thought she might've missed part of the conversation, then realized that Mandy was looking at Justin. But what was she talking about?

Grady spoke before Kayla had a chance to. "Talk about what?"

Justin tried to wave it off. "It's not important right now."

"Yeah, right," Mandy scoffed. "Are you going to tell them or should I?"

"Tell them what?" Justin shoved his hands in his pockets, something Kayla had never seen him do. She supposed there weren't many things that made Justin uncomfortable.

But Mandy looked like she was about to jump out of her skin. "About the, the . . . mind thing!" She waved her hand between her and Justin.

Kayla froze, eyes wide. Had it happened to Mandy and Justin, too?

Grady asked the obvious question. "Uh . . . mind thing?"

Mandy nodded vigorously, her short ponytail bobbing. "Yeah. We could hear each other's thoughts, read each other's minds. It was amazing." She grinned sloppily at Justin, who, to Kayla's surprise, seemed to give in to Mandy's exuberance and grinned as he pulled Mandy closer and laid a sweet kiss on the top of her head. What on earth was going on around here? How long had she been out?

"Wow," came Grady's response, his eyes turning to Kayla. She could almost see him asking if they should share their experience.

And Kayla instantly felt as though she were back in fifth grade, in gym class. When she'd missed the tenth free throw shot in a row. Back before she was good at sports. Back when feeling an inch tall would have been an improvement.

At first, she didn't know why. But then it hit her—reading Grady's mind had felt so personal, so intimate, that she felt somehow uncomfortable talking about it. She didn't really want to share this with anyone but Grady, not yet.

To his credit, Grady seemed to understand whatever look she was giving him and kept quiet. Smart man.

"Well, isn't that pretty cool?" Mandy was sounding more and more like Justin, who was standing next to her, a sad but wide grin on his face.

"It *was* awesome." Justin shrugged as he pulled Mandy to his side.

Grady was still looking at Kayla, his eyes penetrating. She wanted to run to him, then run away with him. The thought was getting more appealing by the minute. She just didn't want to deal with this right now.

Mandy finally changed the subject. "Well, what do we do now?"

Grady stepped in immediately. "Kayla, what did Jack say?"

The question threw Kayla back into the memory of Jack's final moments. The pain of his death was still fresh—she hadn't had enough time to even process the concept of it. But she knew she had to keep going, if only for his sake—she couldn't let Jack's death be in vain. "Jack said someone at the dig is helping Na-um and the Mercenaries, feeding them inside information. Leaking them our whereabouts, keeping them apprised of what we've found . . . and he knew who poisoned everyone here."

Mandy's eyes grew wide. "Who?"

Just then, a twig snapped behind them. The four of them whipped around as Kayla heard Mandy let out a short squeal.

"I didn't mean to startle you," Jackie called as she approached, phone still in hand.

Then her eyes found Kayla. "Kayla! I'm so glad you're awake. Are you okay?"

Kayla forced a smile. "Yes, I'm fine, thank you."

"What is it, Jackie?" Grady asked hurriedly.

She nodded toward the phone she held. "Another call for Justin."

Justin stalked to her in a few long strides and snatched the phone from her hand. He walked away before answering.

Kayla opened her mouth to ask what the first call had been about, then realized she already knew. After being connected to Grady's mind for even just a short time, she unquestioningly felt an abrupt sense of loss . . . but there was something else, a different kind of loss, something hidden away in the background. At the time, she'd ignored it, thinking it not important. But now she knew what it meant; she knew that Justin's father had died, though she wasn't sure how she knew—perhaps she had picked up on Grady's subconscious thoughts without realizing it?

On instinct alone, Kayla pieced the scenario together. Nothing was a coincidence anymore; everything happened for a reason. Na-um's men—Na-um himself—had wanted Roger Stanford dead, so they'd made it happen.

Anger surged through her, and it was all she could do not to explode. She clenched her fist until her nails dug into her palm; her other hand grasped Grady's hand tightly. Grady pulled his hand from hers almost immediately, draping his arm around her shoulders and pulling her to his side.

Kayla knew he could sense what she feeling and was trying to calm her down. But he didn't know the whole story. She knew who was helping Na-um and the Mercenaries, and they were to blame for Roger, for Jack, for everything. And they needed to be stopped.

Holun sped through the forest, heading north. The forest blurred past him as he ran through the dense foliage, fluidly dodging trees and effortlessly bounding through the underbrush. He hadn't told anyone that he was leaving, but he knew they'd soon find out that he was gone.

He had to hurry.

Grady pulled Kayla closer, willing her anger to dissipate. She had every right to be angry. Angry that Na-um and his men had killed so many of their friends, and had tried to kill many more. Angry that she'd been given these visions, visions that had caused what he knew was excruciating pain. He'd never tell her, and he hoped she'd never find out, but he'd felt her pain. He knew how bad it was when she was unconscious. His heart was still aching for her.

But he knew what anger could do to a person, and he didn't want Kayla to give in to it. She was better than that. Her shoulders stiffened beneath his arm, but he refused to let go. He couldn't.

Justin came jogging back, handing the phone to Jackie without a word before rejoining the group. She backed away a few feet, but didn't leave. Grady wondered why, until he saw the look on her face. Eyes wide, mouth slack, jaw quivering. Sheer, unmistakable fear.

Without having to look over, he knew Kayla was causing it. Jackie was staring directly at her, and he could only think that something Jackie saw in Kayla's face had sent that wave of terror through her.

In that moment, his suspicions were confirmed. He knew, beyond the shadow of a doubt, who the traitor was. He knew it by the expression on Jackie's face, by Kayla's fury at her presence. It was suddenly so obvious, he knew he should have figured it out much sooner.

Jackie.

CHAPTER 39

Holun

THEY KNEW.

She was certain of it; she could see it in the way they were glaring at her—especially Kayla, and now Grady, as if he'd just now figured it out. Jackie felt her breath catch as she stared into Kayla's furious eyes. They knew what she was doing. They had discovered her.

Her mind flashed through her options. It didn't take long; there was really only one. She *had* to get away. She still had a chance.

After all, they didn't know everything.

"What's going on?" Justin could clearly see that something was very wrong. He looked at Mandy for answers.

Mandy was staring at Jackie, her expression a slightly milder version of Kayla's. Whatever Kayla was thinking—and Grady now, too, it appeared—Mandy had to be thinking it as well. If only he could still hear her inside his head . . . Justin turned questioning eyes to Kayla.

"Jackie," Kayla growled, and suddenly all the pieces fell into place. *Jackie* was the traitor here. *She* was the one helping the Mercenaries.

Before Justin could react, time seemed to speed up. Suddenly, in the time it took for him to take a breath, Jackie was gone. Justin could've sworn that she'd been standing ten feet away from him only a second ago. Eyes wide, he glanced over at the rest of the group, but they all seemed to be as confused as he was.

"Where is she?" Grady was craning his neck in every direction, his eyes frantically scanning the horizon for any sign of Jackie.

By the looks of it, Kayla had already given up. "She's gone, Grady," she muttered as her shoulders slumped.

"What?"

Kayla shrugged slowly. "She's just gone."

Justin needed to know. "What happened?"

Kayla shook her head as the group moved closer together. "Somehow she affected our minds, or time, or something . . . I'm not sure *what* happened exactly, just that she got away."

Grady nodded, paused for a brief moment, then sighed. "I'll put the dig on alert to watch for her, but there's nothing we can do about it now. Something tells me she won't be coming back."

Kayla nodded in response, then yawned.

Grady continued. "We should all get some rest. Besides, Kayla's been through a lot today."

Justin heard Kayla trying to protest as Grady led her away. *She'll be asleep before she even gets to her tent.* Justin smirked at the thought.

But as Grady and Kayla walked out of sight and he and Mandy started walking back to their tent, Justin's thoughts began to wander. He reviewed the last several minutes and began to analyze everything that had just happened.

Why would she do it? We've known her for years.

Jackie had been with the anthropological department at UCF longer than Justin had. She may have even pre-dated Kayla, who'd been a respected and tenured professor there for more than a few years, if he was remembering correctly. Justin frowned. He tried to understand, but couldn't. How could someone so close to them betray them like this?

A wave of despair washed over him. Someone who knew nearly all their secrets was helping their enemies.

They didn't have a chance.

"Kayla, honey, wake up."

Her eyes slowly fluttered open. They still hurt, still felt like they were being weighed down. Where was she? How long had she been asleep?

"Kayla, someone's here."

Despite being half asleep, she heard the insistence in Grady's voice. She fought to open her eyes and keep them open. She blinked once to clear her vision, then gazed sleepily up at Grady. "Hmmm," she mumbled.

"Someone's here to see us." Grady brushed a strand of hair out of her face.

Kayla nodded, then, after a brief moment, sat up. She started looking around the tent. "Okay, sure . . . uh . . ." She combed a hand through her hair. "I need some clothes . . ."

Grady smiled as he offered a hand to help her to her feet. "You're still dressed."

She looked down at her jeans and t-shirt for a second, then smiled sleepily back up at him. "Let's go."

Mandy and Justin were waiting just outside in the still-sweltering night. Kayla blinked. It was still dark? "How long did I sleep?" She looked down at her wrist, then realized she hadn't worn her watch today.

"Only about twenty minutes. Sorry. I didn't want to wake you, but this is really important. Besides, you're the only one who can translate." Kayla's brow furrowed as Grady took her hand and, with Mandy and Justin in tow, led her to the edge of the surrounding forest.

Kayla saw the dark figure waiting for them only a few seconds before she reached the edge of the trees. As soon as they stepped into the cover of the forest, the figure stepped forward and into the moonlight. Kayla stifled a gasp. The dark figure—a young boy—couldn't have been older than sixteen.

Grady spoke to the young man. "This is Kayla." He turned to Kayla. "He can understand English well, but it's difficult for him to speak. It's easier for him to speak K'iche." He turned back to Holun. "She can translate for us, so you can speak your language."

The boy nodded, then glanced at Kayla, who began translating to the group as soon as the boy started speaking. "This is Holun. He is with"—her eyes narrowed as soon as she heard him speak the name—"Na-um's army."

She glared pointedly at the boy named Holun before he continued.

Kayla kept translating. "He says he can see things that are going to happen." Her eyes widened. She glanced sideways at Holun. "It's why Na-um needs him. He would tell Na-um what was going to happen, then Na-um would try to stop it, but it hasn't worked well so far." To her amusement, Kayla thought Holun's smile looked a little smug.

Holun continued. Kayla paused to listen a moment before translating aloud. "He says the 'Clan' is his family, and he trusted them. He said he thought Na-um was right in what he was doing." Holun was frowning, and Kayla took a breath before continuing. "But Na-um has changed. Na-um's become almost . . . evil . . . and Holun doesn't want to help him anymore."

Holun swallowed, tucking a strand of long black hair behind his ear and offering a tentative smile before ending in English. "Now I here."

Kayla blew out a gust of air. She hadn't even realized she'd been holding her breath. She looked over at Grady and found herself completely speechless, her brain still too foggy to come up with a reasonable response.

Grady stretched his hand out toward the dig. "Come with us, Holun. If what you are saying is true, you are welcome here." He smiled reassuringly at the boy as Kayla looked on, eyes wide. Kayla opened her mouth to translate for Holun, but the boy simply nodded and followed Grady out of the woods and back toward the middle of the dig.

Kayla walked a few paces behind the rest of the group, still trying to process this new information. Was it possible that someone from the Mercenaries—or the Clan, as Holun called them—was offering to help them? She didn't want to let herself hope, but he seemed sincere enough. If it *was* true, if he *was* now on their side, he was quite possibly the key to fighting this battle against the Mercenaries—the battle that, until now, she hadn't even realized they'd been fighting.

She was beginning to believe that they may actually have a chance. Maybe.

Despite her elation over Holun's arrival, Kayla was still drained. Twenty minutes was certainly not enough sleep. She retreated to her tent to try to sleep for a few more hours before meeting with the others to formulate a plan. She wouldn't really have much constructive input on only twenty minutes of sleep anyway.

The brightness of the sun shining through her tent woke her. Still half asleep, she reached blindly for the watch lying on the table at the head of her cot. She smiled tiredly, relieved to find that it was only about eight thirty—she hadn't slept *too* late. She rose up on her elbow and rolled to one side.

There was someone in her tent.

She jerked upright, eyes frozen on the dark figure asleep on the ground next to her. She stepped to the ground gingerly, careful to avoid waking the intruder, and leaned over slowly to catch a glimpse of the intruder's face. But just before she could, the figure stirred, turning to face her.

Kayla exhaled. *Grady.*

Wow, she thought. *I must still be a little edgy, even after Holun's arrival.* She smiled to herself. *Or maybe because of it.*

Grady's eyes blinked open. "Morning," he mumbled, offering a smile in her direction.

She smiled back as she searched the tent for a change of clothes. "Hey." She put her search on hold to lean down and steal a kiss. "Good morning." She reached in her suitcase for a pair of khaki Bermuda shorts and a dark purple t-shirt. "What are you doing here? Not that I mind." Kayla grinned.

Grady smiled back, but his eyes were still droopy. "I gave Holun my tent. Besides, I didn't think you would want to be alone."

Kayla nodded and set her newly-acquired change of clothes on her cot. Then she sat on the ground next to him. "I did like waking up next to you." She reached out to straighten his matted hair.

Grady nodded. "I rather enjoyed it as well." He smiled again, then sat up and rubbed a hand over his face, checking his watch in the process. "What are you doing up so soon? It's still a little early, given the late night we had."

Kayla shrugged. "I'm not really that tired." She glanced around her small tent, finding her toothbrush, then stood. "I'm gonna go get cleaned up a little. You can go back to sleep if you want. Take my cot."

Grady shook his head and rose to his feet. Kayla noticed he was still wearing the same clothes from yesterday. "I think I'll get a quick shower. Meet at the mess tent in twenty?"

Kayla's stomach rumbled in response and she smiled. "Sure. Twenty minutes."

The brilliance of Grady's answering smile lingered in Kayla's mind long after he left.

Holun stirred in the sleeping bag the girl Mandy had given him and stared at an orange canvas ceiling. What was he doing here? He glanced around the tent they'd let him sleep in. What if Na-um found out?

The thought chilled him to his core. There was no telling *what* Na-um would do, but Holun was sure it wouldn't be good. Certainly unpleasant.

But somewhere deep inside him, an inexplicable peace was fighting its way to the surface. Despite his uncertainty, he knew—in a place deep inside—that he had made the right decision. This was what he was supposed to be doing, where he was supposed to be.

And Holun realized that he already knew the truth: this was right. This was Destiny.

"So do you know what Na-um's planning?" Kayla, Grady, and the others were gathered in the mess tent with Holun, who sat staring at the four Americans while casually nibbling on a dried fruit and nut bar they'd given him. The tent was otherwise empty.

"Yes." Holun nodded at Grady, then switched back to K'iche with a quick glance at Kayla, who hurriedly stepped in.

"Holun says there are a few things we need to know first." Kayla saw him smile as the four of them leaned in.

"The Clan's ancestry goes back to the ancient Mayans. No one is allowed to marry outside the Clan, so they are still pure Maya." Kayla paused to listen before continuing. "His family has a lot of stories, but the oldest story of his family is that they guard the secret of the Codex."

Mandy jumped in as soon as Kayla had gotten the final word out. "Codex?"

Holun nodded, answering in English. "Yes. Codex give power." He paused, and Kayla blinked. *What?*

Holun switched back. "One day four men were out in a field and found a book. From the book, they received . . . Holun?" Kayla interrupted herself, then asked in K'iche: "Is that right?"

When Holun nodded, she continued. "From the book, the men received power. Maybe powers." She shook her head once. "Each one had power over one of the four basic elements, just like we thought. They became very strong and ruled the Mayan people." Kayla thought this was sounding oddly familiar. Was Holun telling them the same story from the cavern?

"Men became evil. Hurt many people. People try stop but no." Holun explained in English, frowning.

Kayla translated for him as he switched back to his native tongue. "So his Clan was . . . made, or formed? Some of the Clan received powers, too, and were able to fight who they called the 'Old Ones,' the four men who originally found the book." Kayla heard Holun sigh beside her. "But the power of the Codex was too strong. The Clan lost the fight and retreated to the mountains."

Holun glanced over at Kayla, his eyes sad. "But the power of the Codex was too strong for the Old Ones, too. They eventually went crazy."

Mandy gasped as Holun continued through Kayla. "So they tried to get rid of the power. First, they prayed and sacrificed to the gods for many months so the gods would take away their powers. When that didn't work, they tried to destroy the Codex. But fire wouldn't burn it, and it couldn't be torn apart. So the Old Ones made a plan." Kayla's eyes widened as she translated what Holun said next. "They tried to kill themselves, but the power of the Codex was in them, and it was too strong. They didn't—couldn't—die."

Holun leaned forward. "They were miserable, but they seemed to be stuck with the powers that made them crazy. Until they figured out one thing: they couldn't destroy the book, but they could separate it."

Holun crossed his arms and leaned back in his chair as Kayla finished translating. When she was done, the Four sat for a minute, trying to let it all sink in.

Kayla was the first one to speak. "Into four pieces." It wasn't a question.

Holun smiled and nodded once, switching back to English. "Yes. And you find three."

Holun was almost grinning now.

He watched as the four Americans slowly realized the repercussions of what he was saying. This journey they'd been on would probably be more life-changing than they had ever imagined. He sat quietly so they could digest the information.

It took a few minutes for someone to speak. Grady was first. "So Na-um was trying to stop us from getting all four books . . . so we couldn't reunite them?"

"Yes."

"And . . . if we get all four books together, they become this . . . Codex?"

"Yes."

"And the Codex . . ."

Justin interjected. "I *told* you we'd be getting powers!"

Mandy hit his arm, but laughed anyway.

Holun chuckled along with her. "Yes."

But Kayla seemed to have another concern. "But, Holun, if we get these powers, won't we go crazy too? Like the Old Ones?"

Holun gazed over at her, brows furrowing. "I no think so. Old Ones evil—not like all you. The Power no corrupt them; they corrupt Power."

Kayla nodded, then had another thought. "So if this is your family, Holun, why are you helping us?"

Holun had only just discovered the answer for himself, and nodded at Kayla to translate. "Na-um killed innocent people to stop you. He called it *Destiny*." The last word was in English, and Holun made a face as he spit it out. He continued in K'iche as Kayla translated. "Holun says we would not have found the first three books if it wasn't *our* Destiny." Kayla drew in a deep breath before translating the rest. "And he says it's his Destiny to help us."

Kayla could see he was telling the truth. Or, at the very least, he was telling what he believed was the truth. And she knew, in that instant, that they could trust him.

"So, Holun," Kayla began, "what is Na-um planning?"

Holun's shoulders slumped a little before answering, Kayla translating. "He says he doesn't know the specifics, but he knows it's big. Na-um has a large army—all of the men in the Clan—and they will all fight. Soon. He doesn't know when, but he does know where." Holun was tapping a finger to his temple.

"Where?" Mandy asked.

"Where four book is," Holun answered in English with a shrug of his shoulders, as though the answer was obvious.

Grady, Mandy, and Justin instinctively looked to Kayla. Up to now, Kayla had given them all the answers.

Holun gazed around the group before turning to Kayla. "Kayla, you see what going happen, yes?"

She nodded. "Yes, I have visions."

"Visions." Holun tried the word, then turned to the rest of the group. "I no think she help now. I come help you because I see her vision."

Kayla felt her jaw drop. "What do you mean?"

Holun flashed an endearing half-smile in Kayla's direction, speaking in K'iche so he would be understood. "I saw your vision. It wasn't like it normally is, so I knew it didn't come from me." He looked Kayla directly in the eye. "Are they always so painful?"

Kayla squeezed Grady's hand a little tighter under the table as she dropped her eyes from Holun's piercing gaze. She was glad Grady didn't speak the language, and she wasn't about to translate that. She quickly moved on. "Holun, how would you see my vision? You see visions, too?"

Holun nodded, then continued as Kayla translated for the group. "Holun sees visions, too, but they're not like mine. His aren't fast, or painful." Kayla dropped her gaze for a split second. "He just closes his eyes and sees them. The visions come when he thinks about them. My vision wasn't the same; that's how he knew it wasn't his."

Grady chimed in. "Holun, are the others like you? Can they see visions, too?"

"No." Holun answered in English, shaking his head. "But have other power."

"Like what?" Grady leaned in.

Kayla translated again. "No one can see visions like Holun can, but they can all run very fast. They can hear, see, and smell from very far away, like an animal." Kayla was smiling at Holun sniffing the air. "Some of the Clan—one of them being Na-um—can talk over long distances, in their heads. Like telepathy, I think." Holun was poking his temple.

"Telepathy?" Mandy asked.

Kayla looked at Holun, who tried the word in English, then shrugged, switching back to K'iche. "He said Na-um just talks out loud but hears the response in his head. He thinks it might just be the leaders, to help them in battle." Holun sighed before she was done and frowned.

Kayla fell quiet as she tried to absorb this new information. With all they had just learned, surely they could find a way to defeat Na-um and his Clan.

Then the next logical step occurred to her in the next second. "So, Holun, do you know where the fourth book is?"

Holun's whole countenance changed as he grinned, his smile widening as though he was keeping a secret he couldn't wait to tell. "Yes."

CHAPTER 40

Guide

ACCORDING TO HOLUN, they should reach their location in only a few hours. It wasn't soon enough for Mandy, who had already checked her watch twice since Grady'd started driving. *Only twelve minutes, are you kidding me?*

Mandy rubbed her temples and let her eyes fall closed. Holun, who was supposed to be sitting next to her in the backseat, was currently on the edge of his seat, halfway between Grady and Kayla in the front. He hadn't stopped talking since they'd gotten in the vehicle. She stole a glance at Kayla in the passenger seat and couldn't help but smile at the expression on her face, just a little. She recognized the glazed over, slightly wider-than-normal eyes and the heavy but silent sighs.

Mandy glanced over at Justin, who was staring out the window at the dense foliage rushing past them. Her heart yearned for him, pleaded with her to reach out for him, but she hesitated, her hand twitching slightly on the seat between them before she stopped herself. Why didn't she think she could?

It was almost as if she needed permission. It was stupid, insane even, but she couldn't shake the feeling. Something had come between them.

Maybe it's because of what happened earlier, she reasoned. *Maybe the sudden absence of that close connection just shook us up, and that's what I'm reacting to.*

She kind of hoped it was true. At least then she would have a reason, an explanation as to why things with Justin were just so . . . weird.

But as much as she wanted to believe nothing had changed, she couldn't shake the unsettling feeling that something *had* changed, and drastically. As much as Grady and Kayla had grown closer—as was evidenced by the way Kayla was now gazing at Grady despite Holun's incessant prattling between them and the way Grady was absentmindedly stroking her hand with his thumb as he held it—she and Justin had grown farther apart.

And she hated it.

Justin watched the trees fly by the window and sighed. For some reason, he'd been in a foul mood since the five of them had piled into this rattling, jarring, no-shock-absorbers excuse for a vehicle. His eyes narrowed without thinking. He really wished they could be done with this already.

This "journey"—or whatever Kayla wanted to call it—had cost him the most. His mother and now father were both innocent victims of these vicious mercenaries. Then, without even consulting him, Kayla and Grady had agreed to harbor one of their enemies. What's worse: they *trusted* him! Justin couldn't believe it. He still thought that this kid—so seemingly innocent—was a spy sent to bring them down.

He drew in a deep breath. No, he didn't really believe that. But he sometimes hoped he did. That would make it easy. He just wanted—needed—someone to pay for what had happened. He needed these mercenaries, whoever they were, to pay for the murders of his parents. And if he ever found Jackie . . .

He leaned forward, elbows resting on his knees. He cupped his face in his hands, trying to block out both the kid's jabbering and the jarring of the vehicle so he could think.

He didn't like feeling this way. He hated that his parents were gone. He hated that someone had taken them from him, and much too soon. And he hated how intensely he wished that the men who had killed them would die. He almost hated that the most.

His parents had always taught him that revenge got him nowhere. That taking revenge on someone who wronged him was not only wrong in itself, but it didn't provide the release it promised. It only caused more pain. Ignoring their advice now would dishonor who they were, and all that they'd taught him.

So, though he couldn't help what he was feeling, he could control what he did about it. And he decided, in that moment, that he would not exact revenge. He would only kill in self-defense, and then only if absolutely necessary. He was better than that. He wouldn't allow himself to become the very thing he hated. If not for himself, for . . .

He stole a glance at Mandy, who was staring straight ahead at the back of Grady's seat. He wished that he could talk to her, be close to her again. They had been so close—mere hours ago—but now . . . it seemed like something had come between them. A wide chasm that kept them miles apart.

He needed her. She was the reasonable one. She could've talked him out of this much more quickly than he had. She was the real reason he chose forgiveness instead of revenge, compassion instead of hate.

If only she knew that.

The trip did actually only take a few hours, though to Kayla, Holun's chattering—which had only recently started to wane—made it seem much longer. When they parked the car—a safe distance away from where they were headed, according to Holun—the sun had been overhead for about an hour. Kayla checked her watch to confirm; one o'clock on the dot. She smiled as she reached for the door handle.

Kayla half-jumped out of the SUV, landing silently in the soft grass. She reached back into the vehicle to open the glove box and retrieve a map before flicking the door shut and moving to the hood.

As Mandy came around the other side of the car with sandwiches for everyone and started handing them out, Kayla spread the map out on the hood. When Mandy was done, she leaned against the SUV next to Kayla, tucking a loose strand of hair behind her ear as she peered over at the map Kayla was perusing and bit off a corner of her sandwich. "Any idea where we are?"

Kayla nodded but didn't look up. "Yes. See here," she jabbed at a point in the middle of the forest, "this is roughly where we started." Lamanai was clearly marked on the map, and Kayla was pointing to its eastern edge. "Then we traveled mostly south." Kayla traced her finger along the route they'd just taken, stopping at an obscure location in the middle of the forest about a hundred miles south of Lamanai, according to the map's legend. "And this is approximately where we are."

Mandy leaned over to peruse the map more carefully, so Kayla straightened and stretched her back, then opened her sandwich and took a bite. Grady and Justin, who had already inhaled their sandwiches, were now quietly and carefully pulling the supplies from the back of the vehicle. Holun had actually fallen asleep just before they stopped and was still lying in the backseat of the SUV. Kayla eyed his sleeping form. She couldn't talk herself into waking him up. When he was sleeping, he wasn't talking. Thankfully.

Grady walked around the vehicle to hand Kayla her pack. She hefted it onto her back with a little difficulty, as it was loaded down with hiking gear, rations, and various other supplies that would last her about a week in the forest. She hoped she would at least be back to the dig by then, if not home in her bed. Surely this trip was coming to an end. If they were about to fight their "final battle" wouldn't that mean they were finished? That they'd done everything they were destined to do? She was just tired of all this. Her body—and mind—was exhausted. She didn't think she'd last much longer.

She caught Grady staring at her. Kayla tried to smile reassuringly, but he didn't seem to be buying it. Even when he couldn't read her mind, he could read her.

She mouthed an "I'm fine" in his direction before turning to Justin, who was now approaching them with the rest of the gear. They quickly strapped on their packs, checked and double-checked their gear, and made sure everything was in working order.

Then Kayla remembered the boy in their car, and glanced toward the backseat.

Grady came up beside her and put a gentle hand on her elbow. "Kayla, can I talk to you?"

Kayla nodded, and let him lead her a couple of feet away from the SUV and the sleeping boy. When they stopped, Grady spoke in a whisper. "He can't come with us; it's much too dangerous."

Kayla caught Grady's gaze and matched his hushed tone. "But we can't just leave him here. He'll wake up scared. He'll be alone. Isn't that just as dangerous?"

Grady shook his head. "No. We can't ask him to do this."

Kayla drew a breath. "He *offered* to do this, Grady. He came to us, remember?"

Grady was silent for a moment. Then: "Holun is much too young. Why would Na-um bring a kid into this?" Kayla sensed the question was rhetorical, so she stayed quiet. "These mercenaries are evil, and they undoubtedly must be stopped. Holun can help us—he seems to *want* to help us— but . . ."

"Grady." Kayla interrupted him. "He needs to do this. He believes this is his destiny—he said as much—so who are we to stop it?" Grady bit his lip, so she continued. "When the time comes, we will do everything we can to protect him, to keep him out of danger. But for now—and this is really the biggest reason he should come with us—we need his help."

Grady paused momentarily before nodding. Kayla offered a half-smile, then turned back to the car to awaken their small and unwitting guide.

She hoped he wouldn't start babbling again.

After a few long hours of arduous hiking in excruciating heat, they came to a break in the trees, which revealed to Grady that they were actually a lot higher up than he'd thought. Through the opening in the trees, Grady could see for miles. It was beautiful.

Grady heard a "There!" from behind him. He stopped, grateful for the interruption. Hopefully whatever Holun was indicating was close.

He turned slowly to assess the rest of the group. They looked just as exhausted as he felt. He dropped to a nearby log and looked over at Holun as Kayla took a seat next to him.

Their small guide, who stood pointing off toward an unknown location in the distance, didn't seem tired at all. Perhaps that was because he wasn't carrying any gear.

He felt Kayla smiling beside him, and, for a moment, he wondered if she'd read his thoughts. He sighed. He really missed that.

So he turned to the matter at hand. "What do you see, Holun?"

"There! Where last book." Holun was grinning ear to ear, and nearly bouncing up and down.

Grady wiped his forehead with a sweat-soaked rag as he heard someone come up from his right. He didn't even bother to look to see who it was; he was just too tired. He figured he'd find out soon enough. "Where, Holun?" Mandy came into Grady's line of vision as she spoke and placed her hand on Holun's shoulder, the epitome of patience.

"The mountain!" Holun was so ecstatic that Grady couldn't help but smile.

But his smile faded as soon as he looked at where Holun was pointing. "*That* mountain? It's still miles away!" He wasn't much for complaining, but it'd been a long few days. Who was he kidding—it'd been a long summer.

Kayla folded the map she'd been scanning and shoved it into the side pocket of her backpack before patting his knee dramatically. "Only one and a half. You'll make it."

Grady wrinkled his nose at her as he shook his head. Her answering smile was sweet. Sickeningly sweet.

He looked down at his watch. Three fifteen. He supposed he had a few more hours in him. After all, did he really have a choice?

After a relatively short hike to the mountain's base, Holun led them up the mountain a short way, then started heading back down in another direction. Kayla wondered what he was doing, but thought it best not to question him. If he was telling the truth, he was leading them to the right place. No . . . not if. He *was* telling the truth. She had to trust that. Her heart already trusted him—she just wished her head would catch up.

But a lifetime of trust issues didn't fix themselves overnight.

She gazed up at the light blue sky scattered with wispy, translucent clouds. The sun would be setting in a few hours, and they would be completely at the mercy of Holun. As if they weren't now.

About twenty minutes of downhill hiking later, Kayla saw a break in the trees up ahead. From the distance they had already traveled, and the fact that the ground beneath their feet had leveled out, she estimated that they were probably back at the base of the mountain, just in a different place. What was going on? Where was he taking them?

Once they reached the opening, Kayla began to understand. The clearing now in front of them was nearly a mile across, and about half as deep. In the middle of the clearing, a large collection of boulders stood in a haphazard formation. *This all feels eerily familiar . . .* Kayla thought as she moved toward the edge of the trees.

As she stepped into the open expanse, she began to feel something. Nothing monumental, or even very noticeable— just a small, subtle crawling under her skin. Disconcerting, definitely, but not in a bad way. It was the kind of feeling she remembered from junior high when someone she liked looked at her. An anticipation so unexpected that it sent electricity running through her veins.

Kayla shivered slightly, despite the heat, then stepped forward with a newfound determination.

She understood it now. This was Destiny. Hers, Grady's, Mandy and Justin's—even Holun's. She could feel it in her bones.

She wasn't entirely sure what was coming next, but she smiled anyway. Whatever was coming, she knew deep in her heart that she was right where she was supposed to be.

CHAPTER 41

Distrust

JUSTIN EYED THEIR YOUNG GUIDE as they entered the clearing. Surely something was coming . . . they were almost certainly walking into a trap. There had to be a catch.

Then Justin stepped out of the line of trees into the wide-open expanse and momentarily forgot all about Holun. *Wow. That thing is enormous!* His eyes were automatically drawn up, toward the clouds. He reached for the binoculars Mandy offered in her open hands and stared through them.

In the center of the clearing, soaring to incredible heights, a large rock formation stood tall. After pulling the binoculars away several times to make sure his eyes weren't deceiving him, he slung them around his neck and began to make his way closer.

His eyes widened as he approached. *Certainly this can't be a natural formation . . . Nothing in nature would be this . . . specific. This deliberate. This formation was definitely put here for a reason.*

His thoughts trailed off as he approached the collection of boulders—boulders that were somehow all connected yet separate at the same time. He stood in the shadow of the closest rock and gazed up at the sky. The edge of the boulder was easily five feet above his head. And that was the shortest one.

He headed to the right, along the base of the formation, and began systematically examining the rock face. He wasn't sure what he expected to find; a hidden entrance, maybe, or a way to the top? After a few minutes, he realized he was really just searching for any logical reason this monument before him could exist.

About halfway around the grouping of massive rocks, long after he had lost sight of the rest of the group, he found a collection of smaller rocks: flat, grey stones haphazardly placed in an odd formation against a few sloping boulders—could those be crude steps? Maybe he'd found what he was looking for after all.

He started climbing. The steps were large, with about a foot between each level. He scaled the rocks carefully but quickly, despite the tiresome hike here. Just the idea of a potential discovery had adrenaline coursing through his veins, giving him a newfound strength.

But the climb up was long, and the steps were getting steeper as he neared the top. The adrenaline soon wore off and he started to grow weary. He wished he had saved a little more of his strength.

The summit of the mini-mountain was easily one hundred and fifty feet off the ground. As he reached the top, he sat down on the nearest rock to catch his breath. He slowly raised his head and noticed that he could see for miles; he was above the tree line. He gazed at the horizon to try to catch a glimpse of the soon-to-be setting sun.

That's when he saw it.

Justin jumped to his feet, reaching for the binoculars he had fortuitously slung around his neck just minutes earlier. He rammed them against his face with a force that would have hurt, had he cared.

He scanned the horizon to the south through the lenses of the binoculars, quickly finding again what he had seen moments before. "No . . . no!" He kept his voice as quiet as he could, though he reasoned that he probably wouldn't have been heard even if someone was up here with him. He just wasn't sure how far his voice would carry in this clearing; he was already worried that he would be seen over the surrounding treetops.

"What is it?" Mandy's voice came from behind him. He turned to see her climbing the last few steps with a little effort. Justin put a finger to his lips to signal her to keep quiet before he went over and offered his hand to help her up the rest of the way. He figured she would've had more trouble than he did climbing that makeshift staircase—her legs were much shorter than his.

He smiled to himself as Mandy sat down on the same rock he had rested on just a few minutes ago. He pretended to gaze back through the binoculars as he stole a glance at Mandy out of the corner of his eye. He could stare at her forever . . .

But as he called Mandy over and showed her what was coming, he doubted they would last that long.

Kayla stood very still, a good twenty feet away from the rock formation, loosely holding on to Grady's hand. She was trying to figure out where Justin and Mandy had gone. She had seen them head around the right side of the formation; perhaps they had found something? Maybe an entrance underground?

Grady was nearly motionless beside her. She could feel his pulse through his hand, but little else. What was he thinking? She wished for the thousandth time that she could hear his thoughts again.

She sighed, then began slowly walking toward the rock formation. As she moved forward, Grady clutched her hand tighter, moving with her. She knew he wouldn't let her out of his sight. She didn't have to be able to hear his thoughts to know that.

They approached the formation slowly; Kayla was still trying to decide what to do. Grady suggested they head around to the left, hopefully meet Justin and Mandy in the middle. Kayla shrugged, then turned and headed in that direction with Grady right beside her.

Mandy tucked her hair behind her ear and stared at the ground to the left of her feet. Once Justin had shown her what was concerning him—and with very good reason—he hadn't said a word to her, and had even shushed her when she tried to ask him a question. Why was he ignoring her? This rift between them, whatever it was—and whatever had caused it—was getting really old, and more frustrating by the second.

She sighed, wishing she could do something to fix it. But what would fix something so . . . intangible? So indefinable? The whole thing just seemed hopeless.

But she couldn't lose hope; she wouldn't allow herself to give up. She knew that Justin, despite his shortcomings, was the only man for her. Their relationship wasn't perfect, but whose was? Well, maybe Grady and Kayla's, but then they'd only been together for a few weeks. Just give them a few years.

She smiled bitterly, a single tear escaping her eye. She wiped it away silently, still staring at the grey rock beneath her feet.

"Mandy! Justin!"

Grady's too-loud-for-the-current-situation voice broke into her thoughts from somewhere below. As quietly as she could, she stepped over to the nearest edge. If Justin didn't want her talking, he sure wouldn't want Grady shouting.

She spotted Grady just over the north side of the formation, opposite where Justin was standing. He and Kayla looked up at her almost as soon as she saw them. Instead of calling down to them, she simply put a finger to her lips, signaling them to be quiet. She motioned them toward the steps she and Justin had scaled to get here. Grady and Kayla nodded, then headed out of sight.

Mandy turned around slowly, anticipating Justin's anger at Grady's outburst. She winced just before he came into view.

But Justin was still staring through his binoculars. She tiptoed back to her seat, trying not to distract him. She didn't want him to be angry at her.

Just before she reached the rock, someone grabbed her arm. She gasped, startled.

Mandy whipped around to see Justin at her back.

Justin didn't understand. He stared into Mandy's eyes, which normally held such warmth and innocence, and saw something that sent shivers down his spine. Something he had never wanted to see looking back at him. Not from her.

Fear—stark and very real. And as she stared back at him, eyes slightly wider than normal, he knew in an instant what she was afraid of: She was afraid of *him*.

"Mandy?" he whispered tentatively. He reached out a hand to brush her hair back from her forehead. She cringed away from him for the tiniest instant—but he saw it.

He closed his hand and pulled it away. "What's wrong?"

"Nothing," she mumbled, turning her head away.

No, Justin didn't believe it for a minute. Something about him scared her. And he couldn't live with that. Just the simple knowledge of it was tearing him apart.

"No, Mandy"—he tried to keep his voice light despite the intensity of his emotion—"I need to know. What did I do?" He still held onto her arm, and had to make a conscious effort not to squeeze it too tightly.

Mandy was looking off into the distance, refusing to meet his gaze. He put his free hand on her chin and brought her gaze to his. "Please." His voice was pleading.

The look that crossed her face nearly ripped his heart in two.

She didn't trust him.

He couldn't believe it. He knew something had come between them, but he just figured it was normal couple stuff, something they would work through, like they always did. But, somehow, this felt different. The look in Mandy's eyes was telling him that very clearly.

Justin tried to swallow the lump in his throat. He knew he had to do something to make it right. He wanted to say something, *anything* that might make it better, but nothing came to mind. So, instead, he looked away, dropping his hands to his sides. What could he possibly say that would make her trust him again?

He wanted to cry out, wanted to fall to his knees and beg for her forgiveness, but his body wouldn't move. He wanted so desperately to take away her fear, her distrust, but how could he when he was the thing she feared?

He heard Kayla and Grady coming up the last few steps near where he and Mandy stood. He resolved then, as he watched Mandy move away from him to help their friends up the last few steps, that he would find a way for Mandy to trust him again. He couldn't live with himself if she was afraid of him. He couldn't live without her smile, her laugh. He couldn't live without her faith in him.

He couldn't live without her, period.

Grady could tell something was wrong the minute he and Kayla reached the top of the rock formation, but he knew better than to ask. Whatever was going on between Justin and Mandy was not really any of his business. He didn't want to see them unhappy, but decided it was best not to interfere.

So Grady turned to Justin, who was staring off into the distance through the binoculars still hanging around his neck, and quietly asked, "What'd you find?"

Justin pulled the binoculars and the strap holding them over his head and shoved them into Grady's hands as he pointed south, over the line of the trees. "Look, there."

Grady scanned the horizon. What was Justin talking about? He couldn't find anything out of the ordinary . . . But then, in a startling moment of revelation, he saw it. Or, rather, *them.*

What had to be a good ten or fifteen miles from where they now stood, crossing a wide clearing in the surrounding forest, was . . . well, for lack of a better term, an army. That was the only way he could describe it. A large group of men, dressed in native clothing, appeared to be heading their way —and much more quickly than an army made up of mere men would've been able to. They were even brandishing various ancient weapons: bows and arrows, swords, and the like. There was only one explanation: Na-um and his men were coming.

Grady slowly handed the binoculars to Kayla while still staring at the army of super-charged men.

"Oh . . . no . . ." The distress in Kayla's voice echoed what they were all feeling. They were immensely outnumbered. And Na-um and his men had special abilities.

Grady's stomach tied into knots. They had no chance of winning. No chance of getting out of here alive. No chance except . . .

They *had* to find the book. It was their only hope.

Kayla just stared. She could feel it in the air—sheer terror that threatened to debilitate all of them. What little hope they had left was in the book, and no one knew where that was. There didn't seem to be any clue up here, and they hadn't seen an opening or anything closely resembling one. Shouldn't *something* be here? Holun had led them to this exact spot . . .

Kayla stopped. Where was Holun? She tried to remember the last time she'd seen him. Was it when they first came into the clearing? Had she even seen him in the clearing?

She scanned the clearing, the surrounding tree line . . . there. She hurried over to Grady, then, without explanation, pulled him toward the stairs, barely maintaining her balance as she hurled herself down the rocky steps.

Grady was on her heels. What was going on? He knew that Na-um's army was coming, but how did this improve their situation at all? Why were they about to trip down the world's most uneven flight of stairs?

Then he heard it. *Holun.*

Kayla, is that you? Grady answered back immediately.

Grady! Thank God. We have to get to Holun.

Grady nodded as they finally landed in the grass and sped away toward where Kayla had last seen Holun. They needed to find that kid. What if Na-um had sent a recon team, and they had found Holun? What if he was in trouble?

Or what if he had gone back to Na-um to tell him where they were? He didn't want to believe that, but he had to keep all possibilities in mind.

Kayla shot him a glance as they ran. He knew he shouldn't think Holun was a traitor—or patriot, depending on which side you were on—but he couldn't help it. One of the most important unwritten rules in science: keep an open mind.

Grady spotted Holun only a second later, still standing near the tree line, at precisely the same spot where they'd entered the clearing. He didn't appear to be with anyone.

An open mind only goes so far. Kayla broke into his thoughts as they slowed to a jog. *Sometimes you just have to trust.*

Grady nodded once in her direction, briefly thinking about the irony of her statement before her eyes narrowed in his direction. He shrugged, smirking slightly as they neared Holun. Remembering that their enemies weren't too far away and coming closer by the second, Grady kept quiet until they were within a few feet of him. "Holun, are you okay?"

The boy nodded slowly, a slight frown on his face. "Yes." The frown grew wider. "I see."

Kayla put a hand on his shoulder. "What did you see?"

Holun kept frowning for a few more seconds before answering in K'iche. "I saw the battle. I am not sure that you will win. We need to find the final book."

Grady nodded after he heard Kayla's translation, then addressed Holun. "Did you see Na-um? He and the entire army are here."

Holun nodded slowly, his face much too young for the expression Grady saw there. "Yes. Here soon. We go now."

"Where?" Kayla asked.

Holun nodded toward the middle of the clearing. "There."

Kayla's eyebrows furrowed. "We were just there, Holun. There's nothing there."

Holun simply pointed toward the massive collection of rocks as he repeated himself, more resolutely this time. "There." He started half-walking, half-running toward the middle of the clearing.

Grady returned Kayla's quick glance before they both turned to follow Holun. Grady shrugged as they hurried back toward the formation. What else could they do? Kayla was right.

Sometimes you have to be open to all possibilities—but sometimes you just have to trust that there is only one way.

CHAPTER 42

Earth

MANDY REACHED THE BASE of the stairs just as Holun came running up. Kayla and Grady weren't far behind. Mandy'd left Justin at the top, not caring if he followed. Okay, that wasn't true. She was just telling herself she didn't care. That made it easier. No; that wasn't true either.

Mandy heard Justin come up behind her. She made an effort to ignore him without really knowing why and instead tried to sound cheerful as she addressed the young boy. "Hey, Holun. Where have you been?"

"Has vision of battle." Mandy almost chuckled at the matter-of-fact way he said it. Must be nice to have such clarity at such a young age. She still wasn't entirely sure she knew that she was on the right path.

Grady spoke up, stopping her musings in their tracks. "Where is it, Holun?"

Holun's eyes slid shut. Mandy watched him closely. Was he having another vision?

Then the boy's eyes opened. "Follow me." With a wave of his hand, he headed around the formation.

Mandy figured that Kayla or Grady would've found an entrance if there'd been one. Hadn't they circled the base of these boulders completely between the four of them?

Holun turned toward the formation and started along its base to the right of the stairs. But only a few steps later, he stopped. Mandy looked around him at the rock face. She didn't see anything. Was she missing something? There was nothing here.

Holun closed his eyes for a split second, a little bit longer than a blink. Mandy realized that he was looking for something, maybe calling a vision? He did say his visions worked differently than Kayla's . . . Holun was now staring at the rock face, and held his gaze there for a few seconds before reaching out his right hand. He flattened his palm against the stone.

Nothing happened. Mandy had been expecting *something*—a flash of light, or maybe the sound of grinding rock? But there was nothing.

Holun furrowed his brow, an endearing expression that made Mandy want to smile had the circumstances been different. But as it was, Mandy was starting to get worried. If Holun didn't know what was going on, what hope did they have? They were in the dark. And in another few hours, they would *literally* be in the dark. She was hoping they'd find something by then. And with Na-um's army coming—they really *needed* to find something by then.

"See, I knew it. Holun's working for them! He sent a message to Na-um telling him when we'd be here. This is all just an elaborate trap!" Justin took a step toward their young guide. Mandy rolled her eyes at his childish display.

Grady stepped in, putting a hand on Justin's chest. "Justin, he wouldn't do that."

Justin knocked his hand away as he took another step forward. "You can't know that. He led us here to die!"

Grady moved to stand directly between them, blocking Justin's path to the boy. Justin stopped, his face less than a foot from Grady's.

"Grady, get out of my way. We can't trust him! If you protect him, we will die." Justin leaned in closer, inches away from Grady's face.

Mandy was starting to get worried. Justin was taller than Grady, but, given that Justin was a stick, Grady outweighed him by almost thirty pounds. Mandy hoped Justin would back down. Grady would probably win in a fight, but she was really hoping it wouldn't come to that. They didn't have the time.

"Justin, listen to me. Holun led us here of his own will. He came to *us* without asking for anything in return. All you have to do is look into his eyes to know he's telling the truth." He paused, placing his hand lightly on Justin's shoulder. "Let him show us the way. We can trust him." He cast a quick glance in Kayla's direction. "I believe that completely."

Mandy held her breath as she waited for Justin's response. The silence in the group was thicker than the humidity of the forest surrounding them.

Then she heard Justin sigh. She released her breath in a rush.

When he finally spoke, his voice was much quieter. "Fine," he muttered. "I'll back off. But I don't have to trust him. I just hope you don't get us killed."

Grady nodded once. "Thank you, Justin. We will be fine, I know it."

Justin just shrugged, crossing his arms.

Mandy spoke up then, trying desperately to change the subject. "So, Holun, what do we do now?"

Holun couldn't figure out what went wrong. In his vision, he clearly saw that a hand flattened on this exact spot would open a passageway in the rock. But nothing had happened. And now Justin didn't trust him. He didn't really blame him.

Holun didn't answer Mandy's question; instead, he closed his eyes again, searching the vision for any more clues. But it looked just the same. Except . . . wait. Now he understood.

That wasn't his hand.

"Kayla," he called, reaching in her direction. "I need you."

Kayla stood in the exact spot Holun had, staring at the same rock face. He had told her to reach out her hand and flatten it on the face of the rock, just as he had done. For some reason, he believed that only she could open the secret passage. Of course, with all she'd seen in the past few weeks, she knew it was entirely possible.

She pulled in a breath before slowly reaching out her right hand, offering a silent prayer that this would work.

Just before her hand touched the surface, her mind flashed with the picture of her opening this passageway into the rock formation. Then the picture vanished as quickly as it had come. She smiled and touched the rock in front of her. If they'd had the time, she would've relished the fact that this vision didn't cause her any pain.

But the enemy was coming. And soon.

The rock was warm. It surprised her; she supposed she had expected it to be cool, though she didn't know why. Her fingertips touched it first, then she stretched her arm out further and her palm connected with the stone.

The moment her hand was completely spread out on the rock, the sound of grinding stone reached her ears. She couldn't help but wince and hope that the sound wouldn't carry across the clearing and out into the rainforest. She certainly didn't want to attract the attention of Na-um and his men. Of course, with Na-um's super-hearing, he was probably already listening.

The boulder directly to her left, right next to the staircase, began to open. The progress was slow, and only a crack showed at first. Kayla hoped it would hurry up.

It took almost a full minute for the stone to fully open and stop moving. Kayla was getting nervous. Na-um and his men could be here any minute. They had to find this book.

Kayla bounded into the opening as soon as the grinding stopped, clicking on her flashlight as soon as she stepped inside.

But only a few feet inside, not even far enough for the darkness to have swallowed the sunlight, she stopped at a dead end—or so it appeared. Would this whole thing be full of secret passageways? That would get old really quickly.

She did the first thing she thought of—she reached out her hand and flattened it against the wall in front of her. To her surprise, the wall in front of her swung inward at her touch, just like a door. Hopefully everything would be this easy. Knock on wood.

With the rest of the group following close behind her, Kayla began their not-quick-enough descent underground. The floor started sloping to the left as it descended, creating a ramp leading deep into the earth. She fearlessly hurried down it, eager to find out what was ahead. She could instinctively feel that the worst danger was just behind them—but that their salvation was just ahead.

They descended for a few long minutes before the slope flattened into a long hallway. She shined her flashlight ahead, trying to see what lay ahead of them. Nothing but darkness met her eyes, so she headed into it.

After they had gone a short distance, the hallway began to open up in all directions. The ground sloped down slightly, the ceiling sloped up drastically, and the walls sloped away from her on either side. Her skin started to tingle. This is what she was waiting for. They were close.

The hallway was, in fact, opening up into a large room; her light couldn't reach the other side, or even a close side wall. She stepped into the room and took in her surroundings, trying to make sense of them in the near blackness. As she stood there, she could sense the others come up behind her.

The moment she stepped into the room, Kayla felt something start crawling up and down her skin. For a split second, she thought something might be down here with them, but soon realized that the sensation was coming from inside of her. It was an odd sensation, an inexplicable sense of déjà vu. She could've sworn she'd been here before. Something was so familiar about it.

And suddenly she knew where the book was, without even being able to see the room. She knew what the room looked like, without light to make sense of it. She knew there was a large rock formation in the middle, not unlike the one above them or the one in the first cave at Lamanai. And she knew that at the base of the formation there was a small opening, one where the book was waiting. Waiting for her.

She turned to her left and found what she already knew was there: a small opening carved in the stone wall of the room framed a large torch, ready to be lit. She knew the room was surrounded by identical openings. She had a sudden thought and considered speaking it aloud, mostly for the benefit of Mandy and Justin. It seemed Grady was distracted by trying to figure out how big the room was anyway; she wasn't even sure he'd heard what she'd just realized about this room. "Grady, do you have a lighter or a match or something?" Kayla's voice echoed in what she knew was an enormous room.

Grady said, "Sure, here," as he handed her a small pocket-sized lighter, the ones that were so cheap they were disposable. She idly wondered why he carried it—but before she could complete her thought, Grady offered, *I wanted to be ready for anything.* Kayla smiled. He was back.

After a few attempts at igniting the grass in the torch, the fire caught. Their small corner of the room illuminated slightly, casting ghostly shadows across their faces.

Kayla took charge. "Mandy, Justin, can you take this and light the rest of them?" She tossed the lighter to Mandy, then pulled the torch from the wall and handed it to Justin.

"The rest?" Mandy sounded like she thought Kayla was crazy. Well, yeah, by almost any definition she was.

"They are spaced about ten feet from each other around the circumference of the room. Please hurry." Without offering any further explanation, Kayla started off toward the middle of the room with only her flashlight to light the way.

As she moved toward the center of the massive room, Kayla heard Holun move a good ten feet to the right of the entrance, a careful distance away from the opening should anyone else enter the room, and take a seat. Kayla was grateful. He had done his job, and was now just trying to stay safe.

What aren't you telling them? Grady broke into her thoughts as he followed closely behind her.

I know this place. I think I've been here before, or . . . something. Kayla didn't really know herself why it was so familiar to her, so she couldn't exactly explain it to Grady. So, instead, she recalled the déjà vu she'd experienced just moments ago —and he promptly apologized.

Oh. Sorry I wasn't paying attention earlier.

Kayla smiled. *No problem, Grady. We're still getting used to all this.*

Grady nodded in the semi-darkness. *Just let me know what you need. I will follow your lead.*

Kayla sighed, knowing Grady would somehow understand. *Thank you. I know I'm crazy.*

Not crazy, Grady replied. *Just . . . certain.*

Kayla's smile widened.

Mandy followed Justin quietly, watching him light each torch. He'd only needed the lighter once so far, so Mandy was starting to feel a little useless. She wanted to be able to help, not just trail Justin around the room doing nothing.

They were halfway around the room when Justin turned to her. "I'm sorry."

Mandy's eyes shot to his. "What?"

He sighed visibly. "I scared you earlier; I could see it in your eyes. I don't want you to ever be afraid of me."

Mandy nodded slowly, not sure what she was supposed to say to that. At least he had read her correctly; she *had* been scared of him. Justin grabbing her arm had more than surprised her—she'd been genuinely frightened. And she still wasn't quite sure why.

Justin looked down, blowing out the torch he was holding and setting it carefully against the wall. His next words were a whisper. "You don't trust me."

Mandy's heart tugged at her chest as she looked at the ground. "No, I . . . I don't know. You just . . ." She sighed. "It's not really that I don't . . . I want to trust you. I just . . . can't."

"Why?"

Mandy shook her head slightly, then started speaking without knowing what she was going to say. "You've been so distant. You've been argumentative, or, at best, you've ignored me. I want to be close to you again. I want to trust you. I just feel like . . . like you're pulling away. Maybe it's this thing with your dad, I don't know." Her voice had lowered to a whisper.

Justin sighed and reached a tentative hand toward her face, and this time she didn't pull away. He laid his hand gently on her cheek, his thumb caressing her skin. "I love you. I always have, and always will. I don't know what's going on with me right now, but I still love you. I don't always show it; I know that. But with everything going on, with my dad . . ." His voice broke. "I'm just going through a lot. Then after I couldn't hear your thoughts anymore, it was just . . . I guess it was just easier to ignore you than face the truth about how much it hurt to miss your voice in my head. Or I thought it would be easier. But it's been tearing me up inside. I can't do this alone anymore. I need you. I can't live without you."

Mandy's heart thudded in her chest. She had been trying for hours to figure out what was wrong between them and how to fix it. Justin had just told her everything she needed to hear from him—and she believed him. She knew he'd been through more than any person should have to handle, and she'd wanted to help him through it. Now, finally, he was letting her in.

She swallowed hard and lifted her gaze to his. She touched her hand to his cheek. "I love you, Justin Stanford. Forever."

A serene smile crossed Justin's face. He leaned down and brought his lips to hers. She felt all the concerns and heartache of the past few hours—weeks, really—start to melt away with his kiss. She kissed him back, putting both hands behind his neck and pulling him closer.

He was everything she wanted. He wasn't perfect, but then no one was. They had work to do, trust to rebuild. But somewhere deep inside, she knew that they would become close once again. They would get through this together.

And she knew, with absolute certainty, that he was hers. Whatever was happening between them now would be fixed —and their relationship would be better for it.

But Mandy also knew that sometimes what takes only a second to break can take infinitely longer to heal, and she sensed that she might need a little time. But she still hoped that healing wouldn't take very long. With Na-um and his men coming, she feared that they may not have that kind of time.

Kayla approached the rock formation in the middle of the room in a dead run. She knew that hidden somewhere near this collection of boulders was the last book they needed to find, their only hope of defeating Na-um and his army of mercenaries. She drew in an anticipatory breath as she slowed to keep from crashing into the boulder in front of her. She was so close she could almost taste it.

Grady came up behind her just as she reached the base of the first boulder and placed a hand on the small of her back, encouraging her further. Kayla was tempted to be distracted by his touch, but chose instead to focus on finding that tiny opening. She knew it was here somewhere . . .

But then a sound broke the silence, the painfully recognizable *click, click* of the hammer of a gun sliding into place. Kayla instinctively froze, and Grady tensed behind her. Simultaneously, almost as if they'd rehearsed it, they slowly began to raise their hands.

In that instant, standing only a few feet away from the boulders that held the book they so desperately needed, Kayla realized three horrific things: the hard face of the rock formation was in front of them, a shooter was at their backs, and there was nowhere to run.

They were trapped.

Codex

MANDY AND JUSTIN WERE STILL circling the large room, re-lighted torch in hand, lighting more torches as they went. They had nearly come around the far side of the boulders— even in the dim torch-light, Mandy thought she could see the entrance to this room just beyond the formation—when she heard it.

Mandy.

She froze, staring at the back of Justin's head. The voice wasn't his—she had clearly heard a woman's voice. What on earth was going on?

The voice came again. *Mandy, we need your help.*

Kayla! Mandy wanted to yell out for her, but sensed that if Kayla had made a connection this strong out of nowhere, something had shaken her up pretty badly. Mandy couldn't even imagine what it might be. Was Na-um already here? *What's going on?*

The answer didn't come right away, which didn't make Mandy feel any better. *Someone's here. I think . . . they have a gun.*

Mandy gasped—she couldn't help it—and Justin whipped around at the sound, eyes wide. When he saw Mandy's expression, his eyes flashed; Mandy hadn't seen such genuine concern in a long while. She smiled, a non-verbal *I'm alright* so he wouldn't worry, but she knew he wouldn't be put off so easily. She'd have to explain later, when they had more time.

What do you need from us? Mandy asked, trying to concentrate to make sure her message got through.

Kayla's voice resonated in her mind. *We're not sure what's going on.* Mandy thought she could hear someone else, maybe a male voice, in the background. Was that Grady? This was all too weird.

Kayla continued. *We're blindfolded, and the person's tying our hands behind our backs. Ow!* Whoever it was, they were being rough. *It couldn't be Na-um, could it?* Mandy assumed the question was rhetorical.

She grabbed the torch from a confused Justin, blew it out, then let it drop in the dirt as she grabbed his hand and pulled him toward the center of the room. *We're coming. Hold on.*

Mandy, don't! You don't know who . . .

Mandy cut her off. *It can't be Na-um; we would hear it if the whole army was here with him. This has to be someone else.* Then Mandy had a thought. *Besides, why would they tie you up and blindfold you if they had other people with them? If there were others with them, they would've found the rest of us by now. Maybe it's just one person.* She and Justin had just reached the boulders nearest them and started to head around the massive rocks, toward the entrance. *Kayla, are they still there?*

Kayla's voice answered her, but something was off. *We, uh . . . they're moving us toward the rocks now.*

Mandy did not like her tone of voice; she tried not to picture someone leading her friends up against a rock wall with a gun at their backs. She picked up her pace, still dragging a bewildered Justin along behind her. *Kayla, focus. You will get out of this. We need you to find the book, anyway,* Mandy teased, trying to get Kayla's mind off the situation, if only for a second. Then Mandy heard that male voice again, very softly. *Is Grady here, too?*

Yes. Can you hear him?

Vaguely. Let's just focus on you right now. I'm coming around the formation. I can almost see . . .

A shot rang out, echoing off the massive cavern walls so loudly that it made Mandy's ears hurt. She ducked behind a boulder as quickly as she could, but not before seeing a spray of pebbles and dust burst into the air just inches from her head.

Mandy! Are you okay?!

Mandy drew a shaky breath, trying to collect her thoughts enough to be able to answer Kayla. *Yes, yes, we're fine.* She swallowed hard. *Guess whoever it is is still here.* Mandy drew in another breath, as deep a breath as she could muster, while the echoes in the cavern finally subsided. *I have to try again.*

Don't! It's not safe to . . .

Kayla! I have to do this. It will be okay. Mandy steeled herself, lowering herself near the ground before sticking her head out from behind the boulder again, wincing as she did.

Nothing. Mandy blinked, grateful she wasn't getting shot at but utterly confused. Where did the shooter go? Surely they didn't just vanish into thin air?

Mandy stood and took a tentative step out from behind the boulder . . . still nothing. Maybe the shooter was gone;

she didn't see anyone else in the room. More confidently this time—though still cautious—she took a few more steps, hugging the rock face. When nothing happened, she sped up, circling the boulders quickly until she saw Kayla and Grady sitting on the ground, blindfolded with their hands tied behind their backs. She rushed over to them and ripped their blindfolds off before starting to work at the knots that bound Kayla's wrists. Justin, who had either figured out what was going on or was ignoring it to address more pressing issues, moved to untie Grady's hands.

Once Kayla's hands were untied and her friends were on their feet, Mandy looked around the dimly-lit room. She didn't understand it, but somehow, some way, the shooter was gone, just like that.

Holun—who'd been sitting frozen in place since the moment that shot rang out—was just about to get up and try to find out where Mandy and Justin were when he felt it. A massive gust of wind blew past him, throwing his long hair into his face and sending goosebumps across his skin. Instantly, he knew what it was. Someone had just sped past him in a hurry to get out of here. And he only knew of one group of people that could move like that. Was Na-um already here? He had to warn Kayla . . .

Then it happened. He felt his eyes roll back in his head as his body froze, then went limp. He slumped to the floor, unconscious.

He knew he was unconscious. He'd felt every bit of it—including the bruises that were certainly blossoming under his skin from his collapse to the hard floor—but none of that mattered.

He was having another vision. One so intense that it had rendered him unconscious. He wondered if this was what Kayla had gone through every time she'd had a vision. No wonder she'd looked so drained.

The vision was unlike anything he'd ever seen before. And that was just it—he wasn't really *seeing* anything. He was *feeling*—extremely strong, intense, pervasive emotions. Almost certainly the force that had stolen his consciousness.

And a nearly tangible knowledge flowed into his mind. A knowledge so real that he almost reached out to touch it, as if it were right in front of him. It was as if something was downloading information into his brain without him actually having to see it.

Kayla and Grady were in trouble; Na-um was almost here.

And they hadn't found the book.

Holun's eyes flew open. He jumped up and ran full speed toward the center of the room.

Kayla was at a loss, yet again. She knew the book was here somewhere, but where? She began circling the boulders, hoping that something would jump out at her, but nothing did. She frowned, her shoulders slumping. After all she'd been through this summer, she wanted to believe that the answer would come when she needed it, but she was still worried. Didn't they need that answer right now? What if it didn't come?

It will come to you, Kayla. Just like you were thinking: it will come to you when you need it.

Kayla smiled in Grady's direction. Although she sensed that she could still communicate with Mandy telepathically if she needed to—she and Justin had gone off to light the rest of the torches—Kayla knew that she and Grady were alone with their thoughts. Almost like they could willingly sever the connection between them and Mandy—though Kayla wasn't sure where the off switch was with Grady.

Hey!

Kayla shrugged at him, then grinned. *You know I'm kidding.*

Grady grinned back at her, then took a step toward her and slipped an arm around her shoulders. *Anything?*

Kayla closed her eyes, but it didn't seem to help. Why couldn't she see it? They *had* to find that book. Surely Na-um was almost here, and the book was their only chance.

No sooner than she'd had the thought she felt a sudden gush of air come at them from the entrance. Her stomach dropped.

"Kay . . . la!" Holun shouted, stopping just inches short of running into her. She instinctively took a step back.

"What is it Holun?"

Holun was bent over with his hands on his knees, his chest and back heaving with each drawn breath. "Na-um . . . soon . . . here."

Kayla's eyes flew to Grady's. His wide eyes clearly reflected what she knew was in her own: they were dead.

"Holun, we don't know where the book is. We need your help!" Kayla was yelling and couldn't seem to catch her breath.

Holun offered what Kayla thought was the most sorrowful expression she'd ever seen. "I sorry . . . Kayla." He paused for another breath. "You only know where book."

Kayla sighed. It was all up to her, and she was going to get them all killed.

But then Grady had a thought. *Kayla, since you can't see it on your own, why don't I try too? Maybe our collective brainpower will help.*

Kayla looked up at him and shrugged. *Couldn't hurt.*

She reached for Grady's hands as they faced each other and slid their eyes shut as one. Kayla felt the world fall away, felt Grady enter her mind more completely than he ever had—the sensation was intoxicating and indescribably intimate. Their minds melded into one, creating a stronger consciousness than she could have imagined. She felt something course through her veins, a subtle power trying to push its way to the surface; her skin had started tingling. A smile turned up the sides of her mouth—she couldn't help it. She knew Grady completely now; nothing was hidden. She knew everything in his past, everything he'd been through. She knew all his mistakes and triumphs, all the lies he'd told, all the apologies he'd made. And, despite all his faults, she loved him even more. She didn't love him in spite of them—she loved him *because* of them. He was hers, and she was his; nothing else mattered.

And suddenly they knew where it was. About twenty feet from where they were standing, under an unexceptional place in the floor, was the book they needed.

Kayla's eyes slid open and she met Grady's gaze immediately. He smiled at her as they both turned toward that spot in the floor. Then they were running.

Grady reached it first and placed his hands on the ground, exactly like they'd both just seen. But nothing happened.

Let me try, Kayla thought, and Grady immediately stood and moved out of the way. *Contact Mandy, Grady. Get them over here now.*

Kayla knelt on the ground and placed both hands on the sandy floor. As soon as she did, the ground started moving beneath her. She quickly sat up, pulling her hands away. The sand and dirt started falling, receding into the ground as a hole began opening up just in front of her. For an instant, Kayla saw a flash of what she now knew was coming, how she would be able to do this to any piece of earth anywhere, with just a single thought. The idea both terrified and excited her at the same time.

Mandy and Justin came running up and stood next to Grady and Holun, who'd just joined her. Kayla still couldn't hear Justin, but she assumed that would change once they had the final book in their possession. She suspected *everything* would change once they had the book.

Then the sand stopped moving in front of her and, like an apparition appearing out of the darkness, her book came into view. *Her* book.

Kayla reached down into the hole and grasped the book that seemed to almost be floating in mid-air. Her skin was tingling again; she wasn't really sure when it had stopped, but it was definitely back.

She pulled on the book, praying it would give way. After a few seconds of the book sticking onto whatever was holding it up, the book released. Kayla fell back, now seated on the ground with the book lying on her lap. The second the book was out of the hole, the sand moved in to fill the empty space, and soon the ground looked as though it had never been disturbed.

What happened next was so unexpected, she couldn't have seen it coming in a million years, even with her visions of the future. The book's cover—with the symbol for "earth" emblazoned on it, just as Kayla had expected—flipped open of its own accord and the pages started fluttering, as if in a light breeze. Soon the pages started flipping faster and faster, until Kayla had to clutch the covers of the book in her hands to keep it stable. What was happening?

The ceiling started to crack open, streaming what looked like sunlight through a thousand tiny fissures. The light radiated throughout the room until it was nearly blinding. It hadn't been that bright outside, right?

Through the cracks in the ceiling, tiny pieces of the light broke off and started flying through the air. Soon hundreds of small balls of light were floating like large fireflies around the cavern. One tiny ball of light floated in front of Kayla's eyes as she stood to her feet, the light following her eyes. She gasped as she saw what seemed impossible: in its center were words, images, symbols . . . simply put, information itself was flying around their heads toward the book. Kayla's eyes widened as she took it all in.

The book absorbed all the information swirling through the air until the air was clear, then slammed shut. The bright light from above shut off abruptly, and they were left standing in the dimly lit room once again.

The book was now amazingly much heavier, as if many pages had been added. Kayla could actually feel the weight of all the added information in the book as she struggled to pick it up. She glanced down at it, and her mouth fell open at what she saw.

The cover was no longer emblazoned with the symbol for earth—or, rather, it wasn't *only* emblazoned with the symbol for earth. It was now accompanied by four other symbols. Three of them Kayla had already seen on the other books: water, fire, air. The four symbols of the elements were arranged in each of the four corners, surrounding a single symbol in the center. In her mind, she heard Grady ask her what it was.

As soon as she heard him read the answer in her thoughts, he leaned in closer, his fingers reaching to trace the symbol in the center. His eyes widened.

"What is it, Kayla?" Mandy asked. "What does it say?"

Kayla took a breath before answering her friend's question. When she did, she spoke only one word. "Codex."

"Codex?" Justin asked. "What does that mean?"

In response to Justin's question, Kayla automatically switched into teaching mode. "Literally, 'codex' means 'book.' But for the Mayans, the connotation is different."

"How?" Mandy asked.

"Knowledge was all-important to the Mayans. They valued it above anything else. So in the Mayan language, 'codex' holds a much stronger meaning. A codex for them means, roughly, 'where all knowledge is held.'"

"So what does that symbol have to do with this book? Is this what Holun was talking about?" Justin persisted.

But Kayla didn't answer.

Grady was trying to breathe. He'd heard what Kayla had said, but his brain hadn't quite registered it, not yet. Something else was happening.

Kayla felt it too and stopped talking, despite Mandy and Justin's repeated attempts to ask her questions about the symbol. Something had started sparking through the air, like tiny lightning bolts, vastly different than before. Something that was every bit as foreboding as the lighted spheres of knowledge had been illuminating. Something that made her freeze as the hairs on the back of her neck stood on end.

Mandy noticed Grady and Kayla's expressions and realized something was going on. "What's happening?" As soon as the words were out of her mouth, she felt it, too.

So did Justin.

The four of them stood still in the silence, their skin tingling. Something otherworldly was shooting through the air, something intangible but very, very real. Something was coming.

Holun, staring into the charged air filled with crackles of light, understood what was happening. He knew that they had finally found the Codex, the Great Secret of his Clan. The Codex would give these Americans powers, the powers they needed to defeat Na-um and his army. The Codex would change their lives forever.

He hoped they were ready for it.

Kayla's breathing sped up as her heart started beating out of her chest. Something was flying through the air, headed their way. She could barely see it, and then only intermittently, but she unequivocally knew it was there.

The four of them were standing in a rough circle, with Holun off to the side and Kayla holding the Codex between them. All at once, the Codex flew open and lit up like the sun, shooting what could only be described as lightning out from its pages. Four lightning beams shot out at each of the four in the circle.

Then the lightning was gone, as quickly as it had come. And Kayla had to remember how to breathe.

She felt it. The Power of the Codex. It was flowing through her veins this very moment. And all at once she knew they had the power to defeat Na-um, to defeat his men, to defeat anything in their way. The Power was intoxicating.

Grady's voice in her head brought her back down to earth. He was feeling the same power she was, but he wasn't letting it take him over; he was fighting. *Don't let it control you.* You *control* it.

Kayla nodded, struggling to get herself under control. She could do this. She was born for this, after all; she knew it now, absolutely. This was her Destiny.

CHAPTER 44

Power

MANDY WAS FEELING IT, too. Raw power coursed through her veins, flowed over her skin, enveloped her entire being with crushing force. She struggled to remain standing, struggled to breathe as the power rushed around the cavernous room. She fought to make sense of what was happening.

From what she could tell, the rest of them were feeling it, too. The four of them were still standing in a rough circle, but the fact that something had definitely changed was glaringly obvious. All four of them were giving off an almost perceptible energy which left their skin with a faint glow. Almost as if they were illuminated from within—which Mandy suspected was exactly the case. Mandy stared down at her hands. Her skin was glowing, too.

Kayla's discovery of the final book had given them the Power, just as Holun said it would. Anyone could see that. She could *feel* it. But now what? What happened next?

What was her power supposed to be? She tried to think back to what she knew of the Old Ones . . . she thought she was supposed to have power over the air, but what did *that* mean? Didn't Kayla say something about reading minds . . . ?

But she wasn't hearing anything. She couldn't even hear Justin like she could before, or even Kayla. Only the sound of her own thoughts reverberated in her head. She closed her eyes and concentrated, trying to make it—whatever "it" was —work. Should it be this hard?

Nothing happened. Her eyes flew open. Something was very wrong.

Holun heard it first. With his super-hearing, that wasn't much of a surprise.

Something had just entered the tunnel. From the sounds of it, Na-um and his army of men were almost here.

And by the looks on the faces of his American friends, they had no idea. They were more concerned with the powers they'd just received. Understandable.

He'd heard all the stories of the Old Ones and knew what their powers were—and how they worked. Certainly whoever was able to read minds could hear what he was thinking now, maybe even hear Na-um's thoughts, and could warn the rest of the group.

But whoever it was didn't seem to notice; no one seemed to be reacting. What was going on?

He walked closer to the group, not wanting to make any unnecessary noise. Na-um could probably hear them by now, so it was best not to let him know they knew he was coming.

Holun reached Mandy first, and stepped carefully into her line of view. He didn't want to touch her—she was still glowing.

The terror evident in her wide eyes made Holun freeze. Something was wrong, and she knew it. She stared past him, through him, unseeing. Holun shuddered.

"Mandy?" He whispered tentatively, as quietly as he could.

But he wasn't answered by Mandy. It was Kayla's voice that came from behind him. "Holun, what is it?"

Holun turned. He could see the aura around Kayla illuminating her skin. And he could see, beneath the surface, how hard she was fighting to control it. He stepped toward her, wanting to help. She had received her power last, so the change would be the most abrupt.

But, at this point, that didn't matter. She would have to get her power under control. And by the sounds coming up the tunnel, it would have to be very soon.

Kayla was still straining, fighting to keep herself under control. The Power was threatening to take over.

You've got this, Kayla. Fight.

She nodded once at Grady's comment but kept her eyes straight ahead, knowing he would understand. She saw Holun standing in front of her, and tried to concentrate on him. Maybe focusing on something else would make it easier to control the power beneath her skin, the power that was scratching and clawing its way to the surface.

Holun didn't look well. In the flickering light of the nearby torches, she could see that all the blood had drained from his face.

"Holun, what's wrong?" She took a few steps toward him. It was the first time she'd moved since the powers of the Codex had taken over her body.

The movement seemed to help. Her body was slowly coming out of the initial shock and the power seemed to be ebbing, just a little. She took a few more steps and began to breathe a little easier.

Kayla reached Holun and placed a hand on his shoulder. He slowly looked up at her. The moment their eyes met, she knew. Without him having to say anything, she knew Na-um was almost here.

She jumped back as if Holun had shocked her. Her eyes were wide as she stared at him. The world slowed down, and the only thing her mind could register was the sound of Grady's voice in her head.

Kayla . . .

The world started to spin on its axis, disorienting her. But it wasn't the disorientation that sneaks in just before passing out. She had that heady feeling that comes just moments after realization, and just moments before that realization turns into reality.

Then the world suddenly sped up.

The Four jumped into action, almost as if they'd known what to do all along. They lined up next to Kayla, all facing Holun and the entrance to the cave. Kayla's voice came with a resolute determination. "Na-um and his men are close."

The Four acknowledged her comment, but not by any outward gesture. Kayla just somehow knew they'd heard her, and they were ready.

Grady reached for her hand. Kayla didn't realize until Grady touched her that she was trembling. He held her hand tightly, then looked at their tiny guide standing between them and Na-um's army. "Holun, go."

Holun shook his head furiously.

Grady took a step toward their young friend, dropping Kayla's hand. "Holun, we can't fight them with you here. We can't worry about you while we're fighting. We can't let you get hurt."

"I take care myself." Kayla could've sworn his chin rose up a full inch.

She started to worry. They didn't have time to fight this particular battle, especially not when a much more dangerous one was imminent.

But Grady, diplomatic as always, just nodded. "I know you can, Holun. But we couldn't live with ourselves if you were hurt because of us. Can you understand that?"

Holun hesitated, then nodded reluctantly. "Yes." His shoulders slumped. He turned around to walk away, but froze in his tracks.

He was staring into the eyes of Death itself. Na-um had arrived.

"Holun, go." Grady's voice was a growling command, and Holun didn't argue this time. He snatched up the book, then turned and ran for the wall. He was out of sight in less than a second.

"So nice to see all of you again." Na-um's voice was sickeningly sweet as hundreds of his men flowed into the room like the crashing waves of a violent river. Na-um smirked.

Grady stood unwavering, a step in front of the other three. His hands were out at his sides, palms facing backward as if trying to shield them.

Na-um's mocking laugh echoed throughout the room. "Your show of arrogance will not stop me. You cannot stop me."

Now it was Grady's turn to smirk. Kayla took a step around him and stood at his side. Mandy and Justin followed suit.

Na-um's smile faltered.

No. It couldn't be. Surely they didn't . . .

But looking at the four Americans standing in front of him, Na-um saw it. It was undeniably obvious, painfully so. He saw it on their faces, in the glow of their skin, in the assuredness of their stance.

They had found the Codex.

"NOOOOOOOOO!!" Na-um growled, his voice the sound of the devil himself. "HOLUN! You have BETRAYED your FAMILY! COME OUT AND FACE US!"

Holun cowered behind the rock formation in the middle of the room, out of sight, hugging the Codex close to his chest. Na-um's voice reverberated off every surface in the cavern. The sound chilled him to the bone.

But he wouldn't come out. He wouldn't leave the shelter of these rocks. If he did, Na-um would certainly tear him into pieces, gouge out his eyes, and feed him to the nearest jaguar.

Something he would definitely like to avoid, if possible.

Justin was grinning. Na-um was furious, and he was enjoying every minute of it. But this would soon get ugly, and he had to be ready.

He thought back to everything Kayla'd told them about the powers of the Codex—which was painfully little. But given the symbol on his book . . . he should be able to control fire, right? Made sense. He could harness one of the four elements of nature—fire—and use it against his enemies. Of course.

But how? Did he just think it and it happened? Did he have to concentrate, or would it just come naturally? Could he call it from anywhere, or did some fire source have to be nearby? So many questions needed to be answered, but he knew they wouldn't have time to even ask the questions. When this fight started, using their powers correctly would come down to trial and error.

Their lives depended solely on trial and error. Great.

Na-um turned back to the Four, nostrils flaring. A guttural sound rose up from between his clenched teeth, making the hairs on the back of Kayla's neck stand up a second time. He would attack soon, she was sure of it. And an attack would almost certainly hurt at least one of them. So to protect herself and her friends, she needed to attack before he had the chance.

She took a deep breath then and held it. She concentrated as hard as she could; her eyes squeezed shut, her brows furrowed. Tiny beads of sweat broke out on her forehead. She held her hands out at her sides, palms out, facing Na-um's army. She released the breath she was holding, then began pulling air in and out in a slow, hypnotic rhythm. Her breathing gradually sped up, her chest rising and falling with each gasp. Then, as she summoned all the power of the Codex within her, her body rippled, shuddering once. A quick burst of energy shot through her body to her hands. Her eyes flew open. She could hear it in Grady's thoughts: her eyes were the light brown color of sand.

Grady gasped, but she barely registered it. The Power was flowing through her; she could feel it. Now she just had to release it.

She slowly lifted her hands in front of her, turning her arms so her palms still faced out. Between her outstretched arms, she spotted at least fifty soldiers. After a quick breath, she tightened her arms, straightening them out in one sudden motion. As she did, energy—it couldn't really be explained any other way—shot out from her hands toward the soldiers in front of her. At once the ground underneath the men disappeared—and amid the sound of rushing sand came the screams of several dying men. The earth swallowed them almost instantly. Then their cries for help abruptly cut off.

Kayla slowly lowered her hands. She looked over at Grady, who was staring at her with his mouth open. She blinked a few times, clearing the sandy coloring from her eyes. She knew the moment it did; she could hear it in Grady's thoughts.

She smiled briefly at him, then turned back to look at Na-um. Her less-than-subtle display of power was intended to set Na-um off. He and his men were trained in warfare; the only chance they had was for him to retaliate, react out of anger rather than calculated precision. Perhaps then he would make a mistake, and the Four would have a chance.

Grady was still shocked at Kayla's brutal display of power, but he understood why she'd done it. He could hear her plan as clearly as if he'd come up with it himself. He nodded slowly, fighting to regain his composure, and turned to face Na-um and his men by her side.

Justin was off to the right, still staring at the bare patch of earth that had only seconds earlier held nearly fifty men. He was surprised by Kayla's harsh actions, but quickly realized that she hadn't really had a choice. If she'd waited for Na-um to attack, it could be one of them lying under the ground right now. It was kill or be killed, the most primal of human instincts.

Justin looked over at Kayla and Grady, who were now facing Na-um together, waiting to see how he would react. He wished he knew what the plan was. That would be helpful.

He looked down for a split second. It was the wrong thing to do. All at once, hundreds of flaming arrows filled the room, heading toward the four of them. If he had been looking, he might have seen them aim, might have been able to anticipate the attack, and dodge it. But he'd missed it, and now there was nothing he could do.

Everything flipped into slow motion. He stared as the arrows arched through the room, leaving trails of light in their wake. His stomach dropped as he saw three of them headed right for Mandy.

Mandy, who had moved to the right side of the room during Kayla's attack, saw the arrows coming for her. If only she could call her power, like Kayla had, she may be able to fend them off somehow. It seemed right to her, although she didn't quite know how. She just needed to figure out how to release the power inside her.

She tried to concentrate as Kayla had, tried to replicate what she had seen. But nothing happened. She should have known that it would work differently for her. Of course, that didn't really help anything now. The flaming arrows were headed for her, and she couldn't call her power. There was nowhere to run, and she couldn't stop them.

The second before they hit, she gasped. She felt as though something had hit her, but not the arrows. Almost as if she'd been hit by a brick wall. She staggered back, falling down. The arrows fell, lighting up the ground around her. One arrow grazed by her thigh, setting the leg of her shorts on fire. She screamed.

Justin was already next to her, tearing off his shirt. He threw the shirt over Mandy's leg and smacked it frantically, snuffing the fire out. He pulled the shirt away carefully. The fire had burned a hole through the shorts and had scarred Mandy's leg. Mandy winced.

Justin pulled her close, keeping an eye on the army before them. He would know if they started to attack again.

"What happened?" Justin whispered into her hair without looking at her.

Mandy shook her head. "I don't know. My power's not working; something's blocking it." Whatever she'd felt just before the arrows fell, it was preventing her from being able to use her power. She was certain of it.

She felt Justin freeze against her. Mandy froze in response. She couldn't see Na-um or his men. Were they going to attack again? She looked around Justin. Nope, nothing.

Kayla and Grady were still standing their ground in front of them. So what was wrong?

Then Justin relaxed against her. He leaned in and breathed a quiet "I love you" in her ear.

She certainly didn't expect to hear that. "What?" She choked on the word as it came out.

"I need you to know that I love you."

"I do know that, Justin. Why are we talking about this now?"

"Because you need to trust me again."

"Why now?" She repeated her question.

"If something happens here tonight, I need you to know how I feel. And I need to know how you feel."

It was the perfect opening; Mandy knew that. All she had to say was that she trusted him, that she loved him. But she still wasn't sure herself. She couldn't lie to him, couldn't lie to herself. "Justin . . ." her voice cracked.

His grip on her loosened slightly. He pulled far enough away to look at her face. "Why can't you trust me?"

Mandy shook her head. This was too much. Her leg felt as though it were on fire, and an army of men was about to attack them. She couldn't deal with this right now. "Justin, we can talk about this later." She put a hand on the ground and tried to lift herself up. It didn't work so well. She stumbled; Justin's arms were the only thing that kept her from falling hard on the rocks below. She let him sit her back down. She needed to think.

Kind of difficult considering she was only a hundred feet or so away from hundreds of men who wanted her dead.

CHAPTER 45

Battle

JUSTIN POSITIONED HIMSELF between Mandy and the army, his back to the mercenaries. Screw Na-um and his army. This was the most important thing now; he could feel it. This was why their powers weren't working. She didn't trust him, and it was blocking their powers. They needed the Power of the Four for their powers to fully work, and Mandy was cutting herself off from the Power by not trusting him. And his power was blocked because of what he'd done to lose her trust.

It shouldn't have made sense. He knew that. But it was the truth. He could feel it deep inside his soul. If Mandy couldn't trust him, they could never tap into the full power of the Codex, and would never be able to win against Na-um and his men. Kayla and Grady couldn't fight them alone, especially not at full strength.

He looked over his shoulder at Grady and Kayla. They were keeping Na-um at bay, so far. Kayla and Grady were standing on what could've been the only uncluttered patch of dirt in the whole room—the rest was littered with the remains of spent arrows, including the place where he and Mandy were sitting. Justin watched as Grady drew in a deep breath, then shot his hands toward the rock face on the left side of the large room with a jerk. Justin's breath caught as a flood of water burst out of the side of the rock and poured out over at least a hundred of Na-um's men, drowning them almost immediately. The waterfall grew even larger, catching more and more men in its wake. Na-um was losing men quickly.

But that would change unless he and Mandy could work this out. He was hoping against hope that it would be soon.

Mandy sat there, staring at Justin but not really seeing him. She was thinking.

She'd trusted Justin once; what had changed? She still loved him, she was sure of that. But trust? That was a lot more complicated.

She wasn't quite sure what had happened. She couldn't pinpoint a specific moment where she had stopped trusting him; she just had. And she didn't know why.

So how could she fix something when she didn't know why it was broken?

She sighed. She needed more time. She'd thought she'd have more time. But sitting here, staring at the hundreds of men who wanted to kill her, she knew the time was up. The decision had to be made, yes or no. Could she trust him?

Instantly, she knew. Despite everything that had happened between them, she was willing to trust him. It was no longer a question of if she *did* trust him; it was if she *could* trust him. Asking the question that way, the answer was obvious. The difference was small, but crucial. She knew she *could* trust him, and, whether it was now or later, she was willing to try.

That was all it took. At once she could hear him.

Justin, I love you. I'm sorry.

Mandy, I will always love you. With all my heart.

I've always loved you. I know I can trust you; it may just take awhile for it to be automatic. But for right now, here tonight . . . She paused, drawing in a breath. *I trust you.*

Justin smiled and got to his feet, reaching for her hand and helping her up. The power coursing through her veins had numbed her leg; she could barely feel the burn on her thigh. Maybe this power would come with some beneficial side effects, like faster healing. She could hope.

Justin laughed out loud at the thought. Mandy smiled at him as she grabbed his hand. She pulled him along as they ran toward Kayla and Grady. Their friends needed their help. No sense in making them win this alone.

Grady heard Mandy and Justin come up on his right. He was still controlling the waterfall; he'd tried to let it go, but it had started to dissipate. He sighed. It was going to take him a while to learn everything.

Then, suddenly, something occurred to him. He hadn't really "heard" Mandy and Justin come over, not in the normal sense. He had heard their thoughts as they came running up. He flashed a glance at Kayla. She could hear them, too. Was that supposed to happen?

Kayla simply shrugged in response, but kept an eye on Na-um. He had positioned his army between them and the entrance, blocking any chance of escape. Kayla had been systematically taking out his men with her earth-moving trick, but they were quickly catching on. Once they realized what she was about to do, they just ran to another spot. And they could run *fast*.

So she decided to try something else. If she could make the ground disappear, why couldn't she also raise it? If she could, she could block Na-um's path to them. It might at least buy them time to regroup, get a plan together. It was worth a try.

She raised her outstretched arms, this time with her palms facing up. Na-um's men looked a little confused. Good. She tightened her arms again, this time throwing her arms upward, forcing the power of the earth up instead of out.

It worked. A large mound of dirt started growing between them and Na-um's army. She raised her arms further, coaxing the mound of dirt higher and higher until it nearly reached the ceiling. There. An effectual wall stood between them and Na-um's army.

But Kayla could already hear the men shouting, trying to find ways through the sand wall. They would be here soon.

She turned—with one hand outstretched toward the wall to ensure it stayed standing—to Mandy, who was standing next to her. "How are you?" She looked down at the burn on Mandy's leg. It was hard to miss.

Mandy shrugged it off. "It looks worse than it feels. Doesn't even hurt. I'll be fine."

Grady came over, the waterfall beyond the sand wall abandoned for now. "You can fight?"

Mandy flashed a pointed glance at Justin that Kayla didn't quite understand at first. But once she heard the story flash through Mandy's mind, she got it. "Yeah, our powers are good. We can help." She grinned at Justin before turning back to the group. "What's the plan?"

Grady looked over at Kayla, who nodded slightly. He turned back to Mandy and Justin. "Can you both hear us?"

The couple turned toward each other, brows furrowed, then Kayla watched as their faces relaxed simultaneously. It would have almost been comical if there wasn't an army waiting to slaughter them less than a hundred feet away.

They must not have even noticed in all the confusion. Seemed like it would be hard to do, but Kayla understood. Once she'd been able to hear Grady, it seemed normal. She wondered if she'd start worrying if she *couldn't* hear Grady anymore, like before. Probably.

Mandy's mouth was slightly open; Justin's eyes were wide. Mandy found her voice first. "How is this happening?"

Grady just shrugged. "Probably comes with the powers. Let's hope it doesn't get too intrusive." He glanced at Kayla smugly, allowing just a tiny portion of the passion he felt for her to come to the forefront of his thoughts.

"Hey!" Justin spoke up.

Kayla shot Grady a chastising glance. He just laughed in response.

Mandy smacked him in the arm. "Keep those thoughts to yourself."

Grady just grinned. Then the Four heard sand start to trickle behind them. Kayla turned around. Despite her efforts to keep it standing, the wall was starting to come apart. They would soon be out of time.

So Kayla didn't waste time forming her thoughts into speech as she strained to hold up the wall. *I'll hold them off as long as I can. Grady?*

I'll send some water up the tunnel. I should be able to keep it away from us. Can someone push them out toward the tunnel?

Sure, Justin chimed in. *My pleasure.* Kayla could hear him smiling.

Mandy? Kayla asked.

I'll hold them off. I should be able to trap them. We'll see.

Kayla nodded as the sand in front of her started trickling faster. Sand was now pouring out of numerous holes in the wall. Kayla could see some of the men through the holes. They had to hurry. *Okay, Mandy, take left, Justin take right. Grady and I will take the middle.*

Everyone nodded and moved into position.

Let's hope this works.

Na-um was starting to get irritated. His men were dying off, sometimes hundreds at a time. It wasn't right.

Okay, he was more than just a little irritated. He was losing men, and the four humans were so far unscathed.

Human. Ha. He was lying to himself if he thought they were still human. Sure, they *were* human, technically—they weren't dead, after all—but they were so far beyond human now that they could hardly pass as such. They had been given the Great Secret, the Powers of the Codex, by some cruel twist of fate.

He had to stop them. Surely Destiny did not believe these foolish Americans deserved the Power. It wasn't possible. Right?

But what if they *did* deserve it? What if the Americans were meant to receive these powers all along? Was all his planning, all this fighting for nothing? If he was destined to lose, why even try?

All at once the fight fizzled out of him. Perhaps Destiny had had a different plan all along.

Na-um's men had knocked down most of the wall. Kayla took down the remainder of the wall in a sandstorm, in the hope that the flurry of sand and dirt would disorient them. It seemed to work, for a moment.

Grady, focusing all his attention back on the waterfall that had reduced to nothing but a trickle without his power, started the water rushing again. Any help he could give would be, well, helpful.

Kayla smiled at the thought as she kept the sand swirling through the air. She would let the others get in place, then she would be able to let the sand go.

Then she had a novel idea. She asked Grady what he thought as she mulled it over herself.

It's worth a shot.

Kayla nodded. She collected all the swirling sand above her head, gathering it into a loose, oblong ball, then hurled it at the waterfall. As she expected, the sand turned to mud as it hit the water. It slopped to the ground, but only managed to collect around the feet of a few men.

Grady's thoughts echoed her own. *We need more. A lot more.*

Kayla collected more and more sand and sent it spinning toward the waterfall. Soon the river below the waterfall was an ever-expanding mud pit. The mud was spreading around the feet and ankles of Na-um's men. That would slow them down.

✻

Justin could feel the power flowing through him; it was a great feeling. He shook out his arms, his hands, his neck, then starting jumping up and down. He knew he looked for all the world like an athlete about to make a jump shot, but hey, whatever worked.

He stopped abruptly, letting the power collect in his body until he felt like he was ready to explode. He rode it like a wave, enjoying the feeling. He reached out his hands, palms down. Fire exploded from his hands in a rush, the force of it causing his body to jerk. The fire spread along the ground toward Na-um's men. They started to scream and move away. Justin put more power behind the rush of fire. All at once, the men in front caught on fire. He could hear their screams for only an instant before the fire took them. Luckily, the fire wasn't cruel.

They were winning, no competition; nothing could stop them now.

The minute he thought it, he regretted it. He had just jinxed them all.

Something was about to change; it pretty much had to. Murphy's Law.

✻

Na-um had only about three hundred men left of the five hundred he had brought with him. What would he tell their families? Would their sacrifices all be for nothing?

What had he become? He had been willing to kill the Americans to prevent them from getting the Powers, but they had gotten them anyway. Now they were killing his men. *His* men. This shouldn't be happening.

Then Na-um felt it, a rush of wind pouring into the room from behind him. Despite the cacophony in the cavern, he could clearly hear the sound of someone rushing in, coming up the tunnel, speeding faster than any human could. But all his men were here, the ones that were left, anyway. Was Holun trying to leave? No, it was coming *up* the tunnel, toward them. If it wasn't Holun, was it someone—or *something*—else?

His eyes caught a glimpse of the rush of wind as it entered the illuminated cavern. He saw long, black hair trailing out behind whatever it was. But they were moving too fast for even him to see. And he could see more clearly than most.

The figure stopped, only feet from where the girl called Kayla was standing. A gun was now pointed at her chest.

Na-um smiled wickedly. The tables were turning.

He could now clearly see that the rush of wind was a person, standing so their long hair blocked their face. Who was this intruder? Someone clearly on their side.

Then the person turned, revealing their face.

Na-um's heart stopped.

CHAPTER 46

Intruder

WHERE DID THEY COME FROM? Grady gawked at the person holding the woman he loved at gunpoint. He still couldn't see the intruder's face, only the back of their head.

Grady raised his hand, ready to attack if needed. The person simply shook their head, their long black hair swaying gently down their back. It was as if the intruder knew he was about to attack. What did he know? They probably did.

Don't. Kayla's voice echoed in his head, but it was the look in her eyes that stopped him, and the thought that followed. She recognized their intruder.

Jackie.

Kayla was staring into the eyes of perhaps the most dangerous person in the room. More dangerous than even Na-um,

Jackie's eyes showed no ounce of humanity. A cruel, harsh detachment cooled her otherwise warm countenance. She didn't know how she knew it, but Kayla was looking into the eyes of a heartless and remorseless killer.

One side of her mouth curled up. "Kayla." Her American accent was gone, replaced by the thick accent of the mercenaries. She was one of them? Was that possible?

Kayla's mind ran through the first time she'd met Jackie. She'd been a grad student, just like any other grad student in the Mayan Studies program. She'd received her bachelor's degree at the University of Central Florida before continuing on to her master's degree. Kayla had known her for years. Or she thought she had.

Apparently Jackie—or whatever her real name was—had been planning this for years. She had somehow known that this would happen. But how could she?

"How . . . why . . ." Kayla couldn't seem to form a coherent sentence.

Jackie threw her head back and laughed, a hyenic but oddly feminine laugh that echoed off the cavern walls. The gun didn't waver. "You don't deserve those powers. I'm here to take them back. I'm here to give them back to those who deserve them."

Kayla was over the shock. She found her voice. "We were supposed to be given these powers. Surely you knew that, or you wouldn't have followed us all these years." Kayla's smile was smug. She'd hoped to make Jackie angry, cause her to act rashly and maybe make a mistake, give the others time to attack.

Unfortunately for Kayla, Jackie was as calm as ever. She smiled sweetly. "Perhaps. But I have come to correct Destiny's mistake."

Kayla heard someone coming up on her right. She snuck a peek out of the corner of her eye and saw Na-um approaching. He looked like he'd seen a ghost.

Kayla's eyes flashed back to Jackie's face. She'd seen Na-um approach as well. Her smile wavered.

Na-um stopped a few feet away from them. Kayla risked a glance his way. He was still staring at Jackie. What was wrong with him?

Then Kayla saw it in his eyes. Recognition.

The thought formed in Kayla's mind the second before Na-um spoke.

"Shani?"

Jackie—rather, Shani—turned slowly to face Na-um. Her smile had recovered. "Hello, Brother."

"Brother?" Justin choked out. At the sound of his voice, Kayla realized they might have a serious problem. She mentally took stock of the Four; they were dumbfounded at this new development. Na-um seemed to be sharing the sentiment. For now. But if he recovered more quickly than they could . . .

Pay attention, guys. Be ready for an attack. Just in case. Kayla could still hear the confusion in their thoughts, but they were quickly coming out of it. They could fight if they were attacked. Kayla breathed just a little easier. But only a little. There was still a gun pointed at her chest, after all.

Na-um was still standing frozen a few feet away, eyes wide, staring at Shani. He wasn't getting over the shock as quickly as the rest of them. Understandable. "Shani . . . you . . . the Elders."

Shani smirked. It seemed as though she knew what Na-um was trying to say. "Yes, I've been working with the Elders. They came to me many years ago, before I moved to the States. It seems that you can't run away from our Clan." Her smile turned almost mournful. "I received my powers less than a year after I left. I knew then I couldn't turn away from my people. So when they contacted me, I of course agreed to help them.

"They had learned of a prophesy, one hidden in our religious texts, that explained how the Secret of the Codex would be revealed for the second time, in our time, and the bloodlines of those who would reveal it. So they enlisted my help to stop it. They knew that if they had a person inside, close to the people who would find the Codex"—Shani shot a disdainful look at Kayla—"that we would have a better chance of stopping it. Or so we thought." Kayla was still receiving that disgusted look from Shani. She stood her ground, despite the look, or the gun. If she was going down, she would go down fighting.

"Why did you keep this from me?" Na-um seemed to have found his voice. Kayla couldn't help but notice the hurt in his voice. She almost felt sorry for him. Almost.

Shani looked toward Na-um at the sound of his voice, but kept the gun trained on Kayla. Wow, she was good. Where did she learn to handle a gun like that? "The Elders thought it best you didn't know. You were already squeamish. No need to make the problem worse."

Now Na-um looked angry. Must've been the "squeamish" comment. "I was handling it. I am *not* squeamish." Yeah, it was definitely the "squeamish" comment.

Shani's gaze turned pitilessly mocking. Kayla was again tempted to feel sorry for Na-um. "You were *not* handling it. That's why I was forced to start helping you."

"*You* were our contact at Lamanai?" Na-um couldn't mask the disbelief in his voice.

"Of course." Shani shrugged nonchalantly. "But I would not have had to take such an active role had you stopped them back at Lamanai. I had to clean up *your* mess." She spat the words at him.

Na-um should've been seething, but instead he just looked sad. "You still should have told me. I've . . . wondered about you." Kayla knew he'd been about to say he missed her. It was a good idea to keep that to himself, in her opinion. Shani seemed cruel. Well, not just seemed—she *was* cruel. That wasn't really much of a mystery anymore.

"Well, wonder no longer." Shani smiled wide, a smile too nefarious to be called a grin. "Now, please step aside. I must finish what *you've* started." Each word dripped with contempt.

The hurt in Na-um's eyes tugged at Kayla's heartstrings. He turned and slinked away, head hanging nearly to his chest.

Even monsters have feelings.

Mandy was feeling sorry for Na-um, too. Her heart ached for him, wishing his sister hadn't been so malicious. He didn't deserve much, but surely he deserved a small semblance of compassion from the only family he had.

Wait . . . how did she know that? In an instant, she knew the whole story, how Shani had left the Clan when she was very young with the man she'd loved, how she'd made Na-um lie for her. How Na-um had been carrying around the guilt of the whole situation for years. But how did she know all this?

I loved her. I love her still.

What—where on earth did that come from? Mandy scanned the room, searching for the source of the voice. It didn't seem like the others could hear it; they weren't reacting to it, anyway.

She was working against me, with the Elders. I shouldn't forgive her for that.

Mandy froze. Was she hearing *Na-um's* thoughts?

Mandy, what's happening? The question came from Kayla.

Mandy hesitated, still not sure she believed it herself. *I can hear Na-um.*

After a few seconds of silence, Grady chimed in. *Incredible.*

Kayla didn't respond; she simply kept staring at Shani.

Grady continued. *Can we use this?*

Kayla spoke up. *Mandy, try to find something we can use in his thoughts. Relay it to us when you find something.*

Mandy nodded, knowing the group would understand. She listened more closely to Na-um.

I shouldn't forgive her for lying to me, keeping her plans with the Elders a secret. But I love her. And I hate that I love her. Na-um looked up as he approached his men. Mandy wondered how he would recover his image after the embarrassing display with Shani. *I could just let her handle the Americans, and I could take my men and leave. It would certainly stop any more of my men from dying.* Mandy couldn't let herself hope he'd just give up. It was tempting, though. *Or I can help her. She is my sister, one of us.*

Mandy updated the rest of the group. *He's deciding whether or not to help her. We need to be ready in case he does decide to attack. I'll try to get word to you when he decides. Hopefully it will be in time.*

The rest of the group acknowledged her comment. Justin and Grady were keeping a close watch on Shani, trying to anticipate what she would do. They hadn't had time to test their powers against speeding bullets. Looks like they might get that chance tonight.

Kayla was still staring at Shani, noting her every movement. The moment Shani flinched, she would react. Her mind was already running through the possibilities. Grady could put up a wall of water, or Justin could set Shani on fire; maybe Mandy could read when she was about to pull the trigger . . .

That seemed like the safest option. *Mandy, read Shani. See if she's going to pull the trigger. A heads-up would really help.*

She heard Mandy turn her focus away from Na-um and onto Shani. Maybe she would get a warning after all.

But after several seconds of trying, she heard Mandy sigh. *I can't hear anything. Maybe she's blocking me somehow. Sorry, Kayla.*

Kayla frowned. She would have already had Grady or Justin attack, but she couldn't be sure Shani couldn't move faster than they could. So far, their powers only worked by drawing the power to them and pushing it outward. And that gathering of power took time. Shani would certainly notice.

So they were at an impasse. She couldn't be sure if—or, more likely, when—Shani would pull the trigger. And they couldn't use their powers on her without her knowing about it.

Kayla slowly began to see a solution come into focus. The only solution she could see that would get them out of this mess.

Kayla, no. Grady's pleading voice came through her thoughts. *You can't.*

Kayla fought to ignore him.

Kayla, please. I need you. I love you.

She refused to answer.

Kayla, no!

But her mind was made up. It was the only way.

That didn't mean she had to like it.

You want me to what?!? Justin couldn't have heard Kayla correctly.

Attack Jackie.

No, Kayla, I can't! Justin didn't like where this conversation was heading. He could hear Grady protesting loudly in the back of his mind. What had he missed?

Justin, just do it. Please.

No, Kayla. She'll shoot you!

Justin heard Kayla pause. *That's the plan.*

His stomach dropped.

Kayla, I don't like this. Kayla heard Justin still protesting in her mind, but it was the only chance she had to make it out of this stalemate alive, the only way to take Shani down. She was too fast for a direct attack. They had to catch her off guard.

Justin, please. It's the only way.

Justin hesitated. She knew it would be a hard decision for him, probably one of the hardest decisions he'd ever have to make. That's why she didn't ask Grady.

She knew the instant Justin gave in. He worked to gather his power without making any movement; no need to alert Shani to the plan until absolutely necessary. Kayla steeled herself as Justin raised his hands toward Shani.

Grady screamed an ear-shattering "NO!!!!!" as Kayla felt Justin's power release from behind her. She tensed, anticipating the bullet. She knew that although the Power seemed to allow them to move much more quickly than she thought possible, there was no way she could move fast enough to get out of Shani's way in time.

The bullet hit. Kayla stopped breathing.

CHAPTER 47

End

S HE WAS STILL STANDING. She didn't know how, or why, but she was. Shani was still in front of her, but something had changed. Or, more accurately, everything had changed. The gun was still pointed at her, but it and Shani's arm were on fire. A rush of Justin's power came from behind her, and the fire snaked its way up Shani's arm, lighting her shirt on fire. She couldn't hold her arm steady anymore. She fell to the ground, writhing. The fire was spreading.

Grady grinned diabolically. "Here, let me help you with that." He collected his power, then doused Shani in a torrential flood of water. The fire was out, but now Shani was struggling to breathe. She dropped to her hands and knees, coughing erratically. She was neutralized, for now.

Kayla looked down at her chest, where she was sure the bullet hit. She didn't see anything out of the ordinary. She started patting and pulling at her shirt, at the place where she was sure she saw the bullet make contact.

Nothing.

What? How could that be? She pulled her shirt away from her, looking again for a bullet hole. But the shirt was intact. How did the bullet miss her? She looked at the ground, and there at her feet, only a few feet away from where Shani lay on hands and knees gasping, was the smashed remains of a bullet. It had definitely hit *something*.

Feeling as though the world was in slow motion, Kayla bent down. She picked the bullet up between her thumb and index finger and held it up in the dim light, struggling to see it better, trying to make sense of what had happened. She examined the bullet, but found nothing that would tell her how it hadn't hit her chest.

Kayla, look. Grady was still pouring water over Shani, but once Kayla's eyes met his, he nodded behind her. Kayla stood up and turned around in one motion. Mandy was sitting on the ground, breathing hard, and sweat had lined her forehead and soaked through the top of her shirt. This had been the plan, but Kayla was still stunned that it had actually worked.

Mandy, are you alright?

Mandy nodded at her, trying to catch her breath. *I'm fine.*

That was amazing.

Mandy offered a weak smile. *I wasn't sure it would work.*

But it did. Thank you.

Mandy simply nodded back, then stared at the ground, chest still heaving.

Kayla couldn't think of anything else to say, her mind still trying to make sense of it all. She dropped the bullet next to her would-be murderer. Shani was still on the ground, struggling to breathe. At this point, Kayla couldn't really bring herself to care.

She looked over toward Na-um and his army, but the rest of the room was empty. Na-um and what was left of his army had retreated. The Four had won the battle.

Now they just had to deal with the cleanup.

No one could see it, but Shani was crying. It was making it even harder to breathe, but she couldn't stop herself. She had failed the Elders, had failed her people. But, more importantly, she had failed Na-um, her only brother. Her only family. When the Clan had abandoned her, threatened her into servitude, Na-um had protected her. He'd put himself and his reputation on the line for her, and she had betrayed him. She'd owed him better than that.

She was glad he'd gotten away. If he'd still been here when the four Americans were done with her, they'd most certainly have turned on him and killed him. And, despite all the betrayals and lies, she didn't want to see him hurt. She'd thought she could live with it, thought she could reason it away, but she couldn't. He was her brother, and she'd turned on him. She'd never forgive herself for that.

She needed to get up, get away from this onslaught of water; she hated being on the receiving end of the Power. But to run away, she needed to be able to breathe. And that was proving difficult at the moment.

But she did have one thing. One thing no one else had. As one of the Clan's few female fighters, she was endowed with the ability to defend herself in an attack. She could push anything away from her—human or otherwise, even thoughts— so she could get away. A defensive mechanism, but useful all the same. Especially now.

She was starting to black out; she could feel it coming on. Even with the small pockets of air she was finding in the flowing water, no one can last indefinitely in a rushing flood. Despite all her powers, she still had to be able to breathe. She had to get out of here before she passed out.

Gathering her power to her, she rose up on her knees and pushed her hands outward. The water sprayed away from her hands, leaving her a small area of breathing space. She took a few deep breaths, just enough to run, then got to her feet in one fluid motion. She sped away from the room, heading down the tunnel.

As she emerged from the rocks under the night sky, she realized that she had nowhere to go. Na-um would certainly tell the Elders about her failure, and after tonight, Na-um wouldn't want her anywhere near him. And the man she loved, the one she'd left the Clan for—the one who would be waiting for her back at Lamanai, her sweet Alex—would be in danger if she went back to him. The Clan would most certainly come after them if they were together. He needed to think she was dead.

No one was her ally, not anymore. She was alone.

She ran, tears streaming down her face, to lose herself in the forest. The forest that would now be her home.

Grady wasn't sure how Shani got away, but he wasn't really worried about it. He cut off the stream of water, then sat down on the ground to rest. Keeping that much water flowing for that length of time certainly took a lot out of him.

Kayla walked over to him and joined him on the ground, resting her head against his shoulder. He knew she was just as exhausted as he was.

Justin was tending to Mandy, who was still recovering from her power burst. Grady was grateful for her willingness to push herself to the edge just to save the woman he loved. He owed her his life.

Then he felt Kayla sit up beside him and yell to the nearly empty room, "Holun! You can come out now!"

The young boy scurried out from behind the boulders and started running toward them. Kayla and Grady both stood to meet him.

Holun's grin nearly reached his ears. "You won."

Kayla nodded, chuckling. "Yes, Holun, I suppose we did."

Holun cocked his head to the side then addressed Kayla in K'iche. "Well, I hope it helped."

Kayla stopped. "What helped?"

Holun just stared. "The necklace."

Kayla's eyes widened as she involuntarily glanced down at her shirt.

Holun smiled at her, shrugging. "I had just gotten my visions when I saw that you might need it, so I sent it to you."

Kayla reached for the necklace and pulled it over her head, moving slowly, deliberately. She extended it toward Holun, pleased to feel Grady's arm drape over her shoulders as she did.

Holun took the offered charm. "Thank you." He held it up in the light and examined it for a minute. "Why don't you keep it." He tried to give the charm back to Kayla. "I don't need it."

Kayla blinked, refusing to take it. "Holun, this is yours. Shouldn't you keep it?"

Holun shook his head, dangling the charm even closer to her. "This is the emblem of the Clan. The Clan is not my family anymore; you are."

Kayla smiled with tears in her eyes, taking the necklace and dropping it around her neck once again. Somehow it now felt like it belonged there. "Thank you, Holun. We could not have done this without you."

Holun's grin was back. "I know."

Grady, hearing Kayla's translation in his head, laughed beside her.

Holun glanced over at Mandy and Justin sitting just a few feet away, then at Grady in front of him, then directly at Kayla. "Thank you all for letting me help, for helping me fulfill my Destiny. I will not forget it."

Then he switched to English. "Take care of Power!"

And with that, he was gone.

Grady stood still for a moment, trying to figure out where Holun had gone. He heard Kayla beside him concede ever knowing. He smiled, pulling her toward him for a soft kiss. That was all they had energy for tonight.

After a few lingering seconds, he pulled away slightly to find Mandy and Justin. "Are you guys ready? I think I can get us back in the dark. I have no intention of staying here tonight."

Mandy nodded vigorously. She reached for Justin's hand, pulling him to his feet and rushing over to Kayla and Grady. "Let's get out of here, please."

The Four grabbed their all-but-forgotten backpacks—and the now-complete Codex—and headed for the entrance of the room. Just before they left, Mandy turned and pushed a last burst of air through the room. The torches all flickered out simultaneously, like someone had turned off a light switch. The four of them turned to walk up the tunnel.

The night sky was comforting, a thin, starry blanket on a summer night. A light breeze had cooled the air; the humidity had dissipated with the sunlight.

The hike to the SUV was long and tiring, but Grady was grateful to be headed home, or at least back to the dig. A clean shower, a comfortable bed . . . he had to remind himself to stay awake to drive.

They made it back to Lamanai before sunrise.

Shani

SHE RAN FOR DAYS, ran until she got bored with it, ran north until she hit the ocean. Her lungs fully accommodated her exertion, her breathing as even as if she were merely sleeping.

She ended up on a Northern Canadian beach, a chilly, wind-blown landscape that chilled her to the bone despite the unrealistic prospect of summer warmth.

Shani shivered, finding a seat on a fallen log and wrapping her arms around her torso. Her tears had dried a few days ago, but an overwhelming sadness still threatened to take her over.

She'd lost so much.

She reached up to wipe a stray strand of hair from her face and tried to think of something else, anything else. But life was cruel sometimes; no matter how hard she tried to think of something other than what she'd lost, her mind would conjure up the image of Alex's face. It tore at her heart every time.

But as she wallowed in self-pity and despair, her heart sinking into the lowest depths it had ever known, things gradually started to become very clear. There was only one way to regain everything she'd lost—including the man she loved, the one she'd given up everything for so many years ago.

She'd spent a lifetime studying the Clan's histories; she knew the Elders possessed more power than anyone realized. A power that would overwhelm and make obsolete any other power, perhaps even the power of the Codex.

She knew now what she had to do, knew what would help her get back to her life, to her purpose, to her Alex.

A wide grin spread across her face as she stood and started running again, in the direction she'd come, this time toward something rather than away.

She resolved then, as the miles passing by at lightning speed turned her into a dark and muted blur, that she would succeed, she would prevail. She had to, after all. She had no choice.

Her life depended on it.

Acknowledgments

First of all, I want to say thank you to my wonderfully supportive husband, Andrew, who put up with hours of me holed up in another room, incessant fangirling about the things that just happened in my book (mostly without any context) as I was writing it, and my frequent breakdowns (with lots of tears) when I announced my book launch date and suddenly "What on earth did I do?" was my constant mantra. You ground me, and without you this book would never have been published. (Especially since you offered your editing and formatting services for free . . .) I wrote Grady before I ever knew you, but I think somehow I sensed that kind of love was possible for me, and I found it in you. You will forever be my Grady.

To everyone who helped me get the word out about my book, THANK YOU. You all are AMAZING. Beta readers, reviewers, launch team members, friends—you are all rock stars. Thank you, a million times over.

To the Instagram writing community, I seriously cannot say enough about how much I love you all. Everyone has been extremely supportive, welcoming, and positive, and so much more gracious than I deserve. I feel like I have made friends for life in such a short time—you all are astoundingly incredible. Thank you for all the many likes, comments, and shares, and for letting me fangirl about my book when you'd never even read it! You are THE BEST.

To my dad, who read the first draft of this novel chapter by chapter, as I wrote it. I'm still not sure how you did it—my writing was terrible back then! But you stuck with it, gave me input and advice, and somehow managed not to hate it. That means more than you know.

To my sister, Amanda, the inspiration behind the character of Mandy. If I ever wanted to know how Mandy would react to a situation, I pictured how you would react and wrote that. You helped me tap into her kindness, helped me understand her. Thanks for being you.

To the many authors who came before me, thank you for doing what you do. Because of your bravery, I read your books and believed that I could be an author too. To the ones that unknowingly helped me in writing this book, specifically Dan Brown, Frank Peretti, Stephenie Meyer, and Stephen King, this book exists because of your influence. You all are my heroes.

To all my fellow indie authors, we're all in this together. Thank you for doing what you do and for supporting other indie authors. Keep writing, marketing, and publishing like the bosses you are.

To my Lord and Savior, Jesus Christ, You gave me this story, and I had so much fun discovering it. Our relationship grew, developed, and changed so much over these past ten years, and in that decade You were the only constant. Thank You for saving me, so many more times than I can count.

And finally, to my readers, words cannot describe how much I appreciate you all. This book is in your hands because you chose to support an indie author who had a dream of getting her words out into the world. Thank you, thank you, THANK YOU.

WANT MORE?

Keep reading for an excerpt from Book 2 of The Codex Series, *The Prophecy of the Codex,* coming Spring 2020!

For the latest news on the release, writing advice, and random life updates, sign up at melissafrey.com to stay up to date!

#thesecretofthecodex

Glowing

*Harrington McGready Central American Exhibit Hall,
Central Florida Museum of Natural History, Gainesville,
Florida*

IF THERE'D BEEN ANYONE ELSE around, the incessant click-clacking of the security guard's nightstick against the marble walls would have been irritating. But instead, the museum's sole defender dragged his nightstick at knee level, not caring about the sound. Sometimes that was the only way to stay sane on the night shift: manufacture a distraction to make your mind believe someone else was there. Lonely job.

He really didn't mind it, most nights. He liked the solitude, the lack of micromanaging, and the pay. Plus, he got to carry a gun. Oh, he wasn't stupid about it. He knew how to handle it—in a word, *carefully*—but he liked how it made him feel: powerful. Strong.

Not that he'd admit that to anyone. Least of all his infuriating ex-girlfriend. He wondered what she was doing right now. Probably asleep next to her new *fiancé* . . .

He smacked the nightstick into his left palm, a little harder than he intended. "Ow!"

The nightstick tumbled to the marble floor, sending a clatter reverberating throughout the entire marble-clad museum. He quickly stepped on it to make it stop bouncing and froze.

Because he'd heard something.

With the echoes dissipating, he leaned down slowly, so slowly, and gently lifted the nightstick off the ground. He tilted his head, still bent over. What was that?

He carefully straightened, taking his time to make sure he wouldn't make any extra noise. He gazed across the darkened Incan exhibit, looking for something, anything that could've made the sound he'd heard. Or thought he'd heard.

He shook his head, blinking. Sometimes the mind plays tricks on you at—he checked his phone—three in the morning. Probably just a fluorescent light on somewhere.

His shoulders heaved. Five more hours until the day shift gets here. *They're all probably home, still asleep,* he thought. *Must be nice.*

There it was again.

He froze, every muscle in his body tensing. He turned to the left, toward the room around the corner that housed the rest of the Central American exhibits. Did something move in the Mayan wing? He supposed he should go find out.

He tiptoed around the Incan pyramid replica, the collection of ancient burial masks, and the ceremonial bridal dress before finally spying the doorway to the Mayan collection. Truth be told, this was his favorite room in the whole museum. The curator here had received a generous donation of Mayan artifacts just this past summer—they'd even renamed this section of the museum after the benefactor, though he didn't know who Harrington McGready was—and now it was all on display. Beautiful gems, smooth stones, colorful pottery—it was all here, in living color, and was honestly breathtaking.

And this was for a guy with a high school education.

He rounded the corner, and his view of the entire room opened up. Amid the seemingly endless parade of miscellaneous artifacts, one piece always stood out. It caught his eye whenever he entered the room. *There it is.*

Standing in its own display case, visible from nearly every corner of the L-shaped room, stood the most fascinating thing he'd ever seen. And that was saying something, given that he spent his nights surrounded by the curious and interesting.

It was a sphere, probably less than a foot in diameter, made up of what looked like solid rock. He wasn't really sure what made the object so fascinating, but he found himself drawn to it.

He came up to the display case, eyes fixed on the globe. As he did, his eyes widened. "What the—"

The sphere had started glowing.

That was the last thing he remembered.

Twelve Hours Earlier, Central Florida Museum of Natural History

The olive-skinned, dark-haired woman stepped into the lobby, tossing her long hair to the side as she pulled her handbag to her shoulder. Simon Cortez, the museum's curator, adjusted his thin, knit tie and smoothed his starched collar as he scurried through the glass door with the single word "Offices" painted across it in a muted yellow. He indulged himself a look back through the clouded glass, catching a glimpse of the thin, petite outline of his fiancée. The same thin, petite outline he'd just become intimately reacquainted with in the janitor's closet. For the fifth time this week.

The attractive woman's eyes searched the cavernous room, and Simon pulled at his light gray, perfectly tailored suit jacket as he hurried toward her. He didn't know why, but this woman just screamed VIP.

And he was nothing if he wasn't accommodating.

Her eyes found his and he stumbled slightly as he approached. *How is she doing tha*—the thought died in his brain and suddenly he forgot how to speak. The woman's eyes held his with power of a thousand chains and he tried to swallow without being too obvious. "H–Hello, Miss, may I help you?" Simon clasped his hands in front of him to remind them to be still.

Her voice was as sultry as the summer nights he spent as a child on the Riviera Maya. "Yes, thank you. I am here to view the Mayan exhibit."

Simon exhaled as she broke their gaze and his mind was suddenly clear once again. He blinked once, then directed her toward the Mayan room with a flourish of his right arm. "Of course! Right this way." His quick, staccato steps echoed in the marble room as he led her to the hall immediately to her left.

Simon walked quickly through the Incan and Aztec exhibits as soon as he noticed she was staring straight ahead. Once they passed through the large rectangular opening and into the long, L-shaped room that made up the Mayan exhibit hall, Simon launched into curator mode. Force of habit.

"To your left is a photographic display of the people from Lamanai, an archaeological dig in northern Belize, and the artifacts they found and cataloged. It was said that this particular dig was only open a short time before they found a large number of items with significant value. And next to these photographs"—Simon continued down the wall—"are reproductions of some of the hieroglyphs they found underground at the same site."

The woman was staring intently at the first display. "Are these reproductions a full representation of all the hieroglyphs they found?"

Astute observation, Simon thought. *Beautiful and smart.* "These reproductions simply give us a taste of what they found. The full text is still being analyzed and transcribed. We hope it will be available in the coming months."

The woman was frowning, so Simon quickly changed the subject, pivoting ninety degrees to show the next collection. "And these items are actual artifacts unearthed at the dig." He motioned to the large glass display case behind her. "They found a burial chamber with several pieces of pottery and other items used in the burial process." The case was inhabited by all manner of clay pieces, most only part of their former selves.

Simon turned, moving further into the room toward another display case on their right—this time one with some textiles in it. "The articles seen here are reproductions of period tapestries and garments worn by the native Mayans during the eighth and ninth centuries, just before their civilization realized a drastic decrease in their native peoples. The cause of the Mayan demise has never been determined and is a heavily debated topic among academics."

He glanced at the woman again, whose gaze was fixed on the beige wall on the far side of the room. The plain, empty wall.

He moved on. As they neared the center of the room, Simon sensed that this would be a short tour today. "Along this other wall"—he indicated the other part of the "L" in the room, to their left—"are some rare stones they discovered as well as other pictures of the modern dig, showing the archaeologists who made this discovery and who also donated all the artifacts you see here." He swept his arm in a wide arc, but then noticed the woman was frowning again. Definitely time to wrap it up.

They had reached the center of the room, and now he stopped. "And this, our final stop, is the *crème de la crème*." He moved to stand beside a smaller display standing proudly in the middle of the room. "This is a globe they found underground at Lamanai. It's said to contain a light source from within, though that is simply conjecture at this point—*I've never actually seen it light up*." Simon offered the requisite smile then fell quiet. Though the other cases dwarfed its size, there was something otherworldly about this piece that gave it the most presence in the room. Simon loved to bring patrons in for a tour and watch their reactions.

And he wasn't disappointed. The dark-haired woman leaned in toward the piece, her eyes widening. Simon even thought he saw them sparkle.

"Incredible," the woman breathed and Simon followed her gaze, staring at the artifact next to him. Atop a marble pedestal, at just about chest height and behind four walls—and a ceiling—of glass, a curious globe sat. Simon had always wondered what made this piece so special; it honestly looked like a spherical piece of tan-colored rock.

But as he watched the globe, he noticed something start to happen. As the woman stared into its center, Simon could've sworn the globe was lighting up—*reacting* to her.

No, that would be ridiculous. Simon straightened his back and adjusted his suit jacket again, then cleared his throat. "Would you like to stay here a little longer?"

The woman never took her eyes off the subtly glowing sphere. "Yes, I would like that very much."

Simon nodded once. "Very good." Then he turned on his heels and had to remind himself not to run through the gallery. He suddenly didn't want to be in the same room with that woman and that globe another minute.

CHAPTER 1

The Globe

Anthropology Department, University of Central Florida, Orlando

"Okay, so what's the first step in excavating an archaeological site?"

Dr. Kayla Harrington gazed around at her freshman class, the only class of bright-eyed newbies she had this year. They sat in black wheeled office chairs behind long, off-white tables on four wide, tiered, burgundy-carpeted rows. This was her largest class, but the classroom was cramped; she'd taken to leaving her warmer clothes at home on Tuesdays and Thursdays for this very reason. She made a mental note again to talk to Dean Stewart about changing rooms before the next semester began.

Because the fall semester was almost over—the closer they got to Thanksgiving, then Christmas break, she could see the students' attentiveness exponentially decrease—and she was grateful. She loved to teach, even freshmen, but their naivety sometimes frustrated her. She much rather enjoyed the Masters' students. Not that she'd ever admit that aloud. Probably not even to Grady. Of course, he would know anyway . . .

A tiny, spectacled girl in the second row raised her hand. Kayla nodded at her. "Gretchen?"

The girl swallowed before answering. "We use radar and/or land surveys to find where the artifacts are placed . . . ?" She let the statement hang, ending the sentence with a question.

Kayla nodded once. *At least she was listening at some point this semester* . . . "Very good. Next?" She glanced around the room.

A dark-haired boy named Tommy answered from the fourth row. "We map the site."

Kayla nodded again. "And how do we do that?"

Tommy continued. "We place stakes and twine in a grid pattern, noting the location of every stake."

Kayla smiled. "Very thorough. Someone else want to take the next step?"

Blonde Holly in the back spoke up. "We start excavation. Tools and methods will vary depending on the type of soil, weather conditions, and condition of the artifacts."

Kayla clasped her hands in front of her, nodding once again. "Good." She glanced at the clock on the wall to her left facing the row of windows to her right. "Looks like that's all the time we have for today. The final is two weeks from today. And remember your semester paper is due Tuesday." She always thought it was cruel to have a paper due *after* Thanksgiving, so she liked to collect them the class before the students left for the break.

"I will finish up my lectures in the next class, then we'll have a few of you present your papers the following week. We're in the home stretch." She smiled, and most of the students grinned back. She walked back to her lectern. "See you Tuesday."

Kayla collected her things as her students did the same, but not so quietly. She smiled to herself. *These young kids sure do have a lot of life in them.*

Her phone buzzed on the desk next to her. She glanced over, her smile widening as she read the text that just came through. Grady, wanting to meet for lunch. As always.

She packed her things more quickly.

"Hey, beautiful." Grady stood to pull out the wrought-iron bistro chair for Kayla as she approached. He'd picked this place specifically for her; he knew it was her favorite restaurant on campus.

"You're crazy," she shot back with a smile on her face as she scooted in toward the table.

Grady sat down and reached for her hand, smiling. "Crazy about you." He knew it was cheesy, but he couldn't help himself. Kayla made him feel alive, almost like he hadn't been really living before her. And besides, Grady knew she didn't mind.

Since this past summer, when their relationship had started, things had been moving quickly. And given all that had happened this summer—finding the Codex and receiving its Power, namely—their swift romance made sense.

I love you, Grady McGready. Always will.

Grady grinned at Kayla's thoughts in his head. They'd been able to hear each others' thoughts for several months now, and he honestly loved it. But as his mind started down a path he knew she wasn't ready for yet, he had the realization that sometimes it could be a little problematic . . .

He quickly spoke, pushing the thoughts from his mind. The last five or so months had given him a little practice in being able to surprise Kayla—not a small feat when the woman could hear his thoughts. "So what sounds good today?"

Kayla gave a perfunctory glance at the menu. They came here almost every day, and every day the same song and dance. She'd peruse the menu, pretend to want to try something new, then always settle on one of the three dishes she ordered here. Fish sandwich, soup of the day, or . . .

"Probably the barbecue bacon burger."

Grady grinned. Yep, that was the third one.

"How about you?" Kayla took a sip of her ice water, her eyes smiling at his thoughts in her head.

Grady scanned the menu. He did his best to try new things whenever he had the chance, but sometimes it was exhausting. That's when he decided today was going to be a boring day. "Chicken tenders basket."

Kayla scrunched her nose, smiling, and Grady knew why. Fried food didn't agree with her. Neither did dairy, and she didn't like mushrooms. Or kale. She hated kale.

He loved that he knew nearly everything about her.

Their favorite waiter stepped up to their small jet-black, wrought-iron table in his signature gray high-top sneakers. "Grady, Kayla, hi! How are you both this fine Florida day?"

They smiled up at the skinny, bespectacled young man dressed all in black from his neck to his ankles, his shoes the one aberration management allowed. That and the multiple arm tattoos exposed by the rolled sleeves of his button-up shirt. "Glen, hi! How are your classes going?" Grady knew from their previous conversations that he was a junior economics major, with a minor in statistics. The guy loved business and numbers. Grady's polar opposite.

Glen rested his forearm against his notepad, pen in hand. "Oh, they're going well. Next semester's gonna be crazy, but I'll figure it out." He turned to Kayla. "How are you?"

Kayla smiled up at him. "I'll be glad when this semester's over." She grinned. "And also hungry."

Glen chuckled. "What can I get for you?"

"Barbecue bacon burger, how it comes. With a side salad instead of fries. Olive oil and lemon for the dressing." She handed Glen her menu, who took it and turned to Grady.

"Chicken tenders basket for me, with sweet potato fries. And honey mustard."

Glen nodded, taking Grady's offered menu. He turned to walk away, then quickly flipped back around. "Hey . . . you both were the ones who donated all those artifacts to the Museum of Natural History in Gainesville, right?"

Grady and Kayla nodded in unison.

"It's on the news." He nodded toward the ceiling-mounted flat-screen just inside the open-air restaurant. "Mysterious disappearance, I think."

The three of them stared at the screen, trying to piece together the story from the subtitles on the silent news piece.

After about a minute, Grady asked, "Do you know what happened?"

Glen shrugged. "Not really. I just remembered the name of the museum from that news story last summer, where they interviewed the two of you about all that stuff you'd found in —where was it—Belize?" Kayla nodded and Glen shrugged. "Sorry, that's all I know." He offered a half-smile then walked away to put their order in.

Grady caught Kayla's gaze and held it. *I wonder . . .*

Grady, that's insane. How could anything possibly go wrong?

Kayla, you know better than I do the crazy things that globe did to you.

So you think it's the globe?

I don't know what else it could be. Grady sighed, combing his hair back with his fingers. Then he reached in his pocket for his phone. *I know we promised to keep these away at meals, but . . .*

Kayla nodded once. *We need to find out what happened. This could be nothing—or it could be very bad.*

Grady nodded back, unlocking his phone and quickly searching for and finding the story. He could hear Kayla in his head, trying to understand what he was reading, but apparently having little success. "Grady? What does it say?"

Grady cleared his throat. "Sorry. The story I found doesn't say much, just that a night guard disappeared early this morning. His nightstick was on the ground . . . in the middle of the Mayan exhibit."

Kayla gasped.

"They didn't find any other evidence, and the museum was still locked when his relief got in this morning."

Grady could feel Kayla freeze across from him, and he could sense why. He took a deep breath. "Look . . . our classes are out for the day. I can let the department admin know that we'll be out the rest of the day if you'd like to drive to Gainesville."

Kayla's eyes flew to his. "Really?"

Grady attempted what he hoped was a reassuring smile. "Of course. You won't have peace of mind until we check it out."

Kayla's face relaxed as her shoulders released. She mouthed a quick "thank you" as he dialed the anthropology department.

NOVVEAV RECVEIL

DE LETTRES,

HARANGVES,

ET

DISCOVRS

DIFFERENS;

OV IL EST TRAITE,

De l'Eloquence Françoise, & de
plusieurs matieres Politiques
& Morales.

A PARIS,

Par FRANÇOIS POMERAY, au Palais, en la
gallerie des Merciers, deuant le grand escalier.

M. DC. XXX.

AVEC PRIVILEGE DV ROY.

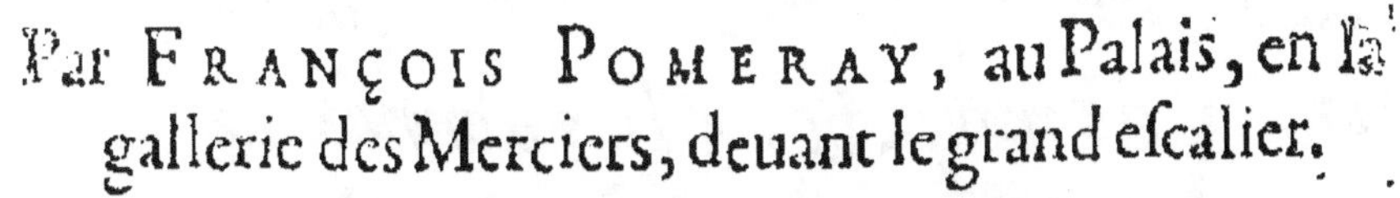

A MESSIRE

NICOLAS LE IAY,
Cheualier, Seigneur de Tilly,
de la Maison - rouge, de
sainct Fargeau & Villiers ;
Conseiller du Roy en ses Conseils d'Estat & Priué, & second
President en sa Cour de Parle-
ment de Paris.

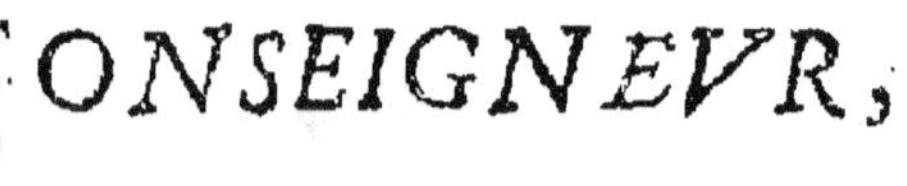

ONSEIGNEVR,

L'Autheur de ce
Liure s'est voulu
seruir de moy, pour luy donner la
lumiere, & ie prends la hardiesse

ã ij

de vous le dedier, afin que vous
luy communiquiez, par voſtre
courtoiſie celle de voſtre nom,
& la protection de voſtre authorité. Ainſi nous auons eſté tous
deux touchez d'vne iuſte paſſion;
luy de donner ſon Liure au public,
& moy de luy choiſir pour ſon
protecteur l'vn des plus grands
Oracles de la Iuſtice, & l'vn des
plus grands Ornemens du lieu
où elle preſide Souuerainement.
Cela eſtant, i'oſe dire que l'Autheur meſme, quelque aduan-
tage de prudence & de iugement
que la nature & les bonnes lettres
luy donnent ſur moy, n'euſt ſçeu
faire en ſa faueur vne meilleure
eſlection que celle que ie prends
la hardieſſe de faire. Si ie croyois

que mes loüanges vous fuſſent auſſi agreables, que celles qu'il ſeroit
capable de vous donner, ce me
ſeroit, MONSEIGNEVR,
un plaiſir extréme de vous loüer:
Car on void reluire en vous tant
de perfections, que les paroles les
plus aduantageuſes qu'on en pourroit dire, ne ſeroient nullement
ſuſpectes de menſonge, ny de flatterie. Ie dirois que vous auez la
Majeſté de ces anciens Senateurs
Romains, que lon prenoit pour
des Roys; que voſtre rencontre
eſt de bon Augure, & qu'elle fait
naiſtre ſoudain, non l'impudence
ou la crainte, mais le reſpect & la
modeſtie dans l'ame de ceux qui
vous approchent. Ie dirois que
vous faictes une des plus nobles,

ã iij

*& des plus excellentes parties du
corps de ce tres-Illustre, & tres-
Auguste Senat; & que iamais homme de longue Robbe n'a mieux que
vous verifié ce que dit Iustinian,*
Qu'il faut que l'authorité souueraine soit appuyée, & mainte-
nuë non seulement par la force
des armes, mais aussi par celle des
Loix: *Car vous estes également
nay à l'vn & à l'autre, & pouuez aussi bien par la generosité de
vostre Courage, que par l'excellence de vostre Esprit aider à maintenir la Puissance, & la Iustice de
nostre* GRAND ROY. *Ie dirois enfin,* MONSEIGNEVR,
*que vous estes & plus Noble, &
plus Illustre dans vostre Famille,
que ne l'est dans l'Histoire de Sa-*

laste ce constant & genereux Ma-
rius, lequel quelque puissant obsta-
cle que la Fortune pût opposer à sa
Vertu, ne laissa pas d'estre sept fois
Consul : car vous pouuez, non seulement produire les Images, & les
Statuës de vos Ancestres (ce qu'il
ne pût, commme il dit luy-mesme:)
mais aussi faire voir les honneurs
& les charges que vos grandes
Vertus, & vos belles Actions vous
ont acquises. Ie dirois tout cela
MONSEIGNEVR, & pu-
blierois beaucoup d'autres loüanges qui vous sont deuës, & des-
quelles l'enuie mesme ne sçauroit
me dementir. Mais il n'appartient
pas à vn homme, qui a plus de Caracteres, que de Lettres; & plus de
Liures que de Sciëce, de les publier.

Ie laiſſe ce deuoir aux meilleurs
Eſprits de ce temps, qui s'en pourront accquiter, ſinon ſelon vos merites, au moins ſans rien dimi-
nuer de l'eſclat de vos Vertus,
ny de la gloire de vos Actions.
D'ailleurs, il me ſemble que i'entens vne voix qui me commande de
me taire, & qui me dit, que ſi les
loüanges ne vous eſtoient point
deſagreables, il faudroit du moins
qu'elles fuſſent prononcées de la
bouche d'vn homme qui meritaſt
luy meſme de les receuoir. Ie vous
ſupplie donc tres-humblement,
MONSEIGNEVR, d'accepter
ce Liure, auec ce viſage & cette courtoiſie dont vous auez accouſtumé de receuoir les bonnes
choſes. Si vous daignez le lire aux

heures destinées aux recreations
& aux diuertissemens de vostre
esprit, ie m'asseure que vous y trouuerez, dequoy le contenter, & le re-
jouyr, estant remply cõme il est, d'v-
ne tres-docte, & tres-agreable diuersité de matieres Politiques &
Morales: En quoy il ressemble à la
table des Princes, & des Grands,
qui est d'autant plus splendide &
plus magnifique en son appareil,
qu'elle est couuerte de diuers Mets
exquis & delicieux. Si vous me
témoignez d'y prendre quelque
goust, & de l'agreer, i'auray sujet
de vous presenter vn autre plus
grand Ouurage, que les veilles des
hommes sçauants me promettent
faire mettre au iour, par le moyen
de mon Art. Car puisque c'est le

propre de l'Imprimerie, d'immortaliſer les grandes & genereuſes
Actiõs; la mienne ne pourroit eſtre
mieux employée qu'à trauailler ſur
les voſtres, qui ſont immortelles:
comme l'affection que i'ay vouée à
voſtre ſeruice, & le deſir que i'ay
de vous témoigner que ie ſuis,

MONSEIGNEVR,

Voſtre tres-humble &
tres-obeyſſant ſeruiteur,
FRANÇOIS POMERAY.

TABLE
DES LETTRES,
HARANGVES,

Et Discours differens, contenus
en ce Volume.

I.

Fin de la Table.

RECVEIL
DE LETTRES
ET DE DISCOVRS
DIFFERENS.

DISCOVRS PREMIER.

De l'Eloquence Françoise, qui va tou-
siours en augmentant contre l'opi-
nion du vulgaire, & à sçauoir si elle
se peut trouuer dedans les lettres.

IE hay ces esprits qui se
laissent plustost gouuerner
par l'opinion que par la
verité. Ie cognoy des hommes de
qui les erreurs ont augmenté leur
force auecque leur âge, encore

que ſuiuant le cours de nature, le temps affoibliſſe toute choſe en nous. Ces gens là ne ſçauroient iamais perdre les premieres impreſ-ſions que l'on leur a donnees, & ſi lors qu'ils eſtoient ieunes, l'on appelloit quelque autheur Prince des Orateurs ou des Poëtes, ils s'i-maginét qu'aucun Vſurpateur n'a pû luy oſter ſa couronne, ny meſ-me que bien qu'il ſoit mort il n'a eu aucun legitime ſucceſſeur. Il ſe peut faire que ç'a eſté leur pere & leur ayeul qui leur ont apris que c'eſtoit ce ſeul eſcriuain qui meri-toit cette dignité: Voila pourquoy s'ils l'attribuoient à vn autre ils croiroient commettre vn ſacrile-ge, & ils ne péſeroient pas que l'of-fence fuſt moins grande, que s'ils auoient contreuenu aux dernieres volontez de ceux dont ils ont pris

leur origine. C'est là vn abus qu'on
doit rejetter, car bien que nos predecesseurs ayent souuent eu plus de
preud'hommie que nous, il ne faut
pas s'attacher superstitieusement à
ce qu'ils croyoient, touchant l'E-
loquence de leur siecle, d'autant
qu'ils n'y estoient pas fort experts,
& que c'estoit en cela que l'authorité de leur âge & de leur vertu
estoit inutile. Nous deuons dire
qu'ils ressembloiét à celuy qui n'a-
uoit iamais veu la Mer, & qui
croyoit que l'on ne pouuoit voir
plus d'eau qu'il y en a au Lac de Ge-
neue. Il ne faut pas laisser de leur
pardonner, puis qu'ils ne pouuoiét
louër que ce qu'ils voyoient, &
qu'ils n'estoient ny Prophetes ny
Deuins pour asseurer quelque chose de l'aduenir. Ie blasme seulement
ceux qui refusent de croire les cho-

fes qu'ils voyent , & qui croyent celles qu'ils ne voyent plus. Ce mal eft fi fort enraciné dans leur efprit que l'on auroit de la peine à l'en arracher. Le degouſt qu'ils ont des choſes de ce Siecle leur vient poſſible auſſi quelquefois de ce que l'âge a corrópu leur eſprit auſſi bien que leur corps, & que n'eſtans plus capables de prédre pláiſir à ce qui leur a pleu dás leur ieuneſſe, ils condánent tout entierement. L'on les peut cóparer à ceux qui ſont dás vn baſteau, & qui s'imaginent que les riuages du fleuue s'enfuyent au lieu que ce ſont eux qui s'en eſloignent. Miſerables qu'ils ſont ! ils penſent que tout le monde va en decadence, & ils ne conſiderent pas que ce ſont eux de qui tous les iours il y a quelque partie qui tombe en ruïne. Si auec la croyance qu'ils ont d'eſtre

capables de iuger de l'Eloquence
& des autres choſes qui ſont les plus
communes entre les hommes, ils
eſtoient encore bons Mathemati-
ciens, il ne faut point douter qu'ils
ne fiſſent leurs efforts pour rendre
leur party ſi vniuerſel qu'il n'y en
euſt point de contraire par toute la
terre. Ils auroient obſerué ce que
l'on dit du Soleil, qui depuis les ob-
ſeruations des premiers Aſtrono-
mes, s'eſt trouué abbaiſſé de beaucoup. Ils diroiét là deſſus que la Nature ſe laſſe, & que l'on void bien
que toutes choſes s'en iront bien
toſt en vn eternel Occidét, mais ils
veulét que l'on les croye ſans qu'ils
ſe ſeruent d'vne ſi haute raiſon qui
pourroit bien encore auoir ſa reſ-
ponſe ſi elle eſtoit neceſſaire en noſtre ſujet. Ils ne ſont pas plus iudi-
cieux que ce vieil homme qui ne

s'eſtant pas miré depuis l'âge de vingt-cinq ans, rencontra vn miroir où il eut la curioſité de ſe regarder, & s'eſtant veu extremement difforme, il le penſa caſſer de deſpit. L'on faiſoit, diſoit-il, de bien meilleurs miroirs en mon ieune âge qui me repreſentoient auec vn viſage gay & vermeil, & non pas auec des rides ſeiches & ſaffrancees. La pluſpart des hommes ſont de cette humeur; ils ne cherchent pas en eux-meſmes la raiſon de ce qu'ils voyent, & ils ont de la peine à ſe perſuader que ce ſont leurs propres difformitez qu'ils croyent voir dedans toutes les choſes qui leur ſont preſentees. N'accuſons point ainſi de noſtre malheur ce qui n'en eſt point cauſe. Nous nous efforçons en vain de le rejetter ſur autruy, il nous ſuit touſ.

iours ; mais pluftoſt il nous accompagne. Si nous ne pouuons tirer les
opiniaſtres de leurs erreurs, ne ſouf-
frons pas qu'ils nous y entraiſnent
auec eux. Il eſt vray que nos forces
diminuent chaque iour ; mais encore que nous ceſſions d'eſtre, les ſcié-
ces & les arts ne laiſſent pas d'atteindre à leur perfection : car en
nous en allant, nous les laiſſons à
nos ſucceſſeurs au pareil eſtat que
nous les auons mis, & ils y adiou-
ſtent ce qu'ils peuuent par le trauail
& l'eſtude. Ne dit-on pas que les
iours s'inſtruiſent l'vn l'autre, pour
monſtrer les enſeignemens eternels
que les hommes ſe peuuent donner
de viue voix ou par eſcrit. Le temps
paſſé n'eſtoit que la ieuneſſe du
monde ; Nous ſommes maintenant
à l'âge viril où toutes choſes tendét
à leur perfection, & où l'on a peu

adiouſter beaucoup de remarques
aux inſtructions precedentes. C'eſt
mal à propos que les Siecles qui
ſont deſia paſſez , ſont appellez le
vieux temps ; Si nous auions commencé de viure deſlors, & que nous
veſcuſſions encore, ce ſeroit nous
que l'on pourroit appeller vieux;
mais pour ce temps-là c'eſtoit encore vne ieuneſſe qui eſtoit ſans experience. Nous voyons par là qu'il
n'eſt point mal à propos de croire
que l'on eſt maintenant plus artifi-
cieux que l'on n'a eſté autrefois, &
par conſequent qu'il y peut auoir
des perſonnes plus eloquentes. Ie ne
veux pas dire pourtant qu'il y ayt
quelqu'vn auiourd'huy que l'on
puiſſe appeller Prince de l'Eloquence; Ce ſeroit faire tort à ceux
qui viendront apres nous, qui pourront peut-eſtre auoir vn ſtile plus

beau que celuy que nous admirons. Aussi difficilement pourroit-
on dire, qui est celuy qui est le
plus eloquent entre tous les autheurs qui sont auiourd'huy en Fráce: car il faut recognoistre ce que
nous sommes, & que la fragilité
humaine est sujete à mille change-
ments dont nous ne sçaurions nous
garentir. Nous ne sommes pas capables de mettre de l'esgalité dans
tous nos ouurages. Tel a bien reüs-
sy en vne chose qui s'est monstré si
foible en vne autre, qu'il ne semble
pas qu'elle soit partie de sa main.
Les sujects nous rient quelquefois,
& nous aident d'eux-mesmes, pource qu'ils ont ie ne sçay quoy de
conforme à nostre nature. Il y en a
d'autres qui nous sont si contraires
que to⁹ nos efforts s'y rendét vains,
& qu'ils ne seruent qu'à faire paroi-

ftre noftre foibleffe. Le hazard
fait quelquefois en cecy plus
que le trauail. On a veu vne
bonne piece partir de la main d'vn
hôme qui ne deuoit rien faire que
cela, s'il vouloit eftre toufiours eftimé. Que fi l'on auoit auffi donné la
palme de l'Eloquence à quelqu'vn
de ceux que nous cognoiffons,
cela feroit poffible honteux pour
luy, d'autant qu'il en pourroit paroiftre en vn inftant vn autre
qui ne s'eft point monftré encore, qui luy pourroit difputer fa
dignité. Si dés que nous voyons vn
difcours qui nous plaift, nous vou-
lions appeller Roy de l'Eloquence
celuy qui l'a fait, la couronne chan-
geroit bien fouuent de tefte, & les
ouurages eftans inégaux comme
nous difons, il y en auroit beaucoup qui fe debufqueroient l'vn

l'autre. Contentons nous de loüer
& de blaſmer en chacun ce qui s'y
trouuera de bon ou de mauuais,
ſans nous empeſcher de croire
neantmoins qu'entre les meilleures
pieces que nous auons, il y en a de
telles qui peuuent ſurpaſſer celles
de l'antiquité contre l'opinion du
vulgaire. Ie ſçay bien que ceux qui
prennent le party des choſes paſſee, m'alleguent que la pluſpart des
Autheurs d'aujourdhuy ſe contentent de faire des Lettres, & ils dou-
tent ſi c'eſt eſtre eloquent que de ſe
meſler de ce genre d'eſcrire: mais
puiſque les Declamations ne ſont
plus guere en vſage, pourquoy
trouuera t'on eſtrange que l'on faſſe des lettres où l'on peut traiter
tant de ſubjets differens? N'y peut-
on pas mettre des accuſations, des
reprehenſions, des propoſitions,

des demandes, des prieres, & des
loüanges, & ne s'en peut on pas feruir pour exprimer toutes les paffions qui peuuent poffeder l'efprit
de l'homme? Ce feroit vne erreur
de les referuer pour donner feulement des aduertiffemens de tout ce
qui fe paffe en vn lieu dont nos amis
font abfens. Ce feroit les abbaiffer
grandement, & les condamner à ne
partir iamais d'vne plus digne main
que celle d'vn Secretaire. Les
Theologiens, les Politiques, & tous
les Philofophes s'en feruent pour
declarer leurs plus hautes conceptions; & l'on ne les doit pas reffer-
rer dans des bornes fi eftroites
qu'elles ne feruent plus qu'à des
Oeconomes ou à de ieunes Ccur-
tifans qui ne les employent qu'à efcrire les nouuelles de la Gazette.
Ceux qui n'en font pas l'eftime

qu’ils deuroiét, nous penfent beaucoup eftonner, lors qu’ils nous difent que quelque beauté de ftile
qu’il y ayt dans les Lettres, ce n’eft
pas toufiours Eloquence, d’autant
que d’eftre eloquent, c’eft parler de
viue voix & tout fur le champ, &
non pas efcrire vne chofe qui n’eft
faite qu’auecque peine. I’auoüe
bien icy que l’Eloquence la plus excellente qui foit au monde, doit
eftre celle des Harangueurs, comme eftoit Demofthene dans Athenes, & Ciceron dedans Rome; mais
il ne laiffe pas d’y auoir vn lieu de
gloire pour Ifocrate qui n’a compofé fes oraifons qu’auec vn long
temps, & qui n’a iamais eu la har-
dieffe de les reciter en public. L’on
dit que ce n’eft là qu’vne Eloquence morte: mais elle n’a pas laiffé de
produire des penfees qui auront

toufiours de la vigueur & de la vie.
Au reſte les choſes ſont elles entierement eſtimables, ſi elles ne ſeruent pas auſſi bien aux hommes de
l'aduenir qu'à ceux qui ont eſté du
temps qu'elles ont eſté faites? Comment peuuent donc ſeruir les Harangues à la poſterité , ſi elles ne
ſont miſes par eſcrit, & ſi elles le
ſont tout de meſme que les Orai-
ſons qui ont eſté faites dás vne eſtude, quelle difference y peut on trouuer? s'il y a quelque diſſemblan-
ce, ie croy pour moy que c'eſt de
la part des Harangues , qui paroiſſent moindres que toutes les autres
pieces, d'autant que l'action & la
prononciation de leur Orateur,
n'eſt pas depeinte dans l'Eſcriture,
bien que ce fuſt quelquefois ce qui
le faiſoit eſtimer d'auantage. Ceux
qui ont faict d'autres Harangues

par escrit, n'ont pas eu besoin de se
releuer par cet esclat: Ils ont employé leur esprit tout entier à rendre leurs ouurages agreables à la
lecture, pource qu'ils ne les faisoiét
que pour cette intention, & s'ils
ont employé dix ans apres vne piece qui n'est pas plus longue que celle qui n'a cousté qu'vn iour à vn autre, il ne nous aparoist rien de cela,
& nous le sçauons seulement pour
l'auoir ouy dire. Voila ce que l'on
doit considerer ce me semble,
pource qui est de l'Eloquence de ce
Siecle. S'il y a encore d'autres raisons à dire, les bons iugemens les
peuuent trouuer d'eux-mesmes; &
ie m'asseure d'ailleurs que nous
verrons bien-tost de si rares pieces
de la main de ceux qui ont pris auiourd'huy l'Eloquence pour leur
seule profession qu'il n'y aura plus

personne qui ne soit entierement
persuadé, & qui ne confesse que la
France a beaucoup d'auantage au
dessus des autres contrees pour produire en peu de temps d'excellens
esprits. Il y en a quelques-vns qui
se plaignent de ce qu'il y a long
temps que l'on a commencé de leur
faire des promesses fort auantageu-
ses, & qu'ils ne voyent point encore qu'elles soient secondees par les
effets; mais qu'ils sçachent qu'il faut
estre long temps à composer vne
chose que l'on veut faire long téps
durer. Il ne semble pas que ce soit la
raison qu'vne piece qui a esté faire
en vn demy quart d'heure, ayt
vingt ou trente Siecles de duree.
D'ailleurs ce ne seroit tenir aucun
compte des hommes que de trauailler comme par jeu à des choses
que l'on leur veut laisser pour de

veritables

veritables enseignemens. Que si
l'impatience nous gaigne , quelle
peine auons nous à la souffrir ? Elle
deuroit estre bien plus grande en
celuy qui trauaille pour nostre sujet, & neantmoins s'il a vne passion
violente pour voir son ouurage ac-
compli , il faut bien qu'il aprenne à
la moderer de peur qu'elle ne luy
fasse faire vne saillie temeraire, &
qu'elle ne luy conseille de mettre
en lumiere des ouurages imparfaites. L'on me peut respondre qu'à
mesure que l'ouurage se polit, son
impatience est moderee , mais en
recompense il s'employe à des trauaux qui ne nous importunent pas,
& nous ne songeons pas si souuent
ce qui est tousiours present dans
son esprit. Cecy nous doit aprendre à ne pas payer d'ingratitude &
de mocquerie les soins continuels

que peuuent quelques-vns de ce
fiecle pour obliger le public. Que
fi les Grands ne les recompenfent
plus par des honneurs & par des
biens de fortune, ne leur oftons pas
la principale fatisfaction qui leur
demeure, qui eft la gloire & la renommee.

De la fauſſe vertu de ceux qui ſe
font auiourd'huy appeller
Eſprits forts.

Es Eſprits des hommes ſont
ſi ſujets à la vanité que les
ſciences meſmes qui n'ont
eſté inuentees que pour les ranger
dans la moderation, leur ſont quelquefois nuiſibles & leur donnent
la liberté de ſe laiſſer emporter dans
l'extrauagance. Nous auons veu les
diſciples ne ſe point contenter des
preceptes de leurs maiſtres, & inué-
ter de nouuelles opinions, afin d'a-
uoir l'honneur d'eſtre chefs d'vne
nouuelle troupe de Philoſophes.
Cela ſe void encore auiourd'huy
non ſeulement parmy les hommes
d'eſtude, mais auſſi parmy des gens

qui n'ont iamais veu les Colleges
que de loin, & qui ne sçauent rien
que ce qu'ils ont apris dans vne legere pratique du monde. Que s'ils
ont pris la peine de lire, ce n'a pas
esté beaucoup de fois, & encore ne
se sont ils pas attachez à des liures
anciens, où l'on trouue les plus belles choses en leur pureté, & où l'on
peut dire que les sciences & les arts
sont comme dans leur source. Ils se
sont seulement amusez à quelque
liure de ce téps qui cache les espines
sous les fleurs, & qui sous quelques
opinions Sophistiques leur presente des aduis fort temeraires. C'est là
dessus qu'ils ont fondé quelques
maximes particulieres, & par ce
moyen ils ont creu qu'ils auoient
beaucoup de raison de se separer
des autres hommes. Ils ont ouy dire
que les Anges estoient diuisez par

des Hierarchies, & que mesmes
parmy les esprits malins il y en
auoit de superieurs & d'inferieurs.
C'est sur ces derniers qu'ils ont deu
chercher l'inuention de leurs ordres, si des desordres veritables se
doiuent appeller ainsi. Ils ont voulu establir des distinctions entre les
esprits des hommes, & en effet ils ne
se sont pas trompez lors qu'ils ont
creu que tous les hommes ne se res-
sembloient pas, car l'on y peut trouuer de merueilleuses differences.
Cela se void dedans les liures où le
temperamēt & le naturel des hommes sont exactement descrits, &
cela se trouue encore mieux dans
quelques traictez de Philosophie
morale où l'on void l'humeur de
chaque personne selon ses vices ou
ses vertus. Nos nouueaux Docteurs
ne s'amusent pas à faire de si belles

diſtinctions. Ils croyent qu'il n'y a
rien de plus beau que de ſe faire appeller Eſprits forts, & ceux qui à
leur aduis leur reſſemblét le moins,
ils les appellent des Eſprits foibles.
Pour ce qui eſt de ceux qui ſont dãs
la mediocrité , ils veulent encore
qu'ils ſoient au deſſous d'eux , ſans
ſonger que la pluſpart des Philoſophes ont ſouſtenu que la vertu tenoit ſa place dans le milieu , & que
l'on ne peut aller dans les deux extremitez ſans qu'il y ayt du trop ou
du trop peu, ce qui engẽdre le vice.
D'ailleurs ils n'entédent nõ plus les
diſtinctiõs de Morale que ceux qui
n'en ont iamais ouy parler, car ils appellent ces Eſprits du milieu des Eſprits ſubtils, & quelquefois des Eſprits doux. Cela eſt extremémét im-
pertinét, car l'on n'eſtablit point vn
milieu entre deux extremitez que

pour des qualitez d'esprit qui regardent vne mesme chose. Comme par
exéple en ce qui cócerne l'vsage des
richesses, l'on dit qu'il y a des auares & des prodigues, & l'on met au
milieu les hommes liberaux. Ainsi
entre le deffaut & l'excez consiste
la mediocrité.　En ce qui est de nostre sujet nous ne trouuons rien de
semblable, & qui plus est les qualitez y sont fortmal attribuées. Quád
nous entendons parler des Esprits
forts, nous croyons d'abord que ce
soient des gents qui se font paroistre aussi bós Stoïques qu'Epictete.
Nous nous imaginós que par ce nó
que l'on leur dóne lóg veut entédre
qu'ils possedent toutes les vertus de
ce Philosophe, & que cóme toute sa
philosophie estoit contenuë sousces
deux mots s'Abstenir & Souffrir, l'ó
la veut encore abreger d'auantage,

la reduisant sous vn seul nom ; car
en effet l'on peut dire qu'il faut de
la force pour s'abstenir des delices
du monde, & qu'il en faut aussi
pour souffrir les aduersitez. Ce sont
là les deux poles sur lesquels roule
toute la vie humaine, & quiconque a l'esprit veritablement fort,
l'on peut dire qu'il est vertueux en
toutes choses. S'il a des richesses, il
ne les côserue que côme des choses
que l'on luy a donnees en depost, &
dont il doit vn iour rendre compte.
Si son corps est en santé, il considere
qu'il ne faut qu'vn petit rheume
pour l'abattre, & que lors qu'il pense quelquefois estre exépt des plus
grandes infirmitez, vne pierre se
forme en ses reins, qui luy donnera des tourmens effroyables. S'il a la
liberté de iouyr de toute sorte de
voluptez, il se modere pourtant &

ne fait rien que ce qui est permis à
vn homme sage. Que si apres cela
il luy arriue vne grande perte ou
quelque maladie incurable, il garde la mesme opinion qu'il auoit
dans sa prosperité. Il croid qu'il est
digne de toutes ces infortunes ; que
Dieu les luy enuoye pour le cha-
stier, ou pour esprouuer sa patience,
& que s'il les souffre de bon cœur, il
en aura beaucoup plus de merite.
C'est de cette sorte que les Esprits
forts de l'antiquité ont vescu ; mais
ceux de ce siecle leur sont si differens qu'ils sont indignes de porter
ce nom. S'ils sont riches, ils ne se seruent de leurs richesses qu'à faire des
despences inutiles, & à estonner
tout le monde de leurs superfluitez, & ils croyent que c'est vne force d'esprit de ne se point soucier de
despendre son bien follement & de

le iouër quelquefois à trois dez
tout en vn coup. Si leur santé
va bien & qu'ils ayent le moyen
de gouster de toutes sortes, de
delices , ils s'y addonnent continuellement & ils s'imaginent
que c'est auoir l'esprit fort de
mespriser les remonstrances que
leurs parens ou leurs superieurs
leur peuuent faire sur ce sujet:
mais , ô impudence inouye! de
la memoire de tous les siecles ,
ils disent encore que c'est a-
uoir l'Esprit fort que de boire tout le long d'vn iour sans
auoir le cerueau troublé. Voylà
la force qu'ils font paroistre pour
la volupté du monde. En ce qui
est des aduersitez ils nous iurent
qu'ils les suportent patiemment.
Il est vray qu'ils les suportent,
mais c'est pourueu qu'elles s'adres-

sent à d'autres; car ils croyent contreuenir aux maximes de leur
Philosophie , s'ils auoient de la
compassion d'autruy. Si quelqu'vn de leurs parents se meurt,
pour garder la force de leur esprit ils ne s'en affligent point: mais
quelque mine qu'ils facent ils
craignent bien de mourir eux
mesmes , & s'il arriue quelque
malheur qui touche leur personne , ils tesmoignent assez par
leurs blasphemes le desespoir
où ils sont reduicts. Ie ne doute point qu'ils ne passent encore plus auant , & que leur force ne consiste encore à ne croire que ce qu'ils veulent touchant
la Religion. Ie ne veux point
entrer dans les particularitez de
leurs meschantes opinions de
peur d'offencer les bonnes ames.

Il faut parler seulement de ceux qu'ils disent estre leurs contraires, & qui veritablement le sont, mais il ne les faudroit pas apeller esprits foibles comme ils les appellent. Ce sont ceux qui temperent leurs plaisirs, & qui s'affligent du malheur des autres. A la verité s'ils ne faisoient autre chose que de plaindre les malheurs de leurs semblables, leur vertu seroit imparfaite ; mais encore qu'ils tachent d'apporter du soulagement aux miseres humaines, les Esprits forts condamnent leur charité, croyans qu'ils doiuent estre mis au rang des esprits foibles. S'ils obeïssent sans murmurer à leurs superieurs, & s'ils ont vne ferme croyance pour tous les mysteres de la foy, ces malheureux appellent cela foiblesse & superstition , au lieu que c'est vne force veritable.

l'aprouuerois bien que l'on tachaſt
de les retirer de leurs erreurs en
particulier par des douces remonſtrances, mais parce qu'ils ont des
maximes deteſtables dont ie ne
veux rien toucher icy, à plus forte
raiſon ne treuueroi-ie pas à propos
que l'on les miſt tout au long dans
quelque volume pour les refuter
en meſme temps, car le ſimple peuple ayāt pris ce liure par meſgarde,
y comprendroit des choſes qu'il
vaut mieux ignorer que ſçauoir.
Auſſi leur fauſſe Philoſophie eſt encore tenuë ſecrette, il ne la faut rendre plˀ manifeſte qu'elle eſt, & quād
elle ſeroit deſcouuerte, & que l'on
l'auroit treuuée auſſi mauuaiſe que
celle des plus pernicieux Athées,
ce ſeroit alors qu'il ſe faudroit abſtenir dauātage d'eſcrire cōtre eux;
car comme dit vn bon Eſprit de ce

fiecle, s'il y a quelqu'vn à qui il
foit permis d'efcrire contre cette
maniere de gens, & qui le puiffe faire iuftemẽt, c'eft le Greffier qui ef-
crira fous fon iuge l'Arreft de leur
condemnation.

Pour moy ie ne veux dire aucune
des raifons dont ils tachẽt d'apuyer
leur mauuaife doctrine. Il fuffit de
declarer qu'ils font tout remplis de
vices & d'impietez fans rien fpeci-
fier. En ce qui eft des Efprits qu'ils
appellent doux & fubtils, ils ne font
pas fi dangereux. Tout ce qu'ils
fçauent ne leur fert qu'à entretenir
les Dames par des cajolleries &
complimẽts. Il y a feulement quelque difference entre la douceur des
vns & la fubtilité des autres. Les
Efprits doux font des gens qui a-
greent à tout ce que l'on dit & qui
donnent des loüages en beaux ter-

mes ; mais pour les fubtils, ils font
vn peu plus mefdifans, & la beauté
de leur difcours confifte pluftoft
dans les pointes & les rēcontres, que
non pas la folidité. Au bout du cópte on ne trouue pas que tous ces
hommes cy foient fort vtiles à l'E-
ftat, & qu'ils facent de grandes a-
ctions, veu qu'ils n'ont foin que de
leurs paroles. Ie confeilleray touf-
jours à tous mes amis de ne fe point
mefler en des femblables conuerfations. Nous ne deuons rechercher
autre compagnie que celles des hó-
neftes gens qui viuent auec plus de
franchife & moins d'affetterie, que
non pas ces faifeurs de fectes, qui
ayment mieux que l'on les eftime
pour l'Eloquence que pour la fageffe.

LETTRE D'ACHANTE

à Philemon, ſur la felicité du Royaume de France & la iuſtice du Roy, auec de fortes perſuaſions pour deſtourner ſon amy de ſes voyages & le faire demeurer dans vn païs ſi heureux que le ſien.

IE ſçay bien, mon cher amy, qu'ayant voyagé par toute l'Europe, comme vous auez faict, vous n'auez pas manqué de remarquer de quelle ſorte l'on vit dans la Cour de tous les grands Princes ; mais vous n'en auez point trouué de ſi celebre que celle de noſtre Roy ; & meſme ie veux bien paſſer plus outre, c'eſt que dedans cette grande lecture à laquelle vous vous eſtes

addonné

addonné dés voftre ieunefle, vous
n'auez point trouué en aucun lieu
de fi beaux exemples. Ce bien eft
d'autant plus grand qu'il n'eft pas
feulement particulier aux lieux où
noftre Monarque refide; mais qu'il
eft commun aufli à tous ceux qui
font rangez fous fa domination.
Vn tel bon-heur commence à naiftre par tout, qu'il n'eft pas poffible
qu'aucune infortune le puiffe ef-
branfler, & ce qui eft de plus beau
en cecy, c'eft que noftre Roy eft la
veritable fource de toutes ces felicitez, & qu'il eft plus digne de commander & d'eftre obey que pas vn
que nous ayôs veu encore. Sa iuftice, fa prudence, & fa valeur vont au
delà de toutes les imaginations des
hommes. Il fait des chofes qui nous
eftoient auparauant incogneuës.
Nous auons bien veu des guerriers,

mais ils eſtoient au deſſous de luy,
& outre cela ils laiſſoient ſouuent
dormir les loix pour n'ouyr que le
ſon de la trompette. Nous auons
auſſi bié veu des Legiſlateurs comme eſtoient Solon, Lycurgue, &
Numa, mais ils n'eſtoiét guere propres à conduire des armees, & l'on
ne trouue point par eſcrit qu'ils
ayent fait de grāds exploicts. Tout
au contraire noſtre grand Roy e-
ſtant Iuſte & valeureux, comme il
eſt, tire de la gloire de ſa Iuſtice &
de ſa generoſité. Il n'a pas ſi toſt
dompté les rebellions de ſon Royaume, qu'il a ſongé à remettre tout
l'Eſtat au plus bel ordre que l'on
pouuoit ſouhaitter. Il a fait des Ordonnances où toutes choſes ſont
reſtablies, auecque des reigles ſi
certaines, que ie ne fay point de
doute que cela ne produiſe vne

tranquilité eternelle. Il me semble desia que ie voy tous les peuples qui l'admirent & qui le reue-
rent, & ie n'entend pas seulement
parler de ceux qui viuent dans les
terres de sa domination, mais aussi
de ceux qui en sont fort essloi-
gnez.

S'il y en a qui prennent leurs Rois
par ellection, ils ne trouueront rien
de plus glorieux pour leur pays
que de les choisir pour leurs Mo-
narques, & ils ne croyront point
que la felicité soit asseuree si l'on ne
se range dessous ses loix. Ces sous-
missions volontaires sont aussi estimables pour celuy qui les reçoit que
les plus grandes conquestes ; mais
que ne doit on point à celuy qui
porte si iustement le tiltre de iuste, & qui fait paroistre vne sagesse
incomparable en toutes ses actions?

Il n'a aussi donné la charge de distribuer sa iustice qu'à des esprits
qui ont toutes les qualitez necessaires pour se rendre recommanda-
bles. Celuy qui a la garde des Seaux
de son Royaume, est si remply de
probité qu'il n'en pouuoit trouuer
vn plus digne de ceste honorable
place. L'on ne void point que les
demandes iniustes de quelques subjets temeraires soient maintenant
accordees. Ce grand esprit qui est
capable de tout, fait en sorte que
ceux qui sont oppressez reçoiuent
du soulagement; & d'vn autre costé s'il y a quelqu'vn qui le veut surprendre, il penetre dans ces subtili-
tez & le renuoye comme il merite,
afin que la seule honte du refus luy
donne le desir de faire mieux. Il
ne se faut point estonner de la vertu de cét homme illustre de nostre

ſiecle, car il eſt ſi fauoriſé de Dieu
que toutes ſes actions ſont dignes
d'eſtre remarquees. Auſſi n'eſt-il
pas de ces hommes d'Eſtat que l'on
a veus autrefois, leſquels ne ſe ſer-
uoient que d'vne ſageſſe mondaine. Il fait aller les maximes de pieté
deuant les maximes Politiques, &
toutes les eſperances humaines ne
luy le ſçauroient faire contreuenir
aux ordonnances diuines. Noſtre
incomparable Monarque teſmoigne ainſi ſon iugement dans l'eſlection de ſes grands Officiers, qui ſe
monſtrans dignes d'vn tel maiſtre,
rendent ſa gloire encore plus illuſtre.

Ie n'aurois iamais fait ſi ie voulois icy raconter les perfections de
tous ceux qui meritent des loüanges & des recognoiſſances. Nous
en auons qui ſont pour la guerre &

pour la paix, lefquels s'acquitent fi bien de leur deuoir que l'on n'y trouue plus dequoy fouhaitter; mais ils me pardonneront fi ie ne leur donne pas la loüange toute entiere de ce qu'ils font de plus remarquable. Ie m'affeure qu'ils fouffriront bien que ie publie que le Roy eft la principale caufe de leurs meilleures actions C'eft luy fans doute qui les a fait tels que l'on les void, c'eft fon exemple qui leur fert pour acquerir vne vertu nompareille. Comme vne verge droicte ne peut faire vn ombre tortu; de mefme ceux qui viuent fous la domination de ce Monarque ne peuuent auoir que de droictes intentions. Ie vous coniure de venir icy vous-mefme, vous en remarquerez d'auantage que ie ne vous en fçaurois dire. Toutes ces

merueilles ont cela de propre qu'elles sont de beaucoup plus agreables
à voir qu'à les ouyr. Quelles excuses me pouuez vous donner pour
vous empescher de quitter la solitude où vous estes, & venir à la Cour
chercher les meilleures cõpagnies
du monde ? Ie me doute desia de ce
que vous me deuez repartir. Vous
me direz que vous n'estes point vn
solitaire & vn ennemy des hommes , comme quelques-vns vous
ont voulu reprocher depuis quelque temps, & que tant s'en faut que
vous le soyez, qu'au contraire vous
auez desia fait plus de 3000. lieuës
pour chercher des hómes qui vous
fussent agreables. Là dessus vous me
representerez que vous auez bié des
voyages dás l'esprit, & que vous ne
serez iamais en repos que vous ne les
ayez accóplis. Ie vo⁹ dis cecy, car i'ay

apris d'vn de nos amis cõmuns, que vous en parliez de la sorte, tellemẽt qu'à son compte vous estes tout prest de partir. C'est vne estrange humeur que la vostre, cher Philemon, pensez vous trouuer le repos de l'esprit dans ces continuelles agitations ? Vous auez desia veu toute l'Europe, que pensez vous qu'il y ayt de beau à voir apres cela ? Si vous auez trouué des trahisons & des tromperies en vn lieu auec vne infinité de complimens inutiles, si vous n'auez veu en vn autre que de la rusticité, & si ailleurs vous n'a-uez remarqué que de l'orgueil & de la vaine apparence, & si vous auez trouué enfin qu'il n'est rien d'esgal à la franchise & à la veritable vertu des François, que pen-sez vous trouuer encore? Vous ver-rez en de certains lieux des hommes ſi cruels qu'il ſemble qu'il ne s'abreuuét iamais que de ſãg. Vous en verrez d'autres qui ont les membres tous velus, & le viſage ſi monſtrueux que l'on peut dire qu'ils reſſemblent à des beſtes brutes, & que s'ils n'auoient point la taille droicte l'on ne les prédroit pas pour des hõmes. Au reſte voſtre plˢ grãd deſſein ne peuteſtre que de les voir; car pour les entretenir de leurs couſtumes, c'eſt vne choſe que vous ne ſçauriez faire. Il vous faudroit auoir eſté vingt ans auec eux pour comprendre la maniere dont ils s'expliquent, qui eſt pluſtoſt vn heurlement qu'vn langage. Que ſi cela eſt, n'aurez vous pas autant de plaiſir de les voir icy en portraict dans quelque cabinet curieux? C'eſt vne choſe que vous pouuez faire ſans peine, & auec fort peu de temps, au lieu que si vous embarquez pour aller voir l'Amerique ou l'Afrique, vous estes en danger de tomber en mille hazards que vous ne craignez pas maintenát. Vostre vaisseau peut faire naufrage auant que vous ayez rienveu de ce que vous desirez, vous pouuez tomber entre les mains des Corsaires plus cruels encore que l'Element où ils habitent. Ils vous mettront à la chaisne cóme l'on y met icy les voleurs. Toutes les belles qualitez de vostre esprit ne serót point cósiderées, elles sont inutiles parmy de semblables gens, l'on ne prendra garde qu'à la bonne disposition & à la force de vostre corps. Ce sera là dessus que l'on reiglera le prix que l'on mettra pour vous lors que l'on vous voudra vendre. Quel regret aurez vous d'estre esclaue des infideles, & de ne pouuoir mander ces triſtes nouuelles à vos parens & à vos amis, qui ne vous pourrót auſſi aſſiſter de lóg-temps, & qui ſeront bié en peine pour enuoyer vne rançon en des Prouinces ſi eſloignées ? Combien maudirez vous voſtre vaine curioſité, qui vo' aura códuit dãs de ſi grãdes infortunes ? Vous ſerez alors ſi mal nourry qu'auec les inquietudes que vo' aurez inceſſãment, cela ſera capable de vous affoiblir & de vous rẽdre malade, & ſi vos maiſtres s'en apperçoiuent, ils vous enuoyeront chercher voſtre tombeau dedans la mer au parauãt meſme que ſoyez mort, pour ce qu'ils iugerót que vous ne leur ſerez pl' qu'vn fardeau inutile.

Voylà les plus grandes extremitez du malheur, Philemõ. Il ſe peut faire de vray qu'elles ne vous arriueront pas, & que voſtre bonne fortune vous accompagnera par tout,

mais quelle asseurance en auez-
vous ? ayez pluſtoſt de la crainte de
la pire choſe qui vous puiſſe aduenir, que non pas de l'eſperance
pour vn plaiſir qui ne ſçauroit eſtre
gueres grand quand vous l'aurez
poſſedé ! Ie vous ay deſia parlé de
la barbarie des gens que vous auez
à voir, mais quand ce ſeroit vn ob-
jeᵗ agreable, quel moyen y a-il de
contéter ſon eſprit en tous les deſirs
qui nous peuuent venir là deſſus ?
Dés que vous aurez veu vne contrée, vous en voudrez encore voir
vne autre; & ainſi voſtre deſir croiſ-
ſant touſiours, vous chercherez
par tout vn contentemét que vous
ne pourrez trouuer nulle part. Que
ſi vous auez veu les Indes Occi-
dentales, pourquoy n'aurez vous
pas autant de deſir de voir les Indes
Orientales? Il y a autant de mer-

ueille aux vnes qu'aux autres, & ie
m'asseure que vous ne voudriez
pas quitter vostre part du voyage
de la Chine, afin de voir si tout ce
que Fernand Pinto en raconte est
veritable. Apres cela il faudra aller
dans la Tartarie, & en beaucoup
d'autres lieux, & vous voudrez faire le tour du monde par mer & par
terre, afin d'estre plus renommé
que le Cheualier Anglois. A quoy
vous seruiront tous ces voyages,
voulez vous augmenter ou corriger le liure des Estats & Empires?
Laissons les choses comme elles
sont, aussi bien ne pouuez vous a-
uoir assez de vie de reste pour aller
en tant de lieux, & pour auoir le
loisir d'y demeurer si long temps
que vous y puissiez apprendre les
diuerses façons de viure. Mais quãd
il se pourroit faire que vous vissiez

toutes ces chofes, il faut que vous
fçachiez que vo° ne feriez pas encore content, car ie cognoy bien que
voftre curiofité eft infatiable. Vous
feriez de l'humeur du grand Alexandre : vous fouhaiteriez qu'il y
euft encore d'autres mondes , & fi
ce n'eftoit pour les conquefter , ce
feroit au moins pour remarquer
leurs differentes polices ; mais fou-
uenez vous de ce bon mot que l'on
a dit contre ce Roy de Macedoine.
Vn homme auffi docte que rem-
ply de pieté a dit fur ce fujet, qu'Ale-
xâdre deuoit bié chercher vn autre
môde, mais nô pas celuy qu'il s'imaginoit, qui eftoit vn mode terreftre
comme celuy dont il auoit defia
conquis vne grande partie : mais
bien vn monde celefte qui s'acquiert par de vertueufes actions,
& non pas par la force des armes.

S'il euſt voulu auſſi aller conquerir
cet autre monde , il n'euſt pas pû
ſortir de celuy - cy ſans auoir le
moyen de s'eſleuer en haut & de
paſſer par le Ciel. Mais c'eſt là qu'il
faut demeurer ſans que l'on deſire
aller plus outre. Vous deuriez y aſ-
pirer ſeulement. Ce deſgouſt que
nous auons de tous les plaiſirs de
la terre auſſi toſt que nous les poſſe-
dons, ne ſçauroit venir d'autre choſe que de ce que noſtre ame eſt hors
de ſa vraye patrie , où elle deſire retourner.

Cela eſtant veritable, comme ie
croy que vous n'en faites plus aucune doute, ne mettez point vos amis
dans le regret de voſtre perte , &
fuyez tant de fatigues & de trauer-
ſes que vous vous eſtiez prepa-
rees. Ce que vous pourriez rechercher de plus doux apres tant

de voyages que vous vous estes figurez, ce seroit de vous repoler &
de palfer vos iours dans les diuertil-
femens qui plailent à voltre humeur : mais à quoy tient il que dés
maintenât vous ne falliez vne femblable vie ? D'ailleurs pour ce qui
eft des contentemens plus folides
que l'on fe propole en l'exercice de
la vertu, où les pouuez vous mieux
trouuer que de la France? Vous deuez employer voltre bel efprit au
fecours du public & du particulier.
C'eft de là que vo tirerez vne veritable fatisfactió. il y a plus de gloire
à feruir fon Roy &le lieu de fa naiffance, qu'à toutes autres occupatiós
que vous fçauriez auoir en des terres eftangeres. Tous les grands hómes de l'antiquité ne font loüez
que pour ce fujet, c'eft par ce chemin qu'ils font paruenus à l'immortalité

mortalité! faites comme eux & vous aurez vne semblable fortune! Les grands voyages ne sont propres qu'à des bannis & à des marchands. Si d'autres personnes les entreprennent, ils les doiuent bien tost terminer sans y vouloir passer toute leur vie. Ie vous ay mõstré en peu de mots le bel ordre qui estoit maintenant estably dedans l'Estat de la France; ç'a esté pour vous faire plus d'enuie d'y demeurer. Ne doutez point que vous n'y trouuiez quelque employ honorable, puisque toutes choses s'y font auecque iustice. Ie ne sçay pas s'il ne peut y auoir que les plus grandes charges qui eschauffent vostre ambition: mais il se faut moderer du commencement. Croyez vous que l'on puisse passer d'vn bout à l'autre sans passer par le milieu? Il y a quelque

honneur dans le second rang, &
aussi dans le troisiesme, & mesme
iusques dans le dernier. C'est assez
pourueu que l'on ne soit point au
nombre de ceux qui sont rejettez,
& qui n'ont point du tout de rang.
La comparaison du monde à la Comedie est fort vieille, mais elle est
des plus excellentes: Ie m'en veux
seruir icy comme en beaucoup
d'autres lieux. Disons donc que celuy qui fait le personnage de valet,
n'est pas moins à priser que celuy
qui fait le personnage de Maistre,
pourueu qu'il s'acquitte bien de sa
charge; & qu'il en est de mesme de
tous nos Offices. Ne desesperez dóc
point tant de vostre bonne fortune, qui sera meilleure icy qu'en
tout autre endroit du monde. Si
vous ne me rendez point vne fauorable response, i'auray tous les re-

grets que l'on se peut imaginer. Ie
veux bien vous aduertir dés maintenant de ce que ie suis en deliberation de faire. Ie m'en vay aduertir
tous vos parents & tous vos amis
de vostre volóté, & nous irons tous
ensemble vous representer tant de
raisons pour vous destourner de
vos voyages, que vous serez honteux de nous refuser ce que nous
vous demanderons, & que vous
nous promettrez de ne plus penser
à vos entreprises dernieres. Ne
croyez pas nous eschaper ; nous serons pluſtoſt à vous, que vous ne
vous imaginez, & pource que voſtre conseruation nous eſt chere, il
ne faudra plus que vous nous quittiez, & nous vous emmenerons
auec vne douce violence.

Lettre de loüanges addreßee à Mon-
seigneur le Cardinal de Richelieu.

ONSEIGNEVR,

On ne doutera iamais que
noſtre ſiecle n'ayt atteint vne felicité ſans exemple, & que tous ces
noms de cruel, d'infidele, d'ignorant, & de fragile que l'on luy a pû
donner auant que de vous y auoir
veu paroiſtre, n'ayent auiourd'huy
tout ſujet d'eſtre bannis de la bouche des hommes. Quels biens ne
pouuions nous pas auoir maintenát
que nous vous auons? & n'eſt-il pas
croyable que la prouidence diuine
ne vous a pas reſerué pour ce temps
cy ſans intention de faire valoir les

rares qualitez qu'elle vous a depar-
ties? Le Monde est vn edifice où il y
a tousiours à refaire, pource que
nous sommes si insensez que nous
demolissons nous-mesmes ce qu'il
y a de plus beau, & nous serions accablez sous ses ruines, s'il ne venoit
de temps en temps des ouuriers
tres-experts pour en reparer les
dommages. Mais maintenát qu'outre ceste perte interieure, il est encore affoibly par sa vieillesse, s'il en
fust venu vn moindre que vous, il
n'y eust trauaillé qu'inutilement.
C'est à vous qu'apartient la gloire
de le rebastir tout à neuf, & de
nos humeurs si destruites & si cor-
rompuës, refaire des inclinations
plus fortes & plus excellentes qu'elles ne furent à leur premier establis-
sement : Soit que l'on considere
vostre doctrine, qui est capable de

D iij

tirer la verité hors des abifmes où
elle eft cachee, foit que l'on regarde voftre pieté qui vous efleue autant pardeffus les chofes de la Terre que fi vous eftiez defia dans le
Ciel, on ne doit attendre de vous
que des chofes nompareilles, & il
ne faut pas douter qu'il n'y ayt
encore des miracles à faire dans le
Monde, puifque vous eftes venu
eftre de fes Citoyens. Et veritablement fi les Chreftiens peuuent e-
ftre ramenez à vne meilleure vie,
& les Infidelles à vne entiere con-
uerfion, il faut efperer d'en eftre
vn iour redeuable à vos paroles &
à vos actions. C'eft vn grand
poinct, MONSEIGNEVR,
que de rendre ces deux chofes fi
conformes l'vne à l'autre comme
vous faictes, & de là vient que les
peuples perdans l'opinion que l'on

les ayt voulu seduire, se sousmet-
tent volontairement au plus seuere ioug que l'on leur puisse impo-
ser. Les Ouurages que l'on ne
peut seulement que commencer
par les preceptes, demeureroient
imparfaits si l'on ne les acheuoit
ainsi par les exemples ; & se mes-
ler d'enseigner ce que l'on ne fait
pas soy-mesme, c'est estre pareil à
ces anciennes Statuës, qui ne faisoient que monstrer le chemin du
bout du doigt sans bouger de leur
place, & non pas ressembler à ces
fidelles guides que vous imitez,
qui s'offrent à nous faire compagnie & courir mesme fortune.
Aussi l'Eglise vous ayant recogneu si prompt à la conduite de
ses enfans, vous a faict vn des
plus precieux membres de son
corps , & vous a mesme cherché

vn si haut lieu que vous puissiez en
estre veu de tous les hommes, afin
de leur proposer vn modele de la
perfection à imiter : Et de fait cette
belle Reyne vous a en telle estime,
que lors qu'elle se voudra rendre
agreable aux yeux de son Espoux,
elle ne s'asseurera point en la valeur d'autres ornements que vos
vertus, qui sont autant de pierre-
ries pour enrichir sa robbe nu-
ptiale.

Mais, MONSEIGNEVR,
ce ne sont pas icy les bornes que vous vous estes prescrit,
& vous croyriez ne mettre en
vsage qu'vne partie des graces que
Dieu vous a conferees au proffit de tout le monde, si outre la
peine que vous prenez pour maintenir la vigueur de la Religion,
vous ne donniez encore vos soins

& vos veilles au gouuernement du plus beau Royaume de la terre. Vous y auez pris naissance cóme au lieu le plus digne de vous receuoir, & à qui les merueilles ont tousiours esté fatales, & d'auātage nous auons vn Prince si iuste, & si puissant à gaigner les volontez, que de quelque costé que vous tourniez les yeux vous ne trouuerez que de douces chaisnes qui vous attachent à la conduite de ses affaires. C'est là que vostre esprit incomparable donne des preuues de foy dont l'on ne peut douter sans crime, & vous monstrez clairemēt que les bons conseils doiuent partager auec la puissance des armes, la gloire de conseruer les Empires en leur splēdeur. Ce sótàn'en point métir des personnages pareils à vous (s'il s'en peut faire encore) qui

doiuent eſtre commis à la conſer-
uation des Eſtats ſi l'on y deſire vn
general reſtabliſſement. Que ſi
l'on compare le monde à vne comedie, il faut que tels hómes ſoyét
les Autheurs des hiſtoires que les
Courtiſans veulent repreſenter ſur
ce grand theatre, qu'ils ayent compoſé les Dialogues de tous les actes,
qu'ils leur ayent apris les démar-
ches, les contenances & les ge-
ſtes, & qu'en outre ils ſoyent touſ-
jours preſens pour leur ſouffler
aux oreilles ce qu'ils oublient,
autrement ils joüeroient fort mal
leur perſonnage, & d'vn ſujet
tout comique ils feroient quelquefois vne Tragedie bien fu-
neſte. Mais ſe peut-on attendre de voir de ces hommes ſi parfaits que leur bonne veuë ſerue à tant d'autres qui n'en ont

point ? N'est- ce pas vne chose
que Dieu ne nous enuoye pas
tous les iours de peur que l'on ne
vienne à mespriser ses miracles
pour estre trop frequens, & cela n'a- il pas donné sujet d'estimer que ces ames accomplies
sont aussi rares que le Phœnix
dont chacun fait assez de contes,
mais que personne n'asseure a-
uoir veu, ou que ces corps,
à qui la vie est conseruee vne
infinité de siecles par la precieu-
se Medecine que promettent les
Philosophes.

Toutefois, Monseignevr,
nous voyons paroistre en vous
ce que nous croyons au para-
uant deuoir plustost souhaitter
que rencontrer, & ce qui nous
estonne encore dauantage, est
que l'effet y va encore au delà

de nos premieres imaginations, &
les vertus que nous nous estiõs proposees sõt iointes à d'autres que no⁹,
ne mettions pas en leur cõpagnie.
C'est certes vne chose bien merueilleuse d'estre pourueu d'vne telle sagesse que l'on ne soit regardé
de tout vn Estat que comme vne
Loy parlante & animée , d'estre
muny d'vne Eloquence si forte que
elle face tout ce que les armes d'vn
puissant Roy pourroient faire, &
d'auoir vne prudence si meure que
les accidens dont elle aduertit, soyét
autant infaillibles comme les promesses de la destinee; Et voyla tout
ce qu'on se figuroit pour vn parfait
Ministre de l'Estat, que l'on n'esperoit non plus de trouuer en estre,
que l'Orateur de Ciceron, ou le
Courtisan du Comte Balthasar.
Mais d'auoir encore d'abondant

vne deuotion ſi ardente enuers
Dieu que vous en attirez ſur vous
toute ſorte de benedictions, & que
voꝰ en obtenez du ſecours pour l'ac-
cōpliſſement de vos conſeils, & de
bruſler d'vne amour ſi paſſionnée
pour le troupeau des fidelles, que ſi
quelque inſenſé s'en eſgare, vous
en auez de pareils reſſentimens que
ſi l'on vous arrachoit vn des membres de voſtre propre corps, c'eſt
à n'en point mentir vne choſe où
la foibleſſe de noſtre eſprit nous
empeſchoit d'arriuer. Où vit-on
iamais enſemble deux Vertus ſi
auantageuſes pour les peuples, de
leur ſçauoir oſter la crainte des plus
effroyables ennemis, les garantir
de toutes ſortes d'oppreſſions, &
mettre leurs biens temporels, &
leurs vies en ſeureté ; & qui plus eſt
de leur ouurir le chemin aux ioyes

eternelles , procurant auſſi bien
le ſalut de leurs ames que celuy de
leurs corps? pour de ſi dignes operations il faut eſtre grand homme   d'Eſtat & grand Prelat
tout enſemble , & c'eſt en ce ſupré-
me degré ſeulement que l'on   ne
veut plus auoir d'intereſts particuliers , & que la Charité ayant
ſa pleine eſtenduë fait tout mettre en oubly pour n'auoir eſgard
qu'aux calamitez publiques. Apres
des remarques ſi conſiderables il
faudroit eſtre ennemy de la raiſon
pour s'eſtonner ſi l'on ne vous appelle point autrement que   l'ornement de voſtre ſiecle & les delices de la France, & ſi les perſonnes dont le merite eſclatte le plus
n'ont point de gloire qu'à vous en
attribuer. Pour moy *Monſeigneur,*
i'auouëray bien que ie ne diſcerne

plus autrement les bons d'auec les mauuais, les illustres d'auec les infames, qu'en m'informât de l'ardeur ou de la froideur qu'ils ont à vous honorer. Aussi craignant d'encourir vn blasme dôt ie menace les autres, ie ferois fort aise de n'auoir plus dorefnauant d'autre exercice que de vous donner toutes les loüãges qui peuuét venir en lapéfee; mais ie fçay qu'indubitablement vous ne goufteriez pas de plaifir à les ouyr, eftans fi fort efpris des charmes de la vertu que vous n'eftes pas encore fatisfait de voftre vie, & que vous ne fçauriez fouffrir que l'on exalte vos actions quoy qu'inimitables, d'autant que vous defirez d'en produire de plus glorieufes dont vous feul auez conçeu l'Idee. D'ailleurs il feroit inutile de les publier aux autres, puis qu'il en eft

de mesme de vous que du Soleil
dont vn certain peuple ne vouloit
iamais s'amuser à raconter les effets que personne n'ignore, & de
qui toute la nature reçoit les commoditez. Ce sera assez quád ie vous
tesmoigneray que ie vous reuere
comme l'vn de ces grands personnages que Dieu nous enuoye, pour
nous monstrer qu'il ne nous a pas
entierement abandonnez, & que
i'ay vne excessiue passion de me
voir au nombre de ceux qui ont
l'honneur d'estre connus de vous.
Mais à dire la verité, pour vne personne si basse comme ie suis, mon
ambition est bien releuée, & ie
n'employe que des moyens bien
foibles pour la mener au but qu'elle se propose, ne vous faisant voir
qu'vne de mes premieres œuures
dont i'ay fait mon apprentissage,
& où

& où ma langue ne faiſant encore que begayer, ie n'auois point de
paroles qui puſſent ſuiure mes penſees. Qu'en dois-ie eſperer ſinon
que de tous ceux qui cherchent la
gloire par ces meſmes voyes l'on
me mettra au moindre prix? Séten-
ce bien rude à vn courage qui a
quelque choſe de genereux, & qui
aymeroit mieux eſtre du tout ignorant d'vne profeſſion que d'en eſtre
eſtimé le dernier. Neantmoins,
MONSEIGNEVR, ie vous offre
aſſeurément ces premiers eſſais de
ma plume, afin que vous remar-
quiez dans les ouurages que ie feray deſormais, combien ie differe-
ray de ce que i'eſtois par cy-deuant,
& que c'eſt vn grand moyen de faire mieux, que d'eſtre eſclairé de vos
regards Que ſi ie ne puis paruenir à
cette beauté & ſtile qui a deſia tant

E

esté cherchee & si peu trouuee,
i'auray au moins cecy pour recon-
fort que les plus esclatantes paroles que puisse estaler l'Eloquence,
ne sçauroient auoir si bonne grace
en ma bouche comme ces mots
aussi veritables que Iustes, que ie
suis,

MONSEIGNEVR,

Vostre tres humble,
& tres-obeïssant
seruiteur.

SVR LE SIEGE DE
la Rochelle.

EN fin ces Rebelles qui se sont tant de fois sousleuez contre l'authorité du Roy, cognoistront que pour estre parfaitement Iuste, il s'exerce autant aux punitions comme aux recompenses, selon les occasions que l'on luy en donne. La ville où ils croyoient estre asseurez contre toute sorte d'attaques, ne leur sert que pour enfermer auec eux toutes les miseres qui peuuét arriuer à des personnes assiegees. S'ils ne veulent point que l'on entre au lieu où ils sont, en recompense l'on leur en

empefche la fortie, & les paffages
font fi bien bouchez par mer & par
terre, que leurs alliez ne les fçau-
roient aller voir, tellement que s'il
leur venoit du fecours, il faudroit
qu'il defcendift du Ciel ; mais il
viendra moins de cet endroit que
de pas vn autre, puifque ceux qui
mefprifent la Royauté & la Religion, ne meritent point que Dieu
les affifte. Tout ce qui leur peut
venir d'enhaut n'eft autre chofe
que de la pluye, mais encore n'eft
elle pas fi frequente qu'ils la defire-
roient, voyans que le cours de leurs
fontaines a efté diuerty. D'ailleurs
la faim qui leur eft vn ennemy do-
meftique, les trauaille continuellement, & le peu de viures qui leur
refte les contraint de ieufner, quoy
que les reigles de leur fauffe Religion ne les y aftraigne poinx. Tout

eſt parmy eux diſtribué au poids &
à la meſure, & ce qu'ils pourroient
bien manger en vn iour eſt reſerué
pour vne ſepmaine,　& ils le reſer-
rent en le deuorant quaſi des yeux.
En conſiderant les choſes qui leur
peuuent ſeruir de nourriture, ils aſ-
ſignent vn terme à leurs forces &
à leur vie, & à la conſeruation de
leur place, quoy qu'ils n'oublient
pas de mettre en ligne de compte
les rats & les ſouris, auſquels ils ont
deſia dreſſé des embuſches. Il eſt
vray qu'ils n'ont point laiſſé de terre inutile dans la Rochelle, & l'on
croid qu'ils ont deſpaué leurs Cours
& leurs ruës pour y ſemer du grain,
mais ils craignent que rien ne prof-
fite dans vne ſi mauuaiſe terre, &
que la moiſſon ne ſoit ſi tardiue,
qu'il leur faille manger leur bled
en herbe. C'eſt parmy eux que ceux

E iij

qui ont le plus d'argent ne font pas
le plus à leur aife, & vn fimple fol-
dat ne leur donneroit pas vn pain
d'vn foul pour dix piftolles, pource qu'il craindroit d'auoir vendu
fa vie, & d'eftre bien toft en eftat
de n'auoir plus befoin de richeffes.
Il n'y a point là de charité qui s'e-
ftende iufques fur fes voifins, ou fur
fes parents. Chacun fonge au falut
de fa perfonne propre, & le mary
ne s'imagine plus que fa femme foit la moitié de foy-mefme.
Le pere a bien du regret de voir
mourir fon fils faute de pain, mais
c'eft vne cópaffion infructueufe, &
il ne l'affifte point à fon dommage, croyant qu'il fe doit d'auantage aymer que celuy qui luy eft
redeuable de fa naiffance, ou que
s'il fe conferue il pourra mettre
d'autres enfans au monde. Voyla

l'estat où l'on iuge que sont les Ro-
chelois, suiuant beaucoup d'apa-
rences indubitables, tellemét qu'ils
seront contraints au bout de quelque temps d'implorer la misericorde de celuy qui les peut sauuer ou
perdre.

L'on pourroit bien battre en ruine tous leurs edifices, & les reduire à se retirer dans leurs caues; mais
cela seroit fascheux que le Roy fist
abbatre des choses qui luy appartiennent. Il en pourra bien vn iour
faire desmolir les fortifications s'il
le trouue à propos, mais pour
maintenant il veut tesmoigner vn
excez de douceur. Vn peu de
patience acheuera ses desseins, &
ie voy desia approcher ce iour
que la Rochelle luy sera ouuerte,
& qu'il y restablira les exercices de
la pieté & ceux de l'obeïssance.

Dieu l'a fauorifé de telle forte iufques à cette heure, qu'il n'eft point
croyable qu'apres l'auoir mené fi
auant, il le vueille fruftrer de ce qu'il
luy promet Les Confeils qu'il reçoit de fes plus fidelles fubjects font
auffi trop certains pour le tromper.
Ce grand Cardinal qui luy fert
comme d'vn Ange tutelaire vifible, luy faict prendre des refolu-
tions fi falutaires, que l'on ne doit
point douter de leur bon euene-
ment. C'eft luy que toute la France regarde auec admiration, & qui
prenant le foin des affaires de la
guerre, bien que fa condition ne
l'oblige qu'à celles de la Paix, monftre que noftre Monarque ne ref-
femble pas feulement en Sainéteté
à Charlemagne & à Sainét Louys,
mais auffi que pour vne entiere
conformité, il le rencontre qu'il

peut auoir aussi des Prelats qui cō-
mandent dans ses armees. Aussi
ayant rangé dans le denoir les rebelles de son Royaume , il pourra
aller faire la guerre aux infidelles,
cōme ces grāds Roys qui ont abbatu l'audace des Sarrazins & des Mo-
res. Ce sera alors que l'on verra l'ac-
complissement de tant de Propheties qui promettent à nostre Roy la
destruction de l'Empire des Maho-
metans.   Comme à l'ayde de ses
guerriers il rangera dās l'obeissance
les plus cruels de tous les Barbares,
tant de Prelats qui fleurissent en
saincteté dedans son Royaume ,
les conuertiront à la foy par leurs
remonstrances. C'est ce que tous
les bons François esperent sans feinte : mais nous ne voulons pas encore estendre nos discours sur ce sujet.   Nos pensées ne s'occupent

qu'aux chofes prefentes, & le cha-
ftiment des reuoltez , eft ce que
nous attendons premierement.
Nous ne voulons pas mefme efcrire de cecy d'vn ftile plus ample,
car il faut attendre la conclufion
de tant de rares chofes pour en
dreffer vne hiftoire parfaite, maintenant qu'elles commécent encore
de s'executer, l'attention & le rauif-
fement nous oftent le moyen de
les defcrire.

Autre description des miseres d'vne Ville assiegee.

E grand Capitaine representa à ses soldats que l'on porteroit tous les iours des viures en cachette dedans la ville si l'on n'y aportoit vn soudain remede, qui estoit de faire vn mur tout au tour; mais que si quelqu'vn pensoit qu'vn si grand ouurage se pust faire sans peine, il se trompoit infiniment veu qu'il n'apartenoit qu'à Dieu seul de faire les choses sans trauail, de sorte que puisqu'ils estoient hommes, il se falloit resoudre à trauailler continuellement. Là dessus il fit encore des exhortations si puissantes à tous les Chefs de ſes compagnies qu'ils partirent incótinent le trauail entre ceux qui marchoient ſous leur conduitte. Les ſimples ſoldats combatoient à qui s'aduáceroit le plus toſt. Chacũ tachoit de complaire au ſergent de bande, les Dizainiers aux Cente-niers lesCéteniers auxTribús, & les Tribuns veuloiét bié méme que les Gouuerneurs principaux fuſſét teſ-moins de leur diligéce,cepédát que leSouuerainauoit l'œil ſur to°,pour iuger de cette loüable contention, & les recompéſer apres ſelon l'affe-ction qu'ils auoient de bien faire.

Le circuit de leur muraille con-tenoit trente neuf ſtades, & par de hors il y eut treize forts baſtis qui auoient dix ſtades de tour. Au reſte cela fut acheué en trois iours, bien que ce fuſt vn ouurage qui ſem-bloit bien digne du trauail de trois

mois. L'on ordonna apres qu'il y
auroit des gardes en chacun fort, &
le Prince voulut prendre la charge
defaire la premiere ronde. Il n'en-
tra depuis aucuns viures dedans la
ville, & les assiegez ne pouuans plus
sortir, commencerent à desesperer
de leur salut. Les munitions qu'ils
auoient de reserue, estoient en si
petit nombre qu'elles ne suffisoient
pas à les nourrir, de sorte qu'il n'y
auoit point de famille qui pour son
plus grand mal ne fust sujette à perir par la faim, & les maisons n'e-
stoient pleines que de femmes & de
petits enfans morts ou prests à ietter le dernier souspir, & les destroits
des ruës estoiét si remplis des corps
des vieilles gens qui y mouroient
de foiblesse, qu'à peine y pouuoit-
on trouuer passage. Les ieunes
hommes n'auoient guere plus de

force. Ils eſtoient enflez comme
des hydropiques pour la mauuaiſe
nourriture qu'ils auoient priſe, &
l'on les voyoit marcher comme des
ombres par les places publiques.
Que s'ils ſe heurtoient l'vn l'autre
par meſgarde, ils tomboient incõ-
tinent. Pour ce qui eſtoit des corps
morts, ils demeuroient la pluſpart
ſans eſtre ſeulement enſeuelis, d autant qu'il n'y en auoit guere qui les
puſſent enterrer , & s'ils auoient
aſſez de force du reſte , ils ſe fa-
choient de prédre ceſte peine, tant
pour le grand nombre des morts,
qu'à cauſe qu'ils ne ſçauoient ce
qui deuoit arriuer à eux meſmes.
Il y en auoit pluſieurs qui eſtoient
deſia tombez tous morts ſur ceux
qu'ils vouloiét enterrer, & d'autres
encore tous viuans, accouroient
aux ſepulchres pour s'y enfermer,

iugeants bien que leur mort eſtoit
prochaine, & que perſonne ne voudroit prendre cette peine pour eux.
Parmi toutes ces miſeres l'ó n'oyoit
point de plaintes ny de ſouſpirspour
le treſpas de quelque parent. La famine que chacũ eſprouuoit ſurmõ-
toit toutes autres afflictions. Ceux
qui mouroiét les derniers eſtoient
ſeulement les gardes de ceux qui a-
uoient finy leurs iours deuant eux,
mais leurs yeux n'auoiét pl'd'humi-
dités pour fournir aux larmes & leur
voix eſtoiét ſi foible qu'à peine pou
uoiét-ils demãder ce qui leur eſtoit
neceſſaire ſãs s'amuſer à plaindre le
malheur d'autruy qui n'eſtoit pas
plus grãd que celuy qui leur eſtoit
arriué. Or il y auoit vn merueilleux
ſiléce par la ville, cõme s'il y euſt eu
vne nuictperpetuelle qui n'euſt eſté
pleine que de fantoſme. Mais il n'y

auoit rié de si cruel à supporter que
la meschanceté des brigands , car
ils alloient despoüiller les corps
morts , & ostoient les meubles de
leurs maisons où ils les laissoient
pour leur seruir de sepulchres , sans
les enterrer ny les couurir. Ils en
sortoient apres auecque des risees
& des mocqueries, & s'ils trouuoiét
quelque pauure homme qui s'en
alloit mourant , ils esprouuoient
sur luy la pointe de leurs espees :
mais leur cruauté estoit si grande
qu'ils ne frapoient que ceux qui
auoient encore quelque espoir
& quelque desir de viure , & si
quelque autre plus ennuyé des miseres de la vie , les eur priez de l'en
deliurer & de luy prester leurs
mains ou l'vne de leurs espees , ils
le laissoient languir & passoient
tout outre auec vne arrogance
inexcusable.

merueilleuse. Tous ceux qui estoiēt
prests de rendre l'esprit leuoient pi-
teusement les yeux vers le Ciel, &
luy demandoient iustice de ces brigands qui estoient cause de la reuolte & du malheur de la ville, & ne
laissoient pas de demeurer en santé!
A la fin ces seditieux ne pouuans
souffrir la puanteur de tant de corps
morts commanderent que l'on les
enterrast aux despens du public;
mais voyans que l'on n'y pouuoit
fournir, ils en firent jetter vne grā-
de partie du haut des murailles. Ce
grand Prince qui les tenoit assiegez
s'aperceut de cecy, & voyant tant
de personnes mortes, il appella Dieu
en tesmoignage, comme il n'estoit
point cause de ce mal. Ce pendant
la misere de la ville augmentoit incessamment. Si la famine estoit grā-
de, la rage des Seditieux l'estoit en-

F

core d'auantage. Ils ne cessoient de
tourmenter les plus notables Citoyens. Que s'ils estoient riches, ils
trouuoient tousiours quelque occasion de les faire mourir, soit qu'ils
voulussent demeurer auec eux, ou
qu'ils se voulussent rendre, car l'on
leur faisoit tousiours acroire qu'ils
auoiët eu dessein de s'enfuyr, pource que le bled estoit failly par tout,
& qu'il n'y en auoit point s'il n'e-
stoit caché, ces Rebelles fouïlloiët
dans toutes les maisons, sans aucun
respect, vsans de force & de violence par tout. Que si par hazard ils
trouuoient quelque chose, ils ou-
trageoient ceux qui l'auoient caché, & s'ils ne trouuoient rien, ils
mettoient tous les domestiques à
la torture, comme s'ils eussent esté
plus malicieux que les autres, & s'ils
eussent caché leurs prouisions plus

secrettemét. Toute la preuue qu'ils auoient pour s'imaginer que ces gés cy fuſſent fournis de bled ou d'autres viures, c'eſtoit quãd ils voyoiét que leurs corps eſtoient vigoureux, d'autant qu'ils croyoient qu'il falloit bien qu'ils euſſent dequoy ſe nourrir. Pour ceux qui eſtoiét maigres & ſecs, ils les laiſſoient en repos, croyans que la faim les feroit bien toſt perir. Il y en eut pluſieurs d'entre les riches qui donnerét tout leur bien pour vne meſure de froment, & quelques pauures donnerent tout auſſi pour vne meſure d'orge. Il y en eut quelques-vns qui s'enfermerent dans les lieux les plus ſecrets de leurs maiſons pour manger du bled pourry & gaſté; tant la neceſſité les cótraignoit. Les autres en faiſoient du pain ſelon que la cómodité leur permettoit. Au reſte il

n'y auoit maifon où l'on vift la nape
mife. On ne donnoit pas feulement
le loifir à la viande de la cuire. L'on
l'empoignoit d'vne grande auidité,
deuorant les morceaux fans les maf-
cher. La famine oftoit toute honte,
& tout refpect. Ceux qui auoient
accouftumé d'eftre amis fe querel-
loient pour vne poignee de farine.
Les femmes rauiffoient à leurs maris ce qu'ils alloiét mettre dans leur
bouche; les enfans faifoient le mefme traictement à leur pere & à leur
mere, & par ce moyen il y auoit en
beaucoup de lieux vne guerre do-
meftique. Pour ce qui eftoit de
ceux qui alloient encore par les
ruës, s'ils voyoient quelque porte
fermee, cela leur eftoit vn figne
que ceux qui eftoient dans la maifon prenoient leur repas, tellement
qu'ils y entroient par force, & ar-

rachoient presque du gosier la via-
de que l'on auoit desia maschee. Le
plus souuent mesme, ils n'adiou-
stoient pas foy à ceux qui s'en alloient rendre le dernier souspir,
quand ils iuroient qu'ils n'auoient
plus rien. Ils les foüilloient pour
voir s'ils n'auoient point encore caché quelque morceau entre les
doubleures de leurs habits, esperans
de pouuoir viure encore. Ils estoiét
tellement insensez qu'ils entroient
par trois ou quatre fois dans vne
mesme maison en vne mesme heure, & y faisoient tousiours la recherche, & bien qu'il y eust de grandes
dissensions entre les Rebelles, tou-
resfois ils s'accordoient ensemble
quand il estoit question de faire
quelque meschanceté. Il n'y auoit
quasi plus qu'eux dedans la ville qui
eussent de la vigueur, car ils auoiét

desrobé toutes les munitions des
autres dont ils se nourrissoient en
cachettes. Les pauures gens ne faisoient plus de difficulté de ramasser
tout ce qu'ils rencontroient pour
s'en nourrir, & il n'y auoit ny cour-
roye ny soulier, qui ne leur seruist
de pasture, iusques là mesme qu'ils
prenoient le cuir de leurs boucliers,
& le faisoient bouillir dans de l'eau,
où ils mettoient seulement vn peu
d'espice pour y donner du goust.
L'on raconte vne chose estrange
qui arriua entr'eux, c'est qu'vn ieune homme qui voyoit que son pere alloit mourir de faim, ne fit pas
comme tant d'autres qui preferoiét
leur salut à celuy de leurs parents.
Comme son sang auoit esté mer-
ueilleusemét eschauffé par vn long
ieusne, il s'en fit tirer quantité, &
voulut persuader à son pere de s'en

nourrir, luy difant qu'il pouuoit iuftement conferuer fa vie, aux defpens de celuy à qui il l'auoit donnée. Il arriua encore des accidens
nompareils, qu'à peine l'on peut
croire maintenant, iufques à ce
qu'enfin cefte ville qui auoit fi peu
de deffence de refte, fut prife par
force, & reduite fous l'obeiffance
du vainqueur.

F iiij

LE PRINCE.

Par M. D. B.

ENCORE qu'il ſoit fort difficile de parler dignement de la vertu de ce Prince que nous venons de perdre, & en dire des choſes eſgales à ſa renommee, ſi eſt-ce que i'ay entrepris de le faire, ne croyant pas qu'il ſoit deffendu de le loüer, à cauſe que l'on ne le ſçauroit loüer autant côme il le merite. Quât à la Nobleſſe de ſa race l'on n'en ſçauroit dire d'auantage que ce qui en a deſia eſté dit. Il ſuffit ſeulement d'aſſeurer icy, qu'il a eſté preferé à plu-

fieurs de fes anceftres, encore qu'ils
euffent tiré leur origine d'vne longue fuitte de Roys, & qu'ils euffent
dominé fur ceux qui eftoient les
maiftres des autres.

Pour ce qui eft des chofes qu'il
a faites en prefence de plufieurs
tefmoins, elles n'ont pas befoin
d'autre preuue, & il faut adioufter
foy aux hiftoires que l'on en publie. Nous en ferons mefme vne
longue narration lors que nous ferons plus de loifir, & pour maintenant l'on fe contentera de ces
pieces feparees que nous offrons
au peuple. Il fe faut efforcer de
monftrer la force de fon efprit qui
luy a ferui pour mettre à fin tant de
belles entreprifes, & pour luy faire aymer la vertu en toutes chofes
& fuyr les occafions du vice. Il gardoit toufiours vne telle integrité,

que ſes ennemis meſmes s'aſſeu-
royét pluſtoſt ſur ſon ſerment que
ſur les traitez qu'ils faiſoyent entre
eux, tellemét qu'ils le choiſiſſoyent
quelquefois pour arbitre de leurs
querelles. Auſſi croyoit-il qu'il e-
ſtoit conuenable à toute ſorte de
perſonnes, mais principalemét à des
Chefs de guerre, non ſeulemét d'e-
ſtre eſtimez iuſtes & fideles, mais
auſſi de l'eſtre veritablement. Nous
cognoiſtrons par ce qui enſuit qu'il
gardoit la meſne iuſtice dans la
diſtribution de ſes finances.

Iamais homme ne ſe plaignit
qu'il luy eut oſté quelque choſe
de ce qui luy appartenoit ; au contraire il y en a eu pluſieurs qui ont
confeſſé qu'il leur auoir fait plus
de bien qu'ils ne meritoient. Que
l'on me diſe donc ſi celuy qui a e-
ſté preſt à donner tout ſon bien

pour secourir ceux qui en auoient
besoin, a pû faire quelque violence
pour enuahir le bien d'autruy?
S'il eust mis ses affections aux richesses, il eust bien plustost gardé
les siennes, que de se donner tant
de peine & de soucy & se mettre au
hasard d'vne infamie eternellé pour
vsurper ce qui ne luy appartenoit
pas. Celui qui fait des presēts aux autres sans qu'il y ayt aucune loy qui
l'y cōtraigne, n'en voudroit pas cō-
mettre des larrecins qui sont deffē-
dus par les loix. Or nostre grand
Prince n'estimoit pas seulement
iniuste celuy qui n'en rendoit pas
dauantage lors qu'il en auoit
le moyen. Au reste comment le
pourroit-on accuser d'auoir pillé
le bien du public, veu qu'il laissoit souuent receuoir par la
Republique les remerciements

& les dons des estrangers qui luy apartenoient en particulier ? Que s'il vouloit donner quelque somme d'argent à ses amis, c'estoit mesme auparauant qu'ils luy eussent rendu quelque seruice, car s'il eust fait autrement il eust creu que les bonnes actions eussent commencé à se vendre, & que l'on ne se fust accoustumé à bien faire que pour de l'argent, de sorte que par ce moyé personne n'eust esté tenu à luy. Il sçauoit bien que ceux à qui l'on fait plaisir gratuitement, se rendent apres fort volontiers, quelques rebelles qu'ils ayent esté, & qu'à toutes heures ils se monstrent seruiables à leur bien-faicteur, tant pour la courtoisie qu'ils en ont receuë, que pour ce qu'ils se glorifient d'auoir este estimez dignes de receuoir des presents, aupara-

uant mesme que d'auoir fait aucune chose en sa consideration, comme si l'on leur auoit donné cela en
depost. Or comme il aymoit mieux
aussi n'auoir guere de chose, pourueu qu'il vesquit auec des hommes
vertueux, que non pas d'en auoir
beaucoup, & n'estre suiuy que par
des hommes meschans : ayant he-
rité de tous les biens de l'vn de ses
predecesseurs il les distribua à de
pauures gentils hommes , quoy
qu'ils fussent parens assez esloignez
du deffunct.

L'on remarque encore qu'estant
dans le païs des ennemis l'on luy
offrit beaucoup d'argent pour l'en
faire retirer. Il fit response que
ceux de sa patrie estimoient estre
vne chose plus honorable à vn Capitaine d'enrichir ses soldats que
de s'enrichir soy mesme , & de

piller pluſtoſt l'énemy que de receuoir ſes preſens. Outre cela bié qu'il
y ayt pluſieurs ſortes de voluptez
qui arreſtent les hommes, l'on ne
marque point qu'il y en ayt aucune
qui l'ayt ſurmóté. Il ne croyoit poit
qu'il y euſtvn plus grãd vice que l'y-
urognerie & la gourmãdiſe, & il ne
s'abſtenoit pas moins de trop boire
que de trop mãger. Que s'il ſe trouuoit en vn feſtin & que l'on luy pre-
ſentaſt double ſeruice, il ſe gardoit
bié de taſter de tout: il en enuoyoit
la plus grande partie à ſes amis, car
il diſoit que ſi l'on donnoit pluſieurs ſeruices à vn Prince, il ne
croyoit pas que ce fuſt afin qu'il
mangeaſt plus que les autres, ce qui
euſt eſté fort deshonneſte, mais
pour en honorer celuy qui luy
plairoit. Pour ce qui eſtoit du
ſommeil, il ne s'y aſſujetiſſoit ia-

mais : il n'en prenoit que ſelon la meſure du temps qu'il faloit reſer-uer pour ſes aſtaires , & encore eſtoit - il quelquefois honteux s'il auoit vn lict meilleur que ceux de ſa compagnie : car il penſoit que le Prince deuoit ſurpaſſer les hommes vulgaires en patience & en force d'eſprit, & non pas en ſes delices Il ſouffroit l'ardeur du Soleil en eſté & l'incommodité du froid en hyuer ſans ſe plaindre , & s'il voyoit que ſes ſoldats euſſent de la laſſitude, il ne ſe repoſoit point , & continuoit de marcher auec eux, afin de leur dóner courage. En fin il ſe plaiſoit à toutes ſortes de trauaux & ne s'ennuyoit que dás l'oyſiueté.

Il faut parler de ſa continence, qui eſt ſi remarquable qu'elle fait voir qu'il n'y a rien que de merueil-leux en toutes les parties de ſa vie.

Ie sçay bien qu'il est facile de s'abstenir des choses que l'on n'ay-me point, mais que dira-on de nostre Prince qui ayma autant Celinde qu'il est possible à vn esprit vehement d'aymer vne belle chose, & qui toutefois encore que ce soit la coustume de baiser les Dames que l'on veut honorer, ne s'aduaça point pour baiser celle cy, lors qu'il la reuit apres vne longue absence ? Celinde s'en fut offencée si elle n'eust bien connu son naturel austere, & vne autre fois comme il la deuoit encore voir, l'vn de ses plus particuliers amis luy demanda s'il ne prenoit point resolution de l'honorer d'auantage qu'auparauant, afin qu'elle n'eust point de mescontentement de luy, & qu'elle ne creust pas qu'il la voulust mespriser. Il se teust quelque

temps, puis apres il parla ainsi.
Quand ie deurois dés l'heure que
ie vous parle, deuenir le plus beau,
le plus fort & le plus agile du monde, ie vous iure que ie ne voudrois
pour chose quelconque entreprendre vn tel combat, car il est si dangereux, que ie n'ose mesme approcher de cette belle ennemie, qui
nous offence en nous plaisant, &
qui nous peut tuer en feignant de
nous donner la vie.

La plufpart de ceux qui entendent cecy n'y adioufteront point
de foy; c'est vne chose dont ie me
doute dés maintenant; mais il est
pourtant tres-certain que noftre
Prince a tenu vn tel difcours, &
qu'il l'a eu auffi dans la penfee, car
il fçauoit bien que plufieurs refi-
ftent pluftoft à leurs plus cruels ennemis qu'aux plus douces atteintes

de l'amour. Au refte ie ne m'eſtonne pas, ſi peu de gens croyent vne
choſe qui peut eſtre faite par ſi peu
de perſonnes. Nous deuons ſeulement conſiderer que ce que nous
diſons peut bien eſtre vray , veu
que les hommes Illuſtres ne font
rien de ſi ſecret que leurs amis ne
prennent plaiſir à le publier apres
leur mort pour augmenter leur
gloire.

Au regard de celuy dont nous
celebrons les loüanges , l'on ſçait
bien que toute ſa vie ſe rapporte à cet exemple de continence
que nous auons remarqué, & iamais l'on ne luy a veu faire aucun
acte deshonneſte, ny meſme l'on ne
l'en a point ſoupçonné ny accuſé:
Auſſi en allant par le païs, il ne ſe logeoit iamais dãs les maiſós priuees,
il ſe tenoit en public auec toute ſa

suite, afin que chacun fuſt teſmoin de ſa continence; ou bien il ſe logeoit dans les Religions, afin qu'en de tels lieux il fuſt obligé à bien faire, & qu'il ne viſt aucune occaſion de peché.

Toute l'Europe ſçait la verité de ces choſes, & ſi ie me trouuois menteur en quelqu'vne, au lieu d'auoir monſtré que ce Prince ſeroit digne d'vne extreme loüange, i'aurois faict voir que ie meriterois vne eternelle infamie.

Ayant aſſez parlé de ceſte force d'eſprit qu'il faiſoit cognoiſtre en ſurmontant les charmes de la volupté, il faut dire quelque choſe de ceſte autre force qu'il teſmoignoit en pleine guerre. Eſtant choiſy d'ordinaire pour abbatre l’orgueil des ennemis de ſa Republique , il eſtoit touſiours le premier qui eſtoit preſt à combattre.

Quand les ennemis auoient enuie de venir aux mains, iamais pour aucune crainte qu’il euſt il ne s’attendit de les vaincre en temporiſant. Il auoit touſiours accouſtumé de les aſſaillir, & de les dompter par ſa valeur. L’on void par tout les Trophees qui ont eſté dreſſez pour eſtre les monuments eternels de ſa vertu. Neantmoins il ne faut pas ſeulement regarder à ceux que l’on rencontre en tant de lieux. Il faut ſonger à beaucoup d’autres qu’il a meritez , & qu’il n’a point eus. Combien de fois a t’il mis les armes bas . lors qu’il a veu que la guerre ſe pouuoit terminer ſans

combattre ? N'est-ce pas là qu'il
a tesmoigné la bonté de son esprit
dans les traictez qui estoient plus
seurs & plus profitables à ses Citoyens que toute autre chose ? De-
uoit-il estre estimé moins victorieux, encore que la guerre n'eut
pas esté fort tragique, veu que mesme c'est la coustume des jeux pu-
blics, de couronner aussi bien ceux
qui obtiennét la victoire sans beaucoup de sueur, que ceux qui la ga-
gnent en combattant violem-
ment?

Quelles autres actions a t'il faites qui ne fussent pleines de sagesse?
Il s'est comporté de telle sorte enuers tout le monde, qu'il n'y auoit
personne qui ne fust tousiours prest
d'aller à la guerre auec luy, & de
tous ceux qui y alloient, il n'y en
auoit pas vn qui ne voulust mou-

rir pour son seruice. Où a-t'on iamais veu de meilleurs Soldats que
ceux qui rendent ainsi vne obeïssance volontaire, & que ceux qui
portent vne telle affection à leur
Chef, qu'ils ne luy demandent iamais vne augmentation de solde,
& se contentent de l'honneur qu'ils
ont de luy obeïr ? Que s'il estoit
eternellement loüé de ceux qui le
seruoient, ceux mesmes qui e-
stoient ses ennemis ne le pouuoient
blasmer, encore qu'ils luy portassent de la hayne.

Pour ce qui estoit de luy, il ne
laissoit pas de fauoriser ceux qui
tenoient leur passion couuerte, &
il les faisoit profiter auecque luy
de la ruine de ses ennemis decla-
rez, les preuenant où il estoit
besoin de vistesse, se cachant où
il ne se falloit pas monstrer, &

faisant toutes choses autremenṭ
enuers eux qu'enuers ceux quị
auoient apparence d'estre ses al_
liez.

Toutesfois il se donnoit garde des
surprises des vns & des autres, sans
faire paroistre sa deffiance. Quand
il estoit besoin de faire quelque entreprise, il se seruoit de la nuict
comme du iour, & du iour comme
de la nuict, & l'on ignoroit souuét
ce qu'il faisoit, & en quel lieu il e-
stoit, ou de quel costé il vouloit aller. Voila pourquoy si les ennemis
tenoient quelquefois vne chose
pour toute certaine, il la rendoit soudain douteuse, quittant
le premier lieu où il s'estoit mis,
& passant par vn autre, puis se
iettant à l'escart promptement.
Quand son armee estoit en cam-

pagne ; il confideroit qu'il n'e-
ftoit forty qu'en intention de combattre, & qu'il fe faifoit tenir dés le
premier iour, afin de ne pas manquer au befoin. Il la faifoit neantmoins marcher pofément, de peur
qu'il n'y euft du defordre, & qu'elle ne tombaft dans quelques embufches. Il donnoit par ce moyen
autant de crainte à fes ennemis,
comme il donnoit de courage à fes
Soldats; de forte qu'il n'a iamais efté
mefprifé ; ny par les eftrangers , ny
par ceux de fa ville, & tant qu'il a
vefcu, il a efté loüé des vns, & aymé
des autres.

Auffi ne fçauroit-on dire tout au
long de quelle affection recipro-
que il recompenfoit fes Citoyens.
Cela feroit trop long pour l'efpace
que nous auons en ce lieu cy. Mais
pour en parler fuccinctement, Ie

croy qu'il ne fit iamais aucune a-
ction qui ne tendit à ce but. Quand
il eſtoit beſoin de ſecourir ſa patrie,
il ne fuyoit aucun trauail & ne craignoit aucun dãger. Il n'eſpargnoit
point l'argent , & ne s'excuſoit
pas ſur la foibleſſe de ſon corps &
les incommoditez de ſa vieilleſſe ;
car il croyoit qu'il ne ſe pouuoit acquitter de la charge qui luy auoit
eſté donnee qu'en apportant du
proffit à tous ceux qui viuoiẽt ſous
ſon obeïſſance. Entre toutes les
perfections qui l'ont rendu recommandable, il eſt fort à admirer de
ce qu'eſtant le plus puiſſant de la
Republique, il ne laiſſoit pas d'o-
beïr à toutes les loix : & c'eſt en cela que la patrie luy eſt extremement obligee, car voyant l'obeïſſance du premier de nos Princes,
qui eſt ce qui euſt voulu eſtre deſ-

obeïſſant ? Qui eſt - ce qui euſt eſté
mal content de ſa condition ? Qui
eſt - ce qui euſt entrepris des nouueautez voyant qu'il conſeruoit les
couſtumes anciennes ? Qui eſt - ce
qui luy euſt voulu contredire,
puiſqu'il ſe monſtroit tel enuers
ceux qui eſtoient en different auecque luy en matiere d'Eſtat , qu'vn
pere auec ſes enfans ？ Il les reprenoit de leurs fautes ſans aucune paſſion, de meſme qu'il les loüoit de
leurs beaux faicts ſans aucune enuie ; & il les aſſiſtoit ſoudain s'il leur
arriuoit quelque infortune. Auſſi
dequelque ſorte qu'ils puſſent viure, il n'y en auoit pas vn qu'il e-
ſtimaſt ſon ennemy. Il les vouloit
aymer tous autant que ſes plus proches parens, & ce luy eſtoit vn grãd
gain de les cõſeruer , & vne grande
perte d'en laiſſer mourir quelque

vn, encore qu'il ne valuſt guere,
d'autant qu'il eſperoit de le rendre
meilleur par des promeſſes & des
remonſtrãces. Il leur diſoit que s'ils
obeïſſoient paiſiblemẽt àleurs loix,
leur ville ſeroit touſiours heureuſe,
& qu'elle ſeroit touſiours puiſſante
tãt qu'ils ſeroiẽt ſages. Au reſte qui
eſt-ce qui a connu iamais aucun
Capitaine qui ne s'efforçaſt de prẽ-
dre vne ville s'il auoit eſperance de
la piller, ou qui eſtimaſt qu'en ob-
tenant vne victoire il peut perdre
quelque choſe? Neãtmoins quand
il ſçeut que dans la bataille qu'il a-
uoit donnée à des rebelles, il n'e-
ſtoit mort que deux cens des ſiens
& mille de ſes ennemis, au lieu de
faire vn cry de ioye il dit en ſouſpi-
rant: O que nous ſommes malheureux ! car de quelque coſté que la
victoire ſoit tournée, nous auons

toufiours beaucoup perdu. Faifons
noftre compte, que nous auós perdu douze cents hommes , qui
eftoient capables de nous ayder à
fubjuguer les barbares. Comme
quelques bannis luy eurent aufſi aſ-
feuré qu'ils luy mettóient vne des
villes rebelles entre les mains, luy
monftrant les moyens par lefquels
on s'en pouuoit emparer & mettre
tout à feu & à fang fi l'on le defiroit, il dit qu'il ne vouloit pas perdre les villes de fa patrie , mais les
chaftier feulement. En effet il auoit
raifon de fonger à la conferuation
de tout le peuple qui eftoit fous fa
conduitte, car encore que le plus
puiffant de fes voifins euft iuré de
luy faire vne guerre eternelle, il ne
vouloit que des forces domeftiques
pour abaiffer fon audace, & il euft
creu eftre iniufte, s'il euft fait re-

uolter contre luy quelques vnes
de ſes Prouinces, ou s'il euſt man-
dié vn ſecours eſtranger. Il ne fut
pas plus malheureux pour auoir eu
de ſi bonnes intentions, & pour ne
vouloir point exercer les trahiſons
& les tromperies. La bonté diuine
eſtoit fauorable à cette bonté humaine, & le petit nombre de ſes
forces eſtant conduit prudemment
a ſouuent deffait de puiſſantes armees qui n'auoient point vn Capitaine ſi ſage.

Il eſt fort à propos de parler
maintenant de ſa courtoiſie nompareille. Encore qu'il euſt parde-
uers luy tout l'honneur & le pouuoir de ſa Republique, & qu'il ſe
fuſt acquis vne ſouueraineté qui e-
ſtoit hors de doute, & qu'il ne tenoit que par l'affection de ſes ſuiets,
ſi eſt-ce qu'il ne s'eſt iamais meſ-

connu , & qu'il a toufiours aduoüé pour fes amis ceux qu'il auoit
recognu pour tels , lors que fa fortune n'eftoit pas en vn degré fi e-
minent. Or pource qu'il auoit
toufiours vn grand courage &
de hautes efperances , il fe mon-
ftroit toufiours ioyeux , de forte
que cela inuitoit plufieurs perfonnes à le venir vifiter, non feulement pour traitter d'affaires auec
luy, mais aufsi pour paffer le temps.
Il eftoit d'vne fi douce conuerfa-
tion qu'encore qu'il fe vantaft
moins qu'hóme du monde, il ne fe
fafchoit point cótre ceux qui par-
loiét d'eux trop aduantageufemét ,
mais pluftoft il leur aduoüoit ce
qu'ils difoient, afin qu'ils s'efforçaf-
fent d'eftre veritablement ce qu'ils
vouloient fembler eftre , & qu'ils
cogneuffent quelles eftoient les re-

compenses d'vne veritable vertu.
Pour ce qui estoit des hommes de
lettres, il leur dónoit vn libre accez
pres de sa personne , & prenoit
plaisir à émouuoir de petites dispu-
tes entres eux, dont puis apres il e-
stoit le Iuge,& quelquefois il recó-
pensoit ceux qui auoient le mieux
parlé.Cela faisoit que l'onse pressoit
pour entrer chez luy quãd il tenoit
de séblables conferences : mais l'on
aymoit mieux pourtãt l'ouyr parler
que ceux qui s'estimoiét les plus doctes; & d'autant qu'il parloit priue-
ment à tout le monde quand il prenoit son repas , c'estoit là qu'il faisoit le meilleur pour les bós esprits ,
& l'on tiroit plus de proffit de l'a-
uoir ouy que d'auoir assisté à la leçon de quelque suffisant Professeur
de science. Il auoit cela d'excellent
qu'il philosophoit sur toute sorte

de ſujets, & que ſur vne choſe de
neant il amenoit vne haute queſtion. Il ne propoſoit rien pourtant
dont il ne dit ſon aduis, & il auoit
vn ſens naturel ſi excellent, qu'il
valoit mieux qu'vn autre qui euſt
eſté raffiné par de longues eſtudes.

Il ne faut pas oublier à faire
quelque remarque de la grandeur
de ſon courage qu'il a monſtree en
diuerſes façons. Ayant receu des
lettres de la part d'vn Roy eſtranger auec lequel la Republique a-
uoit quelque choſe à deſmeſler, il
vid qu'il luy promettoit toute ſorte
d'affection, tellement qu'il ne les
voulut point receuoir, mais il có-
manda au meſſager de dire à ſon
maiſtre qu'il n'eſtoit point beſoin
qui luy reſcriuiſt en particulier, &
qu'il pouuoit eſtre amy s'il n'e-
ſtoit pareillement amy de la Republique.

publique, iusques à ce temps, luy
dit-il, ie le tiendray dans l'indifference, mais s'il continuë à me vouloir seduire par vne infinité de lettres i'auray plustost de la hayne
pour luy que de l'affection. Ce
Prince est fort recommandable
d'auoir mesprisé l'alliäce d'vn Roy
qui luy promettoit de grandes choses, pour n'estre point traistre à sa
patrie, dont il ne tiroit pas de grandes auantages. Aussi ceux qui e-
stoient les plus riches, & qui commandoient à plus de gents, n'estoiët
pas ceux qu'il estimoit le plus ; mais
bien ceux qui estoient les plus vertueux, & qui ne commandoient
aussi qu'à des hommes vertueux. Il
ne pût iamais estre gagné, ny par
presents ny par force. Il faisoit tout
son possible pour garder sa fidelité,
afin qu'à son exemple les plus gräds

H

de l'Eſtat ne quittaſſent point le bõ
party. Neantmoins tous les Princes
qui auoient affaire de luy eſtoient ſi
aueuglez qu'ils amaſſoient des richeſſes de toutes parts, & cherchoient ſi entre leurs pieces les plus
exquiſes, il n'y auroit rien qui luy
pûſt eſtre agreable ; mais il mettoit
vn bon remede à cecy, car il donnoit vn tel ordre à ſa maiſon, qu'il
n'y auoit rien à deſirer, & il viuoit
auec ſi peu de ſomptuoſité, que
tout ce que l'on luy pouuoit offrir
ne conſiſtoit qu'en des choſes ſu-
perfluës. Si quelqu'vn a de la peine
à croire cecy, qu'il regarde de quelle ſorte eſtoit le logement où il de-
meuroit ; qu'il en conſidere les
portes & les feneſtrages faicts à
l'antique ; il verra qu'il n'y a rien
de changé depuis que ſon ayeul
fit baſtir cét edifice. Que l'on voye

auſſi de quelle ſorte eſtoient les
meubles, où il n'y auoit rien d'extraordinaire.

Que l'on aprenne quels eſtoient
ſes feſtins, quel eſtoit ſon equipage
quand il s'en alloit aux champs, l'on
ſçaura bien qu'il a touſiours reglé
ſa deſpence ſuiuant ſon reuenu, &
qu'il n'a eſté contraint de faire aucun acte deshoneſte pour auoir de
l'argent, afin de l'employer en des
ſomptuoſitez.

Ie ſçay bien que l'on eſtime beaucoup ceux qui ont fait de grandes
deſpences pour des baſtiments,
mais il a fait quelque choſe de meilleur. Si c'eſt vne belle choſe de baſtir des murailles imprenables, ce
n'eſt pas doncques vne moindre
gloire de rendre ſon ame inuincible contre l'ambition & l'auarice.

Ie veux reprefenter icy la difference qu'il y auoit entre fa façon
de viure & celle de quelques Princes qui eſtoient fes voiſins & ſes
ennemis. Premierement ceux-là ne
fe monſtroient que fort rarement,
parce qu'ils prenoient beaucoup
de peine à cacher leur mauuaiſe
vie; mais pour luy il vouloit bien
touſiours eſtre veu, croyant que
la lumiere ne faiſoit qu'apporter
de l'ornement aux belles choſes.
Ces gents là eſtoient de fi difficile
accez que perſonne ne les pouuoit aborder ; mais pour luy il
donnoit audience à tout le monde. Si les autres tenoient à honneur de faire languir par des remi-
ſes ceux qui les pourſuiuoient, il
eſtoit bien aiſe au contraire de deſ-
peſcher promptement ceux qui
auoient affaire à luy. Si lon veut

ſçauoir en bref de quelle loüange
on doit honnorer ſa vertu, il faut
conſiderer comment toutes les
commoditez de la vie ont eſté par
luy renduës faciles à recouurer. Il
y a des Gents qui vont iuſques au
bout du monde pour faire boire
leur Roy plus delicieuſement, &
qui trauaillent ſans ceſſe à luy inuenter de nouuelles fauſſes, ou à
trouuer vne inuention pour le faire coucher plus mollement ; mais
noſtre Prince a deliuré ſon peuple
de ces exercices inutiles. Ce qui ſe
trouuoit où il auoit accouſtumé
de demeurer luy ſuffiſoit. Il ſe contentoit de tout ce que ſes Officiers
luy preſentoient ; car il ſe donnoit
tant d'exercice qu'il ne manquoit
iamais d'apetit, & que tout lieu luy
eſtoit propre pour dormir à ſon aiſe. Lors qu'il ſe tenoit ainſi ſatisfaict

H iij

de peu de choses, il s'en resioüissoit
en soy-mesme, & mesprisoit tous
les delices superflus. Il se mocquoit
de ces voluptueux qui viuoiét plus
delicatement que des femmes, &
quand il alloit en voyage il prenoit
plaisir à supporter toutes les iniures
du temps que le Ciel luy vouloit enuoyer, au lieu qu'il y en auoit d'autres qui ne pouuoient supporter ny
les chaleurs ny les froidures, & qui
n'imitoiét poit la vie des hómes genereux, mais celle des bestes les plus
foibles. Si nostre Prínce outre la des-
péce necessaire à sa maisó en a faict
encore quelques autres, elle n'a esté
qu'en des choses honnestes. En téps
de paix il a nourry plusieurs chiens
de chasse, afin de s'addonner à cet e-
xercice, qui est vn' image de la guerre. C'est par ce moyé qu'il s'empeschoit d'estre iamais oysif, & qu'il

s'accouſtumoit à courir de tous les
coſtez par les mótagnes & les foreſts
en toute ſorte de ſaiſons, afin que
cela ne luy fuſt point eſtrange, lors
qu'il ſeroit beſoin de pourſuiure des
ennemis. Il faiſoit auſſi nourrir quátité de cheuaux pour s'é ſeruir quád
la guerre ſuruiendroit. Il perſuada
meſme à ſa ſœur d'employer quelque argĕt à en acheter, ſçachát bien
que l'on n'auroit pas trop de tout.
Ce n'eſtoit pas de cela pourtát qu'il
vouloit eſtre honoré. Il diſoit que
tout cela n'eſtoit que ſigne de richeſſe, & nó pas de vertu, ſi l'on n'a-
uoit des hommes de valeur. Ayant
apris auſſi que les cheuaux qu'il a-
uoit fait eſleuer auoiĕt ſurmonté à
la courſe ceux de quelques particuliers, il dit que ce n'eſtoit pas là encore vn ſujet pour ſe glorifier, &
que s'il ſurmontoit ſa patrie & ſes

H iiij

amis par ses bien-faicts, & s'il trouuoit en mesme téps le moyen de se
váger de ses ennemis, ce seroit alors
qu'il remporteroit la plus belle &
la plus grande victoire du monde,
& qu'il en pourroit acquerir vne
reputation qui l'honoreroit durant
sa vie & apres sa mort.

L'on ne le peut iamais assez loüer
pour tant de bons offices qu'il a
rendus à tous ceux qui se sont rangez sous sa protectió. L'ó ne le peut
pas comparer à vn homme qui ne
seroit riche que pour auoir trouué
vn thresor fortuitement ; car si cettuy-là estoit à son aise, ce ne seroit
pas par son bon mesnage. Si nostre
Prince a vaincu ses ennemis, ce n'est
pas à cause qu'il a trouué toutes
choses à souhait. Si cela estoit il ne
deuroit pas auoir esté loüé pour sa
valeur, mais plustost pour sa bonne

fortune, auſſi n'a-il ſurmóté aucune
difficulté qu'auec des peines extremes. S'il a fallu trauailler, il a eſté pl⁹
patient que les autres, s'il a fallu có-
battre, il a eſté vaillant, & où il a eſté
beſoin de conſeil, il a monſtré que
l'ó luy deuoit dóner le nom de ſage
& de vertueux : & ſi les Princes qui
ne ſont point encore inſtruits en
leur art ſe forment ſur les ouurages
des meilleurs maiſtres, il ne faut
point douter que les actions de ce
grand perſonnage ne ſeruent deſormais à tous ceux qui voudront mener vne vie digne de loüange. Son
exemple profitera merueilleuſement à quiconque le voudra con-
templer. Qui eſt ce qui pourra deuenir meſchant s'il tache vne fois
de ſuiure cet homme qui eſtoit ſi
deuot & ſi iuſte ? Deuiendra-on
inſolent ſi l'on prend garde à ſa mo-

deſtie ? Sera-on addonné à des ſale-
rez , ſi l'on ſe donne pour obiect
ſa nomparcile continence ?   Que
l'on cóſidere qu'il ne s'eſtimoit pas
tant pour dominer ſur les autres,
que pour s'eſtre accouſtumé à có-
mander à ſoy-meſme, & qu'il penſoit qu'il n'auoit pas ſeulement eſté
eſtabl y en la place qu'il tenoit pour
mener ſes ſuiets entre ſes ennemis,
mais pour les guider auſſi au chemin de la vertu.

Or encore que nous en diſions
tant de bien maintenant qu'il n'eſt
plus auec nous , c'eſt pluſtoſt pour
luy faire vn Panegyrique qu'vne
Oraiſon funebre.   Il faut pluſtoſt
employer nos paroles à luy donner
des loüanges qu'à faire des regrets.
L'on dit encore maintenát de luy ce
que l'ó en diſoit de ſon viuát, & puis
y a-il rien plus eſloigné de la plainte

qu'vne vie glorieuse, & vne mort venuë en sa saison? y a-il rien aussi plus digne de loüange, que tant de belles victoires & tant d'actions pleines de vertu? L'on peut veritablement appeller heureux celuy qui n'ayant desiré que de la gloire dés son enfance, en a eu autant qu'il en pouuoit souhaitter, ayant tousiours esté inuincible depuis qu'il a cómencé de manier les armes, & qui ayant vescu longuement, est mort en fin sans receuoir aucun reproche, soit de la part de ceux à qui il a commandé, soit de ceux à qui il a fait la guerre.

Ie veux faire encore icy vn sommaire de ses vertus, afin que l'on les puisse retenir plus facilement. Côsiderós premieremét quenostre Prince estoit si deuotieux, que nó seulemét il alloit d'ordinaire visiter les

Lieux sainčts qui sont en nostre cō-
trée, mais il se destournoit aussi de
beaucoup de chemin pour aller cōme pelerin à ceux qui estoient sur
les terres des ennemis. Aussi n'igno-
roit-il pas que l'on peut dignement
faire ses offrandes en toute sorte
d'endroits. Il n'outrageoit iamais
ceux qui s'estoient retirez dans les
Temples, quoy que ce fussent des
gens qui l'eussent quelquefois offencé : car il iugeoit hors de propos
que l'on appellast sacrileges ceux
qui desroboient quelque chose dãs
vn lieu sacré, & que l'on ne nómast
point de méme ceux qui arrachoiét
des Autels de pauures miserables
qui s'y estoient mis en franchise. Il
chantoit souuent de hymnes à l'hō-
neur de Dieu, sçachant bien que la
diuine Majesté se plaist autant aux
bonnes paroles, qu'aux bonnes

œuures. Lors qu'il eſtoit en proſperité il ne meſpriſoit point ceux
qui eſtoient dans l'infortune. Il rédoit graces à Dieu du bien qu'il luy
auoit fait, & lors qu'il ſe voyoit en
ſeureté, il auoit accouſtumé de dóner de plus grandes offrandes que
celles qu'il auoit promiſes dans le
peril. Il manioit auſſi tellement
ſon eſprit que l'on ne pouuoit cognoiſtre ſi ſes affaires eſtoient en
mauuais eſtat. Il ne laiſſoit pas
de paroiſtre ioyeux lors qu'il auoit
le plus de ſujet de s'attriſter & de
craindre. Que ſi quelque choſe
luy arriuoit ſelon ſon deſir, il de-
meuroit touſiours dans la tranquillité, & ne s'eſchapoit pas tant qu'il
fiſt quelque action cótre les reigles
de la modeſtie. Pour ce qui eſtoit
de ſes amis, il leur faiſoit des faueurs eſgales; mais ſi dans ſon cœur

il y auoit quelque difference d'affection, ce n'eſtoit pas qu'il aymaſt
dauantage ceux qui eſtoient les
plus puiſſants , mais ceux qui e-
ſtoient les plus fidelles , & qui a-
uoient la meilleure volonté. Que
s'il portoit de la hayne à quelques
vns, c'eſtoit à ceux qui demeuroiẽt
ingrats ayans receu quelque bien-
fait , & non pas à ceux qui taſ-
choient d'auoir reparatió de quelque iniure qu'ils auoient receuë.

Il prenoit plaiſir à voir de pauures gens qui aymoient mieux demeurer dans leur pauureté que d'en
ſortir par des remedes des honneſtes , & c'eſtoit eux qu'il enri-
chiſſoit, afin de monſtrer qu'il ne
recompenſoit iamais d'autres que
ceux qui fuyoient l'iniuſtice ; il
parloit bien à toute ſorte de gens
qui l'abordoient, mais il neſe ren-

doit iamais familier qu'auec les bós. Que s'il oyoit quelqu'vn loüer ou blâmer les autres, il auoit autant de desir de le connoistre comme de connoistre ceux dont il parloit, d'autant qu'il esperoit que par ses mœurs il pourroit iuger s'il disoit des veritez ou des mensonges. Au reste il ne blasmoit point ceux qui auoient esté deçeus par leurs a-mys, mais il ne tenoit guere de conte de ceux qui se laissoient tró-per par leurs ennemis. Il estimoit que cestoit vne prudence de se rendre aussi fin que les hommes deffians, mais que c'estoit vne malice de tromper ceux qui se fioyét en nous. Il croyoit aussi qu'il n'y auoit rié de plus honorable, que d'estre loüé de ceux qui sçauoient bien blasmer franchement ceux qui failloient, & iamais il n'auoit pourtant d'inimitié contre ceux qui parloient à cœur ouuert, car il fuyoit les diffimulations comme des embufches fort dangereufes.

Pour ce qui eftoit des calomniateurs, il les hayffoit plus que les larrons, eftimant que ce fuft vn plus grand larrecin d'ofter la bonne reputation aux honeftes gens, que de leur ofter leurs richeffes. Si c'eftoit vn particulier qui fift quelque faute, il la fuportoit plus facilement que celle d'vn grand Seigneur, iugeant que de l'vne il n'arriuoit du dommage qu'à celuy qui l'auoit faite, & de l'autre il en arriuoit outre cela de grands inconuenients au public. Il difoit auffi que la franchife appartenoit pluftoft à vne majefté royale que la fineffe. Quant aux honneurs que l'on luy vouloit rédre, il n'en defiroit point

s'ils

s'ils n'estoient extremément raison-
nables. Il ne vouloit pas mesme
que l'on luy dressaft des Statuës,
pource qu'il trauailloit sans cesse à
laisser des marques de son esprit qui
valoient mieux que les portraicts
de son corps. Il disoit que l'vne de
ces choses pouuoit estre faite par
des Peintres ou des Statuaires, &
l'autre par luy seulement; que l'v-
ne appartenoit aux riches, & l'autre ne pouuoit estre accomplie que
par des hommes vertueux. Que si
là dessus l'on songe aux richesses
qu'il possedoit, l'on verra qu'il
n'en auoit pas tant que sa condition meritoit, & que neantmoins
il en vsoit iustement & liberale-
ment, car nous croyons qu'il suffit à vn homme iuste de s'abstenir
du bien d'autruy & d'employer lo
sien au profit de tous.

Nous deuons encore parler de
sa pieté, qui estoit si grande qu'il ne
croyoit point que les hommes qui
viuoient bien fussent parfaitement
heureux, mais seulement ceux qui
estoient morts en la grace de Dieu,
ayans continué leurs bonnes actiós
iusqu'à la fin. Si vn homme sçauant faisoit vne faute, il le blasmoit
dauantage qu'vn ignorant, d'autant qu'il cognoissoit bien ce qui
estoit bon & ne le faisoit pas, au
lieu que l'autre ne s'estoit fouruoyé
qu'à cause qu'il ne sçauoit pas où
estoit la meilleure voye. En ce qui
estoit de luy, l'on remarque qu'il
prenoit beaucoup de peine à s'informer de ce qu'il pouuoit faire
de loüable, outre ce qu'il auoit
desia fait, & il ne vouloit point
que l'on luy donnast aucune loüange si ce n'estoit pour des choses

qu'il auoit accomplies luy feul. Il me femble auffi qu'entre vn petit nombre d'hommes, il eft de ceux qui ont fouftenu plus fermement qu'il n'y auoit point de trauail à fouffrir en la pourfuitte de la ver-tu: mais que ce n'eftoit que tout plaifir & toute volupté; toutes-fois il difoit que la force de l'ef-prit paroiffoit dauantage dans vn confeil que dans vn peril de guerre, & cela n'empefchoit pas auffi que fa fageffe ne confiftaft dauantage en des actions qu'en des paroles.

Au demeurant s'il moderoit fa ioye dans les profperitez, il gardoit auffi fa conftance dans les aduerfi-tez. Pour ce qui eftoit de fa conuer-fation, elle eftoit infiniment ayma-ble, il n'eftoit pas moins gracieux à fes amis que terrible à fes ennemis

il n'y auoit rien qu'il ne fiſt pour
ceux qu'il affectionnoit, & le meilleur de cela eſtoit que ſes affections
n'eſtoient point iniuſtes, & qu'il regardoit pluſtoſt à la preud'hommie qu'à la bonne mine. Il teſmoignoit par tout qu'il ſçauoit bien
ſon monde, & il ne le faiſoit pas
auec des railleries picquantes ; mais
auec vne grande douceur d'entretien. Auſſi meſpriſoit il tant de vaines cageolleries, & il ne faiſoit eſtat
que des propos graues & ſerieux.
Comme il meſpriſoit fort l'orgueil,
il ſe rendoit quelquefois plus humble que les perſonnes mediocres. Il
n'eſtimoit pas ceux qui ſe faiſoient
ſi braues dans les villes, & qui eſtoiét
ſi peu ſoigneux de leurs armes en
temps de guerre, de ſorte qu'il faiſoit le contraire, & ne monſtroit
iamais ſa ſomptuoſité qu'en des

corps de cuiraſſe & des caſques qu'il faiſoit forger auec vn grand ſoin. Il eſtoit auſſi extremément aſpre au combat, & pourtant l'on l'a touſiours trouué fort doux dans la victoire. En fin il a touſiours eſté auſſi formidable à ſes ennemis, que deſirable à ſes amis, & en deſtruiſant les vns, il a auancé les affaires des autres.

Au bout delà chacun luy a donné des tiltres ſelon ſon ſentiment, & ſelon l'eſpreuue qui auoit eſté faite de ſa vertu. Ses parens diſoient que ſur toutes choſes il eſtoit extremément ſoigneux du ſalut de ceux qui luy apartenoiét. Ses plus familiers amis eſtimoient qu'il n'y auoit perſonne qui gardaſt vne telle franchiſe dans les affaires. Ceux qui luy auoient rendu quelque ſeruice, le loüoient par ſa bonne memoire ; & ceux qui auoient esté outragez, l'appelloiét à haute voix le vray secours de ceux qui se trouuoient en danger, & ils disoient qu'apres Dieu il estoit leur sauueur. Au reste il me semble que luy seul entre tous les hommes a esprouué veritablement que la force du corps se diminuë par la vieillesse, mais que celle de l'esprit ne s'affoiblit iamais en vn homme vertueux: voila pourquoy tant qu'il a eu de la vie il a trauaillé pour la vertu: Aussi n'a-t'on iamais veu de ieunesse plus laborieuse que sa vieillesse, & iamais aucun Capitaine n'a esté plus redoutable à ses ennemis en la fleur de son âge, que cestui-cy ayant prés de cent ans. Qui est-ce qui a donné plus de hardiesse que luy à ses alliez, lors qu'il estoit desia prés de sa fin? Quelle mort aporte plus d'asseurance aux ennemis que

la sienne; & qui est ce en fin qui a
esté plus regretté par ses amis ? I'ay
dit tantost qu'il ne falloit point ietter de larmes pour luy, parce qu'il
estoit mort en vn temps où la vie
commençoit de luy estre ennuyeu-
se; mais la pluspart de nos Citoyens
n'ont pas eu d'esgard à cela ; Ils ont
songé à leur proffit particulier, &
ils ont creu auoir tout perdu dans sa
perte ; mais qu'ils sçachent que
comme nous ne le deuons point
plaindre, à cause qu'il est asseurément en vn lieu où il reçoit la recó-
pense de ses bien-faicts; de mesme
nous ne deuons point nous affliger
de sa mort à nostre cósideration. S'il
nous a esté profitable durãt sa vie, il
le sera encore apres sa mort. Toutes
ses actions seruiront d'exemple aux
Capitaines qui nous meneront de-
formais à la guerre, & ne suiuãs rien

que ſes maximes, il ne leur en pourra arriuer qu'vn tres-bon ſuccez. Par ce moyen les ennemis ne ſeront pas encore où ils penſent, & leurs eſperances ſeront fauſſes; & qui plus eſt, nous auons en cecy vne conſolation merueilleuſe; c'eſt qu'encore que noſtre Prince ne ſoit plus parmy nous, il ne ſçauroit nous auoir oubliez, puis qu'il nous a iuré tant de fois que ſon affection dureroit encore apres ſa premiere vie. Il aura donc ſoin de nous, & nous ne deuons point douter qu'il ne continuë de nous aſſiſter dedans nos neceſſitez. Ses forces ſont mille fois plus grandes maintenant qu'il eſt au Ciel, que lors qu'il eſtoit ſur la terre. Pourueu que par nos bonnes actions & nos prieres, nous obtenions de Dieu qu'il luy permette de nous aſſiſter, nous n'auons plus rien à craindre.   Que l'on crie de tous costez les Cantiques de noſtre ioye, chers Citoyens, nous auons fait vn glorieux eſchange.   Au lieu d'vn Prince mortel, nous en auons vn maintenant qui eſt au nombre des bien - heureux.

EXHORTATION FAICTE
par vn grand Prelat à vn Empereur, traduicte du Grec.

PVuisque vous auez esté esleué en vne dignité qui est au dessus de toutes les autres, tres sage & tres inuincible Monarque, il faut aussi que vous honoriez Dieu sur touts les autres, pource qu'il vous a esleué à ce degré, & qu'il vous a donné sur la terre vne puissance fort approchante de celle qu'il a au Ciel, afin que vous apprissiez aux hommes à garder la iustice, & que vous poursuiuissiez ceux qui l'offencent, obeissant le premier à ses loix & gouuernant vos suiets selon la droicte raison.

Il faut qu'vn Monarque veille
sans cesse des yeux de l'esprit , &
que de mesme qu'vn Pilote , il
tienne tousiours ferme le gou-
uernail de l'Equité , repoussant
courageusement les flots de l'iniustice de peur qu'ils ne heurtent
le vaisseau où est enfermé le salut
du public.

C'est vne diuine leçon laquelle
on nous enseigne auāt toute autre,
de nous cognoistre nous-mesmes;
car quiconque aura acquis la connoissance de soy-mesme,il ne manquera point d'acquerir celle de
Dieu,& quicōque connoistra Dieu
il s'efforcera de luy ressēbler. Or celuy là luy ressemblera qui s'en sera
rédu digne,& celuy là s'en sera rédu
digne qui ne fera rien qui soit indi-
gne de la diuine bōté: qui pésera per
petuellement à elle qui dira aussi ce

qu'il aura en la penſee, & qui fera ce qu'il aura en la bouche.

Que perſonne ne ſe glorifie de la nobleſſe de ſa race, car nous ſommes tous faits du limon de la terre, auſsi bien ceux qui entrent en orgueil pour eſtre couuerts d'or & de poupre, que les pauures qui ſont à demy nuds, & non moins encore ceux qui portent les diademes, que ceux qui ſont ordonnez pour leur garde. Ne nous eſleuons donc point pour eſtre ſortis d'vne illuſtre maiſon, mais pour eſtre ornez de bonnes & loüables mœurs.

Aprenez (ô vous qui eſtes icy vne image de pieté taillée de la main du Tout-puiſſant) que vous luy eſtes d'autant plus obligez & redeuables, que vous auez receus de bien-faicts de ſa bonté. Faites-luy donc les remerciemens que

vous luy deuez, & il les receura non
comme chofe qui luy foit deuë,
mais comme vne gratification , &
il vous en recompenfera encore:
Car il commence toufiours le premier à nous faire du bien, & il nous
recompenfe apres du gré que nous
luy en fçauons, de mefme que s'il y
eftoit obligé; mais fcachez qu'il demande auffi que nous le recognoif-
fions , non pas de parole fimple-
ment, mais par de bonnes œuures.

'Il n'y a rien qui attire plus l'amitié des hommes que de faire pour
eux tout ce que l'on peut , & de
pouuoir faire tout ce qu'ils veulét,
pourueu que l'on ne faffe rien d'ailleurs qui ne leur foit toufiours profitable. Puifque Dieu vous a donc
donné vne puiffance qui en tant
qu'à noftre occafion vous en auez
befoin, efgale noftre defir & la vo-

lonté que vous auez de bien faire,
ne faites rien, & ne souhaittez rien
que ce que vous iugerez estre a-
greable à celuy qui vous a donné
cette puissance.

Les biens du monde ressemblét
aux eaux de la mer, qui vont & viennent incessâment. Ils prennent leurs
cours pour vn téps vers ceux qui pésent les posseder pour tousiours: mais
aussi tost ils les delaissent, & s'en
vont en trouuer d'autres. Quant
aux bonnes œuures, c'est vn tresor
qui ne perit point : d'autant que
le merite en retourne tousiours à
ceux qui les font.

Si la grandeur de la dignité en laquelle vous estes icy parmy nous,
vous peut rédre inaccessible, la force de ceste puissâce qui est au Ciel,
vous doit rédre affable & gratieux
enuers les pauures, elle vous doit có-

nier à prester vne oreille fauorable
à ceux qui sont accablez de misere,
afin que Dieu vous face le mesme;
car nous le trouuerons tel en nostre
endroit que nous aurons esté à l'endroit de ceux que nous aurons eus
en nostre puissance.

Le Monarque qui a beaucoup de
soing, doit auoir l'ame aussi nette
que la glace d'vn miroir, afin que
Dieu l'illumine, & luy face cónoistre
quel jugement il doit faire des affaires qui luy suruiennent; car il n'y
a rien qui luy puisse donner tant de
lumiere de ce qu'il doit faire, que
d'auoir tousiours l'ame pure & nette.

La faute d'vn Matelot importe
peu à ceux qui sont dás le vaisseau où
elle est commise, mais celle du Pilote est de telle importance qu'elle en
cause la perte ou le salut. Le méme
arriue aux villes; car si quelqu'vn

des citoyens commet vne faute , il
ne nuit pas tant au public qu'à foy
mefme ; Mais fi celuy qui cómande à toute la ville vient à faillir , il
preiudicie & fait du mal à tout le
public. Que donc celuy qui en a la
charge foit diligent à faire & à dire
tout ce qu'il doit, comme eftant fu-
ject à eftre recherché de ce qu'il aura deu faire , & qu'il n'aura point
fait.

Les affaires du monde ne font iamais efgales: elles changent perpe-
tuellement , tantoft d'vne façon,
tantoft d'vne autre ; de forte que ce
n'eft rien qu'inconftance , d'autant
qu'il n'y a rien qui demeure touf-
jours en vn méme eftat. C'eft pourquoy en ce perpetuel changement
vous deuez toufiours eftre ferme &
ftable dans la meditation des chofes fainctes & pieufes.

                              Fuyez

Fuyez les discours attrayans des flatteurs, non moins que la cruelle coustume des Corbeaux: car ces derniers creuent les yeux du corps, & ceux-cy aueuglent ceux de l'esprit, ne permettant pas qu'on approfondisse les affaires, & qu'on en cognoisse la verité: car souuent ils loüent ce qui est digne de blasme, & blasment ce qui est si digne de loüange, qu'on ne le peut assez loüer: De sorte qu'ils faillent tousiours d'vne façon ou d'autre, ou en loüant ce qui doit estre blasmé, ou en blasmant ce qui doit estre loüé.

En tout temps & en toutes affaires vn Monarque doit estre esgal à soy-mesme: car de changer selon que les affaires changent, c'est vne marque d'vn esprit inconstant; au lieu que de bien faire tousiours

K

(qui eſt le moyen par lequel vous
auez eſtably voſtre auguſte puiſſance) & n'eſtre iamais inſolent, &
ne perdre iamais courage, c'eſt vne
marque d'vn eſprit fort, qu'on ne
ſçauroit esbranler.

Quiconque conſeruera ſes penſees pures & nettes, & ne les laiſſera
ſurprendre aux fraudes & tromperies du monde ; Quiconque conſi-
derera noſtre neant, la briefueté de
noſtre vie, & à quelles pauuretez
nos corps ſont ſujets, quelque grãd
qu'il ſoit, & en quelque haut degré d'honneur qu'il puiſſe eſtre
conſtitué,il ne tombera iamais dans
vn precipice d'orgueil.

De tout ce qui eſt grand & magnifique en la Royauté,il n'y a rien
qui decore plus vn Monarque, que
la pieté & le culte diuin : car les richeſſes periſſent, & la gloire paſſe,

Mais celle que lon acquiert en bien
seruant Dieu dure eternellement,
& rend immortels ceux qui en sont
ornez.

Il me semble tres absurde, que
pour diuerses causes les riches & les
pauures reçoiuent vn mesme dommage : car les vns creuent de reple-
tion, les autres meurent d'inanitió:
ceux-là possedent toute la terre,
ceux-cy n'ont pas dequoy asseoir la
plante de leurs pieds. Doncques
pour remettre en santé les vns & les
autres, il faut oster aux vns, & don-
neraux autres, & les rendre tous es-
gaux.

C'est de nos iours que nous
voyons fleurir ceste felicité, qu'vn
Ancien a dit deuoir arriuer lors que
les Philosophes regneroient, ou
que les Roys Philosopheroient:
car lors que vous vacquiez à la

Philoſophie, vous fuſtes honoré de
la dignité Imperiale ; & maintenant que vous en eſtes en poſſeſſió,
vous ne laiſſez pas d'y vacquer : car
s'il eſt vray que ce ſoit Philoſopher, que d'aimer la ſageſſe, & ſi la
crainte de Dieu, que vous auez au
cœur, en eſt le commencement, il ſe
trouuera que ce que ie dy eſt tres-
veritable.

Ie recognoy que veritablement
vous eſtes Roy : car vous ſçauez
commander aux voluptez & aux
plaiſirs, vous-vous conſeruez pur
& net de toute impudicité, & vous
vous reueſtez de la pourpre de Iuſtice : auſſi la puiſſance des Monar-
ques qui viuent autrement ſe perd
par le treſpas : mais celle de ceux qui
viuent comme vous, dure à perpe-
tuité : celle des vns finit auecques le
temps : celle des autres les deliure de

la mort eternelle, & les fait regner
au Ciel.

Si vous voulez qu'vn chacun
vous honore, faictes du bien à chacun : car il n'y a rien qui attire tant
la bien-vueillance des hommes, que
de bien faire à ceux qui en ont befoin. Aussi l'obeïssance feruile , &
que l'on rend par crainte est vne
flaterie fardee, laquelle fous vn faux
tiltre d'honneur trompe ceux qui
s'y laissent aller.

Certainement vous meritez que
l'on honore voftre Royale authorité : car par voftre puissance vous-
vous rendez redoutable à vos ennemis, & par voftre douceur vous-
vous faictes aymer de vos fujects:
& vainquant ces premiers par les
armes, vous estes vaincu par ces derniers, non par force , mais par l'a-
mour qu'ils vous portent : car autãt

qu'il y a de difference entre vne be-
lte sauuage & vne brebis, autant y
en a-il entre vos ennemis & vos sujets. Quant au corps, vn Monarque
est semblable à tout autre homme:
mais quant à la dignité il ne ressemble qu'à Dieu, nostre souuerain
maistre & Seigneur: car en toute la
terre il n'y a personne au dessus de
luy. C'est pourquoy de mesme que
Dieu il ne se doit iamais laisser emporter à la cholere, ny s'enorgueil-
lir: car encores qu'il ait l'honneur
d'estre icy bas la viuáte Image de la
Diuinité, pour cela il ne laisse pas
d'estre couuert de terre comme les
autres, & d'estre perissable, ce qui
luy doit apprendre, qu'il est tenu de
garder l'esgalité à l'endroit de chacun. Accueillez ceux qui vous veulent donner de bons conseils, & nõ
pas ceux qui n'ont autre but que de

vous complaire en vous flatrant: car
ceux-là cognoiſſent veritablement
ce qui eſt vtile, & ceux-cy ne regardent qu'à ce qui plaiſt aux Grands:
& de meſme que l'ombre ſuit le
corps', ils ſuiuent & approuuent ce
qui leur plaiſt.

Soyez tel enuers vos domeſtiques que vous deſirez que Dieu
ſoit en voſtre endroit : car de meſme que nous aurons eſcouté , de
meſme nous ſerons eſcoutez ; & de
meſme que nous aurons regardé,
de meſmes nous ſerons regardez de
ce grand Dieu, dont l'œil void tout,
& penetre tout. Il faut donc deuan-
cer ſa miſericorde, & eſtre miſericordieux, afin qu'il nous le ſoit, &
nous rende la pareille.

De meſme qu'vn bon miroër
repreſente le viſage tel qu'il eſt,
ioyeux, s'il eſt ioyeux, & triſte, s'il

est triste: De mesme la diuine Iustice se conforme à nos actions: car
telles qu'elles sont, telles aussi sont
les peines, & les recompenses qu'elle nous en rend.

Soyez long à deliberer de ce qu'il
faut faire: mais si tost que vous l'aurez resolu, executez-le prompte-
ment:car il y a bien du danger à faire les choses temerairement, & sans
y auoir bien pensé. Aussi quiconque aura bien cogneu le mal qui arriue souuent faute d'auoir bien có-
sulté ce que l'on veut faire, il co-
gnoistra le bien qui prouient des
bonnes & longues deliberations:
de mesme qu'apres auoir esté long
temps malade, on iuge bien quel
plaisir c'est que d'estre sain & vigoureux. C'est pourquoy, ô tres-sa-
ge Empereur, vous deuez diligemment rechercher les choses qui sont

vtiles au monde par bons & prudens conseils, & par longues prieres que vous ferez à Dieu.

Vous gouuererez tresbien vostre Empire si vous vo° mettez en peine de sçauoir tout ce qui s'y passe , & si vous ne negligez aucune chose : car ce qui est peu à comparaison de vous n'est point peu quand vous en daignez auoir soin , puisqu'vne petite parole d'vn Prince a beaucoup de poids enuers chacun.

Contraignez-vous vous mesmes d'obseruer les loix , puisqu'il n'y a personne en toute la terre qui vous y puisse contraindre ; car en les reuerant plus qu'aucun autre , vous ferez paroistre la reueréce qui leur est deuë, & ferez que vos sujets estimeront qu'il n'y a pas peu de danger à les enfraindre.

Estimez que c'est vne mesme

chofe que de pecher, & n'empefcher point que l'on peche : car quiconque vit en homme de bien quāt
à foy, & neantmoins adhere à
ceux qui viuent mal, il eft coulpable de leurs mefchancetez enuers
Dieu. Si vous voulez donc remporter vne gloire qui foit double,
honorez ceux qui font bien, & re-
prenez ceux qui font mal.

l'eftime qu'il importe grandement de fuïr la compagnie des
mefchans : car quiconque con-
uerfe d'ordinaire auecques eux, il
eft contraint ou d'endurer le mal,
ou de l'apprendre: au lieu que celuy qui frequẽte auec les bons, apprend à leur exemple à deuenir vertueux, ou moins vicieux.

Puis que Dieu vous a donné le
gouuernement de toute la terre,
prenez garde que vous ne comme-

tiez aux meschans & corrompus
l'administration des affaires : car
vous rédrez compte à Dieu de tout
ce qu'ils feront, puis que vous leur
en aurez donné le pouuoir. Infor-
mez-vous donc diligemment de
ceux que vous appellerez aux dignitez, & ausquels vous confierez
la direction des affaires.

Il me semble que c'est vn mesme
mal, que de se passionner pour les
malices de ses ennemis, & de se laisser aller aux flatteries de ses amis, car
il faut courageusement resister aux
vns & aux autres, & iamais ne s'esloigner de ce qui est honneste, sans se
vanger de la malice enragee des vns
& sans recompenser la feinte bien-
vueillance des autres.

Tenez ceux-là pour vos vrais &
sinceres amis, qui n'applaudissent
pas à tout ce que vous dites,

mais qui s'efforcent de ne rien faire que premierement ils ne l'ayent
trouué iuste & raisonnable, qui se
resioüissent quand vous faites bien,
s'attristent quand vous faites mal:
car en ce faisant, ils tesmoignent
qu'ils vous portent vne vraye &
sincere affection.

Que la grandeur de cest Empire
que vous possedez en terre ne chá-
ge point la magnanimité de vostre
courage, mais vous representant,
que vous regissez vn Empire perissable, & suiect au changement,
soyez ferme & immuable és affaires
muables & changeantes, & ne
vous laissez point emporter à la
ioye, ny abbatre à la tristesse.

De mesme que l'Or, encores
qu'il change de plusieurs figures,
& qu'il soit transformé en diuerses
sortes d'ornemens, demeure tous-

jours en son entier, & ne change
point : Ainsi, ô tres glorieux Empereur, encores que vous ayez
changé de plusieurs dignitez, &
qu'en fin vous en soyez paruenu
iusques au faiste : ce neantmoins
aux affaires qui sont inégales, vous
estes tousiours esgal à vous - mesmes, & vous demeurez tousiours
ferme & stable en ce qui est de vostre deuoir.

Croyez que vous regnerez en
toute asseurance, quand ceux ausquels vous commanderez vous o-
beïront de leur pure & franche volonté, & sans aucune contraincte :
car quiconque obeït contre son
gré, se reuolte toutesfois & quan-
tes que l'occasion s'en offre au lieu
que celuy qui obeït de bône volôté
ne se depart iamais de l'obeïssance
qu'il doit à celuy qui luy cômande.

Afin que vous faciez reüerer voſtre ſouueraine authorité, autant que vous vous mettez en colere contre vos ſujets lors qu’ils faillét, autant mettez-vous y contre vous meſmes quand vous faillirez : car il n’y a perſonne qui puiſſe enſeigner celuy qui a l’authorité que vous a-nez ſi ce n’eſt que ſa raiſon s’émeuue de ſes fautes & les corrige.

Celuy qui a receu vne grande puiſſance (en tant qu’il peut) qu’il imite celuy duquel il l’a receuë; car s’il eſt la viuante image du Tout-puiſſant, & s’il tient ſon Empire de ſa diuine bonté, principale-ment il l’imitera, en ce qu’il n’eſti-mera rien de plus precieux que la miſericorde.

Preferons les œuures de miſe-ricorde à l’or, & aux pierres pre-cieuſes, & amaſſons des treſors,

car c'eſt vne richeſſe qui reſioüit
en ce monde & en l'autre ; en ce
monde par l'eſperance qu'elle donne de la felicité eternelle , & en
l'autre par la douceur qui ſe trouue
en la iouyſſance de ceſte felicité.
Partant que les choſes de ce monde
ne nous delectent ny plus ny moins
que des choſes qui ne nous touchent pas.

Prenez garde à dignement recõ-
penſer ceux qui executent de bon
cœur ce que vous leur cõmandez :
car en ce faiſant vous augmenterez
l'éuie de bien faire qu'ont les gẽs de
bien, & donnerez ſubiect aux meſchans de s'amender : car c'eſt vne
grande iniuſtice de recompenſer
d'vne meſme façon ceux qui ne
font pas les meſmes choſes.

Il n'y a rien de plus releué ny de
plus honorable, que la dignité

Royale : mais c'est alors principalement que celuy qui en est reuestu
n'est point arrogant & outrecuidé,
mais qu'il est doux & gracieux, &
qu'il abhorre l'inhumanité de mesme qu'vne chose brutale , & fait
gloire de l'humanité, comme d'vne
chose toute diuine.

Faictes iustice tant à vos amis
qu'à vos ennemis , & ne gratifiez
point les premiers pour la bien-
vueillance qu'ils vous portent : aussi ne faictes point de tort aux derniers , pour ce qu'ils vous haïssent :
car il est aussi déraisonnable de dô-
ner gain de cause à vostre amy en
chose iniuste , que de condamner
vostre ennemy en chose iuste, dautant que le mal est égal en ces deux
accidents , encores qu'ils soient
contraires.

Il faut que les Iuges soient atten-
tifs,

rifs, d'autant qu'il est difficile de recognoistre ce qui est iuste, & principalement à ceux qui n'y prestent
point l'oreille : Que si mesprisant
l'eloquence de ceux qui parlent deuant eux, & ne s'arrestant point à
l'apparence des raisons qu'ils appor-
tent, ils approfondissent ce qu'on
leur propose, ils comprendront ce
qu'on leur demandera; & en ce faisant ils euiteront deux grandes fautes, l'vne qu'ils ne trahiront point la
Iustice, l'autre qu'ils ne permet-
tront point aux autres de le faire.

Quand vous feriez autant d'actes
de vertu qu'il y a d'estoiles au Ciel;
ce neantmoins vous ne surpasseriez
pas la bonté de Dieu, auquel personne ne sçauroit rien offrir qui ne
luy appartienne. Et de mesme qu'il
est impossible de surpasser son ombre, laquelle tient tousiours le de-

uant, quelque diligence que l'on face: auſſi quelque bien que facent les
hommes, ils ne ſçauroient ſurmon-
ter la bonté de Dieu, laquelle il eſt
impoſſible de ſurpaſſer.

C'eſt vn threſor ineſpuiſable que
celuy de la liberalité: car en donnát
on reçoit, & en ſemant on recueil-
le. Ainſi, ô tres-liberal Empereur,
faites largeſſe à tous ceux qui vous
demandent: car lors que ſera venu
le temps de la remuneration des
bonnes œuures, vous en tirerez des
recompenſes infinies.

Ayant receu de Dieu l'Empire
que vous poſſedez faictes de bonnes œuures, & l'imitez en ce faiſant:
car vous eſtes né pour bien faire
aux autres, & non pas pour en receuoir des bien-faicts. Auſſi n'y a-il
rien qui puiſſe empeſcher les riches de faire du bien aux pauures,

que leur auarice.

Ce que l'œil est au corps, l'Empereur l'est au monde, & Dieu le luy
a donné, afin qu'il prist garde, &
veillast aux choses qui luy sont vtiles. Il faut donc qu'il ait soin de tous
les hommes comme de ses propres
membres, afin que tousiours il leur
arriue du bien, & iamais du mal.

Estimez que c'est vne seure garde, que de n'offenser personne de
vos sujects : car quiconque n'offense personne ne se deffie de personne, & ne craint point qu'on entre-
prenne sur luy : Or si n'offensant
personne on vit en seureté, on y vi-
ura bien dauantage, si l'on se plaist
à faire du bien : car en n'offensant
personne on vit bien sans crainte:
mais on ne gaigne pas les cœurs &
les affections de chacun.

Que vostre souueraine puissance,

ô tres-pieux Empereur, vous rende redoutable à vos suiects; mais que voſtre liberalité vous en face aymer. Et pour en eſtre aymé ne feignez de vous en faire craindre, & pour en eſtre craint ne meſpriſez de vous en faire aymer, mais ſoyez doux & gracieux de telle ſorte que vous ne vous en rendiez point contemptible, vous monſtrant ſeuere à l'endroit de ceux qui abuſeront de voſtre bonté.

Ce que de bouche vous auez commandé à vos ſujets, & leur auez preſcrit de meſme qu'vne loy, vous l'auez executé le premier, leur teſmoignant par là que voſtre vie reſpond à vos paroles, & que vous faictes ce que vous dites : auſſi par ce moyen vous feriez qu'vn chacun approuuera ce que vous commanderez, ſi vous ne dites rien, &

n'enioignez rien aux autres, que
vous ne faciez le premier.

Aymez dauantage, ô tres-sereniſ-
ſime Empereur, ceux qui vous ſup-
plient de leur faire du bien, que
ceux qui ſont deſireux de vous faire des preſens: car en prenant de ces
derniers vous deuenez leur redeuable, où, en donnant aux autres, vous
rendez Dieu voſtre debteur, qui re-
pute fait à ſoy-meſme le bien que
vous leur faictes, & ne laiſſe point
ſans recompenſe voſtre ſaincte &
charitable intention.

C'eſt le deuoir du Soleil que de
reſpandre ſes rayons ſur la terre, &
l'en eſclairer: Et la vertu d'vn Empereur, eſt de faire miſericorde à
ceux qui en ont beſoin. Or vn Empereur miſericordieux eſclate &
reſplendit dauantage que ne fait
pas le grand Aſtre du iour: car ce

dernier se retire, & fait place à la nuict qui luy succede, au lieu que le premier ne cede iamais à la malice des meschans : mais auecques le flambeau de la verité il penetre iusques au fonds, & descouure ce qu'elle a de plus caché.

La dignité de l'Empire a decoré vos predecesseurs, & vous, ô tres-genereux Empereur, en adoucissant l'esclat de sa puissance par vostre douceur, & par vostre bonté, deliurant de crainte ceux qui vous abordent, vous l'auez honoree, & renduë plus illustre. C'est pourquoy tous ceux qui ont besoin de vostre misericorde viennent aborder au port de vostre misericorde, & se voyans guarantis des flots de la pauureté & de la misere, ils vous enuoyent des Hymnes, qui contiennent de tres-humbles actions de graces.

Autant que vous surpassez les autres en puissance, autant efforcez vous de les surpasser en bonnes œuures. Estimez que l'on desire de vous qu'il y ait de la proportion entre ce que vous faictes, & ce que vous pouuez, & que vous faciez autant de bien, que vous estes puissant. Doncques afin que Dieu mesme vous en loüe, ioignez à la couronne inuincible de l'Empire, la couronne de misericorde, qui s'acquiert en secourant les pauures, & leur faisant du bien.

Considerez & contemplez ce que vous voulez faire auparauant que de commander qu'on le face, afin que vous ne commandiez rien mal à propos, & qui ne soit iuste: car c'est vne chose qui va viste que la langue, & qui apporte beaucoup

de dommage à ceux qui n'y pren-
nét pas garde. Preuenez en donc les
mouuemens auec vne pieuſe meditation que vous rendrez ſemblable aux preludes, agreables d'vne
douce Muſique, & alors elle ne re-
ſonnera rien qui diſcorde de l'harmonie des vertus.

Il faut qu'vn Monarque ſoit
prompt en toutes choſes, & principalement au iugement des affaires difficiles, mais il doit eſtre extre-
mémeut tardif à ſe mettre en colere. Mais puis que c'eſt vne choſe
contemptible, que de ne ſe point
colerer iamais, & que c'eſt vne
marque de peu de courage, qu'il
ſe colere quelquefois ; cela n'importe pourueu que cela ſe faſſe
moderément ; mais que d'autre
fois auſſi il ne ſe colere point du
tout.

Il fera cecy pour deux raifons,
la premiere, afin qu'il reprime les
entreprifes des mefchans; la fecon-
de, afin qu'il defcouure les inclinations des bons.

Confiderez en vous mefmes le
plus exactement que vous pourrez
les mœurs & facons de faire de
ceux qui vous frequentent, afin
que vous recognoifliez au vray qui
font ceux qui ont vne vraye & fin-
cere affection à voftre feruice, &
qui font ceux qui vous flattent &
vous trompent: car vne fauffe biĕ-
vueillance porte fouuent grand
dommage à ceux qui la croyent
vraye.

Quand vous entendrez dire
quelque chofe qui vous pourra
profiter, ne vous contentez pas
feulement de l'auoir efcoutee, mais
faictes-la: car vn Monarque ac-

quiert de la reputation, & se rend
celebre lors que de soy - mesme il
se porte aux choses bien seantes,
& les ayât remarquees en autruy ne
les neglige point, mais les apprend
sans en auoir honte , & ne differe
point à les mettre en pratique.

Comme de bonnes & fortes
murailles rendent vne ville impre-
nable: ainsi les œuures de misericorde que fait vostre Majesté , &
les prieres que les gens de bien font
pour elle , rendent vains & inutiles les efforts de ceux qui voudroiét
entreprendre sur vostre puissance
Royale , & font que vous en
triomphez, & en dressez des tro-
phées.

Vsez comme il appartient de la
souueraine authorité que vous a-
uez icy bas , afin qu'elle vous serue
de degré pour monter au Ciel : car

ceux qui en vfent côme ils doiuent
en font reputez dignes. Or ceux-
là en vfent comme il faut qui ref-
moignent à leurs fujets vne affection paternelle , & neantmoins
s'en font craindre comme leurs
Princes fouuerains , en reprimant
les vices par menaces, mais en effet
vfant de mifericorde enuers ceux
qui les commettent.

C'eſt vn veſtement qui ne
s'vfe point que la liberalité, & vne
robbe qui ne deperit point que la
charité qui s'exerce enuers les pauures. C'eſt pourquoy il faut qu'vn
Monarque qui veut regner pieufe-
ment en orne & decore fon ame;
car celuy qui fe veſtira de la pourpre de charité , fera eſtimé digne
du Royaume celeſte.

Puis que par la grace de Dieu
vous eſtes Empereur, regardez cô-

me vous pourrez plaire à sa diuine bonté, qui vous a fait tel, & d'autant qu'elle vous a plus honoré que tous les hommes du monde, portez-luy aussi plus d'honneur & reuerence que nul autre. Or le plus grand honneur que Dieu estime que vous luy sçauriez rendre, c'est d'auoir soin de ses creatures comme de luy mesme, & vous acquitter de l'obligation qui vous astreint à leur faire du bien.

Tout homme qui desire son salut doit reclamer l'ayde de Dieu, & sur tous vn Monarque, comme celuy qui a soin de chacun : car estant en la garde de Dieu, il triomphera genereusement de ses ennemis, & preseruera les siens de tout sinistre accident.

Dieu n'a besoin de chose quelconque, & vn Empereur n'a besoin que de l'assistance de Dieu. Imitez donc celuy qui n'a besoin d'aucune chose, faictes comme luy misericorde à ceux qui vous en requierét, & ne faictes pas rendre compte à vos domestiques iusques au dernier soû, mais satisfaictes à tous ceux qui vous demandent dequoy viure; car il vaut mieux faire misericorde à ceux qui en sont indignes pour l'amour de ceux qui en sont dignes, que de ne la faire point à ceux qui en sont dignes, à cause de ceux qui en sont indignes.

Si vous voulez auoir remission de vos fautes, pardonnez à ceux qui vous offensent : car le pardon est la recompense du pardon, & Dieu nous ayme & se familiarise auecques nous, quand il void que nous - nous reconcilions auecques ceux qui nous ont offen-

fé, qui comme nous sommes fes
feruiteurs.

Quiconque defire regner fans
blafme, il doit prendre garde qu'il
ne coure point de luy de mauuais
bruits, & fur tous autres en particulier il doit auoir honte de foy-
mefme, afin qu'en public, & à caufe des autres il s'abftienne de faillir,
& qu'en particulier il s'en empefche : car fi entre les fubiects d'vn
Roy il y en a quelqu'vn qui foit digne de refpect, le Roy l'eft encores dauantage.

Commettre quelque crime digne de punition, c'eft eftre meschât
quant à vn particulier, mais quant
à vn Monarque, c'eft ne faire pas les
chofes honneftes & falutaires : car il
n'eft pas iuftifié pour ne faire point
de mal, mais il faut qu'il face du bié
s'il veut acquerir de la gloire. Qu'il

ne luy suffisse donc pas de s'abstenir
de mal faire , mais qu'il s'estudie à
faire des choses honnestes & iustes.

L'esclat des dignitez & grandeurs mõdaines n'estonne point la
mort : car elle dõne de la dent à vn
chacun, & le deuore. Auparauant
sa venuë (que nous ne pouuons e-
uiter) thesaurizons au Ciel , & y a-
massons des richesses : car en sor-
tant du monde on n'emportera aucune chose de ce que l'on y aura
amassé , mais y laissant tout ce que
l'on aura acquis , estant nud & de-
spoüillé de toutes choses l'on rédra
raison de tout ce que l'on aura fait
en sa vie. De mesme qu'vn Monarque est Maistre de tous , aussi cóme
to⁵ les autres il est seruiteur du Tout-
puissãt : & alors principalemét est il
apellé Maistre & Seigneur de tous,
quand il se cómande à soy-mesme,

& ne se laisse point maistriser à des voluptez illicites & deshonnestes, prenant pour second vne ame pieuse, & maistresse absoluë des passions desraisonnables, & de pied en cap s'armant des armes de la chasteté pour combattre & dompter les concupiscences qui triomphent de tout le monde.

De mesme que l'ombre suit le corps, ainsi le peché suit l'ame, & au vray en represente les actions. C'est pourquoy lors que nous serons deuant le grand Iuge, il ne nous sera pas possible de nier ce que nous aurons fait : car nos œuures tesmoigneront contre nous, non en parlant, mais en paroissant telles que nous les aurons faictes.

L'estat de ceste vie ressemble à la course d'vn Nauire. Il fait voile insensiblement, & sans que nous

qui en

qui en sommes les Nautonniers, nous en puissiós apperceuoir, nous conduit à nostre fin. Puis que cela est ainsi, outrepassons les choses du monde, qui nous passent, & courons à celles qui sont eternelles.

Que l'homme orgueilleux ne s'esleue pas de mesme qu'vn Taureau hautement encorné, mais qu'il considere qu'il est composé d'vne chair fragile & corruptible, & qu'il abbaisse l'arrogance de son cœur: car encore qu'il soit Prince, ce neātmoins il ne doit pas ignorer qu'il est venu de la terre, & que de la terre estant monté en vn throsne, il y retournera derechef.

Trauaillez sans cesse, ô inuincible Monarque, & comme ceux qui montent par des degrez ne s'arrestent point qu'ils n'en soient au dernier. Ainsi ne desistez iamais de

M

vous addonner aux choſes honneſtes, afin que vous puiſſiez paruenir
au Royaume celeſte, auquel ie prie
le Roy des Roys de vous conduire
auecque voſtre Eſpouſe pour y demeurer eternellement.

De l'excellence de la Solitude, &
les vrays moyens de viure ver-
tueusement à la Cour.

LE s Philosophes Payens ont
arresté que la souueraine felicité de l'ame consiste à se
maintenir en vne puissance reglee
de rendre tous ses mouuements
conformes à la raison, ce qu'ils ont
appellé vertu, & ils n'ont pas oublié à prescrire en quel genre de vie
l'on peut acquerir & conseruer vne
si excellente habitude. Il ne faut
point douter que la pluspart n'ayét
eu opinion que c'est en la vie con-
templatiue qu'elle a plus de lustre,
puisque l'esprit du Philosophe ne
trouue point de si douce nourritu-

M ij

re que celle qu'il tire de ses propres
meditations. Aussi en a t'on veu
plusieurs qui se sont bannis volontairement des villes, se sont priuez
de si peu de richesses mondaines
qu'ils possedoient, & se sont mesmes procuré l'aueuglement des
yeux du corps , afin d'augmenter
la puissance de ceux de l'esprit. Il se
remarque pourtant dans les anciens siecles de bien illustres personnages , & qui estoient veritablement Philosophes, encore qu'ils
n'en eussent point la barbe ny l'habit, lesquels estimans vne telle vie
faineante & mesprisable, ont mis
toute la gloire de l'homme en l'a-
ction. Ceux-cy ont apriuoisé le naturel des peuples barbares, & les
rauissant par des enseignemens diuins, les ont cottisez à la societé. Ce
sont les merueilles de leurs faits

qu'entendent fignifier les Poëtes,
quand ils parlent de ces Heros qui
au fon de leur Lyre ont charmé
les animaux priuez de raifon, ont at-
tiré les pierres à leur fuite pour ba-
ftir les murailles des villes, & ont
tenu les hommes attachez par les o-
reilles à leurs bouches eloquétes. Si
ie me voulois mettre bien auant fur
la recherche des maximes de toutes
les fortes des Philofophes, ie trou-
uerois facilemét quelle forte de vie
a efté la plus aprouuee : mais ce trauail feroit infiniment vain, puifque
ces anciés Sages auoient les efpaules
tournees au Soleil de verité, &
voyoiét vne lumiere dót ils ne pouuoient contépler l'origine fans mé-
dier ailleurs la clarté que le Chre-
ftien a chez foy fi abondamment
qu'elle eft fuffifante pour toute forte de fujets. Voyons ce qui en fem-

ble aux iugemens que la foy efclai-
re le plus. Ceux qu'vn dégouft des
chofes mondaines a faict renoncer
aux pompes de la Cour des Princes,
fouftiendront que ce n'eft que dans
leurs folitudes, que l'on peut rendre
fon efprit ployable, & fe foufmettre
aux loix du deuoir. Les raifós qu'ils
employét pour authorifer leur opi-
nió font particulieremét celles cy.
Dieu ayant donné l'hóme à l'homme, & l'ayant recommandé à luy-
mefme, quand il luy a faict prefent
d'vne liberté de fe tourner au bien
ou au mal, & d'vne raifon qui le
doit conduire au choix de toutes
chofes; c'eft à luy à s'acquiter prudemment de cefte tutelle, & chercher tous les moyens qu'il fe pourra imaginer pour atteindre à la plus
parfaicte felicité. Il eft le milieu du
monde, la liaifon des chofes fupe-

rieures auec les inferieures. Les
deux natures extremes se trouuent
en luy auec esgale puissance. Il a le
corps comme les bestes, & l'esprit
comme les Anges. Il est en luy de
ne cherir que cesse partie brutale,
de ne poursuiure que les delices qui
sont capables de l'assouuir, & se laisser entierement côduire aux fausses
persuasions des sens ; mais s'il a assez
de côsideration pour remarquer de
côbien les choses intellectuelles sur-
passent les sensuelles il fera vne esle-
ction de vie plus auantageuse : tous
ses desseins tédront à rédreso n an. e
la plus pure & la plus affranchie des
pensees terrestres qu'il se pourra faire, afin qu'elle s'aproche insensible-
mét de la nature Angelique. Il y sera
d'autát plus inciré, qu'en ce mesme
endroit, où son bié est establi, la bô-

M iiij

té diuine y a, mais aussi son deuoir.
Outre les obligations qu'il luy a
pour l'auoir creé & racheté apres sa
perte, il luy en a encore de tres-grã-
des pour toutes les choses du monde dont il tire tant de cómoditez.
Où pourra-il donc se ranger plus à
propos que dans vn lieu solitaire
pour payer des debtes si iustes? il
verra là à descouuert les œuures de
Dieu, & en sera d'autant plus en-
flammé à le remercier de les auoir
creées pour le proffit de son corps
& de son ame, afin que l'on en tirast
sa nourriture, & l'autre des ensei-
gnemésts. De là se representant que
ces creatures n'ont ny raison ny instinct qui les porte à remercier celuy qui les a produictes, il iugera
qu'il faut adiouster ceste debte
aux siennes particulieres, & faire cét office pour elles, puis qu'elles

n'ont l'estre que pour luy. L'on est comme hors du monde dedans l'enclos des villes, & bien que l'on y iouysse immoderement de tout ce qui est au monde, c'est ce que l'on y fait le moins que d'en admirer les diuerses productions. Les fruicts de la terre y sont mangez par ceux qui ne sçauent de quelle sorte ils croissent, & n'ont point la curiosité de l'apprendre, ny le desir d'en rendre graces à celuy qui les a produicts.

Le Soleil se leue pour ces lieux-là d'vne heure plustost & se couche d'vne heure plus tard qu'aux chãps; & si les broüillards, les orages & les tempestes ont à s'esleuer, c'est ordinairement pour y venir fondre: ce qui est vn signe euident de l'obscurité & du desordre qui se rencontre bien plus souuent parmy

ceux qui y habitent. Les plus ap-
parens d'entr'eux croyent auoir v-
ne puiſſance abſoluë, mais ils ſe
trompent, ce ſont les vices qui y cō-
mandent. La multitude ne fut iamais exépte de corruptiō: Il ſe faut
retirer de cette preſſe de peur que
la contagion ne nous gaigne comme les autres. Nous ſerions double-
ment coulpables, s'il arriuoit que
nous en fuſſions frappez, ayans eu
les moyens & les inſpirations de
nous en retirer. Comment peut-
on ſe donner à Dieu lors que l'on
n'eſt point à ſoy-meſme, que les
affaires nous poſſedent entierement, & que nous ſommes diuer-
tys de toutes péſees particulieres par
l'importunité des viſites & des rencontres. Ces accidéts ne ſe peuuent
euiter qu'en s'enfuyāt dans la ſolitude, où nos penſees & nos actions

commencent à auoir le champ libre, où nous recognoissons veritablement que nous ne sommes plus esclaues. Vne si pleine liberté fait naistre tant de vertus dans nostre ame que nous pouuons remarquer que de plus belles fleurs sont produittes dans les deserts que dans les parterres des Roys. C'est vn paradis terrestre où l'ame recouure ses premieres beautez , & prenant vne nourriture accomplie vit auec la mesme felicité que nostre premier pere perdit par sa faute.

Les solitaires sont eux mesmes la principale plante de ce miraculeux iardin, & au contraire du cómun des arbres qui poussent aussi auant leurs racines dás la terre qu'ils esleuent en l'air leurs rameaux, bien qu'ils ne tiennent presque point à la terre, ils portent leur sommet iusques dans le Ciel.

Les funestes imaginations, & les vaines terreurs que les mondains se persuadent estre dans la solitude ne troublent iamais leur repos. Iamais ils ne furent moins seuls que depuis qu'ils commencerent à l'estre. Ils ont pour compagnie tous ces saincts personnages qui ont esté Hermites autrefois : Et comme ceux qui desirent aller en quelque païs lointain sont bien ayses d'en apprendre auparauant les coustumes & le langage afin de n'y estre point comme estrangers & d'y pouuoir obtenir vn plus libre accez enuers les plus grands : de mesme nos Solitaires ayans à voyager au Ciel, en cherchent incessamment les addresses dans les liures de ceux qui en ont trouué le chemin, & par des contemplations qui les mettent hors d'eux mesmes ils apprennent

les merueilles de leur vraye patrie
& le parler dont les Anges s'y com-
muniquent leurs penfees.   Ils ne
couchent point au nombre de
leurs iours ceux qui s'écoulent fans
profiter en cefte fcience , & leur a-
me defia tranfportee dãs le Ciel par
la force de fes defirs & de fes imaginations, laiffe leur corps dans leur
cellule comme dans vn fepulchre
où il eft enfermé pour preuenir la
mort.   On ne fçauroit nombrer
combien de grands perfonnages
ont aymé cette vie folitaire. On en
a veu qui fe font retirez fur les plus
hautes montagnes comme de
vrays Atlas pour mieux confiderer
les merueilles du firmament. D'autres fe font tenus dans les boccages
& prés des fontaines prenans plaifir à voir efcouler leurs années ainfi
que les eaux qui iamais ne reuien-

nent ; & plusieurs se sont enfermez
dans les cloistres , où estans logez
au milieu des villes les plus peuplees
ils sont aussi solitairement que dans
les deserts. Les Payens mesmes qui
n'estoient pas enflammez aux bonnes actions par l'espoir d'vne eternelle felicité , n'ont pû se tenir de
rechercher cette douce solitude tāt
elle est attrayante d'elle mesme.

La vie solitaire se peut seruir de
ces raisons pour se mettre en e-
stime, & à dire la verité, es exercices du Chrestien se trouuent si
libres & si accomplies en elles, qu'il
semble que la vie politique soit
toute prophane au prix : mais
ce n'est rien qui n'escoute qu'vne
partie : il faut garder vne oreille
pour sa contraire.

Ceux qui entreprendront cette
deffense , diront : Que les hom-

mes ne font point nez pour fe
fuyr l'vn l'autre , & que c'eſt le
deſſein de nature d'aſſocier toutes
les choſes ſemblables , comme
l'on void aux plantes & aux
animaux d'vne meſme eſpece ,
qui fe trouuent touſiours pluſieurs en vne meſme contree.
Il n'eſt rien de plus ancien , de
plus profitable , ny de plus a-
agreable à Dieu que les Republiques, dont il ietta luy meſme les
fondemens.

Apres la creation de l'homme
ſa main propre a façonné les
nœuds de la premiere & de la
plus parfaicte ſocieté du monde ,
ayant accouplé l'homme à la
femme. Son Fils eſtant venu
ſur terre a tellement fauoriſé ceſte conionction , que ça e-
ſté à des nopces qu'il a produit

le premier de ſes miracles, & qu'il a
voulu auſſi que l'Egliſe ayt porté le
tiltre de ſon Eſpouſe, & que noſtre
mariage, qui n'eſtoit qu'vn effect
de la nature fuſt rendu Sacrement,
capable de multiplier en nous ſes
benedictions. Et comme le ſainct
Eſprit eſt tout amour, cette belle
Vnion n'a pas manqué de luy plaire, & d'attirer ſur elle vne grace
ineſtimable qu'il luy a conferee.

Or de ceſte premiere ſocieté ſont
venuës les familles, des familles les
Republiques, & des Republiques
les Empires. Blaſmera-on des choſes qui ont eu vn ſi diuin commencement, & dont le progrés s'eſt
monſtré ſi conforme à la volonté
de Dieu, qui declare dans l'Eſcriture ſaincte, que c'eſt luy qui e-
ſtablit & qui conſerue les Royaumes, & qui ordonne de la police

des

des Eſtats? Ne voyons nous pas que
nous ſommes nez les vns pour les
autres, & que nous ſommes ſi foibles quand nous ſommes ſeuls qu'il
ne ſçauroit ſortir de nous aucune
operation parfaicte ? Toute terre
ne produit pas toutes choſes, Elles
ont chacune leurs commoditez particulieres dont elles s'entr'aydẽt par
vn traffic mutuel. Celles où croiſt
l'or ſont infertiles pour les bonnes
plantes , tellement qu'il faut que
ceux qui y habitent donnent leurs
richeſſes en eſchange des fruicts qui
les peuuent nourrir. Ceſte meſme
diuerſité ſe trouue parmy les hommes; Les vns s'addonnent à diuerſes
occupations vtiles pour les neceſſitez qui ſe trouuent en la vie, & cependant les autres dont l'ame eſt
plus forte & plus genereuſe veil-
lent pour leur conſeruation. Ils ſe-

donnent mille peines pour faire regner entr'eux vne ferme paix &
vne eternelle iustice, & les amener
au bon chemin par des preceptes si
secourables qu. ils authorisent merueilleusement cette verité : Que
l'homme est vn Dieu à l'homme.

Ce n'est point sás cause que ce cómun dire a eu só cours, puis que veritablemét l'on peut rédre à só prochain de si charitables offices qu'ils
ont beaucoup de ressemblance aux
secours que le Ciel nous dóne Que
peut-on s'imaginer de plus diuin
que de rendre la santé aux malades,
arracher la tristesse du cœur des affli
gez, guarátir les foibles de l'oppression des plus puissants, & de donner
aux simples des cóseils qui les met-
tét en vne parfaite tráquillité? Ceux
qui reçoiuét de telles incómoditez
sçauent bien cognoistre la peine où
ils seroient reduits, s'ils estoiét dans

la solitude qui les en priueroit tout
à fait : Et pour croire que l'on peut
ayſément ſe paſſer d'autruy , il faut
neceſſairement auoir la ceruelle
auſſi bleſſée que le philoſophe Hip-
pias qui eſtoit paruenu iuſqu'à cette ſottiſe de nevouloir point porter
de robbe ny de chauſſes ny de ſou-
liers qui ne fuſſent de ſa façon. On
dit que pour viure dans la ſolitude il faut eſtre ſemblable à Dieu ou
à la beſte : Car ou il faut eſtre ſans
raiſon pour ſe priuer des plaiſirs &
de l'vtilité de la compagnie , ou il
faut auoir vn entendemét doüé de
qualitez plus eminentes que le vulgaire pour s'aſſeurer de toute ſorte
d'aide de la part de Dieu, & n'auoir
point de commerce auec les choſes humaines , bien que l'on y ſoit
encore attaché. Le Ciel fait cette
grace ſi rare de viure en terre ,

N ij

comme si l'on estoit desia dans les Cieux, qu'elle ne sçauroit estre accordee qu'à fort peu de personnes. Dieu veut que nous nous ressentions tous des malheurs qu'Adam a respandu sur sa posterité, & qui sera le presumptueux qui osera se retirer du monde sur l'espoir de viure doresnauant à la maniere des Anges?

Le trauail est le premier appennage de l'homme, & l'on se monstre dautant plus homme que l'on l'ayme le plus, tellement que ceux-là derogent à leur condition qui se veut cacher de peur d'en auoir leur part.

Voylà vne partie des discours que peuuent tenir les personnes qui demeurent dans les villes, si l'on rauale par trop le bon heur de leur condition pour esleuer celle des so-

litaires. Mais de donner vn iugement decifif là deſſus , c'eſt vne
choſe qu'vn eſprit bien ſenſé n'en-
treprendra point de faire. Il n'eſt
point de folie mieux formee que
de ſe figurer que la felicité ne puiſſe
eſtre trouuée autre part que dans la
maniere de viure qu'on a eſleuë, ou
de vouloir induire les autres à imiter tout ce que nous faiſons , ne
priſant rien que nos propres fanta-
ſies.

Dieu imprime en chaſque a-
me de certaines inclinations
differentes que l'on ne peut s'empeſcher de ſuiure , & qui les
voudra forcer ne reuſſira en
pas vne des operations contraires à ſa nature auſquelles il ſe ſera
occupé.

Nous ne ſçaurions douter que

les cloiſtres ne ſoyent des ſeminai-
res pour le Ciel & qu'il n'y ayt touſ-
jours de treſbons Religieux : mais
il s'y en peut trouuer quelquefois
de mauuais.

Nous voyons bien ſouuent des
hommes qui ſe ſont plongez ſi a-
uant dans les vices , qu'ils en ont
perdu leur beauté naturelle , leſquels pour vne petite eſtincelle de
raiſon qui vient à luire en leur eſprit, vont viſtement s'enfermer
dans les Monaſteres à deſſein d'y
faire penitence , & vne infinité
d'autres prennent le meſme chemin auec vne pareille haſte à
cauſe de la perte d'vn amy ou
d'vn office, ou bien pour les
deſdains inuincibles d'vne Da-
me qu'ils ont ſeruie. Sont - ils
au lieu retiré qu'ils ſouhaitoient,
ils recognoiſſent qu'ils s'y ſont

apportez eux-mesmes, cestàdire,
leurs mauuaises affections qu'ils ne
sçauroient abandonner. Ce sainct
mouuement qui les enflammoit
s'est attiedy : Le temps a retranché
les forces de la tristesse, & du desespoir, ou bien a renouuelé celle de
l'Amour. Leurs playes ont esté
mal pensees, & refermees trop ha-
stiuement. Le fer y est encore demeuré qui leur donne assez de douleurs pour les contraindre à les faire r'ouurir. Ainsi les voylà tout
d'vn coup portez à rentrer dans le
gouffre qu'ils pensoient euiter.

Que s'ils ont desia fait vn vœu
qui les retienne, en ce cas le malheur est bien plus sensible, car
les felicitez dont ils s'imaginent
auoir iouy en leur vie passee
leur semblent si regretables qu'au
lieu de la tranquillité qui habite

pour les autres dans ces sainctes maisons, ils n'y trouuent que des ennuys eternels beaucoup plus dommageables que ceux du monde. O qu'ils maudissent de fois leur legereté! & qu'ils aduoüent bien leur erreur d'auoir pensé que s'il ne faut que deux ou trois iours pour arriuer au lieu solitaire qu'ils ont esleu, il n'en faut pas dauantage pour effacer les taches de son ame, & s'esloigner du vice aussi bien que l'on s'esloigne de la ville.

Beaucoup d'autres se sont exposez à de semblables gesnes d'esprit non par leur faute propre, mais par celle de leurs peres, qui les ont voüez au seruice de Dieu, les iugeans inutiles aux affaires à cause de quelque imperfection du corps ou de l'esprit. Ingratitude punissable de n'offrir à Dieu que le re-

ste du môde & le rebut de la famille
à qui, l'on veut faire meilleure part!
Dieu reprouue vne telle action par
la bouche de son Prophete quand
il maudit le trompeur qui luy offre?
le plus foible animal de son troupeau, & quand il deffend au liure
du Leuitique, que l'homme qui a-
uoit quelque deffaut en ses membres ne luy serue de Sacrificateur
en son temple. Cela nous monstre
qu'il faut qu'il y ayt vne vocation
de la part de Dieu pour s'acquitter
heureusement de quelque charge
que ce soit. Il veut bien que l'a-
moureux quitte sa follie, & que celuy qui a perdu ses biens sorte de
son affliction desmesuree, mais il
ne desire pas neantmoins que ny
l'vn ny l'autre s'enferme dans vn
cloistre s'il n'y est propre. Il nous
suffit de suiure la vertu ciuile. Les

vns plaiſent à Dieu en vne condition, les autres en vne autre.

Il tira Dauid du ſoin des brebis,
pour l'appeller à celuy des peuples,
dont il deliura Saul l'en reputant in-
digne. C'eſt ànous à eſcouter atten-
tiuement ce que ſa voix dicte ſans
ceſſe aux oreilles de noſtre eſprit,
pour nous faire comprendre ſes volontez, & quand nous aurons remarqué que pluſieurs accidens ad-
uenus coup ſur coup ſemblent nous
reſſerrer dans les limites de certain
genre de vie, diſons hardiment que
ce ſont des effects de ſa prouidence,
& ne taſchós pas à rópre ces obſta-
cle pour paſſer à des eſtats differens.

Si noſtre naiſſance, la volonté de
nos parens, ou celle du Prince, ou
les qualitez cóuenables à noſtre eſprit, nous portent à donner nos trauaux au ſeruice du public, pourquoi

refuferions-nous vne chofe fi iufte?
feroit-ce pas vne action fort contraire à la charité Chreftienne de fe
deſrober aux autres hommes à qui
Dieu teſmoigne qu'il nous auoit
donnez pour les feruir, puifqu'il a
mis en nous toutes les qualitez que
leurs neceflitez y defirent? Auffi ne
laiffe on pas dans les cloiftres les
Moines que l'on iuge dignes de
quelque Prelature: & mefme en a-
on tiré ceux que la valeur rendoit
neceffaires, lors que les Eftats fe
font veus menacez de ruine par la
fureur des armes.

Ce feroit rompre l'harmonie
que Dieu a voulu eftablir en
l'vniuers que de quitter la partie qu'il nous a donnée à tenir.
Son deffein eft que les chofes y
ayent diuerfes qualitez & que
de toutes ces pieces affemblees

il s'engendre vn accord digne du
maiſtre d'vn tel courage. Or ce ſeroit vne erreur de penſer que l'on
le puſt mieux ſeruir d'vn coſté que
de l'autre, & que nous appellant
à toute ſorte de conditions, il euſt
oublié à en pouruoir quelqu'vne
des moyens aſſeurez d'y acquerir
ſa grace.

La vertu Chreſtienne eſt vne
ſemence ſi bonne qu'il n'eſt point
de terre aſſez infructueuſe pour
luy oſter le pouuoir de germer depuis que la main de Dieu a pris la
peine de l'y reſpandre.

Pour exemple d'vne condition
fort licencieuſe, on me donnera
celle des Courtiſans, & ie veux
bien la receuoir pour telle, mais
c'eſt à la charge que lors que ie parleray cy-apres des vices de la Cour,
on entendera que ie parle en gene-

ral fans vouloir remarquer vne
Cour particuliere, fi ce n'eſt quand
ie parleray de quelques grands vices, car on m'obligera de croire
alors que ie parleray de ceux qui ſe
font commis dans la Cour de quelques anciens Roys ou Empereurs
qui n'eſtoient pas encore fort addonnez à la pieté comme font la
pluſ-part de ceux qui regnent auiourd'huy en Europe No⁹ aduoüe-
rons toutefois à ceux qui blaſment
la Cour, qu'encore que les Princes
ayent eſté extrememeut deuots, il
s'eſt pû trouuer quelques vns de
leurs officiers qui ne l'eſtoient guere, & que par conſequent l'on peut
dire que l'impieté, l'orgueil, l'hypocriſie, l'impudicité & beaucoup de
vices ne font que trop frequens à la
Cour. La ieuneſſ y eſt quelque fois
fans conduite & la vieilleſſe fans re-

pentir. L'on y void des hommes si effeminez qu'ils ne portent l'espee que par contenance. Que si le nom de la vertu a tousiours esté neantmoins en vigueur parmy eux, ç'a esté pour tirer vn mal si preiudiciable qu'il vaudroit mieux que l'on n'en parlast point. Car c'est à des crimes dignes du foudre que l'on donne tous les iours ce beau nom pour abuser les simples ames. La plus effrenée ambitió s'appelle magnanimité, la trahison prudence, la prodigalité Magnificence, la médisance vne belle humeur pour entretenir les compagnies, & les plus dissoluës actions des galanteries d'honneste homme.

Par la licence que chacun se donne de se souiller de toutes ces impuretez, & dauantage par les loüanges que l'on reçoit de les auoir faites, il

semble à plusieurs qu'il soit impossible de resister au cours de ce torrét
qui entraine tout par vn mesme
chemin, & sur cette opinion quelques vns font vne retraicte honteu-
se, n'osants se mettre au hasard de
vaincre ou d'estre vaincus. Mais ce
sont des gens qui ne manquent que
d'vn courage esgal à leurs forces, &
de iugement de les connoistre. S'ils
auoient seulement la patience d'attendre l'ennemy auec vne contená-
ce ferme, ils sentiroient s'esleuer en
eux des mouuemens extraordinaires à son aproche, & comme la necessité de combattre se presentant
aux animaux les plus pesás & les plus
lasches, resueille en eux vne vigueur
qu'ils tenoiét assoupie, il n'est pas si
difficile de resister aux vices que ces
foibles esprits se figurét, encore que
l'on soit enfermé dás les lieux où ils
fót voir des exéples de leur tyránie.

En certains endroits de la mer
se trouue des fontaines d'eau douce
qui se font place malgré la violence de ses ondes, & l'on ne doit
point douter que de mesme au milieu des tempestes de la Cour & de
ces ames corrompues, il ne se trouue qui s'efforcent continuellement
d'adiouster de nouuelles graces à
leurs beautez naturelles à la mesme
proportion que les autres accrois-
sent leur defformité.

Il y en a infailliblement, & il y en
peut auoir encore dauátage, pourueu que ceux à qui de si bónes inspirations seront enuiees veulent oster
leur esprit vne heure seulement du
goust de la mondanité, & considerer les recompenses inestimables
qui sont promises à la vertu. Si les
fatigues de ce chemin que l'on leur
a figurées insupportables, leur en
font

font tenir vn autre tout contraire,
qu'ils ſçachent que ceux qui les ont
ſeduits les ont repeus d'illuſions.
Le Saũueur du monde dit : Qu'il
n'eſt rien de ſi leger que le fardeau
qu'il nous donne, ny rien de ſi doux
que le joug où il nous ſouſmet. Qui
croirons nous pluſtoſt que luy, qui
a marché le premier ſur les eſpines
que nous redoutons, a ſuiuy volon-
tairemẽt les loix qu'il nous a impo-
ſees. Bien que la nature diuine fuſt
jointe en luy à la nature humaine, elle n'vſoit point toutesfois
de ſes priuileges ; & laiſſoit ſouffrir à ſon corps les peines que
l'amour luy faiſoit prendre à noſtre
ſujet, tellement qu'il a conneu noſtre portée, & que ſuiuant ſa Iuſtice
eternelle, il ne nous a rien ordonné
qu'à la meſure de nos forces.

Ceux qui pour colorer leurs fau-

tes difent que parmy la vaine pompe des villes où il font contrainðs
de fe tenir ; il fe trouue d'eternels
obftacles à leur deuotion, témoignent affez qu'ils fe defchargent in-
iuftement fur la corruption du lieu,
& qu'ailleurs ils feroiéꞇ poffible encores. Rien ne nous oblige à eftre
mefchans pour en voir d'autres qui
le font, & quand les iniures & les
mocqueries vniuerfelles feroient à
la Cour la recompenfe des aðions
loüables, il faudroit s'enflammer
d'autant plus à en produire de nouuelles. Mais graces à Dieu, on n'y
eft pas encore affligé de ce malheur
là ; & fi la vraye vertu n'y trouue
vne generale ap'probatió, au moins
y en trouue-elle vne particuliere
entre les efprits finceres que la Diuinité y entretient, afin qu'elle ne
demeure en aucune part fans la

gloire qui luy est deuë. On dit qu'elle a des charmes si puissants que qui
la peut voir en son lustre, côçoit par
elle des affectiôs où iamais il ne mer
de termes. Ne puis-je pas dire aussi
que le vice a de si monstrueuses lai-
deurs, que qui le côsidere en sa naïfueté ne cessera iamais de l'abhorrer ?
Que seruent donc ces injustes plaintes contre les mauuais exemples qui
s'offrent à nos yeux ? remarquons
leurs pernicieuses qualitez, & nous
ferons plustost destournez qu'attirez à les suiure. Chaque chose a plusieurs faces, les vnes agreables, les
autres desplaisantes. Tournons les
de tous costez de peur que nous ne
soyons deceus à la premiere monstre. Ie ne mettray point en vsage
d'autre secret pour prouuer combien il est aysé d'imprimer en soy la
haine du vice, que de monstrer les

deffauts qu'il cache fous vne belle
apparéce, & des exemples mefmes,
à des accidens les plus ordinaires qui
fe trouuent à la Cour, je tireray des
moyens fuffifans de rendre vn courtifan accomply en toutes les vertus
neceffaires à fon falut. Pour fondement d'vn fi glorieux edifice, ie
n'en trouue point de fi neceffaire
que la Pieté que nous confiderons
en fa principale fonction, qui eft de
rendre à Dieu tous les hôneurs que
l'efprit d'vn mortel eft capable de
s'imaginer: Sçauroit on trouuer vn
plus infaillible fujet de faire naiftre
cette vertu que d'eftre à la fuitte
d'vn Prince? Celuy que l'on fert fe
confeffe feruiteur luy mefme, il ne
reçoit l'hommage que l'on luy rend
que comme Lieutenant d'vn maiftre, qui regne abfolument au deffus
de luy. A quel degré de follie feroit

on paruenu pour n'adorer point celuy qu'vn plus grand que nous ado-
re? Outre les enseignemens que
nous produict de toutes parts la
Nature, en qualité d'hommes, &
tant d'autres que nous baille la Religion, s'en peut-on figurer de plus
notables que ceux-cy pour induire
vne ame à reconnoistre son Createur? Que si ceux qui ne cherchent
qu'à s'excuser de bien-faire, m'ob-
jectent qu'il s'est trouué des Empereurs dont le moindre soucy estoit
celuy de conseruer la Religion, &
qui eussét voulu quasi que les vœux
de tous leurs sujets se fussent arrestez à leur throsne, comme s'il n'y
eust eu rien de plus puissant qu'eux;
& qu'en ce cas là on ne reconnoist
point aupres d'eux les bons exemples que ie presuppose. Ie diray que
Dieu n'afflige point tant la Chre-

ſtienté que de luy donner de ſemblables Princes, & que ſi cela arri-
noit, ſa puiſſance feroit rouſiours
manifeſtée en la côſeruation de ſon
Egliſe, qui ſe conſerue malgré toutes impietez , & meſme en la juſte
punition des hommes par vn regne
ſi deteſtable. Rien ne peut dôc nuire aux ſainctes affections d'vne ame
qui prend tout du coſté qu'il faut,
& jamais elle ne ſera tachée des
mauuaiſes inclinations de ceux àqui
c'eſt vn trop grand fardeau d'eſtre
veritablement Chreſtiens, & qui ſe
contentent d'eſtre courtiſans. Ceux
là gardent pour le particulier d'autres actions que pour la monſtre, &
les conuerſations qu'ils ont auec
leurs paroles leur ſembleroient fades & ſans aſſaiſonnement, s'ils n'y
auoient la liberté d'y forger des cô-
tes au meſpris des choſes ſainctes.

Chaque chose dont la passion imprime le desir en leur ame, leur est
vne idole, à qui ils s'asseruissent , &
ne cessent de luy sacrifier. Leur langue s'employe continuellement à
dire des blasphemes, elle qui n'a esté
faicte comme celle de tous les autres hómes que pour dire les loüanges de Dieu. Ils ne croiroient pas
estre au nombre des braues s'il ne se
trouuoit en tous leurs discours
moins de periodes que de iuremēts,
encore qu'il ne soit question de rien
affirmer. Estranges fleurs de Rhetorique que iamais l'Orateur d'Athenes, ny celuy de Rome ne connu-
rent! Mais c'est bien pis quand la colere les transporte ; ils renient , ils
maudissent, ils detestent, & il s'en
est veu mesme qui ne croyans pas
que leur bouche seule peust vomir
contre le Ciel des execratiós dignes

de leur rage, ont donné de l'argent
à leurs valets pour leur ayder à faire
cet office. De semblables rebellions
d'vn ver de terre côtre vne puissance infinie témoignent vn si grand
éloignement de Dieu que ie ne pése pas qu'il les laissast arriuer en vn
homme dont il auroit esté adoré de
bon cœur vne heure seulement. Vn
homme qui n'a pour luy que tout
respect & toute crainte, deffie les
passions de le faire tomber en de tels
accez quoy qu'il viue au milieu de
la Cour, & que les propos que l'on
entend souuent se grauent quelquefois malgré nous en nostre memoire de telle sorte que nous les disons
aussi apres. Il sçait que le nom de
Dieu est si sacré & si redoutable,
qu'à l'ouyr seulement les Anges tré-
blent, & tout ce qui est en la Nature obeyt. Il n'a garde de l'auoir en

la bouche qu'en des occasions qui
le rendent necessaire, & qu'il n'aye
en mesme temps au cœur vne deuotion tres-ardente Que s'il a esté autrefois au rang des aueuglez , &
qu'il en ait retenu cette mauuaise
coustume de iurer, il ne faut point
douter qu'il n'employe tous les efforts pour la quitter , & qu'il n'en
vienne heureusemét à bout De verité ces trois habitudes de iurer, de
iouer & de médire, s'attachent tellement à l'ame, que ceux qui les ont
ne passeroient pas vn moment de
leur vie sans s'adonner à l'vne ou à
l'autre : mais il faut croire que Dieu
gouuerne tout auec vn tel ordre
qu'il ne souffre point de mal au móde qu'il n'y en laisse pareillement le
remede. Ie parleray des deux dernieres habitudes, quãd il sera temps:
& pour ce qui est de la premiere, ie

ne la tiens pas incorrigible, puisqu'il
n'est point d'accoustumance qui ne
se puisse oster par vne accoustumance contraire. Celuy là témoignoit
bien le desir qu'il auoit d'en estre deliuré qui baisoit promptement la
terre dés qu'il s'estoit aperçeu d'a-
uoir iuré. Mais ie ne suis pas d'auis
que celuy qui demeure dans les villes, choisisse vne penitence si publique. Cela ne s'accommode pas aux
mœurs de nostre siecle, & encore y
auroit-il à craindre quelque vanité!
La contrition peut produire d'autres actes fecours qui ne seront pas de
moindre efficace. Ainsi tant plus ira-
t'il auant, tant plus se perfectionne-
ra-t'il, & n'y aura point de journée
qui n'adjouste toufiours quelque
nouuelle grace à son merite.

L'amour qu'il portera à Dieu luy
ostera de l'ame celuy de soy-mef-

me, & par cõsequent les trois bran-
ches qui ont accoustumé d'en sortir, c'est à sçauoir, les affections que
l'on a pour les honneurs, pour les richesses, & pour les voluptez. Les
premiers effects du mespris qu'il aura pour ces choses se monstreront
visiblement au pouuoir qu'il aura
de chasser l'ambition de ses pensées,
& de se donner vne moderation
d'esprit où fort peu de ceux de sa
condition peuuent atteindre, comme il verra que le monde s'appreste
desia de le coucher sur l'estat de ses
esclaues, à la premiere entrée qu'il
faict à la Cour, il ne fera point auecque luy de marché qu'il n'ait consideré prudemment quels sont les gages qu'il luy offre. Il se doit connoistre soy mesme, & sçauoir combien
il se veut vendre. Mais encore que
sa modestie le mette fort bas, quand

il aura connu la nature fragile des biens qui luy font offerts, & que dauantage ils font bien fouuent auffi toft repris que donnez , il auoüera franchement que fa liberté eft trop precieufe pour eftre engagee à fi bas prix, & fe gardera de tomber entre les mains d'vn maiftre fi trompeur & fi perfide. L'erreur qui poffede la plufpart des hommes, leur fait imaginer que de tous les lieux du monde, il n'y en a pas vn où l'on ne s'abftienne pluftoft d'eftre ambitieux que dans la Cour; & qu'indubitablement lors que nous y voyons les autres efleuez aux dignitez eminentes, nous fommes dauátage efmeus à defirer vne pareille felicité, que fi nous eftions priuez de cet object. Mais dites moy quelle paffion defmefurée de s'agrandir pourroit poffeder vn homme qui fçait que la

fortune ne nous rit que lors qu'elle
a enuie de nous faire pleurer, qu'elle ne nous esleue que pour nous faire faire vn plus beau sault, & ne no⁹
pare de tãt d'habits somptueux que
pour nous estouffer plus facilemét?
Il faudroit qu'il fust aueugle pour
ne pas reconnoistre la qualité des
choses qui s'offrent à luy tous les
iours, & ces euenemens estrãges de
la ruine subite des prosperitez que
l'on estimoit les plus fermes, ne luy
peuuent donner que de la crainte
d'estre à la posterité vn exemple de
l'inconstance du monde. Ceux qui
n'ont pas esprouué les faueurs de la
fortune, & qui ne viuent pas dans
les lieux où l'on la peut sonder de
toutes parts, ne sçauent pas comme
luy son amertume, & la souhaitte-
roient bien plustost, n'en esperant
que de la douceur. O qu'il est bien

guary de ces vanitez , ayant veu
que le simple Gentil-homme n'est
point content encore qu'il soit paruenu à estre domestique d'vn Seigneur, ce qui estoit toute son ambition; qu'estant apres en vne qualité
plus remarquable, il souhaite encore, & croit qu'il sera bien-heureux si
son Maistre luy donne vne charge
plus haute, qu'enfin y estant paruenu, le voila aussi miserable & aussi
plein d'agitation qu'en la bassesse
de son premier estat. Ces Meditations sont si puissantes à moderer la
fureur d'vn desir trop haut, qu'il est
impossible d'en vser sans cherir la
mediocrité, & se monstrer de pareille humeur que ce bon Citoyen
qui se consolant sur ce que la charge qu'il auoit briguée auoit esté
donnée à vn autre, disoit qu'il e-
stoit extrememét aysé de ce qu'il se

trouuoit dans la ville de plus gens
de bien que luy. Vn esprit qui n'a
point de sentiments esloignez de la
raison, preferera tousiours ainsi l'v-
tilité publique à la sienne particuliere, & se persuadera qu'il n'estoit
pas propre à la fonction qu'il sou-
haitoit puis qu'on l'en a rejetté. Il
considerera que la fortune n'est pas
obligée de le fauoriser plustost
qu'vn autre, que ce personnage qui
est plus auancé que luy est aussi plus
ancien à la Cour, que la charge
qu'il a obtenuë est la recompense
de mille soufmissions qu'il a renduës. Luy qui s'est garanty de cet es-
clauage ne seroit il-pas iniuste de
vouloir rauir le prix qui y est affe-
œté seulement? Qu'il se contente
d'auoir pour sa part sa franchise
qui vaut bien plus que l'office,

& qu'il prenne garde d'ailleurs, qu'il
est deliuré de beaucoup de soins &
d'ennuys qui sont parauenture inseparables de cette códition, & parmy lesquels son aduersaire se trouuera si empesché qu'il voudroit
auoir changé ses honneurs à la tranquillité d'vne vie champestre. Que
s'il se voit à la fin esleué au degré le
plus eminét que son espoir luy pouuoit promettre , il se souuiendra
tousiours de ce qu'il estoit en sa premiere condition , & se representant
qu'il n'est rien de plus que les autres
hommes, il regardera ce bon-heur
auec vn mesme visage que l'infortune. Il n'a pas mis en oubly le peu
d'estime qu'il faisoit des richesses
mondaines, lors qu'il se reconfor-
toit n'en ayant pas beaucoup , &
maintenant qu'il en a à suffisance, il
change si peu d'opinion , que l'on
connoist

cognoiſt bien que ce qu'il en diſoit
procedoit d'vn veritable meſpris.
Il ne veut rien poſſeder à ceſte heure cy que comme s'il le tenoit par
emprunt, & ſe tient tout preſt à deſ-
loger de ſa place au moindre ſignal
qu'il entendra. S'il eſtoit encore en
vn lieu bas, il ſçait bien que ce ne ſeroit pas merueille de le voir humble, mais qu'eſtant auiourd'huy au
ſommet de la grandeur, c'eſt ce qui
eſt d'admirable & de recommandable enuers toute ſorte d'eſpris, de
ne le voir point auec cét orgueil qui
accompagne d'ordinaire les perſonnes de pareil eſtat. Conſiderant
auſſi que c'eſt le moyen infaillible
de contraindre meſme l'Enuie à ſe
garder de luy nuire. Il s'humilie
d'autant plus qu'il luy arriue de
proſperité. Il reſſemble aux eſpics
qui baiſſent leur teſte, lors qu'ils ont
P

le plus de grains. Les flatteries ont
si peu de credit enuers luy, encore
qu'elles importunét inceſſamment
ſes oreilles, que lors qu'il les entend,
il ſe mocque en luy-meſme de tant
de graces qui diſent le contraire de
ce qu'ils penſent , & de ce qu'ils
voyent , & comme s'ils venoient
joüer vne Comedie deuant luy, pré-
nent d'autres façons & d'autres
langages qu'en leur particulier. Il
eſt le doux ennemy de ſoy-meſme,
& les langues les plus ingenieuſes à
meſdire ne luy ſçauroient tant im-
puter de deffaux qu'il s'en imagine
eſtre en luy, ſi bien que c'eſt perdre
le temps que de le penſer ietter dans
la preſomption. Neantmoins il fait
preſque vn meſme accueil à ceux
qui le flattent & à ceux qui le trai-
tent auecque franchiſe, s'il ſe peut
trouuer de telles gens dans la corruption du lieu, & il ne veut pas

que l'on dise que personne soit
sorty d'aupres de luy sans quelque
satisfaction. S'il a des parents ou des
amis de son ancienne cognoissance, il ne fera pas semblant de les mes-
cognoistre à cause de la petitesse de
leur fortune, mais il les aprochera
de soy pour les rendre participants
de son bon-heur comme ils l'ont
esté de ses aduersitez, sans toutefois
apporter du preiudice au bien de
l'Estat. Car s'il les iuge incapables
de s'acquiter dignement d'vne
charge importante, il se gardera
bien de les en faire pouruoir, &
choisira plustost de les enrichir aux
despens de ses propres facultez.

Icy peut on recognoistre qu'il est
besoin qu'il ioigne à son humilité
vne autre vertu qui n'est pas moins
exquise C'est la liberalité que ie
veux dire, de laquelle il se seruira

pour mettre en vſage les richeſſes
dont Dieu l'a fait le threſorier & le
diſpenſateur. Il ne faut rien chercher de plus puiſſant à l'y conuier
que l'acquiſition qu'il fait en cela
d'vne infinité de courages dont les
vœux ſeruent d'eternel appuy à ſa
fortune, & que ceſte rare proye ſe
gaigne ſans armes, ſans violence,
ſans prieres, & ſans ſe ſouſmettre à
aucune ſeruitude, & ce qui eſt de
plus remarquable, il faict croiſtre
par ce moyen les vertus de pluſieurs
ames genereuſes qui ſe fleſtriroient
ſans la recompenſe. Mais tout cela
ne ſuffiroit pas pour luy oſter la
qualité d'auare, puiſque ceux qui
iouyſſent de ſes bien-faicts, n'ont
que ce qui leur eſtoit deub; il faut
que ſa liberalité s'eſtende auſſi ſur
ceux qui ſe recommandent aſſez à
luy par leur ſeule pauureté, & com-

me il ne manquera pas de ces obiets
de compaſſion , qui ne ſont que
trop frequents, auſſi n'aura t'il pas
faute de charité pour leur bien faire. Les biens qui ſont employez de
ceſte façon luy rendront vn proffit
extreme, il n'y aura iour qu'il n'en
reçoiue des intereſts ſi hauts qu'en
peu de temps le principal ſera plus
que payé. C'eſt ce que l'on deſpenſe
au jeu & aux ſomptuoſitez qu'on
doit eſtimer perdu, & ceſte prodigalité n'eſt pas moins à fuyr que
l'auarice. La Temperance, qui eſt la
regle generale où toutes les vertus
ſe meſurent, nous ordóne le milieu
ſans pancher d'vn coſté ny d'autre, & de toutes les prodigalitez,
celle du jeu luy deplaiſt le plus ; car il
participe tellement des deux extremes que les vns y ſont portez par vn
deſir inſatiable de gagner, & les au-

tres par vne negligence de conseruer quelque heritage paternel qui
ne leur a point donné de peine à acquerir. Le sage Courtisan n'en sera
pas destourné auec peu de force,
quand il aura remarqué que c'est
vne source malheureuse d'où naissent chaque iour les blasphemes, les
meurtres & les desespoirs, sans que
l'on la puisse estancher : Et de faict
quel esprit pernicieux le pourroit
aymer apres auoir veu de quelles
diuerses passions est agité celuy qui
perd? Comment il hazarde son reste
sousvn espoir de regagner qui touf-
jours l'accompagne, & ayant perdu
son argent, son manteau & son cheual, ioué iusqu'à ses Laquais, ce qui
n'a pas encore esté assez pour la rage de plusieurs qui se sont à la fin
joüez eux-mesmes, contents de se
perdre puis qu'ils auoient tant per-

du. Quant à ce qui est de l'inclination que la prodigalité nous donne
au jeu; il ne me semble pas qu'elle
puisse estre mieux corrigee que par
l'inuention que trouua vn certain
Prince pour retrancher les despences trop excessiues de son fils. Il cõ-
manda à son Argentier de ne luy
plus donner aucune somme qu'à la
charge qu'il la compteroit luy-mesme. La premiere fois que ce prodi-
gue eut affaire d'argét pour donner
a quelque bouffon, il n'auoit pas
encore compté le quart de ce qu'il
demandoit, que la lassitude luy fit
quiter ce trauail, & qu'ayant recognu que le don estoit trop grand, il
delibera d'vser d'vne espargne plus
estroite. Si ceux qui ne iouent leur
argent que par sachees, auoient
ainsi pris la peine de le compter, possible n'en seroient ils plus si mau-

uais ménagers. Mais escoutons la
nouuelle Philosophie des plus sçauants Docteurs qui soient sortis de
l'eschole de la mondanité. Ils per-
mettent de bonne heure que leurs
enfans ioüent, & leur baillent tant
d'argent qu'ils ne se peuuent pas affliger de leurs pertes ; leur opinion
estāt que c'est le moyen d'effacer de
leur esprit l'amour des richesses, &
les rendre braues & genereux. Il ne
se faut pas arrester à de si peruerses
maximes, qui sous vne apparence
trompeuse de nous retirer d'vn vice nous iettent dans vne infinité
d'autres. Les pertes accompagnent
tousiours le ieu, soit celles de l'argent, des bonnes habitudes, ou du
temps. Et si les Anciens Sages ne
vouloient point de Musique en
leurs festins, ny qu'on leur aportast
des eschets ou des dez apres le repas, disans qu'ils ne pouuoient trou-

uer de diuertiſſemens plus agreables que leurs diſcours: Ie ne ſçay
comment vn vray Chreſtien pourroit paſſer des iournees en vn entretien ſi brutal que le jeu, ayãt tant de
choſes à s'occuper, qu'à peine ſa vie
y peut elle ſuffire. Noſtre vertueux
Courtiſan a tant de ſerieus diſcours
& tant d'vtiles choſes à faire qu'il
employera bien mieux qu'au jeu &
ſon temps & ſon argent; Et comme
nous l'auons fait autant eſloigné de
l'ambition, qu'humble & liberal, il
eſt à preſumer qu'il eſt auſſi merueilleuſement ennemy de l'enuie.

Il n'eſt pas de ceux qui n'ont point
de maladie plus dangereuſe que
celle que la ſanté de leur voiſin leur
apporte, & qui ne ſe reſiouyſſent
pas tant de leur propre bien, comme ils font du mal d'autruy. Il ne
s'opoſe point au moindre craignãt

qu'il ne vienne à s'efgaler à luy , ny
à l'efgal, afin de le laiffer derriere, ny
au plus grand , afin de ne luy eftre
pas fujet. Ces paffions ne fçauroiét
donner la loy qu'à des efprits infames à qui il ne faudroit qu'ofter la
condition où ils s'eftiment fi malheureux , & la donner à vn autre
pour la faire eftimer qu'elle eft la
plus belle & la plus defirable du
monde. Mais en punition de cefte
iniuftice, il n'y a point de crime qui
trouue vne telle iuftice que ceftui-
cy, & il ne fe rencontre point de Iuges ny de bourreaux fi rigoureux
que l'enuieux eft forcé d'eftre enuers luy-mefme. Tant s'en faut
qu'vn homme genereux foit expo-
fé à ces tourments, qu'au contraire
il fe forme toufiours quelque matiere de ioye aux diuerfes profperitez de fon prochain. S'il void auan-

cer quelque personnage, dont en
conscience on ne sçauroit nier la
visible prud'hommie, il se resiouyt
de ce que les recompenses sont dó-
nees aux merites, & s'enflamme de
plus en plus à bien faire, s'il desire
iouyr d'vn pareil bon-heur. Que si
au contraire vne dignité est accordee à vn autre dont l'insuffisance est
toute cognuë, il se consolera en se
representant que celuy qui se mesle
d'vne charge qu'il n'entend pas, a
tousiours la peine & la honte pour
sa punition, & qu'en fin on sera
contraint d'en receuoir de plus capables. Et quand il n'auroit aucun
espoir de iamais paruenir à vne fortune eminente, vne charité infinie
le portera tousiours à aymer le bié
de ses voisins, & en procurer la conseruation, de sorte que receuant de
la ioye à proportion de leur acroif-

sement, il rendra comme sien ce qu'on luy empeschoit d'obtenir, & par vn moyen miraculeux & iuste, trompant les intentions des Grands, il recueillera les fruicts de leur liberalité, sans estre iouyssant de leur faueur.

Iamais il ne s'efforcera de nuire par ses paroles à qui que ce soit, puis qu'il ne le fait pas par ses actions, ny mesme par ses volontez, & si la médisance n'a point d'autres conseillers que la presomption & l'enuie, elle n'a pas garde de sortir de sa bouche. Ses oreilles sont si bien closes aux pernicieux aduis de ces deux seditieuses, que si tost qu'elles s'apprestent à le tenter, il s'enferme en sa maison propre, & bouche toutes les ouuertures qui regardent chez ses voisins, & n'espiant rien que ce qui est de soy-mesme n'y trouue

que trop de subject de moc̈querie.
Si les yeux de son corps ont ceste
mauuaise qualité qu'ilsvoyent tout,
& ne se sçauroient voir; en recompense ceux de son ame ont leurs
facultez toutes troublees en eux-
mesmes, & se rédent volótairement
aueugles pour toute autre chose.
Il y a de la lascheté & de la bassesse à médire; c'est donner despreu-
ues de la foiblesse de sa cause, &
qu'on a si peu de merite qu'on ne se
sçauroit establir vne ferme reputation que sur les ruines de celle d'autruy. Et de faict si indifferemment
touts ceux d'vne compagnie souffrent auec plaisir la calomnie que
l'on y seme, cela procede de la folle
creance dont chacun est preoccupé
d'estre plus estimable que les autres,
dequoy il pense trouuer de visibles tesmoignages dans ce blasme.

Mais dauantage il n'eſt rien de ſi
abjeɥ que la médiſance, quand l'oɳ
remarque que ceux qui y ont de
l'inclination ayment mieux perdre
vn amy qu'vn bon mot, & ſe ran-
geans aux termes vils de la boufon-
nerie, parlent bien des vices de tout
le monde, mais ils ne donnent point
de preceptes pour s'en corriger, &
les propoſent pluſtoſt comme vn
patron à ceux qui ne s'y addonnent
encore qu'imparfaitement. Que
l'on entend de diſcours de ceſte ſorte en noſtre ſiecle, & qu'à bó droiɥ
l'on les appelle des Satyres, puis
qu'il n'eſt rien de plus laſcif, de plus
puant, ny de plus difforme. O que le
ſage aymeroit bien mieux ſe taire à
peine d'eſtre taxé d'ignorance, que
de monſtrer qu'vne des plus petites
parties de ſó corps euſt tát d'empire
ſur le reſte, qu'on ne luy puſt donner

le frein, & qu'il choifiroit bien pluftoft de fe tronçonner cefte langue
rebelle auec les dents, que la nature femble luy auoir mis pour bar-
riere, & pour correcteurs, que de luy
laiffer efchapper vne parole irreuo-
cable dont il ne luy demeure pour
falaire que le repentir. S'il s'eft rencontré aux mauuaifes actions d'autruy, ou il ne s'y eft point arrefté, ou
il les a oubliees, & fi l'on luy en a
rapporté quelque chofe, ou il ne l'a
point ouy, ou il ne l'a point creu,
tellement qu'à quelque prix que ce
foit il s'exempte toufiours de les publier.

Ignoreroit il que la langue a la
forme du fer d'vn dard, pour monftrer qu'elle eft capable de faire de
dangereufes bleffures, & qu'eftant
de la nature du foudre qui ofte
l'ame fans offenfer le corps, les

playes qu'elle fait sont d'autant plus
incurables, qu'elles ne sont pas
apparentes. Le plus sage d'entre les
Roys luy aprend, que la vie & la
mort sont en la main de la langue,
& sa charité l'oblige à craindre de
voir quelqu'vn outragé de ses
coups, se porte à la colere, & au
discord, ne mesurant pas la foiblef-
se des autres à sa patience. Car pour
luy il s'est bien representé dés qu'il
s'est mis au monde que l'on y reçoit
plus d'iniures en vn iour que l'on
n'en pourroit vanger en vingt annees, & que de vouloir tirer raison
des personnes qui nous les sont, les-
quelles sont pour la plufpart indignes d'estre les objets de la passion
d'vne belle ame, ce seroit vne pareille brutalité que si lors qu'vn
cheual nous a sallis de son escu-
me nous nous efforcions d'en

ietter

jetter aussi dessus luy.

Nostre Courtisan a des armes de si bonne trempe que les traicts de la langue rebouchent contre & retournent vers ceux qui les tirent pour les punir d'vne rage de voir leurs efforts si vains. Il a trouué vne pierre Philosophale de beaucoup plus excellente que celle que les Alchimistes cherchent auec tant de soin , & l'effect que celle là doit auoir sur toute sorte de metaux, la sienne l'a sur toute sorte de fortunes Il les rend toutes d'or, dés qu'elles luy arriuent, se comportant de telle maniere , que ce qui seroit aux autres vn dommage irreparable luy est vn proffit nompareil; & comme la Cour est vn lieu où les amys sont si rares que de tous ceux qui s'y trouueroient en cent Siecles , il n'y en auroit pas assez pour en faire vne

Q

republique, il s'efforce ingenieuse-
ment de tirer de ses ennemis les
mesmes commoditez qu'il tireroit
de ceux qui l'affectionneroient: S'il
n'a personne qui l'aduertisse fide-
lement de ses fautes, il a à tout le
moins ses enuieux qui n'en lair-
roient pas passer vne. Que s'ils en
publient quelqu'autres que iamais
il n'a commises, cela seruira à le garder d'autant plus d'y tomber, afin
de n'estre pas seulement exempt de
crime, mais aussi de soupçon. Cét
auantage luy en reuient de surplus
qu'il y apprend merueilleusement à
souffrir, & que sa vertu y trouue des
occasions de se rendre tousiours
plus illustre. Dans vne tranquilité
d'esprit si generale, il ne se faut pas
attendre que la colere y apporte
quelque trouble, car si ses premieres agitations s'y esleuent pour ac-

corder quelque chose à la foiblesse
de la nature, elles sont au pis aller
en leur plus grande vigueur dés leur
origine, & ne naissent que pour
mourir aussi tost. Celuy qui conseil-
loit à Auguste de reciter l'Alphabet
toutes les fois qu'il entreroit en
courroux, n'auoit pas à mon aduis
tant d'esgard à l'amortissement de
sa passion qui pourroit arriuer cependant, qu'à l'aduertissement taci-
te qu'il luy donnoit, que de ne sçauoir pas dompter l'effort de telles
attaques, c'est n'estre encore que
petit escolier en la vraye science de
l'homme, & se voir reduit à en apprendre les premiers Rudiments.
Quelle honte de trouuer vn Vieil-
lard parmy les enfants aux basses
Classes, où l'on luy enseigne encore que la paix & la societé des hommes ont de si beaux & de si iustes

liens que iamais ils ne les deuroient
rompre , qu'ils doiuent estre tous
attachez au seruice d'vn seul Dieu,
leur seul Createur & Redempteur,
qu'ils ne font tous ensemble qu'v-
ne mesme famille, que leurs corps
sont d'vne mesme matiere , leurs
ames de mesme substance, & leur
dessein vniuersel d'arriuer à la felicité eternelle ; & que par consequét
c'est violer le droict d'vne proximi-
té si estroite de nourrir chez soy ce
dangereux monstre de la hayne , &
sans vouloir ouyr parler de pardon,
mettre son esprit tout entier dans
les desirs & les desseins de la vengeance. Les fumees de la colere
aussi puissantes que celles du vin,
troublent si bien le cerueau de la
pluspart du monde que c'est à se
venger que l'on s'imagine plus de
gloire : mais quelle marque est-ce

de generosité de ne se pouuoir
maintenir aux occasions qu'vn ennemy donne à nostre vertu de s'e-
xercer, & de paroistre & chercher
de l'asseurance en sa mort, comme
si l'on craignoit d'en estre destruit.
O que l'Esprit de Dieu possedoit
plainement celuy de Dauid, quand
il a dit, que les hommes sont trom-
peurs en leurs balances, car ils ne pe-
sent rien comme il faut, & pour
pallier leurs ordures, ils donnent
aux choses mauuaises la valeur des
bonnes, vn faux honneur tenant
parmy eux la place du vray : ils se
croyroient indignes de iamais tenir vne espee s'ils ne s'efforçoient
de tirer esclaircissement des moindres paroles du monde. Ce sont des
ames bien mal saines, puisque si peu
de chose leur fait mal, & si quelques-vns plus robustes le peuuët di-

gerer ayſément, ils ſont neantmoins
contraints de ſuiure le commun
abus, & de demander raiſon par les
armes du tort qu'on leur a voulu
faire. Mais qui croyroit ce que la
rage a bien amené de pire. Vn ieune Gentil-homme n'a pas ſi toſt
paru dans la Cour, que ceux qui s'e-
ſtiment auoir la plus rude eſpee ne
le laiſſent point en repos qu'ils
ne l'ayent fait venir au combat,
craignans que s'il leur reſtoit à eſprouuer la valeur de quelqu'vn, l'on
ne la miſt au deſſus de la leur. Ainſi
dans l'oyſiueté de la paix nous perdons autant de braues Gend'armes
que dans les fureurs de la guerre,
nos membres ſe deſtruiſans l'vn
l'autre. Il n'y a plus que la memoire
de noſtre ancienne puiſſance qui
conſerue de la terreur au cœur de
nos ennemis. Mais vn Courtiſan ſur

lequel la raison tient l'empire, que
la Barbarie exerce sur les autres, ne
s'estudie point à interpreter en tant
de sortes les paroles les plus inno-
centes, qu'il y puisse à la fin trouuer
vne matiere de querelle. Il fournit
d'excuse à toutes iniures, & par les
enchantemens d'vne courtoisie si-
gnalee, il sçait si bien vaincre l'inimitié qu'elle se tueroit plustost de
son venin propre que d'en auoir de-
formais pour luy. C'est pour les iustes occasions qu'il reserue de se hazarder, afin qu'vne mort auenuë
pour vn sujet loüable luy gaigne
des trophees que l'Eternité verra
durer autant qu'elle; il ne satisfaict
point à des passions de vengeance,
pensant se mettre en repos par la
mort d'vn ennemy qui l'expose-
roit aux dangers d'vne fin ignomi-
nieuse, ou la necessité d'abandon-

ner les delices de sa patrie. Les Roys
n'ont point de foudres plus ineuita-
bles que pour ce crime là, & Dieu
les leur a donnez en main auec có-
mandement expres d'en punir la temerité de ceux qui osent desfaire
son ouurage, & mettre fin à la vie
de ses creatures, cóme s'ils auoient
enuie de s'opposer à ses desseins.
Mais outre cela le vray Chrestien
considerant qu'il est obligé de suiure la trace de son Redempteur qui
pardonnoit à ceux qui le cruci-
fioient, arrache de son ame le res-
sentiment des iniures en esperance
de receuoir vn pareil traictement
de la iustice eternelle pour les pechez dont il l'a offensee.

C'est bien vne vertu tres-remar-
quable que ceste patience dont il se
sert à faire passer les affronts pour
des bien-faicts, & ceste modestie

qui esloigne la médisance de ses discours : mais il manque encore vne
picté à leur perfection, c'est que
comme il ne s'efforce point de ter-
nir le lustre de la vertu par des ca-
lomnies, aussi ne doit-il pas s'employer à donner couleur au vice par
la flaterie. La crainte seruile ne se
trouuant point dans ses pensees
qu'est ce qu'il le pourroit empescher de faire voir la verité dans la
Cour, encore qu'à peine y en veuille t'on voir l'image, & lors qu'il aura remarqué des actions contraires au deuoir, par quelles raisons seroit il retenu de condamner leur
iniustice ? A n'en point mentir il se
rencontre des esprits en qui les re-
prehensions & les enseignements
sont aussi mal employez que la se-
mence respanduë sur vn rocher, &
quand il aura reconnu qu'il ne les

fais qu'irriter par ses conseils, il n'est
point de loy qui l'oblige à leur en
donner dauantage. Il ne se quittera
donc point soy-mesme pour se rendre du tout semblable à autruy. Il
ne pleure point pour voir seulemét
pleurer les autres, & ne fait point
paroistre de ioye quand il void naistre la leur, si ces diuers visages ne
se prennent pour l'interest de la vertu; & comme il s'esloigne de la faus-
seté de ceste complaisance, aussi
fait-il de toute autre sorte de mensonge, de peur que les hommes ayás
receu quelque impression qu'il fust
perfide, il ne soit reduit à ce malheur de n'estre pas seulement crû
quand il dira la verité! Il n'est pas
semblable à ces Statuës qui ont bié
vne bouche & toutes les autres parties de dehors de l'homme, mais à
qui le Sculpteur n'a pû tailler de

cœur au dedans ny les autres pieces
neceſſaires. Il agit auſſi bien en effect qu'en apparence, & s'il eſt en
credit il ne fait point vn accueil fauorable à ceux qui le ſuiuét pour les
tromper. Ses promeſſes ſont des ar-
reſts qu'il ne reuoque point, fuſſent ils à ſa ruine.

Apres s'eſtre orné de ſi rares qualitez qui luy font emporter la victoire ſur les vains honneurs, & les
foibles richeſſes du monde, il reſte
à monſtrer comment il ſçait combattre la volupté corporelle. Il faut
auoüer qu'il n'y a point de lieu où
il puiſſe rencontrer des charmes
plus forts que dans la Cour, où chacun eſtime que les beautez des Dames font naiſtre autant de deſirs &
d'amours que l'on les regarde de
fois : mais il ne faut pas nier auſſi
qu'on n'y trouue vn contrepoiſon

tres-ſalutaire, y voyât tous les iours
de notables exemples du peu de
duree de ce beau teint, ſur ces maſ-
ques ridez, couuerts de fard, que
ie ne ſçay ſi ie dois appeller viſa-
ges. La beauté tient vne ſi courte
tyrannie qu'il ne faut pas croire
que Menelaus continua le ſiege de
Troyes l'eſpace de dix ans pour r'a-
uoir ceſte Helene à qui Homere
attribuë tant de graces.

Les perfections que Paris auoit
admirees en elle quand il la rauit
ne pouuoient pas auoir gardé leur
eſclat vn ſi long temps. Il faut pluſtoſt chercher la cauſe d'vne ſi longue guerre dans l'obſtination des
vns & des autres. Quelle ame genereuſe peut tenir pour des beautez des choſes qui ſe doiuent rendre ſi difformes? Se contentera t'elle de n'auoir pour prix de ſa liber-

té qu'vne chose presente & fu-
gitiue, & qui n'a en outre que des
plaisirs si fades qu'à peine le corps
pour l'amour duquel principalement on les recherche, y peut-il
trouuer dequoy se satisfaire? Ceste
passion est vn feu qui amollit ces
courages de fer, qui ne deuroient
point estre employez à d'autre vsage qu'à la guerre. Elle fait que la
constance & la force ne leur sont
plus si familieres.

Tandis qu'elle tient son Empire, les conseils de la raison sont
si peu escoutez que l'on est porté à des folies & des extrauagances qui font rougir de honte quand
l'on reuient en son bon sens, &
l'on recognoist que ce n'estoient
que des resueries que les douceurs que l'on s'imaginoit de
gouster.

Aussi les Syrenes ne sont elles
peintes auec vn visage, vn sein, &
des bras où la iuste proportion & la
viue couleur ont leur accomplisse-
ment, que pour nous signifier les diuerses felicitez que d'abord l'amour
nous fait esperer; & si le reste de
leurs corps ne nous est representé
que comme celuy d'vn monstre,
c'est pour nous faire entendre que
dans ceste ioüyssance que nous
souhaitons, il ny a rien à gaigner en
fin que des difformitez & des malheurs. Il faut donner à l'ame vn obiect plus digne d'elle, & ne chercher iamais les voluptez du corps
qu'auec les conditions qui les rendent legitimes. Les maux qui arriuent de leurs excez sont si frequents
à la Cour, qu'vn homme de iugement qui les remarque n'a pas
besoin d'autre preseruatif contre

ceste fiebure chaude, & que par
consequent il se garantira des sotti-
ses & des vanitez dont elle est la
source. Il ne passera pas les nuicts à
faire des Meditations sur chaque
grace qu'il s'imagine en sa Maistresse, & les matinees à chercher de
nouuelles façons de se parer pour
luy plaire, & le reste du iour à luy
rendre des hommages Idolatres. Il
ne preferera pas à tous les biens du
monde celuy de luy auoir baisé les
mains, & ne s'estimera pas plus heureux d'estre vaincu par elle, que s'il
auoit esté vainqueur de mille Roys,
& aussi de soy-mesme. Il a tant d'autres occupations si graues & si im-
portantes que de telles affections ne
naissent point en son ame, estant
certain que ce sont des plantes toutes contraires aux autres qui viennent mieux quand les terres ont

esté remuees & labourees; car iamais celles cy ne peuuent croiftre
que dans celles que l'on a laiffees en
repos & en friche.

Ie croy auoir remarqué les principaux moyens qui fe prefenteront
chaque iour au Courtifan pour s'acquerir les plus eminentes vertus,
outre lefquels il en pourra encore
trouuer d'autres où il paruiendra
par degrez, & viuant dans le monde comme n'y eftant point, ie fuis
d'auis qu'il faffe comme ce Capitaine qui ayant gagné vne victoire,
& voyant les defpoüilles des ennemis dit à celuy qui le fuiuoit qu'il les
amaffift pource qu'il n'eftoit pas
Themiftocle. Le peuple d'Ifraël ga-
gnant pays vers la terre de Promif-
fion enuoya auffi vers le Roy des
Amortheens quelques Ambaffa-
deurs qui luy firent cefte Harangue.

gue. Nous vous supplions qu'il nous soit permis de passer par vostre terre; Nous n'entrerons point dans vos champs, ny dans vos vignes; nous ne beurons pas mesme l'eau de vos fontaines; Nous irons le long du grand chemin sans nous arrester que nous ne soyons hors de vos frontieres. C'est ainsi qu'il faut passer dans le grand chemin du monde auec vn mespris de toutes les choses qu'on y rencontre, iusques à temps qu'on ayt franchy les barrieres de ceste vie, & il faut laisser ramasser ou cueillir les choses friuoles à ceux qui font moins que nous, & qui font encores esclaues de la mondanité.

En ce passage de la vie le Courtisan inuitera pareillement ceux qui ont à faire vn long & dangereux voyage, & comme ils n'oseroient se

mettre aux champs auec toute forte de perſonnes incognues, de peur
d'eſtre volez, mais attendent à partir auec le Gouuerneur de la Prouince s'il va par ce meſme chemin,
afin d'eſtre aſſeurez contre les plus
mauuaiſes rencontres. Ainſi nous
deuons nous bien garder de tenir la
campagne auec d'autres que les
vrays enfans de noſtre patrie, &
ceux qui y ont beaucoup d'authorité, craignant qu'on ne nous vole
tout ce que nous portons quant &
nous. Mais en quoy penſe t'on que
conſiſtent les richeſſes qu'il faut
auoir? Ce n'eſt pas en pieces fauſſes,
mais en vne bonne monnoye qui
ayt cours en ce pays-là; & c'eſt vne
folie de ſe charger de bagage, puiſque rien ne manque au lieu où nous
aſpirons. Si la Cour nous preſente
ſes plus aymables delices, il faut fai-

re comme ce Roy de Sparte, qui
menant son armee par le pays des
Thasiens retint seulement les fari-
nes qu'ils luy donnerent, & pour
les côfitures & les pastisseries qu'ils
luy apporterent en mesme temps,
il les fit distribuer aux esclaues. Ne
prenons que ce qui est necessaire
pour nostre viure, & nous qui auós
besoin d'vne vertu masle & guer-
riere, ne donnons pas la force de
nous affoiblir aux delicatesses &
aux friandises qui n'appartiennent
qu'à ceux que le monde a rangez
sous sa seruitude. Mais ce n'est pas
assez de mépriser les douleurs qui
nous sont offertes, si l'on ne tesmoigne encore la force de son ame contre les amertumes. Les maux sont
bien aussi frequents que les biens
au lieu où nous sommes, & iusqu'à
tant que nous nous soyons resolus

à les aller mesme chercher pour
sentir quelle est leur nature & leur
puissance, nous les redouterós tousjours de mesme que les enfans ont
peur des masques auparauant qu'ils
les ayent tenus, & se ioüent apres de
ce qui leur sembloit si horrible.
Nous ferons des aduersitez vn pas-
setemps à nostre vertu quand nous
aurons mesuré leur foiblesse auec
la force de nostre courage , &
toutes les fois qu'elles nous viendront assaillir nous nous asseure-
rons qu'elles nous apporteront autant de couronnes & de trophees.
Mais apres la victoire nous ne deuons pas negliger nos forces, comme si elles n'estoient plus necessaires. Ce n'est pas icy comme aux
jeux Olympiques où les Athletes ne
viennent combattre que de cinq
ans en cinq ans. A toute heure il

nous faut recommencer la meslee,
& quand noftre ennemy auroit
perdu le courage pour auoir efté
furmonté, il ne laifferoit pas de
nous venir attaquer encore afin de
nous affliger par ces importunitez.
Le pis que i'y voye c'eft que nous
deuons craindre d'eftre liurez entre
fes mains par nos feruiteurs mefme,
foit par leur trahifon ou par leur
fimplicité. Nos fens qui font la fen-
tinelle peuuét eftre aifément trompez, & prenant pour amis ceux qui
n'en auront que l'apparence, les laif-
feront entrer en noftre ame fans
leur demander le mot du guet qu'ils
ont receu de la raifon. Si nous ne
prenons des confeils là deffus pour
fçauoir fi les nouueaux hoftes que
nous logeons font auffi vtiles qu'a-
greables, nous voila perdus infailliblement, & quand nous y penfe-

ront le moins, ils se rendront maistres absolus du lieu qui ne leur
estoit accordé que par emprunt Le
secret est de ne iamais croire à nos
oreilles ny à nos yeux, ny aux autres sens.   Nostre volonté est comme vne Royne qui a dessus elle
beaucoup d'Officiers différéts , afin
de maintenir son Estat en vne harmonie conuenable. Les plus proches d'elle sont les gens de son
Conseil dont les vns entendent &
comprennent toutes choses & donnent dessus des iugements tres. equi-
tables , & les autres se souuiennent
de ce qui s'est passé & le considerent pour en acquerir vne vraye
prudence. Tant qu'elle croira les
auis de cet entendement & de ceste
memoire, ses affaires iront tousjours bien, mais si elle se laisse subor-
ner par ses flatteurs, qui sont les sens,

au rapport defquels elle eft obligee
de tout ce qu'elle peut fçauoir, on
ne fe fçauroit figurer les erreurs
dont elle fera poffedee. Les yeux
fes courtifans les plus infideles luy
prefentent des objets où toutes les
graces femblent faire leur fejour,
Les oreilles luy font ouïr des contes plaifans, & des perfuafions dont
la force gift en la douceur. Le gouft
luy fait aymer des viandes fauou-
reufes, & l'odorat & le toucher la
font plaire tout de mefme en ce
qu'ils cheriffent. Ainfi fe rend elle
agitee de mille paffions pour acquerir ce qu'elle iuge fouhaitable à
faute de l'auoir faict examiner à
fon confeil. Mais craignant que la
raifon qui la doit affifter ne foit
quelquefois efblouye d'vn vray ef-
clat de quelque pompe mondaine,
& que les hommes en qui nous ne

trouuons pas moins de tromperie
qu'en nos sens quand nous suiuons
leur aduis, ne nous abusent aussi, il
sera fort à propos que nous consul-
tions l'Oracle des bons liures qui
parlent sans enuie, sans dissimulation & sans crainte. Que si nous
n'en pouuions voir d'autres que
ceux qui ont tant la vogue auiour-
d'huy dans la Cour des Princes, ô
qu'il vaudroit beaucoup mieux que
nous n'eussions iamais sceu lire.
C'est là que la vanité trouue de
nouueaux preceptes pour s'accroi-
stre, & que les plus iniustes passions
se voyent honnorées de plus de
loüanges que les gens de bien n'ont
pû s'en imaginer pour les vertus ; Et
bien qu'il s'en rencontre quelques-
vns plus modestes qui ne proposent
point de ces salles exemples de l'as-
ciueté parmy leurs fables, la perte

du temps y est neantmoins infaillible, & l'on n'est pas plus satisfaict
apres les auoir leus, que ces pauures
Romains qui sortoient des ban-
quets d'Heliogabale où il ne leur
auoit fait presenter que des viandes
contrefaires. Il faut chercher d'autres liures qui puissent rassasier nostre ame par leurs bons enseignements, & quitter ceux là qui ne
font que plaire par les diuerses couleurs de leur langage. Mais à la verité il faut auoir le iugemét bon pour
faire vn entier proffit des liures, &
quoy que leurs regles soient tres-
certaines, si est-ce qu'on ne trouue
le moyen de s'en seruir qu'auec vn
long temps, & l'on seroit bien plustost amené à la cognoissance de
ses imperfections par les censures
d'vn amy viuant, que par celles d'vn
mort, comme est vn liure, où l'on

ne voit auiourd'huy que ce que l'on
y voyoit hier, & de qui l'on ne sçauroit auoir de responce sur les difficultez que l'obscurité peut faire
naistre. Les amis que nous auons au
monde sont garentis de ce deffaut,
& s'il nous vient à toute heure de
nouueaux troubles, ils y pouruoiét
aussi tost par autant de nouueaux
remedes. Mais l'on dit qu'vn amy
est vne chose si malaisee à acquerir,
qu'vn hôme n'a pas peu fait quand
en a pû faire vn en toute sa vie, &
principalement dans la Cour où les
affections ne se meslent ordinairement que parmy les interests de la
fortune. Toutefois il ne me semble
pas qu'vn vertueux Courtisan puisse estre priué de ceste felicité, s'il
veut suiure ceste maxime de tourner tousiours les yeux vers quelque
personnage de la pureté de vie du-

quel les sages, les fols, & mesme les
enuieux soient contraints de demeurer d'accord. En luy rendant
toute sorte d'honneurs, il luy doit
donner en outre de visibles marques du desir qu'il a de iouyr de sa
familiarité ; car asseurément cét
homme vertueux aymera en luy
ses bonnes inclinations conformes
aux siennes, & pour l'amour de la
vertu qui l'esloigne de l'ingratitude, il ne luy refusera aucune estroite alliance qu'il puisse souhaiter, &
il luy baillera la main librement
pour l'ayder à franchir les plus difficiles passages. Quand il possedera
ce thresor si rare & si precieux
qu'vn des plus grands Docteurs de
l'Eglise le prefere à tous les dons
que Dieu nous fait apres celuy de
Sagesse, il se representera qu'il ne
doit pas estre au bout de ses veilles,

apres vne telle conquefte, & qu'il
ne la fçauroit conferuer que par
les mefmes forces qu'il l'a gagnee.
Il fe donnera donc plus de foin que
iamais de produire fans cefle de
bonnes actions , afin que ce qu'il
faict encore auecque peine fe change infenfiblement en de parfaictes
habitudes. Et comme les fecours
humains ne font pas affez puiffants
pour cela, il aura recours à Dieu
qui s'eft toufiours referué ce pouuoir au deffus de la nature de donner l'ame aux chofes à qui elle ne
fçauroit donner que le corps : car il
faut auoüer que quand nous aurons formé en nous les plus excellentes vertus, elles demeureroient
imparfaites & fans operation , fi
Dieu ne les viuifioit en leur confe-
rant la grace qui eft veritablement
leur ame. Pour obtenir cét accom-

plissement. Il se seruira de tous les actes de pieté dont on nous recommande l'vsage, iculñant tantost pour rendre les forces corporelles moindres que les spirituelles, faisant des aumosnes pour se tirer de l'amour des richesses, ou s'addonnant à l'Oraison pour dire les louãges de celuy qu'on ne peut assez loüer, & luy demander les choses les plus iustes & les plus necessaires. Mais il faut bien qu'il se garde de laisser couler quelque vanité parmy cela, & que voulant rédre l'œuure vtile à la reputation, il ne la fasse dómageable à son merite. Il ne doit point aussi aller chercher des prieres pleines d'affeteries de langage, veu que les plus beaux ornements qu'elles puissent auoir, c'est la pureté; estans semblables aux eaux qui pour estre bonnes ne doiuent point

auoir de goust, car tandis qu'vn esprit s'occupe à s'imaginer de nouuelles paroles, il perd les moyens de
s'entretenir dans les extases de sa deuotion : il s'ensuit de là que quand
il aura obtenu sur soy de frequenter
dauantage les sermons que les Co-
medies, il ne doit pas fuir ces Predi-
cateurs remplis de zele, qui n'ayans
aucun fard de langage preschét veritablement en stile de Prophete &
d'Apostre, & il ne doit pas faire côme ceux qui s'exposent plustost à la
presse pour en ouyr d'autres qui les
instruisent à l'Eloquence dauantage qu'à la pieté. Ce seroit vne chose
iniuste de donner plus de pouuoir
de nous rauir à la voix humaine
qu'à la diuine, & difficilement tom-
bera-t'il en ce peché, s'il considere
auec combien de regret S. Augustin
se confesse d'vne faute bien moin-

dre, quand il s'accuſe d'auoir ſi fort
laiſſé eſmouuoir ſes ſens à la douceur de la muſique, qu'à grande
peine a-t'il fait autant d'honneur
aux ſainctes paroles des Pſeaumes
que l'on chantoit. Lors qu'vn homme ſera paruenu à tous ces degrez
de perfection dont nous auons parlé; l'on pourra croire que ceux qui
ſe ſont retirez du monde pour y
mener vne meilleure vie, n'auront
guere dauantage ſur luy, & l'on
pourra dire qu'il ſera vn vray
urtiſan Chreſtien.

*Lettre de congratulation à vn grand
personnage qui auoit esté esleue à
vne grande dignité.*

S I apres les compliments que vous auez receus de la part de tous les grands de ce Royaume, ie vous ose tesmoigner le contentement que i'ay receu de vostre promotion à l'office que vous auez maintenãt, vous attribuerez s'il vous plaist ceste hardiesse à l'excez d'vne resioüissance qui n'est pas moins grande qu'elle est iuste. Aussi certes pour n'en auoir point de ioye il faudroit n'auoir point de sentiment, & tenir pour indifferent tous les biens que la France peut esperer quand vne

sagesse

sagesse extraordinaire est honoree d'vne des plus grandes Magistra-tures de l'Estat. Les vertus qui sont nees pour les grands exemples, res-semblent aux parfums qui ne ren-dent aucune senteur, tant que le froid les comprime, & remplissent l'air d'odeurs agreables, aussi-tost que la chaleur a dilaté leurs esprits. Elles sont inutiles au public pen-dant que la fortune les restraint dãs les conditions priuees, & produi-sent des felicitez generales, au mes-me temps qu'elle les esleue en vne grande authorité. Le digne choix que le Roy a faict de vous pour cette fin tesmoigne ainsi que ses au-tres actions, combien le grand iu-gement & la ieunesse sont compa-tibles en sa personne, & qu'il n'a point d'autre but que le repos de ses peuples, ny d'autre conseil que

S

celuy de la raiſon. La loüange qu'il
merite pour ce ſubjet eſt d'autant
plus rare qu'il eſt difficile de borner
ſes volontez en vn pouuoir qui n'a
point de bornes ;　& qu'eſtre bon
Prince eſt vn effet de la prudence , comme eſtre né Prince eſt
vne grace de la nature. Dieu
vous a donné tant de qualitez neceſſaire, pour reformer tous les deſ-
ordres qui peuuent naiſtre dans vn
Royaume, que ſi l'on ne vous euſt
point admis à la charge que vous
poſſedez , on n'euſt pas faict moins
d'iniure au public qu'à voſtre vertu. Ie ne doute point que l'eſperance ne vous en fuſt infaillible apres
le decez de celuy qui vous a prece
dé ; d'autant que vous eſtiez deſia
comme ſon Lieutenant , neantmoins la puiſſance des Roys eſtant
ſi abſoluë qu'elle peut paſſer par

deſſus les loix, & leur prudence e-
ſtant obligee de prendre diuers aduis ſuiuant la diuerſe condition des
temps, vous auez grand ſujet de
loüer Dieu de ce qu'il a inſpiré au
Roy vne ferme reſolution de vous
preferer à tout ce qu'il y a de grands
hommes dans ſon Royaume. Si les
vertus qui rencontrent vn arbitre ſi
fauorable, ne doiuent point d'autels à la fortune de ce qu'elles ſont
eminentes, pour le moins luy ſont
elles redeuables parce qu'elles ſont
heureuſes. Comme iamais eſlection
ne fut faicte plus iuſtement, ainſi
n'en a-t'on point veu de ſi generalement approuuee, tant l'eſtime de
voſtre nom vous a acquis la bien-
veillance publique. Il importe grā-
dement que le Prince qui veut eſtre
aymé, donne les principales charges de ſon Eſtat a des perſonnes

qui foient aimees, & dans le merite defquelles on puiſſe prouuer la
cauſe de leur auancement, autrement la haine dont ſes Miniſtres
ſont chargez, tombe ſur luy-meſme, deſorte qu'à la fin il ſe pourroit voir reduit à conſeruer par la
ſeule force des armes ceſte puiſſance qui ſe peut facilement garder auec l'amour des ſubjeĉts. Mais
en vain les Medecins excellens or-
donnent l'vſage des choſes ſaines
aux malades, ſi ceux auſquels ils
confient le ſoin de les garder leur
en baillent de contraires. Auſſi
quelques bonnes que puiſſent e-
ſtre les intentions des Roys, elles ſont infructueuſes quand elles
ne ſont pas ſecondees par celles
des Miniſtres de leur Eſtat.

Vous eſtes maintenant eſleué

à vne si haute dignité que tout
autre que vous auroit de la peine à
se conseruer l'amour d'vn chacun,
en vne charge où mal-aysément
on peut esuiter l'enuie. Il n'appartient qu'à vous d'acquerir des
seruiteurs au Roy par la douceur,
sans que vostre facilité diminuë
la reuerence qu'on vous doit, ny
vostre grauité l'affection qu'on
vous porte.

L'eminence de l'office qui vous
a esté conferé, m'a quelquefois
mis en doute si ie me deuois con-
iouyr de vostre promotion, mais
au mesme temps que ie me suis mis
vostre dignité deuant les yeux,
ie me suis representé vostre modestie, auec vne ferme croyance
que la fortune qui change les
mœurs de tous les hommes, n'a peu

rien changer en vous que la seule
condition. Vous en estes d'autant
plus loüable qu'il est beaucoup plus
difficile d'vser des prosperitez auec
modestie, que de souffrir les afflictions auec patience, & que rarement les hommes pratiquent
dans l'exercice des grandes charges
les bonnes parties qu'ils font paroistre auparauant que d'y paruenir. En l'incertitude des poursuites ils font dans la complaisance
des Amants; En la seureté de la possession, ils viuent dans la nonchalan-
ce des maris. Vne autre raison qui
m'a donné l'asseurance de vous
rendre ce deuoir, c'est que de long
temps i'ay faict vne profession particuliere de porter à vostre merite le
mesme respect que ie doy à la qualité que vous possedez auiour-
d'huy. I'ay recherché vostre bien-

veillance par toute sorte d'honnestes soins, mais ç'a esté en vn temps
où l'estat des affaires de la Cour,
m'ostoit l'esperance de vous voir
arriuer à cet honneur, tant il est extraordinaire à la fortune d'offrir
deux fois vne mesme faueur à vne
mesme personne. Outre les considerations precedentes, i'ay tant receu de tesmoignage de vostre ame-
tié, qu'en ceste occasion mon silence seroit plustost vne marque d'ingratitude que de respect. Toutefois
ie vous diray que la vraye cause de
ma ioye ne procede pas tant de
ce qu'à present vostre condition
est plus releuee, que parce que celle du public sera plus heureuse.
Ceux-là sont iniustes qui ne tiennent les choses pour grandes ou
pour petites qu'à proportion de
l'vtilité qu'ils en reçoiuent ; Non

que ie vueille exclure du tout
les fentimens que chacun a naturellement de fes interefts. l'eftime fort le Soleil, parce qu'il m'ef-
claire, & me faict voir ce grand
fpectacle du monde; mais ie l'eftime beaucoup plus fans comparai-
fon, alors que ie penfe que cet aftre
n'eft pas fait feulement pour moy;
que fa lumiere eft vniuerfelle, & la
caufe generale de tout ce que la terre produict.

Si ie ne regardois qu'à voftre
intereft , ie croirois que vous auriez plus de repos en vne condition
où vous auriez moins d'affaires.

Les calmes qui font eternels
fur les petites riuieres , ne font
que iournaliers fur les mers. Les
difficultez humaines comme de
vrays Dedales ont tant de tours
& de deftours entrelaffez les vns

dedans les autres , qu'il n'eſt ſorte d'induſtrie capable d'en trouuer le bout. A peine vne prudence telle qu'eſt la voſtre, a terminé ce qu'il y a d'affaires preſentes, que la malice des hommes en forme d'autres , & par de nouueaux crimes luy donne de nouuelles matieres de labeur. Les conditions ſi releuées ne ſont proprement que des miſeres eſclattantes & pompeuſes. Ie ne ſçay ſi les deſirer à ceux que l'on aime,ce n'eſt point faire des vœux d'ennemy. Les grandes charges ſont de grádes ſeruitudes que les Anges tutelaires des Eſtats,ont voulu rendre glorieuſes pour les rendre ſuportables. Ils en ont fait cóme les Princes, qui pour peupler les mauuaiſes regions , en font oublier l'auſterité par les priuileges qu'ils y attachent. Veritablement pour en parler comme il faut,

ce n'eſt point viure, c'eſt ſimplemẽt
eſtre, que de viure dans des occupations qui ne ſe terminent que par les
deux plus grands accidens qui puiſſent iamais arriuer, la mort ou l'é-
loignement.

Ie ne crains point de parler de cette matiere ſans deſguiſer aucune-
ment la verité. Vous auez tant de
lumieres acquiſes & naturelles que
vous ne ſçauriez ignorer l'inſtabili-
té des choſes humaines, & particulierement des proſperitez qui depẽ-
dent de la volonté d'autruy. La force de voſtre eſprit m'eſt trop con-
neuë pour croire que la liberté de
cette lettre vous puiſſe deſplaire.
Non ſeulement les vaillans ſoldats
ne tremblent ny ne palliſſent quand
l'on leur parle de bleſſures ; ils les
cherchent meſme en toutes les occaſions ſignalées qui s'en preſentẽt;

que si d'auenture il arriue qu'ils y
soient blessez, ils regardent couler
leur sang auec la mesme froideur,
que s'ils voyoient espandre le sang
d'autruy. Toutes les belles actions
du monde se font pour la gloire &
par le courage; Et comme en la profession des armes, ceux là meritent
de viure qui ne craignent point de
mourir, de mesme en celle des principaux Ministres d'vn grand Roy,
ceux là sont dignes d'estre maintenus qui ne craignent point d'estre
elloignez, & il ne faut rien attendre
de grand de ces hommes qui ne se
preparent iamais aux grands accidens. Ce n'est point aux seules puis-
sances subalternes que ces peines
sont attachées; Elles sont tout à fait
inseparables d'auec les souueraines,
de sorte que le grand Auguste se
voyant seul arbitre du genre hu-

main, au milieu d'vne paix & d'vne gloire sans exemple, fut contraint de confesser que dans cette lassitude continuelle que luy causoient les soins de l'Empire , il ne trouuoit point de plus grande douceur qu'en la meditation de se despoüiller de ses grandeurs. L'Empereur Charles cinquiesme, dont les vanitez troublerent le repos de tout le monde, n'eust point de contentement qu'apres les auoir quittées.

Ie ne vous tiendrois pas heureux de vostre promotion, si ie ne regardois qu'à vostre interest. Mes pensees vont bien plus auant, quand ie considere que le Roy qui vous a esleué à cet honneur pour recompense de vostre vertu , donne courage à tous ses subjets d'estre vertueux. Naturellement les hommes s'efforcét tous de paruenir aux char-

ges publiques par les voyes qui sont
ouuertes dans les Estats où ils viuét.
Lors qu'elles y sont venales, ils font
tout ce qu'ils peuuent pourles achepter. Quand elles se donnent au merite il n est rien de loüable qu'ils ne
fassent pour y paruenir. Le Roy faisant par ce moyen tous ses subjets
vertueux, les rendra tous obeyssans,
tellement que trouuant vne disposition vniuerselle à faire executer
ses commandemens, il n'aura pas
besoin de recourir à ces remedes
extremes dont l'vsage n'est iamais
sans quelque peril. Ce sont en partie les auantages que sa Majesté
se doit promettre du choix qu'elle a faict de vous. La puissance
de faire ce qui luy plaist luy est
commune auecque tous les Princes Souuerains : mais la moderation de ne faire que ce qu'il

doit , & de borner son pouuoir
par la raison , luy est particuliere
auec les bons Roys. Ses exploicts de
guerre luy ont acquis vn grád nom
tant parmy ses peuples que parmy
les estrangers, mais la gloire de sçauoir choisir les personnes de merite
pour establir vn bon conseil n'est
pas moins estimable que celle de
sçauoir vaincre ses ennemis. C'est
aux grands Princes comme luy à
chercher les grands hommes , non
dans la foule seulement de ceux qui
se pressent pour obtenir quelque
bonne fortune , mais parmy ceux
qui ne demandent rien que les choses dont l'on les aura iugez dignes.
Il ne faut pas vne prudence medio-
cre pour recognoistre la difference
d'entre les Ministres qui sont recó-
mandez par des personnes interes-
sées , & ceux qui sont monstrez par

la seule reputation. Les vns mesna-
gent le bien du Roy auec le mesme
soin que le leur propre, auec la mesme innocence que le bien d'autruy;
les autres font le mesme degast dans
les affaires que s'ils estoient en pays
d'ennemy. Que si iamais il fut necessaire d'auoir vn grand homme
en la charge où vous estes, il faut aduoüer que c'est maintenant. Il y a
de certains maux qui courent aujourd'huy lesquels ne font pas seulemét inueterez, mais qui font mesme si generaux, que ie ne voy guie-
res d'endroicts où ils n'ayent donné
quelques attaques. L'on n'a iamais
veu tant de pompe que l'on en void
par tout. Les meilleures maisons se
consument par le luxe, & il y a plusieurs hommes puissants qui prennent plaisir à tourmenter les miserables, & qui veulent s'attribuer des

miſeres qui ſe trouuent parmy le pauure peuple.

Toutes choſes vous y conuient comme à l'enuy, & particulieremét l'vrgente neceſſité des affaires. La contribution des ſoins de cette Auguſte Princeſſe à qui toute la France eſt ſi redeuable, & ſur toutes choſes les grandes actions du plus puiſſant & du plus juſte Roy qui viue, lequel nous nous deuons touſiours propoſer pour exemple. Conſiderez qu'il n'a pas vne petite opinion de voſtre probité , & qu'il ne conçoit pas auſſi de petites eſperáces de vos ſeruices. Tout le monde arreſte maintenant ſes yeux deſſus vous. Vous auez acquis la bien-veillance de ſa Majeſté par l'eſtime de voſtre vertu; ce ſera par ce meſme moyen que vous la pourrez conſeruer. Pour faire que les bons Princes

continuent à nous bien aymer , il
n'eſt point de meilleur ſecret que de
continuer à les bien ſeruir. Tant
qu'il y a eu des Miniſtres violents,
l'enuie meſme ne vous a point donné de blaſme de ce que vos loüables
deſſeins n'ont pas eu de grands pro-
grez. Doreſnauant comme vous
n'aurez plus d'empeſchement de
quelque part que ce ſoit, auſſi n'aurez vous plus d'excuſe. Faictes que
du meſme Ciel dont l'on void tomber les foudres ſur les coulpables,
on en voye en meſme temps tomber la pluye ſur ceux qui meritent
d'eſtre doucement traictez. Dieu a
faict ſa Majeſté Roy de France, c'eſt
à luy maintenant à faire le reſte, & à
ſe gouuerner de telle ſorte que ſa
bonté le faſſe pere de ſes peuples, &
vous voyez auſſi comme il y proce-

de auec tant d'affection que l'on luy
peut iuftement donner ce tiltre. Il
n'a iamais rien trouué de meilleur
pour augmenter l'affection de fes
fubjets que d'augmenter la felicité
publique, & de faire voir qu'il eft
impoffible qu'on foit fon fubjet &
qu'on ne foit pas heureux. C'eft
pourquoy il faut que tous ceux qui
le feruent tafchent à cooperer de
leur part afin de faire reüffir toutes
fes bonnes intentions. Or ie fçay
bien que long temps auparauant
que vous fuffiez efleué au degré où
vous eftes, ie vous ay fouuent veu
trifte quand les plaintes des pauures
n'eftoient pas quelque fois affez fa-
uorablemét efcoutées par ceux qui
eftoient commis pour ce faire. A
peine fans pleurer vous mefme,
vous pouuiez voir pleurer les op-

preſſez, de ſorte que le plus grand
bien que ie puiſſe ſouhaitter à l'E-
ſtat , maintenant que vous eſtes
dans l'vne de ſes plus illuſtres charges, c'eſt que vous ayez les meſmes
ſentimens que vous auiez eſtant
perſonne priuée.

Harangue d'Alexandre le Grand à ses Soldats: Traduction nouuelle de Quinte Curse.

AYant trauersé tant de contrées dans l'esperance d'vne victoire qui ne se peut gaigner sans combattre, il n'y a plus que cette difficulté à surmonter. Le fleuue Granique, les montagnes de la Cilicie, la Syrie & l'Egypte que nous auons ostez à ceux qui marchent deuant nous, & nous doiuent merueilleusement inciter à la recherche de cette gloire. Les Perses qui ont esté r'alliez apres auoir desia fuy vne fois, ne combattront que pource qu'ils ne peuuent plus fuyr. Il

y a trois iours qu'ils s'arreſtent en
vn meſme lieu , eſtans tranſis de
peur , encore qu'ils ayent leurs armes ſur le dos, qui ne leur ſemblent
qu'vn fardeau inutile. Ie ne demande point vne plus grande marque de leur deſeſpoir , que de ce
qu'ils mettent le feu dans leurs villes, & qu'ils font le degaſt parmy
leurs terres, confeſſant tacitement
que toutes les choſes où ils ne peuuent toucher nous appartiennent,
& que celles meſmes où ils touchḗt
nous doiuent bien toſt appartenir,
puis qu'ils en tiennent ſi peu de
compte.   Ne craignez point maintenant les noms vains de tant de na-
tions inconnuës. Soit que les vns
s'appellent Scythes ou Caduſiens,
cela n'importe de rien au faiĉt de la
guerre. Puiſque tous ces gens là
ſont inconnus , c'eſt ſigne qu'ils

n'ont fait aucune chose digne de remarque. L'on n'ignore pas long
temps la valeur des hommes genereux , mais pour les hommes sans
cœur, lors que l'on les tire des lieux
où ils s'estoient cachez , ils n'appor-
tent rien que leur nom qui ne sert
de rien à la guerre. Pour ce qui est
de vous autres Macedoniens , vous
auez tant fait par vostre vertu, qu'il
n'y a pas vn lieu dans le monde où
l'on ne sçache bien qui vous estes.
Il faut que vous preniez garde au
desordre de l'armée des barbares,
& que l'vn n'a point d'autres armes qu'vn dard , & l'autre n'a
qu'vne fronde & quelques pierres.
Il y en a fort peu qui ayent des armes cópletes. Ie confesse bien qu'il
y a plus de gés de leur costé, mais il y
en a bien plus du nôtre qui sont tous
prests à combattre. Au reste ie ne

desire point que vous vous jettiez
courageusement dans le combat
si ie ne vous en donne l'exemple.
Ie vous promets de me trouuer à la
teste des premieres compagnies, &
que ie croiray qu'autant que ie
pourray receuoir de playes en mon
corps, ce seront autant de marques
d'honneur. Pource qui est du butin,
ie veux estre le seul qui n'y aura
point de part, & il faut que selon ma
coustume ordinaire, i'employe
tout le gain de la victoire à vous
enrichir & à parfaire vostre equipage. Ie ne dy cecy qu'aux hommes
valeureux, & s'il y en a icy qui ne
leur ressemblent guere, ie leur
apprens qu'ils se doiuent monstrer
vaillants malgré qu'ils en ayent, &
qu'ils sont paruenus en vn lieu dont
ils ne peuuent fuyr, ayans trauersé

tant de terres, & laiſſé tant de fleuues & de montagnes derriere eux,
que quand ils voudroient retourner en leur pays, il ſe faudroit faire
paſſage à la pointe de l'eſpee.

Harangue de Darius à ses Soldats.

ENcore qu'il n'y ayt pas long temps que nous a-uons esté les maistres de toutes les terres qui d'vn costé sont arrousées par l'Ocean, & de l'autre fermées par l'Hellespont, il faut maintenant combattre non point pour la gloire, mais pour la cóseruation de la vie, & qui plus est, pour la liberté à qui vous ne croiez pas que la vie soit preferable. Voicy le iour qui doit restablir ou faire finir vn Empire, qui n'a iamais eu son pareil en aucun siecle. Nous sommes venus aux prises auec

l'ennemy prés du Granique, n'ayant
que la moindre partie de nos forces.　Ceux qui ont esté deffaits dans
la Cilicie, ont pû auoir la Syrie pour
retraicte.　Le Tygre & l'Euphrate
feruoient de deffence & de barrie-
re à tout ce qui estoit fous nostre
domination; mais maintenant nous
fommes venus en vn lieu duquel fi
nous fommes chaffez, il n'y a plus
d'endroit pour fuyr. Tout ce que
nous auons laiffé derriere nous a
esté ruyné par vne longue guerre
Nos villes n'ont plus d'habitans , &
nos champs n'ont plus de laboureurs qui les cultiuent. Nos femmes
& nos enfans font auffi à la fuitte de
cefte armee, & c'eft vne proye toute preparee pour les ennemis , fi
nous ne mettons noftre propre
corps en danger pour deffendre des
chofes fi cheres. Quant à moy i'ay

employé tout mõ pouuoir pour af-
fembler vne telle armee qu'à grand'
peine cefte large campagne la peut
contenir. I'ay donné des armes &
des cheuaux à chacun; & i'ay eu
foin de faire vne telle prouifion que
cefte grande multitude ne manque
de rien. I'ay choify vn lieu où ie la
puis mettre en bataille. Tout ce
qui refte apres cela eft en voftre
puiffance. Ayez maintenant affez
de courage pour vaincre, & ne faites point d'eftat de la renommee de
nos ennemis, qui eft vn traict fort
foible pour bleffer des hommes
courageux comme vous. Ce que
vous auez eftimé en eux vne vertu,
& ce que vous auez redouté iufques à cefte heure, n'eft rien qu'vne
temerité qui s'affoupit auffi-toft
qu'elle a fait paroiftre fa premiere
impetuofité, de mefme que font les

mousches quand elles ont perdu
leur aiguillon. Or c'est maintenant
que cette campagne nous descouure leur petit nombre que les
montagnes de la Cilicie nous tenoient caché. Vous voyez leurs
rangs qui sont au large , & leurs
pointes estenduës lors que le milieu de leur arme est vuide & des-
nué. Pour ce qui est de ces derniers
qui sont placez au derriere , ils
tournent desia le dos , & ils peuuent estre escrasez sans doute sous
les pieds des cheuaux , quand mesme ie n'enuoyrois rien contre eux
que mes chariots armez de faulx.
Que si nous gagnons cette bataille , nous aurons gaigné tout
ce qui se peut esperer en cette
guerre ; car il n'y a aucun endroit par où ils puissent fuyr.

L'Euphrate les retient d'vn cofté,
& le Tygre les enferme de l'autre, & ce qui eftoit par cy deuant
de leur party, leur eft maintenant
contraire. Noftre armée eft legere
& prompte à fe remuer, au lieu
que cette là eft chargée de butin.
Nous pourrons maffacrer ayfé-
ment ceux qui fe font embarraf-
fez dans les defpoüilles qu'ils nous
ont prifes, tellement qu'vne mefme chofe fera la caufe & la recompenfe de noftre victoire. Que fi
quelqu'vn de vous eft efmeu par
la renommée de cettte nation,
qu'il s'imagine que les armes
des Macedoniens font bien icy,
mais non pas leurs corps. Auffi
auons nous tiré beaucoup de
fang les vns des autres, & la
perte eft toufiours plus fafcheu-
fe du cofté du plus petit nombre.

Quelque grand qu'Alexandre semble aux foibles & aux timides, ce
n'est pourtant qu'vn homme, &
encore si vous me voulez croire
vous ne le tiendrez que pour vn temeraire & vn insensé, qui s'est iufques à present rendu plus heureux
par nostre crainte que par sa propre
vertu. Or il n'y a rien qui puisse estre
durable de ce qui est priué de sens
& de raison. Bien qu'il semble que
son bon-heur soit aussi haut qu'il
peut desirer, sa temerité n'en sera
pas pourtant satisfaite. Dauantage
le cours des choses du monde est
muable, la fortune ne s'accommode iamais entierement à nos volontez. Les destins ont possible ordonné d'esbranler plustost par quelque
grand mouuement, que d'accabler
l'Empire des Perses qu'ils ont esleué iusques à son periode par l'espace
de

de deux cens trente ans ; & ils font
cela pour nous monſtrer la fragilité humaine, qui eſt par trop oubliee
lors que l'on eſt au milieu des proſperitez. Il n'y a pas long temps que
nous allions faire la guerre aux
Grecs de noſtre bon gré, & maintenant il faut que nous taſchions de
les chaſſer de nos maiſons. Nous
ſommes ainſi agitez l'vn apres l'autre par l'inconſtance de la fortune,
& parce que l'on ne peut ſouffrir
qu'vne ſeule nation commande à
toutes les autres, nous deſirons chacun d'auoir l'Empire. Au reſte quãd
meſme nous aurions perdu toute
eſperance, la neceſſité nous deuroit
toutefois inciter à bien faire. Il faut
conſiderer que nous en ſommes reduits à l'extremité. L'ennemy tient
en captiuité ma mere, mes deux filles, mon fils Ochus qui eſtoit né

auec l'esperance de commander apres moy , & quelques Princes du Sang auec plusieurs de vos Capitaines que vous honoriez autant que des Roys. Ie suis desia prisonnier moy-mesme sans vn reste d'esperance que i'ay en vous. Deliurez mes entrailles des liens ; Rendez moy ces chers gages pour lesquels vous n'auez pas refusé de mourir. Pour ce qui est de ma femme, ie l'ay desia perduë en ceste prison ; mais croyez que ma mere & mes enfans vous tendent maintenant les bras, implorent les Dieux du pays , & demandent vostre secours, taschant de vous esmouuoir à compassion, & de vous faire souuenir de vostre anciéne fidelité, à fin que vous rompiez leurs chaisnes , & que vous les tiriez de seruitude, ne souffrant plus qu'ils viuét par emprût. Croyez-vo⁹ qu'ils puissent de bon cœur rédre du

feruice à ceux dõt ils ne daigneroiẽt
pas eſtre les Rois? Il me ſemble que
ie voy approcher l'armee ennemie,
mais tãt plus ie voy le hazard prochain, tãt moins ſuis-ie ſatisfaiĉt de
ce que i'ay deſia diĉt. Ie vous prie
dõc par les Dieux de noſtre païs, par
le feu eternel qui eſt porté deuant
vous ſur les Autels, par la clarté du
Soleil qui naiſt dedans les bornes de
mon Royaume, par la memoire immortelle de Cyrus qui ayant oſté
l'Empire aux Medes & aux Lydiẽs,
le tranſporta le premier dans la Per-
ſide, de deliurer le nõ & la natiõ des
Perſes d'vn extréme deshõneur. Mar-
chez courageuſemẽt, afin que vous
laiſſiez à vos ſucceſſeurs la meſme
gloire & la meſme reputation que
vous auez heritee de vos anceſtres.
La liberté, le ſecours, & l'eſperance
du temps à venir deſpend de la

V ij

force de voſtre bras. Quiconque meſpriſe la mort, la peut ſouuent euiter. Pour moy ſi ie ſuis monté ſur vn chariot ce n'eſt pas tant pour obſeruer la couſtume de noſtre pays, que pour me faire voir de tout le monde, & ie vous donne toute permiſſion de faire comme moy, ſoit que ie vous monſtre vn exemple de valeur ou de coüardiſe.

Autre *Harangue d'Alexandre à ses Soldats.*

 E n'est pas vne chose estrange, Soldats, si considerant la grandeur des choses que nous auons faites, il vous vient aussi tost vn desir de vous reposer, & si vous estes satisfaits de la gloire que vous auez obtenuë. Ie laisse à part les Sclauons, les Triballes, la Beoce, la Trace, Sparte, les Acheens, & le Peloponese, desquels i'ay dompté les vns par ma conduite, & les autres par ma seule authorité. Ayant aussi cómencé la guerre depuis l'Hellespót, nous auons affranchy l'Ionie & l'E-

olide de la feruitude d'vne barbarie
infupportable. Nous auons rangé
fous noftre pouuoir la Carie, la Ly-
die, la Cappadoce, la Phrygie, la
Paphlagonie, la Pamphilie, la Pifi-
die, la Cilicie, la Syrie, la Phenice,
l'Armenie, la Perfide, & la Medie,
i'ay gagné plus de Prouinces que
les autres n'ont pris de villes, & ie
ne fçay fi en les nommant leur
grand nombre n'a point fait que
i'en aye oublié quelqu'vne. Que
fi ie penfois que la poffeffion des
chofes que nous auons acquifes
auec vne fi grande viteffe nous fuft
affeuree, ie m'en voudrois retourner à mon pays, vers ma mere &
mes fœurs, & tous mes amis (mefme quand vous vous efforceriez de
l'empefcher) afin de iouyr de la
loüange & de la gloire que i'ay ac-
quife auec vous, principalement en

vn lieu où les plus riches recompenſes de noſtre victoire nous attendent, c'eſt à ſçauoir la ioye de nos
enfans, de nos femmes, & de tous
nos parens, auecque la paix & le repos, & la poſſeſſió certaine des choſes que nous auons acquiſes par noſtre valeur. Mais il faut que vous
ſçachiez, Soldats, que dans vn nou-
uel Empire, & meſme ſi nous voulons dire la verité, dans vn Empire
tenu par emprunt où les Barbares
ne l'aſſubjettiſſent encore que par
force, il eſt beſoin de laiſſer eſcou-
ler quelque temps pour addoucir
leurs eſprits, & il faut qu'vne
douce accouſtumance appriuoiſe
ces ſauuages. Les fruicts meſme ne peuuent meurir qu'en
vne certaine ſaiſon, & quoy
qu'ils ſoient priuez de ſentiment,
neantmoins ils ne viennent à

leur perfection qu'auec vn certain ordre. Croiriez vous donc que tant de peuples qui sont accoustumez à vn autre gouuernement & à ouyr le nom d'vn autre maistre, & qui n'ont rien d'aprochant de nostre religion, de nos mœurs, & de nostre langue, puissent auoir esté domptez au mesme combat où ils ont esté vaincus? Ils sont maintenus en leur deuoir par la force de vos armes, & non point par vn respect que leur donne la bonté de leur nature. Que s'ils nous craignent & nous obeissent en nostre presence, ils seront nos ennemis & nous mespriseront quand nous serons absents. Nous auons affaire à des bestes farouches qui ne s'adoucissent qu'à la longue, encore qu'elles soient prises & enfermees, d'autant que leur naturel ne peut estre forcé; Et ie me

gouuerne de la mesme façon que si
j'auois subiugué tout ce qui a esté
sous la puissance de Darius. Na-
burzanes s'est emparé de l'Hyrca-
nie, & le parricide Bessus ne tient
pas seulement les Bactrians sous sa
sujection: mais encore il nous menace. Les Sogdians, les Daheens,
les Massagetes, les Sariens & les Indiens, ne releuent encore que d'eux
mesmes. Ils nous suiuront tous, s'ils
voyent que nous tournions le dos,
car ils ne s'estiment estre tous qu'v-
ne nation, & pour nous nous sommes estrangers. Chacun obeyt plustost à ceux de son pays, & principalement à ceux qui se font le plus
redouter. C'est pourquoy ou il faut
quitter ce que nous auons pris, ou
bien il se faut saisir de ce que nous
n'auons pas encore. De mesme que
les Medecins taschent de purger tel

lement les corps qui font malades
qu'ils ne leur laiſſent rien qui leur
puiſſe nuire, auſſi faut-il que nous
coupions chemin à tous les obſta-
cles qui s'oppoſent à noſtre puiſſance. Bien ſouuent vne petite eſtincelle qui a eſté meſpriſee a allumé vn
grand feu. L'on ne doit rien meſpriſer auec aſſeurance de tout ce que
l'on remarque en ſon ennemy. Celuy que vous meſpriſerez ſe rendra
plus fort par voſtre negligéce. Darius meſme n'a pas eu l'Empire des
Perſes par heritage. Il a eſté eſleué
au trône par l'entremiſe de l'Eunu-
que Bagoas, afin que vous ne penſiez pas que Beſſus euſt beaucoup
de peine à occuper l'Empire s'il
eſtoit abandonné. Pour ce qui eſt
de nous, Soldats, nous aurions
faict vne grand' faute ſi nous a-
uions vaincu Darius pour donner

l'Empire à son esclaue, qui ayant eu l'asseurance de commettre le plus grand de tous les crimes, a pris son Roy prisonnier, lors qu'il auoit besoin d'vn secours estranger, & en vne occasion où nous mesmes qui sommes ses vainqueurs, luy eussions pardonné s'il fust tombé entre nos mains. Laisserez vous regner ce meschant que ie voudrois desia voir pendu en vn gibet, afin que tous les Roys & les peuples soient vangez de ce perfide. Que si maintenant on vous venoit aduertir qu'il faict du rauage dans les villes Grecques ou en l'Hellespont, de quelle douleur seriez vous touchez, voyant qu'vn tel personnage auroit pris pour luy les recompeses devostrevictoire? Alors vous reprendriez les armes, & vous vo⁵ hasteriez de recouurer ce qu'il auroit pris;

mais qu'il est bien plus aisé maintenant d'accabler celuy qui est encore tout estôné apres son forfaict, & qui à peine peut iouyr de sa raison. Il ne nous reste plus que quatre iours de chemin à nous qui auons marché sur tant de neiges, trauersé tant de fleuues, & passé par le sommet de tant de montagnes. Cette mer qui estant enflée bouche le passage auecque ses flots ne retardera point icy nostre voyage. Nous ne sommes pas enfermez dans les destroicts de la Cilicie. Nous voicy dans vne raze campagne. Il me semble que nous tenons desia la victoire. Nous n'auons plus à combattre que contre vn petit nombre de fugitifs, & d'esclaues qui ont tué leur maistre. Ce sera de verité vne belle action qui sera racontée à la posterité par la renommée entre ce que

vous aurez fait de plus glorieux,
qu'ayans esté ennemis de Darius, la
haine que vous luy portïez estant fi-
nie par sa mort, vous ayez pris vengeance de ceux qui l'ont assassiné,
& que pas vn homme qui ayt esté
accusé de quelque meschanceté
n'ayt pû eschapper de vos mains.
De combien pensez vous que les
Perses nous seront rédus plus obeïs-
sans quand cela sera faict, & lors
qu'ils sçauront que vous n'entre-
prenez point de guerre que pour
quelque subject remply de pieté, &
que ce n'est pas contre eux , mais
contre le crime de Bessus que vous
vous estes mis en courroux.

Autre Harangue du mesme Alexan-
dre, à ses Soldats.

IE ne doute point, Soldats, que plusieurs choses n'ayẽt esté semées industrieuse-ment parmy vous ces iours pas-sez, par ceux qui ont demeuré aux Indes afin de vous espouuanter: mais les sots contes de ces diseurs de mensonge ne vous sont pas nou-ueaux. C'est ainsi que les Perses vous rendoient espouuantables les destroicts de la Cilicie, les campa-gnes de la Mesopotamie, & les fleuues du Tygre & celuy d'Euphra-te, bien que nous ayons passé l'vn à gué, & l'autre sur vn pont. La renommée ne faict iamais les choses telles qu'elles sont ; elle nous les donne tousiours plus grandes qu'el-lesne sont veritablemét. Quoy que mesme nostre valeur soit indubitable, si est-ce qu'elle a encore plus de bruit que d'effect. Dittes-moy qui est-ce qui eust pû croire que nous eussions pû soustenir l'effect de ces animaux qui nous estoient opposez comme des ramparts, & que nous eussions pû trauerser l'Hydaspe & tant d'autres lieux dót l'on nous disoit des choses plus grandes que nous ne les auons trouuées? Il y a desia long temps que nous nous en fussions fuys de l'Asie si les fables nous eussent pû vaincre. Croyez vous que les troupeaux des Elephans soient plus grands que ne sont ceux des autres bestes ailleurs, puis que cét animal est fort rare, & qu'il ne se prend pas facilement,

& qu'il eſt encore plus difficile-
ment appriuoyſé. C'eſt par de ſemblables menſonges que les troupes
des gens de pied & de cheual, ont vn
nombre plus grand qu'elles n'ont à
la verité. Pour ce qui eſt du fleuue
dont l'on nous fait peur , où il eſt
plus large , c'eſt là qu'il coule plus
doucement, & qu'il reſſemble à vn
eſtang , car lors que les eaux ſont
reſſerrées dans des riuages eſtroicts,
& qu'elles n'ont pas vn lict aſſez large , elles ſe choquent & s'eſleuent
en forme de torrens; & tout au contraire lors que le lict d'vne riuiere
eſt ſpatieux, la courſe en eſt de beaucoup plus lente. D'ailleurs tout le
danger eſt au riuage où l'ennemy
attend les vaiſſeaux que l'on y veut
faire aborder , tellement que dans
quelque fleuue que ce ſoit le hazard
eſt pareil pour ceux qui veulent gagner

gner la terre. Mais feignons que
tout ce que nous auons ouy dire
foit vray. Qui eft ce qui vous ef-
fraye dauantage ou la grandeur des
beftes, ou la multitude deshommes?
En ce qui eft des Elephans , nous
auons veu depuis peu ce qu'ils fçauent faire. Ils fe font iettez plus fu-
rieufement fur leurs maiftres que
fur nous, & au refte nous auons tail-
lé en pieces ces grands corps auec
des faulx & des haches. Que nous
importe t'il donc s'il y en a autant
qu'en auoit Porus, ou qu'il y en ait
bien trois mille, veu qu'il n'en faut
que bleffer vn pour mettre tous les
autres en fuitte. Outre cela, à peine
en peut-on gouuerner vn petit nó-
bre; & fi l'on en affemble tant de
milliers, ils fe heurteront l'vn l'autre lors que les maffes inutiles de ces
grands corps ne pourront ny s'en-

X

fuyr ny s'arrester. Quant à moy de
verité, i'ay tellement eu à mespris
ces animaux, qu'encore que i'en aye
eu, ie ne les ay point opposez à l'ennemy, sçachant assez qu'ils appor-
tent plus de dommage à ceux qui
sont de leur costé qu'aux autres. Or
ie croy maintenant que c'est le grãd
nombre des gens de pied & de cheual qui vous estonne ; mais n'auez
vous accoustumé de cõbattre que
contre peu de gens , & sera-ce la
premiere fois que vous repousserez
l'effort d'vne grosse troupe toute
en desordre? Le fleuue Granique
a esté tesmoin de la force inuincible des Macedoniens contre vne
multitude , & la Cilicie qui a esté
noyée du sang des Perses, & la campagne d'Arbelle qui a esté semee
des os de ceux que vous auez vaincus, peuuét certifier la mesme chose.

Vous auez commencé bien tard à
cõpter les legions des ennemis, apres
auoir rendu l'Asie toute deserte par
plusieurs victoires. Lors que nous
trauersames l'Hellespont, c'estoit
alors qu'il falloit songer à nostre petit nombre ; mais maintenant les
Scythes nous suiuent, les Bactrians
sont prompts à nous secourir, les
Daheens & les Sogdians combat-
tent auec nous. Ce n'est pas toutefois eñ leurs troupes que ie me fie.
Ie ne considere que la force de vos
bras, & vostre valeur, dont i'ay des-
ja eu tant de preuues, m'est comme
vn gage & vne asseurance des choses que ie doy accomplir. Tant que
ie combattray au milieu de vous, ie
ne cõpteray iamais ny les armees de
mes ennemis ny les miennes. Faites
moy dõc maintenant paroistre que
vos courages sont pleins d'allegresse

& d'esperance. Nous ne sommes pas encore à l'entrée de nos peines & de nos entreprises hardies ; nous en voicy desormais à la fin. Nous sommes arriuez au lieu où le Soleil se leue, & iusqu'au riuage de l'Ocean, pourueu que la lascheté ne nous arreste point. Delà ayant dompté les extremitez de la terre, nous nous en retournerons victorieux en nostre patrie. Ne faictes pas comme ces lasches laboureurs qui par vne grande paresse laissent perdre les fruicts qui sont desia meurs. La recompense qui nous attend est plus grande que le peril : La region où nous allons a beaucoup de richesses & peu de forces ; c'est pourquoy il ne me semble pas que ie vous y côduise tant pour y acquerir de la gloire que du butin. Aussi est-ce vous qui meritez de remporter en vostre

pays les richesses que cette mer jette
à son riuage; C'est vous qui estes dignes d'estre ceux qui ont faict espreuue de tout, & qui n'ont rien
laissé derriere par crainte. Ie vous
prie donc & vous conjure par vous
mesme, & par vostre gloire qui sur-
passe la grandeur ordinaire de celle
des hommes, & par ce que i'ay merité enuers vous, & ce que vous
auez merité enuers moy, ce qui est
vne contention où nous demeurós
tousiours inuincibles, ie vous cóiu-
re, dis-je, que vous n'abandonniez
point celuy que vous auez esleué, lequel est vostre cópagnon de guerre,
& ie ne diray pas vostre Roy, & que
vous ne le laissiez pas aller tout seul
maintenant qu'il a pris dessein d'aller iusqu'au bout du monde. Ie vous
ay cómandé en toutes autres choses,
mais ie vous veux estre redeuable

de cellecy. Confiderez que celuy qui vous prie, eſt celuy qui ne vous a iamais rien commandé qu'il ne ſe ſoit ietté le premier dans le peril, & qui a ſouuent couuert l'armee auec ſon bouclier. Ne rōpez pas la palme que ie tiens deſia dans ma main, & de laquelle ie me ſuis propoſé d'eſgaler Hercule & le pere Liber, ſi l'enuie ne m'y reſiſte. Accordez cela à mes prieres, & faites ceſſer en fin voſtre ſilence obſtiné. Où ſont ces cris dont vous auez accouſtumé de teſmoigner voſtre ioye? Où eſt ce bon viſage que mes Macedoniens prennent d'ordinaire? Ie ne vous recognoy plus, Soldats, & il me ſemble auſſi que vous ne me recognoiſſez plus. Il y a long temps que ie parle icy à des ſourds, & que ie m'efforce de reſuciller des eſprits opiniaſtres & endurcis; ie ne ſçay pas ſi ie vous ay

offencez par mesgarde, mais vous
ne daignez pas mesme me regarder.
Il semble maintenant que ie sois
seul. Personne de ceux à qui ie
parle ne me respond, & il n'y
a aussi personne qui me contre-
dise. Mais qu'est ce que ie demande ? ie ne demande que vostre grandeur & vostre gloire.
Où sont ceux que i'ay veu se battre
il y a quelque temps à qui porteroit
le corps du Roy qui estoit blessé ? ie
suis abãdóné, vous me quittez, vous
me voulez liurer à l'ennemy: mais ie
sçay bien que ie perseuereray dedãs
mes desseins, & que ie m'en iray tout
seul. Exposez moy à des fleuues ra-
pides & à des bestes farouchesou, biẽ
à ces peuples dont vous auez les nós
en horreur, encore que vous me
quittiez, ie trouueray bien qui me
suiue. Les Scythes & les Bactrians

feront auecque moy. Ceux qui eſtoient autrefois mes ennemis, feront maintenant mes Soldats. Il me vaudroit mieux mourir que de n'eſtre voſtre Capitaine que par emprunt. Retournez vous-en en vos maiſons, & vous reſ-jouyſſez d'auoir abandonné voſtre Roy. Quant à moy ie trouueray bien icy vn moyen pour gagner vne victoire que vous n'auez point eſperée, ou pour auoir vne mort honorable.

Responce de Cœnus à Alexandre au nom de toute l'armee.

PLaise ô Dieux de destourner de nous de si mauuaises pensees que celles que vous croyez que nous ayons, ô Alexandre, & de verité ils les ont assez destournees. Nous auons pour vous la mesme affection que nous auons tousiours eüe, c'est assauoir, d'aller par tout où vous nous commanderez de combattre, de nous hazarder & de rendre vostre renommee recommandable à la posterité par la perte de nostre sang. C'est pourquoy si vous perseuerez en vos desseins, nous vous suiurons

tous nuds & sans armes, & n'ayans
presque plus de sang ny de force,
ou bien si vous le desirez, nous
marcherons mesme deuant vous.
Mais s'il vous plaist d'ouyr les paroles de vos soldats qui ne sont
point feintes, mais qu'vne extreme necessité fait sortir de leur bouche, prestez leur ie vous prie vne audience fauorable, puis qu'ils meritent bien cela apres s'estre tousiours
rangez sous vostre conduite, &
estans encore tous prests de vous
suiure en quelque part que vous alliez. Il faut que vous sçachiez, Sire,
que non seulement vous auez vaincu vos ennemis par la grandeur de
vos faicts, mais aussi vos Soldats.
Nous auons accomply tout ce que
les hommes pouuoient faire. Ayãt
trauersé les mers, & les terres. Nous
sçauons mieux tout ce qui s'y trouue que les habitans mesmes, nous

sommes desia quasi au bout du
monde , & vous desirez passer
dans vn autre , & chercher de
certaines Indes qui sont mesmes in-
cognuës aux Indiens. Vous voulez
arracher de leurs cachettes & de
leurs giftes ceux qui demeurent entre les bestes sauuages & les serpens,
afin que voftre victoire vous fasse
descouurir plus de choses que n'en
void le Soleil: C'eft de verité vne
péfee digne de voftre courage,mais
elle eft trop releuee pour le noftre , car voftre valeur va toufi-
jours en augmentant , mais nos
forces sont desia sur le declin. Contemplez nos corps passes & couuerts de playes qui n'eftans point
encore fermees en plusieurs & diuers lieux, font tomber nos membres en pourriture. Nos dards
n'ont plus maintenant de pointe, &
toute forte d'armes nous manquét.

Nous nous sommes veſtus à la mode des Perſes, pource que les habits que nous auions apportez de noſtre pays ſont deſia vſez. Nous auons quitté nos anciennes modes pour nous accouſtumer à celle des eſtrágers. Combien y en a-t'il qui ayent vn corſelet accomply? qui eſt-ce qui a vn cheual? Commandez que l'on faſſe vne recherche pour ſçauoir combien il y en a qui ont encore leurs valets, & ce qui leur peut encore reſter de toute la proye qu'ils ont gagnee. Nous auons tout vaincu, & neantmoins nous ſommes pauures en toutes choſes. Ce n'eſt pas dans des ſomptuoſitez & des braueries que nous nous ſommes ruinez. Nous auons vſé tout noſtre equipage de guerre en faiſant la guerre. Voulez vous expoſer aux beſtes ceſte belle armee toute

nuë, car encore que les Barbares taſ-
chent tout exprez de faire le nombre de ces beſtes plus grandes qu'il
eſt, ſi eſt-ce que dans leurs menſonges meſmes nous pouuions cognoiſtre qu'il ne ſçauroit eſtre petit Que
s'il faut infailliblement aller plus
auant dans les Indes, il y a vn pays
du coſté du Midy qui n'eſt pas ſi de-
ſert que celuy où vous deſirez aller. Lors que vous l'aurez mis ſous
voſtre domination, il vous ſera permis de nauiger ſur ceſte mer que la
nature a donné pour borne à la terre. C'eſt là que les eaux de l'Ocean
flottent pareillement. Si ce n'eſt que
vous aymiez mieux errer de tous
coſtez, nous ſommes paruenus au
lieu où vous deuoit mener voſtre
fortune. I'ay beaucoup mieux aymé
dire ces choſes en voſtre preſence,
que de les compter en voſtre abſen-

ce à mes compagnons, non point
pour acquerir la bonne grace de
l'armee qui m'enuironne, mais afin
que vous entendiez pluſtoſt la voix
de ceux qui parlent franchement,
que les plaintes importunes de ceux
qui ne font que murmurer en ſecret.

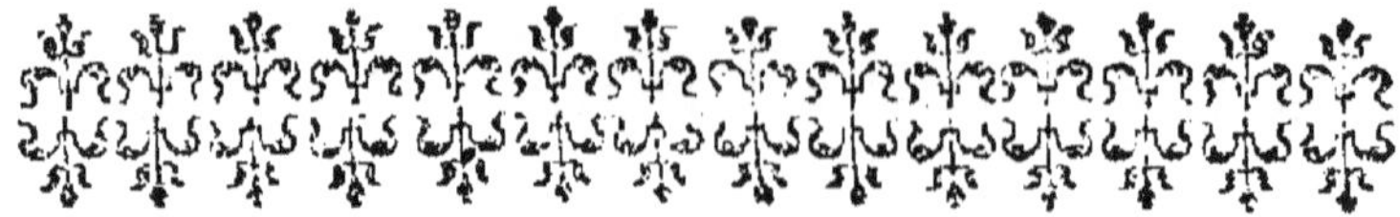

Discours sur l'opinion qu'auoient les Macedoniens de l'entreprise d'Alexandre.

ES Macedoniens faisoient bien cognoistre que quelque affection qu'ils portassent à leur Roy, ils ne desiroient point qu'il les menast plus outre que le lieu où ils estoient paruenus. Ils disoient qu'Alexandre deuoit se contenter d'auoir vaincu iusques au lieu où le Soleil se contentoit de jetter ses rayons ; Que c'estoit dans ces terres là qu'Hercule auoit merité le Ciel ; Que les bornes aussi de son Empire estoient les bornes du monde ; Qu'il n'y auoit rien plus outre que

l’Ocean qui eſtoit plein de monſtres eſpouuantables, & qu’au delà
il n’y auoit point d’autres riuages
de mer, & qu’il ne falloit pas qu’il
s’imaginaſt que l’on y viſt naiſtre
vn autre monde, & que la nature
mere de toutes choſes ne finiſt iamais & n’acheue nulle part ſes ouurages; que de verité cela ſe pouuoit facilement feindre, par ce que
tout l’Ocean ne ſe pouuoit nauiger, mais que ce n’eſtoit pas
à dire que cela fuſt. Qu’Alexandre auoit vaincu tout ce qu’il auoit
cognu, & qu’il deſiroit alors ce
qu’il ne cognoiſſoit pas, mais qu’il
n’y auoit rien ſi grand qu’ils vou-
luſſent aller chercher en danger de
perdre Alexandre, & qu’il eſtoit
temps qu’il s’arreſtaſt où s’arreſtoit
le monde & le Soleil qui l’eſclaire.
En fin diſoient ils encore, Que vou-
lez-

lez-vous, ô grand Alexandre, nous
ne chercherons point le monde,
nous le laifferons fi nous allons où
vous defirez. Nous mettrons nous
fur vne mer infinie où les hommes
n'ont iamais effayé d'aller, d'autant
qu'elle fert comme de foffez à l'en-
tour de la terre ? Irons nous fur ces
eaux qui n'ont iamais efté touchees
par les anciens, & dont les bords
font tantoft couuerts & tourmen-
tez par vne furieufe tempefte, &
tantoft deuiennent deferts lors
que la mer fe retire ? Faut-il aller
chercher ie ne fçay quoy que la nature a caché aux yeux des hommes,
& qui demeure enfeuely fous vne
profonde nuict ? La grandeur des
monftres marins tefmoigne bien
qu'ils n'ont rien laiffé par delà que
nous puiffions vaincre. Ne fçauez
vous pas que comme chaque terre

Y

a ſes bornes, le monde a auſſi les ſiennes? Mettez auſſi de vous-meſme vne borne à voſtre grandeur, encore qu'il ne ſemble point que la fortune ſe ſoucie d'y en mettre. La moderatió eſt honorable à vn grád Prince parmy ſes proſperitez. Alexandre voudra-il donc ſurpaſſer la nature des choſes? Alexandre eſt grand dans le monde & le monde eſt petit pour Alexandre. Nous cognoiſſons auſſi peu qu'il y ayt quelque choſe par delà noſtre Roy, que par delà l'Ocean: Si nous nous mettrons ſi auant ſur les mers, à qui laiſſerons nous les terres? Quitterons nous les choſes aſſeurees pour les incertaines? Dites nous, ô grand Roy, qui c'eſt qui pourra cóſeruer l'Empire que vous poſſedez icy, tandis que vous ſerez paſſé dans vn autre monde pour le ſubiuguer encore.

Ceux mesme qui ont fuy deuant vous ont mieux aymé s'exposer à voftre colere que de s'aller ietter dans les gouffres que vous voulez efprouuer. Nous ferions bien miferables fi nous permettions qu'vn fi grand Prince perdift le fruict de toutes fes victoires, & qu'il s'en allaft fe mettre dans des perils eftranges en des endroicts que l'on ne cognoift point, & dont nos Philofophes difputent tous les iours. Ceux qui ont obferué les iours des Eftoiles, & qui ont reduit fous certaines loix les retours annuels de l'Hyuer & de l'Efté, auoüent qu'encore qu'il n'y ayt aucune partie de la terre qui ne leur foit cognuë, ils ne fçauent pas quelle eft la grandeur de l'Ocean, ny mefme ce qui eft au delà, & s'il enuironne les terres comme vn cercle ou fi

Y ij

eſtant comme lié auec le monde il
s'enfonce dedans des gouffres pour
fournir d'eau de tous coſtez; & que
c'eſt vne choſe encore plus obſcure
de ſçauoir ſi apres luy il y a du feu
ou de l'air dont il tire ſa nourriture.
Conſiderez donc, ô Alexandre, que
ſi nous nous mettons ſur ceſte mer,
nous abandonnerons le monde, &
nous laiſſerons bien loing derriere
nous la lumiere du Soleil, nous irons
errer dans vne perpetuelle nuiĉt, les
vents n'enfleront plus les voiles de
nos vaiſſeaux, & les monſtres qui
les choqueront taſcheront de nous
faire perir. En fin non ſeulement
nous aurons quitté le monde, mais
auſſi la nature. Que trouuerons
nous en fin ? ce ne peut eſtre qu'vn
grand mal, puiſque les Dieux l'ont
caché aux extremitez du monde,
ou s'il y a du bien il n'eſt pas faiĉt

pour nous. C'est peut-estre la demeure de quelques Esprits diuins
qui se fascheront de ce que nous
aurons eu tant de temerité. Croyez
moy que c'est violer vn lieu deffendu que de penetrer iusques à des
endroits qui n'ont esté separez de
nous, que pour nous aduertir que
nous ne deuons pas seulement nous
informer de ce qui s'y trouue. Il
n'y a que trois choses à considerer
en cecy pour vous faire quitter vostre entreprise, le hazard où vous
vous mettez, la perte de vos terres
dont les sujets se reuolteront en vostre absence, & la derniere dont
nous n'auons point encore parlé, &
qui est pourtant la plus forte, c'est
le regret de vostre mere qui vous
tiendra comme perdu, estant sorty
non seulement de l'Asie, mais du
monde.

Voila les principales raisons que
les Macedoniens alleguent à Alexandre pour luy faire quitter le deffein de s'embarquer fur l'Ocean. Il
n'y a point d'Autheur qui les ayt
mifes toutes de fuitte en cefte forte,
mais l'on les a recueillies pour en
faire vn difcours continu. L'on void
en cela vne chofe bien remarquable, qui eft, qu'encore que ces guerriers euffent autant d'efprit que de
courage, ils participoient à la fimplicité de leur fiecle. Ils ne pouuoiét
comprendre que le Ciel & la terre
fuffent ronds, ils ne fçauoiét ce que
c'eftoit que d'Antipodes. Ils s'imaginoient que tout fuft eftendu en
long, & que la mer euft vne grandeur infinie, de forte qu'apres vn
certain efpace le Soleil n'y pouuoit
plus luire. Maintenant que nous
fommes hors de ces erreurs nous

prenons plaisir à voir l'histoire de
ceux qui les suiuoiét encore. Pour
ce qui est du dessein d'Alexandre, il
ne fut pas executé pour la crainte
qu'il eut sur les remonstrances que
luy firent ses Soldats. Il se contenta
de faire dresser des Autels au lieu où
il estoit paruenu & d'y laisser des armees plus grandes que l'ordinaire,
afin que la posterité crust que luy &
tous ceux de sa suitte estoient des
hommes dont les corps estoient
aussi grands que le courage.

Discours sur la faueur des Roys fait pour Epheſtion fauory d'Alexandre.

IL ſemble que les choſes inſenſibles ne ſoient pas meſmes exemptes d'auoir de l'inclination pour quelqu'autre. Les pierres ont vn centre vers lequel elles ſe tournent, & l'on dit qu'il y a des Planettes qui ſe regardent par de certains aſpects de bienveillance : Comment les ames des hommes pourroient elles donc s'abſtenir d'aymer quelque choſe, veu qu'elles ne ſçauroient ceſſer de le faire, ſans ceſſer d'eſtre ce qu'elles ſont, & que l'on void que pour monſtrer que c'eſt leur principale

fonction ces mots d'Amour & d'A-
mitié , ne viennent que de celuy
d'Ame? Que si celle d'vn Roy n'a
point de si petites pensees qu'elles
ne soient autant d'inspirations cele-
stes, afin de representer deuant les
creatures mortelles, ce que Dieu est
deuant les immortelles , il ne faut
point douter que quád il affectionne quelqu'vn, ce ne soit pour imiter
la Diuinité, qui ne fait point mieux
connoistre sa grandeur que lors
qu'elle fauorise les hommes.

Que si l'on se plaint que nostre
grand Monarque ne faict pas à tous
vne part égale de sa bien veillance;
ne sçait on pas aussi , qu'il y a au
Ciel des couronnes & des places les
vnes plus glorieuses que les autres,
& qu'il y a des estoiles à qui Dieu a
donné plus de lumiere & de pouuoir qu'à leurs compagnes, sans que

l'on y puiſſe , ny que l'on y doiue
chercher autre raiſon , ſinon que
c'eſt ſa volonté qui eſt la Iuſtice, &
la raiſon meſme ? Qui ne ſe voudra
ſeruir de ces grands exemples pour
authoriſer vne choſe ſi iuſte & ſi ap-
prouuée , n'a qu'à ſe tenir en terre
ſans monter ſi haut que le Ciel , & à
voir qu'il y a des animaux, qui ont
receu de la Nature des qualitez plus
rares que tous ceux de leur eſpece,
& qu'il n'y a ſi petite famille où le
Maiſtre ne prefere quelque ſeruiteur aux autres.

Puis que des perſonnes, à qui la
baſſeſſe de la condition refuſe preſque tous les plaiſirs de la vie, ne trouuent pas que l'on leur refuſe ceux de
l'Amitié , les voudroit-on oſter à
vn Roy qui ſe doit faire luy meſme ſes Loix ? La plus eminente
condition du monde ſeroit ſans ce-

la la plus defagreable ; & l'on tient
pour certain que les delices mefmes
du Ciel ne nous fatisferoiēt pas entierement, fi nous en jouyffions fans
auoir quelqu'vn à qui nous les peuf-
fions dire. Pour viure heureux, il
nous faut auoir vn confident à qui
nous declarions noftre foin & noftre joye, afin qu'il nous defchar-
ge de l'vn & qu'il nous faffe accroiftre l'autre ; & fi iamais perfonne
a befoin de cecy, ce font les Roys,
qui auffi bien qu'Athlas portoit le
Ciel, font obligez de porter le faix
de leur Empire. Il eft bien vray qu'e-
ftans au deffus de tous les autres, ils
ne peuuent iamais auoir de ces amis
que l'efgalité fait naiftre, mais au
moins ont-ils de fideles fauoris, & ce
n'eft pas vne chofe plus naturelle &
plus equitable d'auoir des Monar-
ques, que de leur voir des perfonnes
qui leur foient confidentes.

Les hommes prophanes ne parlent pas eux mesmes aux Dieux, & ne les interrogent pas sur le succez de leurs affaires : Ils s'addressent aux Prestres initiés aux Mysteres de la Diuinité , par l'entremise desquels ils reçoiuent les Oracles. Aussi tous les sujets d'vn Prince ne sont pas dignes d'approcher de sa personne. Il faut qu'ils entendent la volonté de la bouche qui a esté choisie pour la dire. Nous n'auons pas tous des yeux d'Aigle, pour pouuoir regarder le Soleil sans nous esblouyr, & si nous ne le pouuons considerer que sur quelque glace qui le represente. Il n'est pas plus facile que nous comprenions la grandeur des Roys ; si ce n'est en iettant nos regards sur ceux qu'ils cherissent. Ce n'est que par leurs mains que nous doit estre baillé ce qu'ils nous

accordent; & que l'on quitte toutes ces imaginations de destin & de
fortune, ce sont eux qui font nos
fortunes & nos destins. Qui les honore, honore le Maistre qu'ils seruent, & par la mesme Loy qui nous
oblige d'aymer nostre Roy , nous
sommes obligez d'aymer ceux qu'il
ayme. C'est estre criminel de leze
Majesté de ne les respecter pas , &
qui deschireroit le portraict d'vn
Monarque , & abbatroit sa statuë,
ou mettroit le feu à ses bastimens,
ne seroit pas si coulpable. Aussi les
courages ne témoignent leur generosité que lors qu'ils sont ardens à
deffendre ceux qui sont en faueur,
& l'eloquence n'a point d'empire
sur les esprits, que lors qu'elle parle
de leur merite. Bien qu'ils ne soient
pas nés du Sang des Roys, & que la
Nature ne leur ait pas esté si libera-

le que la Fortune , leurs dignitez leur donnent souuent presqu'
autant d'esclat qu'aux Princes , &
comme les choses où le Soleil jette
ses rayons, renuoyẽt la clarté à tout
ce qui les enuironne , aussi receuans
les faueurs du Souuerain , ils en sont
esclairez, & en esclairent les autres.
Qu'est-ce que nous ne leur deuons
point , lors que nous trouuons en
eux tant de merite qu'il nous lesfaut
seruir autant par inclination que
par deuoir , comme nous voyons
en celuy à qui Alexandre a donné
vne place en son cœur qui n'est de-
stiné qu'à songer à de grandes choses ? L'Enuie ne se doit elle pas im-
poser silence, lors qu'elle considere
que si nous faisonsdes vœux au Ciel
pour le rendre accomply , nos sou-
haits seront vaincus par les perfe-
ctiõs qu'il s'acquiert tous les iours,
& que si l'on veut attribuer au Roy

vne prudéce nôpareille, c'en est vne
bône preuue que de l'auoir pris pour
object de son affection. Le Roy est
estimé sage & prudent pour beaucoup d'autres actiós signalées ; mais
quoy que l'on puisse dire, il n'y en a
guiere qui luy fassent plustost acquerir ce renô que celuy. cy. N'est-
ce pas auoir des conseils qui ne
peuuent venir que du Ciel, d'honorer de ses faueurs celuy qui luy est
aussi bié semblable en naturel comme en âge, & qui estant connû dés
sa jeunesse & esleué par degrez, aura
tousiours pour l'Estat vne fidelité
plus forte que toute sorte d'interest,
& vne moderatió plus puissante que
tout excés de fortune? Mais c'est mal
parler que de dire, que l'affection
que le Roy a pour luy, vienne de
quelque inclinatió particuliere. Il ne
faut pas croire que les Astres môstrét
icy leur pouuoir, & que les signes sé-

blables sous lesquels ils soiēt nés, pro-
duisent cette bien-veillāce. C'est faire tort au bon iugemēt du Roy qui
seroit conduit par vne influence
aueugle. Disons pluftoſt qu'il n'eſt
porté à faire part de ses bonnes graces à celuy qui les poſsede, que par
son merite seulement.　Ce font des
charmes bien forts que les perfections dont il eſt pourueu ; & les
caracteres inconnus, les figures en-
chantées, & les anneaux magiques,
n'auroient pas le pouuoir de le faire
autant aymer. Que les vrays Mace-
doniēs ayent toutes ces veritez auffi bien en leur croyance qu'en leur
difcours, & que l'on fe reprefente
que fi ie ne tafche de les fortifier par
d'autres preuues, c'eſt que ie croirois leur faire tort, tefmoignát que
ie craindrois qu'elles ne fuffent pas
affez connuës ; car ie me doy affeu-
rer

rer qu'elles ont assez de force pour se faire valoir elles mesmes.

Voyla le discours que l'on a pû faire en faueur d'Ephestion au temps qu'il estoit fauorisé d'Alexandre. L'on trouue par tout de grandes preuues de l'affection que ce Prince luy portoit. Lors qu'apres auoir vaincu Darius il voulut aller voir sa mere, qu'il tenoit prisonniere, cette Princesse voyant marcher Ephestion le premier, s'imagina que c'estoit le Roy de Macedoine, tellement qu'elle se vint jetter à ses pieds, & estant aduertie de la faute qu'elle auoit faite, elle en vint demander pardon à Alexandre, mais il luy dit qu'elle ne s'estoit pas beaucoup mesprise, & que cettuy-là estoit aussi Alexandre. C'estoit là vne faueur nompareille, car il vouloit dire qu'ils

n'eſtoient qu'vn & qu'ils s'eſtoient
transformez l'vn en l'autre. Apres
cet exemple il n'en faut point chercher de plus grand pour monſtrer
quelle eſtoit ſa fortune.

Aduis donné à *Ephestion pour se bien gouuerner dans sa faueur.*

Vis que le Roy vous a don-né vne place en son cœur aussi bien qu'aux victoires & aux Empires qui sont les obiects de sa pensée, ie confesse qu'il n'y a personne au móde qui ne soit obli-gé de vous dédier le sien, s'il ne veut témoigner qu'il n'en a point du tout. Mais ie vous auoüeray pourtát que l'esclat de la Fortune qui es-blouït les yeux des autres, ne peut qu'à peine estre veu des miés, & que si vous n'estiez aussi remarquable pour vostre merite que pour vos prosperitez, ie ne serois pas attaché à vous seruir par vne chaine si forte. Ie ne suis pas de ces lasches Courtisás qui ne vousmóstrét point d'affectió

qui ne soit meslee parmy leur interest
& qui ne vo' desirét du bien qu'afin
qu'il leur en arriue. Quand vostre
bon-heur ne seroit pas aussi esleué
qu'il est, ie iure par les choses les plus
Sainctes & les plus venerables, que
le nombre des vœux que ie fay
pour vous ne seroit pas diminué
pour cela ; & qu'estant le seul centre que se deuoient proposer mes
pensées, si ie n'eusse eu le bien de
vous connoistre, ie n'eusse iamais
rien aymé. Si i'auois autrefois recherché vne autre bien-veillance,
& qu'vne autre image que la vostre eust esté grauée en mon ame,
ie ne la tiendrois plus digne de vous
estre offerte. Il ne vous en faut donner qu'vne pure qui n'ait point
quelque reste de ses premieres im-
pressions, & qui ne proteste pas seulement de n'auoir esté voûce qu'à
vous par le passé, mais de ne l'estre

auſſi à l'aduenir. Conſiderez combien il y en a qui auparauant que
vous fuſsiez eſleué où vous eſtes, alloient courtiſer ceux qui iouyſſoiét
d'vne ſemblable proſperité. N'eſt-
il pas croyable que comme ils en
quittent d'autres pour vous, ils vous
peuuent auſsi quitter pour d'autres?
Ils reſſemblent à ces oyſeaux paſſa-
gers qui abandonnent les côtrées où
l'Hyuer reſide, pour venir en la noſtre quand le Printemps y regne ; &
ce n'eſt point voſtre perſonne qu'ils
adorent, mais voſtre fortune. Il ne
faut pas prédre garde aux belles of-
fres de ſeruice qu'ils vous font , ce
ſont pluſtoſt des preuues de leur eloquence que de leur affection ; & l'on
ne doit pas s'eſtonner s'ils y ſont ſi
ſçauans, veu que ce ſont les meſmes
qu'ils ont dés long temps eſtudiées,
& qu'ayās recherché les bónes gra.

Y iij

ces d'autres fauoris, ils les ont appri-
ses à leur escole. Si au lieu de leurs
paroles vous leur demandiez des effets ie m'asseure qu'ils n'en donne-
roient point qu'ils n'eussent receu
la recompense auparauant que d'en
souffrir la peine , ou qu'ils n'y
fussent attirez par quelque esperance auantageuse. Les complimens
dont ils vous importunent, se font
plustost par coustume que par inclination , & quoy que vous ayez
des qualitez capables de gagner
toute sorte d'esprits, possible qu'ils
seroient si aueuglez qu'ils ne les
verroient pas , si elles ne rece-
uoient de la lumiere par vostre
fortune. Prenez garde aussi qu'encore que ceux qui ont esté fa-
uorisez du Roy auparauant vous,
ne semblent pas vous vouloir
moins de bien pour cela , toutes

leurs actions ne font neantmoins
que fard & que feintife , & s'ils
auoient autant de pouuoir que
de mauuaife volonté , ils vous
mettroient hors du lieu où ils defirent eftre. L'inclination que le
Roy a pour vous eft veritablement bien forte. Mais les affaires du monde gardent touf jours
leur inconftance , & s'il y a quelque chofe d'affeuré en elles ,
qu'elles changent à tous momens.
Vous ne deuez donc pas tant vous
fier à fa bien-veillance qu'à celle
du Ciel qui vous peut conferuer voftre felicité; Et le plus feur moyen
que vous fçauriez trouuer pour n'a-
uoir iamais aucun malheur , c'eft
de vous preparer à tout, & de monftrer à vos ennemis & à vos enuieux, que quand vous ne feriez pas

Z iiij

ce que vous estes : vos contentemés ne lairroiét pas d'estre aulsi parfaits. Ce sera pour leur donner vne rage qui accroistra leurs supplices, & il n'y a rien à quoy ils puissent auoir recours, voyant que le changement mesme de vostre fortune ne sçauroit amoindrir vostre constance, & que vostre interest ne vous est pas tant considerable que le seruice de nostre Roy.

Mais à quel excez la passió dót ie vous chery me porte-t'elle? ne m'accuserez vous pas de temerité devous vouloir dóner des auis, moy de qui le iugemét n'a rié qui ne soit au dessous duvostre? Vous sçauez bien discerner ceux qui ne vous seruent pas auec vne affection sincere, & n'auez garde de prophaner vos faueurs les employât vers des personnes qui ne meritêt quevôtre courroux & vôtre

mespris. Aussi estes vous d'vn naturel trop bon & trop iuste, pour ne
pas recognoistre la fidelité de ceux
qui vous honorent comme ie fay,
sans qu'il soit besoin que pour donner de l'esclat à mes actions de mesme que les ombrages aupres des diuerses couleurs les rendent plus viues, ie rapporte les deffaux des autres au mesme discours où ie vous
represente la pureté de mon intention. Toutes les personnes d'esprit
& de valeur ne conçoiuent de vous
que des esperances bien grandes. Ce
n'est plus que pour vous que les O-
racles parlent, & que les presages
nous arriuent.

Les Deuins seroient bien empes-
chez de raconter tout ce que le Ciel
vous promet, & ie m'asseure que ce
sera vn iour le plus bel ornement de
toutes nos histoires. Vous me man-

querez pas à nous faire voir que nos
propheties ont esté tres-veritables,
& qu'il n'y aura plus desormais d'hómes vertueux à la Cour que voſtre
faueur ne recompenſe , ny de vicieux que voſtre equité ne puniſſe.

L'on croid que cet aduertiſſe-
ment fut enuoyé en forme de Lettre à Epheſtion dés le commencement de ſa fortune. Cela fut faict
par vn Courtiſan de ſes amys qui
eſtoit Orateur & Philoſophe tout
enſemble. Les Conſeils en ſont tres-
vtiles pour ceux d'vne pareille condition, & ce qu'il y a d'excellent,
c'eſt qu'il n'y a rien qui ne reſſente
vne veritable preud'hommie. Il eſt
vray que les hiſtoires Grecques ne
rapportent point toutes ces choſes;
mais la nouuelle recherche que l'on
en a pû faire ne ſçauroit eſtre qu'a-
greable.

Discours sur la vie d'vn homme iuste.

NOSTRE vie peut estre comparee à cet ancien jeu des Grecs, où l'on tenoit vn flambeau allumé en courant par vn certain espace, & l'on le donnoit apres de main en main à ceux qui vouloient courir, que si l'on le laissoit esteindre auant que d'estre paruenu au but propo-sé, l'on en receuoit beaucoup de honte. Nous sommes icy tous dans vne lice où il faut que nous couriós sans laisser perdre la flamme du flã-beau qui nous est donné, autrement nous ne gaignerions point la victoi-re, & nous ne serions pas courónez par le souuerain Iuge qui nous re-

garde. Or ce flābeau n'eſt autre choſe que les enſeignemés que nous laiſſons à la poſterité dans nos liures,
afin qu'elle ſçache quels hazards
nous auons eſprouuez, & comment
nous en ſommes ſortis à noſtre honneur, ou bien pluſtoſt ce n'eſt que la
renommee des actions des grands
perſonnages qu'il y a du danger de
laiſſer perir, & qu'il ſe faut bailler
de main en main par vne tradition
continuelle, afin qu'à leur exemple l'on ayt les vices en horreur &
la vertu en eſtime. Quoy que ce
ſoit, il faut que nous faſſions chacun
tout ce que nous pourrons entreprendre de plus vtile pour les autres
hommes, & puiſque nous auons
perdu depuis peu ce grand perſonnage qui tenoit le flambeau de la
vertu haut eſleué, il le faut prendre
apres luy ſi nous pouuons; & com-

me il nous incitoit à la veritable
gloire par l'exemple de ses predecesseurs, il faut que ce soit maintenant par le sien que nous instrui-
sions ceux qui viuent auiourd'huy,
afin que cela soit ainsi transmis à la
posterité. Ce feu que l'on ne doit
point laisser esteindre est aussi pur
que celuy des Vestales. Quand il en
viendroit faute ce ne seroit qu'aux
rays du Soleil qu'il le faudroit r'al-
lumer; c'est à dire qu'il ne faudroit
point se laisser enflamer de l'amour
d'vne autre science que de celle de
Dieu. Pource que nous sommes des
esprits foibles, ie ne sçaurois vser
que d'vne comparaison sensible, en
parlant de ce Createur de toutes
choses, qui est incomprehensible &
infiny. Celuy dont nous admirons
la vie s'est tousiours humilié deuant
ce grand Dieu, & ie croy qu'outre

les enseignemens qu'il auoit receus
de la part de l'antiquité, il auoit des
inspirations particulieres : de sorte
que ie m'imagine que l'on ne peut
rendre maintenant vn meilleur office à ceux de nostre siecle, que de
leur proposer les pensees ordinaires
de cet homme illustre, ainsi que
nous les auons sceuës de ses amis,
ausquels il les auoit confiees, & par
mesme moyen nous dirons aussi de
quelle façon il se gouuernoit en
toute sorte d'occasions, afin que
nous fassions comme vn abbregé de
son histoire.

Il faut sçauoir premierement
que nous l'appellons l'homme Iuste, pource que veritablement il y
auoit de la iustice en toutes ses
actions, & qu'outre cela l'on ne
sçauroit trouuer vn nom qui luy
soit plus propre ; Car le nom de

Iuste comprend toutes fortes de vertus. C'eft par là que nous monftrons qu'il eftoit vertueux en toutes chofes. D'ailleurs le nom de Iufte eft le plus excellent de tous ceux que l'on a iamais donnez à tous les hommes Illuftres. Le nom de Grand eft approprié à des arbres, & à des montagnes, celuy de fort eft donné à des Elephants, à des Lyons, & à des Taureaux, celuy de beau n'eft que pour le corps, & principalement pour ceux des femmes; mais le nom de Iufte, ne peut eftre donné qu'à vn excellent Efprit.

Les principales qualitez que nous remarquions en ce rare perfonnage, eftoient, Qu'il ne paroiffoit point ambitieux ny infatiable en fa fortune, mais qu'il auoit apris à rechercher fõ biẽ dedãs foy-mefme;

Qu'il ne se soucioit d'aucun accident de la vie; Qu'il s'escartoit tousjours du monde bien qu'il fist assez cognoistre qu'il en estoit vn des principaux membres par l'vtilité qu'il apportoit aux autres hommes; Qu'il mesprisoit les plaisirs, & encore plus les desplaisirs qui luy pouuoient arriuer icy bas, ayant gagné ce poinct d'estre asseuré que la mort n'est ny matiere ny occasion d'aucun mal, mais la fin de plusieurs maux; Qu'il auoit dedié toutes ses pensées à la vertu, & tenoit que le chemin pour y paruenir estoit facile & avsé

Ce sont là des choses tres-rares, mais nous deuons croire que sans l'assistance de Dieu, il est impossible de les mettre en pratique. Il falloit qu'il fust introduit au chemin de la vertu par vne puissance superieure. Celuy

Celuy qui pense monter si haut à l'ayde de ses seules forces, se trompe infiniment. Il est en danger de tomber dans des precipices, & de trouuer le chemin extremément mal-aisé, au lieu que ceux qui sont destinez pour paruenir à la vraye felicité, en trouuent toutes les approches fort agreables. Le chemin de la vraye vertu n'est pas seulement comparé à vne montagne, où l'on se peut à la fin esleuer, si haute qu'elle soit en tenant la pointe des roches; l'on dit aussi qu'il est besoin d'vne grande legereté pour y paruenir. C'est dans le Ciel que la vertu reside. Il faut auoir des aisles pour y monter, & ces aisles sont la bonne volonté, qui de verité nous peut esleuer plus haut qu'aucune chose du mōde, mais il faut en mesme temps que nous ayons la foy,

car de ceſte foy naiſtra l'amour de
Dieu, & de cet amour naiſtra la
grace qui nous pourra ioindre à la
vertu. C'eſt ce que noſtre hómeluſte
auoit faict. Il ſçauoit bien que pour
auoir toutes choſes, il ne falloit que
dóner ſon cœur à Dieu. Il n'auoit
ny cœur ny eſprit que pour lui, pour
ce qu'il conſideroit que ce n'eſtoit
que par ſa puiſsáce qu'il auoit le cœur
& l'eſprit & la vie, & que ſás luy il ne
pouuoit ſauuer ſó ame. Il admiroit
la grádeur de Dieu en tous ſes ouurages. Il honoroit ſon pouuoir en tous
les accidéts qui ſuruenoient. Il ado-
roit ſa bóté en tous les biens qu'il receuoit: bref toutes ſes penſees, & ſes
œuures n'auoient autre but que la
loüange de Dieu. C'eſtoit là tout le
ſecret de ſa Philoſophie. C'eſtoit par
ce moyé qu'il meſpriſoit les infortunes, & qu'il ne tenoit guere plus de

côpte des bonnes fortunes. C'eſtoit
ce qui luy faiſoit fouler aux pieds les
honneurs du môde, & c'eſtoit en fin
ce qui luy donnoit l'aſſeurâce de ne
craindre point les hômes, puis qu'il
raſchoit de plaire à vn plus grand
Maiſtre. Il faut maintenât raconter
particulierement de quelle ſorte il
viuoit dans le monde, afin que des
perfections ſi grandes que les ſiennes, nous donnent vn deſir vehement d'en poſſeder de ſemblables. Il
fuïoit premieremét toutes ces actiós
dont l'on taſche quelquefois de deſguiſer ſes péſees. Son cœur, ſa lãgue,
& ſon viſage eſtoient rouſiours de
meſme aduis; Si la ioye ſe liſoit dans
ſes yeux, elle eſtoit auſſi dans ſes diſcours, & pareillemét dedãs ſon ame.
Son entretien n'eſtoit pas remply de
mocquerie. Il auoit moyé de trouuer des reſioüyſſáces plus honeſtes,

que les mal-heurs & les deffaux des
autres hommes. Il ne se vouloit pas
ayder des imperfections d'autruy
pour donner du lustre à ses perfections & les faire esclatter dauantage aupres de leurs contraires. Il regardoit paisiblement les fautes qu'il
ne pouuoit corriger, & il n'entroit
pas en fureur côtre ceux qui les cô-
mettoient, car par ce moyen il se
fust laissé emporter à vn vice lors
qu'il en eust voulu reprendre vn autre. La profession & l'humeur de
ceux qui s'accoustumoient à repré-
dre auec trop de seuerité ne luy plaisoit aucunemét. Il disoit qu'ils n'accordoient rien à la foiblesse humaine, & qu'ils estoient aussi subjets à
pecher contre la bien-seance que
ces anciens Philosophes Cyniques,
lesquels on appelloit Chiens auec
iuste raison, pource qu'ils ne cessoiét
iamais d'aboyer & de mesdire côtre

toute sorte de persónes. Il ne faisoit
mesme aucune estime de ce Céseur
de Rome qui códánoitt out ce qu'il
ne faisoit pas, & qui mesprisoit tout
ce qu'il ne pouuoit pas faire. Que si
l'on me veut surprendre en cecy, &
me dire qu'il estoit dóc de l'humeur
qu'il reprenoit en autruy, puis qu'il
condamnoit ce seuere Censeur dót
il ne faisoit pas les actions ; i'ay m'a
response toute preste. Ie repartiray
qu'il y a difference de reprehensió,
& que si l'on trouue estrange de ce
que ce Romain trouuoit à redire à
tout ce qu'il voyoit, c'estoit pource
qu'il mesprisoit souuent des choses
qui estoient estimables, de sorte que
l'on ne peut point faillir en mesprisant son opinion. C'est ainsi que ie
me puis deliurer des argumens des
Sophistes, qui voudroient s'il leur
estoit possible, nous persuader que

le Soleil a quelque partie tenebreu-
se en soy, & que la vraye vertu a
quelques tasches. Pour continuer
nostre discours, nous sçaurons que
nostre hóme iuste croyoit que Dieu
auoit assez fait pour luy de le garentir des erreurs des autres, sans qu'il
se meslast de leur aller faire des re-
proches. Il ne s'enfloit point d'orgueil pour se faire craindre, mais
aussi il ne rédoit pas son esprit rampant pour se rendre plus accostable.
La iustice qu'il exerçoit enuers tout
le monde ne luy ostoit rien de sa
douceur, & sa douceur ne luy ostoit
rié de son authorité. Toutes les qualitez dont il ornoit son ame, parois-
soient tousiours toutes entieres, &
si quelqu'vne eust fait tort à l'autre
l'on eust pû dire qu'il n'eust eu qu'v-
ne vertu imparfaicte. I'ay monstré
que iamais il ne s'amusoit à parler

des fautes d'autruy, car en effet il vaut mieux en aller aduertir secret-tement ceux qui les ont faictes que de les publier à leur infamie. L'on les met dans le desespoir, & ils ne se soucient plus apres de paroistre tels que chacun estime qu'ils sont. S'il voyoit dóc quelqu'vn qui puist estre corrigé par les remonstrances, il s'y employoit de toute son affection, sans parler iamais à personne de ceste procedure. Aussi disoit-il qu'il auoit apris des hommes à parler, & de Dieu à se taire. En effet le langage n'est qu'vne inuention de la foi-blesse humaine pour se communi-quer ses conceptions, que les esprits bien-heureux voyent les vns dedans les autres sans auoir besoin d'autre organe. Tout ce que nous disons n'est aussi qu'vn jargon ridicule qui n'a ny fondement ny raison, &

A a iiij

le mesme nom que l'on donne à vn
oyseau pouuoit estre donné aussi
iustement à quelque poisson. C'est
ce qui luy faisoit cósiderer que tous
les discours des hommes n'estoient
que vanité, & qu'encore qu'il sceust
beaucoup, s'il eust voulu tousiours
parler, il eust tesmoigné vne temerité insupportable. L'on pouuoit dire de luy comme d'Epaminondas,
que iamais l'on n'auoit veu homme
qui sceust tant, & qui parlast moins.

Non seulement il obseruoit vne
regle en ses discours, mais il vouloit
mesme estre tousiours vestu d'vne
telle sorte qu'il ne donnast point de
mauuais exemple, ny de mauuaises
opiniós au peuple. Ce n'est pas assez
d'estre sage au dedans: il faut encore
le faire paroistre au dehors, afin
qu'il n'y ayt rien en nous qui puisse
offencer les yeux des hómes sages.

Il y en a qui croyent que c’eſt viure en Philoſophe que de ne ſe point ſoucier comment l’on eſt veſtu ; mais ils affectent donc la ſecte de Diogene. L’on ne doit pas ſe negliger tellemét que l’on ſouffre les ordures & les ſalletez : mais il ne faut pas auſſi porter tant d’affection à la vanité que l’on ne ſonge rouſiours qu’à ſe parer comme vne femme. Il ne faut rien auoir de ſuperflu , & d’ailleurs il faut rouſiours eſtre ſelon ſa condition. C’eſt ce qu’il obſeruoit religieuſement , & l’on ne le voyoit iamais par la ville qu’auec les habits propres à ſa charge. Puis que le Roy l’auoit choiſy pour eſtre l’vn de nos Iuges , il vouloit rouſiours faire paroiſtre qu’il deſiroit conſeruer cette dignité, & n’en abandonner pas ſeulement la robbe. Il ne croyoit pas que cela fuſt honneſte

de voir quelquefois vn Iuge qui ne
feroit point habillé d'vne autre façon que fon clerc. Les Magiſtrats
font les Ambaſſadeurs des Princes
vers leurs ſubjets. Ils font depoſitai-
res de la meilleure partie de leur
puiſſance; c'eſt pourquoy il importe de beaucoup qu'ils faſſent touſ-
jours reluire en eux quelques rayons de la Majeſté de leur Maiſtre.

Les Conſuls meſmes qui eſtoient
ſouuerains dedans Rome pour le
temps de leur charge, ne pouuoient pas s'exempter de porter
les habits qui appartenoient à ceux
de leur condition. Tite Liue diſt
dans fon Hiſtoire que le Conſul
Appius Clodius, follicitant quelque affaire pour ſon frere, & fon-
geant ſi peu à toute autre choſe
qu'il n'alloit pas en ſon equipage

ordinaire, le Senat luy manda qu'il
se deuoit souuenir qu'il estoit Con-
ful de Rome , auparauant que de
songer qu'il estoit frere de Publius
Clodius. Quelques Empereurs
mesmes ont depuis ordonné que
les Senateurs qui marcheroient par
la ville auec vn autre habit que le
leur , seroient depossedez de leur
charge. En effect cela sert beaucoup à faire tenir le peuple dans
son deuoir , que de voir à tous
coups passer des Magistrats qu'il
reconnoist pour tels , deuant lesquels l'on n'oseroit commettre aucun crime , & l'on a honte mesme
des plus petites fautes. Ceux qui
sont dans les grandes charges doiuent tousiours monstrer qu'ils sont
plus grands que les autres , quoy
qu'en leur interieur ils n'en reçoiuent aucune vanité , s'ils sont aussi

fages qu'ils doiuent eftre. Les Arcadiens ayans conuié les Thebains d'entrer dans la meilleure de leurs villes pour s'y rafraifchir ; Epaminondas dit aux fiens, qu'ils s'en deuoient bié garder, & que lors qu'ils eftoient armez les Arcadiens les admiroient, mais que s'ils les voyoiét defpoüillez, ils les croiroiét femblables à eux. Auffi les gens de Iuftice ne doiuent jamais quitter leurs robbes, car fi mefme par malheur il y auoit quelque deffaut en eux, il ne paroift pas fi toft, & il n'apporte point de fcandale au peuple. L'on peut dire que les veftemens des Iuges ont quelque fecret de Perfpectiue qui les fait efgaux aux plus grāds hommes de quelque forte qu'ils foient, & que quand ils les defpoüillent, ils deuiennent pareils aux plus petits, & il femble que par quel-

que enchantement non seulement
ils ayent quitté leur pouuoir &
mesme leur dignité, mais aussi
la taille de leur corps Ils s'exposent
ainsi au blasme du vulgaire, & bien
qu'en apparence cela leur semble de
peu de consideration, si est-ce que
c'est en effect la premiere bresche
par où le mespris de leur authorité
entre dãs les esprits de ceux qui sont
sous leur jurisdiction.

Pour ce qui est des affaires du Palais, nostre homme iuste s'y employoit tout entier. Il a tousiours
consideré le monde comme vne
grãde maison dont il estoit l'vn des
principaux œconomes, de sorte
qu'il falloit qu'il employast sa pre-
uoyãce à faire que personne ne mã-
quast de ce qui luy seroit necessaire,
& que les mauuais seruiteurs fussent
punis, & les bõs fussent recõpensez.

Lors qu'il entroit dedans ce lieu où la Iuſtice ſe rend , il gardoit vn auſſi grand reſpect que dans vn Temple , & il faiſoit en ſorte que ſes paroles & ſes actions n'auoient rien de prophane. Il n'y auoit aucun deſir plus preſſant que celuy de terminer la longueur des procez , qui ſont les petites guerres ciuiles qui s'eſmeuuent entre le peuple au milieu de la paix publique. il vouloit que l'auarice & les chiquaneries fuſſent les victimes que l'on immoleroit dedans ce lieu ſacré. Au reſte il ne portoit là aucune opinion du logis, de peur qu'elle ne fermaſt la porte à quelque autre meilleure. Son eſprit eſtoit comme vne table d'attente ou vn papier blanc preſt à receuoir les caracteres que l'on luy donnoit. Il attendoit les inſpira-

tions qu'il plaisoit à Dieu de luy
enuoyer Il cherchoit la verité en
commun sans authoriser aucune
opinion particuliere. Il condamnoit les grands sans enuie, les petits
sans corruption, & tous ceux qui
auoient tort sans animosité. Il sou-
stenoit aussi quelquefois les Grands
sans flatterie, les pauures sans passion, & tout cela se faisoit selon
les differentes causes qui se plai-
doient deuant luy. Il auoit tousjours les yeux fichez sur les fers de
la balance pour voir quel costé
panchoit le plus, mais il ne regardoit iamais ce qui estoit dedans, ou
s'il le regardoit il n'en estoit point
touché, d'autant qu'il faisoit droict
à chacun sans acceptation de personne.

Pour ce qui estoit de sa cópagnie

il taſchoit de la faire viure en con-
corde. Ce n'eſtoit pas la raiſon qu'il
y euſt des querelles parmy eux, puis
qu'ils ſe meſloient d'appaiſer celle
des autres. Cela euſt eſté d'vn pernicieux exemple. L'on leur euſt pû reprocher ce que l'on reprocha à Phi-
lippe de Macedoine , lors qu'il ſe
voulut meſler de mettre la paix, dás
vne Republique. L'on luy dit qu'il
ſongeaſt premierement à terminer
les differens qui eſtoient dans ſa famille , & qu'il s'accordaſt auec ſa
femme & ſon fils. Les Parlemens ſe
doiuent maintenir dans vne harmonie parfaicte. Chacun y doit tenir
ſa partie ſans diſcorder. En quelque
corps que ce ſoit, ſi les mains exerçoient la charge des pieds, & les
pieds celle des mains ou celle de la
teſte, ce ſeroit vne choſe móſtrueu-
ſe, & d'ailleurs il n'y pourroit rien

auoir

auoir de bien faict. Aussi ne faut-il
point que dans les Estats , & dans
quelque compagnie que ce soit ,
personne entreprene sur la fonction
de son voisin. Nostre homme juste
d'vne humeur si douce & si téperée
qu'il ne heurtoit iamais personne,
& mesme il s'en est tousiours absten-
nu en des occasions où l'on l'auoit
mis auec des esprits opiniastres , &
c'est ce qui a fait aussi que chacun l'a
respecté, & que personne n'a desiré
d'auoir de differend auec celuy qui
n'en vouloir point auec personne. Il
n'auoit pas tãt de presomption qu'il
pẽsast que son opiniõ valust autant
que celle de deux autres. Il ne parloit
iamais qu'en sõ ordre, & il n'ouuroit
iamais la bouche que lors que son
grãd esprit luy auoit fait connoistre
qu'il estoit téps. Il croyoit que le cõ-
seil estoit vne chose si sacrée que l'on

ne le deuoit pas prophaner à toute
heure, & mesme lors que l'on ne le
demandoit point. Que si quelquefois il auoit pris vne opinion si saine
qu'il ne pouuoit manquer de la recognoistre, ny de voir que celle des
autres estoit pleine d'erreur, il n'entroit pas pourtát auec eux dans vne
grãde altercation, car il auoit l'artifice de leur proposer doucement ses
pensees, & de les mener où il vouloit
sans aucune violence.

Chacun sçait combien il se monstroit equitable en rendant la Iustice à tout le monde. Les arrests sont
publiez; les conseils qu'il a donnez
aux grãds qui l'ont choisi pour arbitre dans des differéds qui ne se pouuoient terminer cóme les procés du
peuple, témoignét assez que l'on n'a
jamais veu vn homme plus digne du
rãg qu'il tenoit. Parlós maintenãt de
la Iustice qu'il se rendoit à soy-mes-

me. Ne nous imaginôs pas qu'il fuſt
ſeuere aux autres, & indulgent pour
luy ſeul. Il ne vouloit point ſe par-
dóner aucune choſe. Il ſçauoit bien
que ceux qui ſe veulét meſler de iuger autruy, doiuét reſſembler à l'humeur criſtalline de l'œil qui n'a aucune couleur en ſoy afin de pouuoir
diſcerner les autres. Il ne faut point
auoir de deffaut qui ſe veut rendre
capable de cónoiſtre ceux d'autruy,
& ſe móſtrer digne de les condáner.
Les auaricieux excuſét quelquefois
les cóuoitiſes des auares, & ils n'oſe-
roient reprendre vne choſe que l'on
leur peut reprocher. Noſtre vray Iuge entroit dóc ſçauát en ſoy; Il y faiſoit vne reueuë generale de ſes penſees; il demádoit cópte à ſa memoire
de ſes paroles & de ſes actiós; bref il
ſe faiſoit ſon procés à ſoy-meſme Sa
cóſcience luy ſeruoit d'accuſateur,

de teſmoin, & de Iuge. Eſtant l'vn
des meilleurs Catholiques de ce
Royaume, cõmēt ne ſe fuſt-il point
accouſtumé à cét examē, veu qu'vn
Philoſophe Payen, tout aueuglé
qu'il eſtoit, diſoit que tous les ſoirs il
interrogeoit ſon ame, & luy demãdoit, Quel mal eſt-ce que tu as gue-
ry aujourd'huy en toy? à quelle paſſion eſt-ce que tu as reſiſté? en quelle choſe eſt-ce que tu as taſché de
deuenir meilleur? C'eſt ainſi qu'il ſe
faut corriger tous les iours, car les
vices s'amendent ou deuiennēt plus
retenus, quand ils voyent qu'il leur
faut tous les iours cõparoir en perſonne deuant leur Iuge. Mais il y a
vne choſe bien remarquable en ce
que diſoit le Philoſophe Payen; c'eſt
qu'il ſe faiſoit rédre cõpte auſſi bien
des bónes actions que des mauuaiſes, & c'eſtoit afin de voir combien

il profiteroit tous les iours en l'estude de la vertu, & de quelle sorte il se
deuoit comporter pour attaindre à
la perfection.   Aussi ne croyons pas
que si nostre homme Iuste s'exami-
noit si souuent, ce fust qu'il eust
commis de grandes fautes. Ce que
quelques-vns eussent pris en eux
pour des perfections, c'estoit là ses
seuls deffauts. Il s'accusoit de n'auoir
pas fait assez de bien, & non pas d'a-
uoir fait du mal. Au reste l'on peut
dire que son examé estoit cótinuel,
& qu'il songeoit tousiours à la presence de Dieu deuant lequel il eust
esté honteux de ne pas faire tout le
bien qui luy estoit possible. Il se re-
doutoit aussi soy-mesme plus que
toute autre puissance humaine, afin
qu'il n'y eust point pour luy de solitude qui luy donnast la liberté de
s'emanciper quelque fois.

Bb iij

C'eſt de cette ſorte que noſtre homme Iuſte a paſſé les années qu'il a eſté auec nous iuſques à ce que Dieu l'a retiré de cette vie pour le faire iouyr d'vne autre meilleure. Nous croyons qu'apres auoir ſi bien veſcu icy, & apres eſtre paſſé dans l'autre monde auec vne conſtáce merueilleuſe, il a eu la recópenſe de ſes bonnes actions, & qu'il eſt plus capable de prier Dieu pour nous que nous le ſommes de prier Dieu pour luy, de ſorte que nous en pourrons tirer autant de ſecours que lors qu'il eſtoit en noſtre cópagnie. Auſſi les bonnes ames ſont ſemblables aux Aſtres, qui eſchauffent la terre encore qu'ils ſoient attachez dans leur Ciel. Ie voudrois auoir vne eloquence pareille à ſon merite afin d'en parler aſſez dignement; mais ie n'ay pas receu aſſez de faueurs de la Nature.

Quelqu'autre s'efforcera d'y mieux reüssir que moy, & tout le monde sçaura que nous auons eu parmy nous vn si rare personnage, que si nous auions encore des Platons. nous en pourrions faire vn Socrate. Mais il faut croire que ses actions & ses paroles sont bien plus à estimer que celles du Socrate d'Athenes, & si l'on nous auoit faict vne entiere histoire de sa vie, ce nous seroit vne grande consolation, puisque nous auons eu en luy vn Socrate Chrestien.

Bb iiij

Lettre de consolation à vn Gentil-hom-
me qui auoit perdu son fils à
la guerre.

MONSIEVR,
I'ay sçeu en mesme temps
que les autres, l'accidét qui
est arriué à Monsieur vostre fils , &
j'eusse tasché de vous escrire incontinent si j'eusse trouué quelqu'vn
qui eust esté au lieu où vous estes: je
n'eusse pas voulu manquer à vous
mander l'opinion que chacun a de
sa mort , afin que cela vous seruist
de consolation, voyant que ses dernieres actions l'ont faict loüer de
tout le monde. Ie ne desirois pas que
l'on s'imaginast que ie ne voulusse
faire mes efforts pour vous côsoler,

que lors que vous l'auriez desia esté
par de meilleurs esprits que le mien.
Ie ne me soucie pas de ressembler à
ces Medecins que l'on n'estime sça-
uans & habiles en leur profession,
qu'à cause qu'ils ont esté appellez
sur la fin de la maladie. Ie sçay bien
que ceux qui vous ont pû parler ou
escrire les premiers n'ont pas mesme remporté toute la gloire, & que
c'est à vous que l'on en doit la meilleure part. C'est vous qui estes capable d'inuenter de meilleures consolatiõs que toutes celles que nous
vous pouuons donner. Vous auez
veu le monde bien plus que ie n'ay
fait, & vous auez esprouué plus de
fois quelles sont ses diuerses fortunes. Ie ne deurois pas seulement
prendre la hardiesse de vous en parler, si ce n'estoit que d'vn autre costé mon affection me presse, & que

ie ne puis me garentir de vous teſmoigner en toute ſorte d'affaires
que ie n'ay rien de ſi cher comme
les occaſions de vous rendre du
ſeruice. Permettez donc que ie vous
diſe que ie croy que vous n'auez
point de ſujet de regretter celuy qui
eſt mort dans la plus iuſte guerre du
monde apres y auoir rendu des eſ-
preuues ſignalees de ſon courage &
de ſon eſprit. L'on vint dire vne
fois à vn grand perſonnage que ſon
fils eſtoit mort. Il dit qu'il ſçauoit
bien que d'vn homme mortel comme luy il n'en eſtoit pas pû ſortir
vn fils immortel. Voila vne reſolution bien bruſque & bié digne d'vn
homme ſage ; mais en ce qui vous
eſt arriué il ne ſe faut pas ſeulemét
conſoler dans la conſideration de la
foibleſſe de la nature. Le genre de
mort fait beaucoup icy. C'eſt à faire

aux hommes communs à mourir
d'vne mort commune, mais ceux
qui sont elleuez au dessus des autres
ne meurent que pour des sujets ho-
norables. Il y eut autrefois vn Pere
cóme vous qui fut affligé d'abord
quand l'on luy dit que son fils estoit
mort à la guerre, mais ayant demádé si c'estoit en fuyant ou en poursuiuant l'ennemy, comme l'on luy
eut dit que c'estoit en poursuiuant
les ennemis de si pres qu'il s'estoit
trouué enfermé entr'eux & qu'il
n'auoit esté accablé que par la multitude, il se consola alors, & il alla
rendre des actions de graces aux
Dieux plustost que de leur faire des
plaintes : Vous auez de bons tes-
moins cóme M.^r vostre fils n'est pas
mort auec vne moindre generosi-
té. Il estoit de l'humeur du Capitaine Bayard qui mesme en mourant

ne vouloit pas auoir le dos tourné
aux ennemis, de peur que si l'on le
trouuoit en ceste posture, l'on ne
crust qu'il auroit esté poursuiuy par
eux plustost que de les poursuiure.
Que si quelques peuples n'auoient
iamais accoustumé de faire d'oraison funebre, ny de dresser aucun
Epitaphe que pour ceux qui auoiét
esté tuez à la guerre, quelles harangues ne faut il point faire pour celuy qui est mort en vn assaut où il
alloit d'vn si grand courage ? quels
Eloges ne luy faut-il point donner,
& quel marbre sera assez excellent
pour luy dresser vn tombeau ? C'est
à quoy pensent tous ceux qui ont
cognu celuy que vous regrettez.
L'on se represente la valeur qu'il
tesmoignoit dedans les combats, &
l'on songe encore au parfaict esprit
dont il donnoit tant de preuues

quand il estoit besoin de donner
quelque conseil. A peine eust on
pû croire iusques alors qu'vne telle
prudence eust esté compatible auec
vne si grande ieunesse ; mais il n'en
faut plus douter desormais, & vous
deuez vous resiouyr d'auoir eu vn
fils qui a merité des loüanges de
tout le monde. Vous me direz que
vous ne l'auez eu guere long temps,
mais vous l'auez eu assez pour
vous donner de la satisfaction, Dieu
vous le pouuoit oster plustost,
mais il ne l'a pas faict. Rendez luy
grace de ce qu'il vous l'a laissé si
long temps que l'on remarque vne
infinité de rares choses en toutes les
parties de sa vie. Il pouuoit mesme
ne le vous point donner du tout,
ou bien vous en donner vn qui eust
esté de mauuaise complexion , &
de qui vous n'eussiez rien esperé

que du scandale. C'est estre ingrat
de ne sçauoir aucun gré à nostre
bien-faicteur pour les plaisirs que
nous en auons receu, & de nous faf-
cher de ce qu'il ne nous en a point
encore donné dauantage. Nous ne
considerons pas si nous en sommes
dignes , comme en effect nous ne le
sommes pas si nous nous gouuer-
nons de ceste sorte. Outre l'offence
que vous feriez à Dieu si vous vous
faschiez de ce qu'il vous a osté vostre fils , il semble que vous ne tes-
moigneriez point l'affection que
vous auez toufiours portee à nostre
Roy. Vous sçauez bien que ce bra-
ue Gentil-homme est mort pour
son seruice & qu'il ne pouuoit employer sa vie en vne plus belle occasion. Nostre grand Monarque mesme a loüé sa vertu & a dit des paroles à son auantage qui sont dignes

de remarque. Lors qu'elles seront couchees dans l'histoire, elles serui-ront d'vn eternel ornement à vo-stre race. Il n'y aura personne d'en-tre les vostres qui souhaite que les choses se soient passees autrement qu'elles n'ont esté. C'est ce que i'ay consideré moy mesme lors que i'ay sceu les nouuelles de cette mort glo-rieuse. Ie ressétis d'abord vne extre-me affliction, mais ie trouuay de-quoy la moderer. Vous sçauez que i'ay fait mes exercices auec M.ͬ vôtre fils, & qu'encore que ie fusse de six ou sept ans plus âgé que luy, i'ay trou-ué tant de charmes dans son hu-meur que rié ne me pouuoit empes-cher de l'aymer eternellement. Ie m'estimois seul lors que i'estois auec vn autre que luy; Ie ne parlois point; ie ne faisois que resuer & mon esprit n'estoit occupé qu'à

songer aux dernieres paroles qu'il
m'auoit dictes, ou à celles que i'a-
uois à luy dire, ou bien ie m'amusois
à chercher de nouuelles inuentions
de luy plaire, & de luy tesmoigner
que l'affection que ie luy auois iu-
ree estoit fort veritable. Il faut que
ie vous aduoüe qu'il escrit d'vn si
bon naturel que de sa part il me rédoit les mesmes deuoirs. Iamais
nous n'auions de dispute ensemble;
Ie quitois mes opinions pour prendre celles qu'il auoit proposees, & il
me faisoit souuent la mesme courtoisie, de sorte que dedans nos conferences qui estoient exemptes de
contradiction, nous nous rendions
si conformes, bien que ce fust quelquefois par la seule complaisance,
que nous faisions trouuer veritable
ce qu'a dit vn des plus sçauants
d'entre les premiers Chrestiens;
Que

Que l'amitié trouue les hommes
de semblable humeur ou bien qu'elle les rend tels par la conuersation.
Ayant ainsi escoulé fort doucemét
quelques annees auec Monsieur
vostre fils, quel ennuy pensez-vous
que i'aye receu quand l'on m'a asseuré sa mort? Aurois-ie pas eu le
cœur bien dur si ie n'eusse regretté
vne si grande separation qui est
maintenant entre nous, veu que
mesme ie m'affligeois de sa moindre
absence? Neantmoins apres les premiers mouuemens il a fallu reuenir
à soy; Nos secondes pensees valent
mieux que les premieres. A la premiere attaque que l'ennuy donne
à nostre ame nous croyons que tout
est perdu pour nous, & qu'il nous
faut perdre aussi; mais quand les
choses sont venuës en vne parfaicte
maturité, nous en iugeons bien

C c

autrement. I'ay confideré où eftoit
mort celuy que ie regrettois, & pour
quelle occafion & de quelle forte
cela s'eftoit faict. I'ay trouué que
tout eftoit à fa gloire, & que pour ce
qui eftoit de nous fi nous ne deuiós
pas nous refioüyr, nous ne deuions
pas auffi nous affliger. En effect fi
l'on difoit ouuertemét que fa mort
nous contente, il fembleroit que
nous ferions fort aifes de ne l'auoir
plus auec nous, ce qui eft extremément faux; Il faut donc feulement
dire que l'on n'a point de defefpoir
pour l'auoir perdu, & qu'eftant
mort au lict d'honneur, l'on trouue du fubjet de fe confoler de fa
perte.

I'ay fongé à cela plus qu'à
autre chofe, & comme i'ay voulu tantoft vous faire entendre, ie

n'eſtime point vn Gétil-hôme malheureux, lors qu'il meurt pour le
ſeruice de ſon Roy. Mais il faut remarquer outre cela que nous auons
vn Monarque ſi remply de vertu
que rié ne ſçauroit plaire dauantage
à tous ſes ſujects que de le ſuiure en
toutes ſes guerres. C'eſt de luy que
l'on peut dire cóme de l'Empereur
Trajan, que les femmes s'eſtiment
heureuſes d'eſtre fecondes & de luy
auoir engendré des Soldats. Vous
auez encore vn fils qui n'eſt pas ſi
aagé que le deffunct. Tant s'en faut
qu'il ſe faille deſcourager pour
auoir perdu le premier à la guerre,
qu'au contraire il y faut encore
faire inſtruire cettuy-cy, afin qu'il
gagne de l'honneur par la meſme voye que ſon frere. Vous
ſçauez bien qu'en France il n'y

a point de vie plus honorable à vn
Gentil-homme que celle-là. Vous
l'auez touſiours pratiquee iuſques à
ce que vos maladies vous en ont
oſté la force. C'eſt pourquoy ie ne
penſe pas qu'vn homme de voſtre
condition puiſſe s'imaginer que ie
luy donne des conſolations cruelles.
Vous auez meſme deſia penſé à ce
que ie vous dy, & ie ne vous en parle que pour vous monſtrer que ie
n'ignore pas de quelle ſorte voꝰ vous
gouuernez dans l'accident qui vous
eſt ſuruenu. S'il y a quelqu'vn en
voſtre maiſon qui ſoit difficile à
perſuader, i'ay ouy dire que c'eſt la
mere de ce rare fils que vous auez
perdu auec'elle. Les raiſons des hómes de guerre ne peuuent pas ſi toſt
eſtre gouſtees par les femmes. C'eſt
ce qui m'a faict reſoudre à luy eſcrire, & ie croy que vous ne le trouue-

rez point mauuais. Elle m'a autrefois tefmoigné qu'elle auoit quelque creance en moy, fuiuant quelques rapports qui luy auoient efté
faicts à mon auantage. Ie voudrois
que mes perfuafions fuffent maintenant auffi puiffans fur fon efprit,
comme elles ont efté lors qu'il n'e-
ftoit pas fi fort agité. Ie vous affeure
qu'il n'y auroit point en cela de peine que ie ne tinffe pas bien em-
ployce, car ie fuis obligé d'aimer
eternellement le pere & mere dont
i'ay tant aymé le fils, & non feulemét en l'affaire qui fe prefente, mais
auffi en toute autre occafion, ie feray toufiours preft à vous monftrer
que ie fuis,

MONSIEVR,

Voftre tres-humble
& tres-affectionné
feruiteur.

Cc iij

Confolation à vne Dame fur la mort de fon fils.

MADAME,

Ie n'ay point voulu iufqu'à cette heure vous deffendre les larmes; Il eft certain que vous auez fait vne perte felon voftre opinion qui eft la plus grande qui vous pouuoit arriuer, car il vous femble qu'il n'y a rien que vous n'aymaffiez mieux auoir perdu que ce cher fils que vous auiez efleué auec tant de douceur; mais neantmoins il ne faut pas que vous vous perfuadiez que cette playe foit incurable, & qu'il vous foit permis de vous laiffer emporter au defefpoir. C'eft maintenant que ie ne fçaurois plus fouffrir que vous demeuriez dedãs ce dueil, qu'il femble que vous ne

vouliez iamais finir. Il m'est aduis
que sa violence doit estre bien tost
apaisee, & sur l'asseurance que i'en
ay, ie prés la hardiesse de vo° escrire,
afin que mes raisons vous aydent à
sortir d'vne humeur qui vous seroit
à la fin dōmageable. Ie sçay biē que
la tristesse veut estre flattee, la melā-
colie a cela de propre, qu'ēcore que
ce soit vne chose fort fascheuse, il
semble qu'elle nous apporte quelque volupté secrette & incognuë,
qui fait que nous nous faschōs cōtre
ceux qui nous en veulēt retirer. I'ay
dōc fait le complaisant lors que i'ay
creu qu'il estoit besoin de le faire,
mais voicy le iour venu qu'il ne faut
plus escrire que l'on est aussi affligé que vous. Ceux qui sont affligez ne peuuent que fort mal-aysément consoler les autres. Nous auōs
bien auec vous vne grande perte, &

nous le recognoiſſons auſſi claire-
ment, & encore plus ſi ie l'oſe dire,
que lors que la nouuelle nous en fut
apportee, mais nous auons cherché
de tous coſtez le moyen de nous reſoudre, & maintenant que nous l'a-
uons trouué nous ſommes bien aiſe
d'en faire part aux autres, & principalemét à vous qui y eſtes la plus in-
tereſſee. Vo⁹ me direz que ie ſuis bié
rude de vous parler ainſi, mais ne
ſçauez vous pas qu'il faut que les
Medecins qui ont entrepris de guerir quelque faſcheux mal ſoient ſans
compaſſion? Encore qu'ils entendét
crier le malade, il ne faut pas qu'ils
laiſſent de pourſuiure ce qu'ils ont
commencé, & de taſter les endroits
douloureux, & de les faire couper
s'ils s'aperçoiuent que la gangrei-
ne s'y mette ; Car le mal qu'ils
font au patient, n'eſt qu'vn mal

passager, & il en viendra apres vn
bié; au lieu que s'ils estoient trop in-
dulgens, ils seroiét cause qu'il souf-
friroit des douleurs de beaucoup pl⁹
grandes, & que la mort s'ensuiuroit
à la fin. Il faut que ceux qui se meslét
de guerir les maux de l'Ame suiuent
la mesme coustume, & leur humeur ne doit pas toutefois estre appellée cruauté, car il n'en vient apres
que du contentement & de la satisfaction. Ie ne dy pas cecy pour vous
aduoüer qu'il faille de necessité que
ie vous traitte rudement auparauãt
que de vous guerir des douleurs que
vous sentez ; Non, Madame, ce ne
fut iamais mon dessein. Ie n'ay pas
beaucoup de vanité ; mais i'oseray
bien dire sans craindre aucune reprehension, que dans l'occasion qui
se presente ie ne veux pas faire comme ceux qui d'ordinaire se meslent

d'apporter du remede aux affligez.
Ie ne veux point leur reſſembler en
cette rudeſſe qu'ils témoignét; j'en-
trepréd de vous guerir auec vn appareil le plus doux dót l'on puiſſe vſer.
C'eſt l'apprehenſion que vous auez
qui vous fait croire que ie vueille
vſer de quelque cruauté. Sçachez
que ie vous veux mener auec douceur iuſques à vne douceur encore
plus grande, & ie n'y mets point autre condition ſinon que vous vous
diſpoſiez de voſtre part à receuoir
mes remedes, & que vous eſcoutiez
pour vn peu de temps ce que i'ay enuie de vous dire.

Vous auez perdu vn fils qui
eſtoit beau, ieune, adroit, de bon eſprit, & qui en fin eſtoit à ce que vous
dites voſtre meilleure eſperance. Ie
cófeſſe auec vous qu'il auoit toutes
ces qualitez & encore dauantage:

mais deuez vo˒ pourtant vous mettre au defefpoir pour cette perte.
N'auez vous pas toufiours creu que
c'eft Dieu qui gouuerne toutes les
chofes du móde? Si cela eft, cet acci-
dẽt cy n'eft arriué que par fa volóté,
& par confequẽt il n'y a rien de plus
iufte que de fe conformer à ce qu'il
ordonne. Ie fçay que la foibleffe humaine eft fi grãde, qu'il n'eft pas poffible que toutes les ames ayent vne
fi ferme refolution; mais il la faut
prendre en fin quand les premiers
mouuements font ceffez. Confiderez que Dieu ne nous a pas mis en
ce móde cy pour n'y voir iamais riẽ
qui nous fafche. Ce n'a pas efté fon
intẽtion, car fi nous eftiós toufiours
heureux nous l'oublierions dãs cette continuelle profperité : nous
croirions qu'il nous feroit permis de
nous ietter inceffamment dedans

les vices; & d’autant que nous ferons dans vn Paradis terreſtre, nous ne chercherions iamais le Paradis du Ciel: les choſes vont bien d’vne autre ſorte; Dieu nous enuoye des afflictions dans cette vie afin de nous dóner ſubiect d’auoir recours à luy. Il en enuoye aux meſchans pour les chaſtier, & pour les faire ſonger à la repétance, & il en enuoye aux bons pour les eſprouuer. Vous qui eſtes du nombre de ces ames qui luy ont touſiours eſté ſi cheres, ne trouuez pas eſtráge s’il vous donne auſſi voſtre part des afflictions de la terre. Outre qu’il eſprouuera en cela voſtre patience, ſi vous vous diſpoſez à ſuporter le mal facilement, il fera que vous meriterez beaucoup dauantage, & qu’vne place digne de voſtre bonté vous ſera preparée dedans le Ciel. Comment eſt-ce que

l'on connoiſtroit voſtre vertu ſi iamais il ne s'eſtoit preſenté aucune
occaſion dela faire paroiſtre? Ie ſçay
bien que vous l'auez aſſez monſtree
parmy les plus grandes proſperitez,
d'autât que vous ne vous eſtes point
enflé d'orgueil, & que vous n'auez
point pris par excez des voluptez de
la terre; mais ce n'eſt encore là qu'v-
ne moitié du bien que vous pouuez
faire. Il ne ſe faut pas arreſter en ſi
beau chemin, & laiſſer voſtre vertu
imparfaicte. Dieu vous deſire donner vne entiere recompenſe. Faites
paroiſtre auſſi vne entiere vertu.

Il faut que vous conſideriez encore que le malheur qu'il vous a enuoyé n'eſt pas ſi grand comme il
pouuoit eſtre; car outre que la mort
de Monſieur voſtre fils a eu des cir-
conſtance qui en doiuent rendre
l'affliction moindre, & leſquelles ie

vous reprefenteray tantoft , c'eft
qu'il faut prendre garde que vous
pouuiez perdre encore plus que
vous n'auez perdu. Si vous penfez
que ie vous aye tantoft auoüé que
vous auez fait la plus grande perte
du monde, ie vous ay propofé feulement ce que vous penfiez ; car n'a-
uez vous pas encore vn mary &
d'autres enfans, lefquels vous pouuez perdre tous à la fois ? Si cela
eftoit arriué il fe faudroit encore refoudre à la volonté de Dieu, de forte que cela eft encore plus facile
maintenát que le mal n'eft pas fi có-
fiderable. Si vous ne perdez point
vos enfás, vous pourriez auffi perdre
tout voftre bien par des ruines de
maifons, par des larcins, par des procés, & par d'autres accidés, aufquels
vous ne fongez pas , & ce malheur
eftant arriué , poffible diriez vous

que vous seriez extremement miserable de vous voir si pauure , mais
ce qui seroit de plus fascheux en vostre misere, ce seroit d'auoir des enfans, ausquels vous ne pourriez faire
aucun bien", & seriez contrainte de
les voir mesprisez & abandonnez
faute d'auoir dequoy les entretenir
& les faire paroistre dans les grandes charges. Ne connoissez vous pas
des meres qui quelque bonne mine
qu'elles fassent, ne sont pas faschées
lorsque Dieu oste du mõde quelques
vns de leurs enfans quãd elles en sõt
trop chargées, & que leur familleest
en quelque necessité? Cela vous fait
voir que l'on se resout à toutes choses, mais ie nevous conseillerois pas
d'auoir de ces sortes de consolatiõs,
qui n'appartiennét qu'à des ames a-
uaricieuses & desnaturées. I'approuue bien l'affection que vous por-

rez à ceux que vous auez engédrez,
& ie croy que vous les preferez à
toutes les richeffes que vous pouuez
poffeder, mais ie ne laiffe pas de me
tenir dans l'opinion que i'ay , que
vous n'auez pas perdu tout ce que
vous pouuiez perdre, quand ce ne
feroit que vous auez d'autres enfans
de refte, vous auez vne fille qui eft
defia en l'âge où l'on commence à
poruoir celle de fon fexe. Plufieurs
perfonnes de qualité la demandent,
& la defirent auec affection. Vous
n'eftes que fur la difficulté du choix.
Ce n'eft pas peu que d'auoir vne fille fi fage, fi modefte & fi obeïffante
comme eft celle là; mais ce n'eft pas
tout, vous aurez encore par elle vn
gendre que vous choifirez à voftre
gré & qui vous tiendra lieu de fils.
Outre cela ils vous donneront des
enfans, & ils feront augmenter voftre

ſtre famille. Vous me direz que vo⁹
eſtiez bien aiſe de voir chez vous vn
garçon ſi accomply, & qu'vne fille
n'eſt rien au prix ; Que l'affection
que l'on porte à vn gendre eſt plus
forcée & moins naturelle que celle
que l'on a pour vn fils , & pour ce
qui eſt des petits enfans, que l'on ne
les ayme que d'vne amour aueugle,
qui n'a autre raiſon ſinon que ceſt
à cauſe qu'ils viennent de nous, &
non pas qu'ils nous y obligent encore par leur merite. Voyla ce que
vous pouuez me reſpondre ; mais
il y a beaucoup de choſes à repartir
là deſſus, & vous pouuez bien conſiderer vous meſme que les ſentimés
d'affection que vous receurez pour
ceux dont ie vous parle, ſe peuuent
rédre extremes: vous me direz peut-
eſtre que vous ne l'ignorez pas, &
que vous ſeriez encore plus ſatisfai-

Dd

te si vous auiez aussi vn fils. Vous
en auez encore vn de reste : c'est luy
faire tort que de regretter de cette sorte celuy que vous auez perdu , car vous tesmoignez que vous
n'auez pas vne si bonne opinion de
celuy qui vous reste , ie me doute
bien à quoy vous pensez. Vous ne
conceuez pas de petites esperances
de ce fils qui vous est demeuré, mais
vous vous representez que l'autre
estoit desia grand ,   & que cestuy-
cy est encore petit. Vous ne voyez
encore que les fleurs de son enfance, mais l'autre vous produisoit des-
ja des fruicts. Il faut auoir patience
vn peu de temps ; vous aurez le plaisir de le voir croistre, & vous vous
diuertirez à considerer de quelle
sorte il fera son proffit des instructions que l'on luy donnera.

Il me semble que ie vous entends

dire, quãd la jeuneſſe meurt, c'eſt en
effet vne mort plus faſcheuſe que
celle qui arriue ſur le declin de l'âge,
lors que le corps eſt caduque & lan-
guiſſant, d'autant qu'il n'y a pas ſi
grand chemin à faire pour l'vn que
pour l'autre, & que l'on n'a pas tant
de regret lors qu'vn homme à moitié mort, ne fait qu'acheuer de mourir. Ce ſont toutes fauſſes imaginations; Nous ſommes tous auſſi preſts
de la moït les vns que les autres. Il
eſt vray que les vieillards s'en vont
trouuer la mort eux meſmes, & pour
ce qui eſt des ieunes, elle les vient
trouuer quelquefois. Il n'y a que cela de difference, & encore en ce ſubjet vous auez quelque ſorte de conſolation, c'eſt que la mort n'eſt pas
venu trouuer celuy que vous regrettez lorsqu'il y pẽſoit le moins. Il n'eſt
pas mort d'vne ſoudaine maladie. Il

eſt mort dans vne guerre où pluſieurs autres ſont demeurez, & où il n'alloit pas ſans ſçauoir que l'on s'y trouuoit tous les iours au hazard de mourir. Par ce moyen il n'a pas eſté pris au deſpourueu ; & comme il auoit l'ame extremement bonne, il auoit pû ſonger à mettre ſa conſcience en bon eſtat , & à ſe tenir tout preſt comme s'il euſt deu mourir à toutes les heures.

Vous dictes bien ſouuent, Madame , qu'il meritoit de viure dauantage. Il eſt vray qu'il meritoit beaucoup , mais ce qu'il meritoit ne ſe trouuoit pas ſur la terre, & la vie dont il eſtoit digne ſe deuoit paſſer dans le Ciel. Comment iugez vous qu'il n'a pas aſſez veſcu au monde , veu qu'il y a tant laiſſé de marques de ſa vertu , qu'à ouyr compter toutes les

actions qu'il a faictes, il semble
que l'on fasse l'histoire d'vn homme de soixante ans ? Il a si bien
employé ses années que Dieu a veu
qu'il estoit desia meur pour estre
osté de la terre. Vous ne sçauez pas
ce que la Prouidence eternelle tient
caché. Il se peut faire que si Monsieur vostre fils eust vescu dauantage, il luy fust arriué des choses
qui eussent esté bien pires que la
mort. Ie ne veux pas dire que ses
bonnes inclinations se fussent chan-
gees, & qu'il eust commis quelque faute qui eust esté digne de
reprehension. I'ay vne trop bonne estime de sa vertu qui auoit
pris des racines bien fortes dedans
son ame ; mail il y a vne infinité de malheurs que nous ne considerons pas, lesquels s'ils luy fus-

Dd iij

sent arriuez , vous euffent donné
vne fafcherie nompareille.

Or puis qu'il eft mort fans auoir
iamais eu aucune infortune que celle qui l'a fait mourir , laquelle n'eft
pas encore fi grande que l'on penfe,
il faut auoir de la fatisfaction d'vne
fi heureufe vie. Il y a eu vne infinité
de Princes & de grands Seigneurs
dõt l'on admireroit encore auiour-
d'huy la bonne fortune , s'ils fuffent
morts à cet âge là, mais pource qu'ils
ont efté vn peu plus auant , ils ont
rencontré quelques accidens qui
ne manquent point à la vie humaine lors qu'elle eft longue , & depuis l'on les a toufiours appellez
malheureux. N'auez vous iamais
ouy parler de la maiftreffe du Roy
Charles feptiefme ? Pource qu'elle
eft morte en la fleur de fon âge lors
qu'elle poffedoit encore cette mer-

ueilleuſe beauté qui la faiſoit eſtimer par tout, l'on l'appelle encore la
belle Agnes. Que ſi elle euſt encore
paſſé de longues années , il ne luy
euſt pas eſté poſſible de conſeruer
ſon beau teinct , & l'on n'euſt pû
l'appeller belle que par mocquerie,
ſi bien qu'elle euſt ſurueſcu à la perte de ce nom , & parce que l'on ſe
fuſt deſaccouſtumé de le luy donner , elle ne l'euſt pas eu apres ſa
mort, & ſa poſterité ne la nomme-
roit pas de la ſorte.

Conſiderez auſſi que la fortune
reſſemble à cette beauté, & que celuy qui la pert auant que de mourir n'eſt plus eſtimé heureux. Or
cela eſt preſque auſſi infaillible de
perdre ſon bonheur ordinaire en viuant long temps, comme de perdre
la beauté de ſon viſage. Ie croy
que vous trouuez bon que ie vous

entretienne de la forte , & que ie
tire ainſi mes comparaiſons de la
beauté des femmes. Vous eſtes du
ſexe , & d'ailleurs vous poſſedez
la qualité dont nous parlons , &
vous ſçauez bien meſme qu'elle
eſtoit bien plus grande autrefois
en vous , qu'elle n'eſt à preſent.
Ie ne feins point de vous le dire,
car ie ſçay bien que vous faictes
beaucoup moins d'eſtat de cela que
de voſtre ſageſſe. Si ie parlois à
vn homme de guerre, ie luy ame-
nerois quelque exemple des Heros de l'antiquité, mais ie ne vous
ay voulu parler icy que d'vne des
plus renommées femmes de la
France. Pour reuenir au ſubjet de la
fortune de Monſieur voſtre fils , ie
croy que ſi vous y euſſiez remarqué
quelque changement, vous euſſiez

presque eu autant de desplaisir que
vous auez maintenant de sa mort. Ie
sçay bien que vostre dessein estoit
de le marier bien tost, mais que sçauons nous si ce n'estoit point de ce
costé-là qu'il luy eust peu arriuer
quelque chose de fascheux. La femme que l'on luy eust donnee n'eust
pas peut-estre esté de si bonne humeur que luy. Vous eussiez eu beaucoup de regret de l'auoir mis dans
vn si grand martyre, mais pource
que ce nœud ne se peut desnoüer,
vous l'eussiez veu languir dans vne
gesne perpetuelle, & vous n'eussiez
pas moins souffert que luy. N'est-
il pas vray que vous auez dict, qu'au
moins ce vous eust esté beaucoup
de satisfaction si vous l'eussiez veu
marié auparauant que de mourir,
encore qu'il ne l'eust guere esté:
vous vous figurez que vous auez

fait vne grande faute de ne le point
marier l'annee qu'il a esté à la guerre, & en difant cela vous vous imaginez auſſi, que la conſideration
d'vne femme l'euſt empeſché d'aller aux occaſions où ſon deuoir
l'appelloit;mais c'eſt vne fauſſe opinion: Il eſtoit trop genereux pour
manquer de ſe trouuer au lieu où alloit toute la Nobleſſe de ſon âge, &
où les vieillards meſme ſe ſentoient
encore tres-heureux d'aller; Et cela eſtant voſtre affliction euſt elle
eſté moindre lors que l'on vous euſt
apporté les nouuelles de ſa mort?
N'euſsiez vous pas eu vn double
ſubject de vous affliger lors que
vous euſsiez veu vne ieune veufue
qui fuſt venu pleurer auecque vous?
Croyez moy, MADAME, que
Dieu fait les choſes au mieux qu'elles puiſſent eſtre, & que nous n'a-

uons plus que faire d'y rien fou-
haiter. Que si ce cher fils n'eust
point encore esté à ceste guerre, il
pouuoit aller à vne autre quelques annees apres, ou bien il pouuoit mourir autrement, de sorte
que vostre regret n'eust pas esté
moindre, mais plustost il eust esté
plus grand, car si vous regrettez la
mort d'vn ieune homme accomply, vous eussiez regretté celle d'vn
homme parfaict. D'ailleurs il eust
sans doute laissé de petits enfans,
qui vous eussent faict beaucoup de
pitié, les voyant priuez de leur pere.

Ie ne sçay si vous trouuez à redire au genre de mort qu'il a esprouué. Vous estes faschee de ce qu'il est
mort loin de vous, mais eussiez vous
eu le courage de le voir mourir? vo⁹
eusiez voulu mourir auec luy sans
qu'aucune chose vous en eust peu

empefcher. Lors qu'il fut bleffé d'vn coup mortel, l'on l'apporta dans vne tente de guerre, où les Chirurgiens l'ayans vifité, dirent qu'il falloit pluftoft fonger au falut de fon ame qu'à celuy de fon corps qui ne tendoit qu'à la mort. Fuffiez vous pû voir alors les cierges allu-mez, le Preftre à fon cheuet, & les larmes de tous fes feruiteurs, fans vous efuanoüyr? Alors que vous euſsiez prefque efté au pareil eftat que luy, & que l'on n'euft pas moins efté empefché apres vous, à quoy eft-ce que vous euſsiez pû luy eftre vtile? Vous auez v-ne bonne opinion de voftre for-ce; vous croyez qu'elle vous fuft demeuree; mais quand cela euft efté, il ne me femble point que vous luy euſsiez pû feruir en quel-que chofe. Vous auez trop de bon esprit pour estre dans l'erreur des simples femmes qui parlent de la mort comme si c'estoit quelque chose de visible, & qui à cause qu'ils l'ont veüe peinte en squelette, s'imaginent que c'est quelque demon qui est fait ainsi, & qui va fraper de son dard ceux qui sont condamnez à sortir du monde? Si vous eussiez creu cela, eussiez vous voulu lutter contre ceste mauuaise, qui ne feroit rien sans le commandement de son maistre, quand elle seroit veritablement? mais puis qu'elle n'est rien, vous voyez que tous vos efforts eussent esté inutiles, & que vous n'eussiez pû empescher qu'vne ame fust sortie d'vn corps par les ouuertures incurables qu'vn coup de canon luy auoit faictes.

Vous me direz qu'au moins vous eussiez eu le contentement de fermer les yeux à voſtre fils. Ne ſongez point à cela, il n'en ſeroit plus heureux ny vous pareillement. Ce n'a eſté que dans la religion des Payens, que l'on a creu que ces choſes fuſſent abſoluëment necef-ſaires.

Au reſte pour eſtre mort loin de vous, ne croyez pas que l'on ayt moins ſongé à ſon ſalut. Si l'on luy euſt pu ſauuer la vie, cela euſt eſté faict. Il n'y a point eu de negligen-ce de la part des Chirurgiens, qui eſtoient des plus habiles qui ſe trou-uent en France, & qui luy furent meſmes enuoyez par le comman-dement du Roy. En ce qui eſt de ſon ame, ie ne doute point qu'el-le ne ſoit maintenant dans vne ioye parfaicte.

Chacun ſçait quelle eſtoit ſa pieté ordinaire, mais outre cela

pluſieurs bons Religieux & quelques Gentils hommes de marque
qui ſe ſont trouuez à ſa mort, teſ-
moignent qu'auant que de mourir, il a dit des choſes qui euſſent
eſté capables de conuertir les hommes les plus perdus, & qu'ils s'en
ſouuiendront toute leur vie, pour
leur ſeruir de conſolation dans toutes les miſeres qui leur pourront ſur-
uenir.

Si vous conſiderez apres cecy
quelle a eſté l'occaſion de ſa mort,
Ie croy que vous y deuez pluſtoſt
trouuer vne matiere de ioye que
de triſteſſe. Il eſt mort dans vne
guerre qui ſe faiſoit pour le ſeruice de ſon Prince, & pour le
bien de ſa patrie. En quoy eſt-ce
qu'vne vie peut-eſtre mieux employee ? C'eſt vn coup de canon
qui l'a frappé ; Qu'importe t'il

en cela, la mort n'en eſt que plus
glorieuſe. Ce coup eſtoit ineuita-
ble. Il ne le pouuoit pas payer comme vn coup d'eſpee. Il ſuffit que l'on
ſçache qu'auparauant il auoit monſtré ſa valeur en pluſieurs rencontres. Apres tant de belles actions
dont il reçoit la recompéſe au Ciel,
ſa memoire ſera eternelle ſur la terre, & l'on ne parlera iamais de luy
qu'auec honneur. Il eſt vray qu'il
ne laiſſe point d'enfans : mais vous
auez encore vn fils qui empeſchera
que le nom de Monſieur voſtre
mary ne ſe perde. Dauantage vous
deuez croire que les victoires qu'il
a remportees en particulier ſur chacun de ceux contre qui il a combat-
tu, luy tiendront lieu d'vne longue
poſterité, & qu'elles ſeruiront à rendre ſa memoire eternelle. Vn ancié
Capitaine ſe conſoloit en mourant

de

de ce qu'il auoit laiſſé deux filles
immortelles qui eſtoient les deux
victoires qu'il auoit emportees dás
la Grece. Il faut que vous preniez
pour vous vne meſme conſolation.
Il eſt vray que cela vous ſera plus
difficile, d'autant que vous eſtes
d'vn ſexe qui n'eſt pas né pour la
guerre, & qui en euite les hazards;
mais repreſentez vous que celuy
que vous regrettez s'eſt repreſenté
cette meſine choſe, & que luy-meſme il n'a pas eu de regret à mourir.
Quelle gloire auroit il emportee
s'il auoit mené vne vie oyſiue, & s'il
s'eſtoit retiré dans les champs comme ces Eſprits vulgaires qui n'ont
rien de la Nobleſſe que le nom.
A presqu'il euſt eſté mort l'on n'euſt
iamais parlé de luy A peine euſt on
ſceu qu'il euſt eſté au monde. Mais
deſormais encore qu'il ne ſoit plus

E e

icy, l'on parlera de luy dauantage
que lors qu'il eſtoit viuant. Nos hiſtoires ne manqueront pas à faire
mention de ſa valeur, & l'on eſcri-
ra ſes actions au meſme liure qui
n'eſt fait que pour immortaliſer la
vertu des Princes. Ce ſerôt de bons
tiltres pour la Nobleſſe de voſtre
maiſon, & ceux qui viendrôt apres
vous honoreront voſtre race où il
y aura eu vn perſonnage ſi excellét.

Vous voyez donc à ceſte heure
comme vous auez tout ſubjet de
vous conſoler, & que vous ne deuez pas eſtre inceſſamment affligee
pour auoir perdu vn fils, ny pour
conſiderer que ce fils eſtoit extremement vertueux, & qu'il eſtoit en
la fleur de ſon aage, ne faiſant encore que commencer de vous donner
le contentement que vous en deſi-
riez. Qu'il ayt eſté marié ou non,

c'eſt à quoy vous ne deuez point
ſonger, & pour ce qui eſt du genre
de mort, il n'a point de circonſtan-
ce qui puiſſe authoriſer voſtre triſteſſe. Tout ce que vous redites ſans
ceſſe, lors que l'on a reſpondu à vos
principales obiectiós, c'eſt que quoy
que l'on vous puiſſe dire, vous ne
pouuez ceſſer de pleurer la mort
d'vn fils que vous aymiez extremément; Ie vous accorde cela, mais
ſçachez que Dieu ne l'aymoit pas
moins. Il l'a voulu auoir pour ſoy;
ſeriez vous bien ſi temeraire que
de luy refuſer vne choſe qui luy ap-
partiét? Voulez vous eſtre preferable au Createur de toutes choſes? Il
vous auoit dóné vn bien à códition
de vous l'oſter quand il voudroit.
Vous n'en ioüyſſiez que par emprunt, & non point en propre, &
puis en quelle occaſion penſez vous

que Dieu oste les dons qu'il a faicts à ses creatures ? Cela ne se faict point par hasard ; Tout est reglé par vne souueraine prouidence. Asseurez vous que quand Dieu nous oste quelque chose, c'est qu'il preuoit que nous sommes sur les termes d'en mal vser. Vous fiez vous tant sur la force de voftre esprit que de croire que iamais vous n'euffiez pû faillir de ceste forte ? Nous ne recognoiffons pas nous mefmes par quel endroit c'est que nous sommes les plus foibles. C'est souuent en ce que nous croyons auoir de plus asfeuré contre toute sorte d'attaques: Ce qui cause noftre foiblesse, c'est le mefpris que nous faisons de songer à nous conseruer. Les ennemis augmentent leur puiffance cependant que nous negligeons de nous tenir sur la deffensiue & que nous

nous figurons qu'ils n'auront iamais assez de hardiesse pour nous
assaillir. Ie ne veux pas pourtant
vous faire ce tort de vous soustenir
que vous pouuiez faire vne semblable faute.

Si l'on iuge de l'aduenir par ce
qui est desia passé, il faut conclurre
que vous eussiez tasché de vous rendre tousiours semblable à vous-
mesmes, c'est à dire extrememenꞇ
vertueuse, & extrememenꞇ moderee. La prosperité ne vous eust iamais donné d'orgueil & vous n'eussiez pas oublié la puissance de Dieu.
Ie croy bien tout cela, & si ie vous
ay proposé le contraire, ce n'a esté
que pour vous donner vn exemple
de la fragilité humaine. Mais quoy
que nous nous asseurions que vous
n'eussiez iamais abusé de la bonté
de Dieu, ne pouuoit il pas arriuer,

d'autres accidens où vous ne prenez
pas garde, pour lesquels il n'estoit
pas à propos que vostre fils demeu-
rast plus long temps au monde. De
vous dire ce que c'est, c'est vn trop
grand secret qui est reserué à la pro-
uidéce diuine. Nous ne sçauons pas
mesme si cela estoit dómageable à
sa personne propre, ou à celle de ses
plus proches parés de demeurer plus
long temps icy : neantmoins nous
pouuons dire, auec autant d'asseurance comme il est permis d'en prédre à de pauures hommes, que cela
le regarde plustost qu'aucun autre,
& que c'estoit son bó-heur de mourir puis qu'il est mort. Il ne faut
point dire qu'il est mort trop tost
ou trop tard. Personne ne meurt
auant son heure, qui est tousiours
donnee au téps qu'elle estoit le plus
à propos. C'est vne chose que nous

remarquerons facilement ſi nous voulons conſiderer de toutes -façons l'eſtat de ceux qui meurent.

Cela eſtant ainſi, MADAME, ne vous affligez plus d'vne mort qui n'eſt point venüe auãt ſa ſaiſon, puis qu'elle n'eſt arriuee que de la volonté de Dieu qui ſçait mieux que nous tout ce qui nous eſt neceſſaire. Vous me direz à la fin qu'il eſt bien ayſé de parler de la ſorte à ceux qui ne ſont point intereſſez. Ie vous ay deſja dict que ie le ſuis grandement, & il faut que vous ſçachiez que tous mes freres ne le ſont pas moins que moy; car dés que nous eſtions dans les Academies des lettres, & depuis dans celle des armes, nous auions contracté vne ferme amitié auec Monſieur voſtre fils, & cela nous eſt bien eſtrange d'auoir eſté priuez d'vne ſi douce

E e iiij

conuerſation. Neantmoins nous
auons faict ce qui nous a eſté poſſible pour alleger noſtre douleur.
Que ſi cet exemple n'eſt pas encore
aſſez grand, vous en auez vn meilleur aupres de vous. Vous voyez
que Monſieur voſtre mary ſe con-
ſole de luy-meſme, & qu'il ne fait
aucune actió qui reſmoigne du deſeſpoir. Ie luy ay eſcrit auſſi par la
meſme voye que ie vous ay enuoyé
cette lettre, & comme ie ſçay qu'il
a deſia pris de luy-meſme les reſolu-
tions que doit auoir vn homme de
vertu, ie ne luy propoſe pas tout ce
que ie vous ay propoſé. Cela ſeroit
ſuperflu en ſon endroit. Ie le cófirme
ſeulemét en la conſtáce qu'il a priſe.
Vous ne me direz pas qu'il ayt
moins d'intereſt que vous en l'affaire. Celuy qui eſt mort eſtoit auſſi
ſon fils. Il voyoit en luy vne viue

image de ses vertus qui l'incitoit de plus en plus à le cherir. Il est vray que vous me direz qu'il est homme, & que par côsequent il a l'ame plus forte. Ie vous accorde cela & vous dy dauâtage qu'il n'est pas des hommes communs, mais de ceux qui excelent par dessus les autres. Que si vous vous imaginez que l'homme soit la perfection de la nature, taschez d'auoir vn courage viril. Vous ne serez pas la premiere qui a tasché de renoncer à la foiblesse de son sexe. Imitez la generosité de celuy que vous auez tousiours deuant les yeux. Gouuernez-vous de la mesme sorte qu'il fera en ce qui est du mespris des infortunes, & de la resistance que l'on doit faire aux passions. Escoutez de bon cœur les côsolations qu'il vous donnera; c'est à luy que ie vous renuoye encore, si

mes difcours n'ont pas eu affez d'effect. Il eft plus capable de vous fou-
lager que perfonne du monde, & ie
n'euffe pas entreprisde le faire n'euft
efté que i'euffe creu manquer à mon
deuoir fi ie ne vous euffe point efcrit en vne telle occafió; mais quoy
que i'aye fait en cela ie croiray touf-
jours auoir affez faict pour moy, fi
ievous ay pû témoigner que ie veux
eftre eternellement.

MADAME,

> Voftre tres-humble
> & tres-affectionné
> feruiteur.

Autre consolation à vne Dame sur la mort de son mary.

MADAME,
Il est vray que vous auez perdu vn mary qui estoit le plus sage, le plus deuot. & de la plus parfaite amitié du monde. Si quelqu'vn pensoit vous consoler en vous disant le contraire, au lieu de guarir vostre mal, il vous irriteroit contre luy, & ne meriteroit pas le nom & le tiltre d'Orateur, mais celuy du plus meschant de tous les hommes. Tant s'en faut donc que ie vueille abaisser le merite de celui que vous regrettez pour en amoindrir la perte, qu'au contraire ie me tiens

tout preft à luy faire fi vous voulez
vne oraifon funebre, & à luy donner tous les eloges dót vous croyez
qu'il foit digne. C'eft eftre ingrat de
refufer de la loüange à ceux qui en
meritent, & principalement lors
qu'ils font fortis de cette vie & qu'ils
ne poffedent plus rien de tout ce qui
eft fur la terre que de la renommée;
mais encore que ie vous accorde
que le merite du deffunct eftoit in-
eftimable, ie n'approuue pas pourtant l'excez de voftre dueil. Il faut
qu'il y ayt vne mefure à toutes chofes; c'eft de cela maintenant qu'il s'a-
gift. Vous auez bien veu qu'il n'y a
rien qui ne doiue auoir fon terme,
puifque celuy que vous cheriffez tát
l'a bien eu; il faut auffi mettre fin à
voftre deuil. Voulez vous pleurer
eternellement à caufe que voftre
mary n'a pû eftre eternel? C'eft eftre

iniuste de vouloir que la nature faſſe pour nous des loix à part, & que
nous ſoyons exempts des choſes generales. Nous ſommes ſubjects à la
mort depuis le peché du premier
homme. Perſonne ne s'en exemptera; le momēt où nous naiſſons nous
oblige à mourir. Les Payens l'ont
bien cogneu dedans leurs erreurs, de
ſorte que les Chreſtiens ſont encore
plus obligez à le croire. Encore ſi
celuy que vous auez veu mourir
euſt eſté fort ieune, vous diriez
qu'il pouuoit viure encore plus lóg
temps; mais vous ſçauez bien qu'il
auoit deſia paſſé autant d'années
qu'il en faut à vn homme pour le
mettre au rang des vieillards.

Il faut que ie vous raconte vne
choſe qui vous apportera quelque
conſolation. Nous ne ſçaurions tirer d'vn plus bel endroict que de

l’hiſtoire, des remedes pour nos inꞏ
fortunes. Vous pouuez auoir ouy
parler de Thomas Morus qui eſtoit
Chancelier d’Angleterre, & meſme
i’ay trouué ſouuent chez vous quelques vnes de ſes œuures. Cettuy-cy
eſtant en priſon pour n’auoir pas
voulu accorder des choſes qui
eſtoient contre la raiſon & la iuſtice, l’on luy diſoit tous les iours qu’il
changeaſt d’aduis s’il vouloit ſauuer
ſa vie, & ſa femme eſtant aſſeurée
que l’on ne luy feroit aucun mal s’il
deſiroit conſentir aux nouueautez
d’Angleterre, elle luy repreſēta qu’il
ne deuoit point refuſer le pardō que
l’on luy offroit & qu’il ſe deuoit cō-
ſeruer tant pour ſon bien que celuy
de ſa femme & de ſes enfans. Ce genereux homme luy demanda alors
combien elle penſoit qu’il puſt viure encore ſelon le cours de nature

s'il ne souffroit point vne mort violente. Elle luy repartit que voyant
la santé où il estoit & les forces de
son corps qu'il auoit conseruées , elle auoit bonne esperance qu'il pourroit encore viure plus de vingt ans.
Ie vous accorde cela, ma chere femme, luy dit-il, mais voyez quel in-
digne choix ie feray si ie vous croy.
Ie feray eschange de l'immortalité
à vn si petit espace que celuy de
vingt années que vous trouuerez
plus courtes que vous ne pensez. Thomas Morus ayant dict
cela , sa femme vid bien qu'il le falloit laisser dans sa resolution , &
qu'il aymoit mieux mourir que
d'achepter sa vie par de mauuaises
actions.

Vous n'auez iamais esté re-
duicte à ce poinct extréme , mais
neantmoins cet exemple vous peut

beaucoup feruir tant pour vous faire mefprifer la vie, que pour vous
faire eftimer vne mort honorable.
Outre cela vous y pouuez rapporter
quelque chofe à ce qui vous eft arriué; l'on m'a raconté que vous di-
fiez fouuent à voftre mary qu'il fe
deuoit retirer des affaires publiques,
que le foin qu'il en prenoit luy abre-
geoit fes iours; mais qu'il vous faifoit toufiours refpôfe qu'il vouloit
viure & mourir dans fa charge, que
les affaires eftoient fon element, &
qu'il ne les pouuoit quitter que lors
qu'il plairoit à Dieu de l'en retirer.
Vous voyez donc côme il a mieux
aymé mourir auec honneur & eftre
regretté de tout le peuple, que de
tafcher de fe conferuer dans l'oyfiueté: car tout le monde l'euft abandonné alors: Il n'euft plus efté vtile à
aucune chofe, & tant s'en faut qu'il

en euſt veſcu dauantage, que dés le
moment qu'il ſe fuſt retiré des affaires il euſt eſté ſemblableà vn mort,
& l'on l'euſt eſtimé tel, n'ayant plus
aucune fonction; & quand le iour
fuſtvenu que l'on l'euſt enterré tout
à fait, perſonne n'en euſt témoigné
du reſſentiment. Il euſt deſia eſté
mis au nombre des choſes paſſees &
de celles que l'on auoit oubliées. Cela eſt bien arriué d'vne autre ſorte,
car l'on n'a pas ſi toſt ſçeu dans Paris
qu'il eſtoit mort, que to⁹ ceux qui a-
uoiét eu affaire à luy, & qui par cóſe-
quent en auoiét eu de la ſatisfaction
témoignerent vn grand regret de ſa
perte. Ce n'eſt pas tout encore, les
faſcheries ſeruent de peu en cecy, &
c'eſt cela que j'entreprens de vous
perſuader dans cette lettre, mais dauantage, il n'y euſt perſonne qui ne
fiſt des prieres pour luy, & vous eu-

ftes le bien de voir que chacun portoit le dueil dedans l'ame.

Au reſte il ne ſe faut pas meſme
imaginer qu'en effect ſes ſoins &
ſes trauaux l'ayent faict mourir
pluſtoſt qu'il n'euſt faict s'il euſt
quitté ſa charge. L'on ſçait bien
que les affaires eſtoient ſon diuer-
tiſſement auquel il s'eſtoit accouſtumé de jeuneſſe. S'il n'en euſt
plus eu , il n'euſt ſceu de quel coſté ſe tourner ; il fuſt demeuré
dedans vn faſcheux ennuy. D'ailleurs combien en voyez vous qui
viuent dauantage qu'il n'a faict?
Il eſtoit ſur la ſoixante & ſixieſ-
me année de ſon aage. Voudriez
vous qu'il fuſt paruenu iuſques à
quatre vingts dix ans , comme a
faict l'vn de ſes oncles ? Si cela
euſt eſté il euſt ſouffert long temps
les plus grandes miſeres de la vie

humaine qui fe trouuent toufiours
fur la fin. Les gouttes l'euffent
poffible merueilleufement incom-
modé, car il les fentoit depuis quelque temps. C'euft efté vne chofe
bien pitoyable de le voir tant fouffrir fans le pouuoir alleger, puis que
ces fortes de maux font quafi fans remede. Il luy fuft peut-eftre venu
quelque vlcere ou quelque autre
forte de maladie où il euft fallu que
les Chirurgiés euffent operé auffi bié
que les Medecins. Vous euffiez veu
alors ces gens là couper de fa chair
auec auffi peu de pitié que fi elle euft
efté morte, & ils euffent fait deuant
vo⁹ vne anatomie d'vn corps viuãt.
Que fçait-on s'il n'euft point auffi e-
fté malade de la pierre, veu que de
tout téps l'on l'a ouy plaindre d'vne
difficulté d'vrine: Mon Dieu, euffiez
pû foufrir le mal que vous euffiez re-

çeu de le voir entre les mains de ceux
qui luy en euſſent tant fait endurer.
L'on appelle les Chirurgiés les bourreaux des pechez de la Nature. Ils
puniſſent ſans compaſſion les fautes
de noſtre corps, & qui plus eſt ils le
font ſans offence, parce que cela eſt
neceſſaire, & que s'ils ne le faiſoient,
il en arriueroit vn plus grand mal.
Vous n'euſſiez pas oſé leur empeſcher de faire leur charge. Qui eſt-
ce qui nous pourra aſſeurer d'ailleurs, que voſtre mary ne deuint
point paralytique & qu'il ne faluſt
point luy ayder à ſe remuer d'vn coſté & d'autre dans ſon lict cóme s'il
euſt eſté vne ſouche? Commét eſt-ce
auſſi que l'on l'euſt pû empeſcher de
deuenir en enfance & de perdre l'v-
ſage de la raiſon qui eſt la principale
partie des hommes? Quelle differé-
ce eſt-ce que vous euſſiez trouuée

alors entre luy & vn mort? Cóbien
de trauail euſt-il falu prédre pour le
faire manger, & pour luy faire prendre des drogues? vous vous aſſeurez
ſur vos forces, & ie veux bien vous
aduoüer qu'elles ſont auſſi grandes
que voſtre courage; mais neátmoins
la faſcherie que vous euſſiez euë de
le voir en vn eſtat ſi miſerable vous
euſt eſté inſuportable. Pour ce qui
eſt de luy, vo⁹ ſçauez bié qu'il n'euſt
pas eſté en vne códition fort agreable. Or l'on ne ſçauroit ſouhaitter de
l'auoir veu viure plus longuement
ſans l'auoir veu auſſi dans quelqu'vn
de ces maux, car il n'y en a guere à
qui ils n'arriuent L'on deſire donc
ſon mal quand l'on dit que l'on
voudroit que ſa vie euſt eſté plus ló-
gue. Vous ne voudriez pas faire vne
ſi gráde faute que de regretter qu'il
n'ayt point eu des maux dont il s'eſt

exempté en mourant. Ne faites dóc
point des fouhaits pour vne plus ló-
gue vie, veu que d'ailleurs cela eſt
inutile & que l'on ne le peut reſſuſciter.

Vous ne deſirez pas qu'il reuien-
ne au monde. Ce ſeroit le deſir le
plus vain que vous pourriez faire. Il
n'y a que ceux qui ont perdu la raiſon qui deſirent les choſes impoſſi-
bles; mais vous eſtes faſchée pourtant de ce qu'il n'eſt plus icy. Vous
ſçauez bien qu'il eſtoit dás vne mer
perilleuſe; vous n'ignorez pas qu'il
eſtoit au hazard de faire naufrage
puis que chacun y eſt expoſé. Vous
auiez veu deſia que l'on l'auoit voulu choquer quelque fois, & vous ne
croyez pas qu'il ſoit auiourd'huy
fort fort heureux d'eſtre arriué au
port. Non ſeulement ce luy eſt vn
bien d'auoir quitté les miſeres hu-

maines, mais de s'eftre mefme efleué
iufques aux delices du Ciel dont il
ne faut point douter qu'il ne jouyf-
fe pour la recompenfe de fes ver-
tucufes actions.

L'on cognoift affez que ce ne
doit point eftre pour fon fubiet que
vous faites des regrets, c'eft pour le
vôtre. Il eft en vn trop heureux eftat
pour le plaindre, c'eft vous que vous
plaignez, vous regrettez fa compagnie où vous eftiez accouftumée.
Vne feule de fes paroles eftoit capable de vous guerir toute forte d'ennuys. En le voyant feulemét vous e-
ftiez toute cófolee, quelque accidét
qui vo' fuft arriué, mais vous imaginez vous que le lien dót vous eftiez
joints fuft eternel? Ne fongiez vous
point à la mort que vous auez
veuë en tant de lieux depuis que
vous viuez ? Il falloit iuger qu'vn

iour vous la pourriez voir aussi dans
vostre maison & qu'il s'y faudroit
resoudre. Vous estes de l'humeur
de ces mondains qui croyent qu'il
n'en faut iamais parler, & que c'est
vn secret pour viure en repos sans se
tourmenter l'esprit. Si l'on parle
d'vn homme mort, l'on dit seulement, il est trespassé, & ie le trouue
bon si l'on le dit pour monstrer que
la mort n'est qu'vn passage d'vn lieu
à l'autre, & pour auoir vne ferme
resolution; mais si c'est par déguise-
ment & par flatterie, l'on ne parle
pas entierement comme l'on deuroit. Il y a eu autrefois des peuples si corrompus qu'ils dégui-
soient ainsi tous les accidents du
monde, non pour les souffrir
plus constamment ; mais afin de
ne se point affliger lors qu'ils y
songeroient. Ils appelloient l'e-

xil vne retraicte, la prison vne maison asseuree, & le tombeau la maison derniere, il ne faut pas desguiser ainsi les choses. Il en faut parler franchement. Puis que nous sommes subiets à la mort, il le faut dire, afin que nous nous y prepariõs. C'est vn mauuais signe quand l'on n'en veut point ouyr parler; C'est que l'on sent sa conscience chargee de quelques fautes, & que l'on craint d'aller rédre compte au souuerain Iuge qui punira ceux qui n'auront pas voulu quitter leurs vices. Ie ne croy pas que vous ayez iamais adheré à de si pernicieuses maximes.

Ne faites donc point voir en apparéce que vous n'ayez point sceu ce que c'est que de la mort. Il n'est rien arriué d'extraordinaire en vostre famille, & vous-mesme qui regrettez

la mort des autres , vous ferez vn
iour ce qu'ils font. Il ne fe faut donc
pas plaindre de ce que voftre mary
eft allé en vn lieu où vous deuez aller auffi. Si vous auiez vne infinité
de fiecles à paffer dans la folitude du
veufuage, peut eftre que voftre dueil
feroit plus excufable: mais fans vous
flatter, à voir la courte duree de la
vie des autres, vous iugez bien s'il
n'en peut pas autant arriuer à vous.
Employez dóc voftre temps à vous
preparer pour ce grand iour qui eft
le maiftre des autres, & qui fait plus
que pas-vn pour noftre falut ou noftre condamnation. Quittez ces
plaintes inutiles qui font dignes de
blafme lors qu'elles font exceffi-
ues. Refioüyffez-vous de ce que
vous n'auez pas perdu entierement
celuy que voftre affection vous
faifoit nommer la moitié de vous-

mefme. Nous croyons qu'il eft
maintenant dedans le Ciel, où il
ioüyt de toutes les felicitez qu'il a
tafché d'acquerir par fa deuotion.
Puifque voftre moitié eft en vn fi
digne lieu, efforcez-vous d'y mettre auffi le refte. Efleuez vous iufques à cette bien-heureufe région
où les plaifirs font eternels, & où
les ennuys n'ont point de place.
Si vous auez faict des prieres pour
ce cher mary ; il en fera pour vous
en recompenfe. Il vous aydera à
monter iufques au fommet de la
gloire, pourueu que vous faf-
fiez tous vos efforts de voftre
part.

Conuertiffez-vous à Dieu premierement pour vous rendre digne des biens que vous defirez ; Ne fongez plus qu'à cette haufte Majefté qui a creé le

monde. Dites luy dans l'ardeur de vos prieres que vous estes contente d'auoir perdu celuy qui vous auoit esté donné pour espoux, & que ce n'est qu'vne legere afflictió au prix de celles que vous desireriez souffrir pour l'amour de vostre Dieu. Si vous faites cela vous en tirerez plus de satisfaction que de vos souspirs & de vos plaintes. Il ne sera plus besoin de vous consoler; Ce sera vous qui ferez capable de consoler les autres. Vous sentirez tous les iours des ioyes interieures qui vous rauiront, & qui ne vous feront plus regretter autre chose que le temps que vous n'aurez pas employé à de si belles meditatiós. Ie m'asseure bié que vostre esprit se portera infailliblement à toutes ces choses, c'est pourquoy ie n'ay point creu perdre mes peines de vous parler cóme i'ay faict,

Ie vous prie donc d'estre satisfaicte
de la bonne volonté que i'ay euë &
de croire que ie suis,

MADAME,

Vostre tres-humble
& tres-affectionné
seruiteur.

Confolation à vne ieune Dame qui auoit perdu fon mary.

MADAME,
L'on ne fçauroit racheter par les larmes celuy que vous regrettez. Vn feul homme ne peut pas auoir plus d'vne vie. Il faut fe refoudre aux chofes qui font arriuees, puis qu'il n'y a pas moyen de faire qu'elles foient autrement qu'elles ne font. Si vos amys communs ont regretté la perte de voftre mary, voulez-vous qu'ils regrettent encore la voftre? Il n'eft pas befoin que nous perdions tout. Conferuez nous le bien que nous auons de voftre prefence. N'accourciffez point vos iours par

vn ennuy continuel; Ce seroit dommage qu'estant si ieune vous allas-
siez de vous-mesme chercher vostre fin. Nous ne sommes pas en ce
cruel pays où les femmes sont obli-
gees de s'enterrer toutes viues dans
le sepulchre de leurs marys. Prenez
garde que lors que vous pesez vous
monstrer pleine de compassion &
d'amitié, vous faites paroistre que
vous auez de la hayne pour vous-
mesme; vous estes vne creature de
Dieu qui estes vostre propre garde.
Acquitez vous fidellement de la
charge qu'il vous a dónee. Cóseruez
envous l'ouurage de vostre Createur. Ne passez plus les nuicts à pleurer & les iournees sans prédre aucun
repas. Mettez quelque trefue à cette vaine affliction, car à la fin vous
ne trouuerez plus personne qui
escoute vos plaintes librement,

ny qui vueille ioindre les fiennes;
au contraire l'on s'en mocquera, &
pource que voftre dueil eft extraordinaire, l'on dira qu'il eft affecté,
qu'il eft trop grand pour eftre veritable, & qu'enfin il faudra bien que
la ieune veufue ceffe le dernier acte
de fa Tragedie, & qu'elle prenne vn
fubject tout Comique. En effect chacun fçait bien que vous ne perdez
pas tant cóme vous nous voulez faire acroire. Il eft vray qu'il faut eftre
fenfible aux miferes humaines, &
que ce feroit eftre ftupide que de
ne point regretter vn homme qui
vous a beaucoup aymee; mais il fe
faut refoudre à ne le voir plus, puis
qu'il eft forty de cefte vie. Il auoit
beaucoup de merite à n'en point
mentir, mais toute la perfection du
monde n'eft pas morte auecque luy.
Il refte encore icy des hommes que

les

les Esprits les plus difficiles tiennent estimables. Pour ce qui est
des biens de fortune, vous n'en
auez perdu aucun à la mort du
deffunct, il vous a plustost laissé
plus riche que vous n'estiez. Apres
cela ie n'ay qu'vne chose à vous
dire. Vous sçauez bien que lors
que Monsieur vostre pere mou-
rut, & que l'on commença de vous
consoler sur sa mort, vous distes que
cela estoit fort mal-aysé ; & que
vous n'aymiez qu'vn pere, & que
par consequent cela vous estoit fort
fascheux de le perdre, d'autant que
iamais vous n'en pourriez recouurer vn autre, quand mesme vous
viuriez mille ans. Vous disiez alors
vne bonne chose, & bien que
vous fussiez fort ieune, vous fai-
siez desia paroistre la beauté de

G g

voſtre eſprit. Souuenez vous de
cela maintenant , & remarquez
qu'en ce qui ſe preſente, les conſiderations que vous auiez ſont ceſ-
ſees. Vous auez eu vn mary que
vous n'auez plus ; mais vous en
pouuez trouuer vn autre. Il y a
deſia aſſez long temps que vous
portez le dueil. Il n'y a plus de
ſcandale à changer vos habits fune-
ſtes.

Ie ſçay bien que dans peu de
iours il y aura quelqu'vn qui vous
parlera de cela plus amplement ; &
pource que ie croy que vous vous
doutez bien que c'eſt, ie me diſpen-
ſeray de vous en parler. Il ſuffit
que ie vous aye enuoyé ce mot d'eſcrit dans l'occaſion qui ſe preſente, pour m'acquitter de ce que ie
vous dois, & vous faire paroiſtre

que ie cherche toute forte d'occafions pour vous tefmoigner que
ie fuis,

MADAME,

Voftre tres-humble
& tres-affectionné
feruiteur.

Gg ij

L'Eloge de Monsieur de Malherbe.

NO v s n'auons plus auec nous ce rare esprit dont nous faisions tant de compte. Ainsi nous perdons tous les iours quelque chose de ce que nous cherissions iusques à ce que nous nous en allions aussi nous-mesmes. Nous en auons bien veu mourir d'autres qui seruoient d'ornemét à nostre siecle, & le seul bien qui nous reste c'est la consideration de leurs actions glorieuses que nous gardons tousiours dans nostre memoire pour nous seruir

d'vn exéple que nous puissiós imiter.
Mr de Malherbe auoit tant de probité & de vertu que l'on souffrira
bien que ie le mette au nombre de
ceux dont nous deuons honorer le
merite. D'ailleurs, son sçauoir luy a
donné tant de gloire que l'on l'a
tousiours estimé pour l'vn des premiers hommes de son temps.

　Il estoit de la ville de Caën, dont le
sieur du Rosser dit dans ses Poësies,
qu'il est tousiours sorty de grands
hommes, & qu'elle est fertile en
beaux esprits. Il le prouue tout à
l'heure facilement, en nommant
cettui-cy, & Monsieur Bertaud
Euesque de Sees, & encore vne autre de la mesme ville qui est encore
viuant, & qui a eu l'honneur d'estre
autrefois le precepteur de nostre
grand Roy.

　Monsieur de Malherbe estoit de

nos plus anciens Courtifans, il auoit
efté de la Cour du Roy Henry
troifiefme où il y auoit tant de perfonnes fi polies & fi fages. Depuis
il auoit efté de la Cour du Roy Héry
le Grand, & en fin il eftoit paruenu
iufques au regne du Monarque que
nous auons aujourd'huy. Il eft
vray qu'eftant encore ieune du
temps du Roy Henry troifiefme, il
ne paroiffoit pas beaucoup, mais
depuis fous Henry quatriefme fon
merite commença d'efclatter tout
à faiƈt.

La douceur de fa Poëfie l'auoit
faiƈt cognoiftre à quelques Seigneurs de la Cour qui le prefente-
rent à ce grand Roy qui luy donna incontinent vne penfion. Il
feift pour la bien venuë de la Royne cefte belle Ode qui commence ainfi,

Peuples qu'on mette sur la teste
Tout ce que la terre a de fleurs
Peuples que ceste belle feste
A iamais tarisse nos pleurs;
Qu'aux deux bouts du monde se voye
Luire le feu de nostre ioye,
Et soyent dans les coupes noyez
Les soucys de tous ces orages,
Que pour nos rebelles courages
Les Dieux nous auoient enuoyez.

Ceste piece fut si agreable à tout le monde que sans le secours de l'Imprimerie, à peine eust on pû fournir à ceux qui en vouloiét chacun auoir vne copie pour eux. Puis qu'elle courut si tost parmy le peuple, il ne faut pas demander si elle fut veüe par les personnes de consideration : Elle tomba entre les mains de Monsieur Bertaud, qui ne l'eut pas si tost leüe qu'il en fut rauy, & qui la porta à

Monſieur du Perron en luy diſant;
Ho Monſieur, quel homme eſt-ce
que nous auons maintenant parmy
nous? Quel nouueau Poëte eſt-ce
qui vient de naiſtre? Monſieur du
Perron ayant alors veu ces vers en
fit vne eſtime particuliere, & il falloit neceſſairement adiouſter foy à
ce qu'ils en diſoient tous deux, veu
que c'eſtoient des Eſprits qui de
long temps s'eſtoient fais les Maiſtres des autres, & s'eſtoient rendus
capables de iuger de tout ſans flatterie, & ſans enuie. Ils voulurent depuis cognoiſtre l'Autheur dont ils
auoient tant loüé les œuures, & ils
trouuerent encore des choſes plus
aymables dans ſa conuerſation que
dans ſes eſcrits.

Il fit apres quantité de bonnes
pieces à la loüange de Dieu, &
il en fit auſſi à la loüange du Roy,

dont ſa Majeſté fit beaucoup d’e-
ſtat. Il en faiſoit auſſi quelques
autres plus particulieres, & pource
qu’il ne ceſſoit de les preſenter au
Roy, ſa Majeſté s’imagina vne fois
que tout n’auoit pas eſté fait à ſa có-
ſideration. Comme en effect il y a
des Poëtes qui ne reüſsiſſent point à
faire des vers ſi ce n’eſt ſur leurs propres paſſions, d’autant qu’à lors ils
s’enflamment ſans aucune peine, &
leur veine coule facilement. Toutefois Monſieur de Malherbe n’a iamais eu enuie de tromper ainſi ſon
maiſtre, & pour luy móſtrer deſormais que les pieces qu’il luy preſen-
roit eſtoient faites ſeulement pour
luy, il s’efforçoit d’y mettre des choſes, qui tant s’en faut qu’elles fuſſent
propres pour vn Poëte, que nul autre qui viue n’euſt pas eu l’aſſeurance de ſe les attribuer. I’en veux don-

ner vn exemple dans ces vers.

N'ay-ie pas le cœur außi haut
Et pour oser tout ce qu'il faut
Vn außi grand desir de gloire,
Que j'auois lors que ie couury
D'exploicts d'eternelle memoire
Les plaines d'Arques & d'Yury?

L'on sçait bien qui c'est qui pouuoit parler de la sorte. D'ailleurs le
principal mot est à la fin du vers, &
le Poëte luy a donné vne riche rime,
afin de monstrer que ce n'est point
que l'on ait mis vn nom pour vn autre, ce qui eust esté aysé à faire s'il
eust esté au commencement d'vn
vers ou au milieu seulement.

Monsieur de Malherbe acquit incontinent vne telle reputatió dedás
la France par sa Poësie que l'on ne
parloit plus que de luy. Il auoit
faict quelques pieces en son ieune
aage que l'on vouloit mettre en vogue malgré qu'il en eust, à cause de

son nom seulement qui estoit capable de les authoriser, car l'on en a
bien veu l'exemple en plusieurs ouurages de quelques autheurs qui ne
meritent pas que l'on s'y arreste,
& qui neantmoins sont tousiours
rangez parmy les autres à cause du
lieu dont ils sont sortis. Nostre excellét Poëte ne vouloit pas que l'on
fist de mesme de ses œuures. Il aymoit mieux que le volume n'en fust
pas si gros & qu'il en fust meilleur.
Les Lacedemoniens auoiét accoustumé de ne garder que les enfans
qui estoient d'vne assez forte cóple-
xion pour la guerre. Ils les plon-
geoient dás quelque eau froide dés
qu'ils estoiét nés afin de les esprouuer, & s'ils les trouuoient debiles, ils
ne tenoiét cópte de les esleuer & les
alloiét jetter dans vn precipice. Cela
estoit cruel à l'endroit des creatures
humaines qui sót pourueuës d'vne

ame raisónable & immortelle; mais
en ce qui eſt des liures, qui ſont les
enfansde noſtre eſprit,que l'on doit
auſſi conſiderer d'vne autre ſorte, il
eſt fort à propos de leur faire vn
ſemblable traittement, & de les ſup-
primer ſelon noſtre volonté, ſi nous
voyós qu'ils ayent quelque deffaut.
Il ne faut pasiuger auec trop de paſſion de ſes propres ouurages. Nous
auons tous eſté ieunes, & nous ſçauons bien qu'en noſtre bas âge nous
auons pû faire des fautes. Nous ne
ſommes pas obligez de les publier,
& de les rendre eternelles. Ie ne dy
pas que ce qu'auoit fait Monſieur
de Malherbe en ſa ieuneſſe fuſt mauuais; mais cela n'eſtoit pas pourtant
aſſez bon pour luy. Vn autre en euſt
tiré beaucoup de gloire, mais quant
à luy il n'en eſperoit pas tant de ſatisfaction. Quelques vns trouuent

cela fort à leur goust, mais il auoit le
iugement plus subtil & plus delicat.
Il taschoit de plaire à soymesme auparauãt que de plaire au peuple. Les
Sages ne sont iamais de l'opinion du
vulgaire , & l'on tient que tout ce
qu'ils disent n'est qu'vn paradoxe e-
ternel contre les opinions des hommes communs. Il y a bien à dire des
ouurages d'vn aprentif à ceux d'vn
maistre, & il faut que l'on aduoüe
malgré que l'on en ayt, qu'vn Autheur a raison de procurer la perte
des premieres choses qu'il a faictes.
Pour moy ie ne veux pas seulement
nommer les pieces dont Monsieur
de Malherbe n'a tenu compte. Il en
estoit le juste possesseur, & par consequét il en pouuoit disposer de telle maniere qu'il luy plaisoit.

Nous auons de luy assez de choses
de reste pour iuger quel homme il

pouuoit eftre. Il a faict quantité de vers où l'on voit tant de douceur & de maiefté tout enfemble, que nous pouuons dire que c'eft le veritable ornement de la langue Françoife. Ronfard & ceux de fon temps purgerent leur Poëfie de quantité de deffauts qui eftoient dedans celle de Marot: mais Malherbe ayant encore trouué beaucoup de rudeffe dedans les vers de Ronfard, de du Bellay, de Belleau, & de tous ceux de leur bande, a trouué des fecrets qui rendent la Poëfie de beaucoup plus douce, & il en a mefme inuété d'autres encore qui ont feruy à rendre entierement noftre langue plus polie & plus agreable.

Les Poëtes qui l'auoient precedé eftoiét fi plaifáts, qu'au lieu d'accómoder leurs vers felon les mots qui auoiét cours en Fráce, ils accommodoiét leurs mots felon leurs vers. Ils difoient par exemple *mon efpé d'or*, pource que s'ils eufsét mis, *mon efpée* le vers euft efté trop long, & il y euft euvne lettre de fuperflue. Ils ne mettoient iamais, *fi elle eftoit belle; vn fertile chãp*, mais pluftoft *vn fertil chãp*. Il y a plus de mille mots dont ie ne me fouuiens pas, lefquels ils tronquoient de la forte, & il y en auoit d'autres auffi qu'ils allongeoient ou qu'ils chágeoient de prononciatió, afin de venir à leur rime.

Ronfard mettoit toufiours, *la neufaine tropo*, pour rimer auec Calliopo, Il difoit auffi, *le mont à double crope*.

Pour rimer auec *fecouffe*, il parloit, *d'vne femme grouffe*. Il a fait vne elegie où pour rimer auec, *les paifibles oüailles*, il nous importune *les oreilles.* Ie ne luy donne point de blaſme ny à tous ceux qui l'ont ſui-uy; mais quoy, cela eſt; Il le faut dire puis qu'il eſt à propos. Il eſt certain que Monſieur de Malherbe a donné des reigles à ſa Poëſie qui nous empeſchent de croire que cela ſoit bien. Rôſard & ceux de ſa troupe auoient cette couſtume que lors qu'ils mettroient ainſi quelque choſe dans leurs vers qui en effet choquoit la raiſon, ils diſoient, *Que c'eſtoit vne licence Poëtique.* Voyla l'excuſe qui eſt capable de couurir toutes choſes. Nous auons ouy dire cela aſſez de fois aux Pedás qui appellent des licêces toutes les figures extrauagantes qu'ils peuuent trouuer dans les anciens Poëtes, ou bien les mots qui ſont mis ſelon le commun vſage. A Dieu ne plaiſe que nous ſoyós encore dans cette erreur d'appeller.

peller ainsi d'vn beau nom les plus grosses fautes que l'on puisse iamais commettre dans la Poësie.

Nous sçauons bien maintenant comment il faut establir de la difference entre ce qui est bon & ce qui est mauuais. Il n'y a point d'homme si qualifié qui puisse donner de l'authorité à des choses qui sont mal à propos, & quelque credit qu'vn homme ayt acquis par son bien dire, si est-ce que quand il dit de mauuais mots l'on n'est point obligé par aucune loy de les tenir pour excellents.

C'est vne opinion tres-fausse que de croire qu'il soit permis aux grands Autheurs de laisser des fautes dans leurs ouurages: car s'ils n'ont esté estimez que

Hh

pour auoir autrefois bien fait,
pourquoy eſt-ce qu'apres auoir
beaucoup eſcrit , il leur ſera permis de mal faire ? Cela eſt eſloigné de toute raiſon ; car tout au
contraire , depuis qu'vn homme a fait quelque choſe de bien,
l'on s'attend qu'il doit continuer , & s'il commence à dege-
nerer, l'on s'eſtonne de luy pluſtoſt que l'on ne feroit d'vn autre.

Tant plus vn homme s'occu-
pe à quelque art que ce ſoit , tant
plus il y doit eſtre parfait , & il
doit laiſſer aux petits apprentifs
cette honte de faire encore des
fautes, & d'auoir beſoin de s'ex-
cuſer, en diſant qu'ils ont faict
des licences.

Ie ne veux pas nier à la verité
que quelques Poëtes anciens
n'ayent faict des choſes que l'on

dóit apeller des licences poëtiques; mais ce ne font pas des fautes comme celles des modernes:
Ce font des chofes irregulieres
que l'on n'a pas accouftumé de
voir ailleurs, mais leurs extrauagances font agreables, & c'eft
comme ces tableaux où l'on ne
void que des monftres qui encore qu'ils foient horribles, ne laiffent pas de plaire à ceux qui fe
cognoiffent à la peinture, à caufe que l'on y remarque des traits
fort hardis.

Les Poëtes qui font des Peintres parlans, en doiuent faire
de mefme, & quiconque dit des
chofes extraordinaires, a fujeét
de confiderer fi elles font agreables. Il faut faire des coups de
Maiftre qui foient contre les reigles communes de l'art, mais qui

neantmoins ne laiſſent point de plaire à tout le monde. C'eſt cela que l'on doit appeler des licences, & ie n'entens pas parler de ces mauuaiſes licences que ſe donnent les ignorans, qui ne demandent autre choſe que d'auoir la licence de mal faire, ie dy de ces licences genereuſes qui ſont plus difficiles à obſeruer que les loix les plus eſtroictes. S'il n'eſt permis qu'aux grands eſprits de s'en ſeruir, l'on iugera bien que le vulgaire n'y ſçauroit atteindre.

Monſieur de Malherbe qui teſmoignoit touſiours vn genie excellent en tout ce qu'il entreprenoit, a pû eſcrire ainſi quelquefois des choſes qui n'eſtoient pas ordinaires, mais cela s'eſt faict extremement à propos, & l'on aura beaucoup de peine ſi l'on le

veut imiter. Pour ce qui est de
l'abus que l'on commet en croyãt
qu'il soit permis de faillir quelquefois, tant s'en faut qu'il s'y
soit laissé emporter, qu'au contraire il nous a monstré le chemin
de nous en rendre exempts.

Il n'a pas manqué de prendre
garde mesme à tous les mots qui
sont permis dans la prose, mais
qui ne coulent pas assez facilement dedans les vers.

Il a retranché ceux qui estoient
de ce nombre, & il nous en a
enseigné d'autres plus doux &
plus agreables, & qui sont assez significatifs pour exprimer
tout ce que nous voulons dire.

Il y en a d'autres qui de verité ne doiuent pas estre bannis,
mais neantmoins si l'on les veut
faire entrer doucement dedans

vn vers, il faut songer aux obseruations de nostre grande Poëte qui leur a ordonné leur place.

Or ie ne doute point que
les reigles qu'il nous a données
ne soyent eternelles. Elles ne se
peuuent changer si tout le monde ne change, & si le sens commun des hommes ne deuient
tout autre qu'il n'a tousiours e-
sté, & ce qu'il y a mesme d'excellent en cecy, c'est que nos reigles ne sont pas pour nostre langue
toute seule; elles sont faictes aussi
pour toutes les langues estrange-
res. ce qui sert de beaucoup à les
faire trouuer iustes.

Quiconque a des oreilles peut
connoistre aussi qu'elles valent
mieux que les licences que les
ignorans se donnent, & que

sans cela noftre Poëfie eft rude &
fauuage.

Il y en a d'autres qui nous
viennent dire que de faire des
vers felon les loix que Malherbe
a prefcriptes , c'eft fe mettre foy-
mefme dans des gefnes fafcheu-
fes , & que de nous enjoindre
d'obferuer tant de chofes , c'eft
autant faire que fi l'on nous def-
fendoit entierement de faire des
vers.

Cette plainte ne fçauroit for-
tir que de la bouche de quelques
broüillons , qui auroient vne
grande enuie d'eftre Poëtes, afin
d'acquerir de la gloire , mais qui
voudroient que le Palais d'A-
pollon ne fuft pas bafty fur vne
montagne haute & difficile.

Ils fe voudroient faire eftimer
à peu de fraiz , mais nous ne
H h iiij

sommes plus en cette saison où la Renommée se donne à quicon-que la demande.

Monsieur de Malherbe mesme auoit ouy durant sa vie quel-ques semblables discours ; il fit response, que les bons citoyens ne se faschoient point d'aucune Loy que l'on leur pûst donner, parce qu'ils auoient tousiours eu vn extreme desir de bien viure; & qu'aussi ceux qui desiroient bien escrire estoient contens que l'on leur trouuast de nouueaux moyens pour atteindre à la per-fection. L'on n'a iamais acquis beaucoup d'honneur sans auoir eu quelque trauail auparauant.

Pour ce qui est de celuy qui nous est proposé, il est vray qu'il semble grand aux petits esprits; mais l'on en viet à bout par la per-

seurance & l'exercice, & pour ce
qui est des grands Genies ils n'y
trouuent rien de malaysé.

Ceux qui voudroient que l'on
ostast ces difficultez , ne songent
pas qu'ils veulent reduire à neant
l'Art de la Poësie ; car s'il n'auoit
diuerses reigles , ce ne seroit plus vn
Art. Tout le monde pourroit donc
estre Poëte , & les Roquantins &
les Gueridons que les enfans de
ville composent tous sur le champ
auec les Coquettes de Paris , seroient donc pris pour de fort bons
vers.

Il n'en va pas ainsi ; les beaux
ouurages ne se font pas sans indu-
strie , & ceux qui n'ont point iamais appris vn mestier ne sont pas
capables d'y trauailler comme les
maistres.

L'on peut dire qu'il en est de

mesme de la Poësie comme de la musique. Il n'y a personne qui ne chante, pourueu qu'il n'ayt pas le gosier bouché; Les laquais chantent en attendant leur Maistre, & les seruantes en filant leur quenoüille; mais il y a peu de personnes qui chantér de la methode de Boesser & de Bailly.

Voyez vn peu quelle difference il y a entre le chant vulgaire, & celuy de ces parfaicts Musiciens. Vous direz apres la mesme chose de la poësie qui est faicte sans aucune obseruation, & celle qui suit les preceptes de Monsieur de Malherbe.

L'on nous faict encore vne autre plainte. L'on nous dit que si ses obseruations estoient si bonnes, il les falloit donc escrire.

L'on demande en quel lieu elles

se trouuent , & où c'est que l'on a
faict afficher de telles loix ? I'auoüe
que celuy qui les a mises en credit,
n'en a composé aucun liure. Il mesprisoit cette façon d'acquerir de la
gloire. Il aymoit mieux mettre en
pratique ce qu'il enseignoit , & il
laissoit la charge de faire cela pour
luy à quiconque la voudroit entreprendre.

Si l'on ne l'a point faict encore
exactement ; au moins l'on en peut
trouuer quelque chose dans des pieces separées , & il y pourra auoir
quelqu'vn à la fin qui en escrira amplement , & qui fera cette faueur
au public.

Nous ne manquons pas de gens
qui sçauét de poinct en poinct quels
ornemens ont esté apportez à nostre langage par Monsieur de Malherbe. Il n'estoit pas chiche de ce

qu'il sçauoit. Les conferences eſtoient libres chez luy, & il donnoit de la ſatisfaction à tous ceux qui en deſiroient. Il a eu plus de ſectateurs qu'aucun Philoſophe de l'antiquité, & ſes diſciples ſe ſont eſpandus par toute la France.

Il n'y auoit perſonne qui ſe crûſt habile ſans auoir eu ſa connoiſſance & ſa conuerſation, & meſmes l'on n'eſtimoit aucun ouurage qu'apres qu'il l'auoit approuué

Il auoit vn ſi grand iugement que toutes les fautes que pluſieurs perſonnes enſemble n'euſſent remarquées qu'à diuerſes fois, il les rencontroit tout d'vn coup, & vous donnoit en meſme temps le moyen de les corriger.

Ce que les anciés poëtes ont dit par feinte de leur Apollon, pouuoit e-

stre dit de luy auecque verité, car
en effect c'estoit luy qui inspiroit
les Poëtes &les rédoit tels que nous
les voyons. Les meilleurs que nous
ayons aujourd'huy sont encore de
sa façon, & quoy que l'on die d'ordinaire que les Orateurs se font par
leur trauail, & que les Poëtesnaissét
tels qu'ils sont, si est ce que l'on luy
peut donner l'honneur d'auoir fait
des Poëtes.

Ce sont les enfans de son esprit aussi bien que ses Poësies , &
ceux qui ont tant apris de choses
dans son escole, n'oseroient pas le
priuer de l'honneur qu'ils doiuent
luy rendre.

La beauté de son esprit ne pa-
roissoit pas seulement dans les vers.
Tout ce qu'il a fait en prose n'est
pas moindre. L'on y void par
tout des choses extremement po-

lies & fort iudicieuses. Ses lettres
à Caliste sont pleines de douceurs
& de naïfueté : Celuy qui a entrepris de s'en mocquer par vne froide
allusion n'a gaigné autre chose que
d'estre mesprisé pour cét iniuste
mespris : La lettre de cõsolatiõ qu'il
a addressée à Madame la Princesse
de Cõty sur la mort de Monsieur le
Cheualier de Guyse son frere, est
vne piece de si haut prix que l'on ne
la sçauroit trop estimer.

Quelqu'vn a dit, que Seneque
& Malherbe consolent la Princesse de Conty, pour donner à entendre que Malherbe a tiré de Seneque les plusbelles choses qu'il a
dictes : mais si l'on pense le blasmer par là, l'on a entrepris vn mauuais dessein.

Il se peut faire que Malherbe
se soit rencontré dans de mesmes

penſees que Seneque qui a faict
auſſi des conſolations, car il eſt
impoſſible que deux hommes de
bon eſprit parlent de quelque choſe que ce ſoit, ſans alleguer quelques raiſons qui ſont toutes naturelles & qui ſe trouuent dans le ſens
commun de tous ceux qui font
profeſſion de ſageſſe : mais ce n'eſt
pas à dire qu'on les doiue accuſer
de larcin, & pour ce qui eſt de
Malherbe, l'on ſçait bien meſme
qu'il a eſcrit les choſes d'vne autre
ſorte que l'on ne les treuue dans les
anciens autheurs.

Vn Pedant qui aura cité des
paſſages tous entiers de quelque
Philoſophe, pourroit bien amoindrir ſa reputation : Mais ceux qui
eſcriuent en leur propre ſtile, &
qui ne ſongent pas ſeulement
qu'autres qu'eux ayent parlé

du ſujet qu'ils traictent, c'eſt en vain que l'on les ſoupçonne d'emprunter quelque choſe des autres.

Il y a ſi peu de perſonnes qui ayent oſé blaſmer Monſieur de Malherbe, que cela n'eſt pas conſiderable, & d'ailleurs ou ils ne ſe ſont pas nommez, ou ils ne l'ont pas nommé luy meſme, de ſorte que cela ne le pouuoit pas beaucoup offenſer.

Sa reputation eſt vierge: elle n'a iamais eſté attaquee, & l'on la treuue ſi pure qu'elle n'a iamais eſté ſoüillee d'aucun venin de meſdiſance, & nous croyons que ceſte prerogatiue luy demeurera eternellement.

Celuy qui l'a meritee a eu le plus grand bien que puiſſe iamais ſouhaiter vn autheur, c'eſt qu'il a iouy

durant

durant ſa vie; ce qui n'arriue pas
ſouuent, car d'ordinaire l'enuie &
la meſdiſance s'attachent entre
ceux qui viuent encore.

C'eſt par ſa vertu qu'il a acquis
ce bon-heur. Il n'eſtoit pas de ces
petits qui ſe rendent fantaſques &
mal plaiſans dedans leur ſolitude. Il
a touſiours eſté d'vne douce conuerſation, & s'il employoit beaucoup de temps à polir ſes vers, il en
employoit dauantage à polir ſes
mœurs.

Le vulgaire accuſe les Poëtes
de folie, mais il condamne le general pour auoir poſſible eſprou-
ué ſeulement la folie d'vn particulier. Noſtre Poëte eſtoit fort eſtimable pour ſon ſçauoir; mais il l'e-
ſtoit encore plus pour ſa ſageſſe.
L'on ſçait bien qu'il a gouuerné
toutes ſes actions ſelon les reigles

de la raison. Il n'a point commis d'impietez. Il n'a point esté
subject à l'impudicité ; l'on ne dit
point qu'il ayt faict de grandes desbauches , & qu'il y ayt eu de l'excez en aucune chose qu'il ayt faicte,
au côtraire on racóte de luy beaucoup de choses dignes de loüange;
Il n'a pas voulu viure comme ces
Poëtes lascifs qui ne desirent point
d'autre femme que celle de leur
voisin, & qui disent que c'est pour
eux que les autrês se marient. Il a
mieux aymé se marier, afin que l'on
vist qu'il desiroit fuïr toute sorte de
desbauches.

Que si l'on ne me veut pas croire
en cecy, la parfaicte santé qu'il a eüc
iusques à sa mort, tesmoigne assez
qu'il falloit qu'il eust vsé d'vne
grande temperance. Les maladies
sont les interests qui nousfont payez

pour le temps que nous auons employé à la volupté. Si sa ieunesse
eust esté desbauchee, sa vieillesse
eust esté maladiue; mais l'on sçait
que la seule maladie qu'il a eüe
a esté celle qui l'a ainsi faict mourir.

Pour ce qui est de l'ambition &
de l'auarice, qui sont deux passions
qui maistrisent la pluspart des hommes, elles n'ont iamais eu de puissance sur luy.

On me dira qu'elles ne se trouuent guere aussi dans l'esprit de
ceux de sa profession, & que cela n'estoit pas miraculeux en luy;
mais encore qu'il soit vray, que la
pluspart de ceux qui escriuent aujourd'huy soient pauures, ce n'est
pas à dire qu'ils n'ayent vne extreme enuie d'estre riches, & il n'y a

que leur malheur qui les en empefche. Quant à luy il n'auoit pas de
fi baffes penfees. S'il euft voulu faire
fa cour auec affiduité, à fe trouuer
tous les iours au leuer de quátité de
perfonnes, il euft acquis plus de
biens qu'il n'en a pas eu. Il eftoit
content de ce qu'il poffedoit, &
pourueu que le fils qu'il auoit fuft
auancé dans vne honnefte charge,
il eftimoit fa condition affez heureufe.

Quant à l'enuie & à la mefdifan-
ce, il n'en auoit aucune tache. Celuy
qui eftoit au deffus des autres, ne
pouuoit pas enuier les autres ; ny en
mefdire, pource qu'il eftimoit que
c'eftoit vne chofe trop baffe. Il ad-
uertiffoit chacun de fes fautes fans y
proceder auec vne mauuaife volonté, mais auec vne douceur d'efprit,
& vne charité remarquable.

I'ay dit qu'il a esté exempt des maladies du corps : mais il n'a pas sceu garentir son ame de toute sorte de douleurs. Il a eu sa part des afflictions du monde, il a veu mourir deuant luy sa femme qu'il aymoit vniquement, pour laquelle aussi il a fait vn Sonnet inimitable. Apres auoir declaré son ennuy, il dit à ceux qui l'escoutent, que pour recompense de luy auoir aydé à plaindre la mort de celle qu'il aymoit tant, il prie Dieu que iamais autre douleur ne les fasse pleurer. Ce souhait est digne d'vne bonne ame comme la sienne, & il merite de rendre immortel celuy qui l'a faict.

L'assassinat qui a esté faict en la personne de son fils, a encore esté vne autre affliction qu'il a eüe sur ses vieux iours, il vid qu'il auoit per-

du ce fils qui estoit son vnique esperance, & cela luy arriua sur le
poinct qu'il l'alloit faire receuoir en
vne charge de Conseiller. Outre
cela il n'a iamais pû tirer raison des
meurtriers. Les poursuittes qu'il en
faisoit luy deuoient donner beaucoup de peine, & neantmoins il les
souffroit auec vne grande constance, & c'est là qu'il a monstré la meilleure partie de sa vertu.

Pour ce qui est de sa mort elle a
esté aussi belle que sa vie, il n'a point
eu de desespoir; il n'a point eu de
regret au monde, il n'estoit point
de la croyance de quelques Poëtes,
qui viuent dans le libertinage, d'autant que dans leurs Poësies, ils ne
parlent que des fables & des erreurs
de l'antiquité, ils ne sçauent quasi
ce que c'est d'vne pieté veritable,
& comme s'il y auoit vn Paradis

faict pour eux tous feuls, ils ont auſ-
fi des opinions particulieres , &
ne veulent auoir qu'vne religion
Poëtique. Ceſtui-cy n'en eſtoit pas
de meſme ; il eſt mort en bon Chreſtien , & il a donné des teſmoi-
gnages de la pureté de ſa conſcience.

L'on peut encore dire à ſa loüange que dés que l'on a ſceu ſa mort,
il n'y a eu perſonne de tous ceux
qui ſe meſlent d'eſcrire, ſoit en proſe, ſoit en vers , qui n'ayt fait quelque choſe en ſa conſideration.
Les vns des Stances, les autres des
Eloges, & quelques-vns des Poë-
mes tous entiers. Si l'on veut recueillir toutes ces diuerſes pieces , elles pourront faire vn gros
volume, & elles teſmoigneront à la
poſterité que Malherbe a eſté eſti-

mé en France pour celuy qui a donné de la pureté au langage, de la
douceur à la Poëſie, & de la clarté
pour deſcouurir les fautes de iugement qui ſe peuuent commettre
dans vn ouurage.

Voyla ce que j'ay crû que l'on
pouuoit dire à ſa gloire, & ie veux
bien que cela ſoit publié, puis que
c'eſt noſtre deuoir de reconnoiſtre
le merite des grands hommes, &
principalemét à leur mort, afin d'aduertir ceux qui viendrốt apres nous
qu'ils en doiuent faire de l'eſtime, &
qu'ils doiuent croire ceux qui ne
parlent que des choſes qu'ils ont
veuës. Ie penſe que l'on ne peut
manquer d'adiouſter foy à ce que
i'ay dict, car quand ie n'aurois
point d'autres teſmoins du merite de
celuy que i'ay loüé, que ces ouura-

ges incomparables , ce seroit assez
contenter les plus difficiles , & luy
conseruer la grande reputation
qu'il s'est acquise.

De la Poëſie.

Ous m'auez mandé que vous auez ouy parler de quelqu'vn qui a entrepris d'eſcrire côtre la Poëſie. Il y a touſiours à Paris quelque nouueauté, mais ie ne ſçay pas ſi celle là ſera agreable à tout le módé. La Poëſie eſt depuis long téps en poſſeſſion de l'eſtime que l'on fait d'elle; & c'eſt vne choſe que ie puis vous prouuer fort facilement.

Les anciens Oracles eſtoiét autrefois en vers. Les Preſtres qui ſeruoiét les Dieux eſtoiét Poëtes. La Theologie ancienne n'eſtoit traictée que dans la poëſie. Les Grecs faiſoient tant d'eſtime de Pindare que de tou-

tes les victimes que l'on offroit au
Dieu Apollon il en auoit sa part,
comme s'il eust esté le fils ou le frere
ou le copagnon du Dieu de la Poësie & de la Musique. Homere a tant
esté estimé que toutes les villes de la
Grece se sont presque faict la guerre à qui emporteroit l'honneur de
se pouuoir dire le vray lieu de sa naif-
sance. L'on sçait bien quelle estime
faisoit aussi de luy le plus grand des
guerriers, ie veux dire Alexandre de
Macedoine, qui lisoit incessammét
ses ouurages, & les mettoit d'ordinaire sur le cheuet de son lict, afin
que lors qu'il ne pourroit dormir ce
fust son principal entretien. Dix
mille autheurs ont aussi remarqué
dans leurs liures, que luy ayant esté
apporté vn coffret des despoüilles
de Darius, qui estoit la plus riche

pieces que l'on euſt ſçeu voir, l'vn
de ſes courtiſans diſoit, cela ſera propre à mettre des bagues, l'autre diſoit que cela ſeroit fort bon à enfermer les plus ſecrettes miſſiues du
Roy; mais pour luy il dit qu'il n'y
auoit rien qui fuſt digne d'eſtre enfermé là dedans que le liure d'Homere, comme de fait; ce fut à cela
qu'il s'en ſeruit depuis. Comme il
vid auſſi le tombeau d'Achilles, il
s'eſcria que cet Heros auoit eſté tres
heureux d'auoir eu vn tel Trompette de ſes loüanges; & en effect il ne
ſe trompoit pas, car bien d'autres
Princes ont eſté auſſi vaillans qu'A-
chille & qu'Hector &tous les autres
qui ont donné les plus grands coups
dans la guerre de Troye, mais ils
ſont neantmoins demeurez dans
l'oubly, faute de s'eſtre trouué vn
excellent Eſcriuain qui celebraſt

leurs loüanges. Alexandre le Grand
témoigna encore d'vne autre forte
l'eſtat qu'il faiſoit du premier Poete
de la Grece. Vn de ſes Courtiſans
vint vn iour à luy auec vn viſage ouuert & plein de gayeté, luy diſant,
Sire, ie vous apporte les meilleures
nouuelles du monde, comme en effet ce qu'il luy venoit dire le deuoit
fort reſiouyr. Toutefois Alexandre
luy dit auſſi toſt : Ne croyez point
m'apporter vne bonne nouuelle, ſi
vous ne me venez aprendre qu'Homere eſt reſſuſcité. Voila comme il
ſe ſouuenoit touſiours de ce Poëte,
taſchant de l'honorer en toutes façons, pource que tant de villes de la
Grece ſe debattoient à qui ſe diroit
la ſienne, il voulut qu'il y en euſt
vne qui fuſt propre à Homere &
qui portaſt ſon nom. Que s'il ne la
fit point baſtir au meſme pays où il

auoit esté né, cela importe de fort
peu, & c'estoit tousiours pour esté-
dre dauantage sa renommée. Ie sçay
bien que quelqu'vn a desia dit qu'il
ne se faloit pas estonner de cela, &
que c'estoit vne magnificence ordinaire de ce grand Prince, & qu'il
auoit mesme autāt honoré son cheual qu'Homere, puis qu'il auoit fait
bastir vne ville en memoire de Bucephale, laquelle on nommoit Bu-
cephalie. Mais lors que l'on dit cela
l'on a enuie de se railler à quelque
prix que ce soit, & de trouuer
des raisons ingenieuses pour ob-
scurcir la verité. Neantmoins il
est fort aisé d'y respondre, & de
monstrer que lors qu'Alexandre fit
bastir vne ville pour Homere il le
fitauecvne ferme intention de l'honorer, & non point en se laissāt emporter à ses superfluitez sansen cher-

cher aucune raiſon. Ie ne diray pas
qu'il auoit tant fait d'eſtime de ſon
cheual, que ce n'eſtoit pas peu quãd
il eſtimoit autãt vn homme, & qu'il
auoit eu auſſi vn extreme deſir d'en
eterniſer la memoire. Il eſt certain
que Bucephale luy'auoit beaucoup
ſeruy dãs ſes guerres & que c'eſtoit
vn animal qui n'auoit point de prix;
mais c'eſt auoir enuie de ſe gauſſer,
que de dire qu'il n'y euſt point de
difference entre l'eſtime qu'il faiſoit
d'vne beſte & celle d'vn excellent
hóme. Il fit baſtir des villes à la memoire de tous les deux, mais c'eſtoit
qu'il ne ſe pouuoit imaginer vne
autre façon de témoigner l'affectió
qu'il auoit pour quelque choſe dãs
les occaſiós où il ſe récótroit. Au reſte la ville de Bucephale n'eſtoit poſſible pas ſi belle ny ſi bié peupléeque
celle d'Homere. D'ailleurs ie m'en

vay vous dire vne chose qui va couper court à toutes les objections des
mocqueurs; c'est qu'Alexandre n'a
point faict d'honneur à Homere
qu'il n'ait aussi voulu prendre pour
soy-mesme; car l'on sçait bien qu'il
a fait bastir vne ville en son nom laquelle fut appellée Alexandrie. Ne
disons donc point qu'il n'a pas plus
honoré Homere que son cheual,
maisqu'il l'a honoré autát que soy-
mesme. L'on peut encore songer à
l'estime que tous les Grecs ont faite
de ce Poete. Leurs plus grands Philosophes prenoiét quelquefois vne
seuerité excessiue afin de se faire respecter au dessus du vulgaire ; & là
dessus ils se donnoient la licence de
dire que les Poëtes estoiét trop effeminez & qu'ils corrópoient la jeunesse. Toutefois en blasmát la poé-
sie ils ne laissoiét pas de se seruir encore

core des vers d'Homere dedás leurs
escrits pour donner vn exemple des
plus belles choses qu'ils auoient dans
la pésee; Aussi dit- on que la Philosophie & la Poësie sont sœurs; Ce que
l'vne dit ouuertement, l'autre le dit
seulement d'vne façon plus cachée,
& la verité s'y trouue sous des mysteres.

Les Romains n'ont pas fait moins
d'estime de leurs Poëtes. L'on void
dás les Autheurs des marques de l'a-
mitié que le grãd Scipion auoit có-
tractée auec le Poëte Ennius. L'Empereur Auguste qui sçauoit mieux
iuger du merite des hommes & de
leurs ouurages que pas vn autre de
tous les Payens, a faict vn cas merueilleux de la Poësie & des Poëtes,
outre cela il donnoit charge à son
fauory Mecænas de leur faire bon
accueil, & de faire en sorte qu'ils ne

manquaſſent d'aucune choſe qui leur ſeroit neceſſaire. De quelque lieu qu'ils fuſſent ſortis, il ne prenoit point garde à leur baſſeſſe. Il n'auoit eſgard qu'à leur bon eſprit, & bien ſouuent il s'entretenoit auec ceux qui eſtoient de la meilleure conuerſation. L'on ſçait bien qu'il fit beaucoup de faueurs à Virgile, & pour Ouide il l'aymoit tant auſſi, qu'il n'euſt iamais ceſſé de luy faire du bien ſi ce Poëte n'euſt commis vne grande faute pour laquelle il treuua à propos de l'enuoyer en exil, & de ſe priuer de l'obiect d'vn tel homme qui euſt renouuellé dans ſa memoire le ſouuenir d'vne choſe honteuſe & deſagreable à laquelle il ne vouloit iamais penſer. L'on remarque auſſi que le Poëte Oppian a eſté grandement recom-

pensé par vn autre Prince, & que
les vers ayans esté payez chacun
d'vne espece de monnoye qui estoit
la plus grande de ce temps là, l'on
les a depuis appellez les vers dorez.

L'on me dira que ie n'ay rien fait
iusques à cette heure d'auoir allegué tant de choses, & que i'ay employé des paroles inutilement, d'autant que l'on ne se rapporte plus au
iugement des anciens, & que s'ils
estimoient la poësie c'estoit à cause
des fables dont elle estoit pleine, ce
qui estoit leur principale Theologie, à cause qu'ils estoient encore dedans les erreurs du Paganisme. Mais
il se faut representer qu'ils estimoiét
aussi les ouurages des Poëtes à cause
des preceptes moraux & politiques
qu'ils y trouuoient, & en ce cas là
nous deuons deferer quelque chose à l'antiquité, & croire qu'elle ne

s'eſt point abuſee. Il y a eu meſme des Poëtes qui n'ont pas eſté des có-reurs de fables. pythagore auoit mis en vers ſa plus rare doctrine. Le Le-giſlateur Solon n'enſeignoit auſſi les Atheniens que par ſes poëſies, & il eſtoit d'aduis que les loix fuſſent mi-ſes dans des chãſons, afin que le peu-ple ne ceſſant de les chanter, les ap-priſt inſenſiblement & qu'il ne puſt les oublier quand il en euſt eu en-uie. Nous auons veu auſſi chez les Romains les Diſtiches de Caton, qui ſont ſi graues & ſi remplis de moralité, que qui pourroit viure comme ils enſeignent auroit atteint vne veritable preud'hommie.

La Poëſie n'a pas auſſi eſté meſ-priſee du peuple de Dieu. Les Pſeaumes des Hebrieux ont eſté meſurez, & ſi nous ne le pouuons pas reconnoiſtre, c'eſt que nous

ne sçauons pas bien quelles quan-
titez ils obseruoient, & puis c'est
qu'ils changent souuét de metres.
Aufsi Dauid est appellé Poëte sacré, & il a chery esgalement la Poësie & la Musique. Salomon a composé l'Ecclesiaste & les Cantiques
en vers; & l'on tient mesme que le
Cantique d'Esaye est mesuré.

Aufsi deuons nous prendre tant
de peine à ce que nous offrons à
Dieu, que nous pouuons bien prescrire des reigles à nos paroles, & les
enfermer en de certaines mesures.
C'est pour monstrer la difference
qu'il y a d'entre le langage vulgaire
dont les hommes se seruent en leurs
conferences, & celuy qu'ils adres-
sent à Dieu par leurs prieres.

Le credit de la Poësie ne s'est pas
diminué par les années. Il y a eu
toufiours des Poëtes de temps en

temps en toutes les parties de la terre. Les lágues mefmes qui fe font faictes de la corruption des autres depuis la reuolution des Empires, ont trouué des hómes qui ont daigné s'en feruir à declarer leurs conceptions au peuple. Or c'eft icy que l'on peut monftrer l'excellence de la poëfie: car d'autant que de bons efprits s'y font adonnez en toute forte de regions, elle a grandement feruy à faire cultiuer le langage qui fans cela fuft demeuré fi barbare que l'on euft encore eu de la peine à le prononcer. L'on ne peut nier auffi qu'elle n'ait efté caufe que petit à petit l'on a addoucy quantité de mots , où l'on a retranché ceux qui paroiffoient trop rudes , & l'on les a changez à d'autres que l'on a inuentez ou bien que l'on a pris de fes voyfins. L'Italie & l'Efpagne ont

eu leurs Poëtes, & la France a eu aussi
les siens. Ceux d'Italie ont eu des
humeurs extremes. Petrarque a eu
des couronnes & des recompenses.
L'on luy fit vne entrée à Rome cóme à vn Prince ; & pour ce qui est
de l'Arioste & du Tasse , leurs ouurages sont tellement estimez, que
c'est la premiere lecture que font
tous les hommes d'esprit. Pour ce
qui est des Espagnols il est aisé à voir
combien ils ont tousiours faict estat
des Poetes , veu qu'ils ont tant de
Romans & d'autres Poesies dedans
leurs païs; car le nombre des Poetes
n'est augmété que par le bó accueil
que l'on leur fait, & lors qu'on void
qu'vn art n'est plus en estime il faudroit estre hors de iugemét pour s'y
adóner. Les François n'ont pas eu de
tout temps moins d'inclination à la
Poesie. Les plus belles actiós de leurs

Princes n'eſtoient autrefois eſcrites qu'en vers. Les Poëtes les alloient reciter au bout de la table des Grãds, & c'eſtoit vn des plus grands diuertiſſemens de ce temps là que de les ouyr. Lors que toutes choſes ſont depuis montées à leur perfection, noſtre Poëſie s'eſt auſſi renduë plus polie & plus agreable. L'on a commencé de la mettre par eſcrit, & des hommes de reputation ſe ſont meſlez d'y trauailler, & en ont laiſſé de rares pieces à la poſterité.

Nos Roys meſme n'ont pas creu ſe deshonorer s'ils eſcriuoient des vers de la meſme main dont ils tenoient leur ſceptre, pour ſe diuertir quelquefois apres leurs grandes occupations.

François premier a compoſé quelques Epigrãmes & quelques Sónets. Charles neufieſme a auſſi addreſſé

quelques vers à des Poëtes de son
temps, & specialement à Ronsard
qu'il cherissoit par dessus les autres.
Aussi ce Poëte a esté celuy qui a
composé de si beaux ouurages qu'il
n'y a rien au monde qui les puisse es-
galer. Il a parlé de Dieu dans quelques Hymnes & dãs quelques Poë-
mes auec tout le respect qu'il y falloit employer, & il a loüé les Grãds
auec les paroles les plus majestueu-
ses dont ils pouuoient tirer de la satisfaction; & pour ce qui est des autres sujets il y a mis tant de douceur,
& par tout il a tesmoigné tant de
sçauoir, que tous ceux de son temps
ont aduoüé qu'il auoit amené les
Muses en France, & qu'il auoit sur-
passé tous les Poëtes de l'Antiquité.
L'on me dira qu'il ne s'est pas fort
auancé neantmoins, mais ne sçait
on pas aussi que Charles neufiesme

diſoit qu'il ne luy vouloit pas faire
de dons exceſſifs, & qu'il auoit peur
qu'il ne deuinſt comme ces bons
leuriers qui ne valent plus rien pour
la chaſſe lors qu'ils ſont trop bien
nourris. Il ſuffit que les Poëtes ayent
les choſes qui ſont neceſſaires à la
vie. Le reſte n'eſt rien que ſuperflui-
té. Ces conſiderations Philoſophi-
ques qui les entretiennent d'ordinaire les doiuent empeſcher de ſonger à l'auarice & à l'ambition. Tout
ce qu'il leur faut pour bien trauailler, c'eſt de n'auoir que ce qu'il eſt
beſoin à vn homme. Qu'ont ils beſoin d'auoir de grands honneurs,
puis qu'ils doiuent inceſſamét chercher la ſolitude. Pourquoy cher-
cheroiét ils le ſejour des grádes maiſons, veu que d'ordinaire ils ſe plai-
ſoiét à deſcrire vn pauure toiĉt, tels
qu'eſtoiét ceux du ſiecle d'or. Ne di-

sent ils pas souuét qu'ils aimét mieux
voir la nature en sa naïfueté que to⁹
les desguisemés de l'artifice? N'est-ce
pas aussi dans les boccages qu'ils se
plaisét? les rochers, les ruisseaux cou-
lãts, & les cauernes les plus sombres,
ne leur sõt elles pas aussi plus agreables que les bastiméts somptueux où
l'on void les merueilles de l'Archi-
tecture? Tout ce qu'ils aimét est dóc
aisé à acquerir. Ce sont des contéte-
més qui ne sont refusez aux bergers
ny aux laboureurs & aux vignerós;
& mesme les plus miserables hómes
de la terre n'en peuuét pas estre fru-
strez, car quãd ils iroíét d'vne regió
en l'autre, n'ayãt rié pour viure que
des aumosnes, l'on ne leur sçauroit
oster le bié de cõsiderer la beauté des
chãps & de se plaire en to⁹ les lieux où
ils se trouuerõt. L'on ne doit poít se
mettre en peine d'érichir les poëtes.
Puisque la nature est cõtente de peu

de chofe, ils fe tiennent fatisfaicts de
ce qu'ils ont, ayant toufiours fuiuy
les iuftes loix de la nature. D'ailleurs
s'ils cherchoient les richeffes auec
tant de foin il fembleroit qu'ils en
vouluffent faire la vraye recompenfe de leurs ouurages; Et cependant il eft certain, comme tout le
monde le pourra auoüer, qu'ils font
quelquefois des chofes fi rares, que
tous les threfors du monde ne feroient pas capables de les payer. Les
trahifons, les fauffetez, les flatteries,
& mille autres feruices indignes
font payez par l'argent. Il faut chercher vne plus belle recompenfe qui
eft la gloire. C'eft pour elle que l'on
a du foin & que l'on trauaille iour &
nuict. Il y a beaucoup de chofes qui
fans l'efperance que l'on a d'elle demeureroient imparfaictes. Or fi iamais perfonne a aymé la gloire, ce

sont les Poëtes. C'est vne maistresse qu'ils ne cessent tous les iours de
courtiser, & à la fin ils en reçoiuent
des faueurs par la perseuerance.

La Poësie a cela d'excellent que
l'on ne la sçauroit trop loüer pour
les biens qu'elle apporte aux hommes. Outre qu'elle polit les langues,
elle a des inuentions qui diuertis-
sent merueilleusement l'esprit, &
qui allegent les ennuis de la vie.
Apollon a esté estimé Dieu de la
Poësie & de la Medecine tout ensemble, & ce n'est pas sans cause, car
auec la douceur des vers l'on peut
guerir vne fascheuse melancolie
qui sembloit estre vn mal incurable, & qui mesme eust esté dommageable au corps qui se ressent des
afflictions de l'Esprit. Vn ancien
Philosophe disoit que comme la
voix pressee dans le canal d'vne tró-

pette réd vn son plus esclattant. Ainsi les paroles enfermees en de certaines mesures poëtiques ont plus de
puissance que quand elles coulent
laschement dans le discours vulgaires. Cela est si veritable que ie croy
que personne n'en doute; & que ie
ne m'amuseray point à en donner
d'autres preuues.

Ie veux seulement parler de l'opinion que l'on a que la Poësie est vne
fille desbauchee qui a dés long-téps
perdu sa chasteté! Il est vray que
quelques-vns ont abusé d'elle, mais
c'est à eux que la faute en doit estre
attribuee, l'on la peut employer
à des ouurages serieux aussi tost
qu'à des choses prophanes Quelques-vns pésent qu'elle n'est agreable que lors qu'elle parle d'amour;
mais ils se trompent eux mesmes
sans y penser, & pource qu'ils

ne trouuent rien d'aymable cóme les vers amoureux, ils s'imaginent qu'ils auroient beaucoup de peine à en faire ou à en lire d'autres. Ainsi chacun suit sa passion, & s'il est possible qu'vn Poëte soit auaricieux, l'on en pourroit donc voir aussi qui voudroient que la Poësie ne parlast quet de richesses. Elle n'est point coulpable des fautes que l'on luy faict faire.

Le feu est la chose la plus vtile & la plus commode du monde, & neantmoins vn meschant s'en peut seruir à brusler vn Temple. Les espees n'ont esté forgees que pour se deffendre des vsurpateurs estrangers, ou mesmes des larrons domestiques, ou aussi des bestes que l'on rencontre par les champs, & neantmoins voyla vn meurtrier qui en a tué des hommes innocens qui croyoient estre asseurez par le droict du voisinage & la frequentation ordinaire. Ainsi le vray vsage de toutes choses peut-estre peruerty, & il est arriué de mesme à la Poësie; mais ne soyons pas dans l'erreur de ceux qui croyent qu'elle ne peut seruir qu'à descrire de mauuaises passions. plusieurs bons esprits nous ont monstré que c'estoit son vray vsage que les loüanges de Dieu, & apres cela celle des hommes vertueux. Le Legislateur Solon qui en faisoit tant d'estime, auoit mesme deffendu dans la Republique, que l'on ne fist en vers aucune plainte funebre. Il croyoit que ce fust prophaner la poësie, qui ne deuoit seruir qu'à de sainctes resiouysssances, & à des actions de graces que l'on rend à Dieu. Si les payens ont eu

tant

tant de lumiere parmy les tenebres,
nous qui sommes Chrestiens, nous
n'en deuós pas auoir moins qu'eux;
mais pluftoft il les faut furpasser &
tafcher de remettre la Poësie dans
son luftre. Il ne la faut plus employer
aux Satyres ny aux mesdifances. Il
ne s'en faut plus feruir à defcrire des
vilennies qui font mefme de la hôte
à ceux qui les ont faites, veu qu'ils
ne les oferoient auoüer. Il faut que
tout ce que les hommes operét foit
à la gloire de celuy qui les a creés, &
par confequent les vers y doiuent
eftre plusqu'aucune chofe du mòde,
veu que ce font des ouurages libres
où l'on met tout ce qu'on veut, &
qui ne font pas attachez à de certaines chofes qu'il faut toufiours obferuer, comme les meftiers neceffaires à la vie humaine. Or encore que
tous les poëtes n'ayent pas fongé à

L l

cela, si est-ce qu'ils le peuuent faire
& qu'ils peuuent rendre la Poësie la
plus estimable chose du monde, de
sorte que celuy qui a entrepris de la
blasmer n'aura point d'occasion de
persister en son dessein. Toutesfois
s'il n'entend pas parler de la Poësie
en general, mais seulement de celle où l'on a mis des choses ridicules,
il peut se gouuerner de telle sorte
qu'il ne fera rien contre la raison.

De la multitude des Liures.

'AY eu autrefois en-
uie de faire vn Parado-
xe contre l'Imprime-
rie, & souſtenir contre
l'opinion commune,
qu'elle ne nous eſt pas fort neceſſaire, & qu'elle ne nous eſt pas ſi vtile
comme elle nous eſt dómageable.
Il eſt vray que par ſon moyen l'on a
en peu de temps pluſieurs exemplaires d'vn Liure, que l'on ſeroit long
temps à coppier s'il le falloit eſcrire
à la main; mais il faudroit vſer d'vne
inuention pareille à celle des Regéts
qui liſent dans des chaires à quantité d'eſcoliers. L'on auroit vn homme qui prononceroit diſtinctemét
les mots, & qui ſeroit en vn

fiege efleué au milieu d'vne grande
falle, & tout autour de luy il y auroit fix ou fept cens efcriuains qui
efcriroient ce qu'il dicteroit affez
pofément, & de cefte forte ils pour-
roiët bien faire vne fueille ou deux
par iour, lefquelles contiendroient
à peu pres autant de difcours que
celles des Imprimeries. A la fin de la
iournee quelqu'vn liroit encore ce
qui auroit efté efcrit, & chaque ef-
criuain repafferoit les yeux deffus les fueilles pour corriger les fautes qu'il auroit faites, & adioufter ce qu'il auroit oublié. Il ne faut
point douter que les anciens ne fe
foient feruis de cefte inuention, lors
que l'art de l'Imprimerie n'auoit
pas encore efté inuenté. Mais l'on
me dira qu'il y auoit en cela plufieurs difficultez, veu que l'on auoit
bien de la peine à trouuer tant d'hô-

mes qui escriuissent correctement,
& qu'il y en auoit aussi qui n'auoiēt
pas l'oreille si bonne que les autres,
& qui ne pouuoient pas ouyr celuy
qui dictoit lors qu'ils en estoient vn
peu esloignez, tellement que l'on
ne pouuoit donc pas mettre tant
d'Escriuains ensemble, & par consequent l'on ne pouuoit pas auoir
en vn iour tant de copies d'vn liure.
Toutesfois il faut prendre garde
qu'il estoit fort aysé de remedier à
cela, & qu'il coustoit peu d'auoir
trois ou quatre hommes dans des
salles differentespour dicter tout en
vn iour la mesme chose. Pource qui
est de l'escriture ie confesse qu'elle
ne pouuoit estre si lisible ny si belle que les caracteres de l'Impression; mais en recompense ceux qui
auoient apres cela les liures en leur
possession ne les trouuoient-pas

moins agreables ; Car l'on ne se
donnoit point si souuent ceste peine d'escrire les liures comme l'on
faict auiourd'huy en ce qui est de
les imprimer, si bien que les liures
n'estans pas à si bon marché, ny si
faciles à trouuer pour les achepter,
l'on les estimoit comme des choses
precieuses. L'on me demandera si
ceste façon d'escrire des liures se
pratiquoit souuent chez les anciés?
Non ie ne le pense pas. La science
n'estoit pas encore venale comme
elle est, ou si elle l'estoit, ce n'estoit
pas vne chose fort commune. Le
corps des Libraires n'estoit pas alors
aussi grand que celuy des autres
marchands & le trauail des hommes de lettres ne se voyoit pas tous
les iours traisner par les ruës dans
des charettes ou sur les crochets
des portefaix. Quelque homme ri-

che a bien pû entreprendre quelque bon liure en peu de temps, &
par ce moyen il a payé les iournees
des Escriuains qu'il a mis au trauail,
mais ce n'a pas tousiours esté pour
en faire traffic ; C'a esté quelquefois pour faire des presents, & pour
accomplir la Bibliotheque de quelques Esprits curieux. Mais il est certain que les anciens Autheurs qui
ont eu desir que leurs œuures se ren-
dissent publiques, ont bien pris la
peine eux-mesmes d'en aller faire la
lecture dans des lieux qui estoient
destinez à cela, & tous ceux qui a-
uoient desir d'en tirer coppie les
alloient escrire sous eux ; ou
bien ils y enuoyoient de pauures
gens dont ils recompensoient
le trauail. Or cela doit estre certain : car nous voyant dans beau-

coup d'autheurs des preuues de cette couſtume, ou tout au moins d'v-
ne autre qui en approche fort; c'eſt
que lors qu'vn Poëte ou vn Decla-
mateur, ou quelque Sophiſte deſi-
roiét auoir l'approbation du public
pour quelque choſe qu'ils auoient
faicte, ils montoient en chaire & li-
ſoient leurs ouurages deuant ceux
qui les vouloient eſcouter, & meſmes l'on auoit la licence de leur ap-
plaudir ou de les ſiſſler ſelon qu'ils
auoient faict de bonnes ou de mauuaiſes pieces. Que ſi leurs Poëſies,
ou leurs diſcours en proſe, eſtoient
dans vn degré d'excellence dont
perſonne ne pouuoit douter; Il faut
croire auſſi que pluſieurs eſcriuoient ſous eux, & de là l'on tire la conſequence de ceſte inuention d'eſcrire que i'ay alleguee.
A n'en point mentir il falloit bié du

móde pour acheuer vn liure de cette forte. Au lieu que cinq ou fix
hommes feront deux fueilles d'imprimerie en vn iour, dont il y en aura mille de chacune, il euft fallu que
les anciens Efcriuains euffent efté en
plus grand nombre qu'ils n'auoient
de fueilles à faire, & encore ne pouuoient ils pas trauailler auec vne fi
grande diligence.

L'Imprimerie eft doncvne mer-
ueilleufe inuention felon l'opinion
de tous: mais ie dy derechef que i'a-
uois entrepris de móftrer qu'elle eft
dommageable. Ie ne cele point vne
chofe que ie pourrois encore fouste-
nir s'il m'en prenoit l'enuie. qu'ainfi
ne foit, n'eft-il pas vray que cette facilité de faire en peu de temps plufieurs exemplaires d'vn liure , eft
caufe que tout le monde en defire
compofer fans confiderer fa capaci-

té. L'on en void tous les iours naiftre qui ne meritent pas de voir le
iour. Que s'il nous faloit faire encore la grande defpenfe que les anciens faifoient pour leurs efcriuains, il n'y auroit perfonne qui fe
vouluft ruiner à faire tranfcrire plufieurs fois vn mauuais liure. Que fi
les Autheurs montoient encore en
chaire pour lire leurs efcrits,
il y en a plufieurs de noftre temps
qui n'auroient garde de trouuer
perfonne qui en vouluft tirer coppie. L'on ne fe donneroit pas feulement la peine de les aller efcou-
ter , & ces pauures gens ne parle-
roient qu'à des murailles , ou bien il
faudroit que pour contenter leur
vanité ils priffent quelque iour des
auditeurs à loüage , & fi par hazard des honneftes gés alloient paffer quelque apref difnée dans leur

auditoire, ce ne feroit que pour ri-
re aux defpens de leur fottife & de
leur temerité.

Il n'y auroit que les excellents
perfonnages qui feroient efcoutez
& qui auroient l'hôneur de voir de
bons efprits faire eftime de leurs ouurages, & prendre la peine d'en efcrire ce qui leur fembleroit de meilleur. Tant d'impertinences que l'on
void ne feroient pas diftribuees au
peuple fans de bons tiltres qui les
defguifent, & qui les font prendre
pour ce qu'elles ne font pas. L'on
n'en feroit pas moins fçauant quád il
y auroit moins de liures, l'on fe pre-
feroit l'vn à l'autre ceux que l'on
auroit, ou bien l'on fe pafferoit fort
facilemét de ceux qui feroiét inutiles, & l'on tafcheroit de moderer fa
curiofité. Apres que chacun a les liures qui luy font neceffaires felon fa

profession, il n'eſt pas beſoin que
l'on garde ceux qui ne traictent que
de choſes indifferentes. L'on ſe doit
contenter de les lire vne fois & d'en
extraire ce qui nous ſemble de plus
excellent & de plus conforme au
genre de vie que nous auons delibe-
ré de choiſir. Il y a vne conuoitiſe
dommageable en ce qui eſt des liures comme en ce qui eſt des thre-
ſors ou des voluptez mondaines. Il
y faut apporter de la moderation ſi
nous ne voulons qu'elle nous perde.
Le corps & l'eſprit ſe trouuent mal
apres le trauail exceſſif de l'Eſtude.
Le deſir des liures croiſt inceſſamment, & tant plus l'on a leu de choſes, tant moins l'on eſt ſatisfaict, &
l'on ne ceſſe iamais de chercher vne
ſatisfaction qu'il eſt impoſſible de
trouuer en ce monde. Salomon qui
eſtoit le plus ſage de tous les hom-

mes, qui auoit tant leu & tant escrit,
n'aprouue pas luy mesme cette passion que l'on a pour escrire. Que si
la trop grande lecture des bons liures nous peut nuire en quelque sorte, quel dommage ne faut-il point
attendre de ceux où il n'y a rien que
des paroles & point de bon sens, &
mesmes des paroles fort mal arren-
gées ?

Nous receuons ce preiudice de
l'Imprimerie, qu'elle est souuét cause que nous employons si mal le
temps , & que nous ne pouuons
nous abstenir de lire toutes les nouueautez que nous voyons paroistre.
Passe pour celles qui n'outragent
personne, & qui ne touchent ny au
public, ny au particulier ; mais il y a
quelquefois des hommes si passion-
nez qu'ils veulent faire esclatter leur
colere par tout, & semer des calom-

nies estranges parmy le peuple. Ils font imprimer en vne nuict vne Satyre qui se distribuë le lēdemain en moins de rien, & l'on a de la peine quelquefois à trouuer cette mauuaise source, ce qui n'arriueroit pas sans l'impression, car l'escriture faite à la main seroit beaucoup plus aysee à recognoistre.

Quand l'on a consideré cela l'on void quel dommage nous apporte l'Imprimerie, & l'on peut iuger que ie n'auois pas trop mauuaise raison de dresser vne inuectiue contre elle. Toutefois ie n'ay iamais pretendu de le faire que par vne maniere de jeu, & de la mesme sorte que les anciens Declamateurs s'exerçoient à l'eloquence en parlant contre les choses qui estoient generalement approuuées. Ie sçay bien que maintenant l'on met vn tel ordre aux li-

ures que l'on ne permet plus qu'il
s'en imprime d'autres que ceux qui
sont dignes d'estre imprimez , &
pour ce qui est des pieces Satyri-
ques, elles sont generalement ban-
nies. C'est ce qui donnera courage
desormais aux bons esprits de paroistre, & de s'esleuer plus que de coustume, voyant que l'on ne les mettra plus en parallele auec des sots &
des ignorans. Ie souhaitte que cela
se fasse ainsi comme ie le propose, &
que mesme il arriue plus de gloire
& d'honneur aux personnes de lettres qu'ils n'en auoient esperé dedans ce siecle.

De l'vtilité de la science Morale &
de la Politique.

LEs esprits se sont tousiours addonnez à diuerses sciences, selon leurs diuerses inclinations. Ceux qui ont philosophé les premiers n'ont point crû qu'il y eust aucune chose qui meritast mieux d'estre consideree que le cours du Soleil, & des Astres, puis que c'est la premiere chose qui s'offre à nous dans le monde, d'autant que l'homme ne va point rampant comme les autres animaux, & qu'il a la teste leuée pour considerer les merueilles du Ciel. De là vient que les anciens se sont fort addonnez à l'Astrologie & ne croyans pas que

ce fult affez pour leur curiofité, ils
ont auffi remarqué ce qui fe faifoit
plus bas. Ils ont parlé des Comet-
tes, des pluyes, des vents, & des neiges, & ils n'ont pas oublié la nature
des pierres & des metaux. Ils ont
fait auffi des obferuations fur les
parties du corps des animaux, & fur
celles de l'homme; & veritablemét
ils ont faict des recherches fi mer-
ueilleufes, que qui ne les admireroit
auroit vne ftupidité prefque femblable à celle des beftes. Ils ont bien
paffé plus auant, car ils ont mefme
recherché les chofes inuifibles &
furnaturelles, & ils en ont parlé
auec vne doctrine admirable.

Ie ne nie point que leur trauail
ne foit loüable; mais neantmoins il
y a eu depuis des Philofophes qui
leur ont efté contraires, & qui ont
entrepris de retirer les hommes de

la contemplation de ces choses re-
leuees pour ne les occuper qu'à se
bien gouuerner eux-mesmes. Celuy qui a eu plus d'authorité que
tous les autres, est Socrate que Pla-
ton fait parler de cesteforte au Phe-
don. Lors que i'estois encore en
vn fort bas âge, disoit-il, i'auois vn
desir nompareil d'aprendre l'histoire de la nature Ie croyois que cela
estoit fort excellent de sçauoir la
course & l'origine d'vne chose, &
comment elle se maintient , &
pourquoy elle se destruict : C'est
pour ce subjet que i'ay souuent eu
diuerses agitations dans mon esprit
parmy de semblables considerations, comme par exemple à sçauoir si apres que le chaud & le froid
ont receu quelque putrefaction les
animaux en prennent leur nourriture. Outre cela ie m'amusois à considerer, si pour auoir plus de sang

ou de bile ou de pituite, nous estiós
plus sages ou plus fols, & de quelle
forte tous nos sens se raportoient à
l'entendement, mais à la fin ayant
veu qu'il y auoit tant de diuersité
dans toutes ces choses, qu'à peine
y pouuoit on rien establir de certain, i'ay recognu que ie ne profi-
tois de rien en toutes ces choses, &
que ie les desaprenois mesme lors
que ie les pensois sçauoir.

Xenophon confirme la mesme
chose touchant l'opinion de Socrate. Il s'est accordé en cecy auec Pla-
ton, encore qu'ils ne fussent pas fort
bons amys. Il dit au premier liure
de ses Memoires; Que Socrate ne
parloit point de la matiere de toutes choses comme les autres Philosophes, qu'il ne consideroit point
comment le monde auoit esté creé,
mais qu'il monstroit que ceux qui

s'addonnoient à vne telle contemplation, ne faiſoient que perdre leur
temps ; car premierement il s'en-
queroit ſi ces gens-là penſoient deſja cognoiſtre aſſez bien les choſes
humaines pour s'eſleuer aux diuines & aux celeſtes. Il diſoit qu'il ne
ſçauoit comment ils s'imaginoient
d'en pouuoir apprendre la moindre
partie, veu que ceux qui les enſei-
gnoient le mieux en eſtoient inceſ-
famment en diſpute. Il leur demandoit encore ſi de meſme que ceux
qui ont quelque cognoiſſance des
affaires humaines peuuent appro-
prier ce qu'ils ont apris à leur vſage
ou à celuy des autres ; ils eſtimoient
pareillement que s'eſtans enquis des
choſes celeſtes, & en ayans apris
quelque peu, ils pourroient les imiter, & faire pleuuoir quand ils voudroient, & changer les ſaiſons ſelon

qu'il seroit neceſſaire. Que s'ils n'a-
uoient aucune eſperance de faire
cela, il leur remonſtroit que leur recherche eſtoit vaine, & que ce n'e-
ſtoit pas aſſez que de cognoiſtre,
ſans auoir rien que ceſte cognoiſſance.

Voyla l'eſtime qu'il faiſoit de
tout ce qui eſtoit au deſſus de nous.
Il ne vouloit point que les hommes
euſſent d'autres occupations que
celles que l'on prend en fuyant le
vice & ſuiuant la vertu. Il ne ceſſoit
de diſputer de la difference de la iuſtice & de l'iniuſtice, de la pieté &
de l'impieté, de la prudence & de la
folie; & veritablement par ce moyé
là il attiroit les hommes au ſommet
de la perfection, & il les faiſoit viure dans vne tranquillité nompareille.

Toutesfois le chemin de la vertu

est maintenant bien plus facile aux
Chrestiens qu'il n'estoit à ces pauures Payens. I'ay veu quelque part
vne similitude qui est extrememét
propre à ce sujet. C'est que si des
hommes auoient eu perpetuelle-
ment le dos tourné au Soleil, ils ne
croyroient pas qu'il y eust autre lumiere au monde que celle qu'ils
verroient par reflexion, & ils seroiét
fort satisfaicts. Ainsi ces pauures
Philosophes ne voyoient pas la
vraye lumiere de Dieu dont nous
sommes esclairez par la foy, tellement qu'ils se contentoient de la
clarté qui leur estoit seulement en-
uoyee par ses œuures. Nous qui ne
sommes pas dedans les erreurs qui
les ont perdus, nous ne nous ren-
dons pas opiniastres à suiure plustost vne secte qu'vne autre; L'on se
doit mocquer de ceux qui n'esti-

ment que leur Phyſique, & des autres auſſi qui ne veulent point que
l'on aprenne autre choſe que leur
morale. Il eſt certain que la morale eſt la plus vtile ſcience de toutes
les autres ; mais lors que l'on ſera
ſçauant aux choſes naturelles & que
l'on aura recognu les effets de la
puiſſance de Dieu, l'on aura vn plus
ferme deſir de l'honorer & de bien
viure. Il faut ioindre toutes les ſcié-
ces enſemble pour en faire vn eſprit
accomply, mais ie ſuis bien d'aduis
que la ſcience qui aprend à former
les mœurs tienne touſiours le premier rang.

La ſcience Morale eſt la Maiſtreſſe de la vie. C'eſt le vray art des
hommes, les autres ne ſont abſolument neceſſaires que ſelon les pro-
feſſions que l'on veut ſuiure : ainſi
l'on void que les Medecins ne ſçau-

roient se passer de sçauoir la Physi-
que, mais la Morale est propre à
tous les hommes, & en toute sorte
de saisons. C'est elle qui aprend à
souffrir patiemment les iniures, &
à se souuenir incessamment des bié-
faicts. C'est elle qui adoucit les
amertumes de la vie, & qui faict
que les miseres humaines n'abattent
point nostre courage. C'est elle qui
modere nostre conuoitise, qui retient nostre ambition, & qui tem-
pere nostre courroux. C'est elle en
fin qui nous aprend à estre hommes, puis qu'elle nous monstre de
quelle sorte il se faut seruir de la
raison, qui est la qualité qui nous esleue au dessus des bestes.

　　Ceux qui enseignent auiour-
d'huy la ieunesse auec vn extreme
tort de s'amuser comme ils font à
ces menuës obseruations, touchant

la Grammaire, pluſtoſt que de mettre de bonne heure ceſte ſcience
dans l'eſprit des enfans, afin que iamais elle n'en partiſt, & qu'elles fiſt
que leurs plus naturelles inclinations ne tendiſſent qu'à la vertu.

De ceſte ſcience morale depend
la Politique qui eſt encore vne piece exquiſe, mais elle n'eſt principalement neceſſaire qu'à ceux qui
gouuernent les Eſtats. Toutefois
le chemin des ſciences n'a iamais
eſté fermé à perſonne. Quiconque
veut ſçauoir la Politique la peut apprendre, & il verra meſme de quelle ſorte les Princes empeſchent que
les ſeditions ne ſoient produites parmy leur peuple, & comment ils ſe
deffendent des tromperies de leurs
ennemis. Encore que l'on ſoit d'vne
condition extremement baſſe, l'on
peut bien voir cela, & encore

que nous ne soyons point appellez dedans le Conseil des grands,
si est-ce que cette science ne nous
est pas tout à faict inutile : car elle nous apprend à bien obeyr de
mesme qu'elle apprend aux autres
à bien amander ; & puis il n'est
pas arresté qu'il n'y aura que ceux
qui sont desia fort auancez par le
merite de leurs predecesseurs &
par la grandeur de leur race, qui
jouyront de tous les honneurs du
monde.

Ce que nous auons de pro-
pre nous peut seruir, & ceux qui
se monstrent necessaires ne manquent point d'estre esleuez dans
quelque charge, & ils paruien-
nent quelquefois par diuers degrez iusques en des lieux plus eminents que tous les autres.

Tous ces grands legiſlateurs de l'Antiquité ne ſe ſont point mis en en credit que par la ſcience politique. Tant de Princes qui ont auſſi ſurpaſſé les autres ont ſuiuy la meſme profeſſion ; mais outre les preceptes que leur auoient pû donner les liures, ou quelques Philoſophes meſmes qui leur auoient enſeigné ces rares ſecrets, il leur eſtoit beſoin d'vn grand iugement pour les appliquer. C'eſt ce que fait reüſſir tous les deſſeins que l'on entreprend & qui nous donne de la gloire en des occaſions où les autres n'euſſent emporté que de l'infamie.

C'eſt ce qui entretient la paix des Royaumes, ce qui fait gaigner les batailles, ce qui faict que les traittez ſont profitables, & qui attire les benedictions de tout le peuple.

Le plus grand secours de ceste
science ciuile c'est la Morale qui
l'a doit touſiours preceder. C'est ſur
elle qu'il faut prendre ſon fondement. Il faut eſtre vertueux auparauant que d'eſtre bon Politique.
Ceux qui font autrement deguiſent
les vertus, leur prudence n'eſt qu'v-
ne trôperie, leurs paroles ſont fauſſes, leurs actions ſont faictes : ils
n'ont rien en eux qui ne ſoit fardé,
& ils ayment mieux l'apparence
que les choſes veritables. Si nous
voulons donc nous rendre capables
des affaires du monde, n'aprenons
les ſciences Scholaſtiques que pour
monſtrer que nous ne les auons pas
entierement negligees, & que nous
deſirons nous en ſeruir autant côme il ſera beſoin dans les occaſions.
Mais pour la Morale à la vraye Politique, faiſons en ſorte que ce ſoit

noſtre eſtude particuliere , & ne croyons iamais que nous en ſçauons aſſez. Toutesfois ne nous aſſeurons pas entierement ſur les preceptes des Autheurs. Ils ont pû quelquefois ſe tromper, ou bien les choſes qu'ils ont enſeignees ne ſont pas propres dans les accidens qui nous arriuent, comme dans ceux dont ils ont veu des exemples : car il ne faut qu'vne fort petite circonſtáce pour donner beaucoup de peine, & pour nous faire voir que chaque mal veut auoir ſon remede. Seruons nous donc de noſtre eſprit apres que nous l'aurons rendu plus poly & plus ſubtil qu'il n'eſtoit de ſa nature dans des affaires differentes. C'eſt vne dangereuſe choſe lors que les hommes ſans iugement ne veulent croire qu'eux meſmes; mais il n'en eſt pas ainſi de ceux dont la

ſageſſe eſt bien eſprouuee. L'on ne
leur donne pas ſouuent de meilleurs
conſeils que ceux qu'ils prennent
eux-meſmes, car comme les affaires
les touchent de pres, ils les conçoiuent merueilleuſement bien, & ils
iugent mieux que pas-vn quelle en
doit eſtre l'iſſuë. Quand nous aurós
donc vne vraye vertu, & que nous
remarquerons d'vn bon ſens tout
ce qui arriuera, nous nous rendrons
ſages par l'experience qui eſt la plus
grande Maiſtreſſe du monde, &
nous ne pourrons manquer de venir à bout de nos deſſeins, pouruen
qu'ils ſoient bons & iuſtes.

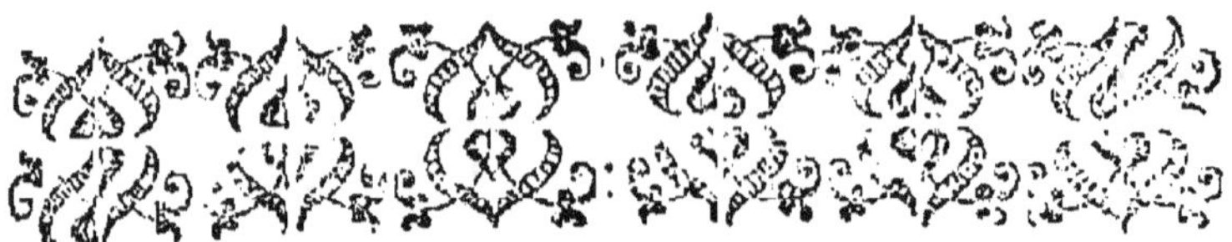

LVCIDOR A PHILANDRE.

Du plaisir de la vie Champeſtre,

LETTRE PREMIERE.

IE ne vous nie pas, Philandre, que ie n'aye autrefois allegué toutes les raiſons qui ſe pouuoient inuenter, pour monſtrer que la ſolitude Champeſtre, ne deuoit point eſtre preferée à la bonne compagnie qui ſe trouue dans les villes. Mais il ne faut pas neantmoins que vous penſiez vous ſeruir aujourd'huy contre moy des meſmes arguments Il faut que vous conſideriez que ie me ſeruois alors

de toutes les puiſſances de la Retho-
rique, & que ie diſois quelquefois
des choſes qui eſtoient plus vray-
ſemblables que vrayes. L'Occaſion
le vouloit ainſi; car il eſtoit queſtion
de ſonder de tous les coſtez vn eſprit opiniaſtre qui ne vouloit bouger des champs toute ſa vie, & ſe
gouuerner auec plus de brutalité
que de bien-ſeance, encore que s'il
euſt voulu il euſt eu le moyen de paroiſtre parmy les honneſtes gens.
Vous ſçauez bien que ie ne ſuis pas
de la ſorte, & que je veux ſeulemēt
demeurer icy iuſques à temps que
mes affaires me rappelleront autre-
part. Il n'eſt pas deffendu de changer de ſtile ſuiuant les occaſions diuerſes, pourueu que l'on ne peche
point contre les reigles de l'honneſte-
té & celles de la bienſeance. Le
joüeur de Luth qui ne ſçait joüer

que

que fur vn ton n'eſt pas maiſtre ac-
cōply. Auſſi l'Orateur qui ne ſçauroit perſuader qu'vne ſeule choſe
n'eſt pas des plus entédus en ſon art.
Il faut ſçauoir parler de diuerſes matieres, & l'on s'exerce meſme bien
ſouuent ſur des choſes extrauagantes, afin que leur difficulté ſerue dauantage à aiguiſer leur eſprit. Que
ſi i'ay parlé contre les plaiſirs des
champs, ç'a eſté de la meſme ſorte
que celuy qui voulût perſuader à vn
auaricieux qu'il deuroit quitter ſon
auarice, s'efforceroit de luy mettre
tout à fait les richeſſes en horreur,
afin de l'en mieux deſtourner,
comme s'il luy vouloit quaſi remō-
ſtrer que ſon or & ſon argent ſont
inutiles, & qu'il les deuroit ietter
dans la riuiere, ainſi que ce Philoſophe qui ietta de meſme tout ce qu'il
auoit, diſant qu'il vouloit perdre ſes

richeſſes , craignant qu'elles ne le perdiſſent. Cependãt l'on ſçait bien que les richeſſes ne doiuent pas eſtre generalement condamnees, & que quand l'on s'en ſert honneſtement, & que l'on en diſtribue à ceux qui en ont beſoin ſelon les occaſions, elles ſeruent de beaucoup à faire paroiſtre la vertu des hommes ; mais pource que ce feroit flatter le vice de luy laiſſer le moyen de s'eſleuer touſiours contre la raiſon, l'on condamne tout à faiĉt deuãt les vitieux les choſes dont l'on permet vn vſage moderé, à ceux qui ſçauent bien ſe gouuerner d'eux meſmes. Voyla comme quoy i'ay parlé abſolument contre les delices champeſtres pour en deſtourner celuy qui les affeĉtiónoit trop ; mais ce n'eſt pas à dire que ie n'entende bien qu'il eſt permis d'en vſer moderement , & ie

croy que maintenant vous commé-
cez de comprendre mon intention
& que vous ne me blasmez plus de
m'estre retiré en ce lieu cy. Il faut
que vous en consideriez encore les
occasions qui sont tres-grandes, &
qui non seulement en auroient fait
retirer quelques-vns dans vne maison pourueuë de toute sorte de cómoditez comme la mienne , mais
plustost dans vn hermitage. Apres la
mort de celle qui m'estoit jointe par
vne affection naturelle autant que
par les liens du mariage, je ne voy
encore qu'à regret les lieux où ie l'ay
perduë. Ie sçay bien qu'à la fin ie
m'y pourrois bien accoustumer, &
que ie modererois mon afflictió par
les conseils de la Philosophie; mais ie
veux bien cótribuer quelque chose
à la foiblesse humaine, & m'esloigner de ce qui peut empescher l'effet

des remedes ; car nous ne sommes
pas touſiours obligez de nous ſeruir
d'vne ſi forte conſtance. Il ne vous
en faut point mentir, Philandre, il y
a eu encore autre choſe qui a cauſé
mon depart, car pour moy qui me
ſuis tant de fois meſlé de donner de
la conſolation aux autres, ce ſeroit
mãquer aux choſes que ie voudrois
enſeigner, que de ne pouuoir donner de terme à la triſteſſe que i'ay
euë, & d'auoir beſoin d'artifice en
cecy. Ie ne veux donc point vous
celer mes intentions ; ce qui m'a
eſloigné de Paris, c'eſt que ie n'y
ſçaurois plus demeurer ſans y receuoir de grãdes importunitez. Vous
ſçauez que mes plus beaux deſſeins
y ont eu vn tres-mauuais ſuccez, &
que de ſi fortes calõnies ſe ſont eſleuées contre moy, que les perſonnes
les plus puiſſantes ont ceſſé de me fa-

uoriſer. Cela fait que ie ne rencôtre
perſonne dans les ruës qui ſoit de ma
cónoiſſance qui ne m'aborde. Chacun témoigne d'auoir vne extreme
curioſité pour entendre la cauſe de
ma diſgrace. Il faut qu'en vn iour ie
rediſe cent fois vne meſme choſe,
& encore ne ſçay-ie ſi chacun me
croit. Ie me deſplais de voir cette
ſotte humeur des hómes qui en ac-
coſtant les autres ne leur parlent de
rien que de ce qui leur eſt plus deſagreable. Ie me ſuis retiré aux chãps
pour euiter cela, & ie pretẽds d'y demeurer iuſques à ce qu'il viéne vne
autre reuolution, & que ie puſſe móſtrer mon innocence aux yeux de
tout le monde.

Ne dites pas que celuy qui s'eſtu-
die à la vertu deuoit meſpriſer toutes
ces cóſideratiós & ſe tenir touſiours
en vn meſme lieu pour y receuoir

toutes les attaques de la fortune. Dieu ne deffend point que les hommes s'aydent lors qu'ils le peuuent faire: au contraire il leur commande de ne se point negliger; d'ailleurs il n'a point esté à propos que i'aye donné plus long temps sujet à tant de personnes de se mettre en peine pour moy. Que si vous croyez qu'il y ait encore vne autre raison de mó esloignement; vous ne vous trompez point. C'est que ie suis las de tant de diuerses poursuites. I'ay voulu me retirer en vn lieu où ie me pûsse reposer à loisir, & où les affaires ne me vinssent point chercher. Ie me suis mis aussi dedans les champs pour les plaisirs que l'on y trouue, & ie ne me cache point de vous en cela. Arrestez là vostre opinion si vous voulez; ie ne vous y contrediray point.

I'ay parlé autrefois du plaisir des

villes, mais ie n'en difois pas les incómoditez , & principalement celles
des grandes cóme Paris. Cette ville
commence maintenant à eftre trop
chargée de fon propre poids; fa grã-
deur luy eft importune, & les chofes mefmes dont les eftrangers la
loüent, ne font pas celles qui luy ap-
portent le plus de commodité. Cela
eft bon pour ceux qui n'y font que
paffer, & qui croyét que leur voyage eft d'autát mieux employé qu'ils
voyent plus de diuers fpectacles;
mais pour ceux qui y demeurent, ils
y peuuent trouuer quantité de chofes qui les fafchent. Toute forte de
gens abordent là, & il s'y faict vne
telle confufion que l'on a de la peine à fe recónoiftre. Les voleurs & les
meurtriers y font plus affeurez que
dans la plus grande foreft du móde,
& s'ils font pris à la fin , il en faut
N n iiij

donner la gloire aux perquifitions exactes de la Iuftice. Au refte quand l'on s'exemptera des tromperies & des larcins de tant de perfonnes in-cogneuës, l'on ne peut euiter l'im-portunité du bruict qui fe fait à tou-te heure. Les vns crient, les autres fe battent, quelques-vns chantent d'v-ne façon importune , & cela dure iufques à plus de la moitié de la nuit: & vous n'auez pas mefme la mati-née libre. Les Marefchaux & les fer-ruriers battent le fer fur leur enclu-me auant qu'il foit iour; les charret-tes commencét à paffer & les petits artifans vous efueillent auffi par leurs fottes chanfons. Que fi vous fortez le long du iour, mille incom-moditez vous accompagnér. Vous rencótrerez vn hóme que fes affaires preffent d'aller treuuer quelqu'vn, qui marchant fans prendre garde à soy, vous donnera du coude dans l'estomach. Vn crochetteur chargé d'vn coffre vous heurtera d'vn autre costé, & vous ne prendrez pas garde que quelque estourdy auan-cera son cheual iusques sur vos talons Si vous allez plus loin, vous trouuerez des charrettes & des carosses tellemét embarrassez ensemble que vous serez là vne heure auát que de pouuoir trouuer passage, & si en quelques lieux ces incommo-ditez ne vous arriuent point, à tout le moins ne pourrez vous vous exé-pter de celle des crottes qui est si grande que l'on a beaucoup de pei-ne à la souffrir, veu que mesmes cela rend vne odeur qui est fort desa-greable à ceux qui n'y sont pas ac-coustumez. Dans tous les lieux pu-blics où l'on peut aller l'on a encore assez de trauail à endurer, & si l'on cherche quelqu'vn pour quelque affaire l'on ne le trouue que difficile-ment. Le malheur eſt que l'on trou-ue bien plus ſouuent ceux que l'on ne cherche pas, & que l'on voudroit pouuoir éuiter. Si l'on vient meſme ſe retirer quelque téps pour s'addó-ner à l'eſtude ou à quelque autre oc-cupation, l'on eſt inceſſamment diuerty. Outre le bruit que l'on ne ſe peut exépter d'entendre, l'on eſt de-ſtourné quelquefois par des viſites de certaines perſonnes qui nous obligeroient fort ſi elles nous vou-loient oublier, & il faut eſtre trois ou quatre heures comme à la geſne dedans leur compagnie.

Vous me direz que l'on ſe peut faire celer, mais cela eſt bien ſouuét impoſſible, & l'on tomberoit dans l'inconuenient de Scipion qui auoit dit à ſa ſeruante qu'elle diſt à Ennius

qui le demãdoit qu'il n'y estoit pas,
ce que le Poëte entendit fort bien,
de sorte qu'vne autre fois que Sci-
pió vint pour le voir il se mit à la fe-
nestre, & luy dit qu'il n'y estoit pas.
Scipion luy dit qu'il se mocquoit
puis qu'il luy parloit luy mesme;
mais Ennius luy respódit pourquoy
ne voulez vous pas me croire aussi
bien cõme vous me vouliez l'autre
iour obliger à croire vne simple ser-
uáte quand elle disoit que vous n'y
estiez pas? Voyla vne petite gaillar-
dise des Anciens, laquelle ie vous
rapporte icy tout expres, & ie veux
en faire quelquefois de mesme pour
vous aduertir qu'il se faut joüer se-
rieusemét, & que l'on peut parler de
ces grãds persónages iusques dãs les
railleries, afin de les auoir tousiours
deuãt les yeux pour s'exciter à la vertu. Pour retourner à nostre propos, il

faut croire qu'il y a des personnes
dõt l'on ne peut honneſtemét euiter
les viſites quand l'on demeure dans
vne meſme ville, & bien ſouuent
dans vne meſme ruë. Il n'y a que
la ſolitude des champs qui nous
puiſſe exempter de ceſte importunité. L'on penſe euiter toutes les
incommoditez des villes quand
l'on va à cheual ou en carroſſe;mais
il ne laiſſe pas d'y en auoir encore
aſſez de reſte, & pour ce qui eſt du
bruit & de la confuſion l'on auroit
bien de la peine à les euiter, car il
n'y a point de quartier qui n'en ayt
ſa part ſoit d'vne façon ou d'vne autre. L'on penſe quelquefois eſtre
loin de toute ſorte d'importunité,
pource que l'on n'eſt pas logé ſur le
chemin des charettes, qu'il n'y a
point de cloches là aupres, & que
l'on ne frappe point du marteau

aux enuirons, mais ce qui eſt bien pis que cela, il n'y a que la muraille entre nous & vne voiſine qui ne ceſſe de crier nuiĉt & iour contre ſon mary. Il ſeroit autant impoſſible de la faire taire comme d'arreſter le vent, d'empeſcher la pluye de tomber, ou de retarder les coups de tonnerre, & de mettre quelque empeſchement à toutes les choſes qui ſont naturelles. Quelle puiſſance auroit-on là deſſus ſi le Miniſtre de la maiſon n'y peut rien? Or ceſte importunité ne ſe trouue point dans vne retraiĉte comme la mienne. Ie ſeray logé tout ſeul quád ie viendray, & ie ne paſtiray point pour les follies d'autruy. Que ſi vous ne croyez point que l'on doiue quitter la ville pour aucune incommodité qu'elle ayt, dautant que l'on s'en peut garentir par des moyens que ie ne m'imagine pas, au moins faut-il eſtimer les champs pour les plaiſirs qui ne leur ſçauroient iamais manquer.

Nous n'auons point icy de mauuais air qui engendre des maladies. Ie ſçay bien que les Elemens ne ſe trouuent guere dans leur pureté, mais ils ſont icy moins meſlez qu'en pas-vn autre lieu, & ils n'y ont pas tant de deſſein de ſe deſtruire. Bien ſouuent noſtre air n'a point d'odeur, ou s'il en a elle ne peut eſtre qu'agreable. Lors qu'il a vn peu pleu, apres vne grande chaleur, la terre nous enuoye vne ſenteur agreable, & il y a des temps où tout eſt parfumé de l'odeur des fleurs, & ie ne dy pas ſeulement de celles de nos iardins, mais de celles qui naiſſent aux hayes. Il y a meſme des herbes dans nos prez qui ont vne odeur excellente. Pour ce qui est du sommeil, nous l'auons icy plus paisible qu'en aucun autre lieu. L'on ne heurte point du matin à nostre porte pour nous aduertir de songer promptement à quelque affaire, & personne ne vient aussi nous faire si matin quelque requeste iniuste & importune. Tout le monde trauaille bien chez nous. Il n'y a personne d'oysif entre tous les hommes, que ie nourris, mais ils ne trauaillent pas pourtant à des mestiers qui fassent tant de bruit que ceux de la ville. Ils ont seulement des occupations champestres qui ne me nuisent point.

Ceux qui meinent la charuë ne s'entendent pas, & encore moins ceux qui coupent les bleds, & pour ce qui est de ceux qui battent dans la grange, ils sont assez esloignez de moy. Les volailles ne sont pas mesme dans la Cour de mon logement; car il y en a vne à part qui sert pour les Laboureurs & les Bergers. Ie ne puis donc estre esueillé que par le chant des oyseaux qui viennent dés le matin iusques sur mes fenestres, ou qui se perchent sur les arbres de mon iardin; mais il faut croire que leur musique est si douce que si ie m'esueille quelquefois de moy-mesme, ou par la nouueauté de leurs chansons, ie me rendors apres auec vne mesme facilité.

Le long du iour ie fay tout ce que ie veux. Il n'y a point de lieu où la liberté soit si entiere Personne ne vient controller mes actions ou me diuertir de ce que i'ay entrepris, ie passeray vne sepmaine de mon humeur retiree, & que l'on s'efforce

de

de ſçauoir à quels nouueaux ouurages ie trauaille. Que ſi ie veux ſortir
quelquefois ie trouue moyen de
Philoſopher à mon aiſe. Ie contem-
ple à nud toute la nature. Ie voy des
choſes que dedans les villes l'on ne
void iamais qu'en portraict. Iuſques
à ceſte heure i'auois bien ouy parler
de toutes les eſtoilles, mais ie n'auois
ſceu en remarquer pas-vne, maintenant ie les puis conſiderer toutes
& remarquer leurs diuerſes grandeurs, & meſme il y en auoit quelques vnes que ie ne pouuois cognoiſtre, leſquelles m'ont eſté mon-
ſtrees par des Payens, car leurs ob-
ſeruations ruſtiques ne ſont pas
touſiours meſpriſables. Les maiſons
qui ſont dans les villes ſont ſi hautes
que l'on ne void iamais qu'vne petite partie du Ciel. Cela m'a long
temps importuné, & ie n'auois ia-

mais pû aussi remarquer le cours
du Soleil. Ie me puis maintenant
contenter en cela tous les iours. Ma
maison est en la plus belle veuë du
monde. Elle est au milieu d'vne
large campagne, & il n'y a que
d'vn costé que l'on void vne colli-
ne qui borne la veuë; mais elle est
si esloignee qu'elle ne nuit point,
& que quand elle n'y seroit pas l'on
n'en verroit pas plus de choses. Ie
voy donc en quel lieu se leue le Soleil vn certain iour, & en quel lieu
il se couche, & comment petit à
petit il se leuera & se couchera plus
loin. Ie remarque en quel lieu il est
au temps de l'Equinoxe, & ie tire
plus de plaisir de ces diuerses obseruations que l'on ne fait pas à considerer tout ce qui se rencontre dans
les villes; car les choses naturelles
qui sont les propres ouurages de

Dieu, nous doiuent plaire dauantage que celles qui sont artificielles,
& qui ne sont que les ouurages des
hommes.

Mettray-ie en ligne de compte
que toutes les choses dont ie me
nourry sont plus pures & plus nettes que celles dont vous vous nour-
rissez. Le pain que ie mange est
faict de mon bled ; Ie sçay bien que
les mains qui l'ont paistry ont accoustumé d'estre nettes, l'on ne met
sur ma table que ce qui a esté esleué
dans ma Cour, & si ie mange des
fruicts , ils ont quelquefois esté
cueillis de ma main. Vne Paysan-
ne mal propre ne les a point desfleu-
rez , & ils n'ont point esté frois-
sez dans vn panier. D'ailleurs
ie reçoy contentement quand
ie me souuiens que les arbres

quiles portent ont esté plantez de la main de mon pere, qui se plaisoit extremement au mesnage, & qui est cause de tous les biens que ie reçoy. Vous ferez estat si vous voulez de ceste sorte de plaisirs, & vous croirez que i'en dois estre touché, & que les autres en doiuent desirer de semblables, mais si vous pensez que l'esprit d'vn Philosophe ne doiue pas prendre garde à si peu de chose, & qu'il se doit donner de plus dignes objets, ie m'accorderay à tout ce que vous en pourrez dire, & nous passerons à d'autres considerations.

Il y en a vne à laquelle ie ne croy pas que personne fasse difficulté de se rendre, & d'aduoüer que la vie champestre est la plus loüable de toutes. C'est que l'on faict veritablement le personnage de l'homme

lors que l'on vit dans les champs.
Dieu a condamné l'homme à gagner son pain à la sueur de son visage. L'Agriculture est le vray trauail de l'homme. Tous les mestiers où il s'occupe ne sont point naturels ny necessaires comme celuy-là, l'on se peut passer des autres, mais la vie depend de cestui-cy. Ie n'estime point vn homme moins noble quand il s'occupe à faire labourer ses terres, ou à les labourer luymesme.

Les Romains ont choisy pour conducteurs d'armee, des hommes qui s'estoient de tout temps adonnez au labourage. Ils esleurent vne fois vn Dictateur que l'on alla trouuer dans ses champs comme il les ensemençoit. Il quitta ceste occupation pour celle de la guerre où il eut vn si bon succez qu'il mit

ſes ennemis ſous le joug auec autant
de facilité comme il auoit accouſtumé d'y ranger ſes bœufs quand
il vouloit labourer ſes terres. Toutefois apres ce grand exploict il s'en
retourna dans ſon village auec vne
extreme promptitude, comme s'il
euſt eu haſte d'aller cueillir la moiſſon dont il auoit eſpandu la ſemence. Ie veux encore vous amener
d'autres exemples. Crocus Duc de
Boheme eſtant decedé ſans enfans
maſles, ſa fille Lybuſſe que l'on
prenoit pour vne Sybille de ſon ſiecle, fut eſtablie dans la principauté
par le peuple.

Ayant commandé l'eſpace de
deux ou trois ans, elle donna vn
iugement contre vn Seigneur qui
n'auoit pas bonne cauſe & qui neät-
moins fut tellement indigné qu'il
publia par tout que c'eſtoit vne

laſcheté d'obeyr à vne femme.
Elle fut donc contrainte de ſe marier, & ne voulut prendre vn mary
que par vne maniere de ſort. Elle
dit que l'on laiſſeroit aller ſeul vn
cheual, & que le premier deuant
qui il s'arreſteroit ſeroit ſon mary.
Il arriua qu'il s'arreſta deuant vn
laboureur lequel l'on luy amena,
& comme elle ne deſdaigna point
de l'eſpouſer, auſſi ceux de Boheme ne refuſerent point de luy
obeïr.

Il y a auſſi dans l'hiſtoire d'Alexandre l'exemple de ce Iardinier
Abdolominus qui fut eſleu Roy;
Que ſi des hommes champeſtres
ont eſté eſleuez de la ſorte aux plus
grandes dignitez, les plus puiſſans
hommes du monde ont quitté
auſſi leur grandeur pour iouïr de la

tranquilité des champs.

L'Empereur Dioclctian qui a-
uoit d'aussi grandes prosperitez
parmy la guerre que parmy la paix,
se deffit volontairement de l'Empire pour se retirer dans vne maison rustique où il s'addonnoit à
toutes les choses que l'on pratique
aux champs, & iamais pour quelque raison que l'on luy sceust alleguer il ne voulut retourner à
Rome.

Comme il vid vne fois que les
Ambassadeurs luy en venoient re-
parler, il leur monstra les laictués
de son iardin, & leur demanda s'il
ne leur sembloit pas plus beau &
plus honneste que celuy qui les
auoit semees eut le plaisir de les
manger en repos, que de s'aller exposer au tumulte des affaires. L'on
fut contraint d'auoüer qu'il auoit

beaucoup de raiſon, & l'on le laiſſa
viure en ce lieu ſans le troubler dauantage. L'on void par là que l'A-
griculture n'a iamais eſté meſpriſée;
mais ſi l'on vouloit remonter plus
haut dans les ſiecles, l'on trouueroit
bien qu'elle auroit eſté plus en honneur qu'elle n'eſt à cette heure. Tous
les hommes indifferemment n'a-
uoient point autrefois de plus grande occupation que celle du labourage; c'eſtoit la principale de toutes,
& ceux meſmes qui commandoient
aux autres ne s'y addonnoient pas
moins que les plus petits, & leurs
richeſſes ne conſiſtoient qu'au reuenu de leurs terres & à la quantité de
leur beſtail. C'eſt ce ſiecle que les
Poëtes ont appellé le ſiecle d'Or,
non pas pource que l'Or y eſtoit en
regne, car le ſiecle où nous viuons,
deuroit bien pluſtoſt porter ce nom

pour cette raison là: mais l'on l'a appellé ainſi pour la bonté & la pureté
des mœurs de ce temps là que l'on
pouuoit comparer au plus excellent
de tous les metaux. L'on void donc
bien que les hômes de toutes ſortes
de rôditions ne peuuent eſtre blaſ-
mez pour aymer la vie champeſtre,
& que quiconque la peut ſuiure
n'ayme pas ſon bien s'il ne le faict.

Quant à moy qui n'en ay iamais
gouſté les plaiſirs ſi à mon ayſe que
ie fay maintenant, j'aurois preſque enuie de vous perſuader que
ie n'ay commencé de viure que
depuis le iour que ie ſuis icy, tellement qu'à mon compte, ie ſuis
de beaucoup plus jeune que l'on
ne penſe. Cette ſuppuration d'â-
ge n'eſt pas extraordinaire. Il y
a eu des Anciens qui l'ont prat-
tiquée, & il y en a eu vn entre au-

tres qui a faict escrire sur son tombeau, qu'il n'auoit vescu que six ans, encore qu'il eust esté soixante & dix ans au mode. Il vouloit dire que iusques à sa soixante & quatriesme année, il estoit demeuré dans le tumulte d'vne republique, mais qu'il auoit seulement eu la commodité de passer le reste du temps dedans le repos d'vne maison champestre.

I'ay presque oublié maintenant la pompe des villes : je ne m'en souuien plus que pour la mespriser, & outre cela si ie m'en souuien, ce n'est que comme d'vn songe dont ie ne sçay si ie doy prendre l'histoire pour veritable ou menteuse. Ie ne voy pas icy tant de monde en vn an comme vous en voyez en vn quart d'heure : mais aussi ie n'ay pas tant de tromperies à craindre.

Entre mille que vous voyez vous n'en connoissez pas vn, & pour moy quand ie verrois icy vn aussi grand nombre d'hommes, il n'y en auroit pas vn que ie ne connûsse ; car j'ay tout loisir de m'informer de l'estat de ceux que ie récontre les vns apres les autres, & ie n'y trouue ny super-cherie ny dissimulation. Il est vray que ceux auec qui vous frequentez ont des paroles fort releuées, mais en mesme temps ils ont quelque fois des actions basses, ils parlent des choses les plus graues & les plus im-portantes du monde : mais c'est sans auoir premedité ce qu'ils disent. Que s'ils proposent de bonnes reso-lutions, c'est plustost par hazard que par prudence : & ils se contentent de dire le bien sans le faire. Ils s'esti-ment chacun plus doctes que tous les autres hommes, mais c'est la va-

nité qui les faict parler, & leur science ne consiste qu'en des remarques
inutiles. Vn paysan ratiocine quelquefois mieux qu'ils ne font, & vne
obseruation qu'il aura faite, ou qu'il
aura veu faire à son pere touchant
l'estat des affaires humaines, vaudra
mieux que les sentences que ces Docteurs tirent de leurs liures, estans
fort satisfaicts quand ils ont seulement chargé leur memoire des ouurages d'autruy sans se mettre en
peine de prattiquer aucun precepte.
L'on dit que les Sages peuuent plus
apprendre des sots, que les sots des
Sages. C'est vne chose qui se monstre tres-veritable : car encore que
les hommes simples ne prennent pas
tousiours garde à ce que nous faisons, & n'en fassent pas leur profit,
si est-ce que nous qui deuons auoir
bien plus de cognoissance qu'eux,

puiſque l'on a pris tant de peineà
nous faire enſeigner, nous auons le
moyen de nous inſtruire encore en
remarquant leurs paroles & leurs
actions qui n'empruntent rien de
l'artifice ; c'eſt pourquoy ne vous
imaginez pas que l'entretien desvil-
lageois me ſoit inutile entierement.
Premierement ie puis apprendre
d'eux tout ce qui eſt du meſnage
champeſtre, & ils me diſent encore
des proprietés des plãtes que les medecins ne ſçauent pas. ils me racon-
tent auſſi la nature des animaux;ce-
la s'entend de ceux de leur contrée,
& ils me font en cela des leçons qui
valent mieux que celles de tous nos
Philoſophes dont nous eſtimons
tant les liures.

Ie vous aduouë qu'auec tout cela
ils ne laiſſent pas d'eſtre fort ſimples,
& qu'ils n'ont qu'vne fort legere

connoiſſance de tous les affaires du móde. Ils n'ont accouſtumé de ſçauoir des choſes paſſees que ce qu'ils en ont appris de leur Curé. Il n'y a que trois jours que les nouuelles leur ſont venuës de la priſe de Troye qui leur a eſté comptée par vn eſcholier eſgaré pour le ſalaire d'vn verre d'eau. Ce qui s'eſt paſſé il y a trois mille ans leur eſt nouueau & extraordinaire. Ces grands noms d'Andromache, de Semiramis & d'Artemiſe, ne leur ſont pas ſi cómuns que ceux de Luce, d'Alix, & de Berthe. Ils s'eſtonnent quand l'on leur parle de la grandeur du monde. Ayant ouy parler ſeulement de l'Italie, de l'Eſpagne & de l'Allemagne , ils croyent que ce ſont toutes les regions de la terre , & qui leur parleroit de l'Amerique ou de la Chine & de la Tartarie, les rendroit

merueilleufement efbahis. Dans
leurs propos ordinaires ils parlent
toufiours du monde comme s'il
auoit vn bout, & ils n'ont garde de
s'imaginer que la terre foit ronde;
l'opinion des Antipodes ne fçauroit
entrer dans leur cerueau. Ils difent
qu'ils ne penfent pas qu'il y ait des
hommes qui marchent à la renuer-
fe. Comme ils voyent le Ciel qui
femble toucher à la terre au bout de
leur plaine, ils croyent qu'il y touche veritablement, mais que c'eft
en vn pays fort efloigné du noftre,
& que c'eft là qu'eft le bout du môde dont ils parlent tant, & que quãd
l'on a rencontré cette muraille l'on
ne fçauroit plus paffer outre. Pour
ce qui eft du Soleil qui s'eftant cou-
ché d'vn cofté fe retreuue le lende-
main de l'autre; ils n'ont pas encore
fongé comment cela fe faict. C'eft
vne

vne estrange humeur des hômes de
ne point admirer vne chose si merueilleuse que le Soleil, bien qu'ils le
voyent tous les iours, mais ce qui
leur donne ce mespris, c'est qu'ils en
jouyssent d'ordinaire. Toutefois à
la premiere occasion ie me veux informer de ce qu'ils en pensent. I'es-
preuueray là dessus la subtilité des
plus entendus. Ne croyez pas, Philandre, que ce soit icy vne matiere
de raillerie à la mode du vulgaire. Il
est vray qu'il y a en cecy quelque
chose de diuertissant, mais cela n'est
faict que pour l'esprit des Philosophes. En s'informant ainsi de plusieurs choses à nos paysans, l'on
connoist la portée de nostre nature lors qu'elle n'est point appuyée
par les instructions. Ce n'est pas
là vne petite curiosité si l'on la
sçait bien comprendre, & si l'on

s'y gouuerne comme il faut.

Ie m'occupe ainſi à des choſes dont il y a vne infinité de perſonnes qui ne tiendroient aucun compte ; mais laiſſons parler le vulgaire.

Ce n'eſt pas d'aujourd'huy que nous ſçauons qu'il ne cognoiſt pas les vrays plaiſirs de la vie dedans leur pureté ! La pluſpart des hommes croyent que pour acquerir de la reputation , il n'y a qu'à ſe tenir touſiours dans l'orgueil , & à faire paroiſtre que l'on ne ſçait ce que c'eſt que de la baſſeſſe.

Ils ſont comme ces petites ſtatuës qui ſont eſleuées ſur vn haut pied-eſtal.

Leur opinion eſt que s'eſtans portez iuſques au ſommet d'vne grandeur empruntée ils paroiſtront plus que les autres , mais c'eſt ce qui les abuſe : car n'eſtans pas grands d'eux meſmes, tant plus ils s'eſleuent, tant plus ils paroiſſent petits. S'ils ne montoient pas ſi haut, ils ſeroient veus en leur grandeur naturelle, mais ils ſont aueuglez en leur propre cauſe, & toutes les remonſtrances que l'on leur ſçauroit donner, ne ſeruent qu'à les irriter contre tout le monde.

Ils veulent meſme chercher vne inuention pour couurir leurs deffauts, & pour cacher les choſes ſur leſquelles ils ſont montez, afin que l'on croye que toute la hauteur qui paroiſt, leur appartient.

Seruons nous de ſimilitudes familiaires à la mode de Plutarque & de tous les plus excellents Autheurs.

N'auez vous iamais veu des bouf-
fons vouloir contrefaire les Geants
pour paroiſtre en quelque maſ-
quarade , ou en quelque deffy de
Cheualiers errans ſelon l'ancienne
couſtume des Tournois. Ils ſont
montez ſur des eſchaſſes auec leſquelles ils ſont accouſtumez de
marcher, en tenant le genoüil bien
ferme, & par là deſſus ils ont vne
longue caſaque qui traiſne depuis
les eſpaules iuſqu'en terre , tellement que le ſimple peuple croit
que la grandeur de leur corps eſt
toute ſemblable ; mais les perſonnes d'eſprit connoiſſent bien leur
deffault qui eſt fort ayſé à deſcouurir : car auecque ce grand corps,
ils ont encore de petits bras , &
vne petite reſte telle qu'il la faut
à vn homme d'vne ſtature ordi-

naire ; car ils ne peuuent point
desguiſer cela , ou bien s'ils taſ-
chent de le desguiſer , la fourbe
eſt encore plus claire , d'autant
que s'ils font les bras plus longs
les mains qu'ils y attachent font
fans mouuement, & s'ils prennent
vn faux viſage d'vne enorme groſ-
ſeur, l'on void bien toſt que ce n'eſt
qu'vn maſque. Il en eſt ainſi de tant
de perſonnages orgueilleux que
nous auons dedans le monde. Leur
courage & leur eſprit , font ſi petits qu'à peine ſe peuuent-ils faire
remarquer. Pour remedier à cela ils
ſe ſeruent de quelque induſtrie pour
auoir vne feinte grandeur. Ils ont
quelquefois des richeſſes qui les
eſleuent : le lieu dont ils font ſortis leur y ſert quelquefois.

Le merite de leurs parens ne leur

est pas auffi inutile ; mais pource
qu'en effect ils font fort petits d'eux
mefmes, & que leur orgueil eft leur
principal fecours qui les guide iufques au lieu où l'on les void, ils tafchent de couurir leurs imperfectiós,
& de cacher auffi leurs artifices.

Ils prennent des qualitez qui ne
doiuent eftre données qu'aux perfonnages les plus eminents de la
terre ; & c'eft ce qui couure mieux
tout ce qu'ils ne veulent point que
les autres voyent, & qui faict naiftre d'abord vne vaine admiration
dedans les fimples efprits.

Mais ceux qui iugent fainement
des chofes connoiffent incontinent
la tromperie. Ils fçauent bien que
ce qui les efleue eft caché fous vn
long veftement. Ils voyent leur tefte qui n'a point de proportion
auec le refte du corps ; c'eft à dire

qu'ils n'ont pas beaucoup de ceruelle ny de iugement. Ils prennent
garde aussi à leurs bras qui sont
trop courts pour auoir autant de
force que ceux d'vn si grand corps
en doiuent auoir, tellement qu'ils
ne sont pas propres à porter vne
massuë pour dompter tous les mon-
stres de la terre comme faisoit Hercule. Voyla ce que j'auois à vous raconter de la vanité des hommes qui
nous pensent estonner par leur suffisance. Ie veux dire que lors qu'ils
se sont esleuez si haut, ils ont si peur
de paroistre petits comme ils sont
en effect, que iamais ils ne daignent
s'abaisser, & qu'ils ne croyent pas
que la terre merite qu'ils luy jettent
seulement vn regard. Ils ne considerent pas qu'encore que Dieu
nous ait faicts pour le Ciel, il veut
que nous esprouuions auparauant

les miſeres de ce monde, & qu'il
a dict de ſa propre bouche qu'il n'y
auoit que les humbles qui meritaſ-
ſent d'eſtre eſleuez.

Nos hommes vains ne veulent
pas ſeulement ouyr parler du village, & ils n'auroient garde de
s'amuſer à entretenir des Payſans.
Ils croyent qu'vne ſi abjecte occupation les deſtourneroit de leurs
penſées ; & que cela leur appor-
teroit plus de honte que de profit.
Ces pauures gens ſçauent bien peu
ce que c'eſt que d'vne veritable
Philoſophie. Ils ne conſiderent pas
que ceux qui ſont grands de nature, ne doiuent point craindre que
leur hauteur ſoit diminuée pour
quelque occaſion que ce ſoit, &
qu'ils ſe peuuent bien abbaiſſer
quelquesfois pour faire des actions
qui ne peuuent pas eſtre fai-

tes d'vne autre sorte. Les hommes les plus illustres du monde, n'ont iamais mesprisé les discours des pauures & des personnes de basse condition Il y a eu des Roys mesmes qui se sont bien souuent déguisez afin d'auoir la liberté de les entretenir pour cognoistre les sentimens qu'ils auoient en chaque chose. Les Sages nous conseillent bien de tirer des instructions des bestes, comme en effet si nous contemplós le naturel different de plusieurs animaux, nous verrons qu'ils nous enseignent vne infinité de secrets pour la conduite de la vie. A plus forte raison nous deuons croire que les plus simples d'entre les hommes, peuuent faire naistre en nous des considerations vtiles. C'est pourquoy ne feignons point de conuerser quelquefois auec eux & de les

interroger sur diuers poincts. C'e-
stoit la coustume ordinaire de Socrate de ne dire presque iamais rien
de soy, & il ne faisoit pas cela seulement lors qu'il estoit auec ses disci-
ples les plus entendus, mais aussi lors
qu'il estoit auec des personnes qui
n'auoiét pas encore gousté les prin-
cipes de la Philosophie. Il ne cessoit
de les interroger & de leur demander la raison d'vne infinité de choses
laquelle il vouloit qu'ils trouuassent
d'eux-mesmes, & il leur aydoit seulement vn petit, sans leur donner
tout en vn coup ses plus beaux preceptes. De là vient qu'il disoit qu'il
exerçoit encore le mestier de sa mere qui estoit sage femme, & qu'il
aydoit les esprits à enfanter leurs
conceptions, mais que pour luy il
ne produisoit iamais les siennes.
Si l'on veut l'imiter l'on peut faire

que toutes nos conuerſations ſoiét
profitables, & qu'elles ſeruent aux
autres ſi elles ne nous ſeruent; car
nous nous gouuernerons de telle
ſorte que ceux qui ne ſeront pas
capables de nous apprendre quelque choſe, exciteront la puiſſance
de leur eſprit pour ſonger à toutes les opinions que l'on doit prendre.

Nous voyons donc que les conuerſations des perſonnes fort baſ-
ſes, ne ſont point à fuyr, & par conſequent que le ſejour champeſtre
ne doit point eſtre meſpriſé pour ce
ſujet.

Que ſi l'on me penſe dire que
l'on ne ſe retire aux champs que
pour paſſer ſa vie dans l'oyſiueté, c'eſt eſtre fort nouueau en
beaucoup de choſes. Ie ſçay bien
qu'il ſe peut trouuer des gens

qui demeurent oyſifs encore
qu'ils ſoient dans vn ſemblable
lieu que celuy où ie ſuis maintenant ; mais n'y en a t'il pas dauantage dans les villes qui paſſent leur
temps à ne rien faire ? Ce n'eſt pas là
le nœud de la queſtion. Il faut ſçauoir ſeulement s'il ſe preſente plus
d'occaſions de trauailler dedans les
villes que dans les champs. Croyez,
Philandre, que tout cela eſt eſgal.
I'ayme mieux vous l'accorder ainſi
auec beaucoup de franchiſe, que de
...re donner de la peine à vous perſuader que l'on ſe peut mieux employer dás la campagne qu'en tout
autre lieu Vous ſçauez bien que
quiconque a volonté de trauailler
ne manque iamais de treuuer de la
beſogne. Bien que l'on ne ſoit pas
reduit à gagner ſon pain à la ſueur
de ſon viſage, ſi eſt-ce que l'on ne

demeurera pas sans se remuer comme vne statuë. Il n'y a guere de difference entre vn homme mort &
vn homme qui ne faict rien. Que
s'il y en a quelqu'vne, l'on ne peut
pas dire neantmoins que celuy qui
est oysif soit veritablement homme. Il ne ressemble point mieux à
aucune chose qu'à vn tronc d'arbre
qui a seulement l'ame vegetatiue,
mais qui n'a point la sensitiue; car ie
ne le voudrois pas mesme comparer à quelques animaux, puis qu'il
y en a beaucoup qui trauaillent, &
qui font des choses qui reüssissent
au bien de tout le monde. Les hommes qui sont oysifs & paresseux ne
font rien que nourrir leurs corps
ainsi que les plantes, & ils ne gagnét
pas seulement l'eau qu'ils boiuent.
Pour moy ie ne croy pas mesme
que ce soit assez de s'addonner à

l’eſtude ſi ie ne prend auſſi ſouuent
quelque autre occupation. Il faut
exercer le corps autant que l’eſprit,
ſi l’on veut qu’ils demeurent en vne
parfaicte harmonie. Bien que ie
n’aye point icy d’affaires à ſoliciter,
ny d’amis à viſiter pour leur donner
du conſeil en toute ſorte d’accidéts.
Ie fay pourtant aſſez d’exercice, ie
vay d’vn coſté voir ceux qui coupent les bleds , & ie regarde auſſi
quelquefois ceux qui les ſerrent, &
ie prend plaiſir à compter les ger-
bes. Ie fay couper du bois tant pour
ſe chauffer que pour baſtir, & ie
conſidere le trauail des ouuriers qui
ont commencé vn petit logement
neuf que ie fay ioindre à l’ancien
pour rendre ma maiſon plus commode. Ie prend plaiſir quelquefois
à planter des arbres ou à faire des
antes, & ie manie bien ſouuent la

befche du iardinier ou les cifeaux
dont il roigne les bordures du par-
terre. Il s'eftonne d'ordinaire de ce
que ie luy veux apprendre fon meftier, & il feroit bien fafché s'il trouuoit que i'en fceuffe d'auantage que
luy. Ie n'aurois de long temps faict
fi ie voulois vous dire en combien
de façons i'euite l'oyfiueté, & combien de fois le iour ie monftre que
ie ne fuis pas ignorant du mefnage
champeftre. Si vous m'auiez veu
vous diriez incontinent que c'eft
moy qui a compofé le liure de la
Maifon Ruftique & le Theatre d'A-
griculture, ou que tout au moins fi
ie n'en fuis l'Autheur, ie fuis de ceux
qui en ont faict vne plus exacte lecture, & qui n'ont rien leu qu'ils
n'ayent efprouué afin de pouuoir
dire qu'ils en ont vne fcience certaine. Ne doutez vous point de ce

que ie vous dy? Philandre. Vous ne
le deuez pas f   si vous vous souuenez de quelle humeur ie suis.
Vous sçauez bien que i'ay de la curiosité pour toutes choses, & que ie
veux pratiquer tout ce que l'on
m'aprend. Vous sçauez d'ailleurs
que ie ne suis pas moins porté au
trauail que i'ay entrepris de vous
dire, & pour vous monstrer que
c'est vne honte extreme d'estre oysif, ie ne veux plus vous remarquer
qu'vne chose : C'est que les Turcs
tout Infidelles qu'ils sont, nous font
en cela vne belle leçon. Vous sçauez
bien s'il y a personne au monde qui
se puisse mieux passer de trauailler
que leur grand Seigneur, & neantmoins pource que Dieu nous a ordonné le trauail, il ne desire point
faire paroistre qu'il s'en veuille exē-
pter; au contraire il pratique tousjours

jours quelque meftier , & il ne fe
paffe pas vn iour qu'il ne s'en ferue.
Il fera de petites cuilliers de bois, &
des manches de coufteau, ou quelque autre gentilleffe felon fon inclination ; & les plus grands de l'Empire les achepteront vn grand prix,
eftans fort glorieux d'auoir les ouurages de leur Prince. Il femble
ainfi qu'il gagne fa vie par ce trauail comme le moindre des hommes, pour obferuer la loy de Maho-
met, qui veut que chacun trauaille
pour auoir dequoy fe nourrir. Il eft
vray qu'encore que nous autres qui
fommes Chreftiens, nous trouuions
là vn fujeð de nous exciter au trauail, puifque les Infidelles mefmes le
croyent fi neceffaire aux hommes,
fi eft-ce que nous ne deuons pas prédre garde entierement à ce qu'ils
en ont ordonné. Ils parlent de cela

auec vne superstition trop grande. Nous sommes bien tous obligez de trauailler pour meriter de viure, mais chacun n'est pas obligé de s'addóner au trauail du corps. Ceux qui gouuernent les autres, qui iugent leurs procez, qui les conseillent en leurs affaires & au mauuais estat de leur santé, font assez pour eux & pour le peuple quand ils occupent seulement leur esprit. Il y a assez d'hommes de reste pour exercer les choses mechaniques, & pour s'addóner aux ouurages qui ne s'accomplissent qu'à l'ayde de la main. Les hommes estans composez de l'ame & du corps, doiuent aussi auoir parmy eux des gens qui s'addonnent aux choses corporelles & les autres aux spirituelles, sans rien entreprendre les vns sur les autres, afin que chacun s'estudie d'auanta-

ge à faire ce qui luy fera propre.
I'ay bien dit que chacun deuoit e-
xercer le corps & l'efprit enfemble,
mais i'entend que ceux qui ont
charge d'exercer leur efprit, ne s'addonnent point à d'autres occupations par vne neceffité qui les y
oblige, mais par vne pure volonté.
Cela ne fe fera que pour noftre
bien. Le profit des autres n'y eft
point engagé.

Nous donnerons de l'exercice à
noftre corps pour nous diuertir
apres les plus grandes fonctions de
l'efprit, & pour accroiftre nos forces. Ce fera auffi pour conferuer
noftre fanté qui feroit grandement
intereffee fi nous ne bougions d'v-
ne place à ne faire que mediter, ou
parler à ceux qui nous interrogent.
L'on peut mefme prendre de l'exercice par paffe-téps feulement, & le

plaiſir ſe peut bien rencontrer quelquefois auec noſtre trauail.

La chaſſe eſt vn des plus grands
diuertiſſements de la vie champeſtre. C'eſt là que le corps s'exerce
auecques plaiſir; Ie ne diray pas auec
proffit, car encore que l'on prenne
quelque choſe, cela n'eſt pas côſide--
ble aux honneſtes gés, qui ne chaſ-
ſent que pour ſe diuertir, & qui ne
viuent pas de meſme que ces chaſ-
ſeurs ordinaires qui ne pourſuiuent
le gibbier & la venaiſon que pour
en auoir tant qu'ils ſe puiſſent enrichir en le reuendant aux autres.
Quelquefois ie cours vn Lieure,
quelquefois ie taſche de prendre
les Perdrix auec la tiraſſe & le chien
couchant. Que ſi la proye m'eſ-
chappe; c'eſt neantmoins autant de
temps paſſé, & i'eſpere que ie ſeray
plus heureux vne autrefois. Ie me

contente de ce que ie trouue apres
à la maison, & ie n'ay pas faict peu
de chose puis que i'ay chassé les
mauuaises pensees qui peuuent naistre dans l'esprit lors que l'on se tiét
dans vne trop longue oysiueté. La
pesche me plaist à de certains iours
quand ie suis dans vne humeur res-
ueuse, mais ie la quitte bien-tost à
cause qu'elle exerce plustost la patience des hommes que leur esprit
ny leur corps. Aussi est-ce vne chose que l'on n'estime pas si noble que
la chasse, où l'on m'a tousiours veu
auoir quelque inclination dés ma
ieunesse. La chasse est le vray plaisir des Roys, & de tous les Gentils-
hommes. C'est vne petite guerre
que l'on faict aux bestes, afin de
s'accoustumer à celle que l'on est
quelquefois cótraint de faire cótre
des ennemis estrangers. Il nous est

mis de pourſuiure ainſi les animaux
& d'en deſtruire quelques-vns de
temps en temps, pource qu'ils ſont
produits à noſtre vſage, & que ſi
l'on ne les attaquoit il y en a entr'-
eux de ſi forts qu'ils ſe rendroient
maiſtres de la campagne, & qu'ils
feroient du dommage dedans les
troupeaux des autres animaux que
l'on a rendus domeſtiques, & qu'ils
outrageroient meſme les hommes.
Nous ne ſommes pas dans l'erreur
des Pythagoriciens, qui croyoient
que ce fuſt vn grand crime de tuer
quelque animal que ce fuſt, & qui
vouloient bien aduoüer qu'ils e-
ſtoient en quelque degré de con-
ſanguinité auec les beſtes. Or l'on
ne peut nier que l'exercice de la
chaſſe ne ſoit ſi aymable que les
plus grands d'entre les hommes
quittent ſouuent les delices des vil-

les pour s'y addonner. Vous le met-
trez si vous voulez au nombre des
contentements qui se treuuent au
lieu où ie suis, sinon vous le passe-
rez comme vne chose indifferente,
& vous croirez que ie sçay bien encore des diuertissements qui me
sont plus agreables.

Au bout de là ie ne sçaurois nier
que l'entretien des hommes doctes
ne vaille mieux que celuy de mes
paysans, & que vous n'ayez vne
grande commodité d'en ioüyr:
mais ne vous imaginez pas que ie
ie me vueille priuer tout exprez
d'vne semblable satisfaction. Ie
vous ay dit dés le commencement
de mon discours qu'il falloit
mettre de la moderation en toutes choses. C'est là que ie reuiens de mon plein gré & ie de-

meure dans ceſte opinion infaillible. Il faut vſer moderement des
plaiſirs champeſtres, & c'eſt ce que
ie pratique tous les iours. Quand
ie veux iouyr du plaiſir des villes,
ie ne fay que monter à cheual & en
vne heure ie me trouue en vne ville des plus agreables de noſtre Prouince. I'y rencontre des hommes
d'auſſi bon entretien qu'à Paris, &
ie dy cela ſans faire tort à la reputation que vous auez d'eſtre de la
meilleure compagnie du monde,
car ie vous tire hors du pair en toutes mes comparaiſons. Quand i'ay
eſté là quelque temps ie reuiens encore iouyr des plaiſirs de ma ſolitude, & c'eſt ainſi que la diuerſité
nous faict trouuer plus de gouſt
à toutes choſes par le changement.

Or vous voyez que ie vous aduoüe que quelque compagnie que j'aye ie cognoy bien que ie n'ay pas la voſtre, & c'eſt icy qu'il faut accorder que ſans vous ma joye ne peut eſtre parfaicte. Mais que voulez vous que ie faſſe ſi ie ſuis obligé de m'eſloigner de vous. Vous n'eſtes pas ſi cruel que de me vouloir oſter les penſées dont je me flatte. A faute d'vn bien accomply ie jouys de celuy que ie puis trouuer, & c'eſt ma ſeule conſolation.

Si nous voulons viure contents nous deuons conſiderer la diuerſité de nos fortunes ; Il ſe faut repreſenter que les choſes ne peuuent pas touſiours eſtre d'vne meſme ſorte, afin que lors qu'elles changeront nous ne nous trouuions pas auſſi eſtonnez que ſi nous auions changé de forme & ſi nous eſtions encore au ſiecle des metamorphoſes.

C'eſt le plus grand ſecret de la vie que de ſçauoir accommoder noſtre humeur de telle ſorte que nous ſupportions toute ſorte d'accidēts, puis que les accidens ne ſe peuuét pas accommoder à nous. Voſtre cōpagnie a beaucoup de charmes; en quelque lieu que vous ſoyez vous banniſſez la triſteſſe; vous ne laiſſez point naiſtre les ſoucis dedans voſtre eſprit, ny vous ne ſouffrez point qu'ils affligét l'eſprit des autres; car vous auez des enchantemens aſſez forts pour les chaſſer. Toutefois ie ne puis aller à vous. Quelques conſiderations me retiennent: tellement que ſi ie veux addoucir l'aigreur de cette mauuaiſe fortune, il faut que ie taſche de me plaire au lieu où ie ſuis, quand il ne ſeroit pas auſsi aymable comme i'ay taſché de vous faire paroiſtre. Puis que toutes les choſes du mon-

de font en perpetuel changement,
j'espere que mon bon-heur pourra
reuenir. Les orages ne tourmentent
pas touſiours la mer, les vēts ceſſent
quelquefois, & lors qu'ils ſoufflent
auec le plus d'impetuoſité, c'eſt lors
que l'on eſt plus proche du calme,
car les contraires s'accordent les vns
aux autres, & vne grande tranquillité eſt incontinent ſuiuie d'vne fu-
rieuſe tempeſte. Ie taſcheray ſi ie
puis de reſiſter à l'vne & à l'autre
fortune ; mais ſur toutes choſes ie
m'efforceray de faire voir que dedans les plus differentes occaſions ie
n'auray rien de ſi vif en l'ame comme le deſir de me monſtrer voſtre
tres humble ſeruiteur.

Il faict des plaintes à son amy de ce qu'il ne luy a point escrit.

LETTRE II.

IE ne sçay quelle excuse vous trouuerez pour ne m'auoir point escrit. Vous ne pouuez pas dire que vous n'ayez pas receu mes lettres. Celuy mesme que j'auois prié de vous les porter est de retour en ce pays cy où il m'a certifié sa diligence, & m'en a donné des marques dont l'on ne sçauroit douter. Ie ne pése pas que vous luy voulussiez contredire, & que pour n'estre point obligé à aucune satisfaction enuers personne, vous

eußiez enuie de nier d'en auoir iamais rien receu. C'est le sommet de
l'ingratitude que non seulement de
ne recompenser pas les bienfaicts
que l'on a receuz , mais de ne les
point auoüer. Ie ne veux pas mettre
au rang des bienfaicts les lettres que
ie vous ay enuoyées. Ce seroit à n'en
point mentir auoir vne trop bonne
estime de moy & de mes ouurages;
mais au moins ie veux bien me persuader, & tascher pareillement de
le persuader aux autres, que ce que
ie vous ay escrit, estoit vn vray tesmoignage de mon affection. Ie ne
sçay donc pas pourquoy vous auez
differé de le reconnoistre , & de
m'en donner des preuues. Il est vray
que vous m'auez escrit vne fois, &
que vous m'auez mandé que vous
vous estonniez de mon depart si
soudain, veu que la ville où ie de

meurois estoit si pleine de delices,
que l'on ne la pouuoit quitter qu'a-
uec regret. Ie croy maintenant
que vous ne m'escriuiez que par curiosité, & que pour sçauoir la raison de mon esloignement; car apres
que ie vous en ay escrit tout ce qui
s'en pouuoit dire, vous n'auez pas
tenu compte de me repliquer, &
l'on ne peut douter en cela que vous
ne l'ayez negligé, puis que celuy qui
vous apportoit de mes nouuelles,
s'offroit à vous pour me rapporter
aussi les vostres, d'autant qu'il ne
vouloit faire guere de sejour à Paris.
Pource que ma derniere lettre a esté
fort longue, auez vous creu que ie
l'auois faite ainsi tout expres, afin de
vous mâder en vn seul coup tout ce
que j'auois à vo⁹ dire, & cesser apres
nostre cómerce? Cela ne peut pas
estre, Philandre. Bien que ma lettre

ne fuſt pas d'vne lôgueur ordinaire,
& qu'elle fuſt plus grâde que celles
du commun, ie ne vous ay toutefois
entretenu que d'vne feule choſe. Si
i'euſſe voulu vous apprêdre en vne
feule fois toutes mes penſées, l'on y
euſt bien trouué vne plus grande diuerſité Que fi i'ay vſé d'vn ſtile qui
n'eſt point ſuccinct côme les autres,
vous n'y deuez pas trouuer des ſujets
d'importunité. I'ay defiré de vous
rendre ſatisfaict en toutes les choſes
dont vous me pouuiez interroger
ſur la matiere qui ſe preſentoit, &
comme vous ſçauez qu'il y a plus de
peine à accomplir les longs ouurages que non pas ceux qui ſont
courts, vous deuez connoiſtre que
ie ne vous affectionne pas peu, puis
que ie n'entreprend point de vous
le teſmoigner à la haſte, & que
ie fay en cela tout ce que ie iu-

ge poſſible. Or en cela vous me
douuiez recópenſer facilement. Les
reconnoiſſances que l'on donne en
ces occaſions ſont d'vne meſme nature que les bien-faits que l'on a receuz. Ie vous ay eſcrit auec autant
de ſoin qu'il m'eſtoit poſſible ; il
vous eſtoit facile de m'eſcrire auſſi.
Sçachez que ie ne vous enuoye de
mes lettres qu'afin d'auoir des voſtres ; & j'ay fait les miennes les plus
longues que i'ay pû , afin de vous
obliger dauantage à reſpondre à celuy qui ne vous eſcrit point par maniere d'acquit , mais qui en faict ſa
principale occupation. Ie n'entends
pas neantmoins que vous ſoyez forcé à m'enuoyer des lettres auſſi longues que les miennes. Vous auez des
affaires plus grandes que moy qui
vous occupent ailleurs ; C'euſt eſté
aſſez ſi vous m'euſſiez ſeulement
enuoye

enuoyé autant de lignes comme ie
vous ay enuoyé de pages. Ie vous
asseure que ie m'en fusse tenu pour
côtent, car c'eust tousiours esté vne
preuue comme vous ne m'eussiez
point mesprisé, & outre cela ie fay
tant de cas de tout ce qui vient de
vous que ie veux bien faire vn eschange à ce prix là de mes ouurages
contre les vostres. Ie m'asseure que
vous voudriez à cette heure cy m'a-
uoir escrit, puisque vous voyez que
vous en eussiez esté quitte à si bon
marché. Ie ne diminuë point en cecy la bonne opinion que i'ay de vostre stile : car encore qu'vne de vos
lettres soit vn grand tresor à ceux
qui la reçoiuent , si est ce qu'elle
vous couste bien peu , & qu'ayant
l'esprit fertile & ingenieux comme
vous l'auez , à peine vostre main
peut suiure vostre esprit, & vos pre-

mieres penſées ſont auſſi bónes que les ſecondes & les troiſieſmes des autres. Que pourrez vous me repartir à ce que ie vous dy ? me direz-vous que maintenant vous n'eſtes iamais libre, & que vous demeurez auec des gens qui veulent que vous leur rendiez compte de toutes vos actions, & qui ne ſe fient pas le plus ſouuent à ce que vous leur en raporteriez, de ſorte qu'ils ſont preſens à tout ce que voꝰ faites? ie me ſouuien d'auoir autrefois demeuré auec des hómes qui eſtoient bien d'vn autre naturel que tous ceux dót vous vous pourriez plaindre. Au lieu que nous paſſons quelquefois desmois à eſtudier, ſans que les honneſtes gens s'en eſtonnent, ceux-cy ne m'euſſent pas veu lire vne heure durãt, qu'ils ne fuſſent entrez dãs vne grãde admiratió, ne ſçachãs de quelle façó ie me pouuois exépter d'auoir vn grãd mal de

teste , & ils estoient si sots qu'ils
croyoiét mesme qu'il n'y auoit rien
qui sist si tost deuenir fol que de trop
lire. Que s'ils me voyoient escrire
quelquefois ils ne pensoiét pas que
ce fust vne plus grâde marque de sagesse, car leur esprit n'estoit addóné
qu'à vne desbauche brutale, dont ils
faisoient plus d'estat que de toute la
sciéce du móde. Ne croyez pas pourtát que ie m'affligeasse beaucoup de
tout ce qu'ils pouuoient dire. Il n'y
eust point eu de malheur pareil au
mien si ie me fusse affligé pour les
deffauts des autres, & si i'eusse voulu
me punir pour leurs pechez. Ie me
riois à tous coups de leurs impertiné-
ces, & malgré toutes leurs railleries
ie ne laissois pas de lire toutes les fois
qu'il me tóboit entre les mains quelque liure nouueau, ny d'escrire aussi
lors que ie voulois mettre par ordre

quelque ouurage que i'auois cóçeu.
Ie fçauois bien comment il leur falloit monſtrer dans de certaines occaſions que le genre de vie que i'a-
uois eſleu n'eſtoit pas ſi meſpriſable
qu'ils ſe l'imaginoient, & que s'il y
auoit des hommes au monde qui
tinſſét de la beſte c'eſtoit eux, car les
metamorphoſes dont les Poëtes parlent s'eſtoient faites en eux, & ſi cela
ne ſe voyoit point au corps, cela ſe
cognoiſſoit en l'eſprit dont le chan-
gemét móſtrueux eſt le plus à craindre, puiſque c'eſt noſtre principale
partie. Ils ne donnoient aucune reigle à leurs paſſions : ſi vn valet ne
mettoit pas vn plat aſſez auant ſur la
table, ou s'il verſoit vn peu trop
d'eau dás leur vin, c'eſtoit aſſez pour
leur faire iurer toute vne iournée.
Pour moy ils voioient que quelque
mauuais accident qui m'arriuaſt, ie

le souffrois auecques patience. L'on
me vint vne fois aduertir que i'auois
perdu vn procez par les chicaneries
& les faussetez d'vn meschát hóme;
ma fascherie ne fut pas si gráde que
celle de l'vn d'eux à qui l'on auoit
cassé vn verre ce iour là. Ils commé-
cerét alors à rentrer en eux mesmes,
& à s'estóner de ce qu'ils voyoiét. Il y
en eut vn qui ne se peut empécher de
me dire. Mais cómét faites vous, Lu-
cidor, pour estre si téperé que vous
estes? Toute sorte de choses vous sót
égales. Vous souffrez sans rien dire
tout ce que l'on vous fait. Ie m'aper-
çoy quelquefois que l'on vous sert
fort mal ceans, mais neátmoins vous
ne vous en plaignez pas. Vous trouuez bon tout ce que l'on vous baille,
& maintenant mesme vous receuez
vne infortune de la mesme sorte
que quelque bon-heur. Ie pris alors

le tɇpsde me faire paroiſtre ainſi que
ie l'auois à ſouhait. Ie luy dy , Monſieur,vous voyez ; cette bonne humeur me vient de la lecture dont
vous me faites tant la guerre, c'eſt
par elle que ie me fuis inſtruict; c'eſt
elle qui me dóne du remede en mes
afflictiõs, & c'eſt elle enfin qui me
rend plus moderé que vous n'eſtes.
Encore qu'il ne me reſpondiſt que
par vn ſouſris, ſi eſt-ce qu'il ſongea
plus d'vne fois à ce que ie luy auois
dit, & il creut que cela pouuoit bien
eſtre veritable. Il ayma ma cõuerſa-
tion plus qu'auparauant, & il commença de s'adóner à lire à mon exéple, en quoy il ſe rendit depuis fort
hóneſte hóme. Cela vous doit mõ-
ſtrer Philádre,que pour quelque cõpagnie que vous avez, vo⁹ ne deuez
point vous empeſcher de lire ny en-

core moins d'escrire. S'il y eut jamais rien de libre, c'est l'esprit d'vn
homme d'estude. Il se doit mocquer
des attaques de ceux qui n'ont pas le
vray vsage de la raison. Quand ie serois auec les plus barbares du móde,
si est-ce que si i'auois enuie d'estudier ou d'escrire à quelqu'vn, ils ne
feroiét pas capables de m'en empescher. Ie me resueillerois plustost la
nuict, i'aurois tousiours vn fusil &
vne bougie sous mon cheuet, i'irois
dans les cachettes les plus asseurées,
ou bien au deffaut d'vne contre-lu-
miere, i'yrois escrire au clair de la
Lune. Mais ie sçay bien que vous
n'estes pas reduit à de semblables
extremitez. Ie ferois tort à ceux qui
demeurent auec vous, si ie me l'i-
maginois. I'ay eu autrefois leur cognoissance, & ie n'ay rien veu en eux

que des marques de tres-bon esprit.
Il est vray qu'ils ne vous abandonnent point, mais c'est pour l'extreme affection qu'ils vous portent, &
s'ils veulent sçauoir ce que vous faictes, quand vous leur direz : i'escry
à vn amy, ils n'y trouuerôt rien d'extraordinaire. Ils sçauent trop ce que
c'est que d'honneur & de courtoisie
pour blasmer vostre dessein. Vous
ne ferez rien pour moy que vous
ne vouluffiez faire pour eux s'ils
estoient absens.

Considerez, Philandre, que ie
languis apres vos lettres, & que
c'est vne cruauté de me traicter
comme vous auez comencé. Vous
pensez que i'aye faict vne grand'
perte en perdant les contentemens
qui se trouuent à Paris. Vous voulez donc me rendre entierement
miserable, puis que vous me priués

encore du plus grand bien qui me
reste en m'ostant le bon heur de vostre amitié, dõt vous me pouuiés af-
feurer par vn mot d'escrit. Me voulez
vous oublier de la sorte, moy qui
vous ay iuré de ne vous oublier iamais, & qui vous monstre des effets
de mes promesses ? Ne voudriez
vous pas donner vn coup de plume
pour vn amy; c'est bien loin de donner des coups d'espee. Qui vous prie-
roit donc d'entreprendre de grands
voyages, ou de former vne grosse
querelle contre quelqu'vn, que feriez vous ? Mais quoy, ie ne vous
prie point de faire vne iniustice. Si
ie le faisois, vous deuriez refuser la
cõtinuation de nostre amitié. L'on
n'est point obligé de garder la foy à
vn autre que tant qu'il nous incite à
faire des choses honnestes & raison-
nables. Vous sçauez bien que ie de-

meure toufiours dans ces termes, &
que i'aymerois mieux mourir que
d'en partir. Ie vous demande vne
chofe que l'on accorde bien quelquefois à des ennemis, car quelque
haine que l'on porte à quelqu'vn,
l'on ne fe peut abftenir de luy efcrire s'il nous a efcrit, & il n'y a
point de fi mauuaifes paroles qu'elles ne meritent vne refponfe, encore que l'opinion du vulgaire n'en
foit pas d'accord. Que faut-il donc
faire pour celuy qui ne tefmoigne
qu'vne extreme affeƈtió, puifque la
vraye recópenfe de l'amitié eft l'a-
mitié mefme? N'eft-il pas vray auffi
que l· vraye recópenfe des Lettres
ne confifte qu'en d'autres Lettres?
Vous le fçauez, Philandre, & ce que
ie vous en dits n'eft que pour vous
monftrer que ie ne l'ignore pas non
plus que vous, tellement que i'ay

tout sujet de me plaindre. Ie voudrois bié sçauoir en quelle humeur
vous estes à ceste heure, & s'il y a
quelque chose qui vous ayt donné
occasion de rompre auecque moy,
& de ne vouloir plus que ie sçache de vos nouuelles. Si cela est,
quittez neantmoins ceste opinia-
streté Faictes moy sçauoir quelle
offence i'ay commise. Ie demande que vous violiez le serment que
vous auez faict de ne me plus escrire, pour ceste fois là seulement.
Vous ferez en cela vne bonne œuure ; vous me tirerez hors de peine, & ie tascheray aussi apres vous
retirer de vostre mescontentement, en vous rendant satisfaict sur
tout ce que vous me pourrez
obiecter. Vous auriez le cœur bien
dur si vous ne vous rendiez point

à mes prieres. Vous vous fou-
uiendrez bien de ce que ie vous ay
esté autrefois, i'ay esté le fidelle cópagnon de vos estudes & de toutes
vos occupations. I'ay autrefois par-
tagé auecque vous tout le bien & le
mal qui vous pouuoit arriuer. Or il
ne me semble point que depuis ce
temps-là i'aye faict aucune chose
qui vous ayt pû desplaire, & tant
s'en faut que ie vous aye offensé ex-
pressement, que ie ne croy pas mesme l'auoir pû faire sans y penser; ou
bien il faut que l'on ayt donné à
mes actions ou à mes paroles vne
autre explication que celle que l'on
leur doit donner. Si cela estoit ainsi,
vous vous feriez rangé du costé de
ceux qui me persecutent. Vous pré-
driez vne fausse apparéce pour vne
verité, & mon bon-heur seroit sans
espoir de retour, puisque ie serois

abandonné de celuy en qui ie met-
tois ma derniere esperance. Mais,
Philandre, ie vous offense veritablement à ceste heure que ie veux
vous persuader que ie ne vous ay
point offencé. Quelle plus grande faute puis-ie faire que de dire
que vous en auez faict vne? Ie fay
icy des propositions qui pourront
possible vous estre desagreables. Il
faut que ie m'imagine plustost toutes les plus estranges choses du
monde, que de croire que vous
me mesprisez, & que vous auez
mis fin à l'affliction que vous auez
accoustumé de me porter. Vous
n'estes pas de ces esprits volages
qui promettent beaucoup plus
qu'ils ne tiennent. Vos effects sur-
passent tousiours vos promesses,
& il faudroit que vous eussiez manqué à estre ce que vous estes, si

vous ne cherchiez plus les occasions de me tesmoigner vostre amitié.

Pardonnez moy si i'ay eu des
paroles trop licentieuses. Ce que
i'ay dict n'a esté que dans le premier
mouuement, & ie n'ay iamais
creu fermement ce que ie propo-
sois. Si vous m'enuoyez seulement
vn billet toute ma fascherie sera
passee ; & au lieu d'auoir crainte
de vous perdre, mon esprit sera
desormais dans vne parfaicte seureté. Il se peut faire que la Lettre que vous m'enuoyez est desia
en chemin, & que dans peu de
temps ie cognoistray que i'ay eu
tort de me plaindre. Ie voudrois
que cela fust & ie ne tiendray iamais si tost ceste Lettre que ie le
desirerois, car comme ie n'ay rien
qui me plaise plus que les preuues

d'affection que ie vous rends ; Aussi
ie chery bien fort les occasions que
vous me donnez de les continuer,
& de paroistre tousiours le meilleur de vos amis.

De l'excellence de l'Escriture.

LETTRE III.

La fin vous m'auez rendu iustice, & vous m'auez monstré que vous ne desiriez point que ie vous aymasse inutilement. Vous m'auez enuoyé vne Lettre où ie tróuue toutes les preuues d'affection que ie pouuois desirer. Ie reçoy les excuses que vous me faictes sur vostre retardement. Il peut bien estre que celuy que i'auois chargé de ma Lettre ne vous la donna que sur le poinct de son depart, tellement que vous n'eustes pas

pas le loisir de luy rendre vne response, car ie l'ay tousiours pris pour
vn homme fort mal soigneux , &
qui à grande peine pourroit songer aux affaires d'autruy , veu qu'il
neglige toutes les siennes. Si vous
voulez l'on ne nous fera plus desormais de semblables tours. Il n'est
pas besoin que pour entretenir nostre amitié nous pratiquions encore d'autres amis qui portent nos
Lettres. L'on ne trouue pas tousjours des hommes à son gré qui fassent voyage , & l'on ne les veut pas
aussi quelquefois importuner d'aucune chose. Il nous faut auoir vn
autre recours plus asseuré. Vous
estes dans la ville de Paris qui est le
Centre de la France. Vous sçauez
bien que l'on y aborde de toutes
parts , & que les plus petits bourgs y
ont leurs messagers. Chargez de vos

lettres ceux de noſtre païs. Ils paſſent touſiours pardeuant ma porte,
& ils ne manqueront point de me
donner ce que vous m'enuoyrez,
ny de me demander à tous coups,
ſi ie n'auray point quelque autre
deſpeſche. Par ce moyen nous nous
pourrons entretenir deux fois chaque ſepmaine; mais ie ne vous veux
pas trop importuner. Puiſque maintenant ie ſuis fort aſſeuré que vous
m'aymerez eternellement quelque
choſe qui aduienne, il me ſuffit de
vous donner ſouuent la peine de
lire mes lettres, ſans que ie vueille
receuoir des voſtres en auſſi grand
nombre. Ie ſçay bien que vous n'a-
uez pas tant de loiſir que moy, &
qu'il faut bien plus de temps pour
eſcrire que pour lire. Ie ſeray content ſi pour deux ou trois lettres que
ie vous enuoyray, i'en reçoy vne
ſeulement.

Ie suis aſſez ſatisfait de voir que vo⁹ commêcez de gouſter le plaiſir que l'on reçoit en s'eſcriuant de la ſorte. Les amis ſe font ainſi entédre leurs penſees par des meſſagers muets, qui diſent neantmoins de meilleu-res choſes que ceux qui parlent, & qui ne manquent point à repreſen-ter les penſees naïfuement & fidel-lement comme ſi c'eſtoit vne vraye peinture de noſtre eſprit. Les lettres ſont le langage des abſents, où l'on void des merueilles qui meritent bien d'eſtre remarquees. C'eſt le plus grand ſecours que les hom-mes ayent entr'eux pour la conſer-uation de leur amitié & de leur cô-merce. Sans cela l'on les tiendroit comme perdus, lors qu'ils ſeroient en voyage, & ceux qu'ils enuoye-roient porter de leurs nouuelles, ne ſeroient pas creus quelquefois.

C’eſt vn miracle de voir que de
certains caracteres arrengez expri-
ment ſi bien le ſon de la parole, que
toutes les fois que l’on les void l’on
entend auſſi toſt ce qu’ils veulent
dire. Ils ſeruent de beaucoup à celuy
qui les faict; car ſa memoire ne peut
pas eſtre ſi heureuſe qu’il ſe ſouuien-
ne touſiours de ce qu’il a ouy dire,
ou bien de ce qu’il a inuenté luy-
meſme, mais par le moyen de ces
marques dont l’vſage a eſté introduit, & où chacun s’eſt exercé; il arreſte pour iamais ce qu’il eſtoit ſur
le poinct de laiſſer eſchaper, & l’ayāt
mis par ordre ſur le papier quand il
ne le reuerroit de dix ans, & qu’il ne
s’en ſouuiendroit plus, dés qu’il le
reuoid il repaſſe dans ſon eſprit les
meſmes péſees qu’il auoit autrefois.
Que l’on cherche toutes les commoditez qui ſe treuuent dans tou-

tes les inuentions des hommes, il ne
s'en trouuera point vne qui soit esgale à celle-cy ; ce qui a donné sujet à vn grand Esprit de l'antiquité,
de dire que l'Escriture estoit vne
chose trop merueilleuse pour sortir de l'Esprit des hommes ; mais
qu'il falloit que ce fussent les Dieux
qui l'eussent inuentee , & qui en
eussent appris le secret aux pauures
mortels pour se soulager dans leurs
miseres, & mesme pour eterniser la
memoire des choses & la faire passer à la posterité, afin que la reputation des grands personnages ne
meure point dedans le monde.
Aussi par le moyen de l'vsage que
l'on a de certaines Lettres dans
chaque païs non seulement l'on
peut recognoistre soy-mesme ce
que l'on a voulu escrire, mais aussi
l'on le faict cognoistre aux autres.

les caracteres estãs communs pour tous ceux qui veulent apprendre à les former & à les distinguer. Il n'y a pas long temps que les Espagnols ayans descouuert vne certaine Prouince du nouueau Monde, trouuerent que les peuples qui y habitoiẽt, ne sçauoient ce que c'estoit que de marques ny de signes pour se faire entendre sans parler, & pour communiquer ses intentions à des personnes absentes. L'on faict des contes qui en seruent de preuue, & qui sont bien dignes d'estre considerez.

Tesmoin est celuy de ce pauure Indien à qui vn Capitaine Espagnol auoit donné vne Lettre à porter auec vn pannier plein de Dattes à vn sien compagnon de guerre qui estoit dans vn Chasteau assez esloigné. L'Indien voulut taster

de ces fruicts en chemin puis qu'il
auoit la peine de les porter, mais il
en mangea tant que lors qu'il fut
au lieu où il luy falloit aller, le panier se trouua à moitié vuide. Celuy
à qui s'addressoit le present l'ayant
receu & ayant leu la Lettre, sceut
le nombre des Dattes que l'on luy
enuoyoit, & comme il vid qu'il y
auoit beaucoup de mescompte, il se
douta que l'Indien en auoit mangé sa part, tellement qu'il le manda
à son Maistre dans la Lettre de re-
merciement qu'il luy enuoya. Le
pauure Indien porta encore cette Lettre, mais son Maistre ne
l'eut pas si tost leüe qu'il luy fit
de grandes reprimendes, & luy dict
mesmement qu'il apprenoit là dedans qu'il auoit mangé ses fruicts,
& que s'il y retournoit plus il
le feroit aussi-tost punir. Il fut

merueilleufement eftonné de cela. Il ne fçauoit comment vn
morceau de papier pouuoit reueler
ce qu'il auoit faict. Il s'imaginoit
que l'on y euft caché quelque Efprit familier, mais ce qui le mettoit
le plus en peine, eftoit que le papier
qu'il venoit de donner à fon Maiftre, n'eftoit pas celuy qu'il portoit
à la main, lors qu'il auoit mangé les
dattes, fi bien qu'il n'en auoit rien
veu, & que ç'eftoit donc le premier qui l'auoit raconté à l'autre
Gentil-homme, lequel auoit chargé cét autre papier d'en faire la narration à fon Maiftre. Voila les penfees que pouuoit auoir vn pauure
homme qui n'entendoit point les
merueilles de l'Efcriture ; Mais
ce n'eft pas là encore le meilleur. Cet Indien eut encore charge de porter d'autres fruicts au

mesme Gentil-homme, & il eut encore enuie d'en taster quãd ce n'euft
esté que pour voir si la lettre qu'il
portoit auecque cela seroit encore
assez fine pour le descouurir. Il se
voulut cacher d'elle, & comme il
eut trouué vne grosse pierre qui e-
stoit creusée par dessous il y mit vn
papier & le couurit aussi de terre &
de cailloux, puis s'estant assis sur la
pierre il tasta si les fruicts qu'il portoit estoient meilleurs que les premiers. Ayant refermé le panier il tira la lettre de sa cachette & côtinua
son voyage. Le Gentil-hôme ayant
encore receu ce present ne manqua
point de considerer si l'on n'y auoit
point faict de tort, d'autant qu'il
auoit desia cogneu l'infidelité du
porteur. Comme il vid donc que le
larcin n'auoit pas esté moins grand
qu'à l'autre fois, il en aduertit son

amy dedans sa lettre, de sorte que
l'Indien se voyant descouuert non-
obstant toutes ses ruses, eut vn
estonnement nompareil. Il creut
que les Espagnols auoient tant de
puissance qu'ils se faisoient seruir par
les demons qui leur apprenoient
toutes choses, si bien qu'il ne voulut pas nier sa faute : mais lors que
son maistre luy eut demádé qui c'e-
stoit qui luy auoit donné l'asseurance de manger ses fruicts, il luy fit entendre commét il auoit creu estre à
sauueté en cachant sa lettre ; Cette
naïfueté fut si agreable à l'Espagnol
qu'il ne le voulut point faire punir.
Bien qu'il y eust beaucoup de sim-
plicité en cet hóme, si est-ce qu'il
témoignoit d'auoir quelque sorte
d'esprit, car ceux qui sont stupides
tout à faict n'admirent point les belles choses. Il y en eut eu d'autres qui

ne se fussent point aduisez de ce que cettuy-cy admiroit. Les plus habiles d'entre nous seroient possible dans vn mesme estonnement que luy, s'ils n'auoient iamais veu de caracteres & s'ils ne sçauoient pas les merueilles de l'escriture.

Outre l'vtilité que l'on en reçoit en communiquant ses pensees aux absents, il y en a encore d'autres qui y sont attachées.

Les choses que l'on escrit se rendent bien plus polies que celles que l'on dit de bouche. Les imaginatiós se presentent quelquefois en desordre dans nostre esprit, & nous les mettons les vnes deuant les autres, sans pouuoir rédre aucune raison de ce que nous faisons. Nostre langage a beaucoup de vices que nous ne no⁹ pouuons abstenir de cómettre dans la promptitude de nostre parole.

Il n'en doit pas estre de mesme de ce que nous escriuons. Le papier est comme vne table où nous estallons quantité de fleurs apresqu'elles sont cueillies , & ayant remarqué leurs diuerses couleurs , nous voyons quelles sont celles qui viendront mieux les vnes auec les autres. Ceux qui vont dans vn jardin & qui en cueillant des fleurs de tous costez font leurs bouquets à la haste , ne font pas vn ouurage si mignard. Ils mettront des pauots auec des tulipes , & ils ne songeront point à la bonne ou à la mauuaise odeur de ce qu'ils auront cueilly. Ils ne feront peut-estre que de gros faisseaux de diuerses plantes, plustost que de faire des bouquets agreables. Ceux qui entendent cét artifice n'y mettent rien qu'auec choix. Outre qu'ils prennent garde à l'odeur ils

considerent aussi la grosseur qui ne
doit pas surpasser la mesure qu'ils
ont establie , & auec cela ils ont
beaucoup d'esgard à la diuersité des
couleurs. Par le bel ordre qu'ils y
donnent , ils font quelquefois des
chiffres auec des fleurs bien arren-
gées, & il y en a eu de si expertsqu'ils
en ont mesme representé des visages. Cela se rapporte fort à ce que
nous disons; car en parlant à la haste
l'on dit souuent des choses qui ne se
rapportét pas: mais si l'on les arráge
sur le papier, ceux qui s'entendent à
cét Art y representent tout ce qu'ils
veulent. Peu de personnes peuuent
parler aussi bien comme ils escri-
roient. L'on n'a pas la liberté d'estre
vne heure à peser vn mot lors que
quelqu'vn nouspreste de l'attention
pour estre instruict de quelque affaire. Il faut dire les choses tout sur le

champ de la mesme sorte qu'elles
nous viennent dans l'esprit. Ce que
l'on escrit doit estre mieux, puis que
l'on le fait d'ordinaire auec plus de
loisir & moins de diuertissement.
N'estans que de pauures hommes
dót la nature est foible & imparfaite en beaucoup de choses, nous n'a-
uons pas des qualitez diuines , & si
nous pouuons faire quelque chose
de bon, ce n'est qu'auec beaucoup
de temps & de trauail. Toutefois il
y en a qui sçauent prononcer d'vn
ton si majestueux les plus mauuaises choses qu'ils puissent dire , &
qui nous esblouyssent tellement
aussi par leur bonne mine & leurs
actions resoluës, que nous croyons
que tout ce qu'ils disent ne peut
estre mieux; mais si l'on despoüille
leur discours de tant d'ornemens
estrangers, & s'il paroist à nud sur

vn papier, l'on remarque incontinent tous ses deffauts , & l'on void
en combien d'endroicts il differe
des choses parfaites. Vn esprit qui
est capable de faire ses ouurages a-
uec ordre & iugement , ne craint
point de mettre ainsi ses pieces en
veuë & de les coucher par escrit. S'il
ne faisoit que les prononcer l'on ne
iugeroit pas ce qu'elles valent, d'autant que l'on n'auroit pas le loisir de
les considerer exactement en toutes leurs parties. C'est leur aduanta-
ge d'estre par escrit , & d'estre en
vn estat constant où l'on les peut
voir plus d'vne fois.

Quiconque est asseuré du prix
d'vn metal ne doit point craindre la
touche. L'espreuue que l'on faict
d'vne chose qui est asseurément
bonne, ne luy sçauroit iamais nuire,

au contraire elle fait que son estime est plus generale, & que ceux qui doutoient de sa bonté en demeurent asseurez.

L'on reçoit encore vne grande commodité de l'escriture & principalement dans les lettres missiues dont j'entrepren de parler icy sur toutes choses, pource que c'est nostre vray subject. Lors qu'vn amy s'en est allé en voyage, il nous a peu parler d'vne affaire dont nous auons oublié les circonstances, mais il ne faut qu'vne de ses lettres pour faire ressusciter les pensées que nous auōs laissé mourir dans nostre esprit; Cette lettre est desormais gardée pour nous seruir de reigle en tout ce que nous auons à faire, & nous ne pouuons plus nous excuser de nous acquitter de nostre deuoir. La memoire est la faculté de nostre ame qui

qui doit retenir tout ce que les sens
luy ont donné en garde , mais elle
n'est pas tousiours fidelle à conseruer tãt de diuerses images. Les vnes
empeschent les autres , & se broüil-
lent tellement que l'on trouue plustost ce que l'on n'y desire pas, que
ce que l'on y cherche. Le lieu n'est
pas tousiours assez grand pour contenir ce que l'on y veut mettre. Ce
qui est de plus ancien en desloge
pour faire place à des nouueautez, & comme vne toile ne sçauroit receuoir vn second portraict
si l'on n'efface le premier, les choses qui auoient esté representées
dans nostre memoire perissent d'elles mesmes, & il y en a d'autres qui
leur succedent. Le plus grand remede que l'on ayt peu treuuer en
cela, c'est l'escriture. L'on peut dire
que ce nous est vne secõde memoi-

re; & veritablemét elle ne nous sert
pas moins que la premiere, & i'oseray bien dire qu'elle nous sert dauã-
tage, puis qu'elle nous rapporte des
choses que nous auions entieremét
perduës , & qu'il estoit impossible
recouurer par vn autre moyen.

Ceux qui parleront pour la memoire, (qui est la troisiesme faculté de nostre ame , auec l'entendement & l'imagination, qui sont les
deux autres) diront qu'il n'y a
point de comparaison de l'escriture à elle, & que sa dignité est bien
plus grande ; d'autant que ce que
nous possedons par elle ne peut iamais nous estre rauy , & se peut appeller nostre propre bien ; mais que
ce que nous ne possedons que par escrit, nous peut estre facilement osté,
& qu'il n'y a personne qui ne se le
puisse aproprier, aussi bien que nous.

Voyla de verité vne grande prerogatiue, mais il faut cõfiderer d'vn
autre coſté que ce que nous gardons
dans noſtre memoire eſt quelquefois reduit à peu de choſe : mais que
ce que nous pouuons garder par eſcrit eſt infiny. Cecy faiȼt beaucoup
pour l'eſcriture, & c'eſt ce qui m'em-
peſche d'en iuger diffinitiuement.
D'ailleurs n'eſt-ce pas vne merueille de voir que des caracteres arran-
gez ſur vn papier, bien qu'ils ne ſoiét
que des choſes mortes, donnent la
vie aux plus belles pẽſées des hómes,
ſoit qu'ils les faſſent naiſtre pour la
premiere fois , ou qu'ils les faſſent
naiſtre pour la ſeconde. Les lettres
ne ſont elles pas auſſi tres-excellentes
en ce qu'elles nous conſolent pendant l'abſence de nos amys, & que
lors que nous les voyons nous

croyons voir leur pourtraict?

Elles seruent aussi merueilleuse-mét pour s'asseurer de la fidelité des hommes. Les paroles s'esuanoüyssent aussi tost qu'elles sont proferées. Alors mesme que nous les entendós proferer, à peine en sommes nous asseurez, car nous ne pouuons nous fier que sur ce que nous entendons, qui est fort peu de chose, & qui ne consiste pas en plus d'vne syllabe, puis que l'on n'en sçauroit pas prononcer dauantage en vn moment.

Or ce qui n'est pas encore dict nous est incertain, & ce qui l'a desia esté est passé, si bien que si nous n'auons de bons tesmoins, celuy qui a parlé se peut desdire en vn instant, & mesme il peut accuser les témoins de mensonge. L'escriture n'est point subjette à ces inconue-

nients. Ce que l'on a vne fois marqué sur le papier y demeure touf-
jours au mesme estat , & quoy que
celuy qui l'a fait chãge d'opiniõ, l'on
luy peut tousiours mettre deuãt les
yeux ses anciennes promesses. Il est
aussi mal aysé de les nier comme il
est aysé de recognoistre l'escriture
de chaque personne , pource que
par vne merueilleuse prouidence de
Dieu, nos escrits manuels sont aussi
differens les vns d'auec les autres, cóme sont nos visages, de sorte que cela bannit les abus qui pourroient in-
teruenir dans le móde sans cette pro-
prieté. Cela fait que beaucoup d'hómes qui se repentent quelquefois de
l'amitié qu'ils ont voüée à vn autre,
demeurent dans les termes où ils se
sont mis eux mesmes , d'autant que
s'ils en sortoient l'on auroit droict
de leur reprocher leur inconstance,

T t iij

& ils feroient en danger d'eſtre ta-
chez d'vne eternelle infamie.

Il y a encore vne autre commodité fort eſtimable que nous apporte l'eſcriture ; c'eſt que nous eſ-
criuons ſouuét des choſes que nous
n'aurions pas l'aſſeurance de dire de
viue voix. Le prouerbe commun
nous apprend , Que le papier ne
rougiſt point , mais pour ce qui eſt
de nous, lors qu'il nous faut parler à
quelqu'vn de quelque choſe fort
importante , nous y ſommes fort
empeſchez , & nous n'y reüſſiſſons
pas comme nous auions eſperé, car
lors que nous ſommes à part nous,
nous nous promettons des miracles , & quand ce vient au faict
& au prendre, nous eſprouuons qu'il
y a beaucoup de choſes qui nous
deſfaillent. Quelquefois la Majeſté d'vn Grand nous eſtonne de tel-

le sorte que de toutes les parole^s
que nous auions premeditées, nous
n'en sçaurions dire seulement la
premiere.   Vne autre fois la façon
rude & austere d'vn Magistrat nous
mettra la crainte dans l'esprit &
nous rendra aussi muets que des
statuës. La colere nous surprendra
de telle maniere en d'autres occasions, qu'à la verité nous dirons bien
quelque chose, mais ce sera sans ordre & sans iugement, & il vaudroit
beaucoup mieux pour nostre honneur que nous eussions appris à nous
taire. Toutes les autres passions sont
capables de nous faire broncher ainsi, & de nous faire parler d'vne autre sorte que nous n'auions projetté
lors que nous auions le vray vsage
de la Raison.

   L'on ne remedie point autremét
à cela qu'en mettant par escrit ses

meilleures penſées , & les enuoyant
à ceux deuant qui l'on ne ſçauroit
paroiſtre ſans eſtre ſurpris.   L'on
peut tellement polir les choſes & les
conſiderer tant de fois, qu'il n'y ayt
rien contre nos ſentiments, & que
nous ne deuions touſiours aduoüer.

Il y a eu des perſonnes qui ont en
effet beaucoup loüé l'inuention de
l'eſcriture ; mais qui ont creu que
nous n'en receuions pas toutes les
commoditez que l'on en pourroit
receuoir, s'il n'y auoit pas tant d'a-
bus dans le monde comme l'on y
en trouue.

Ces gens là nous repreſentent les
diuerſitez des caracteres qui ſont
propres à chaque nation. Ils voudroient qu'il n'y euſt qu'vne ſorte
de caracteres pour tous les hommes qui ſont ſur la terre, puis qu'ils
ſe deuroient tous entr'aymer cóme

freres , ou comme citoyens d’vne
mesme Republique. Ils pensent que
cela nous seruiroit beaucoup , dautant que nous pourrions recognoistre toutes les choses que chacun
auroit inuentees, mais il faudroit
donc souhaiter pareillement qu’il
n’y eust qu’vn langage. Toutefois
à quoy seruiroit cela puisque nous
nous passerons bien d entreprendre
de grands voyages qui nous occupent toute nostre vie, & que nous
auons assez de choses necessaires à
aprendre sans nous soucier des superfluitez, & rascher de rassassier
nostre curiosité en aprenant les affaires des peuples estrangers? Ils
n’ont pas esté en vain separez de
nous par tant de mers, de montagnes & de riuieres : C’est pour nous
monstrer que nous ne deuons point
nous messer de ce qui se passe chez

eux. Penſons nous auoir accomply
toutes les choſes où nous eſtions
entierement obligez , pour aller
chercher des occupations ſi eſloi-
gnees ? La plus grande prudence
qui ſoit au monde pour viure en
tranquilité , c'eſt d'vſer des biens
de la terre ainſi que l'on les trouue,
ſans ſe plaindre de ce qu'ils ne ſont
pas plus parfaicts. Quand meſme à vne lieüe de nous l'on parleroit d'vn langage qui nous ſeroit
incognu, & quand meſme chaque
que ville auroit vne façon de parler & d'eſcrire toute particuliere,
il ne faudroit pas pourtant alterer
ſon repos , & ſe faſcher de voir
que nous ne pourrions pas auoir
du commerce auec tant de ſortes
d'hommes à cauſe que la facilité en ſeroit oſtee.

Ie ne ſerois pas d'aduis de me

troubler l'esprit à retenir tant de
diuerses paroles. Ie croy qu'il vaut
mieux s'addonner à faire de bonnes actions , & qu'il vaudroit
mieux aussi ne parler que par signes , quand l'on seroit auec des
gens qui ne nous entendroient pas,
que de passer toute sa vie en aprenant des choses qui ne sont estimables que dans la fausse opinion des
hommes. Tant de diuerses fre-
quentations ne sont pas les meilleures. Il n'en faut auoir que deux
ou trois ; mais il faut qu'elles soient
choisies par des hommes de grand
iugement , & qu'elles ayent si
l'on peut ces trois qualitez , à
sçauoir qu'elles soient honnestes,
vtiles , & agreables. L'on peut
bien se passer quelquefois de celles qui ne sont qu'vtiles & honne·
stes, d'autant que si elles ne nous

font pareillement agreables, le deffaut ne vient que de noftre mauuaife humeur, & non pas de la chofe qui ne nous femble point eftre à
noftre gré, l'on peut bien rechercher auffi celles qui ne font qu'honneftes & agreables, car nous n'auós
pas toufiours befoin de celles qui
fótvtiles;mais pour ce qui eft de celles qui ne font qu'vtiles & agreables
fans eftre honneftes, il n'y a perfonne de bonne vie qui les eftime. Or à
caufe que les conuerfations qui font
telles qu'il nous les faut,ne fe peuuét
pas trouuer en toute forte de lieux,
l'on doit faire beaucoup de cas des
bonnes, & lors que l'on les a trou-
uees l'on ne doit point perdre fon
temps à en chercher de nouuelles
que le plus fouuent l'on trouue toutes differentes de celles que nous
demandons. De là s'enfuit que nous

n'auons pas befoin de fçauoir tant
de diuers langages, ny de cognoiftre tant de differentes efcritures.
Nous ne deuons pas mefme auoir
la curiofité d'aprendre la diuerfité
des fiecles. Ce font des amufemens
d'vn efprit oyfif, qui en ce qui eft
de toutes les chofes du monde, eft
content de prendre des fueilles
pour des fruicts.

Pourueu que nos amis nous entendent & qu'ils cognoiffent les
caracteres de noftre main nous deuons eftre fatisfaicts, à la charge que
noftre façon d'efcrire leur plaife, &
qu'ils fe feruent d'vne femblable. Ie
veux bien que tous les hómes igno-
rent mes penfees, excepté ceux que
ie chery, & pour ce qui eft des penfees des autres, ie defire auffi qu'elles me foient couuertes fans mettre
perfonne hors du compte que ceux

auec qui ie traicte d'vne familiarité enticre. Qu'en dictes vous, Philandre ; N'ay ie pas quelque apparence de raifon ? Quoy que ceux qui font en France parlent François pour la plufpart, fi eft-ce qu'ils ont chacun des ftiles fi differents que l'on peut dire qu'il n'y a non plus de raport entre ce qu'efcriuent les vns & les autres, qu'entre le Latin & le langage Chinois. Il y en a qui ont toufiours des paroles merueilleufement enflees , & qui ne promettent rien moins que de faire des miracles pour le feruice de leurs amis ; les autres font dans l'autre extremité. Ils ne tefmoignent pas affez d'affection à ceux enuers qui ils font extremement obligez. Ils font fi froids qu'ils ont de la peine à s'enflammer eux-mefmes, & à faire auffi parroiftre leur feu

iusques dans leurs Lettres. Parmy
tous ceux là il y en a quelques-vns
qui n'escriuent rié que des sottifes &
des impertinences, & qui prophanét
l'vfage de l'Escriture qui ne doit e-
ftre employé qu'à des chofes hono-
rables & vtiles, & ie n'entends pas
parler icy d'vne vtilité de fortune,
qui n'eft que pour le bien du corps,
mais de celle qui eft pour le vray bié
de l'ame. L'Escriture eft vne chofe
fi excelléte que Dieu s'en eft voulu
feruir pour aprendre aux hómes de
quelle forte ils deuoient viure. Il a-
uoit efcrit de tout téps dás nos cœurs
ce qui eftoit neceffaire pour cét effet, mais la plufpart auoient efté fi
miferables qu'ils auoient effacé fes
belles marques; tellement qu'il a dóné fa loy à Moyfe auec vne Efcriture vifible ; & depuis au fiecle
de grace, les Euangeliftes nous

ont eſcrit ſon nouueau Teſtament.
Apres cela quantité de grands perſonnages ont employé dignement
l'eſcriture en des diſcours de pieté
qu'ils nous ont laiſſez. Ceux meſme
qui ont veſcu dans l'erreur n'ont oſé
prophaner cet artifice diuin. Ils nous
ont eſcrit des diſcours où nous ne
voyons point de choſes inutiles. Ils
ne contiennent que les ſecrets de la
Philoſophie, & de toutes les ſciences, & ce qui eſt de plus excellent
l'on y rencontre auſſi en quelques-
vns des preceptes de moralité où les
ames les plus Chreſtiennes ne ſçauroient trouuer à redire tant l'on les
trouue conformes à la vraye religion. Que ferons nous donc nous
autres qui auons eu ceſte grace d'e-
ſtre nez en vn ſiecle, & en vne contree où nous auons pû receuoir de
ſi bonnes inſtructions que nous ne
deuons

deuons pas ignorer de quelle sorte
l'on doit rendre hômage à la Diuinité? Il ne faut pas employer nos discours à traicter d'vne matiere prophane & inutile, d'autant que nous
ne sommes icy que pour trauailler à
nostre salut, il faut tascher de faire
que toutes nos operations y tendêt.
Les ouurages de nostre esprit y
pourrôt beaucoup seruir non moins
que les autres choses. Ie me delibere
dôc pour ce qui est de mon particulier, de ne trauailler iamais en vain,
& de faire que le trauail de l'estude
me meine s'il est possible au chemin
de la vertu, au lieu que la pluspart
ne songent à autre chose qu'à leur
plaisir & à leur diuertissement. Pour
ce qui est du stile de mes lettres, ie
ne veux pas qu'il soit ny trop mai-
gre ny trop enflé. Ie m'efforceray
de me tenir dans vne mediocrité

loüable. Ie ne me rendray pas en-
nuyeux en vſant trop ſouuent d'v-
ne meſme figure de Rhetorique,
Les meilleures choſes ſe rendent
à la fin mauuaiſes, lors que l'on s'en
ſert hors de ſaiſon. Il faut diuer-
ſifier ſes ouurages afin de contenter toute ſorte d'eſprits, & il y a des
occaſions où l'on peut dire que
l'inconſtance n'eſt point à blaſmer.
Qui demeureroit touſiours ſur vn
meſme ſubjet, ne pourroit pas emporter beaucoup de gloire. Il ne
s'inſtruiroit pas auſſi ſur toute ſorte d'accidents, & ſi la fortune met-
roit quelque changement dedans
ſes affaires, il ne ſçauroit pas de
quelle ſorte il y faudroit remedier.
Il ſe trouueroit auſſi nouueau dedans le monde que s'il ne faiſoit
que de naiſtre, & au lieu d'aprendre aux autres, il ſeroit reduit à la

condition d'vn diſciple. Voila comme il en prend à ceux qui ne font
pas marcher la prudence deuant
toutes leurs actions. Taſchons de
nous gouuerner d'vne autre ſorte,
puiſque nous auôs entrepris de vous
eſcrire, faiſons que nos lettres nous
ſoient profitables en quelque maniere. Pour moy ie vous dy derechef que ie ſuis bien aiſe de voir
que l'Eſcriture ſoit employee à des
bonnes choſes. Ie vous aduoüeray
bien ſans vous flatter, que ſi en vous
eſcriuant ie vous puis perſuader que
ie ſuis voſtre ſeruiteur tres humble,
ce n'eſt pas auoir faict peu de choſe;
mais il faut encore faire dauātage ſi
l'occaſion s'en preſente. Outre les
aſſeurances de mon affection que ie
vous donne dans mes lettres, & auec
toutes les promeſſes de ſeruice que
i'y adiouſte, il vous y faut rendre

des seruices mesme. Quand l'on joinct les effects auec les promesses c'est le moyen de n'auoir que faire d'autres preuues ny d'autres cautions pour asseurance de ce que l'on dit. Ie tascheray donc desormais d'employer ainsi mes escrits, pouruveu que ceste maniere de proceder vous soit agreable.

Qu'il est bien aisé d'escrire des choses Morales.

Lettre IV.

VOVS auez touché le but où ie vous atten- dois, & vous ne me laissez plus rien à desi- rer. Ie n'ay point de paroles assez puissantes pour vous tesmoigner le contentement que ie reçoy de voir que vous commencez d'adherer à mes opinions. Pour les asseuran- ces de vostre amitié que vous me reiterez, c'est vne chose que ie de- uois attendre de vous ; car vous n'eussiez pas voulu vous desdire

d'vne chofe que vous m'auez iui ce.
Voftre ferment a efté trop folénel
& d'ailleurs il y a long-temps que ie
fuis defia en poffeffió de ce que vous
permettez que ie garde. Mais
vous m'auez tefmoigné de furplus
que vous defiriez entrer auecque
moy dans vne grande familiarité,
& que ie ferois caufe que vous de-
uiendriez plus diligent à m'efcrire
que vous ne fuftes iamais. Vous ap-
prouuez auffi le deffein que i'ay de
rendre nos lettres inutiles, & vous
eftes fort ayfe que i'empliffe les mié-
nes de toutes les penfees qui me
pourront venir dans l'efprit, pourueu qu'elles nous feruent à nous
rendre plus fçauans ou plus fages.
Vous me dictes là deffus que vous
me ferez quelquefois des objectiós
tout exprez pour me donner vn fu-
ject de difcourir, & que vous me

ferez entrer insensiblement dedans les choses qui seront le plus à vostre goust. C'est ce que ie desire, Philandre, mais ie voudrois bien aussi que de vostre part vous m'escriuissiez quelquefois vos sentimens. C'est en vain que vous prenez tant de peine à vous abbaisser. Ie ne vous deliureray pas de la peine que vous deuez prendre à m'escrire de bonnes choses, car ie sçay bien que vous estes capable d'en faire. Vous n'y manquerez pas aussi quelque chose que vous puissiez dire. Vous auriez plus de peine à mal escrire que beaucoup d'autres n'en auroient à escrire bien. Vous-vous estes accoustumé de vostre ieunesse à mettre vos ourages dans la perfection, & de les accomplir mesme en fort peu de temps. Vous ferez donc

V u iiij

de voſtre part autant comme
ie pourray faire de la mienne, &
par ce moyen noſtre commerce ſera parfaiĉt. & il n'y aura perſonne qui ne ſoit content. Pour moy
ſi ie vous eſcry quelque choſe qui
ſemble deuoir eſtre pris pour des
preceptes, ce n'eſt pas que ie me
donne vne authorité de maiſtre. Ie
ne parleray iamais qu'auecque franchiſe, & mon intention ſera de
m'inſtruire en inſtruiſant les autres.
Or afin que nous ne manquions
iamais d'occaſion de tirer du profit de ceſte façon d'eſcrire, nous eſ-
crirons tout ce qui nous viendra
dans la fantaiſie, pourueu que cela touche la Morale & les autres
ſciences. Nous ne ferons point
auſſi difficulté de raconter des petites hiſtoires, ou de citer meſme des
Autheurs ſi cela vient à propos, car

nous voulons nous prescrire vne autre reigle que celle des lettres ordinaires.

Nous ne ferons pas les premiers qui fe font meflez de cét exercice. Il y a eu de grands perfonnages dans l'Antiquité qui nous peuuent feruir d'exemple.

Ie ne parleray point de tant de Philofophes de la Grece ; je n'iray pas plus loin que les Latins, entre lefquels nous auons Senecque qui a efcrit quantité de lettres à vn feul homme, lefquelles ne feruoient point pour l'aduertir du iugement de quelque procés ou de la diligence qu'il falloit apporter à quelque autre chofe. Ce ne font point des lettres d'affaires, elles ne parlent que de tous les poincts de la Philofophie morale qui leur pouuoient venir dans l'efprit. Il eft vray que tout le monde n'a pas faict eſtat des ouurages de Seneque. Les vns ont dit que l'on les pouuoit cóparer à des brins de jonc ou d'ozier que l'on auroit fagottez enſemble, & les autres ont aſſeuré que c'eſtoit comme vn baſtiment ſans chaux & ſans plaſtre, dont les pierres eſtoiét ſeulemét arrágées les vnes ſur les autres. L'on a voulu móſtrer par là que ſes diſcours n'ont aucune liaiſon, & que ce ſont toutes ſentéces ramaſſées qui ſemblét pluſtoſt eſtre les tiltres de quelques chapitres que des diſcours parfaits. Il y en'a auſſi qui aſſeurent qu'eſtant extremement riche, il auoit achepté quantité d'eſclaues fort ſçauans cóme il y en auoit touſiours dans l'Italie, & qu'il les faiſoit trauailler ſans ceſſe à recueillir les paſſages de tous les bons Autheurs qui auoient eſcrit en toute ſorte de langues , & que

lors qu'il vouloit escrire de l'ambition ou de quelque autre vice, il leur
demandoit ce qu'ils auoient trouué
sur ce sujet, de sorte qu'ayant quantité de lieux communs il y choisis-
soit ce qui luy venoit le plus à gré,
& il en bastissoit des discours à sa
mode sans se donner beaucoup de
peine à joindre ces diuerses pieces.
C'estoit emporter de la gloire du
trauail d'autruy, & c'est par là que
l'on nous veut faire cognoistre
qu'il ne se faut pas estonner si les
discours de Seneque ont si peu de
liaison ; mais ie ne croiray iamais
qu'vn si grand personnage voulust permettre à ses valets d'estudier
pour luy. Il aymoit assez l'estude
pour s'y adonner luy mesme , &
s'il n'eust esté sçauant que pource
que les autres l'estoient, il n'eust pas
esté asseuré dans la connoissance

d'aucune chofe, & l'on euſt bien toſt
recogneu ſes tromperies.

Tant de bons eſprits qui eſtoient
à Rome de ſon temps ne ſe fuſſent
pas laiſſé prendre pour des duppes,
& s'il ne ſe fuſt glorifié que d'vne
fauſſe capacité l'on euſt bien toſt
ſondé ſon eſprit iuſques au fonds &
l'on l'euſt faict viure dans vne eternelle infamie. Il n'eſt point croyable que celuy qui s'eſt trouué aſſez
ſuffiſant pour manier de grandes affaires dás l'Empire, & mettre à execution les plus importantes choſes
du monde, fuſt ſi peu auiſé que de
vouloir compoſer des liures d'vn ra-
mas de ſentéces priſes de diuers Autheurs. Son larcin euſt eſté bien toſt
deſcouuert, & nous le recognoi-
ſtrions encore, car nous trouuerions
dans d'autres Autheurs ſes meilleures penſées ; ce qui ne ſe void pas

neantmoins, bien que les ouurages des plus grands Philosophes de l'antiquité soyent paruenus iusques à nous. Au reste ses escrits ne sont pas si deliez, cõme il y en a eu quelques vns qui l'ont voulu persuader. Il a faict de fort longs traictez où l'on void des periodes qui ont leur iuste mesure, & puis il n'est pas icy question de l'eloquéce, nous ne faisons estat que de ses preceptes moraux, qui sont si excellens que l'on n'en trouue point ailleurs qui meritent d'estre estimez dauantage. Il a aussi parlé sur tant de subjects & en tant de manieres differentes que ie ne pense pas que l'on puisse rien enseigner touchant les bonnes mœurs dont il n'ayt dit quelque chose dans ses liures.

Il ne faut pas conclurre pourtant que l'on ne doiu plus escrire apres

luy sur cette matiere: car il a accom-
modé les choses à la mode de só téps,
& si nous voulós que le public fasse
son profit d'vne semblable lecture il
faut composer des ouurages qui res-
pondent à nos coustumes nouuelles.

C'est ce que ie voudrois bien faire si i'auois la puissance esgale à mes
desirs; mais parce que ie ne m'asseure pas beaucoup sur mes forces, ce
qu'vn autre voudroit donner à tous
les hommes ensemble ie ne pretends
point le donner à autre qu'à vous.

Ce que l'on veut rendre public a
besoin d'estre merueilleusement
poly. Cela passe par tant de mains
qu'il ne se peut autrement qu'il n'y
ayt quelqu'vn qui y treuue quelque chose de rude , & il y a tant
d'yeux qui espluchét de pres tout ce
quis'y rencontre , qu'il n'y a point
de si petit deffaut qui leur puisse es-

chapper. En ne donnant ſes ouurages qu'à vn amy côme vous l'on ſe
garentit de tant de perſecutiós que
l'on ſouffre par les attaques de tant
de diuerſes perſonnes. Noſtre vie
n'eſt pas trauerſée de tant d'inquietudes, & l'on eſcrit auec vne plus
grande franchiſe. Quelquefois auſſi
cette grãde liberté n'eſt pas la moindre cauſe de ce que nous faiſons de
meilleur. Nous ne nous cognoiſsós
pas touſiours nous meſmes, & pour
la crainte que nous auós que nosou-
urages ne plaiſent pas au vulgaire,
nous en retranchons des choſes qui
eſtoiét les meilleures que nous y puſ-
ſiós mettre, & nous y laiſſons au lieu
des extrauagances qui ne plaiſent
qu'aux eſprits mal faits. Quiconque
ſuit ſon propre genie ne tôbe point
dãs vn ſéblable malheur, & ſes premieres boutades valét mieux ſouuét

que tant de choses contrainctes.

Or si l'on veut esprouuer sa force
naturelle il se faut exercer de la mesme façon que nous auons entrepris.
Vn si beau & si honneste trauail ne
sçauroit iamais reüssir qu'à nostre
loüange & à nostre gloire; mais ce
n'est pas là encore ce que nous cherchons principalement. Nous ne ti-
rons pas nostre bien de l'applaudisse-
ment du peuple. Nous cherchons
quelque chose de plus solide qui
n'est rien que les fruicts de la vertu.

Que les autres emplissent leurs lettres d'vne longue suitte de compliments; Qu'ils ne s'estudient qu'à escrire par poinctes, & à faire des rencontres sur les mots; Qu'ils cherchér
des gentillesses & des allusions sur
les fables, & qu'ils taschent s'ils veulent de faire les Poëtes en prose, tout
cela n'a rien qui nous touche, ny
que

que nous voulons imiter.

Il n'est plus de besoin de vous redire que ie suis prest à vous rendre
toute sorte de seruices, & que ie ne
croy pas mesme que la mort puisse
terminer l'affection que i'ay pour
vous. Vous ne doutez point d'vne
chose si claire.

Il faut employer le temps en de
meilleures occupations qui sont
celles que nous auons commencées,
& que vous m'auez prié de continuer.

Que pour bien viure, il faut touſiours
ſonger que Dieu nous regarde.

LETTRE V.

E veux vous commu-
niquer vne penſee que
i'ay euë ce matin tou-
chât l'eſtat de ce móde.
Il me ſemble que l'Vni-
uers n'eſt rien qu'vn grand Amphitheatre. La terre eſt la place du có-
bat, & les hommes s'y trouuent
pour lutter contre diuers maux qui
ne ſont pas leurs ſeuls ennemis,
car ils ont auſſi quelquefois des querelles à demeſler les vns auec les autres.

Si l'on suiuoit l'opinion des Payés
qui croyoient que les Astres fussent
des Dieux, l'on diroit que les Planettes ne se sont mises en leur rang que
pour se donner le plaisir de voir la
meslée: mais sans aller si auant, disons seulement que ce sont les flam-
beaux qui esclairent à ce spectacle
& pource qu'il y a des Philosophes
qui donnent des intelligences à chacun des Cieux, nous dirons bien
qu'elles ont esté placées ainsi les
vnes au dessus des autres, de mesme
que l'on estoit aux theatres anciens.
Tous les esprits bien heureux sont
aussi rangez par ordre pour prendre
part à ce contentement. Nostre grãd
Dieu qui cõprend toutes choses sans
estre compris, est non seulement
au dessus de toutes ces choses, mais
il est dedans elles, pource qu'il est

par tout & qu'il eſt infiny.

Les eſprits ſubalternes ne font auſſi que conſiderer nos combats, mais
pour luy il en iuge diffinitiuement.
Ils nous donnent bien quelquefois
courage de bien faire & nous enſeignent le moyen de vaincre nos
ennemis, mais ce n'eſt que par la
permiſſion qu'il leur en a dónée. Ils
ne feroient pas calpables de nous
aſſiſter en aucune choſe ſans cela. Or
nos cóbats ſont fort dangereux d'ordinaire: mais faiſons reſſuſciter noſtre valeur en nous repreſentant que
nous auós tant d'illuſtres ſpectateurs
Taſchons de paroiſtre vaillans deuant eux, ils diront du bien de nous
au ſouuerain Iuge qui nous donnera des palmes & des couronnes.

Ie ne treuue rien Philandre qui
ſoit plus capable de nous exciter à
bien viure que de conſiderer qu'en-

core que les hommes ne nous regardent point, les Anges nous voyent
sans cesse & que nous deurions estre
honteux de nous soüiller dedans les
pechez deuant des Esprits si purs. Ils
ne sont pas encore seuls qui nous
voyent. Ce ne seroit rien que cela
puisqu'ils n'ont pas le pouuoir de
nous absoudre ny de nous punir;
mais nostre grand Iuge nous void
pareillement, & quand il n'y auroit
point de tesmoins contre nous il est
assez capable de nous conuaincre.

Il y a long temps que l'on a dict
que la vie de l'homme estoit vn
combat perpetuel, & ce ne sont pas
seulement les Chrestiens qui l'ont
reconnu. Les peuples qui ne sçauoient ce que c'estoit que du vray
Dieu ont eu de semblables imaginatiós. Lors que le Philosophe Diogene estoit tourmenté d'vne forte

fiéure, il appelloit vers luy ceux qui
s'en alloient au theatre voir le combat des beftes farouches ou quelque
autre debat felon la couftume du
fiecle, & il leur difoit, O hommes
fans efprit & fans iugement où cou-
rez vous de la forte ? Qu'eft il befoin d'aller au theatre pour voir les
lutteurs les plus adroicts ? Arreftez
vous icy pour voir Diogene qui
combat contre la fiebure. En effet il
faut auoir beaucoup de courage
pour refifter à l'effort des maladies.
Il y en a qui ont l'efprit fi foible
qu'ils fe laiffent abbatre du premier
coup & qui fe negligent eux mefmes fe faifans plus de mal que de
mal mefme.   Pour ce qui eft de
ceux qui fouffrent toute forte d'attaques auec vne patience inuincible il y a beaucoup de plaifir à les
voir fouffrir ; & ne croyez pas que

ce que ie dy prouienne d'vne humeur farouche & cruelle qui se plairoit au mal d'autruy & qui ne tascheroit point de le soulager.

Ce n'est pas à voir le mal que l'on doit auoir de la satisfaction, mais à voir la constance de celuy qui le souffre.

Cela ne faict point de tort à la compassion que l'on doit auoir, mais cela la modere seulement, & pource qui est du secours que l'on est obligé d'apporter à ceux qui souffrent, cela ne le retarde en aucune maniere.

Les combats que nous entreprenons dans le monde ne se font pas seulement contre les maladies du corps ; l'esprit n'est pas moins sujet à estre affligé.

Les passions nous attaquent quelquefois toutes les vnes apres

les autres, & ce qui est bien plus à
craindre, c'est que les maladies corporelles se font grandement sentir à
ceux qui les ont, & se font aussi cognoistre à tous ceux qui les rencontrent, mais nous auons souuent des
maux dans l'Ame où personne ne
prend garde pour nous en aduertir,
& dont nous ne pouuons pas
mesme nous apperceuoir d'autant que cela est accompagné
d'vn certain plaisir qui nous char-
me, & qui nous faict croire que
nous sommes au vray estat où nous
deuós estre pour estre parfaictemét
sage? L'on ne se persuade qu'auecque peine d'auoir faict quelque
faute de iugement.

Les erreurs qui nous enuiron-
nent ont des flatteries qui nous
trompent.

Ce sont comme des nuages qui

offuſquent la lumiere de noſtre eſprit. Quiconque les peut diſſiper eſt
celuy qui eſt preſt à reſiſter à tant de
dangereux ennemis. Il deſcouure
les embuſches que l'on luy dreſſe. Il
reſiſte à tous les aſſauts que l'on luy
donne, & il ne ceſſe point de combattre qu'il n'ayt obtenu vne victoire entiere. L'ambition, l'auarice, & l'amour n'ont iamais de pouuoir ſur luy. Il a des armes qui ſont
à l'eſpreuue de leurs atteintes, &
pour s'entretenir touſiours dans ſa
valeur il ſonge ſans ceſſe qu'il eſt en
la preſence du Createur de toutes
choſes qui le doit punir ou recompenſer ſelon ſes bonnes ou mauuaiſes actions.

Ie ſuis maintenant dans vne ſolitude ſi grande que ie pourrois bien
faire de mauuaiſes choſes ſans que
les hommes les viſſent, neantmoins

Philandre, ie tafche de mettre vne
bonne reigle à ma vie, & ie ne veux
pas mefmes que mes penfées foient
originelles. Dieu penetre iufques
dans les cachettes des cœurs & les a-
bifmes les plus profonds luy font
defcouuerts. Pour ceux qui font dedans les villes, ils peuuent bien s'abftenir des vices a caufes de la honte qu'ils ont eftans veus de toutes
parts, & pour crainte auffi d'vne
punition: mais ce n'eft pas là feulement ce qui nous doit empefcher
de faillir, & ce qui nous doit amener au bon chemin. Nous deuons
tafcher de bien viure pour le feul a-
mour des chofes eternelles.

Or ne croyez pas Philandre que
les conuoitifes que l'on a pour les
richeffes ou pour les honneurs &
pour les voluptez du corps, foyent
les feuls ennemis que nous auons

à combattre. Il y a de deux sortes de passions ; les vnes sont comprises sous les desirs , & les autres sous la fuite & l'auersion que l'on a pour quelque chose. Nous auons parlé de celles qui nous font desirer, & celles qui nous font fuyr & euiter quelque chose, c'est la hayne & la colere qui sont deux dangereuses maistresses quand elles peuuent auoir de l'ascendant sur l'esprit d'vn homme.

Le vray moyen de s'en garentir, c'est de ne point mettre son cœur aux choses de la terre : car si nous les perdons nous ne serons point en danger de nous perdre aussi par la fascherie & le desespoir. Si nous ne voulons point sortir de nostre similitude du theatre, considerons que les anciens Athletes se mettoient tous nuds pour aller au combat, afin que l'ennemy n'euſt point de priſe ſur eux. Il nous faut ainſi deſpoüiller de l'affection des choſes mondaines, ſi nous ne deſirons point que l'ennemy qui nous attaque, nous arreſte par ces veſtemens inutiles, & qu'il nous faſſe tomber.

I'ay voulu vous entretenir auiourd'huy des penſees que i'ay eües ſur l'Amphitheatre du monde, en conſiderant l'ordre des creatures. Cela vous ſera d'autant plus agreable. Si vous auez veu quelquefois ces tables des Cabaliſtes où ils arrangent tout ce qui eſt en l'Vniuers pour en monſtrer l'harmonie. Vous voyez la rondeur du monde, & ces diuers degrez qui font beaucoup à ceſte ſimilitude. Ie ſçay bien que c'eſt ce qui ſe peut dire de meilleur ſur ce ſubjet, & pour n'eſtre point

loüé aux despens d'autruy, je vous
confesse ingenuément que ceste
imagination ne vient pas de moy,
mais qu'à cause que ie l'ay souuent
passee pardeuant mes yeux, i'en ay
faict comme de mon propre. Ie ne
doute point que vous n'ayez maintenant vne extreme curiosité de
sçauoir en quel autheur i'ay faict
cét heureux larcin : mais premierement ce n'est pas vn larcin, puisque
ie veux que celuy qui est le maistre
d'vne si belle chose ioüisse du principal fruict qui est la gloire. D'ailleurs
ie ne luy ay point pris cela en cachettes; c'est luy qui me l'a commu-
niqué, & qui apres me l'a donné
gratuitement, auec vn pouuoir bien
ample de m'en seruir en toute sorte d'occasions. Au reste si en le nommant Autheur vous le pensez mettre au nombre de tant d'hommes

impertinens qui eſcriuent auiour-
d'huy encore que ce ſoit le meſ-
tier où ils ſont le moins propres;
c'eſt ce que ie ne puis ſouffrir ſans
quereller. Celuy qui m'aprend les
plus belles choſes que ie ſçache eſt
exempt de la corruption de ce ſiecle. C'eſt vn maiſtre ſans orgueil
& ſans vanité, à qui ie defere plus
qu'à tous les hommes du monde,
& dont i'eſtime plus l'entretien que
la lecture de tous mes liures. Vous
ſçauez à peu prez de qui ie parle;
C'eſt de ce grãd eſprit qui demeure
à trois licuës de ma maiſon, & que
ie vay quelquefois viſiter auec vne
reuerence auſſi grande que celle
que les anciens auroient quand
ils s'en alloient à l'Oracle. Il couche bien quelquefois par eſcrit ſes
meilleures penſées, mais ce n'eſt
que pour les monſtrer plus facile-

ment à ceux qui les defirent ; car
pour auoir l'ambition d'en faire
des liures quife vendent publique-
ment; c'eft à quoy il ne fe peut refoudre. Il ne fe foucie pas d'eftre
cognu des hommes pourueu qu'il
foit cognu de Dieu, & il ne fonge
qu'aux delices du Ciel tant il a peur
de s'arrefter aux recompenfes de
la terre.

De la Colere.

Lettre VI.

QVAND ie vous ay escrit quelque chose, ie ne suis pas si impor-tun que de desirer que vous me respondiez sur chaque article. Il faut laisser les discours que vous croyez que i'aye finis de moy-mesme, & prendre quelquefois ceux qui vous sont les plus agreables, & dont vous croyez me pouuoir mieux entretenir. En parlant de la colere dans ma dernie-re lettre, ie vous ay donné subject de me raconter les mauuaises actiós

qu'vn

qu'vn de vos amis a faictes estant
maistrisé de cette passion. Cela me
faict entrer sur cette matiere ; car ie
me reserue la mesme liberté que
vous d'escrire tout ce qui me viendra dans l'esprit. Il me semble donc
que la colere est vne agitation si ve-
hemente, que nous deuriós tascher
de nous en garétir à cause des maux
dont elle est cause non seulement à
ceux que nous deurions cherir, puis
qu'ils sont hommes comme nous,
mais aussi à nous mesmes ; car lors
que nous sommes en colere nous ne
prenons point garde à ce que nous
faisons , & nous ressemblons les
chiens qui mordent les pierres que
l'on leur a iettées. Nous ressemblons
aussi au serpent dont il est parlé dans
les fables, lequel estant entré dans la
boutique d'vn serrurier se fascha de
ce qu'vne lime luy estoit cheute sur

le dos, de forte qu'il fe mit à la mordre de rage & s'y vfa toutes les déts. Nous attaquons ainfi quelquefois des ennemis qui font plus puiſſans que nous, & nous procurons noſtre propre dommage. Il y a eu meſme des hommes qui fe font mis en colere contre des choſes infenfibles. Vn Roy de Perfe fit foüetter la mer qui auoit ſubmergé ſes nauires, & vn autre fit diuiſer vn fleuue en pluſieurs petits ruiſſeaux, à cauſe que quelques vns de ſes cheuaux s'y eſtoient noyez. C'eſtoit là vn courroux barbare & inutile qui n'aportoit que de la honte à ceux qui en eſtoient poſſedez; car la mer ſe pouuoit encore eſleuer au meſme téps qu'elle eſtoit foüettée pour engloutir dans ſes abiſmes, ceux qui la penſoient corriger en la puniſſant comme vn enfant. Le fleuue qui auoit

esté diuisé pouuoit aussi rompre les
digues, & faire plus de dommage
en noyant la platte campagne, qu'il
n'eust sçeu faire si l'on l'eust laissé
dans son canal ordinaire.

Ie sçay bien que ceux qui faisoient de semblables impertinences, ne pensoient pas auoir trauaillé en vain, car s'ils sçauoient que les
eaux de la mer & des riuieres estoiēt
insensibles, ils croyoient au moins
que les Dieux qui y presidoient ne
l'estoient pas, & par consequent
que l'on leur faisoit vn grand affront
en les allant assaillir dans leur Royaume, & en taschant de perdre les
choses qui leur appartenoient: mais
s'il eust esté vray qu'il y eust eu vn
Neptune au monde, il se fust bien
peu soucié de la sottise de ces petites
gens qui n'estoient pas capables de
resister à sa puissance.

La honte eſtoit grande pour ceux qui auoient faict vn tel exploict. Ie m'aſſeure qu'ils ſe repentirent apres de s'en eſtre meſlez. La colere a cela qu'elle eſt hôteuſe de ſa laideur lors qu'elle ſe conſidere, tellement qu'il y a quelque moyen pour la moderer.

Il y a des animaux qui ſe laiſſent prendre par l'artifice des miroirs. Ils ſont trompez croyans voir leurs ſemblables, & lors qu'ils s'aprochét ils ſont ſoudain arreſtez. Il en faut faire de meſme à ceux qui ſont en colere. Il leur faut remonſtrer naïfuement la laideur de leur vice afin que l'ayans recognu ils ſe laiſſent prendre par où l'on voudra & s'apriuoiſent ſans aucune peine.

Si l'on leur pouuoit auſſi monſtrer vn miroir, le ſecret ne ſeroit pas de peu de conſideration ; & ſe

n'entens pas vn miroir myſtique,
comme celuy que l'on leur preſente
dans le diſcours, en leur racontant
quelques exemples.

Ie veux parler d'vne glace naturelle où leur viſage puiſſe eſtre repreſenté; car la colere met des rides
ſur noſtre front, rend nos yeux eſ-
garez, faict changer pluſieurs fois
de couleur à noſtre teinct, & nous
rend quelquefois ſi horribles que
nous ſommes hôteux de nous trouuer en cet eſtat.

Ce n'eſt pas moy ſeulemét qui có-
ſcille les autres de ſe regarder dans
les miroirs, & qui a creu que ce que
les perſonnes mondaines faiſoient
vn inſtrument de leur vanité, pouuoit ſeruir à de meilleures inuentions & nous retirer de nos vices.

Socrate donnoit conſeil à toute
ſorte de perſonnes de ſe mirer bien

Y y iij

fouuent, mais il ne vouloir pas que
ce fuſt pour ſe farder le viſage, ou
pour ſe parer auec trop de ſuperflui-
té. Il diſoit qu'il faloit que les
beaux ſe miraſſent afin de reconnoiſtre leur beauté & de s'empeſcher de rien faire qui fuſt capable
de leur faire perdre l'honneur que
chacun leur rendoit. Il ne conſeil-
loit pas moins auſſi aux laids de ſe
mirer, pource qu'il faut qu'en voyât
leur laideur ils s'excitent à rendre
leur ame plus belle que leur corps,
& faire que leur conuerſation ſoit
plus aymable que l'on ne la iugeroit
pas à l'abord. Il faut adiouſter à cela
que de quelque ſorte que ſoit noſtre viſage, ſi nous nous imaginons
qu'il y ait des deformitez, c'eſt ſelon l'vſage que nous auons pris de
nous plaire en vn certain aſſembla-
ge de proportion & de couleurs ſans

pouuoir definir au vray quelle doit
estre la parfaicte beauté , de sorte
que nous ne deuons pas croire qu'il
y ait aucun visage qui ait tant de
choses à reprendre , & nous nous
deuós representer que c'est l'ouurage de Dieu qu'il faut cóseruer en son
naturel. Or toutes les passiós y alte-
rét quelque chose,à la colere principalement , si bien qu'aussi tost que
nous verrons qu'elle y aura apporté
quelque mutation nous deuós songer à la chasser de nostre ame. Les A-
theniés ont aussi fait beaucoup d'e-
stime de la coustume que l'on a de se
mirer. Ils croyoiét que Minerue qui
estoit la patróne de leur ville,s'estoit
voulu vne fois adóner à joüer de la
fluste, mais que s'estát mirée dás vne
fótaine,elle auoit veu qu'elle se des-
figuroit le visage en soufflant , tellement qu'elle en auoit jetté sa fluste

de colere, la laiſſant pour les Satyres
& le Dieu Pan, qui eſtoient deſia ſi
laids qu'ils ne ſe ſoucioient point
de le paroiſtre dauantage.

Il faut ainſi prendre garde aux
mauuaiſes habitudes que nous pre-
nous, & taſcher de les quitter comme eſtans indignes de nous, qui ne
ſommes nés que pour nous addonner à des choſes loüables & honneſtes.

Si tous les hommes viuoient
comme ils doiuent, lors qu'ils verroient que quelqu'vn ſeroit maiſtri-
ſé de ſa paſſion, ils taſcheroient de
l'en retirer par toute ſorte de remedes. Lors qu'ils verroiẽt vn homme
en colere ils y deuroiẽt courir comme au feu pour l'eſteindre; car veritablement cette agitation nous eſ-
chauffe de telle ſorte que d'vne petite eſtincelle il en vient de grandes

flâmes, qui paſſent meſmes d'vn eſprit à l'autre, & qui ſont capables de
perdre toute vne ville & toute vne
contrée. Tant s'en faut que l'on jette de l'eau ſur ce grand feu, qu'au
contraire l'on y fournit le plus ſouuent de matiere pour l'accroiſtre,
ce qui eſt cauſe de la ruine d'vne infinité de perſonnes. Vous n'eſtes pas
de ceux qui ſont ſi peu charitables.
Il y a long temps que ie ſçay qui
vous eſtes, & ie me reſiouy d'auoir
veu encore depuis peu de grandes
preuues de voſtre bonté. Mais taſ-
chez de faire que tous ceux qui vo⁹
cognoiſſent vous reſſemblent, &
que non ſeulement ils arreſtẽt l'impetuoſité de leur colere, mais qu'ils
s'efforcent auſſi d'arreſter celle des
autres. Il ne faut pas regarder auec
plaiſir la querelle de ceux que nous
deurions tous aymer comme nos

freres. L'on ne doit pas faire comme ceux qui pouſſent les chiens les vns contre les autres, & qui les animent par vn frappement de mains. Nous n'eſpargnons point les beſtes qui ſont eſloignées de noſtre nature; mais pour ce qui eſt des hommes qui ſont compoſez d'vne meſme matiere & d'vne meſme forme que nous, il leur faut rémoigner plus d'amour & de charité.

La colere eſt comme vne fiéure chaude qui nous faict dire vne infinité de choſes ridicules, & nous fait entreprendre beaucoup de ſottes actions dont nous nous repentons lors qu'elle eſt paſſee. C'eſt ce qu'il faut repreſenter à ceux qui en ſont poſſedez, & ſi l'on tient qu'il eſt impoſſible de ne ſe point colerer, au moins faut il croire que l'on peut bien ne ſe pas tant colerer que les au-

tres & se moderer insensiblement.
Nous auons de meilleurs preceptes
que ceux des Philosophes Stoiques,
qui ne vouloient pas qu'vn homme
s'esmeust non plus qu'vne pierre.
Nostre Oracle Chrestien nous a dit,
Soyez en courroux, mais ne pechez
pas. C'est à dire que nous pouuons
bien auoir quelque premier mouuement qui nous excite à la colere;
mais que l'on le peut abbatre & par
ce moyen ne point pecher; Car tant
s'en faut que ce soit vn peché s'il
nous vient vne mauuaise pensée,
qu'au contraire c'est vn subject de
meriter beaucoup si nous la rejet-
tons, & si nous faisons que le Soleil
ne se couche point sur nostre colere.

Comme ie parlois vne fois de cecy à ce grand Philosophe de nostre
siecle, que ie vous ay tant estimé, je
luy demanday si ceux qui s'addon-

noient à la Philosophie ancienne,
auoient trouué de bons remedes côtre la colere ; il me fit estat de quelques vns qui veritablement ne sont point à rejetter , mais il se mocqua ouuertement des autres. Comme par exemple tous nos Pedans qui ne disent iamais rien d'eux mesmes , & qui se contentent seulement d'alleguer ce qu'ils trouuent dans leurs liures ne tombent iamais sur le propos de la colere, qu'ils ne parlent du Roy Cotis qui à leur aduis a donné vn bel exemple pour moderer ses passions Or ils ne considerent point si ce qu'il fit estoit bien ou mal; car ils ne penetrent pas si auant dans les choses Ils se contentent de transcrire diuers exemples dans leurs liures auec moins d'ordre qu'il n'en faudroit mesme dans des lieux cómuns que l'on ne feroit que pour son vsa-

ge, Il faut tascher de trauailler plus
exactement & de faire icy des re-
cueils qui nous soient plus vtiles. Le
Roy Cotis ayant donc receu vn magnifique present d'vn buffet de verre dont toutes les pieces estoient in-
genieusement faites, recompensa li-
beralement l'ouurier selon la beauté de son ouurage & aussi selon la
grandeur d'vn tel Prince que luy;
mais il ne voulut pas garder neantmoins de si beaux vases , pource
qu'ils estoient trop fragiles, & qu'il
craignoit que ses valets les ayás cas-
sez il ne se mist en colere côtre eux.
Il les cassa donc incontinent luy
mesme , & l'on croid que par ce
moyen il euita de grádes occasions
de se laisser emporter à sa passion.
Mais tant s'en faut que je loüe cette
action, qu'au contraire ie la blasme
extremement , car elle témoigne

vne grande deffiance de ſes forces,
& vne extreſine laſcheté de ne s'oſer
eſprouuer contre les premiers mouuemens de la colere qui luy fuſſent
ſuruenus. Quelle niaiſerie de n'auoir
pas voulu garder vne ſi belle choſe!
car il ſe peut faire que ſes ſeruiteurs
en euſſent eu tant de ſoin, que meſme lorsqu'il s'en fuſt voulu ſeruir ils
n'y euſſent fait aucun dommage, &
puis quand ils en euſſent caſſé quelque piece, il en fuſt encore demeuré beaucoup d'autres, & tout le reſte n'euſt eſté de long temps caſſé.
Poſſible que de ſa vie il n'en euſt
veu la fin ; & quand il l'euſt veu,
touſiours euſt il eu le plaiſir d'auoir
iouy long temps d'vne choſe dont
il n'auoit eu la iouyſſance que l'eſpace d'vn inſtant. D'ailleurs il pouuoit faire ſerrer cette vaiſſelle dans
vn cabinet de raretez où perſonne

n'euſt iamais touché, & ie ne ſçay
quelle ſorte precaution il auoit de
vouloir caſſer vne choſe de peur
qu'à l'auenir elle ne fuſt caſſée, car
quand il l'euſt gardée, qu'eſt-ce qu'il
en pouuoit arriuer de pire? Il deuoit
pluſtoſt reſſembler à ce Gentil-homme à qui vn de ſes amys enuoyoit
deux beaux verres de criſtal de Ve-
niſe ainſi qu'il luy mandoit par ſa
lettre. Le laquais qui les portoit en
caſſa vn en chemin l'ayant laiſſé tõ-
ber de ſes mains en ſongeant à autre
choſe Quand il fut deuant le Gentil-homme qui d'abord leut la lettre
qu'il luy preſentoit, il n'en fut point
plus eſtonné Comme il luy deman-
da l'autre verre, il luy dit qu'il l'auoit
caſſé, & le Gentil-homme luy ayãt
demandé encore, comment il auoit
fait pour le caſſer , il laiſſa tomber
celuy qu'il auoit dans ſes mains & le

caſſa encore. Il y euſt eu des hommes qui ſe fuſſent extremement faſ-
chez de cela, & qui euſſent fait donner les eſtriuieres au laquais, mais ce
Gentil-hôme admira ſeulement la
naïfueté de ce garçon, & cogneut
qu'il ne faloit point interroger vn
lourdaut que de bonne ſorte, ny luy
rien dire d'ambigu de crainte de luy
faire commettre de grandes fautes
en prenant les choſes au pied de la
lettre. Ce conte vaut bien celuy de
Cotis qui ne deuoit pas auoir ſi peur
de la colere, encore que les Philoſophes nous la depeignêt comme vne
dangereuſe beſte, car nous auons aſ-
fez de ſecrets pour l'apiuoiſer.

Ce Philoſophe ancien qui diſoit
auſſi qu'il ne vouloit point battre
ſon valet pource qu'il eſtoit en colere, n'eſtoit pas moins ridicule. Il
prioit ſon voyſin de le battre pour

luy

luy à cauſe que s'il l'euſt battu luy-
meſme il l'euſt outragé auec excez,
& euſt commis vne injuſtice rendât
la punition plus grande que la faute.
Il penſoit teſmoigner en cela qu'il
eſtoit vn fort habile hóme, & qu'il
ſçauoit bien monſtrer de quelle ſorte l'on ſe pouuoit exempter de paſſion, mais s'il auoit cette puiſſance,
pourquoy craignoit-il d'entrer en
colere. Quand il auoit le foüet ou le
baſton à la main deuenoit-il bour-
reau au lieu d'vn Philoſophe? Voyla
vn homme bien laſche de ſe laiſſer
maiſtriſer de la ſorte. N'employons
pas ainſi tout noſtre ſoin à des choſes qui ne ſont pas bien ſeantes à vn
homme ſage S'il nous vient des occaſions de nous faſcher, ayans les remedes tous preſts, il nous eſt permis
d'en vſer pourueu que ce ſoient des
remedes genereux & dignes d'vn

homme de vertu, & autres que ceux
du Roy Cotis.

Il est vray qu'il y a beaucoup de
des-honneur à estre vaincu ; mais ce
n'est pas à dire qu'il s'en faille fuyr
de peur de l'estre , car c'est par ce
moyen que l'on est vaincu veritablement & d'vne autre maniere
que l'on ne pense. Quiconque veut
emporter de l'honneur se doit presenter au combat, & receuoir les attaques, mais il ne faut point paroistre foible & abbatu , il faut estre
tousiours debout sans fleschir d'vn
costé ny d'autre , & c'est alors que
l'on merite d'estre couronné Aussi
pour auoir l'hóneur de n'estre point
sujet aux passions, ce n'est pas assez
d'euiter toutes les occasions qui les
peuuent faire esleuer contre nous. Il
faut s'estre esprouué contre leurs efforts, & leur auoir long-temps re-

siflé fans qu'ils ayent peu rien gaigner deſſus noſtre conſtance.

Il y a des hommes qui font ſi ſimples que de croire abſolument tout
ce que leur diſent leurs Medecins,
Ils penſent que leur naturel n'eſt
point reiglé que par l'vne des quatre humeurs qui domine ſur les autres, & que s'ils ont plus de pituite
que de bile, ils ſont plus pacifiques
que coleres. Ils ſe fient au raport que
l'on leur faict de la diuerſe couleur
de leurs excrements, & ils s'imaginent que par des purgations rejet-
tées, ils ſe deſchargeront de beaucoup d'afflictions & d'inquietudes,
& s'abſtiendront de ſe faſcher pour
quelque choſe que ce ſoit Il y en a
d'autres qui croyent auſſi, que s'ils
ſe font tirer du ſang, cela pourra
moderer les chaleurs de leur eſprit,
mais ie leur aſſeure que tous ceux

qui leur perſuadent cela les trôpent,
meſmes qu'ils doiuent trouuer vne
aſſez forte medecine pour purger
leur mauuaiſe humeur. Leur mal eſt
attaché ſi fermement à l'Ame, que
c'eſt en vain que l'on le veut guerir
par le corps. Pour faire cela il faudroit eſtre auſſi ſçauant que Para-
celſe & ſes diſciples qui gueriſſoient
les playes du corps en appliquant les
remedes ſur le pourpoinct. En effet
le corps n'eſt que le veſtement de
l'ame, & il faut paſſer iuſques à elle
ſi l'on luy veut donner vne entiere
guerifon. Ne voyez vous pas ſouuent des hommes qui releuent de
maladie, eſtre auſſi coleres qu'auparauant. Neantmoins ils ont quelquefois pris tant de medecines, que
l'on croit qu'ils ont eſté parfaicte-
ment purgez. L'on leur a auſſi tiré
tant de ſang, qu'ils n'ont plus que de

la froideur & de la foiblesse, & pourtant à cause que leur esprit s'est accoustumé à se mettre en colere, il est
encore assez chaud & assez fort
pour cela. Ces pauures gens sont si
aueuglez qu'ils s'imaginẽt que pour
monstrer qu'ils ne sont pas encore
morts, comme leurs heritiers auoiẽt
desia pensé, ils crient, ils tempestent
contre chacun, & ils n'agissent plus
que par la colere. Leurs seruiteurs
patissent de leur mauuaise humeur,
& ils sont cause de les faire tomber
en peché, car il y en a tel qui souhaitte de les voir encore au mesme
estat où ils ont esté lors qu'ils
auoient perdu le mouuement & la
parole.

Ce qu'il y a de pire en cecy, c'est
que l'on void des hommes que le
vulgaire prend pour des Anges,
pource qu'ils ne cessent de parler des

choſes ſainctes, & de frequenter les
lieux ſacrez ; mais ils ont quelquefois de l'hypocriſie pluſtoſt qu'vne
vraye deuotion , & ſi quelqu'vn
faict quelque petite choſe qui les
offenſe, ils ne luy pardónent iamais,
& la colere leur fait deſirer quelque
vengeance remarquable. Ils s'imaginent eſtre dauantage que les autres à cauſe qu'ils ont acquis quelque ſorte de reputation par leurs artifices. Ils font les grands & les ſerieux, & à leur aduis tout le monde
eſt réply d'impieté, & il n'y a qu'eux
qui ſoient les fauoris du Ciel. Que
s'ils ont quelque pouuoir , ils ne má-
quent pas de le faire paroiſtre, & de
ruiner s'il leur eſt poſſible ceux
qu'ils ont pris pour object de leur
paſſion. Encore croyent-ils en cela
faire vne œuure agreable à Dieu. Ils
s'imaginent que ceux à qui ils font

du tort sont des meschans, & que
c'est bien faict de les punir. Mais, ô
foibles hommes , qui pensez vous
estre pour vouloir ainsi tirer vengeance du peché des autres? faut-il
vsurper vne puissance que Dieu se
reserue a luy seul? Il est vray que la
justice du monde punit quelques
crimes, mais ce n'est que ceux qui
sont apparents , & dont il y a des
tesmoins qui peuuent conuaincre le
coulpable , mais vous voulez bien
aller plus outre, & vous desirez punir les pensees, ou bien quelques autres fautes legeres qui ne meritent
pas que l'on y songe.

Si l'on vous a rendu vn mauuais
office en quelque affaire , taschez
d'euiter ce coup ; cela n'est point
deffendu ; mais ne vous efforcez
point de rendre la pareille a celuy
qui vous a fait du tort. La vengean-

ce est deffenduë aux particuliers. Ils
se peuuent pouruoir pardeuant la
justice des Roys s'ils ont droict de le
faire. Que s'ils ne l'ont point, ils se
doiuent consoler eux mesmes, &
laisser faire au grand Iuge qui recó-
pensera chacun selon ses merites, &
qui donnera des supplices à ceux
qui nous ont faict injure, cependant
que nous receurons le prix de nostre patience.

F I N.

www.ingramcontent.com/pod-product-compliance
Lightning Source LLC
Chambersburg PA
CBHW070704100726
47907CB00001B/44